THE BORDER

Don Winslow is the author of nineteen acclaimed, award-winning, inter-national bestsellers – including the No.1 international bestseller *The Cartel*, *The Power of the Dog*, *The Force*, *Savages*, and *The Winter of Frankie Machine*. *Savages* was made into a critically acclaimed film by three-time Oscar-winning Oliver Stone. *The Cartel* is scheduled to begin production in 2019 and *The Force* has been adapted by Pulitzer Prize winner David Mamet and Oscar nominee Scott Frank for director James Mangold and 20th Century Fox. A former investigator, anti-terrorist trainer, and trial consultant, Winslow lives in California and Rhode Island.

 @donwinslow

/DonWinslowAuthor

www.don-winslow.com

Also by Don Winslow

The Force
The Cartel
The Kings of Cool
The Gentlemen's Hour
Satori
Savages
The Dawn Patrol
The Winter of Frankie Machine
The Power of the Dog
Looking for a Hero (with Peter Maslowski)
California Fire and Life
The Death and Life of Bobby Z
Isle of Joy
While Drowning in the Desert
A Long Walk Up the Water Slide
Way Down on the High Lonely
The Trail to Buddha's Mirror
A Cool Breeze on the Underground

DON WINSLOW

THE BORDER

HarperCollins*Publishers*

HarperCollins*Publishers*
1 London Bridge Street
London SE1 9GF

www.harpercollins.co.uk

First published in Great Britain by HarperCollins*Publishers* 2019
1

First published in the United States by William Morrow,
an imprint of HarperCollins*Publishers* 2019

Stephen King, excerpt from Introduction to *The Shining* (New York: Pocket Books, 2001).
Copyright © 2001 by Stephen King. Reprinted by permission.

Tom Russell, excerpt from "Leaving El Paso" (Frontera Music / BMG Firefly).
Reprinted by permission. All rights reserved.

Don Winslow asserts the moral right to
be identified as the author of this work

A catalogue record for this book
is available from the British Library

ISBN: 978-0-00-822753-1 (HB)
ISBN: 978-0-00-822754-8 (TPB)

Printed and bound in Great Britain by
CPI Group (UK) Ltd, Croydon, CR0 4YY

MIX
Paper from
responsible sources
FSC™ C007454
FSC
www.fsc.org

This book is produced from independently certified FSC™ paper
to ensure responsible forest management.

For more information visit: www.harpercollins.co.uk/green

In memory of
Abel García Hernández, Abelardo Vázquez Peniten, Adán Abraján de la Cruz, Alexander Mora Venancio, Antonio Santana Maestro, Benjamín Ascencio Bautista, Bernardo Flores Alcaraz, Carlos Iván Ramírez Villarreal, Carlos Lorenzo Hernández Muñoz, César Manuel González Hernández, Christian Alfonso Rodríguez Telumbre, Christian Tomás Colón Garnica, Cutberto Ortiz Ramos, Doriam González Parral, Emiliano Alen Gaspar de la Cruz, Everardo Rodríguez Bello, Felipe Arnulfo Rosa, Giovanni Galindes Guerrero, Israel Caballero Sánchez, Israel Jacinto Lugardo, Jesús Jovany Rodríguez Tlatempa, Jhosivani Guerrero de la Cruz, Jonás Trujillo González, Jorge Álvarez Nava, Jorge Aníbal Cruz Mendoza, Jorge Antonio Tizapa Legideño, Jorge Luis González Parral, José Ángel Campos Cantor, José Ángel Navarrete González, José Eduardo Bartolo Tlatempa, José Luis Luna Torres, Julio César López Patolzín, Leonel Castro Abarca, Luis Ángel Abarca Carrillo, Luis Ángel Francisco Arzola, Magdaleno Rubén Lauro Villegas, Marcial Pablo Baranda, Marco Antonio Gómez Molina, Martín Getsemany Sánchez García, Mauricio Ortega Valerio, Miguel Ángel Hernández Martínez, Miguel Ángel Mendoza Zacarías, Saúl Bruno García, Daniel Solís Gallardo, Julio César Ramírez Nava, Julio César Mondragón Fontes and Aldo Gutiérrez Solano.
And dedicated to
Javier Valdez Cárdenas
and all journalists everywhere.

And when anyone builds a wall, behold, they plaster it over with white-wash; so tell those who plaster it over with whitewash, that it will fall.

—Ezekiel 13:10

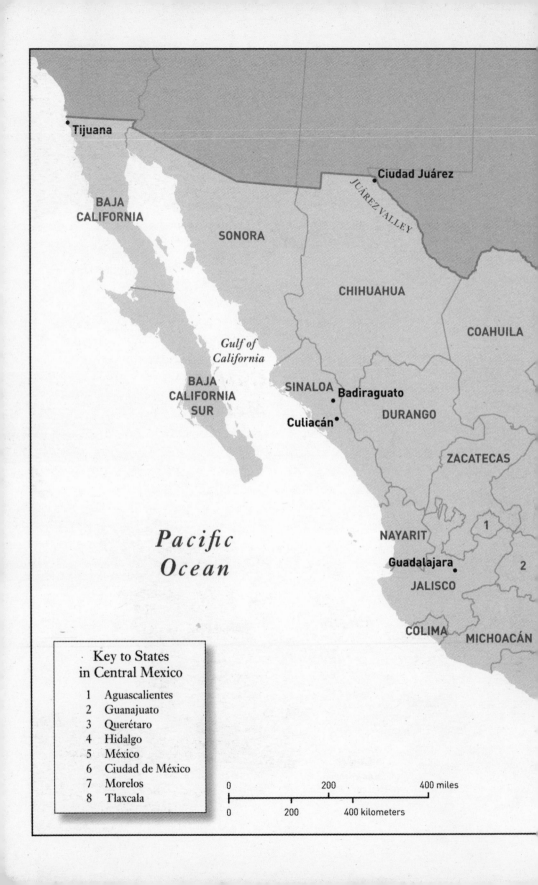

Tijuana

BAJA
CALIFORNIA

SONORA

Ciudad Juárez

JUÁREZ VALLEY

CHIHUAHUA

COAHUILA

*Gulf of
California*

BAJA
CALIFORNIA
SUR

SINALOA

Badiraguato

Culiacán

DURANGO

ZACATECAS

*Pacific
Ocean*

NAYARIT

Guadalajara

JALISCO

COLIMA

MICHOACÁN

1

2

Key to States
in Central Mexico

1   Aguascalientes
2   Guanajuato
3   Querétaro
4   Hidalgo
5   México
6   Ciudad de México
7   Morelos
8   Tlaxcala

0		200		400 miles

0	200	400 kilometers

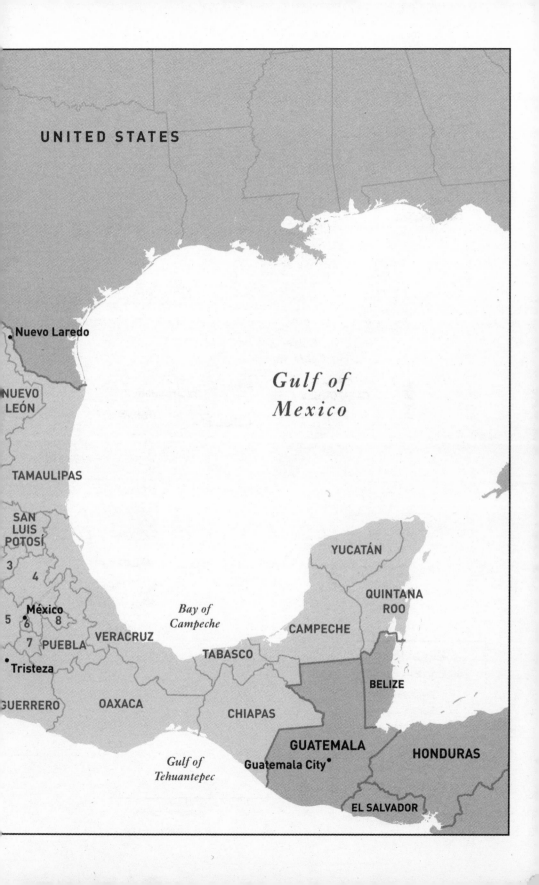

THE BORDER

THE BORDER

Prologue

Keller sees the child and the glint of the scope in the same moment.

The little boy, holding his mother's hand, gazes at the names etched into the black stone, and Keller wonders if he's looking for someone—a grandfather, maybe, or an uncle—or if his mother just brought her son to the Vietnam Veterans Memorial as the end of a walk down the National Mall.

The Wall sits low in the park, hidden like a guilty secret, a private shame. Here and there, mourners have left flowers, or cigarettes, even small bottles of booze. Vietnam was a long time ago, another lifetime, and he's fought his own long war since then.

No battles are inscribed on the Vietnam Wall. No Khe Sanhs or Quảng Trịs or Hamburger Hills. Maybe because we won every battle but lost the war, Keller thinks. All these deaths for a futile war. On previous trips, he'd seen men lean against the Wall and sob like children.

The sense of loss heartbreaking and overwhelming.

There are maybe forty people here today. Some of them look like they might be vets, others families; most are probably tourists. Two older men in VFW uniforms and caps are there to help people locate their loved ones' names.

Now Keller is at war again—against his own DEA, the US Senate, the Mexican drug cartels, even the president of the United States.

And they're the same thing, the same entity.

Every border Keller once thought existed has been crossed.

Some of them want to silence him, put him in prison, destroy him; a few, he suspects, want to kill him.

Keller knows that he's become a polarizing figure, embodying the rift that threatens to widen and tear the country in two. He's triggered a scandal, an investigation that's spread from the poppy fields of Mexico to Wall Street to the White House itself.

It's a warm spring day, a little breezy, and cherry blossoms float in the air. Sensing his emotion, Marisol takes his hand.

Now Keller sees the boy and then—to the right, back toward the Washington Monument—the odd, random glint of light. Lunging for the mother and the child, Keller shoves them to the ground.

Then he turns to shield Mari.

The bullet spins Keller like a top.

Creases his skull and whips his neck around.

Blood pours into his eyes and he literally sees red as he reaches out and pulls Marisol down.

Her cane clatters on the walkway.

Keller covers her body with his.

More bullets smack into the Wall above him.

He hears shouts and screams. Someone yells, "Active shooter!"

Peering up, Keller looks for the origin of the shots and sees that they're coming from the southeast, from about ten o'clock—from behind a small building he remembers is a restroom. He feels for the Sig Sauer at his hip but then remembers that he's unarmed.

The shooter flips to automatic.

Bullets spray the stone above Keller, chipping away names. People lie flat or crouch against the Wall. A few near the lower edges scramble over and run toward Constitution Avenue. Others just stand, bewildered.

Keller yells, *"Down! Shooter! Down!"*

But he sees that's not going to help and that the memorial is now a death trap. The Wall forms a wide V and there are only two ways out along a narrow path. A middle-aged couple run to the east exit, toward the shooter, and are hit right away, dropping like characters in some hideous video game.

"Mari," Keller says, "we have to move. Do you understand?"

"Yes."

"Be ready."

He waits until there's a pause in the fire—the shooter changing clips—then gets up, grabs Mari and hefts her over his shoulder. He carries her along the Wall to the west exit, where the Wall slopes down to waist level, tosses her up and over and sets her down behind a tree.

"Stay down!" he yells. "Stay there!"

"Where are you going?!"

The shooting starts again.

Jumping back over the Wall, Keller starts to herd people toward the southwest exit. He puts one hand on the back of a woman's neck, pushes her head down and moves her along, yelling, *"This* way! *This* way!" But then he hears the sharp hiss of a bullet and the solid *thunk* as it hits her. She staggers and drops to her knees, clutching at her arm as blood pours through her fingers.

Keller tries to lift her.

A round whizzes past his face.

A young man runs up to him and reaches for the woman. "I'm a paramedic!" Keller hands her across, turns back and keeps shoving people ahead of him, away from the gunfire. He sees the boy again, still clutching his mother's hand, his eyes wide with fear as his mother pushes him ahead of her, trying to screen him with her body.

Keller wraps an arm around her shoulder and bends her down as he keeps her moving. He says, "I've got you. I've got you. Keep walking." He sees her to safety at the far end of the Wall and then goes back again.

Another pause in the firing as the shooter changes clips again.

Christ, Keller thinks, how many can he have?

At least one more, because the firing starts again.

People stumble and fall.

Sirens shriek and howl; helicopter rotors throb in deep, vibrating bass.

Keller grabs a man to pull him forward but a bullet hits the man high in the back and he falls at Keller's feet.

Most people have made it out the west exit, others lie sprawled along the walkway, and still others lie on the grass where they tried to run the wrong way.

A dropped water bottle gurgles out on the walkway.

A cell phone, its glass cracked, rings on the ground next to a souvenir— a small, cheap bust of Lincoln—its face splattered with blood.

Keller looks east and sees a National Park Service policeman, his pistol drawn, charge toward the restroom building and then go down as bullets stitch across his chest.

Dropping to the ground, Keller snake-crawls toward the cop and feels for a pulse in his neck. The man is dead. Keller flattens behind the body as rounds smack into it. He looks up and thinks he spots the shooter, crouched behind the restroom building as he loads another clip.

Art Keller has spent most of his life fighting a war on the other side of the border, and now he's home.

The war has come with him.

Keller takes the policeman's sidearm—a 9 mm Glock—and moves through the trees toward the shooter.

BOOK ONE

Memorial

Only the dead have seen the end of war.

—Plato

1

Monsters and Ghosts

Monsters are real, and ghosts are real, too. They live inside us, and sometimes, they win.

—Stephen King

November 1, 2012

Art Keller walks out of the Guatemalan jungle like a refugee.

He left a scene of slaughter behind him. In the little village of Dos Erres, bodies lie in heaps, some half burned in the smoldering remnants of the bonfire into which they'd been tossed, others in the village clearing where they'd been gunned down.

Most of the dead are *narcos*, gunmen from rival cartels that came here allegedly to make peace. They had negotiated a treaty, but at the debauched party to celebrate their reconciliation, the Zetas pulled out guns, knives and machetes and set to butchering the Sinaloans.

Keller had literally fallen onto the scene—the helicopter he'd been in was hit by a rocket and spun to a hard landing in the middle of the firefight. He was hardly an innocent, having planned with the Sinaloa boss, Adán Barrera, to come in with a team of mercenaries and eliminate the Zetas.

Barrera had set up his enemies.

The problem was, they set him up first.

But the two main targets of Keller's mission, the Zeta leaders, are dead—one decapitated, the other turned into a flaming torch. Then, as they'd agreed in their uneasy, evil truce, Keller had gone off into the jungle to find Barrera and bring him out.

It seemed to Keller that he'd spent his whole adult life going after Adán Barrera.

After twenty years of trying, he'd finally put Barrera in a US prison, only to see him transferred back to a Mexican maximum-security facility from which he promptly "escaped" and then made himself more powerful than ever, the godfather of the Sinaloa cartel.

So Keller went back down to Mexico to go after Barrera again, only to become, after eight years, his ally, joining with him to bring down the Zetas.

The greater of two evils.

Which they did.

But Barrera disappeared.

So now Keller walks.

A handful of pesos to the border guard gets him into Mexico and then he hikes the ten miles to the Campeche village from which the raid had been staged.

More like he staggers.

The adrenaline from the gunfight that started before dawn has dropped, and now he feels the sun and the close heat of the rain forest. His legs ache, his eyes hurt, the stench of flame, smoke and death sticks in his nose.

The smell of burning flesh never leaves you.

Orduña waits for him at the little airstrip hacked out of the forest. The commander of FES sits inside the bay of a Black Hawk helicopter. Keller and Admiral Orduña had formed an "anything you need, anytime" relationship during their war against the Zetas. Keller provided him with top-level American intelligence and often accompanied his elite special-forces marines on operations inside Mexico.

This one had been different—the chance to decapitate the Zeta leadership in a single stroke came in Guatemala, where the Mexican marines couldn't go. But Orduña provided Keller's team with a staging base and logistical support, flew the team into Campeche, and now waits to see if his friend Art Keller is still alive.

Orduña smiles broadly when he sees Keller walk out of the tree line, then reaches into a cooler and hands Keller a cold Modelo.

"The rest of the team?" Keller asks.

"We flew them out already," Orduña says. "They should be in El Paso by now."

"Casualties?"

"One KIA," Orduña says. "Four wounded. I wasn't so sure about you. If you didn't come in by nightfall, *a la mierda todo*, we were going over to get you."

"I was looking for Barrera," Keller says, sluicing down the beer.

"And?"

"I didn't find him," Keller says.

"What about Ochoa?"

Orduña hates the Zeta leader almost as much as Keller hates Adán Barrera. The war on drugs tends to get very personal. It had gotten personal for Orduña when one of his officers was killed on a raid against the Zetas, and they came in and murdered the young officer's mother, aunt, sister and brother the night of his funeral. He had formed the Matazetas—"Zeta Killers"—the morning after that. And kill Zetas they did, every chance they got. If they took prisoners, it was only to get information, and then they executed them.

Keller had different reasons to hate the Zetas.

Different, but sufficient.

"Ochoa's dead," Keller says.

"Confirmed?"

"I saw it," Keller says. He'd watched Eddie Ruiz pour a can of paraffin all over the wounded Zeta boss and then toss a match on him. Ochoa died screaming. "Forty, too."

Forty was Ochoa's number-two man. A sadist like his boss.

"You saw his body?" Orduña asks.

"I saw his *head*," Keller says. "It wasn't attached to his body. That good enough for you?"

"It'll do," Orduña says, smiling.

Actually, Keller didn't see Forty's head. What he saw was Forty's *face*, which someone had peeled off and sewn to a soccer ball.

"Has Ruiz shown up?" Keller asks.

"Not yet," Orduña says.

"He was alive the last time I saw him," Keller says.

Turning Ochoa into a highway flare. Then standing on some old Mayan stone courtyard watching a kid kick a very bizarre soccer ball around.

"Maybe he just took off," Orduña says.

"Maybe."

"We should get in touch with your people. They've been calling about every fifteen minutes." Orduña punches some numbers into a burn phone and then says, "Taylor? Guess who I have here."

Keller takes the phone and hears Tim Taylor, the DEA chief of the Southwest District, say, *"Jesus Christ, we thought you were dead."*

"Sorry to disappoint you."

They're waiting for him at the Adobe Inn in Clint, Texas, on a remote highway a few miles east of El Paso.

The room is your standard motel "efficiency," a large living room with a kitchen area—microwave, coffee maker, small refrigerator—a sofa with a coffee table, a couple of chairs and a television set. A bad painting of a sunset behind a cactus. A door at the left, open now, leads into a bedroom and bathroom. It's a good, nondescript place to hold their debrief.

The television is on low, tuned to CNN.

Tim Taylor sits on the sofa, looking at a laptop computer set on the coffee table. A satphone stands upright by the computer.

John Downey, the military commander of the raid, stands by the microwave, waiting for something to heat. He's out of cammies, Keller sees, showered and shaved, wearing a plum polo shirt over jeans and tennis shoes.

Another man, a CIA guy Keller knows as Rollins, sits in one of the chairs and watches the television.

Downey looks up when Keller comes in. "Where the fuck have you been, Art? We've done satellite runs, helicopter searches . . ."

Keller was supposed to have brought Barrera out safely. That was the deal. Keller asks, "How are your people?"

"*Phwoom*." Downey makes a gesture with his hands, like a flushed covey of quail. Keller knows that within twelve hours the spec-ops will be scattered all over the country, if not the world, with cover stories about where they've been. "The only unaccounted for is Ruiz. I was hoping he came out with you."

"I saw him after the firefight," Keller says. "He was walking out."

"So Ruiz is in the wind?" Rollins asks.

"You don't have to worry about him," Keller says.

"He's your responsibility," Rollins says.

"Fuck Ruiz," Taylor says. "What happened to Barrera?"

Keller says, "You tell me."

"We haven't had any word from him."

"Then I guess he didn't make it," Keller says.

"You refused to get on the ex-fil chopper," Rollins says.

"The chopper had to take off," Keller says, "and I still had to find Barrera."

"But you didn't find him," Rollins says.

"Special ops aren't room service," Keller answers. "You can't always get exactly what you order. Things happen."

Right from the jump.

They'd helicoptered onto a firefight that was already in progress as the Zetas were butchering the Sinaloans. Then a surface-to-air rocket hit the lead chopper that Keller was in, killing one man and wounding another. So instead of going down the ropes, they made a hard landing onto a hot zone. Then they had to shuttle the team out on the surviving chopper.

We were lucky to have gotten out at all, Keller thinks, never mind completing the main mission of executing the leading Zetas. If we didn't manage to bring Barrera out with us, well . . .

"The primary mission, as I understood it," Keller says, "was to take out the Zetas' command and control. If Barrera was a collateral casualty . . ."

"All the better?" Rollins asks.

They all know Keller's hatred of Barrera.

That the drug lord had tortured and murdered Keller's partner.

That he'd never forget, never mind forgive.

"I won't shed any crocodile tears for Adán Barrera," Keller says. He knows the situation in Mexico better than any of the people in that room. Like it or not, the Sinaloa cartel is key to stability in Mexico. If the cartel falls apart because Barrera is gone, the tenuous peace could fall apart with it. Barrera knew that, too—this *après moi, le déluge* attitude allowed him to drive a tough bargain with both the Mexican and American governments to lay off him and attack his enemies.

The microwave bings and Downey takes out the tray. "Stouffer's lasagna. A classic."

"We don't even know Barrera's dead," Keller says. "Have they found a body?"

"No," Taylor says.

"D-2 is on the scene now," Rollins says, referring to the Guatemalan paramilitary intelligence agency. "They haven't found Barrera. Or either of the primary targets, for that matter."

"I can personally confirm that both targets were terminated," Keller says. "Ochoa is basically charcoal, and Forty . . . well, you don't want to know about Forty. I'm telling you, they're both past tense."

"We'd better hope Barrera isn't," Rollins says. "If the Sinaloa cartel is unstable, Mexico is unstable."

"The law of unintended consequences," Keller says.

Rollins says, "We had a very specific agreement with the Mexican government to preserve Adán Barrera's life. We guaranteed his safety. This isn't Vietnam, Keller. It isn't Phoenix. If we find out that you violated that agreement, we'll—"

Keller stands up. "You'll do exactly shit. Because that was an unauthorized, illegal operation that 'never happened.' What are you going to do? Take me to trial? Put me on the witness stand? Let me testify under oath that we had a deal with the world's biggest drug dealer? That I went on a US-sponsored raid to eliminate his rivals? Let me tell you something that those of us who do the actual work know—never draw your weapon unless you're prepared to pull the trigger. Are you prepared to pull the trigger?"

There's no answer.

"Yeah, that's what I thought," Keller says. "For the record, I *wanted* to kill Barrera, I wish I *had* killed him, but I didn't."

He gets up and walks out.

Taylor follows him. "Where are you going?"

"None of your business, Tim."

"To Mexico?" Taylor asks.

"I'm not with DEA anymore," Keller says. "I don't work for you. You can't tell me where to go or not to go."

"They'll kill you, Art," Taylor says. "If the Zetas don't, the Sinaloans will."

Probably, Keller thinks.

But if I don't go, they'll kill me anyway.

He drives into El Paso, to the apartment he keeps near EPIC. Strips out of his filthy, sweaty clothes and takes a long, hot shower. Then he goes into the bedroom and lies down, suddenly aware that he hasn't slept for coming on two days and that he's exhausted, depleted.

But he's too tired to sleep.

He gets up, throws on a white button-down shirt over jeans and takes the little Sig 380 compact out of the gun safe in the bedroom closet. Clips the holster onto his belt, puts on a navy-blue windbreaker as he's headed out the door.

For Sinaloa.

Keller first came to Culiacán as a rookie DEA agent back in the '70s, when the city was the epicenter of the Mexican heroin trade.

And now it is again, he thinks as he walks through the terminal toward the taxi stand. Everything has come full circle.

Adán Barrera was just a punk kid then, trying to make it as a boxing manager.

His uncle, though, a Sinaloa cop, was the second-biggest opium grower in Sinaloa, striving to become the biggest. That was back when we were burning and poisoning the poppy fields, Keller thinks, driving peasants from their homes, and Adán got caught up in one of those sweeps. The *federales* were going to throw him out of an airplane, but I intervened and saved his life.

The first, Keller thinks, of many mistakes.

The world would have been a much better place if I had let them go Rocky the Flying Squirrel on little Adán, instead of letting him live to become the world's greatest drug lord.

But we were actually friends back then.

Friends and allies.

Hard to believe.

Harder to accept.

He gets into a cab and tells the driver to go into *centro*—downtown.

"Where exactly?" the driver asks, looking at his face in the rearview mirror.

"Doesn't matter," Keller says. "That will give you time to call your bosses and tell them a strange *yanqui* is in town."

The cabdrivers in every Mexican city where there's a strong narco presence are *halcones*—"falcons"—spies for the cartels. Their job is to watch the airports, train stations and streets and let the powers that be know who's coming in and out of their town.

"I'll save you some effort," Keller says. "Tell whoever you're going to call that you have Art Keller in your cab. They'll tell you where to take me."

The driver gets on his phone.

It takes several calls and the driver's voice gets edgier with each one. Keller knows the drill—the driver will call his local cell leader, who will call *his*, who will kick it up the chain, and the name Art Keller will take it to the very top.

Keller looks out the window as the cab goes into town on Route 280 and sees the memorials left on the roadside to fallen narcos—mostly young men—killed in the drug wars. Some are simply bunches of flowers and a beer bottle set beside cheaply made wooden crosses, others are full-color banners with photographs of the deceased stretched between two poles, while others are elaborate marble stiles.

But there will be more memorials soon, he thinks, when news of the "Dos Erres Massacre" reaches the city. A hundred Sinaloan *sicarios* went down to Guatemala with Barrera; few, if any, are coming back.

And there will be memorials in the Zeta heartlands of Chihuahua and Tamaulipas in the country's northeast, when *their* soldiers don't return.

The Zetas are a spent force now, Keller knows. Once a genuine threat to take over the country, the paramilitary cartel made up of former special forces troops is now leaderless and hamstrung, its best people killed by Orduña or lying dead in Guatemala.

There is no one now to challenge Sinaloa.

"They say to take you to Rotarismo," the driver says, sounding nervous.

Rotarismo is a neighborhood at the far northern edge of the city, hard by the empty hills and farmlands.

An easy place to dump a corpse.

"To an auto body shop," the driver says.

All the better, Keller thinks.

The tools are already there.

To chop up a car or a body.

You can always spot a conclave of high-ranking narcos by the number of SUVs parked out front, and this has to be a major meeting, Keller thinks as they roll up, because a dozen Suburbans and Expeditions are lined up in front of the garage with guns poking out like porcupine quills.

The guns train on the cab and Keller thinks that the driver might piss himself.

"*Tranquilo*," Keller says.

A few uniformed *sicarios* patrol on foot outside. It's become a thing in every branch of all the cartels, Keller knows—they each have their own armed security forces with distinctive uniforms.

These wear Armani caps and Hermès vests.

Which Keller thinks is a little fey.

A man hustles out of the garage toward the cab, opens the rear passenger door and tells Keller to get the fuck out.

Keller knows the man. Terry Blanco is a high-ranking Sinaloa state cop. He's been on the cartel's payroll since he was a rookie and now there's some silver in his black hair.

Blanco says, "You don't know what's going on around here."

"It's why I came," Keller says.

"You know something?"

"Who's inside?"

"Núñez," Blanco says.

"Let's go."

"Keller, if you go in," Blanco says, "you might not come back out."

"Story of my life, Terry," Keller says.

Blanco walks him through the garage, past the work bays and the lifts, to a large empty area of concrete floor that seems more like a warehouse.

It's the same scene as the motel, Keller thinks.

Just different players.

Same action, though—people on phones, working laptops, trying to get information as to the whereabouts of Adán Barrera. The place is dark—no windows and thick walls—just what you want in a climate that is baking hot from the sun or chilled by the north wind. You don't want the weather or prying eyes penetrating this place, and if anyone dies in here, goes out screaming or crying or pleading, the walls keep that inside.

Keller follows Blanco to a door in the back.

It opens to a small room.

Blanco ushers Keller in and shuts the door behind them.

A man Keller recognizes sits behind a desk, on the phone. Distinguished-looking with salt-and-pepper hair, a neatly trimmed goatee, wearing a houndstooth jacket and a knit tie, looking distinctly uncomfortable in the greasy atmosphere of a garage back room.

Ricardo Núñez.

El Abogado—"The Lawyer."

A former state prosecutor, he had been the warden of Puente Grande prison, resigning his position just weeks before Barrera "escaped" back in 2004. Keller had questioned him and he pleaded total innocence, but he was disbarred and went on to become Barrera's right-hand man, making, reportedly, hundreds of millions trafficking cocaine.

He clicks off the phone and looks up at Blanco. "Give us a moment, Terry?"

Blanco walks out.

"What are you doing here?" Núñez asks.

"Saving you the trouble of tracking me down," Keller says. "You're apparently aware of Guatemala."

"Adán confided to me your arrangement," Núñez says. "What happened down there?"

Keller repeats what he told the boys in Texas.

"You were supposed to have brought El Señor out," Núñez says. "That was the arrangement."

"The Zetas got to him first," Keller says. "He was careless."

"You have no information about Adán's whereabouts," Núñez says.

"Only what I just told you."

"The family is sick with worry," Núñez says. "There's been no word at all. No . . . remains . . . found."

Keller hears a commotion outside—Blanco tells someone they can't go in—and then the door swings open and bangs against the wall.

Three men come in.

The first is young—late twenties or early thirties—in a black Saint Laurent leather jacket that has to go at least three grand, Rokker jeans, Air Jordans. His curly black hair has a five-hundred-dollar cut and his jawline sports fashionable stubble.

He's worked up.

Angry, tense.

"Where's my father?" he demands of Núñez. "What's happened to my father?"

"We don't know yet," Núñez says.

"The fuck you mean, you don't know?!"

"Easy, Iván," one of the others says. Another young guy, expensively dressed but sloppy, shaggy black hair jammed under a ball cap, unshaven. He looks a little drunk or a little high, or both. Keller doesn't recognize him, but the other kid must be Iván Esparza.

The Sinaloa cartel used to have three wings—Barrera's, Diego Tapia's, and Ignacio Esparza's. Barrera was the boss, the first among equals, but "Nacho" Esparza was a respected partner and, not coincidentally, Barrera's father-in-law. He'd married his young daughter Eva off to the drug lord to cement the alliance.

So this kid, Keller thinks, has to be Esparza's son and Adán's brother-in-law. The intelligence profiles say that Iván Esparza now runs the crucial Baja plaza for the cartel, with its vital border crossings in Tijuana and Tecate.

"Is he dead?!" Iván yells. "Is my father dead?!"

"We know he was in Guatemala with Adán," Núñez says.

"Fuck!" Iván slams his hand on the desk in front of Núñez. He looks around for someone to be angry at and sees Keller. "Who the fuck are you?"

Keller doesn't answer.

"I asked you a question," Iván says.

"I heard you."

"*Pinche gringo* fuck—"

He starts for Keller but the third man steps between them.

Keller knows him from intelligence photos. Tito Ascensión had been Nacho Esparza's head of security, a man even the Zetas feared—for good reason; he had slaughtered scores of them. As a reward, he was given his own organization in Jalisco. His massive frame, big sloping head, guard-dog disposition and penchant for brutality had given him the nickname El Mastín—"The Mastiff."

He grabs Iván by the upper arms and holds him in place.

Núñez looks at the other young man. "Where have you been, Ric? I've been calling everywhere."

Ric shrugs.

Like, *What difference does it make where I was?*

Núñez frowns.

Father and son, Keller thinks.

"I asked who this guy is," Iván says. He rips his arms out of Ascensión's grip but doesn't go for Keller again.

"Adán had certain . . . arrangements," Núñez says. "This man was in Guatemala."

"Did you see my father?" Iván asks.

I saw what looked like your old man, Keller thinks. What was left of the bottom half of him was lying in the ashes of a smoldering bonfire. "I think you'd better get your head around the probability that your father's not coming back."

The expression on Ascensión's face is exactly that of a dog that's just learned it has lost its beloved master.

Confusion.

Grief.

Rage.

"How do you know that?" Iván asks Keller.

Ric wraps his arms around Iván. "I'm sorry, 'mano."

"Someone's going to pay for this," Iván says.

"I have Elena on the phone," Núñez says. He puts it on speaker. "Elena, have you heard anything more?"

It has to be Elena Sánchez, Keller thinks. Adán's sister, retired from the family trade since she handed Baja over to the Esparzas.

"Nothing, Ricardo. Have you?"

"We have confirmation that Ignacio is gone."

"Has anyone told Eva? Has anyone been to see her?"

"Not yet," Núñez says. "We've been waiting until we know something definitive."

"Someone should be with her," Elena says. "She's lost her father and maybe her husband. The poor boys . . ."

Eva has twin sons by Adán.

"I'll go," Iván says. "I'll take her to my mother's."

"She'll be grieving, too," Núñez says.

"I'm flying down."

"Do you need transportation from the airport?" Núñez asks.

"We still have people there, Ricardo."

They've forgotten I'm even here, Keller thinks.

Oddly enough, it's the young stoned one—Ric?—who remembers. "Uhhh, what do we do with him?"

More commotion outside.

Shouts.

Punches and slaps.

Grunts of pain, screams.

The interrogations have started, Keller thinks. The cartel is rounding people up—suspected Zetas, possible traitors, Guatemalan associates, anyone—to try to get information.

By any means necessary.

Keller hears chains being pulled across the concrete floor.

The hiss of an acetylene torch being lit.

Núñez looks up at Keller and raises his eyebrows.

"I came to tell you that I'm done," Keller says. "It's over for me now. I'm going to stay in Mexico, but I'm out of all this. You won't hear from me and I don't expect to hear from you."

"You walk away and my father doesn't?" Iván asks. He pulls a Glock 9 from his jacket and points it at Keller's face. "I don't think so."

It's a young man's mistake.

Putting the gun too close to the guy you want to kill.

Keller leans away from the barrel at the same time that his hand shoots out, grabs the gun barrel, twists, and wrenches it out of Iván's hand. Then he smashes it three times into Iván's face and hears the cheekbone shatter before Iván slides to the floor like a robe dropped at Keller's feet.

Ascensión moves in but Keller has his forearm wrapped around Ric Núñez's throat and puts the gun to the side of his head. "No."

El Mastín freezes.

"The fuck did *I* do?" Ric asks.

"Here's how it's going to work," Keller says. "I'm going to walk out of here. I'm going to live my life, you're going to live yours. If anyone comes after me, I'll kill all of you. *¿Entienden?*"

"We understand," Núñez says.

Holding Ric as a shield, Keller backs out of the room.

He sees men chained to the walls, pools of blood, smells sweat and urine. No one moves, they all watch him go outside.

There's nothing he can do for them.

Not a damn thing.

Twenty rifles point at him but no one is going to take a chance on hitting their boss's son.

Reaching behind him, Keller opens the passenger door of the cab, then pushes Ric to the ground.

Sticks the gun into the back of the driver's seat. "*Ándale.*"

On the drive back to the airport, Keller sees the first memorial to Adán on the side of the highway.

A banner spray-painted—

ADÁN VIVE.

Adán lives.

Juárez is a city of ghosts.

What Art Keller thinks as he drives through the town.

More than ten thousand Juarenses were killed in Adán Barrera's conquest of the city, which he ripped from the old Juárez cartel to give him another gateway into the United States. Four bridges—the Stanton Street Bridge, the Ysleta International Bridge, the Paso del Norte and the Bridge of the Americas, the so-called Bridge of Dreams.

Ten thousand lives so Barrera could have those bridges.

During the five years of the war between the Sinaloa and Juárez cartels, more than three hundred thousand Juarenses fled the city, leaving the population at about a million and a half.

A third of whom, Keller has read, suffer from post-traumatic stress disorder.

He's surprised there aren't more. At the height of the fighting, the citizens of Juárez got used to stepping over dead bodies on the sidewalk. The cartels would radio ambulance drivers to tell them which wounded they could pick up, and which they had to let die. Hospitals were attacked, as well as homeless shelters and drug treatment houses.

The city center was virtually abandoned. Once vibrant with its famous nightlife, half the city's restaurants and a third of its bars shut their doors. Stores closed. The mayor, the town council and most of the city police moved across those bridges to El Paso.

But in the past couple of years the city had started to come back. Businesses were reopening, refugees were coming home, and the murder rate was down.

Keller knows that the violence receded for one reason.

Sinaloa won the war.

And established the Pax Sinaloa.

Well, fuck you, Adán, Keller thinks as he drives around the Plaza del Periodista, with its statue of a newsboy hawking papers.

To hell with your bridges.

And to hell with your peace.

Keller can never drive by the plaza without seeing the scattered remains of his friend Pablo.

Pablo Mora was a journalist who had defied the Zetas by persisting to write a blog that exposed narco crimes. They'd kidnapped him, tortured him to death, dismembered him and arranged the pieces of his body around the statue of the newsboy.

So many journalists murdered, Keller thinks, as the cartels realized that they needed to control not only the action, but the narrative as well.

Most of the media simply stopped covering narco news.

Which is why Pablo started his suicidal blog.

And then there was Jimena Abarca, the baker from a little town in the Juárez Valley, who had stood up against the narcos, the *federales*, the army, and the entire government. Went on a hunger strike and forced them to release innocent prisoners. One of Barrera's thugs shot her nine times in the chest and face in the parking lot of her favorite Juárez restaurant.

Or Giorgio, the photojournalist beheaded for the sin of taking images of dead narcos.

Erika Valles, slaughtered and cut up like a chicken. A nineteen-year-old girl brave enough to be the only cop in a little town where narcos had killed her four predecessors.

And then, of course, Marisol.

Dr. Marisol Cisneros is the mayor of Valverde, Jimena Abarca's town in the Juárez Valley.

She took the office after the three previous mayors had been murdered. Stayed in the job when the Zetas threatened to kill her, then again after they gunned her down in her car, putting bullets in her stomach, chest and legs, breaking her femur and two ribs, cracking a vertebra.

After weeks in the hospital and months of recuperation, Marisol came back and held a press conference. Beautifully dressed, impeccably coiffed and made up, she showed her scars—and her colostomy bag—to the media, looked straight into the camera and told the narcos, *I'm going back to work and you will not stop me.*

Keller has no way to account for that kind of courage.

So it makes him furious when American politicians paint all Mexicans with the broad brush of corruption. He thinks about people like Pablo Mora, Jimena Abarca, Erika Valles and Marisol Cisneros.

Not all ghosts are dead—some are shades of what might have been.

You're a ghost yourself, he tells himself.

A ghost *of* yourself, existing in a half life.

You've come back to Mexico because you're more at home with the dead than the living.

The highway, Carretera Federal 2, parallels the border east of Juárez. Keller can see Texas, just a few miles away, through the driver's-side window.

It might as well be a world away.

The Mexican federal government sent the army here to restore the peace, and, if anything, the army was as brutal as the cartels. Killings actually rose during the military occupation. There used to be army checkpoints every few miles on this road, which the locals dreaded as the locations of shakedowns, extortion and arbitrary arrests that too often ended in beatings, torture and internment in a hastily built prison camp that used to exist farther up the road.

If you didn't get killed in a cartel cross fire, you could be murdered by the soldiers.

Or just disappear.

It was on this same road that the Zetas gunned Marisol down, left her for dead at the side of the road, bleeding out. One of the reasons Keller had made his temporary alliance with Barrera was because the "Lord of the Skies" promised to keep her safe.

Keller glances into the rearview mirror just to make sure, but he knows there's no need for them to follow him. They already know where he's going and will know when he gets there. The cartel had *halcones* everywhere. Cops, taxi drivers, kids on the corners, old women in their windows, clerks behind their counters. Everyone has a cell phone these days, and everyone will pick it up to curry favor with Sinaloa.

If they want to kill me, they'll kill me.

Or at least they'll try.

He pulls into the little town of Valverde, twenty or so blocks arranged in a rectangle on the desert flat. The houses—the ones that survived, anyway—are mostly cinder block with a few adobes. Some of them, Keller notices, have been repainted in bright blues, reds and yellows.

But the signs of war are still there, he also notices as he drives down the broad central street. The Abarca bakery, once the social center of the town, is still an empty pile of char, the pockmarks of bullets still scar walls, and some of the buildings are still boarded up and abandoned. Thousands of people had fled the Juárez Valley during the war, some afraid, others forced by Barrera's threats. People would wake up in the morning to find signs draped across the street from phone pole to phone pole, with lists of names, residents who were told to leave that day or be killed.

Barrera depopulated some of the towns to replace their people with his own loyalists from Sinaloa.

He literally colonized the valley.

But now the army checkpoints are gone.

The sandbagged bunker that was on the main street is gone, and a few old people sit in the gazebo in the town square enjoying the afternoon warmth, something they never would have dared to do just a couple of years ago.

And Keller notices the little *tienda* has reopened, so people have a place again to buy necessities.

Some people have come back to Valverde, many stay away, but the town looks like it's making a modest recovery. Keller drives past the little clinic and pulls into the parking lot in front of town hall, a two-story cinder-block rectangle that houses what's left of the town government.

He parks the car and walks up the exterior staircase to the mayor's office.

Marisol sits behind her desk, her cane hooked over the arm of her chair. Poring over papers, she doesn't notice Keller.

Her beauty stops his heart.

She's wearing a simple blue dress and her black hair is pulled back into a severe chignon, setting off her high cheekbones and dark eyes.

He knows that he'll never stop loving her.

Marisol looks up, sees him, and smiles. "Arturo."

She grabs her cane and starts to get up. Getting in and out of chairs is still hard for her and Keller notices the slight wince as she pushes herself up. The cut of her dress hides the colostomy bag, an enduring gift from the round that clipped her small intestine.

It was the Zetas who did that to her.

Keller went to Guatemala to kill the men who ordered it, Ochoa and Forty. Even though she begged him not to seek revenge. Now she wraps her arms around him and holds him close. "I was afraid you wouldn't come back."

"You said you weren't sure if you wanted me to."

"That was a terrible thing for me to say." She lays her head against his chest. "I'm so sorry."

"No need."

She's quiet for a few seconds, and then asks, "Is it over?"

"For me it is."

He feels her sigh. "What are you going to do now?"

"I don't know."

It's true. He hadn't expected to come back from Dos Erres alive, and now that he has, he doesn't know what to do with his life. He knows he isn't going back to Tidewater, the security firm that conducted the Guatemala raid, and he sure as shit isn't going back to DEA. But as for what he *is* going to do, he doesn't have a clue.

Except here he is in Valverde.

Drawn to her.

Keller knows that they can never have what they once had. There's too much shared sorrow between them, too many loved ones killed, each death like a stone in a wall built so high that it can't be breached.

"I have afternoon clinic hours," Marisol says.

She's the town's mayor and its only doctor. There are thirty thousand people in the Juárez Valley and she's the one full-time physician.

So she started a free clinic in town.

"I'll walk you," Keller says.

Marisol hangs the cane on her wrist and grabs the handrail as she makes her way down the exterior staircase, and Keller is half-terrified she's going to fall. He walks behind with one hand ready to catch her.

"I do this several times a day, Arturo," she says.

"I know."

Poor Arturo, she thinks. There is such a sadness about him.

Marisol knows the price he's already paid for his long war—his partner murdered, his family estranged, the things he has seen and done that wake him up at night, or worse, trap him in nightmares.

She's paid a price herself.

The external wounds are obvious, the chronic pain that accompanies them somewhat less so, but still all too real. She's lost her youth and her beauty—Arturo likes to think that she's still beautiful, but face it, she thinks, I'm a woman with a cane in my hand and a bag of shit strapped to my back.

That isn't the worst of it. Marisol is insightful enough to know that she has a bad case of survivor's guilt—why is she alive when so many others aren't?—and she knows that Arturo suffers from the same malady.

"How's Ana doing?" Keller asks.

"I'm worried about her," Marisol says. "She's depressed, drinking too much. She's at the clinic, you'll see her."

"We're a mess, aren't we? All of us."

"Pretty much," Marisol says.

All veterans of an unspeakable war, she thinks. From which there has been—in the pop-speak of the day—no "closure."

No victory or defeat.

No reconciliation or war crimes tribunals. Certainly no parades, no medals, no speeches, no thanks from a grateful nation.

Just a slow, sodden lessening of the violence.

And a soul-crushing sense of loss, an emptiness that can't be filled no matter how busy she keeps herself at the office or the clinic.

They walk past the town square.

The old people in the gazebo watch them.

"This will start the rumor mill grinding," Marisol says. "By five o'clock I'll be pregnant with your baby. By seven we'll be married. By nine you'll have left me for a younger woman, probably a *güera*."

The people of Valverde know Keller well. He lived in their town after Marisol was shot, nursing her back to health. He went to their church, to their holidays, to their funerals. If not exactly one of their own, he isn't a stranger, either, not just another *yanqui*.

They love him because they love her.

Keller feels more than sees the car cruise behind them on the street, slowly reaches for the gun under his windbreaker and keeps his hand on the grip. The car, an old Lincoln, crawls past them. A driver and a passenger don't bother to disguise their interest in Keller.

Keller nods to them.

The *halcón* nods back as the car drives on.

Sinaloa is keeping an eye on him.

Marisol doesn't notice. Instead, she asks, "Did you kill him, Arturo?"

"Who?"

"Barrera."

"There's an old, bad joke," Keller says, "about this woman on her wedding night. Her husband inquires if she's a virgin and she answers, 'Why does everyone keep *asking* me that?'"

"Why *does* everyone keep asking you that?" Marisol knows an evasion when she hears one. They had made a promise that they would never lie to each other, and Arturo is a man of his word. By his not answering directly, she suspects what the truth is. "Just tell me the truth. Did you kill him?"

"No," Keller says. "No, Mari, I didn't."

Keller has been living in Ana's house in Juárez only a couple of days when Eddie Ruiz shows up. He made the veteran reporter an offer and she took it—the house had too many memories for her.

"Crazy Eddie" was on the Guatemala raid. Keller had watched as the young narco—a *pocho*, a Mexican American from El Paso—poured a can of paraffin over the wounded Zeta boss Heriberto Ochoa and then set him on fire.

When Eddie walks into Keller's house in Juárez, he isn't alone.

With him is Jesús Barajos—"Chuy"—a seventeen-year-old schizophrenic battered into psychosis by the horrors he endured, the horrors he witnessed, and the horrors he inflicted on others. A narco hit man at eleven years old, the kid never had a chance, and Keller found him in the Guatemalan jungle, calmly kicking a soccer ball onto which he had sewn the face of a man he had decapitated.

"Why did you bring him here?" Keller asks, looking at Chuy's blank stare. He'd almost shot the kid himself down in Guatemala. An execution for murdering Erika Valles.

And Ruiz brought him here? To me?

"I didn't know what else to do with him," Eddie says.

"Turn him in."

"They'll kill him," Eddie says. Chuy walks past them, curls up on the couch, and falls asleep. Small and scrawny, he has the feral look of an underfed coyote. "Anyway, I can't take him where I'm going."

"What are you going to do?" Keller asks.

"Cross the river and turn myself in," Eddie says. "Four years and I'm out."

It's the bargain Keller had arranged for him.

"How about you?" Eddie asks.

"I don't have a plan," Keller says. "Just live, I guess."

Except he has no idea how.

His war is over and he has no idea how to live.

Or what to do with Chuy Barajos.

Marisol vetoes his idea of turning the boy in to the Mexican authorities. "He wouldn't survive."

"Mari, he killed—"

"I know he did," she says. "He's sick, Arturo. He needs help. What kind of help will he get in the system?"

None, Keller knows, not really sure that he cares. He wants his war to be over, not to drag it around with him like a ball and chain in the person of a virtual catatonic who had slaughtered people he loved. "I'm not you. I can't forgive like you do."

"Your war won't end until you do."

"Then I guess it won't end."

But he doesn't turn Chuy in.

Mari finds a psychiatrist who will treat the kid gratis and arranges for his meds through her clinic, but the prognosis is "guarded." The best Chuy can hope for is a marginal existence, a shadow life with the worst of his memories at least muted if not erased.

Keller can't explain why he undertook to care for the kid.

Maybe it's penance.

Chuy stays around the house like another ghost in Keller's life, sleeping in the spare room, playing video games on the Xbox Keller bought at the Walmart in El Paso, or wolfing down whatever meals Keller fixes for them, most of which come out of cans labeled HORMEL. Keller monitors Chuy's cocktail of medications and makes sure that he takes them on schedule.

Keller escorts him to his psychiatric appointments and sits in the waiting room, leafing through Spanish editions of *National Geographic* and *Newsweek*. Then they take the bus home and Chuy settles in front of the television while Keller fixes dinner. They rarely speak. Sometimes Keller hears the screams coming from Chuy's room and goes in to wake him from his nightmare. Even though he's sometimes tempted to let the kid suffer, he never does.

Some nights Keller takes a beer and sits outside on the steps leading down to Ana's small backyard, remembering the parties there—the music, the poetry, the passionate political arguments, the laughter. That's where he first met Ana, and Pablo and Giorgio, and El Búho—"The Owl"—the dean of Mexican journalism who edited the newspaper that Ana and Pablo had worked for.

Other nights, when Marisol comes into the city to visit a patient she's placed in the Juárez Hospital, she and Keller go out to dinner or maybe go to El Paso for a movie. Or sometimes he drives out to Valverde, meets her after clinic hours, and they take a quiet sunset walk through town.

It never goes further than that, and he drives home each time.

Life settles into a rhythm that is dreamlike, surreal.

Rumors of Barrera's death or survival swirl through the city but Keller pays little attention. Every now and then a car cruises slowly past the house, and once Terry Blanco comes by to ask Keller if he's heard anything, knows anything.

Keller hasn't, he doesn't.

But otherwise, as promised, they leave him alone.

Until they don't.

Eddie Ruiz flushes the steel toilet bolted to the concrete wall. Then he sticks an empty toilet paper roll into the toilet drain and blows into it, sending the water lower into the trap. That done, he takes his foam mattress pad off his concrete bed slab, folds it over the toilet and presses on it as if he were giving it CPR. Then he takes the mattress pad off, stacks three toilet paper rolls into the john, puts his mouth against the top one and hollers, "El Señor!"

He waits a few seconds and then hears, "Eddie! *¿Qué pasa, m'ijo?*"

Eddie isn't Rafael Caro's son, but he's glad that the old drug lord calls him that, maybe even thinks of him as a son.

Caro's been in Florence virtually since it opened back in '94, one of the first guests of the supermax. It fucking amazes Eddie: since 1994 Rafael Caro has been alone in a seven-by-twelve-foot concrete box—concrete bed, concrete table, concrete stool, concrete desk—and he still has all his marbles.

Kurt Cobain goes room temp, Caro's in his cell. Bill Clinton gets his cigar smoked, Caro is in his cell. Fuckin' ragheads fly planes into buildings, we invade the wrong fuckin' country, a black dude gets elected president, Caro is sitting in that same seven-by-twelve.

Twenty-three hours a day, seven days a week.

Fuck, Eddie thinks, I was fourteen years old, a freshman in high school jerking off to *Penthouse Letters,* when they closed that door on Caro, and the guy is still here and he's still sane. Rudolfo Sánchez did just eighteen months and left his balls here. I'm just coming on my second year in the place and I'm about to lose my shit. Probably would have already, I didn't have Caro to talk to through the "toilet phone."

Caro is still sharp as a blade—Eddie can see why he was once a major player in the drug game. The only mistake Caro made—but it was a terminal one—was to back the wrong horse in a two-pony race: Güero Méndez against Adán Barrera.

Always a bad bet, Eddie thinks.

Caro got what a lot of Adán's enemies get—extradition to the US, which had major wood for him as they suspected he'd had a hand in the torture-murder of a DEA agent named Ernie Hidalgo. They couldn't prove it, though, so he got the max on drug-trafficking charges—twenty-five-to-life instead of the LWOP.

Life without possibility of parole.

But the feds were jacked enough to send him to Florence, where they put cats like the Unabomber, Timothy McVeigh before they did him, and a slew of terrorists. Osiel Contreras, the old boss of the Gulf cartel, is here, along with a few other major narcos.

And me, Eddie thinks.

Eddie freakin' Ruiz, the first and only American to head up a Mexican cartel, for what that's worth.

Actually, he knows exactly what it's worth.

Four years.

Which is kind of a problem, because some people, not a few of them inhabitants of this institution, wonder why it's *only* four years.

For a guy of Eddie's stature.

Crazy Eddie.

The former "Narco Polo," glossed for his choice of shirt. The guy who fought the Zetas to a standstill in Nuevo Laredo, who led Diego Tapia's *sicarios* first against the Zetas, then against Barrera. Who survived the marines' execution of Diego and then headed up his own outfit, a splinter of the old Tapia organization.

Some of these people wonder why Eddie would come back to the States—where he was already wanted on trafficking charges—why he would turn himself in, and why he would get only a double-deuce in a federal lockup.

The obvious speculation was that Eddie was a rat, that he flipped on his friends in exchange for a light bit. Eddie denied this emphatically to other inmates. "Name me one guy who has gone down since I got popped. *One.*"

He knew there was no answer to that because there hasn't been anyone.

"And if I was going to make myself a deal," Eddie pushed, "you think I'd deal myself into Florence? The worst supermax in the country?"

No answer to this, either.

"And a seven-million-dollar fine?" Eddie asked. "The fuck kind of rat deal is that?"

But the clincher was his friendship with Caro, because everyone knew that Rafael Caro—a guy who's taken a twenty-five-year hit without mumbling a word of complaint, never mind cooperation; would never deign to as much as look at a *soplón*, never mind be friends with one.

So if Eddie was good with Rafael Caro, he was good with everyone. Now he shouts back through the tube, "It's all good, Señor. You?"

"I'm fine, thank you. What's new?"

What's *new*? Eddie thinks.

Nothing.

Nothing is ever new in this place—every day is the same as the last. They wake you at six, shove something they call food through a metal slot. After "breakfast," Eddie cleans his cell. Religiously, meticulously. The purpose of solitary confinement is to turn you into an animal, and Eddie isn't gonna cooperate with that by living in filth. So he keeps himself, his cell, and his clothes clean and tight. After he wipes off every surface in his cell, he washes his clothes in the metal sink, wrings them out and hangs them up to dry.

Isn't hard to keep track of his clothes.

He has two regulation orange pullover shirts, two pairs of khaki slacks, two pairs of white socks, two pairs of white underwear, a pair of plastic sandals.

After doing his laundry, he works out.

One hundred push-ups.

One hundred sit-ups.

Eddie is a young dude, still only thirty-two, and he doesn't intend to let prison make him old. He's going to hit the bricks at thirty-five in shape, looking good, with his mind still sharp.

Most of the guys in this place are never going to see the world again.

They're going to die in this shithole.

His workout done, he generally takes a shower in the tiny cubicle in the corner of his cell and then lets himself watch a little TV, a tiny black-and-white he earned by being a "model prisoner," which on this block pretty much means not screaming all the time, finger-painting on the walls with your own shit, or trying to splash urine out the slot at the guards.

The television is closed-circuit and closely controlled—just educational and religious programs, but some of the women are reasonably hot and at least Eddie gets to hear some human voices.

Around noon, they shove something they call lunch through the door.

Sometime in the afternoon, or at night, or whenever the fuck they feel like it, the guards come to take him for his big hour out. They mix up the time because they don't want to get in a routine so maybe Eddie could call in an airstrike or something.

But when they do decide to show up, Eddie stands backward against the door and puts his hands through the slot for cuffing. They open the door and he kneels like he's at First Communion while they shackle his ankles and then run a chain up through the handcuffs.

Then they walk him to the exercise yard.

Which is a privilege.

His first couple of months here, Eddie wasn't allowed outside but instead was taken to an indoor hall with no windows that looked like an empty swimming pool. But now he can actually get some fresh air in a twelve-by-twenty cage of solid concrete walls with heavy wire mesh attached to red beams across the top. It has pull-up bars and a basketball hoop, and if you haven't fucked up and the guards are in a good mood, they might put a couple of other prisoners in there and let you talk to each other.

Caro doesn't get to go out there.

He's a cop killer, he doesn't get shit.

Usually, though, Eddie is alone. He does pull-ups, shoots some hoops or tosses himself a football. Back in high school, Eddie was a star linebacker in Texas, which made him a big fuckin' deal and got him a lot of prime cheerleader pussy. Now he throws a ball, runs after it, catches it, and no one cheers.

He used to love making guys cough up the ball. Hit them hard and just right so the air went out of their lungs and the ball popped out of their hands. Rip the hearts right out of their fucking chests.

High school ball.

Friday nights.

A long time ago.

Five days a month, Eddie doesn't go to the exercise yard but out in a hallway where he can make an hour of phone calls.

Eddie usually calls his wife.

First one, then the other.

It's tricky, because he never got officially divorced from Teresa, whom he married in the US, so technically he's not really married to Priscilla, whom he married in Mexico. He has a daughter and a son—almost four and two, respectively—with Priscilla and a thirteen-year-old daughter and ten-year-old son with Teresa.

The families are not, shall we say, "mutually aware," so Eddie has to be careful to remember who he's on the phone with at any given time and has been known to write his kids' names on his hand so he doesn't fuck up and ask about the wrong ones, which would be, like, awkward.

Same with his monthly visits.

He has to alternate them and make some excuse to either Teresa or Priscilla about why he can't see her that month. It goes pretty much the same with either wife—

"Baby, I have to use the time to see my lawyer."

"You love your lawyer more than your wife and kids?"

"I have to see my lawyer so I can come home to my wife and kids."

Yeah, well, which home and which family is another tricky question, but nothing he has to figure out for another three years. Eddie's thinking of maybe becoming Mormon, like that guy on *Big Love,* and then Teresa and Priscilla could become "sister wives."

But then he'd have to live in Utah.

He does sometimes use the monthly visit to consult with his lawyer. "Minimum Ben" Tompkins makes the trip out from San Diego, especially now that his former biggest client is among the missing.

Eddie was there in Guatemala when El Señor got croaked.

But Eddie didn't say nothin' to no one about that. He wasn't even supposed to have been down there in Guatemala, and he owes that motherfucker Keller a solid for bringing him along and letting him kill Ochoa.

Sometimes Eddie uses that memory to get him through the long hours—him pouring a canful of paraffin over the Zeta boss and then tossing a match on him. They say revenge is a dish best served cold, but this tasted pretty good hot, watching Ochoa go all Wicked Witch of the West and screaming like her, too.

Payback for a friend of Eddie's who Ochoa burned to death.

So Eddie owes Keller to keep his mouth shut.

But shit, he thinks, they should have given me a medal for doing Ochoa instead of throwing me in ADX Florence.

Keller, too.

We're motherfuckin' heroes, him and me.

Texas Rangers.

Barrera was ant food and Tompkins needed a new paycheck, so he was perfectly happy to take Eddie's messages about what to do with the money stored in offshore accounts all over the world.

Seven million in fines, fuck you, Uncle Sam, Eddie thinks. I've had that much fall out of my pockets into the sofa cushions.

Eddie owns four nightclubs in Acapulco, two other restaurants, a car dealership, and shit he's forgotten about. Plus the cash getting a tan on various islands. All he has to do is complete his time and get out and he'll be set for life.

But right now he's in Florence and Caro wants to know what's "new."

Eddie thinks, Caro don't want to know what's new in Florence, but what's new out in the world, which Eddie hears about when he's in the exercise cage or by standing up on his bed and talking through the vent to his neighbors.

Now Caro asks, "What do you hear from Sinaloa?"

Eddie doesn't know why Caro even cares about this shit. That world passed him by a long time ago, so why is he thinking about it? Then again, what else does he have to think about? So it's good for him to just shoot the shit like he's still in the game.

Like those old guys back in El Paso, hanging around the football field, telling war stories about when they played and then arguing about who this new coach should start at quarterback, whether they should dump the I for a spread formation, that sort of thing.

But Eddie respects Caro and is happy to kill the time with him. "I hear they're ramping up their *chiva* production," Eddie says.

He knows Caro won't approve.

The old *gomero* was there back in the '70s when the Americans napalmed and poisoned the poppy fields, scattering the growers to the winds. Caro was present at the famous meeting in Guadalajara when Miguel Ángel Barrera—the famous M-1 himself—told the *gomeros* to get out of heroin and go into cocaine. He was there when M-1 formed the Federación.

Eddie and Caro talk bullshit for another minute or so, but it's cumbersome, communicating through the plumbing. It's why narcos are scared to death of extradition to an American supermax—on a practical level, there's no way to run their business from inside, like they can do from a Mexican prison. Here they have limited visitation—if any at all—which is monitored and recorded. So are their phone calls. So even the most powerful kingpin can only receive bits of information and give vague orders. After a short while, it breaks down.

Caro has been in a long time.

If this were the NFL draft, Eddie thinks, he'd be Mr. Irrelevant.

Eddie sits across the table from Minimum Ben.

He admires the lawyer's style—a khaki linen sports jacket, blue shirt and a plaid bow tie, which is a nice touch. Thick snow-white hair, a handlebar mustache and a goatee.

Tompkins would be Colonel Sanders if it were chicken, not dope.

"BOP is moving you," Tompkins says. "It's standard operating procedure. You have a good record here so you're due for a 'step-down.'"

The American federal prison system has a hierarchy. The most severe is the supermax like Florence. Next comes the penitentiary, still behind walls but on a cell block, not solitary. Then it's a correctional facility, dormitory buildings behind wire fences, and finally, a minimum-security camp.

"To a penitentiary," Tompkins says. "Given your charges, you're not going lower than that until your release date is close. Then they might even move you to a halfway house. Jesus, Eddie, I thought you'd be happy about this."

"Yeah, I am, but . . ."

"But what?" Tompkins asks. "You're in solitary confinement, Eddie, locked down twenty-three hours a day. You don't see anybody—"

"Maybe that's the point. Do I have to explain it to you?" Sure, here he's in solitary and solitary is a bitch, but he's handling it, he's gotten used to it. And he's safe in his own cell, where no one can get to him. You put him on some cell block somewhere, the snitch cloud might rain all over him. Eddie doesn't want to say this out loud, because you never know what guard is on whose payroll. "I was promised protection."

Tompkins lowers his voice. "And you'll get it. Do your time and then you go into the program."

I have to *live* through my time to serve it, Eddie thinks. If I get moved, my paperwork goes with me. They can keep my PSI under wraps here, but in a penitentiary? Those guards would sell their mothers for a chocolate glazed. "Where are they sending me?"

"They're talking Victorville."

Eddie wants to swallow his teeth. "You know who runs Victimville? La Eme. The Mexican Mafia. They might as well transfer me to Culiacán."

La Eme does business with all the cartels except the Zetas, he thinks, but they're thickest with Sinaloa. They get a look at my pre-sentence interview, they'll shank me in the eyes.

"We'll get you housed in a protective unit," Tompkins says.

Eddie leans across the table. "Listen to me—if they put me in AdSeg, they might as well announce I'm a rat over the PA. You think they can't get to me in segregation? You know how hard that is? A guard leaves a door unlocked. I'll slash my wrists here before I let them put me in protection."

"What do you want, Eddie?"

"Keep me where I am."

"No can do," Tompkins says.

"What, they need the cell?"

"Something like that," Tompkins says. "You know the Bureau of Prisons. Once they start the paperwork . . ."

"They don't care if I die." It was a stupid thing to say and he knows it. Of course they don't care if you die. Guys die in prison all the time and most of the admin write it off as a no loss, addition by subtraction. So does the public. You're already fucking garbage, so if someone takes you out, all the better.

"I'll do what I can," Tompkins says.

Eddie's pretty sure that what Tompkins can do is exactly nothing. If his papers follow him to V-Ville, he's a dead man.

"You gotta call someone for me," Eddie says.

Keller answers his phone and it's Ben Tompkins.

"What do you want?" Keller asks, not happy.

"I represent Eddie Ruiz now."

"Why doesn't that surprise me?"

"Eddie wants to speak with you," Tompkins says. "He says he has valuable information."

"I'm out of the game," Keller says. "I don't care about any kind of information."

"He doesn't have valuable information *for* you," Tompkins says. "He has valuable information *on* you."

Keller flies to Denver and then drives down to Florence.

Eddie picks up the phone to talk through the glass. "You gotta help me."

He tells Keller about his imminent transfer to Victorville.

"What's that have to do with me?" Keller asks.

"That's it? YOYO?" *You're on your own.*

"We pretty much all are, aren't we?" Keller says. "Anyway, I don't have any swag anymore."

"Bullshit."

"Truth."

"You're pushing me into a corner," Eddie says. "You're pushing me someplace neither of us want to go."

"Are you threatening me, Eddie?"

"I'm asking for your help," Eddie says. "But if I don't get it, I have to help myself. You know what I'm saying here."

Guatemala.

The raid that never happened.

When Keller stood there and did nothing while Eddie turned Heriberto Ochoa into a road flare.

Then Keller walked into the jungle to find Barrera.

And only Keller walked out.

"You talk about certain things," Keller says, "maybe I have enough swag left to get you moved to Z-Wing, Eddie."

Z-Wing.

Basically, *under* ADX Florence.

Z-Wing is where they toss you if you fuck up. They strip you, shackle you by the hands and feet, throw you in and leave you there.

A black hole.

"You think you can do three years in Z-Wing?" Keller asks. "You'll come out a babbling idiot, yapping about all *kinds* of shit that never happened. No one will believe a word you say."

"Then keep me where I'm at."

"You're not thinking this through," Keller says. "If you stay in Florence, the same people you're worried about are going to wonder why."

"Then you think of something better," Eddie says. "If I get fucked, it's not going to be by myself. Just so you understand—my next call's not *to* you, it's *about* you."

"I'll see what I can do," Keller says.

"And you gotta do something else for me," Eddie says.

"What?"

"I want a Big Mac," Eddie says. "Large fries and a Coke."

"That's it?" Keller asks. "I thought you'd want to get laid."

Eddie thinks for a second, then says, "No, I'll go with the burger."

Eddie hears the toilet bang and knows that Caro wants to speak to him. He goes through the whole rigmarole of flushing water out of the toilet and then puts his ear to the toilet paper roll.

"I hear they're moving you," Caro says.

That didn't take long, Eddie thinks. And Caro's more hooked up than I thought he was. "That's right."

"To Victorville."

"Yeah."

He's not as scared about going there anymore since he got a call from Keller telling him that his paperwork was squeaky clean. Anyone looking at it could read through the lines and decide that Eddie got four years because his lawyer was a lot stronger than the government's case.

"Don't worry," Caro says. "We have friends there. They'll look after you."

"Thank you."

"La Mariposa," Caro says.

Another name for La Eme.

Caro says, "I'll miss our talks."

"Me too."

"You're a good young man, Eddie. You show respect." Caro is quiet for a few seconds, then he says, "*M'ijo*, I want you to do something for me in V-Ville."

"Anything, Señor."

Eddie doesn't want to do whatever it is.

Just wants to do his time and get out.

Out of the joint, out of the trade.

He's still toying with producing a movie about his life, what do they call it, a "biopic," which would have to be, like, a huge hit if they got someone like DiCaprio to play him.

But he can't say no to Rafael Caro. If he does, La Eme will give him another kind of welcome to V-Ville. Maybe shank him on the spot, or maybe just shun him. Either way, he won't survive without being cliqued up with a gang.

"I knew that would be your answer," Caro says. He lowers his voice so Eddie can barely hear him say—

"Find us a *mayate*."

A black guy.

"From New York. With an early release date. Put him in your debt," Caro says. "Do you understand?"

Jesus Christ, Eddie thinks. Caro is still a player.

He does the math—Caro has done twenty years on his twenty-five-year sentence. Federal time, they can make you do every day or they can knock it down to 85 percent, maybe even less.

Which makes Caro a short-timer, looking at the gate.

And he wants back in the game.

"I understand, Señor," Eddie says. "You want to put the arm on a black guy who's going to get out soon. But why?"

"Because Adán Barrera was right," Caro says.

Heroin was our past.

And our past is our future.

He don't need to tell Eddie *that*.

Keller gets on the horn to Ben O'Brien. "Call me back on a clean line."

The first time Keller met O'Brien was in a hotel room in Georgetown a few weeks before the Guatemala raid. They didn't exchange names, and Keller, who was never much of a political animal, didn't recognize him as a senator from Texas. He just knew that the man represented certain oil interests willing to fund an operation to eliminate the Zeta leadership because the "Z Company" was taking over valuable oil and gas fields in northern Mexico.

The White House had just officially rejected the operation but sent O'Brien to authorize it off the record. The senator arranged a funding line through his oil connections and helped put together a team of mercenaries through a private firm based in Virginia. Keller had resigned from DEA and joined Tidewater Security as a consultant.

Now O'Brien calls him back. "What's wrong?"

Keller tells him about Eddie's threat. "You have any leverage at BOP? Get Ruiz's PSI scrubbed?"

"In English?"

"I need you to reach out to someone in the Bureau of Prisons and get Ruiz's records cleansed of any trace of his deal," Keller says.

"We're letting drug dealers blackmail us now?" O'Brien asks.

"Pretty much," Keller says. "Unless you want to answer a lot of questions about what happened down in Guatemala."

"I'll get it done."

"I don't like it any more than you do."

Goddamn Barrera, Keller thinks when he clicks off.

Adán vive.

Elena Sánchez Barrera is reluctant to admit, even to herself, that her brother is dead.

The family held out hope through the long silence that lasted days, then weeks, and now months, as they tried to glean information as to what had happened in Dos Erres.

But so far they've come up with no new information. Nor, apparently, have the authorities disseminated what they do know down the ranks—it seems as if half of law enforcement believe that the rumor of Adán's death was put out as a smoke screen to help him evade arrest.

As if, Elena thinks. The federal police are virtually a wholly owned subsidiary of the Sinaloa cartel. The government favors us because we pay them well, we retain order and we're not savages. So the idea that Adán staged his own death to avoid capture is as ludicrous as it is widespread.

If it wasn't the police, it was the media.

Elena had heard the term *media circus* before, but she never fully realized what it meant until the rumors about Adán's death began to swirl. Then she was besieged—reporters even had the nerve to set up post outside her house in Tijuana. She couldn't go out the door without being harassed by questions about Adán.

"How many ways can I say 'I don't know'?" she had said to the reporters. "All I can tell you is that I love my brother and pray for his safety."

"So you can confirm he's missing?"

"I love my brother and pray for his safety."

"Is it true your brother was the world's biggest drug trafficker?"

"My brother is a businessman. I love him and pray for his safety."

Every fresh rumor prompted a new assault. *"We've heard Adán is in Costa Rica." "Is it true he's hiding in the United States?" "Adán has been seen in Brazil, Colombia, Paraguay, Paris . . ."*

"All I can tell you is that I love my brother and pray for his safety."

The pack of hyenas would have eaten little Eva alive, torn her to shreds. If they could have found her. It wasn't for lack of trying. The media flooded Culiacán, Badiraguato. An ambitious reporter in California even tracked down Eva's condo in La Jolla. When they couldn't find her, they pestered Elena.

"Where is Eva? Where are the boys? There are rumors they've been kidnapped. Are they alive?"

"Señora Barrera is in seclusion," Elena said. "We ask you to respect her privacy in this difficult time."

"You're public figures."

"We're not," Elena said. "We're private businesspeople."

It was true—she had retired from the *pista secreta* eight years ago, when she agreed to turn over the Baja plaza to Adán so he could give it to the Esparzas. She had done so willingly—she was tired of the killings, of the death, that went along with the trade and was happy to live off her many investments.

And Eva knows as much about the drug trade as she does about particle physics. Goodhearted, beautiful, and stupid. But fecund. She served her purpose. Gave Adán sons and heirs. The twin boys—Miguel and Raúl. And what will become of them? Elena wonders.

Eva is a young Mexican woman, a young Sinaloan woman. With her father and husband apparently dead, she probably feels that she has to obey her older brother, and Elena wonders what Iván has been telling her.

I know what I would tell her, Elena thinks. You're an American citizen and so are the boys. You have enough money to live like a queen the rest of your life. Take your sons and run back to California. Raise your children away from this business, before you and they are trapped in it for another generation. It will take some time, but eventually the media circus will pack up and move to the next town.

Hopefully.

The bizarre social alchemy of this vulgar age has turned Adán into that most precious of public commodities—a celebrity. Images of him—old mug shots, random photos taken at social events—are plastered over television screens, computer monitors, front pages of newspapers. The details of his 2004 escape from prison are recited with titillated delight. "Experts" join panels of talking heads to assert Adán's power, wealth and influence. Mexican "witnesses" are interviewed to testify about Adán's philanthropy—the clinics he built, the schools, the playgrounds. ("To you he is a drug trafficker. To us he is a hero.")

Celebrity culture, Elena thinks.

An oxymoron.

Even if you could control the traditional press, corralling social media is like grabbing mercury—it slips out of your hand and breaks into a thousand more pieces. The internet, Twitter, Facebook are electric with "news" about Adán Barrera—every rumor, whisper, innuendo and bit of misinformation went viral. Behind the screen of digital anonymity, people inside the organization who know they shouldn't be talking are leaking what information they have, mixing little bits of truth into a stew of falsehood.

And the most pernicious rumor of all—

Adán is alive.

It wasn't Adán at all in Guatemala, but a double. The Lord of the Skies outsmarted his enemies yet again.

Adán is in a coma, hidden away in a hospital in Dubai.

I saw Adán in Durango.

In Los Mochis, in Costa Rica, in Mazatlán.

I saw him in a dream. The spirit of Adán came to me and told me everything will be all right.

Like Jesus, Elena thinks, resurrection is always possible when there's no body. And just like Jesus, Adán now has disciples.

Elena walks from the living room into the enormous kitchen. She's thought of selling and downsizing now that her sons are grown and out. The maids busy preparing breakfast look away and seem even busier as they try to avoid her glance. The servants always know first, Elena thinks. Somehow they always hear of every death, every birth, every hurried engagement or secret affair before we do.

Elena pours herself a cup of herbal tea and walks out onto the deck. Her house is in the hills above the city and she looks down at the bowl of polluted smoke that is Tijuana and thinks of all the blood that her family shed—in both the active and passive sense—to control this place.

Her brother Adán and her brother Raúl—long dead—had done that, taken the Baja plaza and turned it into the base of a national empire that had risen and fallen and risen again, and now . . .

Now Iván Esparza has it.

Just as he will have Adán's crown.

With Adán's sons mere toddlers, Iván is next in the line of succession. The news of Guatemala had barely reached their ears before he was ready to declare his father and Adán dead and announce that he was taking over.

Elena and Núñez talked him down from that tree.

"It's premature," Núñez said. "We don't yet know for a fact that they're dead, and you really don't want to step up to the top position anyway."

"Why not?" Iván demanded.

"It's too dangerous," Núñez said. "Too exposed. In the absence of your father and Adán, we don't know who will stay loyal."

"Some ambiguity over their deaths has its uses," Elena said. "The doubt about whether they might be alive keeps the wolves at bay for a while. But if you announce that the king is dead, everyone from the dukes to the barons to the knights to the peasants will see a weakness in the Sinaloa cartel as a chance to seize the throne."

Iván reluctantly agreed to wait.

He's a classic, almost stereotypical third-generation spoiled narco brat, Elena thinks. Hotheaded, violently inclined. Adán didn't like or trust him and worried about his taking over when Nacho died or retired.

So do I, Elena thinks.

But the only alternatives are her own sons.

They're Adán's true nephews, the Barrera blood flows through them. Her oldest son, Rudolfo, has done his time, figuratively and literally. He went into the family business young, trafficking cocaine from Tijuana into California, and did well for years—bought nightclubs, owned top recording bands, and managed champion boxers. A beautiful wife and three beautiful children.

No one loved life more than Rudolfo.

Then he sold 250 grams of coke to a DEA undercover at a motel in San Diego.

Two hundred and fifty grams, Elena thinks. So stupid, so small. They've moved tons of cocaine in the States, and poor Rudolfo went down for less than half a pound. The American judge sentenced him to six years in a federal prison.

A "supermax."

Florence, Colorado.

Because, Elena thinks, he bore the name "Barrera."

It took everything the family had—money, power, influence, lawyers, blackmail and extortion, but they got him out—well, Adán got him out—after only eighteen months.

Only eighteen months, she reflects.

A year and a half in a seven-by-twelve cell, twenty-three hours a day, alone. An hour a day for a shower, or exercise in a cage with a glimpse of the sky.

When he returned, coming across the Paso del Norte Bridge into Juárez, Elena barely recognized him. Gaunt, pale, haunted—a ghost. Her life-loving son, at thirty-five, looked more like sixty.

That was a year ago.

Now Rudolfo focuses on his "legitimate" business, nightclubs in Culiacán and in Cabo San Lucas, and music—the various bands that he produces and promotes. Sometimes he talks about getting back into *la pista secreta*, but Elena knows he's afraid of ever going back to prison. Rudolfo will *say* that he wants the chair at the head of the table, but he's lying to himself.

Luis, her baby, she doesn't worry about. He went to college to become an engineer, God bless him, and wants nothing to do with the family business.

Well, good, Elena thinks now.

It's what we wanted, isn't it? It's what we always intended—for *our* generation to make the family fortune in the trade so that our children wouldn't need to. Because the trade has brought us riches beyond imagining, but it has also brought us to the cemetery time and again.

Her husband, her uncle—the patriarch "Tío" Barrera—her brother Raúl, and now her brother Adán is dead. Her nephew Salvador, and so many cousins and in-laws and friends.

And enemies.

Güero Méndez, the Tapia brothers, so many others that Adán defeated. They fought for "turf," she thinks, and the only turf they eventually, inevitably, inherit and share is the cemetery.

Or the prisons.

Here in Mexico or El Norte.

In cells for decades or for the rest of their lives.

A living death.

So if Rudolfo wants to run a nightclub and play at making music, and Luis wants to build bridges, so much the better.

If the world will let them.

"We're all going to die young anyway!" Ric Núñez announces. "Let's make legends while we're doing it!"

It's been a night of Cristal and coke at Rudolfo Sánchez's new club, the Blue Marlin. Well, that's where they wound up; part of the group informally known as Los Hijos—Ric, the Esparza brothers, Rubén Ascensión—and a host of girls had been hitting all the trendy clubs in Cabo, going from VIP room to VIP room, usually comped but leaving hefty tips, and then they were in a private room at the Marlin when Ric got the idea to "take it to the next level."

He takes out his .38 Colt and sets it on the table.

Can you imagine the songs they'll write? Ric thinks. The corridos about young people, the scions of the drug cartels, decked out in Armani, Boss, Gucci; driving Rolls, Ferraris; snorting primo blow through hundred-dollar bills, throwing it all away on a game?

They've been together forever, Los Hijos. Went to school together in Culiacán, played together at their parents' parties, went on vacations together to Cabo and Puerto Vallarta. Snuck off and drank beer together, smoked weed, picked up girls. A few of them did a couple of semesters of college, most went straight into the family business.

They knew who they were.

The next generation of the Sinaloa cartel.

The sons.

Los Hijos.

And the girls? They always get the best girls. Ever since middle school, even more so now. Of course they do—they have looks, clothes, money, drugs, guns. They have the swag—they go to the VIP rooms, get the best tables at the best restaurants, front-row seats and backstage passes to the hot concerts; shit, the bands sing songs to them, *about* them. Maître d's open doors and women open up their legs.

Los Hijos.

Now one of Iván's bitches takes out her phone and screams, "It would be a million YouTube hits!"

Fucking *awesome*, Ric thinks. Someone blowing his brains out on a vid-clip, over a dare. Show the world we just don't give a shit, we're capable of anything, *anything*. "Okay, whoever the barrel points to puts it to his head and pulls the trigger. If he survives, we do it again."

He spins it.

Hard.

Everyone holds their breath.

The barrel points right back at him.

Iván Esparza explodes in laughter. "Fuck you, Ric!"

The oldest Esparza brother has always been pushing him, since they were little kids. Daring him to jump off the cliff into the quarry pond. *Go on, do it, I dare you. I dare you to break into the school, steal your* papi's *whiskey, unbutton that girl's blouse.* They've chugged bottles of vodka, raced speedboats straight at each other, cars to the edge of cliffs, but this . . .

Amid chants of "Do it! Do it! Do it!," Ric picks up the pistol and puts it against his right temple.

Just like that *yanqui* cop did.

The one who did a number on Iván's face.

It's been what, a year, and the scar is still angry on Iván's cheek, even after the best plastic surgeons money can buy. Iván is cool about it, of course, claiming that it makes him look even *more* macho.

And swearing that one day he will kill that gringo Keller.

Ric's hand shakes.

Drunk and stoned as he is, all he wants in the world right then is to not pull the trigger. All he wants is to go back a few minutes to the moment when he had this insanely stupid idea, and to not suggest it.

But now he's trapped.

He can't punk out, not in front of Iván, Alfredo and Oviedo, not in front of Rubén. Especially not in front of Belinda, the girl sitting beside him in a black leather jacket, a sequined bustier and painted-on jeans. Belinda is as crazy as she is beautiful; this girl will do anything. Now she smiles at him and the smile says, *Do it, boyfriend. Do it and I'll make you so happy later.*

If you live.

"Come on, man, put it down," Rubén says. "It was a joke."

But that's Rubén. The cautious one, the careful one, what did Iván call him once—the "Emergency Brake." Yeah, maybe, but Ric knows that Rubén is his father's son—El Cachorro, "The Puppy," is absolutely, totally lethal, like his old man.

He doesn't look lethal now, though; he looks scared.

"No, I'm doing it," Ric says. They're telling him not to, and he knows they mean it, but he also knows they'll think less of him. He'd be the one who chickened out, not them. But if he pulls the trigger and it doesn't go off, *he'll* be the man.

And it's great to see Iván freaking out.

"It was a joke, Ric! No one expected you'd *do* it!" Iván yells. He looks like he's going to lunge across the table but is afraid to make the gun go off. Everyone at the table is frozen, staring at Ric. From the corner of his eye, he sees their private waiter sneak out the door.

"Put the gun down," Rubén says.

"Okay, here goes," Ric says. He's starting to tighten his finger when Belinda grabs the gun from his hand, sticks it in her mouth and pulls the trigger.

The hammer clicks on the empty chamber.

"Jesus fucking Christ!" Iván yells.

They all freak out. The crazy *chava* actually did it, and then she calmly sets the gun back on the table and says, "Next."

Except Rubén picks up the gun and sticks it in his pocket. "I think we're done."

"Pussy," Belinda says.

If it were a guy who'd said that, Ric knows, it would be on, a reason to go, and Rubén would either pull the trigger on himself or on the mouth that called him that. But it's a girl, a *chica*, so it's all good.

"What a rush," Belinda says. "I think I came."

The door opens and Rudolfo Sánchez walks in. "What the hell is going on in here?"

"We're just having some fun," Iván says, assuming leadership.

"I heard," Rudolfo says. "Do me a favor? You want to kill yourselves, don't do it in my place, okay?"

He asks politely, but if it were any other club owner, there'd be a problem. Iván would feel a need to face him, maybe slap him down, or at least cause some damage, break some shit up, throw down some bills to cover the damage, and walk out.

But this isn't any club owner.

Rudolfo is Adán Barrera's nephew, his sister Elena's son. A little older, but an Hijo like them.

Rudolfo looks at them like, *Why are you in my club raising dust? Why did you have to pick* this *place?* And he says, "What would I say to your fathers if I let you blow your brains out in my club?"

Then he stops, looking embarrassed, only now remembering that Iván's father is dead, killed by the Zetas in Guatemala.

Ric feels bad for him. "Sorry, 'Dolfo. We're fucked up."

"Maybe we should just get the check," Rubén says.

"It's comped," Rudolfo says.

But Ric notices he doesn't say anything like, *No, please stay. Have another round.* They all get up, say good night to Rudolfo, thank him—show some respect, Ric thinks—and walk out onto the street.

Where Iván goes *off.* "That *malandro, pendejo, pinche* motherfucker *lambioso* fuck! Does he think he's funny?! 'What would your fathers think?'"

"He didn't mean anything," Rubén says. "He probably just forgot."

"You don't forget something like that!" Iván says. "He was stepping on my dick! When I take over . . ."

Ric says, "The guy hasn't been the same since he got back."

Unlike any of them, Rudolfo had gone to prison. Did time in an American supermax and the word was that it wrecked him, that he came home messed up.

"The guy is weak," Iván says. "He couldn't take it."

"None of us know what we'd do," Rubén says. "My old man says prison is the worst thing that can happen to you."

"He came out of it okay," Ric says. "Your dad is tough."

"None of us know," Rubén repeats.

"Fuck that," Iván says. "This is our life. If you go, you go. You have to hold it together, like a man."

"Rudolfo did," Ric says. "He didn't bitch up, he didn't flip."

"His uncle got him out," Iván says.

"Good," Ric says. "Good for Adán. He'd have done the same for you."

They all know that Adán did it before, too, when his nephew Sal got busted for killing two people outside a club. Adán made a deal to get the charges dropped, and the rumor they all heard was that he flipped on the Tapia brothers, launching the bloody civil war that almost destroyed the cartel.

And Sal got killed anyway.

Blown to shit by Crazy Eddie Ruiz.

Sal should be here tonight, drinking with us, Ric thinks.

Go with God, 'mano.

Iván notices the girls staring at him. "What are you looking at?! Walk ahead, get in the fucking cars!"

Then, just as quickly as he got furious, he gets all happy again. Throws his arms around Ric's and Rubén's shoulders and yells, "We're brothers! Brothers forever!"

And they all shout, "¡Los Hijos!"

Coked, drunk, and orgasmed out, the girl falls asleep.

Belinda shakes her head. "No stamina. I wish Gaby was here."

She rolls over and looks at Ric.

Shit, he thinks, she wants to go again. "I can't."

"I'll give you a few minutes," Belinda says. She finds a blunt on the nightstand, lights it up, takes a hit and offers him one.

He takes it. "That was crazy tonight, what you did."

"I did it to bail you out," she says. "You talked yourself into a trap."

"You could have died."

"Could have," she says, gesturing to get the joint back. "Didn't. Anyway, it's my job to protect you."

Belinda Vatos—La Fósfora—was the *jefa* of FEN, Fuerza Especial de Núñez, the armed wing of the Núñez faction of the Sinaloa cartel. It's unusual to have a woman in that position, but God knows she earned it, Ric thinks.

Started as a courier, then a mule, then took a major step up when she volunteered to kill a Zeta operative who was playing hell with their people in Veracruz. The guy didn't expect a young, beautiful woman with big round tits and a head of wavy black hair to walk up and put two bullets in his face, but that's what Belinda did.

She and her girlfriend, Gabriela, had a technique. La Gaby would go into a bar, stay awhile, then leave pretending to be drunk. She'd fall down on the sidewalk, then when the target bent over to help her, La Fósfora would come out of the alley and blast him.

Ric soon learned that she had more exotic tastes. She and Gaby and a few of her men liked to kidnap victims, chop them up into deli meat, and then drop the pieces off at their families' doorsteps, as a message.

The message got through.

La Fósfora became a narco rock star, posing in sexy garb for Facebook photos and YouTube videos, having songs written about her, and Ric's father moved her up to the top spot after the previous head of security was sent to prison.

Ric first fucked her on a dare.

"It would be like sticking your dick into death," Iván said.

"Yeah, but a *chava* that crazy has to be great in bed," Ric said.

"If you live," Iván said. "She might be like one of those spiders who, you know, kill the male after mating. Anyway, I hear she's a lesbian."

"She's bi," Ric said. "She told me."

"So go for it," Iván said. "You can maybe get a threesome out of it."

"That's what she said she wants," Ric said. "Her and that girl Gaby, I can dick them both."

"You only live once."

So Ric went to bed with Belinda and Gaby, and the fucked-up thing is that he fell for one and not the other. He still fucked a lot of different women, including even sometimes his wife, but what he had with Belinda was special.

"We're soul mates," Belinda explained to him. "In the sense that neither of us has one."

"You don't have a soul?" Ric asked her.

"I like to get high, I like to fuck guys, I like to fuck girls, and I like to kill people," Belinda said. "If I have a soul, it's not much of a soul."

Now Belinda looks at him and says, "Anyway, I couldn't let the crown prince blow his own brains out."

"What are you talking about?"

"Think about it," she says, handing back the joint. "Barrera's probably dead. Nacho's dead for sure. Rudolfo is a zero. Your father? I love your father, I kill for him, I'd die for him, but he's a placeholder. You're the godson."

Ric says, "You're talking crazy. Iván's next in line."

"I'm just saying." She takes the joint from him, sets it down and kisses him. "Lie back, baby. If you can't fuck me, I'll fuck *you*. Let me fuck you, baby."

She licks her finger and then snakes it into his ass. "You like that, don't you?"

"Fuck."

"Oh, I will, baby," she says. "I'll fuck you. I'll fuck you good."

She does.

With her mouth and her fingers, and when he's about to come she takes her mouth off him, shoves her fingers in deep and says, "It could be yours, all of it. The whole cartel, the whole country, if you want it."

Because you're Adán Barrera's godson, he hears her tell him.

His rightful heir.

The anointed one.

El Ahijado.

Weeks went by, then months, then a year.

The anniversary of the reputed battle in Guatemala coincides with the Day of the Dead, and makeshift shrines to Adán Barrera—photos of him, candles, coins, little bottles of booze and *papel picado*—spring up all over the country, even in Juárez. Some are left intact while others are torn down by angry adherents claiming there's no need for shrines because "*Adán vive.*"

For Keller, the Christmas holidays come and go with little fanfare. He joins Marisol and Ana for a subdued dinner and an exchange of small gifts, then goes back to Juárez and gives Chuy a new video game that the kid seems to like. The next morning's newspapers carry stories of toys magically appearing for poor children in rural villages and city barrios in Sinaloa and Durango from their "Tío Adán." Baskets of food arrive in town plazas, gifts from "El Señor."

Keller barely acknowledges New Year's Eve. He and Marisol share an early dinner, a glass of champagne, and a chaste kiss. He's in bed asleep before the ball drops in Times Square.

Two weeks into the new year, Chuy disappears.

Keller comes back from grocery shopping, the television is off, the Xbox cables unhooked.

In Chuy's room the backpack Keller had bought him is gone, as are the few clothes Chuy owns. His toothbrush is missing from the ceramic rack in the bathroom. Whatever storms blew inside Chuy's head, Keller thinks, have apparently driven him to leave. At least, as Keller discovers when he searches the room, he took his meds with him.

Keller drives around the neighborhood, asking at local shops and internet cafés. No one has seen Chuy. He cruises the places downtown where teenagers hang out, but doesn't see Chuy. On the off chance that the kid has decided to go out to Valverde, he calls Marisol, but no one has seen him there, either.

Maybe, Keller thinks, he's crossed the bridge back into El Paso where he grew up, so Keller goes over and drives around the barrio, asks some reasonably hostile gangbangers who instantly make him as some sort of cop and tell him that they haven't seen any Chuy Barajos.

Keller reaches out to old connections with the El Paso PD narcotics squad and finds out that Chuy is a person of interest in several local homicides back in '07 and '08 and they'd like to talk with him. In any case, they'll keep an eye out and give Keller a call if they pick him up.

Going back to Juárez, Keller finds Terry Blanco at San Martín over on Avenida Escobar downing a Caguama at the bar.

"Who is this kid?" the cop asks when Keller explains the favor he wants.

"You know who he is," Keller says. "You see him when you scope my house."

"Just checking on your welfare," Blanco says. He's drunk more than one beer. "Tough times here, Keller. We don't know who to report to anymore, who's in charge. You think he's alive?"

"Who?"

"Barrera."

"I don't know," Keller says. "Have you seen this kid?"

"You know how many fucked-up kids we got running around Mexico?" Blanco asks. "Shit, just in Juárez? Hundreds? Thousands? What's one more? What's this one to you?"

Keller doesn't have an answer for that. He says, "Just pick him up if you find him. Bring him to me."

"Sure, why not?"

Keller leaves some money on the bar for Blanco's next beer. Then he gets back in his car, calls Orduña and explains the situation.

"This Barajos was in Guatemala?" Orduña asks.

"Yeah."

"Was he a witness?"

"To what, Roberto?"

"Okay."

"Look, you owe this kid," Keller says. "He killed Forty."

After a long silence Orduña says, "We'll take good care of him. But, Arturo, you know the odds of finding him are . . ."

"I know."

Infinitesimal.

The long drug war has left thousands of orphans, shattered families and dislocated teenagers. And that doesn't include the thousands fleeing gang violence in Guatemala, El Salvador, and Honduras, passing through Mexico to try to find sanctuary in the United States. A lot of them don't make it.

Chuy is now both a monster and a ghost.

Senator Ben O'Brien calls.

He's in El Paso, phones Keller and asks for a meeting. What he actually says is "Keller, let me buy you a beer."

"Where are you staying?"

"The Indigo. On Kansas Street. You know it?"

Keller knows it. He drives up to the city and meets O'Brien at the hotel bar. The senator has gone back to his roots, wearing a denim shirt and Lucchese boots. His Stetson is perched on his lap. Good as his word, he brings a pitcher of beer, pours one for Keller and says, "I saw something interesting driving through El Paso today—a homemade sign that read '*Adán Vive*.'"

Keller isn't surprised—he's seen the same signs in Juárez and heard that they're all over the place in Sinaloa and Durango. "What can I tell you? The man has a following."

"He's becoming Che Guevara," O'Brien says.

"I guess absence does make the heart grow fonder."

"You heard anything more?" O'Brien asks. "About his death?"

"I don't follow that world anymore."

"Bullshit."

Keller shrugs—it's true.

"Do you read the American papers?" O'Brien asks.

"The sports pages," Keller says.

"Then you don't know what's been happening up here?" O'Brien asks. "With heroin?"

"No."

"A lot of people in the law enforcement community have been celebrating Barrera's alleged demise," O'Brien says, "but the truth is that it hasn't slowed the flow of drugs at all. In fact, it's only gotten worse. Especially with heroin."

From the year 2000 to 2006, O'Brien tells him, fatal heroin overdoses stayed fairly stable, about 2,000 a year. From 2007 to 2010, they rose to about 3,000. But in 2011, they rose to 4,000. Six thousand in 2012, 8,000 in 2013.

"To put it in perspective," O'Brien says, "from 2004 to now we lost 7,222 military personnel in Iraq and Afghanistan combined."

"To put it in perspective," Keller says, "in the same period of time, over a hundred thousand Mexicans were killed in drug violence, with another twenty-two thousand missing. And that's a conservative estimate."

"You're making my argument," O'Brien says. "The loss of life you cite in Mexico, the heroin epidemic here, the millions of people we have behind bars. Whatever we're doing, it's not working."

"If you asked me here to tell me that," Keller says, "you've wasted both our time. Thanks for the beer, but what do you want?"

"I represent a group of senators and congressmen who have the power and influence to fire the current DEA administrator and appoint a new one," O'Brien says. "We want that to be you."

Keller has never been easily shocked, but he is now. "With all respect, you're out of your goddamn mind."

"The country is flooded with heroin, use is up over eighty percent, and most of it's coming from Mexico," O'Brien says. "I have constituents who go to cemeteries to visit their children."

"And I've seen Mexican kids buried with bulldozers," Keller says. "Nobody up here gave a damn. There's a 'heroin epidemic' now because *white* kids are dying."

"I'm asking you to give a damn now," O'Brien says.

"I fought my war," Keller says.

"Kids are dying out there," O'Brien says. "And I don't think you're a guy who can just take your pension, sit on your ass and let it happen."

"Watch me."

"Think about it." O'Brien slides off the barstool and hands Keller his card. "Call me."

"I won't be calling."

"We'll see."

O'Brien leaves him sitting there.

Keller does the math—O'Brien said that heroin deaths rose slightly in 2010, but then spiked in 2011. Then rose again by half in 2012.

All while Adán was alive.

Motherfucker, Keller thinks. Barrera put it in place—his last malignant gift to the world. Keller remembers his Shakespeare: "The evil that men do lives after them."

Ain't that the truth.

The ghost and the monster.

They eat at Garufa, an Argentine place on Bulevar Tomás Fernández. It's expensive as hell but he wants to take her someplace nice. Keller has steak, Marisol has salmon and eats with an unabashed appetite, something he's always liked about her.

"What aren't you telling me?" Marisol asks, setting down her fork.

"Why do you think there's something I'm not telling you?"

"Because I know you," Marisol says. "So what is it? Spill."

When he tells her about his meeting with O'Brien, she sits back in her chair. "Arturo, oh my God. I'm stunned."

"Right?"

"I thought you were persona non grata," Marisol says.

"So did I." He tells her what O'Brien said and how he'd responded.

Marisol is quiet.

"Christ, you don't think I should accept, do you?" Keller asks.

She's still quiet.

"*Do* you?" Keller asks.

"Art, think of the power you'd have," Marisol says. "The good you could do. You could actually effect change."

Keller sometimes forgets her political activism. Now he remembers the woman who had camped out in the Zócalo in Mexico City to protest election fraud, her marches down the Paseo de la Reforma to protest police brutality. All part of the woman he fell in love with.

"You're completely opposed to virtually everything DEA does," he says.

"But you could change policies."

"I don't know," Keller says.

"Okay," she says. "Let's play it the other way. Why wouldn't you?"

Keller lays out the reasons for her. One, he's done with the war on drugs.

"But maybe it's not done with you," she says.

Forty years is more than enough, he tells her. He's not a bureaucrat, not a political animal. He's not sure he can even live in the US anymore.

She knows that Keller's mother was Mexican, his father an Anglo who brought them to San Diego and then abandoned them. But he grew up as an American—UCLA, the US Marines—then the DEA took him back to Mexico and he's spent more of his adult life there than in the States. Marisol knows that he's always been torn between the two cultures—Arturo has a love/hate relationship with both countries.

And Marisol knows that he moved to Juárez almost out of guilt—that he thought he owed something to this city that had suffered so much from the US war on drugs, that he had a moral obligation to help its recovery—even if it was as small a contribution as paying taxes, buying groceries, keeping a house open.

And then taking care of Chuy, his personal cross to bear.

But Chuy is gone.

Now she asks him, "Why do you want to live in Juárez? And tell the truth."

"It's real."

"It is that," she says. "And you can't walk a block without being reminded of the war."

"Meaning what?"

"There's nothing for you here now but bad memories and—"

She stops.

"What?" Keller asks.

"All right—*me*," she says. "Proximity to me. I know you still love me, Arturo."

"I can't help what I feel."

"I'm not asking you to," Marisol says. "But if you're turning this down to be near me, don't."

They finish dinner and then go for a walk, something they couldn't have done a couple of years ago.

"What do you hear?" Marisol asks.

"Nothing."

"Exactly," Marisol says. "No police sirens, ambulances screaming. No gunshots."

"The Pax Sinaloa."

"Can it last?" she asks.

No, Keller thinks.

This isn't peace, it's a lull.

"I'll drive you home," Keller says.

"It's a long drive," Marisol says. "Why don't I just stay at your place?"

"Chuy's room is free," Keller says.

"What if I don't want to stay in Chuy's room?" Marisol asks.

He wakes up very early, before dawn, with a cold Juárez wind whipping the walls and rattling the windows.

It's funny, he thinks, how the big decisions in your life don't always follow a big moment or a big change, but just seem to settle on you like an inevitability, something you didn't decide at all but has always been decided for you.

Maybe it was the sign that decided it.

ADÁN VIVE.

Because it was true, Keller thinks that morning. The king might be gone, but the kingdom he created remains. Spreading suffering and death as surely as if Barrera were still on the throne.

Keller has to admit another truth. If anyone in the world could destroy the kingdom, he tells himself—by dint of history, experience, motivation, knowledge and skills—it's you.

Marisol knows it, too. That morning he comes back to bed and she wakes up and asks, "What?"

"Nothing. Go back to sleep."

"A nightmare?"

"Maybe." And he laughs.

"What?"

"I don't think I'm ready to be a ghost yet," Keller says. "Or live with ghosts. And you were right—my war isn't over."

"You want to take that job."

"Yes," Keller says. He puts his hand to the back of her head and pulls her closer. "But only if you'll come with me."

"Arturo . . ."

"We wear our sorrow like it's some sort of medal," Keller says. "Drag it around like a chain, and it's heavy, Mari. I don't want to let it beat us, make us less than we are. We've lost so much, let's not lose each other, too. That's too big a loss."

"The clinic—"

"I'll take care of it. I promise."

They get married in New Mexico, at the Monastery of Christ in the Desert, have a brief honeymoon in Taos, then drive to Washington, where O'Brien's Realtor has lined up houses for them to look at.

They love a house on Hillyer Place, put in an offer and buy it.

Keller's at work the next morning.

Because he knows that the ghost has come back.

And with it, the monster.

The Death of Kings

Come, let us sit upon the ground and tell sad stories of the death of kings.

—Shakespeare
Henry VI, Part One

**Washington, DC
May 2014**

Keller looks down at the photo of the skeleton.

Blades of grass poke up through the ribs; vines wrap around the leg bones as if trying to strap the body to the earth.

"Is it Barrera?" Keller asks.

Barrera's been off the radar for a year and a half. Now these photos have just come in from the DEA Guatemala City field office. Guatemalan special forces found the bones in the Petén, in the rain forest about a kilometer from the village of Dos Erres, where Barrera was last seen.

Tom Blair, the head of DEA's Intelligence Unit, lays down a different photo on Keller's desk, this of the skeleton lying on a gurney. "The height matches."

Barrera is short, Keller knows, a shade under five seven, but that could describe a lot of people, especially in the undernourished Mayan regions of Guatemala.

Blair spreads more photos on the desk—a close-up of the skull next to a facial shot of Adán Barrera. Keller recognizes the image: it was taken fifteen years ago, when Barrera was booked into the Metropolitan Correctional Center in San Diego.

Keller put him there.

The face looks back at him.

Familiar, almost intimate.

"Orbitals match," Blair is saying, "brain case measurements identical. We'd need dental and DNA analysis to be a hundred percent, but . . ."

We'll have dental records and DNA samples from Barrera's stay in the American prison system, Keller thinks. It would be highly doubtful that any useful DNA could be pulled from a skeleton that had been rotting in the rain forest for more than a year, but Keller can see in the photos that the jaw is still intact.

And he knows in his gut that the dental records are going to match.

"The way the back of the skull is blown out," Blair says, "I'd say two shots to the face, close range, fired downward. Barrera was executed, by someone who wanted him to know it was coming. It would match the Dos Erres theory."

The Dos Erres theory, a particular pet of the DEA's Sinaloa Working Group, postulates that in October 2012, Adán Barrera and his partner and father-in-law, Ignacio Esparza, traveled with a large, armed entourage to Guatemala for a peace conference with their rivals, an especially vicious drug cartel known as the Zetas. There was a factual precedent for this—Barrera had sat down with the Zeta leadership at a similar conference back in 2006, divided Mexico into territories, and created a short-lived peace that fell apart into an even more violent and costly war. The theory continues that Barrera and the Zeta leader Heriberto Ochoa met in the remote village of Dos Erres in the Petén District of Guatemala and again carved up Mexico like a Thanksgiving turkey. At a party to celebrate the peace, the Zetas ambushed and slaughtered the Sinaloans.

Neither Barrera nor Esparza had been seen or heard from since the reputed meeting, nor had Ochoa or his right-hand man, Miguel Morales, also known as Forty. And there was intelligence to support the theory that a large gunfight occurred in Dos Erres—D-2, the military unit that controls Guatemalan intelligence, had gone in and found scores of corpses, some in the remnants of a large bonfire, which was consistent with the Zeta practice of burning bodies.

The Zetas, once the most feared cartel in Mexico, went into steep decline after the alleged Dos Erres conference, further suggesting that their leadership had been killed and that they had suffered mass casualties.

The Sinaloa cartel had not experienced a similar decline. To the contrary, it had become the undisputed power, by far the most dominant cartel, and had imposed a sort of peace on a Mexico that had seen a hundred thousand people killed in ten years of drug violence.

And Sinaloa was sending more drugs than ever into the United States, not only the marijuana, methamphetamine and cocaine that had made the cartel wealthy beyond measure, but also masses of heroin.

All of which argued against the Dos Erres theory and for the rival "empty coffin theory" that Barrera had, in fact, decimated the Zetas in Dos Erres, then staged his own death and was now running the cartel from a remote location.

Again, there was ample precedent—over the years several cartel bosses had faked their deaths to relieve relentless DEA pressure. Cartel soldiers had raided coroners' offices and stolen the bodies of their bosses to prevent positive identification and to encourage rumors that their *jefes* were still on the right side of the grass.

Indeed, as Keller has often pointed out to his subordinates, none of the bodies of the leaders alleged to have been killed in Dos Erres have ever been found. And while it is widely accepted that Ochoa and Forty have gone to their reward, the fact that Sinaloa just keeps humming along like a machine lends credence to the empty coffin theory.

But the absence of any appearances by Barrera over the past year and a half indicates otherwise. While he always tended to be reclusive, Barrera usually would have shown up with his young wife, Eva, for holiday celebrations in his hometown of La Tuna, Sinaloa, or for New Year's Eve at a resort town like Puerto Vallarta or Mazatlán. No such sightings have been reported. Furthermore, digital surveillance has revealed no emails, tweets, or other social media messages; phone monitoring has revealed no telephonic communications.

Barrera has numerous *estancias* in Sinaloa and Durango in addition to houses in Los Mochis, along the coast. The DEA knows about these residences and there are doubtless others. But satellite photos of these locations have shown a decided lessening of traffic in and out. Ordinarily, when Barrera was moving from one location to another, there would be an *increase* in traffic of bodyguards and support personnel, a spike in internet and cell-phone communications as his people arranged logistics, and a heavier communications footprint among state and local police on the Sinaloa cartel payroll.

The absence of any of this would tend to support the Dos Erres theory, that Barrera is dead.

But the question—if Barrera isn't running the cartel, who is?—has yet to be answered, and the Mexican rumor mill is full to capacity with Barrera sightings in Sinaloa, Durango, Guatemala, Barcelona, even in San Diego where his wife (or widow?) and two small sons live. "Barrera" has even sent texts and Twitter messages that have fueled a cult of "*Adán vive*" disciples, who leave hand-painted signs along roadsides to that effect.

Members of Barrera's immediate family—especially his sister, Elena— have gone to some lengths to *not* confirm his death, and any ambiguity surrounding his status gives the cartel time to try to arrange an orderly succession.

The Dos Erres theory believers aver that the cartel has a vested interest in keeping Barrera "alive" and is putting out these messages as disinformation—

a living Barrera is to be feared, and that fear helps keep potential enemies from challenging Sinaloa. Some of the theory's strongest adherents even posit that the Mexican government itself, desperate to maintain stability, is behind the Adán Vive movement.

The confirmation of Barrera's death, if that's what this is, Keller thinks, is going to send shock waves across the narco world.

"Who has custody of the body?" Keller asks.

"D-2," Blair says.

"So Sinaloa already knows." The cartel has deep sources in all levels of the Guatemalan government. And the CIA already knows, too, Keller thinks. D-2 has been penetrated by everybody. "Who else in DEA knows about this?"

"Just the Guat City RAC, you, and me," Blair says. "I thought you'd want to keep this tight."

Blair is smart and loyal enough to make sure that Keller got this news first and as exclusively as possible. Art Keller is a good man to have as a boss and a dangerous man to have as an enemy.

Everyone in DEA knows about the vendetta between Keller and Adán Barrera, which goes all the way back to the 1980s, when Barrera participated in the torture-murder of Keller's partner, Ernie Hidalgo.

And everyone knows that Keller was sent down to Mexico to recapture Barrera, but ended up taking down the Zetas instead.

Maybe literally.

The watercooler talk—more like whispers—speaks of the ruins of a wrecked Black Hawk helicopter in the village of Dos Erres, where the battle between the Zetas and Barrera's Sinaloans allegedly took place. Sure, the Guatemalan army has American helicopters—so does the Sinaloa cartel for that matter—but the talk continues about a secret mission of American spec-op mercenaries who went in and took out the Zeta leadership, bin Laden style. And if you believe those rumors—dismissed as laughable grassy knoll fantasies by the DEA brass—you might also believe that on that mission was one Art Keller.

And now Keller, who took down both Adán Barrera and the Zetas, is the administrator of the Drug Enforcement Agency, the most powerful "drug warrior" in the world, commanding an agency with over 10,000 employees, 5,000 special agents, and 800 intelligence analysts.

"Keep it tight for now," Keller says.

He knows that Blair hears the dog whistle—that what Keller really means is that he wants to keep this away from Denton Howard, the assistant administrator of the DEA, a political appointee who would like nothing more than to flay Keller alive and display the pelt on his office wall.

The chief whisperer of all things Keller—*Keller has a questionable past, Keller has divided loyalties, a Mexican mother and a Mexican wife (did you know that his first name isn't actually Arthur, it's Arturo?), Keller is a cowboy, a loose cannon, he has blood on his hands, there are rumors that he was even there in Dos Erres*—Howard is a cancer, going around the Intelligence Unit to work his own sources, cultivating personal diplomatic relationships in Mexico, Central America, Colombia, Europe, Asia, working the Hill, cuddling up to the media.

Keller can't keep this news from him, but even a couple of hours' head start will help. For one thing, the Mexican government has to hear this from me, Keller thinks, not from Howard, or worse, from Howard's buddies at Fox News.

"Send the dental records to D-2," Keller says. "They get our full cooperation."

We're talking hours, not days, Keller thinks, before this gets out there. Some responsible person in D-2 sent this to us, but someone else has doubtless put in a call to Sinaloa, and someone else will look to cash in with the media.

Because Adán Barrera has become in death what he never was in life.

A rock star.

It started, in of all places, with an article in *Rolling Stone*.

An investigative journalist named Clay Bowen started to chase down the rumors of a gun battle in Guatemala between the Zetas and the Sinaloa cartel and soon tripped over the fact that Adán Barrera had, in the snappy hip language of the story, "gone 414." The journalistic Stanley went in search of his narco Livingstone and came up with nothing.

So that became his story.

Adán Barrera was the phantom, the will-o'-the-wisp, the mysterious, invisible power behind the world's largest drug-trafficking organization, an elusive genius that law enforcement could neither catch nor even find. The story went back to Barrera's "daring escape" from a Mexican prison in 2004 ("Daring," my aching ass, Keller thought when he read the story—the man bought his way out of the prison and left from the roof in a helicopter), and now Barrera had made the "ultimate escape" by staging his own death.

In the absence of an interview with his subject, Bowen apparently talked to associates and family members ("anonymous sources say . . . unidentified people close to Barrera state that . . .") who painted a flattering picture of Barrera—he gives money to churches and schools; he builds clinics and playgrounds; he's good to his mother and his kids.

He brought peace to Mexico.

(This last quote made Keller laugh out loud. It was Barrera who started the war that killed a hundred thousand people, and he "brought peace" by winning it?)

Adán Barrera, drug trafficker and mass murderer, became a combination of Houdini, Zorro, Amelia Earhart, and Mahatma Gandhi. A misunderstood child of rural poverty who rose from his humble beginnings to wealth and power by selling a product that, after all, people wanted anyway, and who is now a benefactor, a philanthropist harassed and hunted by two governments that he brilliantly eludes and outwits.

The rest of the media took it up during a slow news cycle, and stories about Barrera's disappearance ran on CNN, Fox, all the networks. He became a social media darling, with thousands playing a game of "Where's Waldo?" on the internet, breathlessly speculating on the great man's whereabouts. (Keller's absolute favorite story was that Barrera had turned down an offer from *Dancing with the Stars,* or alternatively, was hiding out as the star of an NBC sitcom.) The furor faded, of course, as all these things do, save for a few die-hard bloggers and the DEA and the Mexican SEIDO, for whom the issue of Barrera's existence or lack thereof wasn't a game but deadly serious business.

And now, Keller thinks, it will start again.

The coffin is filled.

Now it's the throne that's empty.

We're in a double bind, Keller thinks. The Sinaloa cartel is the key driver behind the heroin traffic. If we help take the cartel down, we destroy the Pax Sinaloa. If we lay off the cartel, we accept the continuation of the heroin crisis here.

The Sinaloa cartel has its agenda and we have ours, and Barrera's "death" could create an irreconcilable conflict between promoting stability in Mexico and stopping the heroin epidemic in the United States.

The first requires the preservation of the Sinaloa cartel, the second requires its destruction.

The State Department and CIA will at least passively collude in Mexico's partnership with the cartel, while the Justice Department and DEA are determined to shut down the cartel's heroin operations.

There are other factions. The AG wants drug policy reforms, and so does the White House drug czar, but while the attorney general is going to leave soon anyway, the White House is more cautious. The president has all the courage and freedom of a lame duck, but doesn't want to hand the conservatives any ammunition to fire at his potential successor who has to run in 2016.

And one of those conservatives is your own deputy, Keller thinks, who would like to see you *and* the reforms swept out in '16 and preferably before. The Republicans already have the House and Senate, if they win the White House the new occupant will put in a new AG who will take us back to the heights—or depths, if you will—of the war on drugs, and one of the first people he'll fire is you.

So the clock is ticking.

It's your job, Keller thinks, to stop the flow of heroin into this country. The Sinaloa cartel—Adán's legacy, the edifice he constructed, that you *helped* him construct—is slaughtering thousands of people and it has to die.

Check that—it won't just die.

You have to kill it.

When Blair leaves, Keller starts working the phones.

First he puts in a call to Orduña.

"They found the body," Keller says, without introduction.

"Where?"

"Where do you think?" Keller says. "I'm about to call SEIDO but I wanted you to know first."

Because Orduña is clean—absolutely squeaky clean, taking neither money nor shit from anyone. His marines—with Keller's help and intelligence from the US—had devastated the Zetas, and now Orduña is ready to take down the rest, including Sinaloa.

A silence, then Orduña says, "So champagne is in order."

Next, Keller phones SEIDO, the Mexican version of a combined FBI and DEA, and speaks to the attorney general. It's a delicate call because the Mexican AG would be offended that the Guatemalans contacted DEA before they contacted him. The relationship has always been fragile, all the more so because of Howard's incessant meddling, but mostly because SEIDO has been, at various times, in Sinaloa's pocket.

"I wanted to give you a heads-up right away," Keller says. "We're going to put out a press release, but we can hold it until you put out yours."

"I appreciate that."

The next call Keller makes is to his own attorney general.

"We want to get a statement out," the AG says.

"We do," Keller says, "but let's hold it until Mexico can get it out first."

"Why is that?"

"To let them save face," Keller says. "It looks bad for them if they got the news from us."

"They *did* get the news from us."

"We have to work with them," Keller says. "And it's always good to have a marker. Hell, it's not like we captured the guy—he got killed by other narcos."

"Is that what happened?"

"Sure looks like it." He spends five more minutes persuading the AG to hold the announcement and then calls a contact at CNN. "You didn't get this from me, but Mexico is about to announce that Adán Barrera's body has been found in Guatemala."

"Jesus, can we run with that?"

"That's your call," Keller says. "I'm just telling you what's about to happen. It will confirm the story that Barrera was killed after a peace meeting with the Zetas."

"Then who's been running the cartel?"

"Hell if I know."

"Come on, Art."

"Do you want to get out ahead of Fox," Keller asks, "or do you want to stay on the phone asking me questions I can't answer?"

Turns out it's the former.

Martin's Tavern has been in business since they repealed Prohibition in 1933 and has been a haven for Democratic pols ever since. Keller steps inside next to the booth where legend says that John Kennedy proposed to Jackie.

Camelot, Keller thinks.

Another myth, but one that he had profoundly believed in as a kid. He believed in JFK and Bobby, Martin Luther King Jr., Jesus and God. The first four having been assassinated, that leaves God, but not the one who'd inhabited Keller's childhood in the place of his absent father, not the omnipresent, omniscient, omnipotent deity who ruled with stern but fair justice.

That God died in Mexico.

Like a lot of gods, Keller thinks as the stale warmth of the cozy tavern hits him. Mexico is a country where the temples of the new gods are built on the gravesites of the old.

He climbs the narrow wooden stairs to the upstairs room where Sam Rayburn used to hold court, and Harry Truman and Lyndon Johnson twisted arms to get their bills passed.

O'Brien sits alone in a booth. His full face is ruddy, his thick hair snow white, as befits a man in his seventies. His thick hand is wrapped around a squat glass. Another glass sits on the table.

O'Brien is a Republican. He just likes Martin's.

"I ordered for you," he says as Keller sits down.

"Thanks," Keller says. "It *is* Barrera's body. They just confirmed it."

"What did you tell the attorney general?" O'Brien asks.

"What we know," Keller says. "That our intelligence about a battle between the Zetas and Sinaloa turned out to be accurate, and that Barrera was apparently killed in the gunfight."

O'Brien says, "If Dos Erres becomes a real story, we can be connected to Tidewater."

"We can," Keller says. "But there's nothing to connect Tidewater to the raid."

The company had dissolved and then re-formed in Arizona under a different flag. Twenty people went on the Guatemala mission. One KIA. His body was extracted, the family informed that he was killed in a training accident, and they agreed to an out-of-court settlement. Four wounded, also successfully extracted and treated at a facility in Costa Rica, the medical records destroyed and the men compensated according to the contractual terms. Of the remaining fifteen, one has been killed in a car accident, a second while under contract to another vendor. The other thirteen have no intention of breaching the confidentiality clauses in their contracts.

The Black Hawk that went down had no markings, and the guys blew it up before they exfilled. D-2 came in the next day and laundered the scene.

"I'm more worried about the White House getting nervous," Keller says.

"I'll keep them steady," O'Brien says. "We got guns to each other's heads, what we used to call 'mutually assured destruction.' And shit, when you think about it, if the public found out that POTUS went cowboy and whacked three of the world's biggest drug dealers? In the current environment—the heroin epidemic—his approval rating would go through the roof."

"Your Republican colleagues would try to impeach," Keller says. "And you'd vote with them."

There's been talk of O'Brien running for president in 2016, most of it started by the senator himself.

O'Brien laughs. "In terms of sheer treachery, backstabbing and cutthroat, hand-to-hand combat—in terms of pure lethal killing power—the Mexican cartels have nothing on this town. Try to remember that."

"I'll keep it in mind."

"So you're satisfied this won't come back on us."

"I am."

O'Brien raises his glass. "Then here's to the recently discovered dead."

Keller finishes his drink.

Two hours later Keller looks at the image of Iván Esparza on the big screen of the briefing room. Esparza wears a striped *norteño* shirt, jeans, and shades, and stands in front of a private jet.

"Iván Archivaldo Esparza," Blair says. "Age thirty. Born in Culiacán, Sinaloa. Eldest son of the late Ignacio 'Nacho' Esparza, one of the three principal partners in the Sinaloa cartel. Iván has two younger brothers, Oviedo and Alfredo, in order of seniority, all in the family business."

The picture changes to a bare-chested Iván standing on a boat with other motor yachts in the background.

"Iván is a classic example of the group that has come to be known as Los Hijos," Blair says. "'The Sons.' Replete with *norteño*-cowboy wardrobe, oversize jewelry, gold chains, backward baseball caps, exotic boots and multiple cars—Maseratis, Ferraris, Lamborghinis. He even has the diamond-encrusted handguns. And he posts photos of all this on social media."

Blair shows some images from Iván's blog:

A gold-plated AK-47 on the console of a Maserati convertible.

Stacks of twenty-dollar bills.

Iván posing with two bikini-clad young women.

Another *chica* sitting in the front seat of a car with the name Esparza tattooed on her long left leg.

Sports cars, boats, jet skis, more guns.

Keller's favorite photos are of Iván in a hooded jacket bending over a fully grown lion stretched out in front of a Ferrari, and then one with two lion cubs in the front seat. The scar on Iván's face is barely visible, but the cheekbone is still a little flattened.

"Now that Barrera is confirmed dead," Blair says, "Iván is next in line to take over. Not only is he Nacho's son, he's Adán's brother-in-law. The Esparza wing of the cartel has billions of dollars, hundreds of soldiers and heavy political influence. But there are other candidates."

A picture of an elegant woman comes on the screen.

"Elena Sánchez Barrera," Blair says, "Adán's sister, once ran his Baja plaza but retired years ago, yielding the territory to Iván. She has two sons: Rudolfo, who did time here in the US for cocaine trafficking, and Luis. Elena is reputed to be out of the drug business now, as are her two sons. Most of the family money is now invested in legitimate businesses, but both Rudolfo and

Luis occasionally run with Los Hijos, and as Adán's blood nephews, they have to be considered potential heirs to the throne."

A photo of Ricardo Núñez comes up.

"Núñez has the wealth and the power to take over the cartel," Blair says, "but he's a natural born number two, born to stand behind the throne, not to sit in it. He's a lawyer at heart, a cautious, persnickety legalist without the taste or tolerance for blood that a move for the top demands."

Another picture of a young man goes up on the screen.

Keller recognizes Ric Núñez.

"Núñez has a son," Blair says, "also Ricardo, twenty-five, with the ridiculous sobriquet of 'Mini-Ric.' He's only on the list because he's Barrera's godson."

More pictures go up of Mini-Ric.

Drinking beer.

Driving a Porsche.

Holding a monogrammed pistol.

Pulling a cheetah on a leash.

"Ric lacks his father's seriousness," Blair says. "He's another Hijo, a playboy burning through money he never earned through his own sweat or blood. When he isn't high, he's drunk. He can't control himself, never mind the cartel."

Keller sees a photo of Ric and Iván drinking together, raising glasses in a toast to the camera. Their free hands are tossed over each other's shoulders.

"Iván Esparza and Ric Núñez are best friends," Blair says. "Iván is probably closer to Ric than to his own brothers. But Ric is a beta wolf in the pack that Iván leads. Iván is ambitious, Ric is almost antiambitious."

Keller already knows all this, but he asked Blair to give a briefing to the DEA and Justice personnel in the wake of the discovery of Adán's body. Denton Howard is in the front row—finally educating himself, Keller thinks.

"There are a few other Hijos," Blair says. "Rubén Ascensión's father, Tito, was Nacho Esparza's bodyguard, but now has his own organization, the Jalisco cartel, which primarily makes its money from methamphetamine.

"This kid—"

He shows another picture of a young man—short black hair, black shirt, staring angrily into the camera.

"—Damien Tapia," Blair says, "aka 'The Young Wolf.' Age twenty-two, son of the late Diego Tapia, another one of Adán's former partners. Was a member of Los Hijos until his dad ran afoul of Barrera back in 2007, touching off a major civil war in the cartel, which Barrera won. Used to be very tight with Ric and Iván, but Damien doesn't hang with them anymore, as he blames their fathers for *his* father's killing."

Los Hijos, Keller thinks, are sort of the Brat Pack of the Mexican drug trade, the third generation of traffickers. The first was Miguel Ángel Barrera—"M-1"—and his associates; the second was Adán Barrera, Nacho Esparza, Diego Tapia, and their various rivals and enemies—Heriberto Ochoa, Hugo Garza, Rafael Caro.

Now it's Los Hijos.

But unlike the previous generation, Los Hijos never worked the poppy fields, never got their hands dirty in the soil or bloody in the wars that their fathers and uncles fought. They talk a good game, they wave around gold-plated pistols and AKs, but they've never walked the walk. Spoiled, entitled and vacuous, they think they're just owed the money and the power. They have no idea what comes with it.

Iván Esparza's assumption of power is at least ten years premature. He doesn't have the maturity or experience required to run this thing. If he's smart, he'll use Ricardo Núñez as a sort of consigliere, but the word on Iván is that he's not smart—he's arrogant, short-tempered and showy, qualities that his buttoned-down father had only contempt for.

But the son is not the father.

"It's a new day," Keller says. "Barrera's death didn't slow down the flow for even a week. There's more coming in now than ever. So there's a continuity and stability there. The cartel is a corporation that lost its CEO. It still has a board of directors that will eventually appoint a new chief executive. Let's make sure we're privy to that conversation."

He's the image of his old man.

When Hugo Hidalgo walks through the door, it takes Keller back almost thirty years.

To himself and Ernie Hidalgo in Guadalajara.

Same jet-black hair.

Same handsome face.

Same smile.

"Hugo, how long has it been?" Keller walks out from behind the desk and hugs him. "Come on, sit down, sit down."

He leads Hugo to a chair in a little alcove by the window and takes the seat across from him. His receptionist and a number of secretaries had wondered how a junior field agent had managed to get an appointment with the administrator, especially on a day when Keller had canceled everything else and basically locked himself in his office.

Keller has been in there all day, watching Mexican news shows and satellite feeds covering the announcement of Adán Barrera's death. Univision broadcast footage of the funeral cortege—scores of vehicles—as it snaked its way down from the mountains toward Culiacán. In villages and towns along the way, people lined the road and tossed flowers, ran up to the hearse weeping, pressing their hands against the glass. Makeshift shrines had been constructed with photos of Barrera, candles and signs that read ¡ADÁN VIVE!

All for the little piece of shit who murdered the father of the young man who now sits across from him, who used to call him Tío Arturo. Hugo must be, what, thirty now? A little older?

"How are you?" Keller asks. "How's the family?"

"Mom's good," Hugo says. "She's living in Houston now. Ernesto is with Austin PD. One of those hippie cops on a bicycle. Married, three kids."

Keller feels guilty that he's lost touch.

Feels guilty about a lot of things involving Ernie Hidalgo. It was his fault that Ernie got killed when Hugo was just a little boy. Keller had spent his entire career trying to make it right—had tracked down everyone involved and put them behind bars.

Devoted his life to taking down Adán Barrera.

And finally did.

"How about you?" Keller asks. "Married? Kids?"

"Neither," Hugo says. "Yet. Look, sir, I know you're very busy, I appreciate you taking the time—"

"Of course."

"You once told me if there was anything you could ever do, not to hesitate."

"I meant it."

"Thank you," Hugo says. "I haven't wanted to take advantage of that, of our relationship, it's not that I think I'm owed anything . . ."

Keller has followed Hugo's career from afar.

The kid has done it the right way.

Military. Good service with the US Marines in Iraq.

Then he went back and finished college, degree in criminal justice from UT, and then caught on with Maricopa County Sheriff's Office. Put up a good record there and kept applying to DEA until he was finally hired.

He could have done it differently, Keller knows. Could simply have walked in and said he was the son of a fallen DEA hero, and they would have given him a job right away.

But he didn't do that.

He earned it, and Keller respects that.

His father would have, too.

"What can I do for you, Hugo?"

"I've been on the job for three years now," Hugo says, "and I'm still investigating marijuana buys in suburban Seattle."

"You don't like Seattle?"

"It's about as far as you can get from Mexico," Hugo says. "But maybe that's the idea."

"What do you mean?"

Hugo looks uncomfortable, but then sets his jaw and looks straight at Keller.

Just like Ernie would have done, Keller thinks.

"Are you keeping me out of danger, sir?" Hugo asks. "If you are—"

"I'm not."

"Well, someone is," Hugo says. "I've put in for FAST assignments five times and haven't gotten one of them. It doesn't make any sense. I speak fluent Spanish, I look Mexican, I have all the weapons qualifications."

"Why do you want FAST?"

FAST is an acronym for Foreign-Deployed Advisory and Support Team, but Keller knows they do a lot more than advise and support. They're basically the DEA's special forces.

"Because that's where it's happening," Hugo says. "I see kids dying of overdoses. I want in on that fight. On the front lines."

"Is that the only reason?" Keller asks.

"Isn't it enough?"

"Can I be honest with you, Hugo?"

"I wish someone would," Hugo says.

"You can't spend your life getting revenge for your father," Keller says.

"With all respect, sir," Hugo says. "*You* did."

"Which is how I know." Keller leans forward in his chair. "The men who killed your father are all dead. Two died in prison, one was killed in a gunfight on a bridge in San Diego. I was there. The last one . . . they're about to hold his wake. The job is finished, son. You don't have to take it up."

"I want my father to have been proud of me," Hugo says.

"I'm sure he is."

"I don't want to be advanced because of who my father was," Hugo says, "but I don't want to be held back, either."

"That's fair," Keller says. "I tell you what, if someone is blocking your transfer to FAST, I'll unblock it. You pass the test, you get through training— only half do—I'll oil the wheels for assignment to Afghanistan. Front lines."

"I speak Spanish, not Urdu."

"Be realistic, Hugo," Keller says. "There's no way in hell we're going to let you go into Mexico. Or Guatemala, or El Salvador, or Costa Rica or Colombia. DEA is simply not going to risk those headlines, if something happened to you. And something would—you'd be a marked man."

"I'll take my chances."

"I won't." I had to tell Teresa Hidalgo her husband was dead, Keller thinks. I'm not going to tell her that her son has been killed. He makes a mental note to find out who has been keeping Hugo out of harm's way and thank him. It was solid thinking. "You don't want Kabul, name me something you would want. Europe—Spain, France, Italy?"

"Don't dangle shiny objects in front of me, sir," Hugo says. "Either I get moved to the front lines or I leave DEA. And you know I'll catch on with a border-state police force and you also know they'll put me UC. I'll be making drug buys from Sinaloa before you take my name off the Christmas card list."

You are your father's son, Keller thinks. You'll do exactly what you said, and you'll get yourself killed, and I owe your dad more than that.

"You want to take down the cartel?" Keller asks.

"Yes, sir."

"I might have a job for you right here," Keller says. "As my aide."

"Pushing paper," Hugo says.

"You think you're going to take down the cartel by buying a few keys of coke in El Paso or gunning down a few *sicarios* in El Salvador, you might be too stupid to work here," Keller says. "But if you want to be in the real war, fly back to Seattle, pack your things, and be here ready to work first thing Monday morning. It's the best offer you're going to get, son. I'd take it if I were you."

"I'll take it."

"Good. See you Monday."

He walks Hugo to the door and thinks, Shit, I just got stood down by Ernie Hidalgo's *kid*.

He goes back to the television.

They've brought Adán's body back to Culiacán.

If Ric has to sit there five more minutes, he *will* blow his brains out.

For sure, this time.

Death would be preferable to sitting on this wooden folding chair staring at a closed coffin full of Adán Barrera's bones, pretending to be grieving, pretending to be contemplating fond memories of his godfather that he really didn't have.

The whole thing is gross.

But kind of funny, in a Guillermo del Toro kind of way. The whole concept of a *velorio* is so people can view the body, but there *is* no body, not really; they just tossed the skeleton into a coffin that probably cost more than most people's houses, so it's kind of like going to a movie where there's no picture, only sound.

Then there was the whole discussion of what to do with the suit, because you're supposed to dress the deceased in his best suit so he's not walking around in the next life looking shabby, but that clearly wasn't going to work, so what they did was they folded up an Armani they found in one of Adán's closets and laid it in the coffin.

Even funnier, though, was the dilemma about what else to throw in, because the tradition is you put in stuff that the dead guy liked to do in life, but no one could think of anything that Adán did for fun, anything that he actually liked.

"We could put money in there," Iván muttered to Ric as they stood on the edge of this conversation. "He sure as shit liked money."

"Or pussy," Ric answered.

The word was that his godfather was a major player.

"Yeah, I don't think they're going to let you kill some hot bitch and lay her in there with him," Iván said.

"I dunno," Ric said. "There's plenty of room."

"I'll give you a thousand bucks to suggest it," Iván said.

"Not worth it," Ric said, watching his father and Elena Sánchez in earnest discussion on the topic. No, his dad would not be amused and Elena already didn't like him. And, anyway, he wouldn't say anything like that in front of Eva—speaking of hot bitches—who looked . . . well, hot . . . in her black dress.

Ric would definitely fuck Eva, who was, after all, his own age, but he wasn't going to say that, either, not in front of her brother Iván.

"*I'd* fuck her," Belinda had said to Ric. "Definitely."

"You think she goes both ways?"

"Baby," Belinda said, "with me, they *all* go both ways. I get anyone I want."

Ric thought about this for a second. "Not Elena. She has ice down there."

"I'd melt it," Belinda said, flicking out her tongue. "And turn it to tears of joy."

Belinda never lacked for confidence.

Anyway, what they finally decided to put in the coffin was a baseball, because Adán sort of liked baseball—although no one there could remember him going to a single game—an old pair of boxing gloves from Adán's teenage days as a wannabe boxing promoter, and a photo of the daughter who died so young, which made Ric feel a little bad about wanting to put a dead chick in with him.

So that was *that* discussion—the more serious debate had been where to hold the *velorio* in the first place. At first they thought they'd do it at Adán's mother's house in his home village of La Tuna, but then they reconsidered that it might be too much on the old lady and also—as Ric's father had pointed out—"the rural location would present a host of logistical difficulties."

Okay.

They decided to hold it in Culiacán, where the cemetery was, after all, at someone's house. The problem was that everyone had a house—actually, houses—in or around the city, so an argument started about whose house they should do it in because it seemed to have some *significance*.

Elena wanted it at her house—Adán was her brother, after all; Iván wanted at the Esparza family home—Adán was the son-in-law; Ric's dad suggested their place in the suburbs of Eldorado, "farther away from prying eyes."

The fuck difference does it make? Ric wondered, watching the debate get heated. Adán's not going to care, the guy is dead. But it seemed to matter to them and they really got into it until Eva quietly said, "Adán and I also had a home. We'll do it there."

Ric noticed that Iván didn't look too thrilled about his little sister speaking up. "It's too much to ask you to host this."

Why? Ric wondered. It's not like Adán's going to be too busy laying out bean dip or something to enjoy his own wake.

"It really is too much, dear," Elena said.

Ric's dad nodded. "It's so far out in the country."

They finally agree on something, Ric thought.

But Eva said, "We'll do it there."

So Ric and everyone else had to drive all the way out to East Buttfuck to Adán's *estancia,* up twisting dirt roads, past blockades of state police providing security. Fucking caravans of narcos coming to pay their respects, some out of love, some out of obligation, some out of fear of not being seen there. You got an invitation to Adán Barrera's *velorio* and you no-showed, you might be the guest of honor for the next one.

His dad and Elena had made most of the arrangements, so of course it was perfect. Helicopters circling overhead, armed security prowling the grounds, parking valets with nines strapped to their waists.

Guests crowded the sloping front lawn. Tables with white cloths had been set out and were heavy with platters of food, bottles of wine, and pitchers of beer, lemonade, and water. Waiters walked around with trays of hors d'oeuvres.

One of Rudolfo Sánchez's norteño bands played from a gazebo.

The walkway up to the house was strewn with marigold petals, a tradition in a *velorio*.

"They really went all out," Ric's wife, Karin, said.

"What did you expect?"

Ric had attended the Autonomous University of Sinaloa for all of two semesters, majoring in business, and all he really learned about economics was that a cheap condom can be far more expensive than a good one. When he told his father that Karin was *embarazada*, Ricardo told him he was going to do the right thing.

Ric knew what that was: get rid of the thing and break up with Karin.

"No," Núñez said. "You're going to get married and raise your child."

Ric Sr. thought the responsibility of having a family would "make a man" out of his son. It sort of did—it made a man who rarely came home and had a mistress who would do everything his wife wouldn't. Not that he asked her—Karin, while pretty enough, was as dull as Sunday dinner. If he suggested some of the things that Belinda did, she would probably burst out crying and lock herself in the bathroom.

His father was unsympathetic. "You spend more time running around with the Esparzas than you do at home."

"I need a boys' night out now and again."

"But you're not a boy, you're a man," Núñez said. "A man spends time with his family."

"You've met Karin?"

"You chose to have sex with her," Núñez said. "Without adequate protection."

"Once," Ric said. "I don't have to worry about sex with her much now."

"Have a mistress," Núñez said. "A man does that. But a man takes care of his family."

Although his father would shit bricks sideways if he knew Ric's choice of a mistress—an out-and-out psycho who is also his head of security. No, Dad would not approve of La Fósfora so they've kept it on the down low.

His old man had more to say. "To disrespect your marriage is to disrespect your godfather, and that I cannot allow."

Ric went home that night, all right.

"Have you been bitching to my father?" he asked Karin.

"You're never home!" she said. "You spend every night with your friends! You're probably fucking some whore!"

Whores, plural, Ric thought, but he didn't say that. What he said was "Do you like this big new house? How about the condo in Cabo, do you like that? The Rosarito beach cottage? Where do you think all that comes from? The clothes, the jewelry, the big flat-screen your eyes are always glued to. The nanny for your daughter so your telenovelas won't be interrupted. Where do you think all that comes from? Me?"

Karin sneered. "You don't even have a job."

"My *job*," Ric said, "is being that man's son."

Another sneer. " 'Mini-Ric.' "

"That's right," he said. "So someone who's not acting like a dumb bitch might think, 'Hmm, the last thing I want to do is run my husband down to his dad and risk cutting all that off.' Of course, that's someone who's *not* acting like a dumb bitch."

"Get out."

"Jesus Christ, make up your mind," Ric said. "You want me home or you want me out, which is it? One fucking night with you and it turns into a life sentence."

"How do you think I feel?" Karin asked.

That's the best she can do, Ric thought. If he'd called Belinda a dumb cunt, she would have shot him in the dick and then sucked the bullet out.

"Here's the point," Ric said. "You want to bitch, bitch to your girlfriends over one of your lunches. Complain to the housekeeper, complain to the worthless little piece of shit dog I paid for. But you do not, *ever*, complain to my father."

"Or you'll what?" She got right in his face.

"I would never hit a woman," Ric said. "You know that's not me. But I will divorce you. You'll get one of the houses and you'll live in it alone, and good luck trying to find a new husband with a kid on your hip."

Later that night he crawled into bed, drunk enough to soften a little. "Karin?"

"What?"

"I know I'm an asshole," Ric said. "I'm an Hijo, I don't know any different."

"It's just that you . . ."

"What?"

"You just play at life," she said.

Ric laughed. "Baby, what else is there to do with it?"

As an Hijo, he's seen friends, cousins, uncles killed. Most of them young, some younger than he is. You have to play while life gives you the time to play, because sooner or later, probably sooner, they're going to be putting your favorite toys in a box with you.

Fast cars, fast boats, faster women. Good food, better booze, best drugs. Nice houses, nicer clothes, nicest guns. If there's anything more to life than that, he hasn't seen it.

"Play *with* me," he said.

"I can't," she said. "We have a child."

Now that she's settled into young motherhood, raising their little girl, their marriage has evolved from open hostility to dull tolerance. And, of course, she had to accompany him to Adán's *velorio*, anything else would have been "unseemly" in his father's eyes.

But it didn't help that Belinda was there, too.

On the job.

Karin noticed her. "That girl. Is she security?"

"She's the *head* of security."

"She's striking," Karin said. "Is she a *tortillera*, do you think?"

Ric laughed. "How do you know that word?"

"I know things. I don't live in a cocoon."

Yeah, sort of you do, Ric thought. "I don't know if she's lesbian or not. Probably."

Now Karin sits next to Ric, looking every bit as miserable as he feels, but gazing dutifully at the coffin (Karin does duty like a nun does a rosary, Ric thinks) as befits the wife of the godson.

Which reminds Ric that he became Adán's godson on the happy occasion of his wedding, an old Mexican tradition in which a man can "adopt" a godson on the celebration of a major event in his life, although Ric knows that Adán did this to honor his father more than to express any particular closeness to him.

Ric has heard the story of how his father hooked up with Adán Barrera at least a thousand times.

Ricardo Núñez was a young man then, just thirty-eight when Adán was brought to the gates of the prison, having been given "compassionate extradition" from the US to serve the remainder of his twenty-two-year sentence in Mexico.

It was a cold morning, Ric's dad always said when relating the story. Adán was cuffed by the wrists and ankles, shivering as he changed from a blue down issue jacket into a brown uniform with the number 817 stitched on the front and back.

"I made a sanctimonious speech," Núñez told Ric. (Does he make any other kind? Ric thought.) *"Adán Barrera, you are now a prisoner of CEF- ERESO II. Do not think that your former status gives you any standing here. You are just another criminal."*

That was for the benefit of the cameras, which Adán completely understood. Inside, he graciously accepted Núñez's apology and assurances that everything that could be done to make him comfortable would be done.

As indeed it was.

Diego Tapia had already arranged for complete security. A number of his most trusted men agreed to be arrested, convicted and sent to the facility so that they could guard "El Patrón." And Núñez cooperated with Diego to provide Adán with a "cell" that was over six hundred square feet with a full kitchen, a well-stocked bar, an LED television, a computer, and a commercial refrigerator stocked with fresh groceries.

On some nights, the prison cafeteria would be converted into a theater for Adán to host "movie nights" for his friends, and Ric's dad always made it a point to relate that the drug lord preferred G movies without sex or violence.

On other nights, prison guards would go into Guadalajara and return with a van full of ladies of the evening for the Barrera supports and employees. But Adán didn't partake, and it wasn't long before he started his affair with a beautiful convict, former Miss Sinaloa Magda Beltrán, who became his famous mistress.

"But that was Adán," Núñez told Ric. "He always had a certain class, a certain dignity, and appreciation for quality, in people as well as things."

Adán took care of people who took care of him.

So it was just like him when weeks before Christmas he came into the office and quietly suggested that Núñez resign. That a numbered bank account had been opened for him in the Caymans and he'd find the paperwork in his new house in Culiacán.

Núñez resigned his position and went back to Sinaloa.

On Christmas night, a helicopter whisked Adán Barrera and Magda Beltrán off the roof and rumors circulated that the "escape" cost more than four million dollars in payments to people in Mexico City.

Part of that was in a numbered account in Grand Cayman for Ricardo Núñez.

Federal investigators came to question Núñez but he knew nothing about the escape. They expressed moral outrage over Adán's favored treatment in prison and threatened to prosecute Núñez, but nothing came of it. And while Núñez became unemployable as a prosecutor, it no longer mattered—Adán was as good as his word and reached out to him.

Put him into the cocaine business.

Núñez became respected.

Trusted.

And discreet. He wasn't showy, stayed out of the spotlight and off social media. Flew deliberately under the radar so even SEIDO and DEA—in fact, few people in the cartel—knew just how important he'd become.

El Abogado.

Núñez, in fact, became Adán's right-hand man.

Ric himself actually spent little time at all with Barrera, so it's weird sitting there pretending to mourn.

Adán's coffin is set on an altar built at the end of the great room for the occasion. Piles of fresh flowers are heaped on the altar, along with religious icons and crosses. Unhusked ears of corn, squash, and *papel picado* hang from a bower of branches constructed above the coffin. Open containers of raw coffee have been set out, another *velorio* tradition, which Ric suspects had more to do with killing the smell of decomposition.

As a godson, Ric sits in the front row along with Eva, of course, the Esparzas, and Elena and her sons. Adán's mother, ancient as the land, sits in a rocking chair, clad in black, a black shawl over her head, her shriveled face showing the patient sorrow of the Mexican *campesina*. God, the things she's seen, Ric thinks, the losses she's suffered—both sons, a grandson killed, a granddaughter who died young, so many others.

He knows the expression about cutting the tension with a knife, but you couldn't cut the tension in this room with a blowtorch. They're supposed to be sitting there exchanging fond stories about the deceased, except no one can think of any.

Ric has a few ideas—

Hey, how about the time Tío Adán had a whole village slaughtered to make sure he killed the snitch?

Or—

What about that time Tío Adán had his rival's wife's head sent to him in a package of dry ice?

Or—

Hey, hey, remember when Tío Adán threw those two little kids off a bridge? What a stitch. What a great, funny guy, huh?

Barrera made billions of dollars, created and ruled a freaking empire, and what does he have to show for it?

A dead child, an ex-wife who doesn't come to his wake, a young trophy widow, twin sons who will grow up without their father, a baseball, some smelly old boxing gloves and a suit he never wore. And no one, not one of the hundreds of people here, can think of one nice story to tell about him.

And that's the guy who *won*.

El Señor. El Patrón. The Godfather.

Ric sees Iván looking at him, touching his nose with his index finger. Iván gets up from his chair.

"I have to piss," Ric says.

Ric shuts the bathroom door behind him.

Iván is laying out lines on the marble-top vanity. "Fuck, could this get any more tedious?"

"It's pretty awful."

Iván rolls up a hundred-dollar bill (of course, Ric thinks), snorts a line of coke, then hands Ric the bill. "None of this shit for me, *cuate*. When I go, big fucking party, then take me out on a cigarette boat and, *bam*, Viking funeral."

Ric leans over and breathes the coke into his nose. "Goddamn, that's better. What if *I* go first?"

"I'll dump your body in an alley."

"Thanks."

There's a soft knock at the door.

"*¡Momento!*" Iván yells.

"It's me."

"Belinda," Ric says.

He opens the door, she slides in quickly and shuts it behind her. "I knew what you assholes were doing in here. Share."

Iván takes the vial out of his pocket and hands it to her. "Knock yourself out."

Belinda pours out a line and snorts it.

Iván leans against the wall. "Guess who I saw the other day? Damien Tapia."

"No shit," Ric says. "Where?"

"Starbucks."

"Christ, what did you say?"

"I said 'hello,' what do you think?"

Ric doesn't know what he thought. Damien had been an Hijo, they were kids together, played together all the time, partied, all that shit. He was as close to Damien as he was to Iván, until Adán and Diego Tapia got into a beef, which turned into a war, and Damien's father was killed.

They were all just teenagers then, kids.

Adán, of course, won the war, and the Tapia family was thrown out of the fold. Since then they had been forbidden to have any contact with Damien Tapia. Not that he wanted anything to do with them anyway. He was still around town, but running into him was, well, awkward.

"When I take over," Iván says, "I'm going to bring Damien back in."

"Yeah?"

"Why not?" Iván says. "The beef was between Adán and Damien's old man. Adán's dead, as you might have noticed. I'll make it right with Damien, it will be like before."

"Sounds good," Ric says.

He's missed Damien.

"That generation," Iván says, jutting his chin at the door, "we don't have to inherit their wars. We're going to move ahead. The Esparzas, you, Rubén and Damien. Like before. Los Hijos, like brothers, right?"

"Like brothers," Ric says.

They touch knuckles.

"If you guys are done being gay," Belinda says, "we better get back out there before they figure out what we're doing. Snorting coke at El Patrón's *velorio*? Tsk, tsk, tsk."

"Coke built this place," Iván says.

"Selling it, not snorting it," Belinda says. She looks at Ric. "Wipe your nose, boyfriend. Hey, your wife is cute."

"You've seen her before."

"Yeah, but she looks cuter today," Belinda says. "You want to do a three-some, I'll teach her some things. Come on, let's go."

She opens the door and steps out.

Iván grabs Ric by the elbow. "Hey, you know I have to take care of my brothers. But let things settle down for a few days and we'll talk, okay? About where you fit in?"

"Okay."

"Don't worry, *'mano,*" Iván says. "I'll be fair with your father, and I'll take care of you."

Ric follows him out the door.

Elena sits between her sons.

She saw a documentary on television, a nature show, and learned that when a new male lion takes over a pride, the first thing he does is kill the previous ruler's cubs. Her own cubs still carry the Barrera name and people will assume that they have ambitions even if they don't. Rudolfo has a small retinue of bodyguards and a few hangers-on, Luis even fewer. Whether I want to or not, she thinks, I'll have to take on a certain level of power to protect them.

But the top spot?

There's never been a female head of a cartel, and she doesn't want to be the first.

But she'll have to do something.

Without a power base, the other lions will track down her cubs and kill them.

Looking at her brother's coffin, she wishes she felt more. Adán was always very good to her, good to her children. She wants to cry, but the tears won't come and she tells herself that's because her heart is exhausted, played out from all the loss over the years.

Her mother, perched in her chair like a crow, is virtually catatonic. She's buried two sons, a grandson and a granddaughter. Elena wishes that she could get her to move to town but she insists on staying in the house that Adán built for her in La Tuna, all by herself if you don't count the servants and the bodyguards.

But she won't leave, she'll die in that house.

If my mother is a crow, Elena thinks, the rest are vultures. Circling, waiting to swoop down to pick my brother's bones.

Iván Esparza and his two equally cretinous brothers, Adán's horrible lawyer Núñez, and a flock of smaller players—plaza bosses, cell leaders, gunmen—looking to become bigger players.

She feels tired, all the more so when she sees Núñez walking toward her.

"Elena," Núñez says, "I wonder if we could have a word. In private."

She follows him outside to the grand sloping lawn she walked so many times with Adán.

Núñez hands her a piece of paper and says, "This is awkward."

He waits while she reads.

"This is not a position I relish," Núñez says, "certainly not one that I wanted. In fact, I prayed that this day would never come about. But I feel—strongly—that your brother's wishes should be respected."

It's Adán's writing, no question, Elena thinks. And it quite clearly declares that Ricardo Núñez should take over in the event of Adán's untimely death until his own sons reach the age of responsibility. Christ, the twins are barely two years old. Núñez will have a long regency. Plenty of time to turn the organization over to his own offspring.

"I realize that this might be a surprise," Núñez says, "and a disappointment. I only hope that there's no resentment."

"Why should there be?"

"I could understand that you might think this should have gone to family."

"Neither of my sons is interested, and Eva—"

"Is a beauty pageant queen," Núñez says.

"So was Magda Beltrán," Elena says, although she doesn't know why she feels a need to argue with him. But it's true. Adán should have married his magnificent mistress. The beautiful Magda met Adán in prison, became his lover, and then parlayed that and her considerable business acumen into creating her own multimillion-dollar organization.

"And look what happened to her," Núñez says.

True enough, Elena thinks. The Zetas suffocated her with a plastic bag and then slashed a Z into her chest. And she was carrying Adán's unborn child. Magda had confided in Elena and now she wonders if Adán ever knew. She hopes not—it would have broken his heart.

"Obviously Eva is not the person to take over," Elena says.

"Please understand," Núñez says, "that I believe I hold this position in trust for Adán's sons. But if you think that you would be the better choice, I am willing to ignore Adán's wishes and step down."

"No," she says.

Letting Núñez take the throne means shoving her own sons aside, but Elena knows that they're secretly happy to be pushed. And, frankly, if Núñez wants to make himself a target, all the better.

But Iván . . . Iván is not going to like it.

"You have my support," Elena says. She sees Núñez nod with a lawyer's graciousness at having won a settlement. Then she drops the other shoe. "I just have one small request."

Núñez smiles. "Please."

"I want Baja back. For Rudolfo."

"Baja is Iván Esparza's."

"And before it was his, it was mine."

"In all fairness, Elena, you gave it up," Núñez says. "You wanted to retire."

It was *my uncle*, M-1, who sent *my brothers* to take the Baja plaza from Güero Méndez and Rafael Caro, Elena thinks. That was in 1990, and Adán and Raúl did it. They seduced the rich Tijuana kids and turned them into a trafficking network that co-opted their parents' power structure on our behalf. They recruited gangs from San Diego to be gunmen, and they beat Méndez, Caro and everyone else to seize that plaza and use it as a base to take the entire country.

We made your Sinaloa cartel what it is, she thinks, so if I want Baja back, you're going to give it to me. I won't leave my sons without a power base with which to defend themselves.

"Baja was given to Nacho Esparza," Ricardo is saying. "And with his death, it passed to Iván."

"Iván is a clown," Elena says. They all are, she thinks, all the Hijos, including your son, Ricardo.

"With a legitimate claim and an army to back it up," Núñez says.

"And *you* now have Adán's army," Elena says, allowing to go unspoken the obvious—*if I back you up*.

"Iván is already going to be very disappointed that he's not getting the big chair," Núñez says. "Elena, I have to leave him with something."

"And Rudolfo—Adán's nephew—gets nothing?" Elena asks. "The Esparza brothers have plenty—more money than they can waste in their collective lifetimes. I'm asking for one plaza. And you can keep your domestic sales there."

Núñez looks surprised.

"Oh, please," Elena says. "I know young Ric is dealing your drugs all over Baja Sur. It's fine—I just want the north and the border."

"Oh, that's all." Elena wants one of the most lucrative plazas in the narcotics trade. Baja has a growing *narcomenudeo*, domestic street sales, but that's dwarfed by the *trasiego*, the products that run from Tijuana and Tecate into San Diego and Los Angeles. From there the drugs are distributed all over the United States.

"Is it so much?" Elena asks. "For Adán's sister to put her blessings on her brother's last wishes? You need that, Ricardo. Without it . . ."

"You're asking me to give you something that's not mine to give," Núñez says. "Adán gave the plaza to Esparza. And with all respect, Elena—my domestic business in Cabo is none of yours."

"Spoken like a lawyer," Elena says. "Not a *patrón*. If you're going to be El Patrón, *be* El Patrón. Make decisions, give orders. If you want my support, the price is Baja for my son."

The king is dead, Elena thinks.

Long live the king.

Ric sits out by the pool next to Iván.

"This is better," Ric says. "I couldn't stand another fucking minute in there."

"Where's Karin?"

"On the phone with the nanny," Ric says, "probably discussing the color of poop. It'll be a while."

"You think she's figured out you and Belinda?" Iván asks.

"Who gives a fuck?"

"Uh-oh."

"What?"

"Look," Iván says.

Ric turns to see Tito Ascensión walking toward them. About as tall as a refrigerator but thicker.

The Mastiff.

"My father's old attack dog," Iván says.

"Show some respect," Ric says. "He's Rubén's dad. Anyway, you know how many guys he's killed?"

A lot, is the answer.

Triple digits, at least.

Tito Ascensión used to be the head of Nacho Esparza's armed wing. He fought the Zetas, then the Tapias, then the Zetas again. Tito once killed thirty-eight Zetas in a single whack and hanged their bodies from a highway overpass. Turned out it was a whoops—they weren't Zetas after all, just your average citizens. Tito donned a balaclava, held a press conference and apologized for the mistake, with the caveat that his group was still at war with the Zetas so it would be prudent not to be mistaken for one.

Anyway, Tito played a big role in winning the wars for Sinaloa, and as a reward Nacho let him start his own organization in Jalisco, independent but still a satellite of Sinaloa.

Tito loved Nacho, and when he heard the Zetas had killed him down in Guatemala he grabbed five of them, tortured them to death over the course of weeks, then cut off their dicks and stuffed them in their mouths.

No, you don't disrespect El Mastín.

Now the man's shadow literally falls over both of them.

"Iván," Tito says, "may I have a word?"

"I'll catch you later," Ric says, trying not to laugh. All he can think of is Luca Brazi from the wedding scene in *The Godfather*, which he's had to watch with Iván about fifty-seven thousand times. Iván is obsessed with the movie to only a slighter lesser degree than he is with *Scarface*.

"No, stay," Iván says, and when Tito looks dubious, adds, "Ric is going to be my number two. Anything you can say to me, you can say in front of him."

He talks a little slow, like Tito is stupid.

Tito says, "I want to move my organization into heroin."

"Do you think that's wise?" Iván asks.

"It's profitable," Tito says.

He's got that right, Ric thinks. Sinaloa is making millions off smack while Jalisco is still slinging cocaine and meth.

"The two don't always go together," Iván says, trying to sound like his father. "For one thing, it would put you into competition with us."

"The market's big enough for both of us," Tito says.

Iván frowns. "Tito. Why fix what isn't broken? Jalisco makes plenty of money on meth, doesn't it? And we don't even charge you a *piso* to use our plazas."

"That was the arrangement I had with your father," Tito says.

"You paid your dues," Iván says, "no question. You've been a good soldier, and you got your own organization as a reward for that. But I think it's better to just leave things as they are, don't you?"

Christ, Ric thinks, it's almost as if he's patting the man's head.

Good dog, good dog.

Sit.

Stay.

But Tito says, "If that's what you think is best."

"It is," Iván says.

Tito nods to Ric and walks away.

"Rubén got his brains from his mother," Iván says. "His looks, too, thank God."

"Rubén's a good guy."

"He's a great guy," Iván says.

Doesn't Ric know it. Rubén is Tito's solid number two, runs his security force in Jalisco and is heavily involved in the transport of their product. How many times has Ric heard his own father say, *If only you were more like Rubén Ascensión. Serious. Mature.*

He's made it pretty clear, Ric thinks. Given a choice, he'd rather have Rubén for his son than me.

Tough luck for both of us, I guess.

"What?" Iván asks.

"What what?"

"You got a look on your face like someone just ass-fucked your puppy."

"I don't have a puppy," Ric says.

"Maybe that's it," Iván says. "You want me to get you one? What kind of dog do you want, Ric? I'll send someone out right now to get it for you. I want you to be happy, 'mano."

That's Iván, Ric thinks.

Ever since they were kids. You told him you were hungry, he went out and got food. Your bike got stolen, a new one appeared. You said you were horny, a girl showed up at the door.

"Love you, man."

"Love you, too," Iván says. Then he adds, "It's our turn now, 'mano. Our time. You'll see—it's going to be good."

"Yeah."

Ric sees his father approaching.

But it's not Ric he wants to see.

Núñez says, "Iván, we should talk."

"We should," Iván says.

Ric sees the look on his face, the smile, knows that this is the moment he's been waiting for.

His coronation.

Núñez glances down at his son and says, "In private."

"Sure." Iván winks at Ric. "I'll be back, bro."

Ric nods.

Leans back in the chair and watches his best friend and his father walk away from him.

Then he does have a memory of Adán.

Standing on the side of a dirt road in rural Durango.

"Look around you," Adán said. "What do you see?"

"Fields," Ric said.

"*Empty* fields," Adán said.

Ric couldn't argue with that. On both sides of the road, as far as he could see, marijuana fields lay fallow.

"The US has, de facto, legalized marijuana," Adán said. "If my American sources are right, two or more states will soon make it official. We simply can't compete with the local American quality and transportation costs. Last year we were getting a hundred dollars for a kilo of marijuana. Now it's twenty-five. It's hardly worth our growing the stuff anymore. We're losing tens of millions of dollars a year, and if California, for instance, legalizes, the loss will be in the hundreds of millions. But it's hot out here. Let's go get a beer."

They drove another ten miles to a little town.

A lead car went in first, made sure it was all clear, and then went into a tavern and emptied it out. The nervous owner and a girl who looked to be his daughter brought in a pitcher of cold beer and glasses.

Adán said, "Our marijuana market, once a major profit center, is collapsing; meth sales are falling; cocaine sales have flattened. For the first time in over a decade, we're looking at a fiscal year of negative growth."

It's not like they were losing money, Ric thought. Everyone there was making millions. But they made less millions than they had the year before, and it was human nature that, even if you're rich, being less rich feels like being poor.

"The present situation is unsustainable," Adán said. "The last time this occurred we were saved by the innovation of crystal meth. It became, and remains, a major profit center, but there is small potential for growth that would compensate for our marijuana losses. Similarly, the cocaine market seems to have reached its saturation point."

"What we need," Ric's father said, "is a new product."

"No," Adán said. "What we need is an *old* product."

Adán paused for dramatic effect and then said, "Heroin."

Ric was shocked. Sure, they still sold heroin, but it was a side product compared to weed, meth and coke. All their business had started with heroin, with opium, back in the days of the old *gomeros* who grew the poppy and made their fortunes selling it to the Americans to make the morphine they needed during World War II. After the war, it was the American Mafia that provided the market and bought up as much opium as they could grow for heroin.

But in the 1970s, the American DEA joined forces with the Mexican military to burn and poison the poppy fields in Sinaloa and Durango. They sprayed pesticides from airplanes, burned villages, forced the *campesinos* from their homes and scattered the *gomeros* to the winds.

It was Adán's uncle, the great Miguel Ángel Barrera—M-1—who gathered the *gomeros* at a meeting similar to this one and told them that they didn't want to be farmers—farms could be poisoned and burned—they wanted to be traffickers. He introduced them to the Colombian cocaine market and they all became wealthy as middlemen, moving Cali and Medellín coke into the United States. It was also M-1 who introduced crack cocaine to the market, creating the greatest financial windfall the *gomeros*—now known as *narcos*—had ever known.

Millionaires became billionaires.

The loose confederation of narcos became the Federación.

And now Adán wants them to make opium again? Ric thought. He thinks heroin is the answer to their problem?

It was insane.

"We have an opportunity," Adán said, "even greater than crack. A ready-made market that's just waiting for us to take advantage of. And the Americans have created it themselves."

The giant American pharmaceutical companies, he explained, had addicted thousands of people to legal painkillers.

Pills.

Oxycodone, Vicodin and others, all opium derivatives, all the fruit of the poppy.

But the pills are expensive and can be hard to obtain, Adán explained. Addicts who can no longer get prescriptions from their doctors turn to the street, where the bootleg product can cost up to thirty dollars a dose. Some of these addicts need as many as ten doses a day.

"What I propose," Adán said, "is to increase our production of heroin by seventy percent."

Ric was skeptical. Mexican black tar heroin had never been able to compete with the quality of the purer product that comes in from South Asia or the Golden Triangle. More than doubling production would only lead to massive losses.

"Our black tar heroin is currently around forty percent pure," Adán said. "I've met with the best heroin cookers in Colombia, who assure me that they can take our base product and create something called 'cinnamon heroin.'"

He took a small glassine envelope from his jacket pocket and held it up. "Cinnamon heroin is seventy to eighty percent pure. And the beauty of it is, we can sell it for ten dollars a dose."

"Why so cheap?" Núñez asked.

"We make up for it in volume," Adán said. "We become Walmart. We undercut the American pharmaceutical companies in their own market. They can't possibly compete. It will more than compensate for our marijuana losses. The yield could be in billions of new dollars. Heroin was our past. It will also be our future."

Adán, as usual, had been prescient.

In the time since just three American states legalized weed, the cartel's marijuana sales dropped by almost forty percent. It's going to take time to complete, but Núñez started to convert the marijuana fields to poppies. Just over the past year, they've increased the heroin production by 30 percent. Soon it will be 50 and by the end of the year they'll reach the 70 percent goal.

The Americans are buying. And why not? Ric thinks now. The new product is cheaper, more plentiful and more potent. It's a win–win–win. Heroin is flowing north, dollars are flowing back. So maybe, he thinks, the Adanistas are right—Barrera lives on.

Heroin is his legacy.

So that's a story you could tell.

3

Malevolent Clowns

I had a friend who was a clown. When he died, all his friends came to the funeral in the same car.

—Steven Wright

Their house is a brownstone on Hillyer Place east of Twenty-First in the Dupont Circle neighborhood. They chose it because Dupont is "walkable," for Marisol; there are coffee shops, restaurants, and bookstores nearby; and Keller likes the historical resonance of the neighborhood. Teddy Roosevelt lived around here; so did Franklin and Eleanor.

And Marisol loved the crepe myrtle tree that grew up to the third-story window, its lavender blooms reminding her of the vivid colors back in Mexico.

She's waiting up when Keller gets home, sitting in the big armchair by the living room window, reading a magazine.

"We're a 'power couple,'" she says when Keller comes through the door.

"We are?" He bends over and kisses her forehead.

"It says so right here," she says, pointing to the copy of *Washington Life* in her lap. "'Washington power couple Mr. and Mrs.'—actually, Doctor—'Art Keller showed up at the Kennedy Center fund-raiser. The DEA director and his stylish Latina wife'—that's me, I'm your 'stylish Latina wife' . . ."

Keller looks at the page, not thrilled that she's been photographed. He doesn't like her image being out there. But it's almost inevitable—she *is* stylish and interesting, and the story of the DEA hero with the Mexican wife who was once gunned down by narcos is irresistible to both the media and the Washington society types. So they get invitations to the chic parties and events, which Keller would by inclination turn down, but Marisol says that whether they like it or not, the political and social connections are extremely useful to his work.

She's right, Keller thinks. Mari's charm has proved to be an effective antidote to what has been referred to as his "anticharm," and she has opened doors (and kept them open) that would otherwise be closed to him.

When Keller needs to talk with a representative, a senator, a cabinet official, a lobbyist, an editor, an ambassador, a shaker-and-mover—even someone in the White House—the chances are that Mari just had lunch or breakfast or served on a committee with the spouse.

Or she does the talking herself. Marisol is fully aware that people who would say no to Keller find it much harder to refuse his charming, fashionable wife, and she's not above picking up the phone when an appropriations vote is needed, a critical piece of information has to go out in the media, or a project needs to be funded.

She's busy—already on the board of the Children's National Medical Center and the Art Museum of the Americas and has worked on fund-raisers for the Children's Inn, Doorways for Women and Families, and AIDS United.

Keller worries that she's too busy for her health.

"I love those causes," she said to him when he expressed his concern. "And anyway, you need to put political capital in the bank."

"It's not your job."

"It *is* my job," she said. "It's *exactly* my job. You kept your promise to me."

He had. When he first called O'Brien to accept the offer, he said he had one condition—a replacement for Mari at her clinic had to be found and funded. O'Brien called him back the same morning with the news that a Texas oil firm had stepped up with a qualified physician and a big check, and was there anything else he needed?

Marisol started her diplomatic campaign to help him. Joined the boards and the committees, went to the lunches and the fund-raisers. Over Keller's objections she was profiled in the *Post* and the *Washingtonian*.

"The cartels already know what I look like," she told him. "And you need me doing these things, Arturo. The Tea Party troglodytes are already out to hang you, and the liberals don't love you, either."

Keller knew that she was right. Marisol was "politically perspicacious," as she once put it, her observations and analysis usually dead-on, and she was quick to discern the nuances of the increasingly polarized American scene. And he had to admit that his desperate desire to escape politics and "just do his job" was naive.

"*All* jobs are political," Marisol said. "Yours more than most."

True enough, Keller thought, because he was the top "drug warrior" at a time when the current administration was seriously questioning what the war on drugs should mean and what it should—and, more importantly, shouldn't—be.

The attorney general, in fact, had ordered DEA to stop using the phrase *war on drugs* at all, stating (rightly, in Keller's opinion) that we shouldn't wage war on our own people. The Justice Department and the White House were reevaluating the draconian drug laws passed during the crack epidemic of the '80s and '90s that legislated mandatory minimum sentences that put nonviolent offenders behind bars for thirty years to life.

The result of that legislation was that more than two million people—the majority of them African American and Hispanic—were in prison, and now the administration was reviewing a lot of those sentences, considering clemency for some of them, and exploring ending mandatory minimum sentences.

Keller agreed with these efforts but wanted to stay out of the controversies and focus on the mandate to end the heroin epidemic. In his opinion, he was the head of the Drug *Enforcement* Administration, and while he was willing to put less emphasis on enforcing, say, marijuana laws, he preferred to defer policy statements to the drug czar.

Officially the director of the White House Office of National Drug Control Policy, the "drug czar"—as the position had been tagged—was the guy who spoke for the president on drug policy and was in charge of seeing the White House's intentions implemented.

Well, sort of.

The current czar was a hard-liner who was somewhat resistant to the AG's reforms that POTUS supported, so he was on his way out to become the boss of US Customs and Border Protection (so Keller would still have to work with him), and a new guy—more amenable to the reforms—was on his way in.

To Keller, it was just another strand of bureaucracy in an already tangled net. Technically, Keller's immediate boss was the attorney general, but they both had to take the drug czar into account, as the AG served at the behest of the White House.

Then there was Congress. At various times, DEA had to consult with and report to the Senate Judiciary Committee, Appropriations Committee, Budget Committee, the Homeland Security and Government Affairs Committee.

The House was even worse. It had its own Budget, Appropriations, and Homeland Security and Government Affairs Committees, but its Judiciary Committee also had subcommittees—Crime, Terrorism, Homeland Security and Investigations, and Immigration Policy and Border Security.

So Keller had to confer and coordinate with the Justice Department, the White House, and the Senate and House committees, but there were also the other federal agencies whose missions coincided with his—Homeland Security; CIA; FBI; Bureau of Alcohol, Firearms and Tobacco; ICE; Bureau of Prisons; the Coast Guard and the Navy; the Department of Transportation; the State Department . . . the list went on and on.

And that was just federal.

Keller also had to deal with fifty state governments and state police forces, over three thousand county sheriff's departments and more than twelve thousand city police departments. Not to mention state and local prosecutors and judges.

That was the United States, but Keller also had to communicate, confer and negotiate with government officials and police from foreign countries— Mexico, of course, but also Colombia, Bolivia, Peru, Cambodia, Laos, Thailand, Myanmar, Pakistan, Afghanistan, Uzbekistan, Turkey, Lebanon, Syria, and all the European Union countries where heroin was bought, sold and/or transshipped. And any of those dealings had to be run through the State Department and sometimes the White House.

Of course, Keller delegated most of this—in many ways the DEA was a perpetual motion machine that functioned on its own momentum—but he still had to handle the major issues personally and was determined to sharpen its blade and point it straight at the heroin problem.

Keller took over a DEA that was deeply wary of him as a former undercover operative, a field agent and a hard charger with a reputation for ruthlessness.

We got us a real cowboy now was pretty much the overall take, and a number of midlevel bureaucrats started to pack their personal belongings because they thought the new boss would bring in his own people.

Keller disappointed them.

He called a general meeting at which he said, "I'm not firing anybody. The knock on me is that I'm not an administrator and don't have a clue how to run a gigantic organization. That rap is accurate—I don't. What I do have is you. I will give clear, concise direction and I trust you to make the organization work toward those objectives. What I expect from you is loyalty, honesty and hard work. What you can expect from me is loyalty, honesty, hard work and support. I will never stab you in the back, but I will stab you in the chest if I catch you playing games. Don't be afraid to make mistakes—only slackers and cowards don't make mistakes. But if we have a problem, I don't want to be the last to know. I want your thoughts and your criticisms. I'm a big believer in the battleground of ideas—I don't need the only word, just the last word."

He set priorities.

Next he called in the deputy administrator, Denton Howard, and the chiefs of Intelligence and Operations and told them that their first priority was heroin.

The second priority was heroin.

The third priority was heroin.

"We'll sustain our efforts on all Schedule I drugs," he told them, "but our overriding emphasis on the enforcement side is ending the heroin epidemic. I don't care about marijuana, except where it can lead us up the ladder to the heroin traffickers."

Which meant focusing on the Sinaloa cartel.

Keller's approach is something of a departure—historically, Sinaloa hadn't been greatly involved with heroin production since the 1970s, when the DEA and the Mexican military had burned and poisoned the poppy fields (Keller was there), and the growers turned to other products.

The Barrera wing of the cartel had made most of its money from cocaine and marijuana, the Esparza wing from methamphetamine, the Tapia faction from a combination of all three.

"It's a mistake to put all our efforts into fighting them in Mexico," Keller told his people. "I know, because it's a mistake I made. Repeatedly. From now on we put our priority on hitting them where we can hit them—here in the United States."

Howard said, "That's a piecemeal approach that will require coordination from dozens of metropolitan police departments."

"Set it up," Keller said. "Within the next month I want face-to-face meetings with the chiefs of narcotics from New York, Chicago and Los Angeles. If they can't or won't come to me, I'll go to them. After that, I want Boston, Detroit and San Diego. And so on. The days of standing at the urinal pissing on each other's shoes are over."

But great, Keller thought, I have a deputy who's looking to sabotage me. I'm going to have to starve him out, and the way to starve a bureaucrat is to deprive him of access and information.

Keller kept Blair after the meeting. "Does Howard have a hard-on for me?"

Blair smiled. "He expected to get your desk."

The administrator and deputy administrator of the DEA are political appointees—all the rest are civil servants who come up through the system. Keller figured that Howard probably thought O'Brien and his cabal fucked him.

The organizational chart has all the department heads reporting directly to Howard, who then reports to Keller.

"Anything significant," Keller told Blair, "you bypass Howard, bring directly to me."

"You want me to keep a double set of books."

"You have a problem with that?"

"No," Blair said. "I don't trust the son of a bitch, either."

"It blows up, I'll cover your ass."

"Who's going to cover yours?" Blair asked.

Same person who always has, Keller thought.

Me.

"Let's look at the *velorio* again," Keller says.

Blair puts up the photos from Barrera's wake, taken by an incredibly brave SEIDO undercover working as a waiter for the catering company that serviced the event. Keller stares at the dozens of photos—Elena Sánchez sitting by the coffin; the Esparza brothers; Ricardo Núñez and his son, Mini-Ric; a host of other important players. He studies photos taken in the house, on the lawn, out by the pool.

"Can you order them by time sequence?" Keller asks.

The cliché is that every picture tells a story, but a sequence of pictures, Keller thinks, can be more like a movie and tell a different story. He's a big believer in chronology, in causation, and now he studies the photos with that sensibility.

Blair is smart enough to shut up.

Twenty minutes later, Keller starts to select a series of photos and lay them out in line. "Look at this—Núñez goes up to Elena. They walk outside, let's say it's to talk in private." He highlights a series of photos that show Elena and Núñez walking closely together, in what seems to be intense conversation. Then—

"Shit," Keller says, "what's this?"

He zooms in on Núñez's hands, on a piece of paper that he gives Elena.

"What is it?" Blair asks.

"Can't make it out, but she's sure as hell reading it." Keller zooms in on Elena's face—reading, frowning. "It could be the catering bill, who knows, but she isn't happy."

They look at pictures of Elena and Núñez in conversation and then check the time log. The conversation lasted for five minutes and twenty-two seconds. Elena gave Núñez the paper and went back inside the house.

"What I wouldn't give for some audio," Keller says.

"They were jamming," Blair says.

Keller goes back to his timeline series of photos and notes Iván and Mini-Ric in what looks to be a casual conversation by the pool. Then Núñez comes out and walks away with Iván, leaving Ric sitting there. Half an hour later, by the time log, Iván comes back out and talks to Ric.

And it doesn't look casual.

"Am I imagining things," Keller says, "or are they in an argument?"

"Iván sure looks angry."

"Whatever got his panties in a wad," Keller says, "it had to have been when he was with Núñez. I don't know, maybe I'm reading too much into this."

And maybe not, he thinks.

All the drumbeats said that Iván was next in line to take control of the cartel, merging the Barrera and Esparza wings of the organization. But now we seem to be seeing Ricardo Núñez summoning Elena Sánchez and Iván Esparza to personal talks, after which Iván appears to be angry.

Jesus Christ, could we have missed something here?

Keller had thought of Ricardo Núñez as a midlevel functionary, at most some kind of adviser to Barrera, but he's been playing an outsize role in the *velorio* and the funeral and now he seems to be some kind of go-between from Elena to Iván.

Negotiating what, though?

Elena's been out of the trade for years.

Keller tries a different theory—maybe Núñez isn't simply providing "good offices," but has become a power in and of his own.

Stay tuned, Keller thinks.

¡ADÁN VIVE!

Elena Sánchez Barrera looks at the graffiti spray-painted on the stone wall of the Jardines del Valle cemetery.

She saw the same thing on the ride into the city, painted on walls, the sides of buildings, on billboards. She's been told that the same phenomenon has occurred in Badiraguato and that little shrines to "Santo Adán" have shown up on roadsides in smaller towns and villages all across Sinaloa and Durango—the deeply felt, passionate wishful thinking that Adán Barrera— the beloved El Señor, El Patrón, the "Godfather," the "Lord of the Skies," the man who built clinics, schools, churches, who gave money to the poor and fed the hungry—is immortal, that he lives in flesh or spirit.

Saint Adán, indeed, she thinks.

Adán was many things, but a saint wasn't one of them.

Elena looks out the window and sees the entire power structure of the Sinaloa cartel, in fact of the whole Mexican trafficking world, gathered. If the government really intended to stop the drug trade, it could do so in one fell swoop.

A single raid would net them all.

It will never happen—not only are there hundreds of cartel *sicarios* posted around and inside the cemetery, but it's been cordoned off by the Sinaloa state police and the Culiacán municipal police. A state police helicopter hovers overhead, and, in any case, the federal government is not serious about shutting down the drug trade, it's serious about *managing* the drug trade, so it's not going to disrupt this service.

Ricardo Núñez stands in his impeccably tailored black suit, rubbing his hands together like some kind of Latino Uriah Heep, Elena thinks. The man insisted on inserting himself into the planning of every element of the funeral, from the selection of the coffin to the seating arrangements to security, and Núñez *sicarios* in their trademark Armani caps and Hermès vests guard the gate and the walls.

Elena spots the notorious La Fósfora, somewhat subdued in a black suit jacket over black pants, supervising the *sicarios*, and she has to admit that the girl is quite striking. Ricardo's son, "Mini-Ric," stands beside him with his mousy wife, whose name Elena cannot recall.

The Esparza brothers stand in a row like crows on a telephone line. For once they aren't dressed like extras in a cheap telenovela, but respectfully garbed in black suits and real shoes with actual laces. She nods to Iván, who curtly nods back and then moves a little closer to his sister as if asserting his ownership.

Poor Eva, Elena thinks, standing there with her two small boys, who are now pawns in a game they know nothing about. As is Eva, of course—Iván will take control of her as leverage against Núñez. She can hear it already—*See*, we *are Adán Barrera's real family, his true heirs, not some jumped-up assistant, some clerk.* If Eva is too weak to go back to California, Iván will roll her and the twins around like stage props.

Speaking of props, he has his guard dog close at hand. El Mastín is sweating at the collar, looking distinctly uncomfortable in a jacket and tie, and Elena knows that he was brought here as a reminder that Jalisco is allied to the *Esparza* wing of the cartel and that if it comes to a fight, this brutal mass murderer and all his troops are loyal to Iván.

But hopefully it won't come to that.

Ricardo had phoned her to say that Iván had—albeit grudgingly and bitterly—accepted Núñez's leadership of the cartel and—grudgingly and bitterly—the transfer of Baja to Rudolfo.

It must have been some scene, Elena thinks, at least as Ricardo described it. Iván had yelled, cursed, called Elena every name in the book and a few that hadn't been memorialized yet, had threatened war, promised to fight to the death, but was finally worn down by Ricardo's steady, monotonous, Chinese-water-torture application of logic and reason.

"He agreed to a two percent *piso*," Ricardo told her.

"The standard is five."

"Elena . . ."

"Very well, fine." She would have agreed to zero, if that's what it took.

Ricardo couldn't help but slip the knife in a little. "And shouldn't I be having this conversation with Rudolfo?"

"You phoned me."

"So I did," Ricardo said. "Slip of the speed dial."

"I'll run it past Rudolfo," she said. "But I'm sure he'll agree."

"Oh, I'm sure he will," Ricardo said.

Rudolfo sits beside her in the back seat of the limousine. He had claimed nothing but enthusiasm when she told him that he was the new boss of Baja, but she could tell he was nervous.

He has reason to be, she thinks.

There's hard and uncertain work to be done. Traffickers and gunmen who had once been "Barrera people" had been transferred to the Esparzas and would now be asked to come back. Most will, she knows, eagerly; but others will be reluctant, even rebellious.

A few examples might have to be made—the first person who vocally objects will have to be killed—and she worries if Rudolfo has it in him to order that. If he ever did—her poor sweet son likes to be liked, a useful trait in the music and club businesses, not so much in *la pista secreta*.

Elena has people who will do it, and do it in his name, but sooner rather than later he will need to have his own armed wing. She can and will give him the people, but he will have to command.

She puts her hand over his.

"What?" Rudolfo asks.

"Nothing," Elena says. "Just that it's a sad occasion."

The car slows as one of Núñez's people tells them where to park.

The mausoleum, Elena thinks as she takes her seat next to her mother, is a monument to tasteless excess. Three stories high in classic churrigueresque architecture with a dome roof tiled with mosaic; marble columns; and stone carvings of birds, phoenixes and dragons.

And it's air-conditioned.

I doubt, Elena thinks, that Adán will feel the heat.

A Dolby sound system is encased in the columns, running a continuous loop of corridos about Adán; inside the crypt, a flat-screen monitor shows videos of the great man and his good works.

It's hideous, Elena thinks, but it's what the people expect.

And it wouldn't do to let the people down.

The priest had actually hesitated to perform the service for "a notorious drug lord."

"Look around you, you sanctimonious little prick," Elena said when they met in his office. "That desk you're sitting behind? We paid for it. The chair your flabby ass sits in? We paid for it. The sanctuary, the altar, the pews, the new stained-glass windows? All straight from Adán's pocket. So I'm not asking you, Padre, I'm *telling* you—you will perform this service. Otherwise—my hand to the Virgin Mary—we will send people in to remove everything from this church, starting with you."

So now Father Rivera says some prayers, gives a blessing, then a little homily about Adán's virtues as a dedicated family man, his generosity toward the church and the community, his deep love of Sinaloa and its people, his faith in Jesus Christ, the Holy Ghost and God the Father.

Adán had faith in money, power and himself, Elena thinks as the priest moves to wrap it up. That was his Holy Trinity, he didn't believe in God.

"I do believe in Satan, though," he had told her once.

"You can't believe in one without the other," she said.

"Sure you can," Adán said. "The way I understand it, God and the devil were in a giant battle to rule the world, right?"

"I suppose."

"Right," Adán said. "Look around you—the devil won."

The whole thing is a joke, Ric thinks.

He's also thinking about how badly he has to piss and wishes he had before this endless service began, but it's too late now, he'll just have to hold it.

And endure Iván's stink eye.

His friend hasn't stopped glaring at him since it started. Just as he had glared at him when he came out of his meeting with Ricardo Sr. at the *velorio,* walked up to Ric at the pool, glared down at him and said, "You knew."

"Knew what?"

"That Adán made your father the new boss."

"I didn't know."

"Fuck you."

"I didn't."

"You father called me a clown," Iván said.

"I'm sure he didn't say that, Iván."

"No, that bitch Elena did," Iván said. "But your father repeated it. And you knew, Ric. You *knew.* You let me talk, go on and on about what I was going to do, and all the time, you knew."

"Come on, Iván, I—"

"No, you're the guy now, right?" Iván said. "Your father is the *jefe,* that makes you what, Mini-Ric, huh?"

"Still your friend."

"No, you're not," Iván said. "We're not friends. Not anymore."

He walked away.

Ric called him, texted him, but got no answers. Nothing. Now Iván sits there staring at him like he hates him.

Which maybe he does, Ric thinks.

And maybe I can't blame him.

After talking to Iván, his father had called Ric in.

Ric read the paper that his old man slid across the glass top. "Jesus Christ."

"That's all you have to say?"

"What do you want me to say?"

"I was hoping for something more along the lines of 'Let me know what I can do to help, Dad,'" Núñez said, "or 'Whatever you need from me, I'm there.' Or 'Adán chose wisely, Dad, you're the man for the job.'"

"All that goes without saying."

"And yet I had to say it." Núñez leaned back in his chair and put his fingertips together, a gesture Ric had hated since he was a child, as it always meant that a lecture was coming. "I need you to step up now, Ric. Take more of an active role, lend a hand."

"Iván thought it was going to be him." Every other word out of Iván's mouth had been how things were going to be when he took over, and now here was Adán reaching out from the grave to snatch that from him.

"His happiness is not my concern," Núñez said. "Or, for that matter, yours."

"He's my friend."

"Then perhaps you can help persuade him to be reasonable," Núñez said. "He'll still run the Esparza wing of the organization."

"I think he had something more in mind."

"We all have to live with our disappointments," Núñez said.

Ric had an idea he was talking about *him*.

"Iván will have to run the entire Esparza operation," Núñez said. "He wouldn't have time for Baja anyway."

"He was going to give it to Oviedo."

"The same Oviedo I saw on Facebook driving a motorcycle with his feet?" Núñez asked.

"I didn't know you went on Facebook."

"Aides keep me in touch," Núñez said. "In any case, you have Elena's permission to keep selling in Baja."

"Elena's or Rudolfo's?"

"Are you being funny with me?"

"I *had* an arrangement," Ric said. "With Iván."

"Now you have it with Rudolfo," Núñez said. "Show me some success on the *narcomenudeo*, I might give you the *trasiego*. From there, who knows?"

"Show you some success."

"For God's sake, Ric," Núñez said, "show me *something*. You're Adán Barrera's godson. With that comes certain privileges, and with privilege comes responsibility. I have a responsibility to see that his wishes are carried out, and you share in that."

"Okay."

"Here's something else you should think about," Núñez said. "We're holding this position for Adán's sons to come of age, but that will be years from now. Suppose something happens to me in the interim? That leaves you."

"I don't want it," Ric said.

There it was again—that trace of disappointment, even disgust, as his father asked, "Do you want to be 'Mini-Ric' your whole life?"

Ric was surprised by his father's ability to hurt him. He thought he was over it by now, but he felt a stab in his heart.

He didn't answer.

One of the things Ric is expected to show his father is a speech, a eulogy, at the funeral service.

To which Ric had objected. "Why me?"

"As the godson," Ricardo said, "it's *expected*."

Well, if it's *expected*, Ric thought. He had no idea what he was going to say.

Belinda offered some ideas. "'My godfather, Adán, was a ruthless cocksucker who killed more men than ass cancer—'"

"Nice."

"—and married a hot *chica* less than half his age who we would all like to fuck, if we're being honest with ourselves. What's not to love about Adán Barrera, a man's man, a narco's narco, a godfather's godfather. Peace. Out.'"

She hadn't been much more help about his Iván problem.

"You know Iván," she said. "He runs hot. He'll get over it, you'll be doing shots together tonight."

"I don't think so."

"Then so be it," Belinda said. "You got to start looking at the facts. Fact: Barrera named your father the boss, not Iván. Fact: you're the godson, not him. Maybe you should start acting like it."

"You sound like my father."

"He's not always wrong."

Now Ric really has to piss. The fucking priest finally gets offstage and then a singer comes on. One of Rudolfo's older recording hacks who starts in with a corrido he wrote "especially for El Señor," and it has more downer lyrics than an Adele tune.

After that, a poet comes up.

A poet.

What's next, Ric thinks, puppets?

Actually, it's him.

His father gives him what could be called a "significant" nod and Ric walks up to the altar. He's not stupid—he knows it's a moment, an announcement of sorts that he has leapfrogged Iván to the head of the line.

Ric leans into the microphone. "My godfather, Adán Barrera, was a great man."

A general murmur of agreement and the audience waits for him to go on.

"He loved me like a son," Ric says, "and I loved him like a second father. He was a father to us all, wasn't he? He—"

Ric blinks when he sees a clown—a full-fledged *payaso* with white makeup, a red curly wig, a rubber nose, baggy pants and floppy shoes come prancing down the center aisle blowing on a kazoo and carrying a bunch of white balloons in one hand.

Who ordered this up? Ric wonders, thinking he's seeing things.

It couldn't have been laugh-a-minute Elena or his old man, neither of whom is exactly known for whimsy. Ric glances over at both of them and neither is laughing.

Elena, in fact, looks pissed.

But, then again, she always does.

Ric tries to pick up his speech. "He gave money to the poor and built . . ."

But no one is listening as the clown makes his way to the altar, tossing paper flowers and little *papel picado* animals to the astonished onlookers. Then he turns, reaches inside his patched madras jacket, and pulls out a 9 mm Glock.

I'm going to get killed by a fucking clown, Ric thinks in disbelief. It's not fair, it's not right.

But the *payaso* turns and shoots Rudolfo square in the forehead.

Blood flecks Elena's face.

Her son falls into her lap and she sits holding him, her face twisted in agony as she screams and screams.

The killer runs back up the aisle—but how fast can a clown run in floppy shoes—and Belinda pulls a MAC-10 from her jacket and melts him.

Balloons rise into the air.

. . .

Adán Barrera's Pax Sinaloa ended before he was even lowered into the ground, Keller thinks, watching the news on Univision.

Reporters outside the walls of the cemetery described a "scene of chaos" as panicked mourners fled, others pulled out a "proliferation" of weapons, and ambulances raced toward the scene. And with that touch of surrealism that so often seems to pervade the Mexican narco world, early reports indicate that Rudolfo Sánchez's killer was dressed as a clown.

"A clown," Keller says to Blair.

Blair shrugs.

"Do they have an ID on the shooter?" Keller asks, unwilling to say *clown*.

"SEIDO thinks it's this guy," Blair says, throwing a file up on the computer screen. "Jorge Galina Aguirre—'El Caballo'—a player in the Tijuana cartel way back in the nineties when Adán and Raúl were first taking over. A midlevel marijuana trafficker with no known enemies, and no known grudges against the Barreras."

"Apparently he had a grudge against Rudolfo."

"There's some shit running around that Rudolfo nailed Galina's daughter, or maybe his wife," Blair says.

"Rudolfo was a player."

"The wages of sin," Blair says.

Yeah, but Keller doubts it.

The old "honor killing" ethos is rapidly fading into the past, and the insult—the almost unbelievably offensive act of murdering one of Barrera's nephews in front of his family at his funeral—argues that this is something more.

It's a declaration.

But of what, and by whom?

By all accounts, Rudolfo Sánchez was a spent force, the juice drained out of him by the stay in Florence. He was involved with nightclubs, restaurants and music management, cash businesses handy for laundering money. Had he fucked someone on a deal, lost someone a serious amount of cash?

Maybe, but you don't kill a Barrera over something like that, especially not at El Señor's funeral. You negotiate a settlement or you eat the loss because it's better for business and your odds for survival. Again, intelligence had it that Rudolfo—or any of the Sánchez family—wasn't trafficking anymore, so he shouldn't have been killed over turf.

Unless the intelligence is wrong or things have changed.

Of course things have changed, Keller thinks. Barrera is dead and maybe this was the opening shot in the battle to replace him.

Rudolfo didn't want to be buried in the cemetery, he wanted to be cremated, his ashes tossed into the sea. There will be no grave, no crypt, no gaudy mausoleum to visit, just the sound of waves and an endless horizon.

His widow—we have so many widows, Elena thinks, we are our own cartel—stands with her son and daughter, ten and seven, respectively. Who saw their father murdered.

They shot my son in front of his wife and children.

And his mother.

She's heard the joke going around—*Did they catch the clown who did it?*

They did.

He never made it out of the mausoleum. One of Núñez's people gunned him down in the aisle. The question, Elena thinks, is how he made it in. There was so much security, so much security. Barrera security, Esparza security, Núñez security, city police, state police—and this man walked right through it all.

The shooter was Jorge Galina Aguirre, a marijuana trafficker with no known enemies, and no known grudges against the Barreras.

Certainly not against Rudolfo.

That night, after she had seen Rudolfo to a funeral home, Elena went to a house on the edge of town where the entire security contingent was held in the basement, sitting on the concrete floor, their hands tied behind their backs.

Elena walked down the row and looked each one in the eye.

Looking for guilt.

Looking for fear.

She saw a lot of the latter, none of the former.

They all told the same story—they saw a black SUV pull up. With just the driver and the clown, in the passenger seat. The clown got out of the car, and the guards let him in because they thought he was some bizarre part of the ceremony. The SUV drove off. So it was a suicide mission, Elena thought. A suicide mission that the shooter didn't know was a suicide mission. The driver watched him go in and then took off, leaving him there.

To do his job and die.

When they went back upstairs, Ricardo Núñez said, "If you want them all dead, they're all dead."

Members of his armed wing were already in place, locked, loaded and ready to perform a mass execution.

"Do what you want with your men," Elena said. "Release mine."

"You're sure?"

Elena just nodded.

She sat in the back of a car, flanked by armed guards, her own people flown in from Tijuana, and watched the local Barrera men walk out of the house.

They looked surprised, stunned to still be alive.

Elena said to one of her men, "Go out there, tell them they're fired. They'll never work for us again."

Then she watched Ricardo's people go in.

They walked back to their cars an hour later.

Now she watches her daughter-in-law step ankle-deep into the ocean and pour Rudolfo's ashes out of a jar.

Like instant coffee, Elena thinks.

My son.

Whom I laid on my chest, held in my arms.

Wiped his ass, his nose, his tears.

My baby.

She talked to her other baby, Luis, that morning.

"It was the Esparzas," she said. "It was Iván."

"I don't think so, Mother," Luis said. "The police say that Gallina was insane. Delusional. He thought Rudolfo had slept with his daughter or something."

"And you believe that."

"Why would Iván want to kill Rudolfo?" Luis asked.

Because I took Baja from him, Elena thought. Or thought I did. "They killed your brother and now they're going to try to kill you. They'll never let us out alive, so we have to stay in. And if we stay in, we have to win. I'm sorry, but that's the cold truth."

Luis turned pale. "I've never had anything to do with the business. I don't want to have anything to do with the business."

"I know," Elena said. "And I wish it were possible to keep you out of it, my darling. But it's not."

"Mother—I don't want it."

"And I didn't want it for you," Elena said. "But I'm going to need you. To avenge your brother."

She watches Luis looking at his brother's ashes float on the surface of the water and then disappear into the foam of a gentle wave.

Just like that.

The poor boy, she thinks.

Not a boy, a young man, twenty-seven now. Born to this life from which he can't escape. It was foolish of me to think otherwise.

And that foolishness cost my other son his life.

She watches the wave go out, taking her child with it, and thinks of the song she sang on his birthdays.

The day you were born,
All the flowers were born,
And in the baptismal fountain
The nightingales did sing,
The light of day is shining on us,
Get up in the morning,
See that it has already dawned.

A sharp, heavy blade presses down on her chest.

Pain that will never go away.

Keller sits down on the sofa across from Marisol.

"You look tired," Marisol says.

"It's been a day."

"Barrera," she says. "It's been all over the shows. What a scene, huh?"

"Even dead, he's still getting people killed," Keller says.

They talk for a few more minutes and then she goes up to bed. He goes into the den and turns the television on. CNN is covering the Barrera story and doing a recap of his life—how he started as a teenager selling bootleg jeans, how he joined his uncle's drug business, his bloody war with Güero Méndez to take over the Baja plaza, his succeeding his uncle as the head of the Mexican Federación. As the scant photos of Barrera appear on the screen, the reporter goes on to talk about "unconfirmed rumors"—that Barrera was involved in the torture-murder of DEA agent Ernie Hidalgo, that Barrera had thrown the two small children of his rival Méndez off a bridge, that he'd slaughtered nineteen innocent men, women and children in a small Baja village.

Keller pours himself a weak nightcap as the reporter provides "balance"—Barrera built schools, clinics and playgrounds in his home state of Sinaloa, he had forbidden his people to engage in kidnappings or extortion, he was "beloved" by the rural people in the mountains of the Sierra Madre.

The screen shows the signs reading ¡ADÁN VIVE! and the little homebuilt roadside shrines with photos of him, candles, bottles of beer, and cigarettes.

Barrera didn't smoke, Keller thinks.

The profile relates Barrera's 1999 arrest by "current DEA head Art Keller," his transfer to a Mexican prison, his 2004 "daring escape" and subsequent rise back to the top of the drug world. His war with the "hyperviolent" Zetas, and his betrayal at the peace conference in Guatemala.

Then the scene at the funeral.

The bizarre murder.

The lonely lowering of the coffin into the ground, with only his widow, his twin sons and Ricardo Núñez present.

Keller turns off the television.

He thought that putting two bullets into Adán Barrera's face would bring him peace.

It hasn't.

BOOK TWO

Heroin

They left at once and met the Lotus-eaters,
who had no thought of killing my companions,
but gave them lotus plants to eat, whose fruit,
sweet as honey, made any man who tried it
lose his desire ever to journey home . . .

—Homer
The Odyssey, book 9

1

The Acela

This train don't carry no liars, this train . . .
—Traditional American folk song

New York City
July 2014

Keller looks out the train window at abandoned factory buildings in Baltimore and wonders if some of them are now shooting galleries. The windows are shattered, gang graffiti is sprayed on the redbrick walls, fence posts lean like drunken sailors, and the chain links have been cut.

It's the same story all the way up the Amtrak line, on the outskirts of Philadelphia, Wilmington, and Newark—the factories are shells, the jobs are gone and too many of the former workers are shooting smack.

A huge sign over a decrepit building outside Wilmington says it all. It originally read GOOD BUY WORKS, but someone spray-painted it to GOOD BYE WORK.

Keller's glad he took the train instead of flying. From the air he would have missed seeing all this. It's tempting to think that the root causes of the heroin epidemic are in Mexico, because he's so focused on interdiction, but the real source is right here and in scores of smaller cities and towns.

Opiates are a response to pain.

Physical pain, emotional pain, economic pain.

He's looking at all three.

The Heroin Trifecta.

Keller is riding the Acela, the three-hour train from Washington, DC, to New York City, from the governmental power center to the financial one, although sometimes it's hard to know which rules which.

And hard to know what he can do about Mexico from Washington when the real source of the opiate problem might just be on Wall Street. You're standing on the Rio Grande with a broom, he thinks, trying to sweep back the tide of heroin while billionaires are sending jobs overseas, closing factories and towns, killing hopes and dreams, inflicting pain.

And then they tell you, stop the heroin epidemic.

The difference between a hedge fund manager and a cartel boss?

Wharton Business School.

He looks over to see Hugo Hidalgo lurching down the aisle with a card-board tray in his hand, bringing back coffee and sandwiches. The young agent plops down in the aisle seat beside him. "I got you a ham and cheese panini. I hope that's all right."

"It's fine. What did you get?"

"A burger."

"Brave man."

A good man, actually.

In a few short months, Hidalgo has become a rock star. He's the first one to arrive in the morning and the last to leave at night, although Keller suspects that Hugo sometimes sleeps on a cot in the office if he's monitoring something.

Hugo is immersed in cell phone traffic analysis, email tracking, satellite pickups, field reports, anything he can look at to assemble a picture of the changing, fluid nature of the Sinaloa cartel.

He's become Keller's personal briefer, his last report coming before they left this morning to catch the train: three Tijuana street dealers found hang-ing from a bridge.

"They were Esparza's people," Hugo said. "Elena's answer to her son's murder."

"Is he still denying responsibility for Rudolfo's murder?"

"He is," Hugo said, "but the street says that he's using Elena's hostility as an excuse for not handing over Baja, so she hits his street dealers."

The Mexican street sales are a relatively small profit center compared to the cross-border trade, but they're essential to holding the border turf. To hold a plaza, a boss needs local gunmen, and the gunmen make most of their money from local street sales.

Without the street sales, no army.

No army, no plaza.

Hence, no local street sales, no international trade.

So unless Núñez can enforce peace, Elena and Iván will fight it out locally in Baja for control of the border crossings.

"Does Elena have the troops?" Keller asked.

Hugo shrugged. "Hard to say. Some old Barrera loyalists are going back to Elena now that she's raised her flag. A lot of them were Rudolfo's friends looking for revenge. Others are holding with the Esparzas, scared shitless Iván will bring Tito Ascensión and his Jalisco people in to keep them in line."

It's a reasonable fear, Keller thought. Nacho's old guard dog El Mastín is as brutal as it gets. "Núñez?"

"Staying neutral," Hugo said. "Trying to keep the peace."

Keller's suspicions about Núñez had proved to be true—Barrera had named the lawyer as his successor, as the "first among equals" to run the cartel. Núñez is in a tough position—if he lets Iván keep Baja, he looks weak, which in the narco world is the top of a slippery slope. But if he forces Iván to give it up, he'll have to go to war against him. Either way he goes, his organization fractures. While most of the old Barrera wing is staying loyal to Núñez, some are reported to be looking hard at Elena or Iván as options.

Núñez will have to either force Iván and Elena to the peace table or choose a side.

In the aftermath of Adán Barrera's death the Pax Sinaloa is dissolving.

Maybe it's all deck chairs on the *Titanic,* Keller thinks. Maybe it doesn't matter who's sending the heroin, only that it's coming in. The narcos can play musical chairs all they want; hell, we can empty the chairs with the so-called kingpin strategy—arresting or killing cartel bosses—but the top chair always gets filled and the drugs keep coming.

Keller had been one of the main executors of that strategy, having had a hand in taking out the *jefes* of the old Federación, the Gulf cartel, the Zetas and Sinaloa, and what's been the result?

More Americans than ever are dying from overdoses.

If you asked the average citizen to name America's longest war, he'd probably say Vietnam and then quickly amend it to Afghanistan, but the true answer is the war on drugs.

Fifty years old and counting.

It's cost over a trillion dollars, and that's only one part of the financial equation—the legitimate, "clean" money that goes for equipment, police, courts and prisons. But if we're going to be really honest, Keller knows, we have to account for the dirty money, too.

Tens of billions of drug dollars—in cash—go down to Mexico alone every year, so much cash they don't even count it, they *weigh* it. It has to go somewhere, the narcos can't stick it under their pillows or dig holes in their backyards. A lot of it is invested in Mexico, the estimate being that drug money accounts for 7 to 12 percent of the Mexican economy.

But a lot of it comes back here—into real estate and other investments.

Into banking and then out to legitimate businesses.

It's the dirty secret of the war on drugs—every time an addict sticks a needle into his arm, everyone makes money.

We're all investors.

We're all the cartel.

Now you're the commanding general in this war, Keller thinks, and you have no idea how to win it. You have thousands of brave, dedicated troops and all they can do is hold the line. You only know how to do the same old thing you've been doing, which isn't working, but what's the alternative?

Just give up?

Surrender?

You can't do that, because people are dying.

But you have to try something different.

The train goes into a tunnel on its way to Manhattan.

By design, no one is there to meet them. No one from DEA or the AG's office. They go out of Penn Station by the Eighth Avenue exit and hail a cab. Hugo tells the driver, "Ninety-Nine West Tenth."

"We're not going there," Keller says, and before Hidalgo can ask why not, adds, "Because if I take a piss in the New York DEA office, Denton Howard knows how much and what color before I finish washing my hands."

Leaks are going out from DEA, Keller knows—to the conservative media and also to the Republican politicians now vying for the presidential nomination, Ben O'Brien among them.

One of the potential candidates is right here in New York, although Keller has a hard time believing he's for real.

Real estate tycoon and reality TV star John Dennison is making noise about running, and a lot of the noises he's making have to do with Mexico and the border. All Keller needs is Howard feeding Dennison half-truths and insider information, including that Keller is meeting privately with the chief of the New York City Police Department's Division of Narcotics.

"Where are we going?" Hidalgo asks.

Keller tells the driver, "Two-Eighty Richmond Terrace. Staten Island."

"What's there?" Hidalgo asks.

"You ask a lot of questions."

Brian Mullen is waiting for them on the sidewalk outside an old house.

Keller gets out of the cab, walks up to him and says, "Thanks for meeting me."

"If my chief finds out I'm doing this on the down low," Mullen says, "he'll hand me my ass."

Mullen came up the hard way, as an undercover, working Brooklyn during the bad old crack days and coming out of a dirty precinct squeaky clean. Now he's breaking every protocol by agreeing to meet with Keller without informing his superiors.

The visit of the head of DEA would be an occasion, replete with media and photos taken with a gang of brass in dress uniform at One Police Plaza. There'd be assistants and cupbearers and PR flaks and a lot of talk and nothing would get done.

Mullen is wearing a Yankees jacket over jeans.

"Does it bring back your UC days?" Keller asks.

"Sort of."

"What is this place?" Keller asks.

"Amethyst House," Mullen says. "A halfway house for female addicts. If I get spotted by some cop from the One Twenty, I can say I was meeting with a source."

"This is Hugo Hidalgo," Keller says. He can see Mullen isn't thrilled to see someone else there. "His father and I worked together back in the day. Ernie Hidalgo."

Mullen shakes Hugo's hand. "Welcome. Come on, I have a car. There's a deli at the corner, you need coffee or something."

"We're good."

They follow Mullen to an unmarked black Navigator parked on the street. The guy behind the wheel doesn't look at them as they get into the back. Young guy, black hair slicked back, wearing a black leather jacket.

"Meet Bobby Cirello," Mullen says. "He works for me. Don't worry. Detective Cirello is professionally deaf and dumb. Just take us for a drive, Bobby, okay?"

Cirello pulls out onto the street.

"This is the St. George neighborhood," Mullen says. "Used to be the epicenter of the heroin epidemic in New York, because it's closest to the city, except now heroin is everywhere on the island—Brighton, Fox Hills, Tottenville—hence the name 'Heroin Island.'"

St. George looks like junkie turf, Keller thinks, if there is such a thing, and he sees what look like addicts from the car, hanging out on the corner, in parking lots and vacant lots.

But then they drive into what could be any suburb in any town in the United States. Residential areas of single-family homes, tree-lined streets, well-kept yards, swing sets and driveway basketball hoops.

"Smack is killing kids here now," Mullen says. "Which is why we have an 'epidemic.' When it was blacks and Puerto Ricans, it wasn't an illness, it was a crime, right?"

"It's still a crime, Brian."

"You know what I mean," Mullen says. "It's this new 'cinnamon.' Thirty percent stronger than the black tar the Mexicans used to sell, that the addicts were used to. That's why they're overdosing—they're shooting the same amount they used to and it's taking them out. Or they were used to taking pills, but the heroin is cheaper, and they shoot too much."

As the drive moves south into even more suburban areas, Mullen points out houses—*a son from this house, a daughter from this one, these people lucked out, their kid ODed but survived, is in rehab now, who knows, we'll see, I guess.*

"We're talking triage here," Mullen says. "The first step is to treat the wounded, right? See if we can save them on the battlefield. New York State just gave us a grant to equip twenty thousand officers with naloxone."

Keller knows the drug, commercially known as Narcan. It's like an EpiPen—if an overdosing addict is treated in time, you can practically bring them back from the dead. A Narcan kit costs all of sixty bucks.

"But DEA has expressed 'reservations,' right?" Mullen says. "You're concerned it will just encourage addicts to shoot up, or kids will start using it to get high. You're worried about 'Narcan parties.'"

That's Denton Howard shooting his mouth off to the media, Keller thinks, but he doesn't say it. He's not about to lay it off with a "that ain't me" excuse.

"I'd put Narcan kits out on the street like fire extinguishers," Mullen says. "Maybe the addicts could save their friends, because by the time my cops or first responders get there, it's often too late."

It makes sense, Keller thinks. It's also political suicide—if he came out for open Narcan distribution, *Fox and Friends* would chop him to pieces. "Okay, triage—keep going."

"Cutting down on overdose deaths is the first step," Mullen says, "but when the addict comes to, he's still an addict, right? You're just saving him so you can save him again, until one day you can't. What you have to do is get him into rehab."

"So rehab's the answer?"

"I know jail isn't the answer, prison isn't the answer," Mullen says. "They're getting high in there, only it costs more. Drug courts, maybe— bust them, have a judge force them into rehab? I don't know that there's *an* answer. But we have to do *something* different. We have to change the way we think."

"Is this you?" Keller asks. "I mean, are you expressing a shift in the department's thinking or are you an outlier?"

"A little bit of both," Mullen says. "Look, you go to the chief, some of the older guys with this stuff, they look at you like you're some bleeding-heart mugger hugger, but even some of the guys at One Police are starting to look for different answers, they see what's going on now. Hell, we had a *detective* overdose two years ago, did you know that? Guy got hurt on the job, started taking pain pills. Then smack. Then he ODed. An NYPD gold shield, for Chrissakes. It makes people think. Look for new solutions. You heard of SIFs?"

Supervised injection facilities, Keller thinks. Places addicts can go and shoot up. Medical personnel supervise the content and the dose. "De facto legalization of heroin?"

"Call it what you want," Mullen says. "It's saving lives. The revolving door of bust-and-convict doesn't. I arrest addicts, they shoot up in jail. I take dealers out, new ones take their place. I seize heroin, more comes in. Bobby, let's head up to Inwood, show this man what he needs to see."

"Jersey or Brooklyn?" Cirello asks.

"Take the Verrazano," Mullen says. He looks at Keller. "I don't like going out of my jurisdiction."

They take Route 278 into the Bay Ridge section of Brooklyn, then Sunset Park and Carroll Gardens. Mullen says, "This used to be called Red Hook, but Carroll Gardens sounds better for real estate. You're not a New York guy, are you?"

"San Diego."

"Beautiful there," Mullen says. "Great weather, right?"

"I haven't been there much the past few years," Keller says. "Mostly El Paso and Mexico. Now DC."

They cross the Brooklyn Bridge into lower Manhattan, over to the West Side Highway almost all the way up the island until they turn off at Dyckman Street, then take a left and go up Broadway.

"Where are we?" Keller asks.

"Fort Tryon Park, Inwood area," Mullen says. "The northernmost tip of Manhattan, and heroin central."

Keller looks around at the well-tended redbrick apartment complexes. Parks, ballfields, nannies pushing babies in strollers. "Doesn't look like it."

"Exactly," Mullen says. "There aren't a lot of users up here, but what you have here in Inwood and Washington Heights, just downtown from here, are heroin mills. This is where your Mexicans bring the shit in, sell it to wholesalers who cut it up, put it into dime bags and ship it out. Sort of an Amazon fulfillment center."

"Why here?"

Location, location, location, Mullen explains. Easy access to Route 9, right up to the little towns on the Hudson that are getting hammered with the shit. A short hop to 95 and the Bronx, or out to Long Island or up to New England. Harlem is just down Broadway, and you're close to the West Side Highway *and* the FDR to go to the boroughs.

"If you were UPS or FedEx," Mullen says, "and wanted to serve the Northeast Corridor, this is where you'd be. You can get in your car, be on the Jersey Turnpike or the Garden State in minutes and you're on your way to Newark, Camden, Wilmington, Philly, Baltimore, Washington. If you're moving less weight, you put it in a backpack, you take the One or the Two train to Penn Station and get on the Acela. Go south to the towns I just mentioned or north to Providence or Boston. No one is going to stop you, no one's going to search your bag, and they have Wi-Fi on the train, you can catch up on *Narcos*.

"Your people are onto this, too. We've busted mills here . . . fifteen pounds, twenty, thirty-five, millions in cash . . . but the narcos write it off as the cost of doing business, and the shit keeps coming."

"You feel like you're trying to sweep back the ocean," Keller says.

"Something like that."

"Are you getting what you need from my agency?" Keller asks.

"In the short term?" Mullen says. "Pretty much. Look, there's always the tension between feds and local police, let's not kid ourselves. Some of your people are afraid to share information with us, either because they want the busts for themselves or they think all local cops are dirty. My people will play hide-the-ball with your guys because *they* want the busts and they don't want the feds tromping over their turf and jacking it up."

Coordination is tricky, Keller knows, even when there's the best of intent, which isn't always the case. It's too easy for different agencies to run across each other's informants or protected witnesses, jam up or cut short a promising investigation, even get informants killed. And he knows DEA can be high-handed with local police forces, telling them to stay away from investigations, just as he knows the local guys are too often more than willing to freeze his people out of valuable intelligence.

Professional jealousy is a real problem. Everyone wants to make busts themselves because busts are the route to promotions. And good publicity— everyone wants to stand in front of that table loaded with drugs, guns, and money and get their picture taken. It's become a cliché but not a harmless one, Keller thinks, because it gives the impression that we're winning a war we're not winning.

The drugs on the table are like photos of dead Vietcong.

"But for the most part," Mullen is saying, "I think we're working pretty well together. It could always be better, of course."

Which is Mullen opening the door, Keller thinks. Asking the question— what are you really doing here?

"Why don't you and I talk away from the kids," Keller says.

"You ever been to the Cloisters?"

Keller and Mullen walk along the pillared arches of the Cuxa Cloisters in the park not far from Inwood. The structure was once part of the Benedictine Abbey of St. Michel in the French Pyrenees, was moved to New York in 1907 and now surrounds a central garden.

Keller knows that Mullen is making a statement by coming here. And, sure enough, Mullen says, "I heard you liked monasteries."

"I lived in one for a while."

"Yeah, that's what I heard," Mullen says. "In New Mexico, right? What was that like?"

"Quiet."

"They said you were in charge of, what, the beehives or something?" Mullen asks.

"The monastery sold honey," Keller says. "What else do you want to know, Brian?"

Because if Mullen has doubts about him, it's better to know now.

"Why did you leave it?" Mullen asks.

"Because they let Adán Barrera out of prison."

"And you wanted to put him back in," Mullen says.

"Something like that."

"I like it here," Mullen says. "I like to come here, walk around and think. It gets me away from all the shit. I'm not sure I like the modern world, Art."

"Me neither," Keller says. "But it's the one we have."

"Hey, we're at the chapel, you want to go in?" Mullen asks. "I mean, if we're going to have a come-to-Jesus talk, we might as well come to Jesus."

They go through the heavy oak doors, which are flanked by carvings of leaping animals. The large room is dominated by an apse at the end with a hanging crucifix. The side wall contains frescoes honoring the Virgin Mary.

"They moved this here from Spain," Mullen says. "Beautiful, huh?"

"It is."

"Why are you really here?" Mullen asks. "I know it's not for me to give you a tour and show you things you already know."

"You talked about triage," Keller says. "Short-term and long-term solutions. I want you to know my long-term intentions. I'm going to move DEA onto a new course, more in the direction of what you were talking about earlier. Away from the revolving door of arrest and incarceration, more into rehabilitation. I want us to back local initiatives with federal power and re-move federal obstacles."

"Can you?" Mullen says. "Your people aren't going to like it."

Keller knows what Mullen isn't saying but what he's thinking, that DEA has a vested interest in keeping the drug war going—its own existence.

"I don't know," Keller says. "But I'm going to try. If I'm going to succeed, I'll need support from police forces like NYPD."

"And the short term?"

"Until we change the baseline," Keller says, "we have to do everything we can to slow the flow of heroin."

"No argument from me."

"I've come to the conclusion that I can't do much in Mexico," Keller says. "They're too protected. If I'm going to attack the problem, it has to be here in New York, which has become the heroin hub."

Mullen smiles. "Any other epiphanies, Art?"

"Yeah," Keller says. "We can't answer the question of why people *do* drugs. But we do know why people *deal* them. Very simple—money."

"So?"

"So if we really want to do something, we go after the money," Keller says. "And I don't mean down in Mexico."

"You know what you're talking about here."

"Yeah, I do," Keller says. "And I'm ready to go there. I guess the question is, are you?"

Keller knows what he's asking of the man.

It's a potentially career-ending move.

You go after junkies and street dealers, they don't have a way to fight back. You attack the centers of power, they have more than enough ways of fighting back.

They can bury you.

Mullen doesn't look scared.

"Only if you're going to go all the way," he says. "I'm not interested in sending a few patsies to Club Fed for a few years. But if you're going to take this wherever it goes, then . . . what do you need?"

A banker, Keller tells him.

A Wall Street banker.

On the train back, Hidalgo has another burger and tells Keller that actu-ally it isn't so bad.

"That's good," Keller says.

Because you're going to be spending a lot more time on the Acela.

It's the start of Operation Agitator.

Guerrero, Mexico

Heroin reminds Ric of Easter.

The poppies shimmer vibrant purple in the sunlight, and the flowers that aren't purple are pink, red and yellow. Set against the emerald-green stalks, they look like candy baskets.

The plane banks hard against the Sierra Madre del Sur as it angles for its landing at a private airstrip outside the Guerrero town of Tristeza. Ric's father has brought him here as sort of a tutorial, "to learn the business from the ground up, as it were." It's part of his ongoing "Your Generation" lecture series, along the lines of "Your generation is separated from the soil that has made you all rich."

As if, Ric thinks, my lawyer father spent a single day in the fields. His closest brush with being a *campesino* was a thankfully brief attempt to grow tomatoes in the backyard that ended in a declaration that it was more "economically efficient" to buy them at the market, notwithstanding a previous installment in the lecture series entitled "Your Generation Doesn't Know Where Its Food Comes From."

Yes, we do, Ric thinks.

Calimax.

The plane lands with a hard bounce.

Ric sees the Jeeps full of armed men beside the airstrip, waiting to take them up the winding dirt roads into the mountains. A convoy is necessary because this part of Guerrero is increasingly "bandit country," relatively new to the Sinaloa cartel.

The cartel's fields in Sinaloa and Durango can't keep up with the growing demand for heroin, so the cartel has expanded into Guerrero and Michoacán.

Both states are producing more and more opium paste, Ric knows. The problem is that the infrastructure hasn't yet caught up to the production and they have to rely on smaller organizations as middlemen between the growers and the cartel.

Not a bad thing in itself, if the middlemen weren't at war with each other. So this beautiful country, Ric thinks as the Jeep passes through stands of tall *ocote* pines, is rife with gunmen on the hunt for one another.

First there are the Knights Templar, mostly in Michoacán, the survivors of the old La Familia organization, still possessed (and that *is* the word, Ric thinks) with a crazy quasi-religious zeal to eradicate "evildoers." Sinaloa tolerated them as long as they were helping to fight the Zetas, but now their utility is fast coming to an end and they're more trouble than they're worth.

Especially as these "do-gooders" are heavily involved in meth, extortion and murder for hire.

The Knights insist on fighting Los Guerreros Unidos, a splinter group of the Tapia organization founded by the old Tapia gunman Eddie Ruiz, now residing in an American penitentiary.

Ruiz was the first American to be the head of a Mexican cartel. Ric met him once or twice as a kid, but mostly knows him from the famous YouTube videos when "Crazy Eddie" filmed himself interviewing four Zetas before he executed them. Then he sent the tapes to all the television stations and put the clip out on the internet.

It started a trend.

Now "Eddie's Boys," as Guerreros Unidos are sometimes known, are running amok in Guerrero, Morelos and Edoméx, killing rivals, kidnapping for profit, extorting businesses and just generally being a pain in the ass.

We can't step on them because we need them, Núñez has told Ric. Especially here in Guerrero, where they control Tristeza. A city of about a hundred thousand people, Tristeza has importance beyond its size because it sits on the crossroads of several highways, including the all-important interstate down to Acapulco. The mayor of Tristeza is a longtime member of GU, and we need, at least for the time being, to stay in her good graces.

GU has a blood feud with Los Rojos, yet another splinter group of the Tapia organization, which, it should be fairly noted, was itself a splinter group of the Sinaloa cartel.

"The conflict is over smuggling routes," Núñez explained, "but when you really analyze it, what they're fighting over is us. It's a flaw in the system that we set up, and Adán was too busy fighting the Zetas to repair it, and since his death, it's only gotten worse."

The Sinaloa cartel, Ric has learned, doesn't actually own heroin farms in Guerrero. Most of them are just a few acres large, tucked away deep in the mountains, and are owned by small farmers who harvest the poppy and then sell the opium gum to middlemen, such as GU and Los Rojos, who transport it north—mostly hidden on commercial buses out of Tristeza to Acapulco and then to labs in Sinaloa or closer to the American border.

So they're killing each other, Ric thinks, his breath getting tight as they climb up past the ten-thousand-foot mark, for the right to sell to us.

Then there's his old friend Damien Tapia.

Now glossing himself the Young Wolf and making himself another pain in Sinaloa's ass.

Damien has reassembled some of his father's old loyalists and started to sell cocaine and methamphetamine in Culiacán, Badiraguato, Mazatlán, and even Acapulco, where he's reportedly based, protected by some of Ruiz's former people, extorting bars and nightclubs. There are rumors that he's been spotted in Durango and here in Guerrero, and, if that's the case, he's going to try to get into the heroin market as well.

"Such a nice young man," Núñez had said about Damien. "It was a shame that his father went insane and had to be put down like a mad dog."

The convoy comes into a sharp curve and Ric sees a flash of color ahead—hidden behind a stand of tall pines on a steep slope are the bright blooms of the poppy. He can see and smell the charred stumps where the farmer burned down the trees to create land for opium cultivation.

The field is maybe only two acres, but Núñez tells his son not to be deceived. "A well-irrigated, skillfully tended acre in Guerrero can yield as much as eight kilos of opium sap in a season, which is enough to produce a kilo of raw heroin.

"Just last year," he says, "that kilo of sap sold for about seven hundred dollars; already the price has doubled to fifteen hundred dollars as demand has grown, and we've only managed to keep the price that low by being the sole buyer, Walmart, if you will.

"This farmer might have as many as eight to ten of these patches scattered around the mountainside, hidden from the army helicopters that patrol the terrain in order to spray herbicides. At three thousand dollars a patch, you're starting to talk real money."

Three thousand dollars is lunch money to my old man, Ric thinks, but a fortune to a poor farmer in rural Guerrero.

He gets out of the Jeep to watch the *rayadores* work the patch.

They make good money, he learns. A productive worker can make thirty to forty dollars a day, seven times what her parents can make working in fields of corn or avocado groves. The *rayadores* are mostly teenagers and mostly girls, because their hands are smaller and nimbler. Wearing small razor blades attached to rings on their thumbs, they carefully slice tiny slits into the opium pods until the gum seeps out like a teardrop.

It's delicate work: Cut too shallow and you get no sap. Cut too deep and you ruin the pod, a disaster to profitability. The *rayadora* will come back to the same plant again—a pod can be scored as many as seven or eight times to produce the maximum amount of sap.

Once the cut is made, the seeping liquid is allowed to harden into brown gum and the *rayadores* use the razors to gently scrape the gum into pans, then take it to sheds or barns where other workers roll it into balls or cakes, which can be stored, for years if necessary.

When the farmer has harvested enough opium paste, he contacts the middleman, who comes and collects it, pays for it, and takes it to a lab to be processed into cinnamon heroin. From there it goes to a transshipment point like Tristeza, where it's loaded onto buses for what's called "shotgun shipping" north.

The middleman marks it up by as much as 40 percent—up to $2,100 a kilo—and then sells it to the cartel, which, again, controls the price by being virtually the only buyer.

A kilo of raw heroin will sell for somewhere between $60,000 and $80,000 in the States.

"The margin is excellent," Núñez says, "and even when you factor in the costs of transport, smuggling, security and, of course, bribes, we can still undersell the American pharmaceuticals and make a healthy profit."

Ric is a city kid, but he can't help but appreciate the beauty of the scene in front of him. It's idyllic. The air is crisp and clean, the flowers beautiful, and the sight of the young girls with their white smocks and long black hair moving quietly and efficiently as they do their work is peaceful beyond description, beautiful, really, in its simplicity.

"It's gratifying to know," Ric hears his father say, "that this business gives so many people gainful employment at a salary they could never otherwise realize."

There are hundreds of these farms scattered around Guerrero.

Plenty of work for everyone.

Yeah, Ric thinks, we're social benefactors.

He gets back in the Jeep and the convoy snakes its way down the mountain, the *sicarios* on the lookout for bandits.

Damien Tapia, the Young Wolf, watches the convoy through the telescopic sights of a sniper rifle.

From the cover of trees on the facing slope, he has the head of the Sinaloa cartel, Ricardo Núñez—one of the men who made the decision to kill his father—literally in the crosshairs.

When Damien was a boy, his father was one of the three bosses of the Sinaloa cartel, along with Adán Barrera and Nacho Esparza, two men Damien thought of as his uncles. The Tapia brothers were powerful then— Martín as the politician, Alberto the gunman, and his father, Diego, the undisputed leader.

When Tío Adán was captured in the States, it was Damien's father who took care of the business. When Tío Adán was transferred back to Mexico, to Puente Grande prison, it was Damien's father who arranged for his protection. When Tío Adán got out, it was Damien's father who fought alongside him to take Nuevo Laredo from the Gulf and the Zetas.

They were all friends then, the Tapias, the Barreras, the Esparzas. In those days, Damien looked up to the older boys like Iván and Sal and Rubén Ascensión and Ric Núñez, who was closer to him in age. They were his buddies, his *cuates*. They were Los Hijos, the sons who would inherit the all-powerful Sinaloa cartel, and they would run it together and be brothers forever.

Then Tío Adán married Eva Esparza.

Little Eva is younger than I am, Damien thinks now as he centers the sights on Ricardo Núñez's graying temple; we used to play together as kids.

But Tío Nacho wanted Baja for Iván, and he pimped his daughter out to get it. After Eva married Tío Adán, the Tapia wing of the cartel became the stepchild—slighted, ignored, pushed to the side. The very night Adán was popping little Eva's cherry, his tame *federales* went to arrest Damien's uncle Alberto and shot him dead. It turned out that Adán had sold out the Tapias to save his nephew Sal from a murder charge.

My father, Damien thinks, was never the same after that. He couldn't believe the men he called his *primos*, his cousins—Adán and Nacho—would betray him, would kill his flesh and blood. He started to get deeper and deeper into the Santa Muerte, deeper into the coke. The anger, the grief, ate him alive and the war he launched to get revenge tore the cartel to pieces.

Shit, Damien thinks, it tore the whole country to pieces, as Diego allied the Tapia organization with the Zetas to fight the Barreras and the Esparzas, his old partners in the Sinaloa cartel.

Thousands died.

Damien was only sixteen that day, just after Christmas, when the marines tracked his father down to an apartment tower in Cuernavaca, went in with armored cars, helicopters, and machine guns, and murdered him.

He keeps the photo on his phone as a screen saver. Diego Tapia, bullet holes in his face and chest, his shirt ripped open, his pants pulled down, dollar bills tossed over him.

The marines did that to his father.

Killed him, mocked his corpse, put the disgusting photos out on the net.

But Damien always blamed Tío Adán.

And Tío Nacho.

His "uncles."

And Ricardo Núñez, Ric's father.

What they did to Diego Tapia is unforgivable, Damien thinks. My father was a great man.

And I am my father's son.

He wrote a *narcocorrido* about it, put it out on Instagram.

I am my father's son and always will be
I'm a man of my family
A man of the trade
And I'll never turn my back on my blood
This is my life until I die.
I'm the Young Wolf.

His mother has begged him to get out of the business, do something else, anything else, she's already lost too many loved ones to the trade. *You're handsome*, she tells him—*movie star, rock star, Telemundo handsome, why don't you become an actor, a singer, a television host?* But Damien told her no, he wouldn't disrespect his father that way. He swore on Diego's grave to bring the Tapias back to where they belong.

At the top of the Sinaloa cartel.

"They stole it from us, Mami," Damien told his mother. "And I'm going to take back what they stole."

Easy to say.

Harder to do.

The Tapia organization still exists, but with only a fraction of the power it used to have. Without the leadership of the three brothers—Diego and Alberto dead, Martín in prison—it operates more like a group of franchises giving nominal allegiance to the Tapia name while they each operate independently, trafficking coke, meth, marijuana and now heroin. And they're scattered, with cells in southern Sinaloa, Durango, Guerrero, Veracruz, Cuernavaca, Baja, Mexico City and Quintana Roo.

Damien has his own cell, based in Acapulco, and while the other cells give him a certain level of respect because of who his father was, they don't view him as the boss. And Sinaloa—maybe out of guilt over what they did to his family—tolerates him as long as he's subservient and not looking to get revenge.

And the truth, Damien knows, is that he's not much of a threat—hopelessly outgunned by the combined forces of the Barrera and Esparza wings of the cartel.

Until now, he thinks.

Now Tío Adán and Tío Nacho are dead.

Iván and Elena Sánchez are at war.

Game changer.

And now he can pull the trigger on Ricardo Núñez.

"Shoot," Fausto tells him.

Fausto—squat, thickset, mustached—was one of his father's loyalists who went with Eddie Ruiz after Diego's death. Now, with Eddie in prison, he's back with Damien.

Based in Mazatlán, Fausto is a stone killer.

What Damien needs.

"Shoot," Fausto repeats.

Damien's finger tightens on the trigger.

But stops.

For several reasons.

One, he's unsure of the wind. Two, he's never killed anyone before. But three—

Damien shifts the scope onto Ric.

Ric is sitting right next to his dad, and Damien doesn't want to take the chance on missing and killing his friend.

"No," he says, lowering the rifle. "They'd come after us too hard."

"Not if they're dead." Fausto shrugs. "Shit, *I'll* do it."

"No, it's too soon," Damien says. "We don't have the power yet."

It's what he tells Fausto, what he tells himself.

He watches the convoy turn into the next switchback, out of sight and out of range.

The plane takes an unexpected turn.

Ric expected that they'd fly directly back to Culiacán, but the plane banks west toward the ocean to Mazatlán.

"I want to show you something," Núñez says.

Ric figures he already pretty much knows Mazatlán, which has been a major playground for Los Hijos. They've been coming to the carnival here since they were kids, and when they got older would frequent the beachside bars and clubs and hit on the *turista* women who flocked from the US and Europe for the sunshine and sand. It was in Mazatlán where Iván taught Ric how to say, "Would you like to sleep with me tonight?" in French, German, Italian and, on one occasion that lives only hazily in Ric's memory, Romanian.

That might have been the night—Ric is unclear—when he and the Esparza boys and Rubén Ascensión were arrested on the Malecón for some forgotten transgression, taken to the city jail and immediately released, with apologies, when they revealed their last names.

Ric is vaguely aware that Mazatlán, like a lot of towns in Sinaloa, was settled by Germans and still has a kind of Bavarian feel about it in its music and its affinity for beer, a heritage that Ric has partaken in more than he should have.

A car is waiting at the airstrip and drives them not to the boardwalk or the beach but down to the port.

Ric also knows the port well because that's where the cruise ships come, and where you have cruise ships you have available women. He and the Esparzas used to sit on the boardwalk above the piers and rate the women as they got off the ships, then pretend to be local tour guides and volunteer to take the top scorers to the best bars.

Although there was that time when Iván looked a tall, striking Norwegian woman straight in her blues eyes and stated flatly, "Actually, I'm not a guide. I'm the son of a cartel boss. I have millions of dollars, speedboats and fast cars, but what I really like to do is fuck beautiful women like you."

To Ric's surprise, she said okay, so they went off with her and her friends, rented a hotel suite, guzzled Dom, did a ton of coke and fucked like monkeys until it was time for the girls to get back on the cruise ship.

Yeah, Ric could show his father a few things about Mazatlán.

But they don't go to the cruise ship docks. They pass right by them and go to the commercial docks where the freighters come in.

"A business," Núñez says as they get out of the car next to a warehouse, "can never stand still. If you are static, you are dying. Your godfather, Adán, knew this, which is why he moved us into heroin."

A guard standing at the door of the warehouse lets them in.

"Heroin is good," Núñez says as they go in, "it's profitable, but like all profitable things, it attracts competition. Other people see you making money and they copy you. The first thing they try to do is undersell you, driving the price down and reducing everyone's profits."

If the cartel were truly a cartel, he explains, in the classic sense—that is, a collection of businesses that dominate a commodity and have agreed to meet set prices—it wouldn't be a problem.

"But 'cartel' is really a misnomer in our case; in fact, it's oxymoronic to speak of 'cartels' in the plural." They have competition, he explains—the remnants of the Zetas, bits and pieces left of the Gulf "cartel," the Knights Templar—but what worries Núñez is Tito Ascensión.

Ascensión asked Iván for permission to get into heroin, Iván smartly refused, but what if Tito does it anyway? Jalisco could become, quickly, the Sinaloa cartel's biggest competition. He'd undersell them, and Núñez is not of a mind to be forced into reducing profit margins. So . . .

They step into a back room.

Núñez closes the door behind them.

A young Asian man sits behind a table, on which are stacked several tightly wrapped bricks of . . .

Ric doesn't recognize whatever it is.

"The only good response to lower prices," Núñez says, "is higher quality. Customers will pay a premium for quality."

"So this is a higher-grade heroin?" Ric asks.

"No," Núñez says. "This is fentanyl. It's fifty times stronger than heroin."

A synthetic opiate, fentanyl was originally used in skin patches to relieve the pain of terminal cancer patients, Núñez explains. It's so powerful, even a small dot can be lethal. But the right dose gets the addict much higher, much faster.

He leads Ric out of the office to the back of the warehouse. A number of men are gathered there, some of whom Ric recognizes as high-ranking people in the cartel—Carlos Martínez, who operates out of Sonora; Héctor Greco, the plaza boss of Juárez; Pedro Esteban from Badiraguato. A few others that Ric doesn't know.

Behind them, along the wall, three men are tied to chairs.

One look at them, Ric knows they're junkies.

Emaciated, shaking, strung out.

A guy who looks like a lab tech sits at a chair by a small table, on which three syringes are set.

"Gentlemen," Núñez says. "I've told you about the new product, but seeing is believing. So, a little demonstration."

He nods at the lab tech, who takes one of the syringes and squats next to one of the junkies. "This is our standard cinnamon heroin."

The tech ties off the junkie's arm, finds a vein and injects him. A second later, the junkie's head snaps back, and then lolls.

He's high.

"The next syringe is the heroin laced with a small amount of fentanyl," Núñez says.

The tech injects the second junkie.

His head snaps, his eyes open wide, his mouth curls into an almost beatific smile. "Oh, God. Oh, my God."

"How is it?" Núñez asks.

"It's wonderful," the junkie says. "It's so wonderful."

Ric feels like he's watching QVC.

And sort of he is. The myth, he knows, is that cartel bosses are dictators who simply issue commands and expect them done. That's true with the *sicarios,* the gunmen and the lower levels, but a cartel is made up of businesspeople who will only do what's good for their businesses, and they have to be sold.

"The next," Núñez says, "is just three milligrams of fentanyl."

The last junkie strains against the ropes, screams, "No!"

But the tech ties him off, locates a vein, and then shoots the full syringe into his arm. The same snap of the head, the same wide eyes. Then the eyes close and the man's head falls forward. The tech holds two fingers against the junkie's neck and then shakes his head. "He's gone."

Ric fights the urge to throw up.

Jesus, did his father just do that? Did his father just really do that? He couldn't have used a lab rat, or a monkey or something, he just had a human being killed for a sales demo?

"Any addict who tries this new product," Núñez says, "would never go back, *could* never go back to the more expensive and less potent pharmaceutical pills or even cinnamon heroin. Why take the local, when you can take the express?"

"What's the cost to us?" Martínez asks.

"Four thousand US per kilogram," Núñez says. "Although by buying bulk we can probably get that down to three. But each kilo of fentanyl will produce twenty kilos of enhanced product worth over a million dollars at the retail level. The margin isn't the problem."

"What is the problem?" Martínez asks.

"Supply," Núñez says. "The production of fentanyl is tightly controlled in the US and Europe. We can buy it in China, however, and ship it into the ports we control, such as Mazatlán, La Paz and Cabo. But that means we have to control the ports.

"Gentlemen, thirty years ago, the great Miguel Ángel Barrera—M-1, the founder of our organization—introduced a derivative product of cocaine at a similar gathering. That derivative, 'crack,' made our organization wealthy and powerful. I'm now introducing a derivative of heroin that will take us to an even higher level. I want to take the organization into fentanyl and I hope you'll get behind me. Now, I've arranged for dinner at a local restaurant, and I hope you'll join me in that as well."

They go out to dinner at a place on the shore.

The usual drill, Ric thinks—private room in the back, the rest of the place bought out, a ring of guards circling the restaurant. They dine on ceviche, lobster, shrimp, smoked marlin, and bearded tamales washed down with quantities of Pacífico beer, and if any one of them gave a thought to the dead junkie in the back of the warehouse, Ric doesn't notice.

• • •

After the banquet, the plane flies Ric and his father back to Culiacán.

"So what do you think?" Núñez asks on the flight.

"About . . ."

"Fentanyl."

"I think you sold them," Ric says. "But if fentanyl's that good, the competition will also get in on it."

"Of course they will," Núñez says. "That's business. Ford designs a good pickup truck, Chevy copies and improves it, Ford designs an even better one. The key is getting there first, monopolizing the supply chain, establishing dominant sales channels and a loyal customer base, and continuing to service them. You can be very helpful by assuring that La Paz remains ours exclusively."

"Sure," Ric says. "But there's a problem you haven't thought of. Fentanyl's a synthetic?"

"Yes."

"Then anyone can make it," Ric says. "You don't need farms, like you do with heroin. You only need a lab, which you can put up anywhere. It will be like meth was—every asshole with a couple of bucks and a chemistry set will be making it in his bathtub."

"There'll be cheap knockoffs, no doubt," Núñez says. "But it will be an annoyance at the edge of the market, at most. The bootleggers won't have the sales reach to create a serious problem."

If you say so, Ric thinks.

But you won't be able to control it at the retail level. The retailers won't have the discipline to limit the doses, and they'll start to kill off the customer base. People are going to start dying, just like that poor guy in the warehouse, and when they start dying in the US, it's going to bring heat and light on us.

Pandora's box has been opened.

And the demons have flown out.

Fentanyl, Ric thinks, could kill us all.

Staten Island, New York

Jacqui wakes up sick.

Like she wakes up every morning.

That's why they call it a "wake-up shot," she thinks as she rolls out of bed. Well, it's not exactly a bed, it's an air mattress on the floor of a van, but I guess if you sleep in it . . . on it . . . it's a bed.

Nouns, after all, are based on verbs. Which is sort of too bad, she thinks, because her nickname, Jacqui the Junkie (a noun), lends itself far too easily to alliteration based on what she does, shoot junk, a verb.

Now she fights off an urge to puke.

Jacqui hates puking. She needs a wake-up.

Elbowing Travis, she says, "Hey."

"Hey." He's out of it.

"I'm going out to score."

"'Kay."

Lazy prick, she thinks, I'm going out to score for you, too. She pulls on an old UConn sweatshirt, slips into her jeans, then puts on a pair of purple Nikes she found at a yard sale.

Slides the door open and steps out into a Staten Island Sunday morning.

Specifically Tottenville, down on the south end of the island across the river from Perth Amboy. The van is parked in the lot at Tottenville Commons, out behind the Walgreens along Amboy Road, but she knows they'll have to move this morning before the security guys throw them out.

She walks into the drugstore, ignores the cashier's dirty look and goes to the back to the restroom because she really has to pee. Does her business, washes her hands, splashes water on her face and is pissed at herself because she forgot to bring her toothbrush and her mouth tastes like day-old shit.

Which is pretty much what you look like, Jacqui thinks.

She doesn't have any makeup on, her long brown hair is dirty and stringy and she's going to have to find a place to deal with that before she goes to work today but right now all she hears is her mother's voice: *You're such a pretty girl, Jacqueline, when you take care of yourself.*

What I'm trying to do, Mom, Jacqui thinks as she walks out of the store and gives the cashier a *fuck you* smile on her way out.

Fuck *you*, bitch, *you* try living in a van.

Which is what she and Travis have been doing since her mom threw them out, what, three months ago, when she came home from the bar early— miracle of miracles—and found them shooting up.

So they moved into Travis's van and live basically as gypsies now. Not homeless, Jacqui insists, because the van is a home, but they're . . . what's the word . . . peripatetic. She's always liked the word *peripatetic*. She wishes it rhymed with something so she could use it in a song, but it really doesn't. It sort of rhymes with *pathetic*, but Jacqui doesn't want to go there because it has the ring of truth.

We are, she thinks, kind of pathetic.

They want to get an apartment, plan to get an apartment, but so far the first—and last—and the damage deposit have been going up their arms.

Back out in the parking lot she starts working the phone and calls her dealer, Marco, but it goes right to voice mail. She leaves a quick message— *It's Jacqui. Looking for you. Call back.*

She really wants to hook up by phone because she's starting to feel seriously sick and doesn't want to have to get in the van and go all the way over to Princes Bay or way the hell up to Richmond, where the street dealers work.

It's too far and it's too risky, because the cops are clamping down, chasing the slingers inside. Or worse, you buy from some narc and get busted and what Jacqui really, really doesn't want is to get arrested and detox at Rikers.

She's about to go back to the van and drive down to Waldbaum's parking lot where you can usually score and then her phone buzzes and it's Marco and he isn't happy. "It's Sunday morning."

"I know, I need a wake-up."

"You should have saved some from last night."

"Yes, Mom."

"What do you need?" Marco asks.

"Two bags."

"You want me to come out for twenty bucks?"

Jesus, why is he hassling her? Her nose is starting to run and she thinks she's going to puke. "I'm getting sick, Marco."

"Okay, where are you?"

"The Walgreens on Amboy."

"I'm at Micky D's," Marco says. "I'll meet you behind the Laundromat. You know where that is?"

Yeah, she does her laundry there all the time. Well, not all the time, when she thinks about it. When it gets too disgusting. "Duh, yes."

"Half an hour," Marco says.

"To walk across the parking lot?"

"I just got my food."

"Okay, I'll come there."

"Ten minutes," Marco says. "Behind the Laundromat."

"Bring me a coffee," Jacqui says. "Milk, four sugars."

"Yes, Lady Mary," Marco says. "You want, like, a McMuffin or something?"

"Just the coffee." She's just going to be able to keep that down, never mind greasy food.

Jacqui crosses the parking lot and walks out to Page Avenue, then up to the next strip mall, which has a CVS, a McDonald's, a grocery store, a liquor store, an Italian restaurant and the Laundromat.

She walks behind the CVS and waits out the back of the Laundromat.

Five minutes later, Marco pulls up in his Ford Taurus. He rolls down the window and hands her the coffee.

"You *drove* across the parking lot?" Jacqui asks. "Global warming, Marco? Ever heard of that?"

"You have the money?" Marco asks. "And don't tell me you'll get it, you're totally out of credit right now."

"I have it." She looks around and then hands him a twenty.

He reaches into the console and then slips her two glassine envelopes. "And a buck for the coffee."

"Really?" Marco's gotten kind of salty since he started dealing. Sometimes he forgets he's just another addict, slinging shit so he has the money to get himself well. A lot of people are doing that these days—every dealer Jacqui knows is a user. She digs into her jeans pocket, finds a dollar bill and gives it to him. "I thought you were being a gentleman."

"No, I'm a feminist."

"Where are you going to be later?"

Marco holds his little finger to his mouth and his thumb to his ear—"Call me"—and pulls away.

Jacqui puts the envelopes in her pocket and walks back to the van.

Travis is awake.

"I scored," Jacqui says, pulling the envelopes out.

"Where?"

"From Marco."

"He's an asshole," Travis says.

"Okay, *you* go the next time," Jacqui says.

Fuck the lazy bastard, she thinks. She loves him, but, Jesus, he can be a pain in the ass sometimes. And speaking of Our Lord and Savior, Travis looks a little like Jesus—shoulder-length hair and a beard, all slightly tinged with red. And thin like Jesus, at least like he looks in all the pictures.

Jacqui finds the cut-out bottom of a soda can she uses instead of a spoon for a cooker and pours the heroin into it. She fills her syringe out of a water bottle, squirts it into the heroin, then flicks on her lighter and holds it under the cooker until the solution bubbles. Taking the filter out of a cigarette, she dips it in water and gently lays it into the solution. Then she puts the tip of the needle into the filter and sucks the liquid into the syringe.

She takes a skinny belt she keeps for the purpose, wraps it around her left arm, and pulls on it until a vein pops up. Then she places the needle into the vein and pulls the plunger back so there's a little air bubble in it and moves the needle around until a little blood shows up in the needle.

Jacqui hits the plunger.

Unties before she pulls the needle out and then—

Bam.

It hits her.

So beautiful, so peaceful.

Jacqui leans back against the van wall and looks at Travis, who just finished shooting up himself. They smile at each other and then she drifts off into heroin world, so vastly superior to the real world.

Which isn't that high a bar to clear.

When Jacqui was little, when she was little, when Jacqui was a little girl, she saw her daddy in every man on the sidewalk, on the bus, every man who came into the restaurant where her mommy worked.

Is that my daddy? Is that my daddy? Is that my daddy? she'd asked her mom until her mom got tired of hearing it and told her that her daddy was in heaven with Jesus and Jacqui wondered why Jesus got him and she didn't so she didn't like Jesus very much.

When Jacqui was little she stayed in her room and looked at picture books and made up stories and told herself stories, especially when Mommy thought she was asleep and brought home some of the men who came into the restaurant where Mommy worked. She'd lie in her bed and make up stories and sings songs about when Jacqui was little, when she was little, when Jacqui was a little girl.

She wasn't so little, she was nine, when Mommy married one of the men who came into the restaurant where she worked and he told Jacqui he wasn't her daddy, he was her stepdaddy, and she told him she knew that because her daddy was with Jesus and he laughed and said yeah maybe, if Jesus is holding down a barstool in Bay Ridge.

Jacqui was eleven the first time Barry asked her if she was going to grow up to be a whore like her mother and she remembers that he pronounced it "who-are," like "Horton Hears a Who-Are," and Jacqui would go around the house muttering *I meant what I said, and I said what I meant. Barry's an asshole, one hundred percent.* And one time he heard her and smacked her in the face and said *You may not love me but you're sure as shit going to respect me* and her mother sat there at the kitchen table and did nothing. But then again she did nothing when he hit *her* and called *her* a who-are and a fucking drunk and Jacqui would run and hide in her room ashamed she didn't do anything to stop him. And when Barry stormed out to go to the bar, Jacqui came out and asked her mother why she would stay with a man who was mean to her and her mother answered that someday she'd understand that a woman has needs, she gets lonely.

Jacqui didn't feel lonely, because she had books. She would shut herself up in her room and read books—she read all of *Harry Potter* and the idea that they had been written by a woman led her to go to the library and find Jane Austen, the Brontës, Mary Shelley and George Eliot and then Virginia Woolf and Iris Murdoch and poems by Sylvia Plath and Jacqui decided that someday she'd leave Tottenville and move to England and become a writer and live in a room of her own where she didn't have to block out the sounds of shouting and crying and hitting outside the door.

She started listening to music—not the pop shit her few friends listened to but good shit like the Dead Weather, Broken Bells, Monsters of Folk, Dead by Sunrise, Skunk Anansie. She bought an old guitar at a pawn shop, sat in her room and taught herself (in both literature and music Jacqui is an autodidact) chords and started to write songs when Jacqui was little (C), when she was little (F), when Jacqui was a little girl (C).

Jacqui is playing her guitar one afternoon when her mother is at work and Barry comes in and takes the guitar from her hand and says *This will be our secret, our little secret, I'll make you feel so good* and lays her back on the bed and lies on top of her and she doesn't tell her mother and she doesn't tell anyone *This will be our secret (D), our little secret (G), I'll make you feel so good (Em)* even when her mother says *I can tell you've been having sex you're a little whore who's the boy I'll have his ass thrown in jail* and Barry keeps coming into her room until one day one early morning she hears her mother screaming and runs and sees Barry hunched over on the toilet and her mother screams *Call 911* and Jacqui walks slowly to her room to get her phone and sings *This will be our secret (D), our little secret (G), I'll make you feel so good (Em)* before she punches in the number and by the time the EMTs get there Barry is dead.

By this time Jacqui is in middle school, smoking a little weed, drinking some beer, some wine with her friends but mostly she stays in and reads or plays guitar, discovers Patti Smith and Deborah Harry, even Janis Joplin, writes songs with sardonic lyrics *This will be my secret / My little secret / I killed my stepfather / Passively aggressively / And it makes me feel good / So good* and her mother says she needs to get a job to help out so she becomes a barista at Starbucks.

Jacqui gets good grades in high school, almost out of spite because she hates high school and everything about it except study hall. Her grades are good enough to get a scholarship, but not good enough for Columbia or NYU or Boston University and there's no money to send her anywhere she wants to go and she's never going to live in England and be a writer and have a room of her own and her mother wants her to go to cosmetology school so she can make a living but Jacqui holds on to a shred of dream and enrolls at CUNY Staten Island.

It starts with pills.

She's a freshman at CUNY, living at home with her mother, and it's Christmas break and someone offers her some Oxy and she's a little drunk and a lot bored so she thinks what the fuck and downs it and she likes it and the next day she goes out and gets some more because if you can't find pills in Tottenville your seeing-eye dog probably can. They're selling it in schools, on corners, in bars, shit, they're even selling it from ice cream trucks.

The pills are everywhere—Oxy, Vicodin, Percocet—everyone is selling or buying or both. For Jacqui, it takes the edge off, the edge off having no fucking idea what she wants to do with her life, the edge off knowing that she was born in Tottenville and is going to live in Tottenville and die in Tottenville, working minimum-wage jobs no matter what degree she gets from CUNY. The edge off keeping the secret that her stepfather had turned her into a matinee.

The pills make her feel good and she doesn't have a drug problem; what Jacqui has is a money problem. Not at first, when she was doing a little Oxy on weekends, not even when it was a pill a day, but now it's two or three at thirty dollars a pop.

Some of the money she gets from her job at Starbucks, then some from her mother's purse, sometimes she doesn't need money at all if she wants to fuck guys who have pills. Fucking is nothing, she's used to lying there letting a man fuck her and it might as well be somebody who can get her high if he can't get her off.

Jacqui is basically high her second semester of college, then all summer, and then she kind of stops going to class her sophomore year as she goes from a 3.8 GPA to Incompletes, and then she just gives up the sham and drops out.

She drifts into working and getting high and fucking dealers and then she meets Travis.

Who turns her on to heroin.

It would be easy to blame him—her mother certainly does—but it wasn't really Travis's fault. They met at a club, one of those grungy coffeehouses where the neo-Kerouac crowd hangs out and plays guitars, and Travis had just been laid off from his construction job—he was a roofer—because he'd hurt his back and couldn't really work and his disability ran out.

That was Travis's story—he started taking Vike for the back pain—

prescribed by a doctor—and never really stopped. On the age-old theory that if one was good, fifteen is better, Travis started chucking pills like M&M's.

They were both high when they met but it was like—

BAM.

Love.

They fucked in the back of his van and Jacqui got off like she'd never gotten off; he had a long skinny dick like his long skinny body and it touched her in a place she'd never been touched.

It was Travis for her after that, and she for him.

They liked the same art, the same music, the same poetry. They wrote music together, busked together up in St. George for people getting off the ferry. They were having a blast, but it was the money.

The money, the money.

Because they had a habit together, too, a habit that cost up to three hundred dollars a day, and that was just unsustainable.

Travis had the answer.

"H," he said, "it takes less to get you high and it costs, like, six or seven bucks a hit."

Instead of thirty.

But Jacqui was afraid of heroin.

"It's the same shit," Travis said. "They're all opiates, whether it's a pill or a powder, it's all the fruit of the poppy."

"I don't want to get addicted," Jacqui said.

Travis laughed. "Shit, you're addicted *now*."

Everything he said was true, but Jacqui argued she didn't want to use a needle. Cool, Travis said, we can just snort.

He did it first.

It really got him off.

He looked beatific.

So Jacqui snorted and it was so good, so good, so good. Better than anything, until they discovered smoking the shit, which was so much better, better, better.

Then one day Travis said, "Fuck this shit. Why are we messing around? It's so much more efficient to shoot it, I'm not letting trypanophobia get in the way."

Trypanophobia, Jacqui thought—the fear of needles.

They both loved words.

But she didn't think she had a phobia, she thought she had a reasonable fear—needles gave you hep C, HIV, God knows what.

"Not if you're clean, not if you're careful, not if you're . . . meticulous," Travis said.

At first he was, using only fresh needles he bought from nurses and guys who worked at drugstores. He always swabbed his arm with alcohol before he shot up, always boiled the heroin to get any bacteria out.

And he got high.

Higher than Oxy, higher than snorting or smoking, he got mainlining-in-your-blood, in-your-brain high. Jacqui was jealous, felt left behind, earthbound while he flew to the moon, and one night he offered to shoot her up and she let him do it. Stuck a needle instead of his dick in her and it got her off more than he ever did.

Once she did that she knew she was never going back.

So you can blame Travis all you want, but Jacqui knows it's her, it's in her, the heart and soul of an addict, because she loves it, loves the H, loves the high, it's literally in her blood.

"You're too smart to be doing this," her mother would tell her.

No, I'm too smart *not* to, Jacqui would think. Who would want to stay in this world when there's an alternative?

"You're killing yourself," her mother would wail.

No, Mom, I'm living.

"It's that rotten bastard's fault."

I love him.

I love our life.

I love . . .

It's two hours later when Jacqui looks at her watch and thinks, Shit, I'm going to be late.

She gets out of the van and walks to CVS this time because she likes to switch it up. Goes into the restroom, locks the door behind her, takes some shampoo from her purse and washes her hair in the sink. Dries off with paper towels, and then puts on eyeliner and a little mascara and changes into her work clothes, reasonably clean jeans and a long-sleeved plum polo shirt with a name tag on it.

Back in the van, she rouses Travis. "I have to go to work."

"Okay."

"Try to score for us, okay?"

"Okay."

I mean, how hard can it be, Travis? It's easier to find H on Staten Island than it is to find weed. It's everywhere. Half the people she knows are users.

"And move the van," Jacqui says.

"Where?" Travis asks.

"I dunno, just move it."

She gets out and takes the bus to the Starbucks on Page Avenue. Hopes the manager doesn't see her come in five minutes late because it would be her third time in the last two weeks and she really needs this job.

There's the Verizon bill, gas money, food money and she's up to fifty bucks a day now just to stay well, never mind get high.

It's like a train that just keeps picking up speed.

There are no stops and you can't get off.

Keller steps out of the Metro at Dupont Circle sweating.

The Washington summer is typically hot, humid, and sweltering. Shirts and flowers wilt, energies and ambitions flag, blazing afternoons yield to sticky nights that bring small relief. It reminds Keller that the nation's capital was actually built on a drained swamp, revives the rumor that old George chose the location to rescue himself from an ill-advised real estate investment.

It's been an ugly summer everywhere.

In June, a radical Islamic group called ISIS emerged in Syria and Iraq, its atrocities rivaling those of the Mexican drug cartels.

In Veracruz, Mexico, thirty-one bodies were exhumed from a mass grave on property owned by the former mayor.

The Mexican army fought a gun battle with Guerreros Unidos and killed twenty-two of them. Later, a story came out that the narcos had actually been taken into a barn and executed.

In the post-Barrera era, violence in Mexico has just gone on and on and on.

In July, a group of three hundred flag-waving, sign-wielding protesters chanting "USA, USA" and screaming "Go home!" surrounded three buses full of Central American immigrants—many of them children—in Murrieta, California, and forced them to turn around.

"Is this America?" Marisol asked when she and Keller watched the news on television.

Two weeks later, NYPD cops on Staten Island put a black man named Eric Garner in a lethal headlock, killing him. Garner had been selling illegal cigarettes.

In August, a cop in Ferguson, Missouri, fatally shot eighteen-year-old African American Michael Brown, triggering, as it were, days of violent rioting. It reminded Keller of the long hot summers of the '60s.

Later that month, potential presidential candidate John Dennison—

without a trace of evidence, never mind actual proof—accused the Obama administration of dealing guns to ISIS.

"Is he insane?" Marisol asked.

"He's throwing mud at the wall and seeing what sticks," Keller said.

He knows from experience—Dennison has thrown some mud at him, too. Keller's advocacy of naloxone prompted the barrage.

"Isn't it a shame," Dennison said, "that the boss of the Drug Enforcement Administration is soft on drugs? Weak. Not good. And isn't his wife from Mexico?"

"He's right about that," Marisol said. "I am from Mexico."

The conservative media picked it up and ran with it.

Keller was furious that they'd brought Marisol into it, but he didn't issue a response. Dennison can't play tennis, he thought, if I don't hit the ball back. But he brought another attack on himself when he said, in response to a question from the *Huffington Post,* that he basically agreed with the administration's review of maximum sentences for drug offenses.

Pathetic, Dennison tweeted. DEA boss wants drug dealers back on the streets. Weak Obama should say, "You're fired!"

Which apparently is a catchphrase Dennison uses on his reality TV show, which Keller has never seen.

"B-list celebrities go around running errands for him," Mari explained, "and the one who does the worst job every week gets fired."

Keller doesn't even know what a "B-list celebrity" is, but Mari does, having become shamelessly addicted to *Real Housewives* shows. She informed him that there are "real housewives" of Orange County, New Jersey, New York, Beverly Hills, and that what they do is go out to dinner, get drunk, and call each other names.

He was tempted to suggest *Real Housewives of Sinaloa*—a few of whom he'd actually known—in which they go out to dinner, get into arguments and machine-gun each other, but wisely decided to leave that one alone— Marisol can get very protective of her American pop culture.

On a serious level, his efforts to move DEA toward more progressive policy positions is running into resistance inside the agency.

Keller gets it.

He was one of the original true believers, a real hard-liner. He's a hard-liner *now* on the cartels that bring heroin, coke and meth into the country. But he's also a realist. What we're doing now isn't working, he thinks; it's time to try something different, but it's hard to sell that to other people who've also spent *their* lives fighting this war.

Denton Howard picks up Keller's statements like rocks and throws them at him. Like Keller, he's a political appointee, and he's lobbying inside and outside DEA, making sure that potential supporters on the Hill and in the media know that he disagrees with his boss.

It gets out there.

Two days later, *Politico* comes out with a story about "factionalism" inside DEA. According to the story, the agency is splitting between a "Keller faction"' and a "Howard faction."

It's no secret that the two men don't like each other, the story reads, *but the issue is more philosophical than personal. Art Keller is more liberal, wants to see a relaxation of drug prohibition laws, reduction of mandatory sentences and more focus placed on treatment than prohibition. Howard is a hard-liner on prohibition, a "lock 'em up and throw away the key" conservative.*

Factions are forming around the two positions, the story goes on to say:

But it's more complicated than a bipolar political struggle. What makes it really interesting is what might be called an "experiential divide." A lot of the veteran, old-school personnel, who might otherwise support Howard's more hard-core stance, don't respect him because he's a bureaucrat, a politician who never worked the field, while Keller is a veteran field agent, a former undercover, who knows the job from the street up. On the other hand, some of the younger personnel, who might otherwise be sympathetic to Keller's more liberal positions, tend to see him as something of a dinosaur, a street cop with a "shoot first, ask questions later" history who lacks administrative skills and tends to spend too much time on operations to the detriment of policy.

It might all be a moot point, anyway, decided not in the halls of the DEA but in the voting booth. If the Democrats win the next presidential election, Keller is almost certain to keep his job and will in all likelihood move to dump Howard and purge his faction. If a Republican candidate takes the White House, Keller is almost as certainly out the door, with Howard taking his desk.

Stay tuned.

Keller gets the writer on the phone. "Who did you talk to for this story?"

"I can't reveal sources."

"I know the feeling," Keller says. Marisol has schooled him that the media is not the enemy and that he needs to play nice. "But I know you didn't talk to *me*."

"I tried. You wouldn't take my call."

"Well, that was a mistake," Keller says. Or sabotage, he thinks. "Look, here's my cell number. Next time you want to do a story about my operation, call me directly."

"Is there anything in the story you want to correct or comment on?"

"Well, I don't shoot first and ask questions later," he says. That was Howard, he thinks, building a narrative. "And I'm not going to conduct any 'purges.'"

"But you would dump Howard."

"Denton Howard is a political appointee," Keller says. "I couldn't fire him if I wanted to."

"But you do want to."

"No."

"Can I quote you?"

"Sure."

Let Howard look like the asshole.

Keller clicks off and walks out to the reception area. "Elise, did I get an incoming call from *Politico*?"

He is an old undercover guy, so the slight trace of hesitation in her eyes tells him what he needs to know.

"Never mind," Keller says. "I'm reassigning you."

"Why?"

"Because I need someone I can trust," Keller says. "Have your desk cleaned out by the end of day."

He can't afford to have a Howard loyalist screening his phone calls.

Not with Agitator going on.

Keller has kept knowledge of, and access to, Agitator on a highly select need-to-know basis, the intelligence on which is restricted to Blair, Hidalgo, and himself.

On the NYPD side, Mullen has laid his neck on the chopping block by running the op from his own desk, not informing his superiors or anyone else in the Narcotics Division except for one detective—Bobby Cirello, the cop who drove them around on the New York City heroin tour.

This was part of the "top-down/bottom-up" strategy that Keller and Mullen developed over their intense discussions. Cirello would be sent out to penetrate the New York heroin connection from the lowest level and work his way up. At the same time, they'd try to find an opening at the top of the financial world and work their way toward a connection between the two.

Agitator is a slow burn, it's going to take months, if not years. Keller and Mullen have promised each other that they will make no premature arrests or seizures, no matter how tempting.

"We won't pull the string on the net," Mullen said, "until we have all the fish."

Cirello is already on the street.

Finding a target in the financial world has taken longer.

They can't put an undercover cop into the financial world, because the learning curve at the level they want would be too steep and it would take too long.

That means finding a snitch.

It's ugly, but what they're looking for is a victim. Like any predators, they're scanning the herd to find the vulnerable, the injured, the weak.

It's no different from finding an informer in the drug world, Keller thinks; you're looking for someone who has succumbed to weaknesses or is in trouble.

The vulnerabilities always come in the same categories.

Money, anger, fear, drugs, or sex.

Money is the easiest. In the drug world, someone has received some dope on credit, then got it busted or ripped. He owes a lot of money he can't pay. He flips in exchange for cash or refuge.

Anger. Someone doesn't get the bump he wanted, the deal he wanted, the respect he thinks he deserves. Or someone screws someone's wife or girl-friend. Or, worse, someone kills someone's brother or friend. The aggrieved doesn't have the power to extract his own revenge, so he goes to law enforcement to do it for him.

Fear. Someone gets word he's on the list, his head is on the block. He has nowhere to run but to the cops. But he can't come empty-handed, the law doesn't give protection from the goodness of its heart. He has to come with information, he has to be willing to go back and wear a wire. Then there's the fear of going to prison for a long stretch—one of the biggest motivations for ratting out. The feds used that particular fear to rip the guts out of the Mafia—most guys can't deal with the fear of dying in the joint. There are the few who could—Johnny Boy Cozzo, Rafael Caro—but they're few and far between.

Drugs. It used to be axiomatic in organized crime that if you do dope, you die. It makes guys too unpredictable, too talkative, too vulnerable. People do crazy, fucked-up things when they're high or drunk. They gamble stupidly, they get into fights, they crash cars. And an addict? All you have to do to get information from an addict is to withhold the drug. The addict will talk.

And then there's sex. Carnal misdeeds are not such a big deal in the drug world—unless you screw someone's wife, girlfriend, daughter, or sister, or unless you're gay—but out in the civilian world, sex is the undefeated champion of vulnerabilities.

Men who will confess to their wives that they cheated on their taxes, embezzled millions, hell, *killed* somebody, won't cop to something on the side. Guys who make sure their buddies know that they're players—that they have girlfriends, mistresses, hookers, high-priced call girls—would practically die before letting those same buddies find out that they don the girlfriends' lingerie, the mistresses' makeup; that the hookers and the call girls get a bonus for spanking them or pissing on them.

The weirder the sex, the more vulnerable the target is.

Money, anger, fear, drugs and sex.

What you're really looking for is a combo plate. Mix any of the five and you have a guy who is on the fast track to being your victim.

Hugo Hidalgo takes a cab from Penn Station to the Four Seasons Hotel.

He spends most of his time in New York now, because that's the new heroin hub and because, in the words often attributed to bank robber Willie Sutton, "That's where the money is."

Mullen is waiting for Hugo in the sitting room of a penthouse suite.

A guy in his early thirties, Hidalgo guesses, sits on one of the upholstered chairs. His sandy hair is slicked straight back, although a little disheveled as if he's run his hands through it. He's wearing an expensive white shirt and black suit pants, but he's barefoot.

His elbows are on his knees, his face in his hands.

Hidalgo is familiar with the posture.

It's someone who's been caught.

He looks at Mullen.

"Chandler Claiborne," Mullen says. "Meet Agent Hidalgo from DEA."

Claiborne doesn't look up, but mumbles, "Hello."

"How are you?" Hidalgo says.

"He's had better days," Mullen says. "Mr. Claiborne rented a suite here, brought up a thousand-dollar escort, an ounce of coke, got shall we say 'over-excited,' and beat the hell out of the woman. She, in turn, called a detective she knows, who came up to the room, saw the coke and had the good career sense to call me."

Claiborne finally looks up. Sees Hidalgo and says, "Do you know who I am? I'm a syndication broker with the Berkeley Group."

"Okay . . ."

Claiborne sighs, like a twenty-year-old trying to teach his parents how to use an iPhone app. "A hedge fund. We have controlling interest in some of the largest office and residential building projects in the world, over twenty million square feet of prime property."

He goes on to name buildings that Hidalgo knows, and a bunch he doesn't.

"What I think Mr. Claiborne is trying to indicate," Mullen says, "is that he's an important person who has powerful business connections. Am I representing that correctly, Mr. Claiborne?"

"I mean, if I didn't," Claiborne says, "I'd be in jail right now, wouldn't I?"

He's a cocky prick, Hidalgo thinks, used to getting away with shit. "What's a 'syndication broker' do?"

Claiborne is getting comfortable now. "As you can imagine, these properties cost hundreds of millions, if not billions of dollars to finance. No single bank or lending institution is going to take that entire risk. It takes sometimes as many as fifty lenders to put together a project. That's called a syndicate. I put syndicates together."

"How do you get paid?" Hidalgo asks.

"I have a salary," Claiborne says, "mid–seven figures, but the real money comes from bonuses. Last year it was north of twenty-eight mil."

"Mil would be millions?"

Hidalgo's DEA salary is $57,000.

"Yeah," Claiborne says. "Look, I'm sorry, I did get carried away. I'll pay her whatever she wants, within reason. And if I can make some sort of contribution to a policemen's fund, or . . ."

"I think he's offering us a bribe," Mullen says.

"I think he is," says Hidalgo.

Mullen says, "See, Chandler . . . may I call you Chandler?"

"Sure."

"See, Chandler," Mullen says, "money isn't going to do it this time. Cash isn't the coin of my realm."

"What is the 'coin of your realm'?" Claiborne says. Because he's confident that there's some kind of coin—there always is.

"This idiot's getting snarky with us," Mullen says. "I don't think he's used to taking crap from a mick or a Mexican. That isn't the way you want to go here, Chandler."

Claiborne says, "If I call certain people . . . I can get John Dennison on his private cell right now."

Mullen looks at Hidalgo. "He can get John Dennison on his private cell."

"Right now," Hidalgo says.

Mullen offers him his phone. "Call him. And then here's what's going to happen: We take you right down to Central Booking, charge you with felony possession of a Class One drug, soliciting, aggravated assault, and attempted bribery. Your lawyer will probably bail you before we can get you to Rikers, but you never know. In any case, you can read all about it in the

Post and the *Daily News*. The *Times* will take another day but they'll get to it. So call."

Claiborne doesn't take the phone. "What are my other options?"

Because Claiborne is basically right, Hidalgo thinks. If he was your basic Johnny Jerkoff, he'd be downtown already. He knows he has options—rich people always have options, that's how it works.

"Agent Hidalgo is up from Washington," Mullen explains. "He's very interested in how drug money makes its way through the banking system. So am I. If you could help us with that, we might be willing to forestall arrest and prosecution."

Hidalgo thinks that Claiborne is already about as white as white gets, but now he turns whiter.

Like ghost white.

Pay dirt.

"I think I'll take my chances," Claiborne says.

Hidalgo hears what Claiborne *didn't* say. He didn't say, *I don't know anything about drug money.* He didn't say, *We don't do that.* What he did say was that he would take his chances, meaning that he does know people who deal in dope money, and he's more scared of them than he is of the cops.

"Really?" Mullen asks. "Okay. Maybe your money people get to the hooker and she drops the assault charges. Then you hire a seven-figure lawyer and maybe, *maybe* he keeps you out of jail on the coke charge. But by then it's too late, because by that time your career is fucked, your marriage is fucked and you are fucked."

"I'll sue you for malicious prosecution," Claiborne says. "I'll destroy your career."

"Here's the bad news for you," Mullen says. "I don't care about my career. I've got kids dying on my watch. I only care about stopping the drugs. So sue me. I have a house in Long Island City, you can have it—the roof leaks, by the way, full disclosure.

"Now, here's what's going to happen—I'm going to have a DA up here in about thirty minutes. She can take your statement, which will be composed of a full and forthright confession, and write a memorandum of agreement for your cooperation, the details of which you will work out with Agent Hidalgo here. Or she can charge you with the full monty and we'll all go to the precinct together and get this war started. But, son? I'm telling you this right now, and I beg you to believe me, I am not the guy you want to go to war with. Because I will fly the last kamikaze mission right into your ship. So you have a half hour to think about it."

Hidalgo and Mullen step out into the hallway.

"I'm impressed," Hidalgo says.

"Ahhhh," Mullen says. "It's an old routine. I have it down."

"Do you know what we're taking on here?"

Because Claiborne's not entirely wrong. You start fucking with people who control billions of dollars, they fuck back. And a John Dennison could do a lot of fucking back.

"Your boss said he was willing to go the whole way," Mullen says. "If that was bullshit, I need to know now, so I can kick this asshole."

"I'll call him."

Mullen goes back in to babysit.

Hidalgo gets on the phone to Keller and fills him in. "Are you sure you want to do this?"

Oh, yeah.

Keller is sure.

It's time to start agitating.

Keller testifies in front of Ben O'Brien's committee to brief them on his strategy for combatting the heroin epidemic. He started by dismissing the so-called kingpin strategy.

"As you know," Keller says, "I was one of the chief supporters of the kingpin strategy—the focus on arresting or otherwise disposing of the cartel leaders. It roughly parallels our strategy in the war on terror. In coordination with the Mexican marines, we did an extraordinary job of it, lopping off the heads of the Gulf, Zeta, and Sinaloa cartels along with dozens of other plaza bosses and other high-ranking members. Unfortunately, it hasn't worked."

He tells them that marijuana exports from Mexico are down by almost 40 percent, but satellite photos and other intelligence show that the Sinaloans are converting thousands of acres from marijuana to poppy cultivation.

"You just said that you decapitated the major cartels," one of the senators says.

"Exactly," Keller says. "And what was the result? An increase in drug exports into the United States. In modeling the war against terrorists, we've been following the wrong model. Terrorists are reluctant to take over the top spots of their dead comrades—but the profits from drug trafficking are so great that there is always someone willing to step up. So all we've really done is to create job vacancies worth killing for."

The other major strategy of interdiction—the effort to prevent drugs from coming across the border—also hasn't worked, he explains to them. The agency estimates that, at best, they seize about 15 percent of the illicit drugs coming across the border, even though, in their business plans, the cartels plan for a 30 percent loss.

"Why can't we do better than that?" a senator asks.

"Because your predecessors passed NAFTA," Keller says. "Three-quarters of the drugs come in on tractor-trailer trucks through legal crossings—San Diego, Laredo, El Paso—the busiest commercial crossings in the world. Thousands of trucks every day, and if we thoroughly searched every truck and car, we'd shut down commerce."

"You've told us what doesn't work," O'Brien says. "So what will work?"

"For fifty years our primary effort has been stopping the flow of drugs from south to north," Keller says. "My idea is to reverse that priority and focus on shutting down the flow of money from north to south. If money stops flowing south, the motivation to send drugs north will diminish. We can't destroy the cartels in Mexico, but maybe we can starve them from the United States."

"It sounds to me like you're surrendering," one says.

"No one is surrendering," Keller says.

It's a closed hearing but he wants to keep this on the broadest possible terms. He sure as hell doesn't tell them about Agitator, because if you sneeze in DC someone on Wall Street says gesundheit. It's not that he doesn't trust the senators, but he doesn't trust the senators. A campaign year is coming up, two of the guys sitting in front of him have set up "exploratory committees" and PACs, and they're going to be looking for campaign contributions. And like me, Keller thinks, they're going to go where the money is.

New York.

Blair has already tipped him that Denton Howard is crawling into bed with John Dennison.

"They had dinner together at one of Dennison's golf clubs down in Florida," Blair said.

Keller guesses he was on the menu.

Dennison, still flirting with running, tweeted, DEA boss wants to let drug dealers out of prison! A disgrace!

Well, Keller thinks, I do want to let some drug dealers out of prison. But he doesn't need Howard talking out of school. After the hearing, he collars O'Brien in the hallway and tells him he wants Howard out.

"You can't fire him," O'Brien says.

"You can."

"No, I can't," O'Brien says. "He's a Tea Party favorite and I'm facing a revolt from the right in the next election. I can't win the general if I lose in the primary. You're stuck with him."

"He's stabbing me in the back."

"No shit," O'Brien says. "That's what we do in this town. The best way for you to deal with it is to get results."

The man is right, Keller thinks.

He goes back to the office and calls Hidalgo in.

"How are we doing with Claiborne?"

"He's given us shit," Hidalgo says. "'This broker does coke, this hedge fund manager is heavy into tree . . .'"

"Not good enough," Keller says. "Lean on him."

"Will do."

The "bottom-up" half of Agitator is going well—Cirello is climbing the ladder. But the "top-down" half is stalled—this cute piece of shit Claiborne thinks he can play them by giving them bits and pieces.

They need to bring him up short, make him produce.

No more free ride.

He pays the fare or he's off the bus.

They meet on the Acela.

"What do you think we are, Chandler, assholes?" Hidalgo asks. "You think you can just blow us off and go on with your life?"

"I'm trying."

"Not hard enough."

"What do you want me to do?" Chandler asks.

"Bring us something we can use," Hidalgo says. "New York's fed up with your act. They're going to prosecute."

"They can't do that," Claiborne says. "We have a deal."

"Which you haven't lived up to."

"I've been doing my best."

"Bullshit, you have," Hidalgo says. "You've been playing us. You think you're so much smarter than a bunch of dumb cops who buy their suits off the rack, and you probably are. You're so smart you're going to smart your way right into a cell. You're going to love the room service in Attica, mother-fucker."

"No, give me a chance."

"You had your chance. We're done."

"Please."

Hidalgo pretends to think about it. Then he says, "All right, let me get on the phone, see what I can do. But no promises."

He gets up, walks out of the car and stands in the next one for a couple of minutes. Then he walks back in and says, "I bought you a little more time.

But not, like, infinity. You give us something we can use, or I let New York hump you."

Keller takes a call from Admiral Orduña.

"That kid you're looking for," Orduña says, "we might have a sighting."

"Where?"

"Guerrero," Orduña says. "Does that make any sense?"

"No," Keller says. But when has anything to do with Chuy Barajos made any sense?

They're not sure it's him, Orduña says, but one of his people in Guerrero was surveilling a group of student radicals at a local college and spotted a young man hanging around the fringes who meets the description, and he heard one of the students call him Jesús.

Could be anybody, Keller thinks. "What college?"

Chuy never finished high school.

"Hold on," Orduña says, checking his notes. "Ayotzinapa Rural Teachers' College."

"Never heard of it."

"That makes two of us."

"I don't suppose your guy—"

"It's on its way, *cuate*."

Keller stares at his computer screen.

Christ, the odds are . . .

The photo comes across.

Keller sees a short, scrawny kid in torn jeans, sneakers and a black ball cap. His hair is long and unkempt.

The photo is a little blurry, but there's no question.

It's Chuy.

Heroin Island

Let me have a dram of poison, such soon-speeding gear
As will dispense itself through all the veins . . .

—Shakespeare

Romeo and Juliet, act V, scene 1

Staten Island, New York
2014

Bobby Cirello is thirty-four.

Young for a detective.

Chief Mullen is his hook and he's worked for the man for a long time, first as a UC out in Brooklyn when the boss was running the Seven Six. Cirello made a shitload of cases for him. When Mullen got the big job at One Police, he brought Cirello with him, and a gold shield came with the ride across the bridge.

Cirello's glad to be out from under UC. It's no way to live, hanging out with skels, junkies and dealers all the time.

You can't have your own life.

He likes his new job, his little efficiency apartment in Brooklyn Heights, just big enough for him to be able to keep clean and trim, and at least semi-regular hours, although there are a lot *of* them.

Now he sits in Mullen's office on the eleventh floor of One Police Plaza.

Mullen has the remote control in his hand and clicks from news channel to news channel on the television mounted to the wall. Every one of them is running the story of a famous actor's overdose, and every one of them refers to the "flood of heroin" and the "heroin epidemic" rampant in the city. And they each maintain that NYPD "seems powerless to stop it."

Cirello knows Mullen isn't one to take the description "powerless" passively. Nor the phone calls from the chief of D's, the commissioner, and Hizzoner the Mayor. Shit, about the only big shot who hasn't piled weight on Mullen is the president of the United States, and that's probably only because he doesn't have his phone number.

"So now we have a heroin epidemic," Mullen says. "You know how I know? The *New York Times*, the *Post*, the *Daily News*, the *Voice*, CNN,

Fox, NBC, CBS, ABC, and, let us not forget, *Entertainment Tonight*. That's right, people, we're getting ass-fucked by *ET.*

"All that aside, people are dying out there. Black people, white people, young people, poor people, rich people—this shit is an equal opportunity killer. Last year we had 335 homicides and 420 heroin overdoses. I don't care about the media, I can deal with the media. What I do care about is these people dying."

Cirello doesn't speak the obvious. *ET* wasn't there when it was blacks dying out in Brooklyn. He keeps his mouth shut, though. He has too much respect for Mullen and, anyway, the man is right.

There *are* too many people dying.

And we're a few brooms trying to sweep back an ocean of H.

"The paradigm has shifted," Mullen says, "and we have to shift with it. 'Buy and bust' works up to a point, but that point is far short of what we need. We've had some success busting the heroin mills—we've seized a lot of horse and a lot of cash—but the Mexicans can always make more heroin and therefore more cash. They figure these losses into their business plans. We're in a numbers game we can never win."

Cirello's done some of the mill busts.

The Mexicans bring the heroin up through Texas to New York and store it in apartments and houses, mostly in Upper Manhattan and the Bronx. At these "mills" they cut the H up into dime bags and sell it to the retailers, mostly gangbangers, who put it out in the boroughs or take it to smaller towns upstate and in New England.

NYPD has made some big hits on the mills—twenty-million-, fifty-million-dollar pops—but it's a revolving door. Mullen's right, the Mexican cartels can replace any dope and any money they lose.

They can also replace the people, because most of the personnel at the mills are local women who cut the heroin and low-level managers who work for cash. The cartel wholesalers themselves are rarely, if ever, present at the mills except for the few minutes it takes to bring the drugs in.

And the drugs are coming in.

Mullen is in daily touch with DEA liaisons who tell him the same thing is happening all over the country—the new Mexican heroin is coming up through San Diego, El Paso and Laredo into Los Angeles, Chicago, Seattle, Washington, DC, and New York—all the major markets.

And the minor ones.

Street gangs are migrating from the cities into small towns, setting up and doing business from motels. It's not just urban dwellers hooked on opiates now—it's suburban housewives and rural farmers.

They aren't Mullen's responsibility, though.

New York City is.

Mullen cuts right to it. "If we're going to beat the Mexicans at their game, we have to start playing like the Mexicans."

"I'm not following you."

"What do the narcos have in Mexico they don't have here?" Mullen asks.

Primo tequila, Cirello thinks, but he doesn't say it. He doesn't say anything—Bobby Cirello recognizes a rhetorical question when he hears one.

"Cops," Mullen says. "Sure, we have some dirty cops. Guys who'll look the other way for cash, a few who do rips, a rare few who sell dope themselves, even serve as bodyguards for the narcos, but they're the exception. In Mexico, they're the rule."

"I don't get where you're going with this."

"I want you to go back undercover," Mullen says.

Cirello shakes his head. His UC days are over—even if he wants to go back under, he can't. He's too well known as a cop now. He'd get made in thirty seconds, it would be a fuckin' joke.

He tells Mullen this. "They all know I'm a cop."

"Right. I want you to go undercover as a cop," Mullen says. "A dirty cop."

Now Cirello doesn't say anything because he doesn't know what to say. He doesn't want this job. Assignments like this are career killers—you get the rep for being dirty, the stink stays on you. The suspicion lingers, and when the promotion lists are posted, your name isn't on them.

"I want you to put it out there that you're for sale," Mullen says.

"I'm a thirty-year man," Cirello says. "I want to pull the pin from this job. This is my life, Chief. What you're asking will only jam me up."

"I know what I'm asking."

Cirello grabs at straws. "Besides, I'm a gold shield. That's too high up the chain. The last gold chains who went dirty were all the way back in the eighties."

"Also true."

"And everyone knows I'm your guy."

"That's the point," Mullen says. "When you get a high-enough buyer, you're going to put it out that you represent me."

Jesus Christ, Cirello thinks, Mullen wants me to put it out that the whole Narcotics Division is up for sale?

"That's how it works in Mexico," Mullen says. "They don't buy cops, they buy departments. They want to deal with the top guys. It's the only way we get in the same room with the Sinaloans."

Cirello's brain is spinning.

It's so goddamn dangerous, what Mullen's suggesting. There's so much that can go wrong. Other cops get word he's dirty and run an op against him. Or the feds do.

"How are you going to paper this?" he asks. Document the operation so that if it goes south, their asses are covered.

"I'm not," Mullen says. "No one is going to know about this. Just you and me."

"And that guy Keller?" Cirello asks.

"But you don't know about that."

"If we get popped, we can't prove we're clean."

"That's right."

"We could end up in jail."

"I'm relying on my reputation," Mullen says. "And yours."

Yeah, Cirello thinks, that's going to do a lot of good if I run into other cops who are dirty, who are taking drug money, doing rips. What the hell do I do then? I'm not a goddamn rat.

Mullen reads his mind. "I only want the narcos. Anything else you might come across, you don't see."

"That's in direct violation of every reg—"

"I know." Mullen gets up from behind his desk and looks out the window. "What the hell do you want me to do? Keep playing it by the book while kids are dying like flies? You're too young, you don't really remember the AIDS epidemic, but I watched this city become a graveyard. I'm not watching it again."

"I get it."

"I don't have anyone else to go to, Bobby," Mullen says. "You have the brains and the experience to do this and I don't know who else I could trust. You have my word, I'll do everything I can to protect your career."

"Okay."

"Okay, you'll do it?"

"Yes, sir."

"Thank you."

Riding down in the elevator, Cirello wonders if he's not completely, utterly and totally fucked.

Libby looks at him and says, "So you're a nice Italian boy."

"Actually, I'm a nice Greek boy," Cirello says.

They're sitting at a table at Joe Allen, near the theater where she's working, bolting down cheeseburgers.

"'Cirello'?" she asks.

"It doesn't hurt to have an Italian-sounding name on the job," Cirello says. "If you can't be Irish, it's the next best thing. But, yeah, I'm a Greek boy from Astoria."

Almost a stereotype. His grandparents came over after World War II, worked their asses off and opened the restaurant on Twenty-Third Street that his father still runs. The neighborhood isn't so Greek anymore, but a lot of them still live there and you can still hear "Ellenika" spoken on the streets.

Cirello didn't want to go into the restaurant business, and it's a good thing he has a younger brother who did so his parents weren't heartbroken when Bobby went first to John Jay and then to the police academy. They came to his graduation and were proud of him, although they always worry, and never really understood when he was undercover and would show up with shaggy hair and a beard, looking thin and haggard.

His grandmother looked him straight in the eyes and asked, "Bobby, are you on drugs?"

"No, Ya-Ya."

I just buy them, he thought. It was impossible to explain his life to them. Another reason undercover is such a tough gig—nobody understands what you really do except other undercovers, and you never see them anyway.

"And you're a detective," Libby says now.

"Let's talk about you."

Libby is freaking beautiful. Rich red hair Cirello thinks they usually describe as "lustrous." A long nose, wide lips and a body that won't quit. Legs longer than a country road, although Cirello wouldn't know much about country roads. He saw her at a Starbucks in the Village, turned around and said, "I have you for a low-fat macchiato type."

"How did you know?"

"I'm a detective."

"Not a very good one," Libby said. "I'm a low-fat latte."

"But your phone number," Cirello said, "is 212-555-6708. Am I right?"

"No, you're wrong."

"Prove it."

"Let me see your badge," Libby said.

"Oh, you're not going to turn me in for sexual harassment, are you?" Cirello asked.

But he showed her his badge.

She gave him her phone number.

He had her down as a cop groupie, except it took him about eighteen phone calls to get her to this table.

"There's not much to tell," she says. "I'm from a little town in Ohio, I went to Ohio State and studied dance. Six years ago I came to the big city to make it."

"How's that going?"

"Well," she says, shrugging, "I'm on Broadway."

Libby's in the chorus of *Chicago*, which Cirello figures is probably the dancer equivalent of a gold shield. And she's looking at him with those green eyes, letting him know that she's his equal.

Cool, Cirello thinks.

Very cool.

"You live in the city?" he asks.

"Upper West Side," she says. "Eighty-Ninth between Broadway and Amsterdam. You?"

"Brooklyn Heights."

"I guess we're not geographically compatible," Libby says.

"You know, I've always thought geography was overrated," Cirello says. "I don't think they even teach it in school anymore. Anyway, I *work* in Manhattan, down at One Police."

"What's that?"

"NYPD headquarters," he says. "I work in the Narcotics Division."

"So I shouldn't smoke weed around you."

"I don't care," Cirello says. "I'd do it with you, except they test us from time to time. Let me ask you something, you have roommates?"

"Bobby," she says, "I'm not sleeping with you tonight."

"I didn't ask you to," Cirello says. "Frankly, I'm offended. What do I look like, some cheap whore, you can let him buy you a burger and you think it means you can have your way with him?"

Libby laughs.

It's deep and throaty and he likes it a lot.

"Do *you* have roommates?" Libby asks.

"No," Cirello says. "I have an efficiency, you have to step outside to change your mind, but I like it. I'm not there a lot."

"You work all the time."

"Pretty much."

"What are you working on now?" she asks. "Or can you tell me?"

"We were going to talk about you," Cirello says. "For instance, I didn't think dancers ate cheeseburgers."

"I'll have to take an extra class tomorrow, but it's worth it."

"Class?" Cirello asks. "I thought you already went to college for this."

"You have to keep working," Libby says, "to stay in shape. Especially if you're going to indulge in late-night meat binges, and I realized how gross that sounded the second it came out of my mouth. How about you? Do you eat healthy?"

"No," Cirello says. "I eat like a cop, whatever I can grab on the street at the moment."

"Like doughnuts?"

"Don't profile me, Libby."

"What about all that wonderful Greek food?"

"Not so wonderful when you grow up on it," Cirello says. "Don't tell my ya-ya, but I'd take Italian every time. Or Indian, or Caribbean, anything, as long as it's not wrapped in a grape leaf. Let me ask you something else: Indians or Reds?"

"Reds," Libby says. "I'm all about the National League."

"Should Rose get in the Hall?"

"Absolutely," Libby says. "I bet on myself every day. I'll bet you do, too."

"You know, this could work out."

"Mets?"

"Of course."

She takes a french fry off his plate and pops it in her mouth. "Bobby, about this cheap whore thing . . ."

Cirello spoons coffee into the *briki* and turns the gas stove to medium. He stirs the coffee until the foam rises, pours it into two cups and walks over to the bed. "Libby? You said wake you at seven."

"Oh shit," she says, "I have to get to class."

He hands her the coffee.

"This is wonderful," she says. "What is it?"

"Greek coffee."

"I thought you said you hated Greek food."

"I'm so full of shit . . ."

She walks into the bathroom, apparently unbothered by her nudity. Yeah, I wouldn't be bothered either, Cirello thinks, a body like that. When she comes out, her red hair is in a ponytail and she has a sweatshirt and leggings on.

"Time to do the walk of shame," she says.

"Let me drive you."

"I'll take the subway."

"Is that your way of saying this was a one-night stand?" Cirello asks.

"Look at you, Mr. Big-Shot Detective, all insecure," she says. She kisses him on the lips. "It's my way of saying that the subway is faster."

He tosses his coffee down. "Come on, I'll walk you."

"Yeah?"

"Like I said, I'm a nice Greek boy."

At the top of the subway entrance she says, "You'd better call me."

"I'll call you," Cirello says.

She kisses him lightly and goes down the stairs.

Cirello stops at a newsstand, buys the papers, and walks to a diner for breakfast. He sits down at a booth, has a big cheese omelet with rye toast, and looks through the *Times*. There's a prominent story about the actor who overdosed.

And now, Cirello thinks, I have to reach out and sell myself to the people who killed him.

Easy to say, harder to do.

These people aren't billionaires because they're idiots. They don't own cops in Mexico just because Mexican cops are easier to buy—they own cops because they have leverage on them. The offer isn't "take it or leave it," the offer is "take it or we kill you and your family." That way they know they can trust the cop they bought—he isn't going to flip on them.

Doesn't work that way up here.

No wiseguy in his right mind would kill a New York City cop, much less threaten his family, because he knows he'd have thirty-eight thousand angry police up his ass. Even if he survived his arrest—which is unlikely—the Irish and Italian prosecutors and the Jewish judge would see that he did the rest of his life under the worst prison in the state. Worse, it would fuck up business, so the bosses make sure their troops don't do that shit.

The black and Latino gangbangers know better than to kill a cop, because it would shut their businesses down.

Cops get killed, all right, too many, but not by OC.

The Mexicans are going to be hinky about buying an NYPD cop because they won't have the insurance policy on him.

So you have to give them some.

He goes to the garage, picks up his car, a 2012 Mustang GT, and drives out to Resorts World Casino.

A week later he's at a Starbucks in Staten Island listening to the barista sing the theme song from *Gilligan's Island*.

"You're too young to know that show," he says.

"Hulu," she answers. "What can I get you?"

He looks at her name tag. "A latte, please, Jacqui."

"Just a latte?" she asks. "No annoying adjectives?"

"Just a latte," he says, thinking, And maybe some smack. The girl wears long sleeves and her eyes look as if she's high.

Staten Island is one of the heroin hot spots. They're seeing three times the smack they did only two years ago. Used to be the drug was just in the northern, more urban part of the island, where it came on the ferry from Manhattan or over the bridge from Brooklyn, and you found it in the projects.

Not anymore.

Now it's down to the single-family neighborhoods in the central and southern parts of the island, working-class neighborhoods with a lot of cops, firefighters, and city employees.

And let's be honest about it, Cirello thinks.

White neighborhoods.

Blue-collar neighborhoods.

Why he's here now.

Because he's white.

Up in Manhattan and out in Brooklyn, drug trafficking is pretty much a gang thing. The black and Latino gangs dominate the trade in and around the projects and he knows he's not going to break in with them.

Not a white cop.

Not even a dirty white cop.

But out here the heroin trafficking is different—you have a lot of independent dealers, most of them users themselves, selling dime and even nickel bags they're buying from wiseguy retailers who buy it from the mills uptown.

Twenty years ago, maybe even ten, it would be worth your life to deal H to white kids in Staten Island, which is as mobbed up as it is copped up. Shit, Paul Calabrese himself lived out here, and there's still a mob presence but it's different. They don't look out for their own like they used to, and that thing about the mob protecting white kids from dope is a long-gone myth.

Cirello has heard that John Cozzo's fucking grandkid is slinging dope out here. Which is really no big surprise when you consider that Cozzo killed Calabrese to clear the way for importing Mexican heroin.

Anyway, Cirello knows he isn't going to find his hook in the Bronx, Brooklyn, or Manhattan. He's going to find it out here in white Staten Island—Heroin Isle—with users like Jacqui here.

To lead him to the sharks.

He's thrown out the chum. Went to Resorts World and dropped three large at the blackjack table, betting stupid. Then he chased it with basketball bets—college and pro—and dropped five more. Then he drove up to Connecticut—Mohegan Sun and Foxwoods—dumped a few grand more and got drunk and loud so the word would get around the northeast OC community that a New York detective was off the leash, gambling heavy, losing heavy, drinking heavy.

Blood in the water.

Now he drinks his latte and watches Jacqui work behind the counter. She's got a smile on her face and does her job but she looks a little shaky, walks a little jumpy, and Cirello knows she has *maybe* three hours before she needs a get-well fix.

She has to be what, nineteen? Twenty, tops?

What a world.

Young people dropping like it's World War I out here. Parents burying their kids. It's unnatural.

Other than this jacked-up assignment, his new life is pretty good. He's been seeing Libby for a few weeks now and so far it's working out. Their schedules match—she's not available until late night or early in the morning and right now they're both content with a triweekly late dinner and subsequent sex. She isn't making any further demands and neither is he.

It's easy.

He finishes his coffee and walks up the block to Zio Toto.

The bar is empty and he pulls out one of the black stools, sits down and orders a Seven and Coke.

Angie is late and Cirello knows it's a power play.

Make the other guy wait.

Angie comes in about five minutes later.

If he's been a regular at 24 Hour Fitness, he's hiding it pretty well, Cirello thinks. Angelo Bucci is still the same doughy slob he was when they went to Archbishop Malloy together in Astoria. He has his hair cut short now and wears a Mets jacket with jeans and a pair of loafers.

Gives Cirello a hug, sits down at the bar and says, "The fuck did I have to come down to Alabama for?"

"Don't you live in Richmond now?"

"Still a haul," Angie says. "What, you don't want to be seen with your old friends, now you're a gold shield? What are you drinking? What's that, a Coke?"

"And Seven."

"I'll have what he's having," Angie says to the bartender, "only make it a vodka straight up. And give this *mezzo fanook* another soda."

Cirello points at his empty glass to indicate he'll have another. "How's Gina?"

"Well, she hasn't stopped bustin' balls, that's what you're asking," Angie says. "The kids are growing like weeds. But you didn't ask me down here to talk about my domestic life, Bobby."

The bartender brings the drinks. Angelo juts his chin, meaning he should find something to do at the other end of the bar.

"I need to borrow some money," Cirello says.

"I was afraid of that," Angie says. "How much?"

"Twenty large."

"What the *fuck*, Bobby?"

"Blame St. John's," Bobby says.

"Who are you into?"

"No one," Bobby says. "I'm paid up but I'm broke. Little shit like rent, car payments, food . . ."

"More bets . . ."

"I need cash, Angie. Not a lecture."

"You put money on St. John's, maybe you need a lecture," Angie says. "Jesus, Bobby, I don't want to lend you money. I'd have to charge you vig."

"I know."

"And you go chasing that and lose . . ."

"I make good money," Cirello says.

"Which is why you're coming to me?" Angie asks.

"Yeah, well, I thought we were friends."

"We are," Angie says. "Which is why I don't want to see you dig a deeper hole, for yourself, and . . ."

"And what?"

"How do I put this, Bobby?" Angie says. "Lending money to an NYPD detective . . . if you don't pay me, how am I supposed to get my money back? I mean, I can't lean on you, can I?"

"First of all," Cirello says, "I'm going to pay you back. But if I don't, what you do is, you drop a dime to Internal Affairs, and my career is fucked. It's good leverage."

"Yeah, maybe. I didn't think of that."

"Good thing *I'm* here, then."

"Yeah, not so much," Angie says. "Okay, thirty days at twenty points, the vig every Friday, regular as a priest with an altar boy. You miss, it compounds on the principal."

"I know how it works, Angie."

"I live off gamblers," Angie says. "They put food on my table, clothes on my kids' backs. I don't want to live off you, Bobby. Shit, what would I say to your ya-ya? How is she, by the way?"

"Good. Cantankerous."

"I should swing by there, say hello," Angie says. "It's been too long."

"She'd like to see you."

Angie gets up, finishes his drink. "Little League practice, would you believe that? You parked out front?"

"Down the block."

"Come outside."

They walk out to Angie's black Land Rover. Cirello gets into the passenger seat. Angie opens the console, takes out a stack of hundred-dollar bills and counts out twenty grand. "Don't fuck me on this, Bobby."

"I won't."

"You want a ride to your car?"

"It's just at Starbucks."

"Okay," Angie says. "See you Friday. Pier 76, a bar up in St. George. You know it?"

"I can find it."

"Five p.m. Don't be late."

"This is just between us, right, Angie?"

"Of course," Angie says, looking hurt. "The fuck you think?"

Getting out of the car, Cirello knows what happens next—Angie makes a beeline to his bosses to brag he has an NYPD detective on the hook. They're going to ask him what this detective works and he's going to tell them narcotics. The bosses file that piece of information away. Because that's what they do.

Cops and criminals, information is currency.

Cirello goes back to his car and sits.

Because that's what *I* do, he thinks. I sit. A lot of cop work is a matter of sitting and waiting for something to happen. Sometimes it does, which is the same as saying that sometimes it doesn't.

But he has a hunch about Jacqui.

She's going to score and she's going to score soon.

Which would ordinarily be no big deal—a few thousand addicts are going to score soon, and it's really a matter for the uniforms or maybe the plain-clothes, if they need some arrests for the quotas that supposedly don't exist.

But Cirello needs a Goldilocks bust.

Not too big, not too small.

Popping Jacqui's score is too small, but it might lead him to the midlevel bust he's looking for.

So he sits and waits.

In ambush.

Like the predator he's become.

A cop hunting for a payday.

Jacqui has texted Travis about fifty-seven times and her manager has started getting raggy about it.

Where the hell is he?

Why doesn't he at least answer? If he hasn't scored, she thinks, he could at least tell me that so that I can try to reach Marco or someone. She signals the manager that she's taking a bathroom break and he looks at her like, *What, again?* She goes into the restroom and is about to call Marco when a text finally comes in from Travis. Pulling in now. Come on out.

When she comes out, the manager stops her. "Are you sick?"

"No, why?"

"You seem sick."

"I'm fine," Jacqui says.

"No, why don't you check out," he says. "It's slow."

"I need the hours."

"Go home, Jacqui."

She walks out into the parking lot. Travis is waiting in the van, parked along the edge of the lot. She gets into the back and Travis gets out of the driver's seat and joins her.

"You score?" Jacqui asks.

"Yeah."

She's cooking up when there's a banging at the door.

"It's the fucking manager," Jacqui says. "I'll deal with him."

She slides the door open a crack.

It's not the manager. It's the latte-no-adjectives.

Holding up a badge.

"Hello, kids," he says. "What are we doing in here?"

Cirello makes his pitch.

"I arrest you both now," he says. "It's simple possession, so you probably get drug court, but you'll still go to Rikers for a couple of weeks unless you can make bail, which I'm guessing you can't. Or . . ."

He pauses for effect.

Hold out a little hope.

"You give me your dealer."

The guy shakes his head. Cirello had his plates run, so he already knows his name is Travis Meehan, no priors.

He feels bad for the kid.

"We can't do that," Travis says.

"That's too bad," Cirello says, "because you're going to get really sick in jail. You love this girl?"

Travis nods.

"If you do," Cirello says, feeling like shit, "you don't want to see what can happen to her in the bullpen at Rose Singer."

"We can't be rats," Jacqui says.

"I hear you," Cirello says. "I really do. The thing of it is, I don't even want your dealer, ultimately. I'm betting he's a friend of yours, a user himself, right? Come on, am I right?"

He gets grudging nods.

"I don't want to hurt your friend," Cirello says. "I don't want to hurt *you*. I'm after people you don't even know, the people who sold the shit to your friend, and I'll bet they're not friends of his."

"We have to live here."

"If you make it back here," Cirello says, "from Rikers. You've never been in the system, you don't know. It's iffy. Could go either way. You get the wrong judge, he's having a bad day . . . But look, I get your point. We can do this so no one ever knows it was you. But, if you want, I pop you and then I put it out on the street you flipped. Not good."

"You're a prick," Jacqui says.

"Yup."

She's jonesing, he sees. They both are.

And he has the most persuasive tool available to anyone dealing with an addict. "I'm not asking you to set him up. Just give me a name, a description, a car, where he hangs, and I'll let you fix."

Winner, winner.

Chicken dinner.

He gets Marco that night.

Easy pickings, the dumb shit is dealing from the Micky D's parking lot. ("Would you like fries with that, sir?" "No, thanks, just the smack.")

Cirello watches a deal go down from Marco's Ford Taurus, walks right up and gets into the passenger seat.

"NYPD, Marco," Cirello says, showing his badge. "Do not make me pull my weapon, just set your hands on the wheel."

Marco tries to tough it out. "Do you have a warrant?"

"Don't need one," Cirello says. "I have probable cause. I just saw you sling a dime bag. I don't even have to ask you if I can search the car, I can just search the car, but first I'm going to ask you, do you have any weapons on you, especially any firearms?"

"No."

"That's good, Marco," Cirello says, "that will save you four years on this beef. Now let's see what we do have."

He opens the console and sees a stack of dime bags.

"Uh-oh," Cirello says. "Possession with intent to distribute. Felony weight. Rockefeller law shit. Fifteen to thirty, mandatory."

Marco starts to cry. He's a skinny, scared, pathetic junkie and Cirello feels like a piece of shit.

"I'd cry, too," Cirello says. "You have priors, Marco?"

"One."

"For?"

"Possession," Marco says.

"What did you get?"

"Probation," Marco says. "Court-ordered counseling, methadone program."

"Didn't take, huh?" Cirello says. "Well, now you're double fucked, Marco. The judge is going to go flamenco on you. They're very serious about heroin slingers these days, and you, my dumb young friend, are dealing in a white neighborhood that's had a lot of overdose deaths. You know how many COs live in Staten Island? They're going to be waiting for you inside."

Cirello's just making this shit up, but it sounds good. And the guy is terrified, his hands quivering on the wheel.

"I want my lawyer."

"What a lawyer is going to get you is *maybe* the minimum fifteen," Cirello says, seeing this slip right out of his hands. "That means you're, what, forty when you get out? Best-case scenario. Worst-case, sixty? But yeah, let's call him. Only thing is, once you do, I can't help you anymore."

"What can you do to help me?"

"That depends on you," Cirello says.

"I know what you want."

"What do I want, Marco?"

"You want me to give you the guys who sold this to me," Marco says.

"You're not as stupid as you look," Cirello says. "That's good. Now before you say something that proves you *are* as stupid as you look, let me ask you something: if those guys were in your position, would they do fifteen to thirty upstate to save you? Think before you answer."

"They'll kill me."

"Not if we do it right," Cirello says. "Look at me, Marco. Marco, look at me."

Marco looks at him.

"Son," Cirello says, looking all fatherly. "I am the way, the truth and the life. I am your one chance at still having some kind of future, but I can't do it on my own. I need your help. Work with me here. Give me what I need and you walk."

Marco hesitates.

The deal is on the tipping point.

Cirello says, "The guys who sold you this shit know you don't know how to do time. They know you'll be jonesing. You think they're going to sit around worrying about whether you're going to flip?"

Marco thinks about it.

The last thing Cirello wants is Marco thinking. You let a skel think, he comes up with all kinds of happy shit to make your life complicated. "No, you know what? I'm full of shit. Let's get you booked so you can call your lawyer."

"No."

"No?"

"No," Marco says. "Please help me."

Yeah, that's what I'm here to do, Cirello thinks.

I'm in a helping profession.

Cirello follows Marco's car west on Arden Avenue across the southern end of Staten Island.

To Cirello, who's done most of his narcotics work in the ghettos of Brooklyn, it's surreal driving past strip malls and blocks of single-family homes on one side and the green of Arden Heights to his left. He feels like he's in the suburbs—some ardent New Yorkers might call it "the country"—as they pass under the Korean War Veterans Parkway through leafy Edgegrove, then turn north onto Amboy Road at the northeast corner of Blue Heron Park. Amboy is mostly residential for the next ten blocks or so, then opens into a commercial area in Eltingville—the post office, a couple of banks and the Eltingville Shopping Center on the left, another strip mall to the right, where Marco pulls into a parking lot.

Cirello passes him and pulls into the far end of the lot near a Smashburger and gets on the phone. "Where are you meeting them?"

"Out in front of Carvel."

"The ice cream store?" Cirello asks.

"Yeah."

"That makes the cakes?"

"Yeah, Carvel."

Jesus Christ, Cirello thinks. Ice cream cakes and smack. The Professor *and* Mary Ann . . .

He watches Marco pull into a parking slot. A couple of minutes later, a red Ford Explorer pulls up next to him. Marco hands some money across, a package comes back in return.

Marco, as per their deal, pulls out.

Cirello follows the Explorer as it takes a right onto Amboy and heads north into Great Kills and past Ocean View Cemetery (although why a view would be important in a cemetery is beyond him), then past Frederick Douglass Park (which is a little weird, because Cirello hasn't seen a black person all day) into Bay Terrace.

Normally he'd call in the plates but he doesn't want to be on the record and he already has an ID from Marco—the car should belong to a Steven DeStefano.

Then right on Guyon Avenue—east toward the beach—a left onto Mill Road and then a right onto Kissam Avenue, where the houses thin out into a marsh that flanks the road on both sides. The Explorer pulls into a driveway on the north side of the road by a shotgun house with no other houses for two lots on either side.

Privacy, Cirello thinks.

Good.

Cirello drives past the house and takes Kissam to its end where it hits Oakwood Beach at Lower Bay. There's nothing here, he thinks, nothing but beach to the right or left as far as he can see.

He takes his Glock from its holster, sets it on the seat beside him, pins his shield on the lapel of his jacket, turns around and drives back to the house. Taking a deep breath, he opens the door, gets out and walks up to the front door.

There is nothing about this that is even slightly regulation.

Proper procedure would be to have marked the address, gone back to Division and reported it, obtained a warrant, and then come back in force—several detectives, some uniforms—maybe SWAT, maybe ATF—coordinate with DEA.

It's definitely not one detective with a Glock and no paper, and probable cause that wouldn't hold up five minutes in an evidentiary hearing. This is stupid shit, the kind of stupid shit that gets you fired, maybe indicted, maybe killed.

But he doesn't know any other way to do it.

Cirello raps the gun butt on the wooden door. "NYPD!"

He can hear the scrambling inside, the kind of chaos he's heard a few dozen times as drug skels panic and try to figure out what to do. Flush their stash? Run? Fight?

"I said open the fucking door, Steve!" he yells, then steps to the side in case Steve decides to shoot through the fucking door instead.

He doesn't.

Cirello reaches in and tries the knob.

The fucking door is unlocked.

These assholes are confident.

Taking another deep breath, Cirello slows down his heartbeat, kicks the door open and steps in, the Glock held in front of him.

Two guys stand there looking at him.

Deer in the headlights.

A strip of the wood-paneled wall is open and Cirello can see the heroin stash inside. The idiots were trying to decide whether to go out the back with it but didn't decide quick enough. It looks like about a kilo cut into bags.

"You move your fucking hands, I'll splatter your fucking brains all over the room," Cirello yells, hearing how adrenaline jacked his voice is.

"Take it easy, take it easy!" This comes from the fatter one. Looks to be in his young thirties, beefed up from the gym, classic Staten Island goombah short-on-the-sides haircut. From Marco's description, this is DeStefano.

The other one is about the same age, same uniform haircut, not as active on the bench press. They each have Yankees caps on backward, track suits, gold chains.

Where do they find these guys? Cirello wonders.

Neither of them look to be heroin users.

Anadrol, maybe.

"Sit down," Cirello says. "Cross your legs in front of you."

They do it.

"Now stretch your legs out, roll over on your stomachs and put your hands behind your backs," Cirello says.

"Come on," DeStefano says. "Is this really necessary?"

"Depends on you," Cirello says.

He sees the wiseguy smirk come across DeStefano's face. Mob guys always think everyone is like them—everyone has an angle, everyone is for sale—and Cirello has just confirmed his deeply held beliefs.

The smirk widens into a smile. DeStefano juts his chin toward the wall. "There's twenty-seven large in a bank deposit bag in there. Take the money, walk away, have a Coke and a smile."

Keeping his gun trained on DeStefano, Cirello steps over to the loose panel, feels inside and comes out with the bag. "What about the smack?"

"You want it, take it," DeStefano says. "But where are you going to lay it off?"

Cirello sticks the bag into the waistband of his slacks in the small of his back, under his jacket. "I'm not going to lay it off, *you're* going to lay it off. Business as usual, except now you have a partner."

"Yeah? How big a partner we got?"

"Ten grand a week."

"Five."

"Seven."

"Done," DeStefano says. "But I like to know my partners' names."

"Bobby Cirello. Narcotics Division."

"What precinct?" DeStefano says. "Because I haven't seen you around."

"One Police."

DeStefano lets himself look impressed for a second. "So if I have a problem with one of the local cops, I can come to you."

"I'll straighten it out."

"Out of your cut."

"I said I'd take care of it," Cirello says.

"Okay, Bobby," DeStefano says. "I can call you that, right? I give a guy twenty-seven K, I can call him by his first name, can't I? So, Bobby, how'd you get onto us?"

"You kidding?" Cirello asks. "You been slinging out of that parking lot for weeks. You need to mix it up a little."

"I told you," the skinny guy says.

"Shut the fuck up."

"So, Steve," Cirello says. "I want to see you every Friday. Your Carvel parking lot. You don't show up, I'll find you. If I have to find you, I bust you. We understand each other?"

"That twenty-seven gives me three weeks and change, though, right?"

"No," Cirello says. "The twenty-seven is a fine for being stupid and lazy. Mix it up from now on. See you Friday."

He goes out the door.

There's no going back now, Cirello thinks.

Now I'm a dirty cop.

He drives back out to Tottenville and meets Marco in the parking lot by Mickey D's. He gets into the Taurus and hands the kid two thousand in cash. "Don't put this up your arm. Drive. You have people anywhere outside of New York?"

"My sister's in Cleveland."

"Go inflict yourself on her," Cirello says. "Whatever you do, don't come back here, okay?"

He gets out of the car and Marco takes off.

Cirello doubts he'll get any farther than Jersey, but you can always hope. Except he knows junkies, and if anyone's capable of doing something stupid, counterproductive, and self-destructive, it's a junkie.

It's what they do.

The loan shark is surprised.

Maybe even disappointed. He doesn't make money by people paying off the whole principal in one shot.

But that's what Cirello does. Finds Angie among the happy hour crowd at the Pier 76 bar and slips him a heavy envelope. "That's all of it. Principal and vig."

Angie tucks it into his jacket. "You get lucky?"

"You could say that," Cirello says. "Can you lay me ten on North Carolina–Louisville? I want the Heels and the points."

"Jesus, Bobby, you just got out of the hole, why do you want to jump back in?" Angie asks.

"You want the action or you don't?"

Angie shrugs. "Yeah, I can lay it for you."

"You the man."

"No, *you* the man."

Cirello refuses the offer of a drink.

Over the next few weeks, he chases his money like a pathetic middle-aged man going after a young chick he isn't ever going to catch.

He bets basketball, college and pro.

He goes to the casino, plays blackjack.

He bets *baseball*, for Chrissakes, and no one in his right mind bets baseball, except for a degenerate gambler.

Which is what he is.

Angelo tells him so when he comes in light for the third consecutive week, uses those exact words. "You're a degenerate gambler."

"You're a bookie and a loan shark."

They're back on their customary stools at Pier 76.

"I'm a bookie and a loan shark who pays his bills," Angelo says. "You're into me for thirty-two large and you can't even cover the vig."

"Georgia Tech–Wake Forest—"

"Georgia Tech–Wake Forest my aching balls," Angelo says. "We're right where I said I didn't want to be. I'm supposed to hurt you, but how can I hurt a friend and a fucking NYPD detective to boot?"

"I'll get you your money."

"Gold shield or no gold shield," Angelo says, "we can't just let you walk, Bobby."

"Who's 'we'?"

"I can't afford to carry you for thirty-two," Angelo says. "I laid your account off. I'm sorry, but you didn't leave me any choice."

Meaning Angelo sold Cirello's debt to someone higher in the organization.

"So it's like that," Cirello says.

Angelo swirls the vodka around his glass. Then he says, "The Play Sports Bar. On Sneden. Go there."

"What are you talking about?"

"Just go there, Bobby." Angelo polishes off his drink, gets up and leaves.

Cirello parks the car on Sneden and walks into the Play Sports Bar.

There's a guy in a booth, eating. Midforties, thin, black hair with streaks of silver. He looks up and says, "You Cirello?"

"Who's asking?"

"Mike Andrea." He gestures at the bench across from him, but Cirello doesn't sit. "You want a panini? They're good here. I like the Trio—*prosciutto, sopressatta, capocollo* . . . You should eat something, you look thin."

"The fuck are you, my mother?"

"Right now I'm your best friend, Bobby boy," Andrea says. He takes another bite of the panini and wipes his mouth with the back of his hand. "I can throw you a rope, pull you out of the shit you're in."

"What shit am I in?"

"Angie Bucci sold your paper to me," Andrea says. "Angie's a nice guy, I love him. I'm not a nice guy, I didn't go to high school with you, I don't know your grandmother, I don't have a problem hurting you."

"It might be more of a problem than you think."

"Yeah, I know—gold shield, tough guy," Andrea says. "We don't have to go there. Sit and have a little something to eat, act like a human being, listen to me."

Cirello sits down.

Andrea signals the waitress to come over. "Lisa, my handsome young friend here will have a Trio and a beer."

"Have you had a chance to look at our beer menu?" she asks.

"'Beer menus,'" Andrea says. "This is what our world has come to."

"I'll have a Sixpoint," Cirello says.

"The ale or the pilsner?"

"The pilsner, thank you," Cirello says.

The waitress smiles at him and walks away.

"I'll bet you could fuck her, you play your cards right," Andrea says. "No, I forgot, you *don't* play your cards right. You play them stupid, and you want to know why?"

"No."

"You *want* to lose," Andrea says. "All degenerate gamblers, what they really want is to lose. Something about punishing themselves, I don't know."

"What do you want?"

Andrea says, "Maybe you do a favor for some people."

"What kind of favor and what people?"

"People who are willing to stop the collection process on your loan," Andrea says, "you don't need to know who exactly. And just for some information. These people are thinking of getting into business with someone sometime, they want to know if he's clean, they're not walking into a sting."

"Getting that kind of information is risky."

"Not as risky as owing thirty-two K you don't have," Andrea says. He slides a slip of paper across the table.

It's an empty threat, Cirello thinks. The problem with owing a loan shark money isn't owing too much, it's not owing enough. You owe five grand to a wiseguy, you're in trouble. You owe ten or more, he can't afford to clip you. He'll send a bodyguard to keep you safe because he needs you to pay that money. You want to live forever? Get into a shy for a hundred K. He'd donate a kidney if you need it.

Cirello glances at the paper, sees three names written down. "I won't give up CIs."

"Don't get your panties in a wad," Andrea says. "No one's asking you to get anyone killed. These are people we aren't in business with yet. Think of it as job screening. Due diligence. That's all."

"How do I know you're not wearing a wire?"

Andrea says, "Yeah, you got me, Cirello. Lisa the waitress is an undercover agent. Those tits are microphones. You want to get well or not?"

"You'll suspend the vig."

"The vig is still there," Andrea says, "but it stops growing. And no one comes to collect, we work out some kind of payment plan."

"This *is* the payment plan." Cirello takes the paper. "And dinner's on you."

"Every little bit helps, right?" Andrea says. "Fucking cops—nickel-and-dimers."

Lisa brings the food over.

Andrea was right, Cirello thinks. It's good—*prosciutto, sopressatta, capocollo.*

He has breakfast at Mullen's house out in Long Island City.

Judy Mullen made them French toast and they sit at the kitchen table, the sound of the chief's two boys playing *Halo* drifting in from the den.

"Mike Andrea is a capo in the Cimino family," Mullen says. "Out of Bensonhurst. If he picked up your account from Bucci, it's serious. OC likes him for at least a dozen murders."

"The Ciminos are out of the dope business," Cirello says. "Have been for years."

"Maybe Andrea is in business for himself."

"Then who are these 'people' he says he reps?"

"That's what we're going to find out," Mullen says. He looks back at the list Andrea gave Cirello. "I'm betting they already know about these guys. They're testing you."

"That's my read, too."

Mullen looks at the paper again. "Markesian and Dinestri are clean. Tell him we have eyes on Gutiérrez."

"Do we?" Cirello asks.

Mullen smiles. "We will."

Cirello asks, "You want me to push Andrea on meeting these people?"

"Too soon," Mullen says. "You'll scare them off. Just keep doing what you're doing."

Mullen knows he's asking a lot. He's already getting blowback about Cirello. Just two days ago, his lieutenant came in to talk to him, shut the door behind him. "Organized Crime is hearing shit about one of our guys. Bobby Cirello has been seen with a loan shark named Angelo Bucci."

He laid out surveillance photos of Cirello sitting at a bar with Bucci.

"Maybe he's working a case," Mullen said.

"I hope so," the lieutenant said. "I hope it's just that, but there's word that Cirello's been gambling. And losing. Drinking hard, coming in looking like shit . . ."

"Okay, let's keep an eye on it."

"Look, I know he's your guy."

"I said keep an eye on it. Keep me informed."

It's the kind of word you want going out, an operation like this; at the same time, Mullen feels bad because it does compromise Cirello's career. That kind of stink is hard to get back in the bottle. On a practical level, if Internal Affairs gets onto Cirello, it could compromise the whole operation.

Cirello's ahead of him. "What I need from you is assurance that OC doesn't have Andrea up, I'm walking into a recording studio, I go home and IAB is waiting on the stoop."

"If I go asking questions to OC," Mullen says, "I have to tell them why. I'm not ready to bring them in yet."

"Yeah, okay."

"I'm sorry," Mullen says. "If you get confronted by OC, IAB, anyone else, you tell them you need to speak to your rep, and you come straight to me. At that point, I promise you I'll straighten everyone out."

"Okay."

"This is great work, Bobby," Mullen says. "This takes us up another level. Let's ride it out."

Us, Cirello thinks. It's not *us,* boss, it's *me* with my ass on the line. Me having to play out being a dirtbag.

It's costing him, too.

The hanging out in casinos, the drinking . . . it isn't him.

And Libby doesn't like it. That relationship's going good, it's turning into something. Except lately she says he's "different," he's "changing."

"Like how?" Cirello asked when she brought it up.

They were having brunch (he does "brunch" now, since he got with Libby, what happens, he guesses, when you date a dancer) at the Heights Café over on Hicks Street and she said, "I don't know. You seem kind of distant."

"I'm right here, Libby."

"Like, where do you go when I'm working?" she asked. "What do you do?"

"I don't know," Bobby said. "I watch TV, I work . . . I'm not cheating on you, if that's what you're asking."

"That's not what I'm asking," Libby said. "You just seem, I don't know, stressed. And you're drinking more than . . ."

"More than what?"

"Than when I met you."

"It's the job."

"Tell me."

"Can't," he said. "Look, Libby, neither of us has traditional, nine-to-five, how-was-your-day-honey, fine-thank-you jobs, you know?"

"Mine's pretty straightforward."

"Well, mine isn't," he said. Then realized it sounded harsher than he intended. "I'll watch the drinking; you're right, I'm hitting it a little hard."

"I don't want to be the nagging girlfriend."

"You're not," Cirello said. "It's just that . . ."

"What?"

"Where I go is where I go," Cirello said. "It's the job."

"Okay."

But she doesn't like it and it's putting stress on their relationship. Cirello doesn't want to lose this woman. Now he says to Mullen, "No, look, we're just starting to get somewhere. Of course I want to see it through."

"Okay, good. I appreciate it, Bobby."

"Sure." He gets up from the table. "Tell Mrs. Mullen thanks for breakfast. It was really good."

"I'll tell her," Mullen says. "Come over for dinner sometime soon. Bring . . ."

"Libby."

"We'd like to meet her," Mullen says. "And, Bobby, be careful, right?"

"You got it."

He meets Andrea again, gives his report, gets his envelope. The next week, Andrea says, "Your stuff checked out."

"Yeah, I know."

"It was helpful." Andrea slips him another piece of paper.

Two more names.

"You guys on a hiring jag?" Cirello asks. He doesn't pick up the paper.

"What?" Andrea asks. "They ain't gonna wipe the tab clean, that's what you're thinking."

"I want the vig forgiven."

"You want forgiveness, see a priest," Andrea says. "He'll give you ten Hail Marys. You don't do them, he'll stack on another ten. Even the Catholic Church charges vig."

"I'm Greek Orthodox."

"You're not exactly in the strongest bargaining position here," Andrea says.

Yeah I am, Cirello thinks, because your people would rather have a gold shield on the arm than their money.

He slides the paper back. "Google these."

They forgive the vig.

Cirello runs the names.

Then another set, then he clears a location, then he runs some license plate numbers to see if they're cop cars.

All the time he keeps gambling until he loses, his debt goes up and down like a yo-yo, but the net is that it goes up, vig or no vig. He keeps drinking, looking more and more like what he's supposed to be, an out-of-control cop on a downward spiral.

Mullen keeps getting complaints about him—Cirello came in hungover again, Cirello didn't come in at all, Cirello has an attitude, Cirello's been seen with a bookie again, Cirello is off the reservation.

The lieutenant wants to piss-test him, hook him up to a polygraph, at the least send him to a department shrink.

Mullen says no.

The lieutenant wonders why the chief of Narcotics is running interference for a cop who seems to be running off the rails.

Libby wonders what happened to the sweet guy she met.

It only helps a little when they go to Mullen's house for dinner. Mullen and his wife are wonderful, the kids are great, but Bobby is tense and preoccupied during the whole meal, almost to the point of being rude.

They fight about it on the way home.

"I like your boss," she says.

"Yeah?"

"You don't?"

"Yeah, sure," Bobby says. "I mean, he's a boss."

"What's that mean?"

"What, you on his side now?"

"I didn't know there were sides," Libby says. "I'm just saying I like him."

"Good for you."

"Fuck you, Bobby."

"Yeah, fuck me."

"Self-pity is so attractive," Libby says. "I just want to get you home and jump your bones right now."

Cirello knows what he's doing, knows how he is. Knows the brutal truth of undercover work—you pretend to be something long enough, you're not pretending anymore, you are that thing.

That's why he's so glad when Andrea says, "My people want to meet you."

"Where's the meet?" Mullen asks.

"Prospect Park," Cirello says. "Place called Erv's, Flatbush and Beekman."

"One of those millennial hipster places," Mullen says. "Craft cocktails, that kind of shit."

Cirello doesn't know how Mullen knows this stuff, but he seems to know everything.

"The meeting won't be there," Mullen says. "Andrea will meet you there and take you somewhere else. I'm sending backup."

"They'll sniff it out."

"Look, we don't know what this is."

"They're not going to kill a New York cop," Cirello says.

"We'll wire you," Mullen says, "and lay off a little. Then if you get in trouble, we can get there."

"I haven't gone all this way to blow it now."

"I'm not putting you on an island, Bobby," Mullen says.

Where the hell do you think I am now? Cirello thinks.

He meets Andrea at Erv's.

Mullen called it—urban hipsters "doing" cute cocktails and bespoke coffee drinks.

"I didn't make you for a place like this," Cirello says.

"We're not staying."

So Mullen called it again. Cirello follows Andrea to his Lincoln Navigator and gets in.

"I have to pat you down."

"Save you the trouble," Cirello says. "I have my service weapon, a Glock nine, and I'm not giving it over."

"I'm talking about a wire."

"Fuck you, a wire."

"Come on, Cirello."

"Put your hands on me, I'll smash your face into that windshield," Cirello says.

"Why do you have a problem with this?"

Because I'm wearing a fucking wire, Cirello thinks. But it's a small mike, like Mullen promised, state-of-the-art, glued between the heel and the sole of the Chelsea boot that Libby had him buy. So he backs down. "Okay, pat me down. But you spend one more second than you have to around my package, I'm telling."

Andrea pats him all over.

"Happy now?" Cirello asks.

"And horny," Andrea says. He starts the car and pulls out onto Flatbush.

"Where are we going?" Cirello asks.

"That would defeat the point of all this clever subterfuge," Andrea says. "You'll see."

He takes Eastern Parkway to the Van Wyck and turns south.

"We going to Kennedy?" Cirello asks, more for Mullen's benefit than his own.

"Jesus, you're worse than my kids," Andrea says. "'We there yet? We there yet?' You don't have to pee, do you?"

"I wouldn't mind."

"Hold it in," Andrea says. He keeps looking into the rearview mirror.

"There's no one following us," Cirello says. "Unless *you* have someone following us. And if you do, Mike, I'm going to blow your fucking head off."

"Relax."

They get to Kennedy and Andrea pulls into the Dollar Rent-A-Car return lane.

"Dollar?" Cirello asks, to let Mullen know where he is. "Not Hertz, not even Avis? Things that bad with you guys?"

"Come on."

Cirello gets out of the car and follows him over to a parking slot where another Lincoln sits.

"In the front passenger," Andrea says. He gets in on the driver's side.

Cirello gets in.

Kennedy Airport is a smart choice for a meet, Cirello thinks. Since 9/11 only Homeland Security can do audio surveillance around an airport, and Homeland Security doesn't give one shit about the mob. And with the planes taking off and landing, the mike in his boot is useless. Mullen won't be able to hear a thing. He must be shitting bricks.

No, something goes south here, you're on your own.

Unless the chief freaks out and comes charging in, which Cirello hopes he doesn't do.

Too much work down the drain.

Still, Cirello doesn't like being in the front passenger seat, the "Italian electric chair." Two pops in the back of the head, they get out and into another rental car, and he becomes a cold case. He can hear Andrea in the interview room now: *A dirty cop, he asked me to take him to the airport. After that, what can I tell you?*

So now Cirello asks, "Okay if I turn around?"

The guy behind him says, "Well, this is supposed to be a face-to-face."

Cirello turns around.

It's a fucking kid—you'd card him if he came into your store to buy a six-pack.

Brown hair and a brown beard. Wide face with high cheekbones. His leather jacket wears tight across a heavy chest and shoulders.

Looks like his grandfather Johnny Boy.

Johnny Boy Cozzo was the last of the old-school gangsters—didn't plead out, took his case to juries (two of which acquitted him), didn't rat when he finally got life without parole.

Died of throat cancer in a federal lockup.

They make movies about the guy.

Cirello knows his mob history—knows it was Johnny Boy who broke the long-standing Cimino family "you deal, you die" commandment and brought cocaine in from Mexico. Killed his boss to do it, took his chair, and the Cimino family made millions from the coke.

Until Giuliani and them took down the Ciminos and the rest of the Five Families and now they're, as the saying goes, shells of their former selves. And the "no drugs" order is back on, ordered by Johnny Boy's son, Junior, because guys were ratting out when faced with the long sentences.

Except now here's another John Cozzo sitting next to Steve DeStefano in the back of a car.

"Do you know who I am?" he asks Cirello.

"Don't you know who you are?" Cirello asks. "We have an amnesia thing going on right now?"

"Hey, we got open mike night here," Cozzo says. "Do yourself a favor, don't quit your day job. I'm John Cozzo—yeah, he was my grandfather—people call me Jay."

"What are we doing, Jay?"

"You've been shaking down my friend Steve, here."

Cirello still has his weapon, but there's no way he's going to be able to reach it, cramped like he is in this seat, before one of them can get a shot off. And out of the corner of his eye, he sees Andrea shift his hand toward the waistband of his pants.

If they really want to do me, Cirello thinks, I'm dead. He asks, "Does your uncle know you're here?"

"What's my uncle got to do with it?"

"Doesn't Junior have a rule about slinging dope?"

"There's only one rule now," Cozzo says. "Make money. You make enough money, you make your own rules. My grandfather taught me that. I'm more like him than my uncle is, no disrespect."

"Of course not." Yeah, of course not. Just about everybody disrespects Junior. His own people call him "the Clown Prince" and "Urkel." He's just about run what's left of the family into the ground. And now one of his capos has gone off the reservation, running interference for his nephew's drug deal.

"You're a piece of work," Cozzo says. "You shake down one of my people for seven grand a week and you don't pay the money you owe."

"You've been taking it out in trade."

"That's why I wanted to meet you in person," Cozzo says. "Look you in the eye, see what I've bought."

"More of a rental."

"Whatever gets you through the day, Detective," Cozzo says. "I've taken a controlling interest in Steve's business. Given the new arrangement, I don't think we need to pay you for protection anymore. Here's the question: Do we need to kill you now, or can we do business?"

"We've *been* doing business," Cirello says, trying to keep the fear out of his voice.

"See, when I said I bought you, that's what I meant," Cozzo says. "Bucci sold your paper to Mike, Mike sold it to me. All sales are final."

He wants something, Cirello thinks, and he wants it badly. Otherwise he'd have stopped talking and Andrea would have pulled the trigger.

"What if I tear up the paper?" Cozzo asks. "What does that buy me?"

"Principal and vig?"

"Principal and vig."

"What do you want?" Cirello asks. This is what it's been building to, this is the reason for all the games up to now.

"I'm looking at a major piece of business with someone," Cozzo says. "I have to know it's safe. Listen to me now, Cirello—I'm going to bring my family back to its proper place. This deal is a major piece of that and I cannot have it fucked up."

"Are you talking heroin?"

"You don't need to know that," Cozzo says.

"Yeah, he does, Jay," Andrea says. "It might make a difference where he looks."

"Is that right?" Cozzo asks.

"It is," Cirello says. "There are different units in Narcotics. There's a Heroin Task Force, for instance. Then you have the separate precincts . . ."

"Yeah, heroin," Cozzo says. "I need this cleared. I need to know local, state, federal . . ."

"I can give you NYPD," Cirello says. "State and DEA, I don't have access."

"*Get* access."

"*If* I can," Cirello says, "it will cost you more."

"Greedy motherfucker."

"I can't go empty-handed," Cirello says. "State is one thing, the fucking feds . . ."

"How much?"

"Fifty maybe. Cash."

"What the fuck?"

"The cost of doing business, Jay," Andrea says.

"And you're going to take, what?" Cozzo asks. "Fifteen as a finder's fee?"

"I'm thinking more like twenty," Cirello says. "I gotta live, too."

"You gotta gamble, you mean."

"Same thing."

Cozzo thinks about it for a few seconds and then says, "I'll get you your fifty. You get me the information. But it comes with a guarantee—your motherfucking life, Cirello. Cop or no cop, this goes bad, I'll kill you."

"Who's the guy?"

"Mike will give you that," Cozzo says, opening the door. "Have a safe drive back. And, Cirello, remember what I said."

He and DeStefano get out of the car.

Cirello watches them walk to another one, get in, and drive off.

On the way back, Cirello asks Andrea, "Isn't this going to jam you up with Junior?"

"Junior has narrowed the income stream like an old man pissing," Andrea says. "I have kids in college, you know what that costs these days? I don't want them coming out, they're already upside down."

"You trust this Cozzo kid?"

"Trust," Andrea says. "You *are* a comedian."

"Who am I checking out?"

Black guy out of East New York, Andrea tells him.

Name is Darius Darnell.

3

Victimville

When the prison doors are opened, the real dragon will fly out.
—Ho Chi Minh

Eddie sees the blade and knows he's dead.

Cruz is coming down the corridor, a *pedazo*—a razor blade melted into a toothbrush—held low at his hip and a smile on his face because he's wanted to kill Eddie for a while and now it looks like La Eme has given him the green light.

Eddie curses himself because he has nothing but his fists and he should have been ready.

Caro has fucked him.

And now Cruz is right up on him and there's not a goddamn thing he can do to save himself.

It was different when he first got to Victorville.

He came onto the yard seven months ago with the endorsement of Rafael Caro and got an instant introduction to Benny Zuniga, the Eme *llavero*, the shot caller. Zuniga has been the *mesa* for all of USP Victorville forever, twenty-five years now into a thirty-to-life sentence.

He gives the orders inside and on the streets.

So Eddie got instant status when Zuniga greeted him personally on the iron pile.

"I've heard good things," Zuniga said.

"Mutual," Eddie said, holding back a sigh of relief. Keller had laundered his PSI, but you never knew. Zuniga would have had one of his people take a good long look at the report.

The cell was a small improvement on Florence—thirteen by six—but it had to be shared by two guys. Eddie didn't mind; the prison is 50 percent over its max and a lot of the *vatos* are in triples, the weakest guy sleeping on the floor.

There was a bunk bed, a stainless-steel toilet and sink combo, and a small table with a single stool bolted into the floor.

And it's air-conditioned, Eddie noticed.

It was the freaking Four Seasons compared to Florence.

When he first went into his new cell, a young *vato*—skinny, tall, his head shaved—sat nervously on the lower bunk, looking up at Eddie.

"Hi," he said. "I'm Julio."

"The fuck you doing, Julio?"

"What do you mean?"

"I mean," Eddie said, "the fuck you doing on my bunk?"

"I thought maybe you'd want the top," Julio said.

"Who told you to think?" Eddie asked.

Julio hustled up to the top bunk.

"Did Zuniga talk to you about me?" Eddie asked.

"I'm supposed to do whatever you need," Julio said. "Keep the cell clean, do your laundry, get your commissary. Whatever you want . . ."

Eddie saw Julio was looking at him funny.

"Chill," Eddie said. "I don't play that. I'm not your daddy and you're not my bitch. When I want pussy, I'll get real pussy. But you're my cellie, so no one fucks with you. That wouldn't reflect good on me. Anyone bothers you, you come to me, no one else, you understand?"

Julio nodded, relieved.

Eddie asked, "Whose car are you in?"

"I'm doing my bones with Eme now."

"If this works out," Eddie said, "I'll try to get you off the bumper."

"Thank you."

"Make my bed up."

That night in the dining hall Eddie got a seat at the head table, with Zuniga and the other shot callers.

"This is a Mexican prison," Zuniga said. "You got about a hundred *güeros*, most of them Aryan Brotherhood, five hundred *mayates*, but a thousand border brothers. Say three hundred are *norteños*, but the rest are in line. The warden is Mexican, most of the guards are Mexican. We run this place."

"Good to know."

"It ain't like it is in state," Zuniga said. "We work with the *güeros* and we fight with the *norteños*, but we all hate the blacks. Even the guards hate the blacks. It's *todo el mundo* against the *mayates*."

"Got it."

La Eme, the Mexican Mafia, was formed all the way back in the '50s, but it was a Southern California gang, *sureños*, mostly made up of convicts from LA and San Diego—city guys who abused their country cousins, fruit pickers from the rural northern part of the state.

So to protect themselves the northerners formed Nuestra Familia, and almost thirty years later the feud between the *sureños* and the *norteños* was more vicious than between the races. In fact, La Eme—which ran the various *sureño* gangs—was closely allied with the Aryan Brotherhood.

Brown hated brown more than it hated white.

La Eme, the Aryan Brotherhood, and the Black Guerrillas all started when the prisons desegregated and threw the races together on the same cell blocks and yards. People being what people are, they started killing each other right away and quickly formed into the gangs to protect themselves. When the prisoners got out, they took the gangs to the streets, spinning a revolving door that never stopped.

Same with the big Central American gangs.

In the late '80s, a lot of Salvadorans, Hondurans and Guatemalans started to run away from the shitholes their countries had become and came to California. Without jobs, schooling or connections, a lot of their young men ended up in the system, where they weren't black, white, *norteño*, or *sureño*.

They were just fucked.

The Mexicans, the blacks, the Aryans turned them out, robbed them, hooked them on junk, extorted them. It was good business at first, but then the totally expected happened.

Some of these guys turned out to be pretty tough—former soldiers or guerrillas in their countries' civil wars—and they decided to get organized and fight back.

A Salvadoran named Flaco Stoner founded Wonder-13, soon to be known as Mara Salvatrucha. An old '50s gang called 18th Street revived itself as Calle 18, and together they became some of the most violent gangs in the prison system. Some of the *mareros* were fucking *crazy*—they had done some serious shit back home during the wars—beheadings, disemboweling—and they just let that crazy loose in the joint.

Even La Eme backed off them.

And just like the other prison gangs, the ones who made it home took the gang with them, established *clicas* of Mara Salvatrucha and Calle 18 not only in LA and other American cities, but also back in San Salvador, Tegucigalpa and Guatemala City.

Eddie laughs his ass off when he hears dumbass ignorant politicians like John Dennison say they're going to send the gangs "back to where they came from."

They were *hecho en los Estados Unidos*.

Made in the USA.

And the prison administrations were never serious about curbing prison violence. It was exactly the opposite—they wanted the prisoners fighting one another instead of the guards.

Shit, they needed the gangs to run the prison.

Needed them to maintain discipline and order.

And if a bunch of white trash, beaners and niggers killed one another, it was no loss, was it?

"What kind of job you want?" Zuniga asked.

Eddie didn't know. He'd never had a *j-o-b* in his fucking life. He didn't know how to do anything but sling dope and shoot people, and his job in Florence was basically to jerk off. "I dunno. The kitchen?"

"You don't want the kitchen," Zuniga said. "You really have to work there. You want custodial."

"A fuckin' janitor?"

"*Tranquilo.* Your partner will do the work."

So Eddie got a job on the custodial crew, watching some peasant mop the floors and clean toilets. The sheer fucking monotony of prison life settled in. It was different monotony than Florence, but monotonous all the same.

He didn't "get married"—officially join La Eme—but his status as a cartel man gave him the prestigious status of *camarada*—a comrade, an associate—and that was enough. Even though he didn't get the black hand tattoo, he was accepted into *la clica*—the inner circle.

And he lived by *las reglas*—the strict rules La Eme had established for its members in prison.

No fighting with other members.

No ratting.

No cowardice.

No hard drugs.

You could drink, you could smoke a little *yerba*, but you couldn't do *chiva* because no one can trust a junkie and a junkie is useless in a fight.

No "baseball"—homo shit.

They were allowed to turn other inmates out—sell them to suck cock or put out for the Aryans, for instance. If you were a "baby," a bitch, if you wouldn't or couldn't fight, Zuniga or the others would rent you out, but the Eme *carnals* or *camaradas* weren't allowed to use your services. That was for peckerwoods or *mayates*, not for proud, macho Mexican men of *la raza*.

You didn't do that and you didn't interfere with another member's business. And you sure as shit didn't disrespect his *ruca* or his girlfriend, you didn't cast a lustful eye in the visiting room, and when you got out, you didn't mess with a member's woman.

You broke any of the *reglas*, you made it on a list you didn't want to be on. It took the votes of three full members to put your name on *la lista*, but once it was on, you were as good as dead.

It was strict, but Eddie understood the reasons. They needed *las reglas*, needed the discipline to maintain their dignity, their self-respect in a place that was designed to take it from them.

Las reglas kept you strong when you wanted to break down.

He came off the exercise yard back to his cell one day and watched Julio make "clear."

The kid stripped the insulation from a piece of wire and dunked it into the "stinger," a batch of old, strong wine in a plastic bucket on the floor of the cell. Then he plugged the other end of the wire into a wall socket.

The wine began to heat.

It took a while, but the alcohol distilled and then ran through a length of rubber hose into a second bucket, producing a drink twice as powerful as the standard homemade prison hooch.

Julio offered Eddie a sip.

"It's good," Eddie said.

Julio shrugged. "Of course it's good, I'm the best hooch maker in Victimville, at least among the Mexicans."

Eddie was on the yard, waiting his turn at the bench press, when Zuniga came up to him. "I was wondering if maybe you could do some work, *campa*."

"Anything," Eddie said, hoping it wouldn't be too heavy. He catches a murder beef in here, his deal with the feds is gone and he never gets out. But he can't say no to the *mesa*, so he just hoped.

"A lop just checked in," Zuniga said. "One of us. Been going around talking about he's in for armed robbery, but a wood in the office pulled his card—turns out he's a chester."

A child molester, Eddie thought. A white clerk found his real rap sheet and took it to the Mexicans to handle. It was a rule—white disciplines white, black disciplines black, brown disciplines brown.

It's that jacked-up prison justice. A guy from one race can't put his hands on a guy from another. If a white guy jumped this Mexican chester, the Mexicans would have to first beat up the white guy, touching off an endless cycle of retaliations, then they'd have to beat up the chester, too. So this makes its own weird kind of sense; the whites hand it over to the Mexicans to take care of their own.

But discipline *was* expected. If Zuniga knew he had a short-eyes on his yard and didn't do something about it, he would lose massive respect. The whole *raza* would, if it got out they tolerated a *vato* like that.

"I was wondering if you'd walk the dog on him," Zuniga said.

"No problem," Eddie said, intensely relieved it was just a beating. "Shit, if you want to green-light him . . ."

"No, just a beating," Zuniga said. "I want him off my yard."

And you want to see if I'm legit, Eddie thought. You have a few hundred guys you could give this to, but you want me to pass a heart check.

Okay.

You want me to do it out in the open, Eddie thought.

Make a show of it.

"You'll do a bit in SHU," Zuniga said, "but they won't pile charges on you."

"I just did Florence," Eddie said. "It was *all* SHU. Besides, I got kids of my own."

"Respect, *'mano.*"

Zuniga gave him the name and walked away.

Why wait, Eddie thought, so the next morning at breakfast he sat and listened to the chester over at another table with other lowlifes bragging about how he pulled his gun but it jammed so the cops got him, and Eddie thought, Who is this stupid fuck?

So when the guy got up from his chair Eddie got up from his, and as the guy was coming toward him Eddie swung his tray like an ax into the guy's throat and the guy would have gone down like a felled tree except Eddie had already dropped his tray, grabbed him by the front of the shirt, and started pumping rights into his face—*bam, bam, bam, bam*—four straight shots, and then Eddie drove him to the floor, landed on top of him and whaled away until his arms got tired and then he started slamming knees into the guy's ribs and then his crotch and then rained elbows and forearms onto his face.

Eddie felt himself getting winded and the guards didn't seem to be in any particular rush to break this up—they had kids of their own, too—and the rest of the guys were all hooting and hollering and shouting encouragement— "Fuck him up, mess him up, *ese!*"—and the guy was whimpering and crying and bleeding and begging for Eddie to stop, but Eddie knew the rules—you don't stop until the monkeys pull you off—so he just kept busting up the guy's face until finally he felt hands grab the back of his shirt and he let himself be hauled up as the rest of the guys cheered for him.

The chester was lying there curled up but Eddie got another kick into his balls and stomped on his knee. Saw Zuniga nod his approval, and one of the AB shot callers gave him a respectful nod, too, on his way out.

At his disciplinary hearing the CO asked him what started the fight and Eddie said, "With all respect, sir, you know what started it. Y'all tried to hide that guy's PSI, gave him some idiot cover story, but you know that's not going to go here."

The CO gave Eddie thirty in SHU and Eddie waived his right to an appeal.

The fuck could he appeal? There was video of it and, anyway, he wasn't denying it, he was proclaiming it. The word got out—Eddie Ruiz was not only a narco big shot, he was a tough guy in his own right and in the car with La Eme.

The administration didn't push for assault charges, the chester refused to file and got sent to protective custody so was off Zuniga's yard, and Eddie did his thirty like a man.

La Eme took care of him in the hole, too, sent down sandwiches and Little Debbie cakes through a guard they had on the arm, and one time he even brought Eddie a bottle of Julio's clear so Eddie could just sit in there and get pleasantly shit-faced.

Eddie shared it with his SHU cellie, Quito Fuentes, an ancient Mexican narco doing an LWOP for his role in the Hidalgo thing all the way back in '85. Turns out that motherfucking Art Keller had literally pulled him through the border fence so he could arrest him in the States.

Quito wasn't ever getting out and the monkeys threw him in the hole every chance they got because he was a cop killer and they didn't ever forget that. He was half a babbling lunatic by then, carrying on a virtually nonstop conversation with something or someone he called "the honey-dripper," so Eddie was happy to get him drunk if it would shut him and the honey-dripper up for a little while.

But fuckin' Keller, man, right?

Through the fuckin' fence?

It didn't seem that long before a monkey opened the door and said, "Ruiz, you're going back to main street."

"Hey, Quito," Eddie said, "give the honey-dripper my regards, okay?"

"The honey-dripper, he says good luck."

"Who's the honey-dripper?" the monkey asked as he walked Eddie back to his old unit.

"The fuck do I know?"

He got back to his cell, it was spick-and-span and Julio was waiting for him like the fucking butler. "Welcome home."

"Thanks for the clear."

Julio almost blushed.

"We need to talk about that," Eddie said. "We're leaving money on the table. How much can you get for this shit?"

"Fifty bucks for a twenty-ounce water bottle."

"I'll get the okay from Zuniga," Eddie said. "We'll go into business and I'll let you keep twenty percent."

Eddie walked down to the *mesa*'s cell—a "birdbath," an end-of-the-row cell on the ground floor. Three Emes were with him but Zuniga gestured for one of them to get up so Eddie could sit on the stool.

"Thank you for the goods," Eddie said.

Zuniga nodded. "I heard they had you with Quito. How is he?"

"Crazy. Totally spun."

"That's too bad."

"I want to sell some hooch," Eddie said.

Zuniga laughed. "That fuckin' Julio can cook, huh? It's lunch money. Go with God."

Eddie went and started a business selling clear.

The stinger itself, though, like a good bread yeast, never got touched but was carefully hidden away behind the wall of a little-used storage shed and only taken out when it was time to make another batch of clear.

Eddie started other businesses.

There were two babies on his tier, one a real B-cat complete with mascara, lipstick and long curly hair.

Eddie sought out their daddy. "They work for me now."

The guy totally bitched, didn't as much as say shit, but what was he going to do? Eddie had MM's blessing.

Eddie took the B-cat aside. "What's your name?"

"Martina."

"Well, Martina, I'm your daddy now," Eddie said. "If I can find a long-term lease for you, I'll do that. Otherwise, I'm turning you out by the throw. I'll let you keep a third, the rest goes to me. You have a problem with that, I give you to the blacks as a pass-around pack. That's *after* I beat you so ugly they'll shove your face into the pillow while they fuck you."

Martina had no problem with it.

Neither did the other bitch, a skinny little guy named Manuel.

"You're Manuela now," Eddie said. "And you need to up your game. Shave, for Chrissakes, and I'll get you some fucking makeup."

Eddie found a nice old lifer and leased Martina out to him for six months in exchange for a third of the lifer's commissary. Manuela he put out on a one-off basis for cigarettes and stamps, both of which he could turn over for a profit.

Or Julio could—Eddie put him in charge of the small shit.

And the still.

Eddie tipped a guard for the little wall space in the storage shed to hide the stinger and then got that boy to cooking every chance he got. When he wasn't cooking, Julio was out selling the bottles.

No cash, ever.

All stamps, phone cards and commissary.

Eddie sipped on a new batch of clear and figured that life was good.

But what he really wanted was to get laid.

Her name was Crystal and she was pure white Okie trash from Barstow.

Early thirties, maybe, not bad-looking. Red hair, freckles, a skinny nose, skinny mouth and a bowling pin figure. Little tits on top, a big ass on the bottom.

Being a CO was the best job she could get.

Paid better than Costco.

And came with health insurance.

Crystal put up with a lot of shit in V-Ville. The Mexican guards gave her a hard time because they thought a Latina should have the job, not a featherwood. And the cons looked at her like they wanted to fuck her.

Eddie, he didn't do that.

He treated her with respect, talked to her like she was a human being, looked into her eyes like there was something behind them. All the time, of course, thinking about fucking her, but he kept that shaded because he knew women don't like that.

Later, yes, but not at first.

"You know what the most sensitive part of a woman is?" Eddie asked Julio. "Her ears."

"I heard that." Julio stuck out his tongue and licked.

"No, asshole," Eddie said. "I mean you *talk* to her. Then you use *your* ears—you listen. You want to get her wet, listen to her."

That's how he started with Crystal. Little things at first, like literally, "Hi," then "How are you?," then, a week later, "You look nice today, CO Brenner." She needed some boxes moved, Eddie was there; she needed someplace cleaned up in a hurry, Eddie was there, about the only time he ever picked up a mop.

One day, passing her in the corridor, she looked upset, her eyes a little puffy.

"You okay, CO Brenner?" Eddie asked.

"What?"

"Are you okay?"

"Move it along, Ruiz." But she didn't move. Then she said, "Sometimes this place . . . I don't know . . . it gets to you."

"Tell me about it."

"Sure, you know."

"No, I mean tell me about it," Eddie said. "If someone is giving you a problem . . ."

Crystal laughed. "What, are you going to straighten it out?"

"Yeah, maybe."

She looked at him for a long moment. "No, it's just, you know, the other guards . . . First, I'm a woman, then I'm white . . . No offense, Ruiz."

"I know what you mean," Eddie said. "When I lived in Texas, I was a 'Mexican,' when I lived in Mexico, I was a *yanqui*. Look, I can't straighten out the COs, but if a con is giving you a problem, talk to me."

"Okay."

"I mean it."

"I know you do," she said. "Look. We'd better get going."

Eddie smiled. "Fraternization."

"Frowned upon."

The next day, Eddie went up to another con on his tier. "Ortega, do me a solid."

"What do you want?"

Eddie told him.

"What's in it for me?" Ortega asked.

"A bottle of clear?"

The next day Crystal saw Eddie in the corridor he was supposedly cleaning. She looked worried.

"What's the matter?" Eddie asked.

Crystal hesitated.

"Come on, you can tell me."

"This con on C Wing, Ortega," Crystal said. "He's been giving me a real hard time. Every stand-up count, he's insolent. Lockdown, he lingers at the door, gives me the eye, mumbles shit under his breath. I don't want to write him up, but—"

"I'll talk to him."

"Yeah?"

"Yeah."

Two days later, Crystal collared Eddie coming out of the dining hall. "What did you do?"

"I just talked to him," Eddie said. "It's all good now?"

"Yeah. Thank you."

"You're welcome," Eddie said, then pushing it a little, added, "*mamacita*."

The next day, passing her in the corridor, he didn't say anything but slipped a small piece of paper into her uniform pocket. On it he had written, *Thinking about you*. It was a big risk; if she turned it in, he'd be back in the hole.

When she saw him later that day she didn't say anything either, but slid a piece of paper into his hand. Eddie waited until he was back in his cell to take it out and saw that it read, *Thinking about you, too*.

Eddie knew he was in. It wasn't a matter of *if* now, it was a matter of *where* and *when*.

He got the answer the next morning when he passed her in the corridor.

"Chapel," she whispered. "In back."

Eddie got religion.

He went into the chapel, which was empty that early in the morning, and walked around the back of the altar into a narrow passageway. Crystal was standing there waiting for him. She said exactly what he knew she would say. "We can't be doing this."

And he said exactly what he knew he'd say: "We can't *not* be doing this."

He pulled her into him and they kissed. Then he turned her around, pushed her against the wall and pulled her pants down. Unzipped himself, took out his dick, and put it in her. She came before he did, which surprised him. He finished, zipped up, and turned her back around.

"Now what?" she asked.

More of the same, was the answer.

They had quick, sweaty, breathless encounters in the chapel, in storerooms. Furtive glances and smiles in the hallways, notes passed back and forth. It was fun, it was dangerous, and Eddie knew what really got her off—dangerous sex with a dangerous guy. The sex got even better. He taught her a few things they didn't know about in Barstow.

Zuniga looked out past the uniformed men walking the yard, playing basketball, lifting weights or just standing around. Past the chain-link fence, the coils of barbed wire, the towers, out onto the empty high desert.

"What are we doing this for, Eddie?" he asked over the clang of iron on the metal racks. "I've spent most of my life in places like this. I'll never leave *this* place unless it's to go to someplace worse. I have millions of dollars, but the richest I can ever get is the two-hundred-ninety-dollar monthly max in my commissary account, which I use to buy noodles, cookies—food for a child, not a man. I have a wife, kids, grandkids I see a few hours a month. Every now and then I fuck some slut of a guard, I remember how her hair smells, but mostly I have the stink of men in my nose. I can order life and death, but I have to jerk myself off. And still, I do business. Why is that?"

"I don't know."

What Eddie did know was he had to find a black guy.

Caro had asked him for that favor, Eddie had said he'd do it, and you don't go back on your word to a guy like Rafael Caro because that would get you a blade in the eye on any yard in the US or Mexico.

And anyway, Caro said they were going to make millions.

You wouldn't think finding a black guy in prison would be a problem, but brown don't socialize with black, and if you do, you better have a good reason.

Eddie went to Crystal. "I need you to look at some paper for me, baby."

"Eddie, if I get caught . . ."

"Then don't get caught," Eddie said. "Come on, a CO looking through the PSIs? What's the problem?"

He told her what he needed. It was pretty specific—a black guy out of New York in on a drug conviction but close to the door. It takes her a week, but she comes back with it: Darius Darnell, aka DD. Thirty-six years old, on the back end of a dime for coke slinging. Due out mid-2014.

Eddie threw a little extra affection into their quickie fuck to express his appreciation. He still had a problem, though—how to get next to a black guy for a serious conversation.

So it was lucky for Eddie that the riot broke out.

Which is a time when the races, you know, *mix*.

Prison riots don't just happen.

The most spontaneous ones require forethought, planning and specific intent. What looks to be a sudden burst of violence, coming from nowhere onto a peaceful yard, is anything but.

Zuniga planned this one to remind the *mayates* of their place.

"It has to happen every once in a while," Zuniga told Eddie. "This time, though, they give us an excuse."

The usual stupid shit, Eddie thought. Testosterone shit. A Mexican named Herrera was walking off the yard and got brushed by a black guy. Words were exchanged, which, inevitably, led to racial slurs.

Eddie had played against a lot of black guys in high school—shit, some of those teams from Houston and Dallas were all black guys, and some of the Tex-Mex guys liked to toss around "nigger" and "*mayate*," but Eddie never much went in for that, never seeing the sense of making guys who were generally bigger and faster angrier as well.

Anyway, the black guy—DuPont, some newbie up from Louisiana—and Herrera started to go at it, the monkeys broke it up, but not until DuPont said he wanted to go "one-on-one" with Herrera.

At first, Zuniga thought to keep the peace and told Eddie, "You worked with the *mayates* before, didn't you?"

"I sold them some *yerba* back in the day."

"Go talk to Harrison, tell him to have his guy back off."

Eddie wandered over to the edge of the yard, near the black basketball court, and stood there with his arms crossed over his chest. It got the attention of the black shot caller, a lifer named Harrison, who sent two of his people over.

"What you want?"

"A word," Eddie said.

They led him over to the weight rack, where Harrison was sitting with a bunch of his homeboys and DuPont, who was still running hot. He's a big motherfucker, Eddie thought, one of those big black southern motherfuckers like the ones who used to come out of east Texas.

"Eddie Ruiz," Eddie said.

"What do you want?" Harrison asked. He had eyes like the freakin' ages, Eddie thought. Eyes that know they're never going to see anything outside this desert shithole.

"This six o'clock set-to," Eddie said. "Benny Z thinks it's a bad idea. Says why don't we let it go, chalk it up to the heat."

"I don't want to let it go," DuPont said.

Harrison looked at him like, *Who the fuck asked you what you wanted?* But he turned back to Eddie and said, "Your boy called him a nigger."

"And he called our guy a beaner," Eddie said. "It ain't worth blood being spilled."

An expression Eddie has never really understood. He'd never seen blood actually spilled, like it's chocolate milk or something. He'd seen it run, he'd seen it flow, he'd seen it shoot out the back of someone's head, but spilled? No.

"*He* thinks it's worth blood," Harrison said, jutting his chin at DuPont.

"And you care what he thinks?" DuPont is a new boot, Eddie thought, a do-rag cotton picker who probably fucks his own sister in the ass as a form of birth control.

"The man has his rights," Harrison said.

This is true, Eddie thought. A man has a right to be a fucking idiot, which is what DuPont is if he thinks this is really going to be one-on-one. He shrugged, walked back to Zuniga and reported on his conversation.

"Fucking *mayates* don't know their place," Zuniga said.

Eddie knew he was pissed because he had lost face. An Eme *mesa* can't afford to lose face. If it got out that Benny Z let himself get stood down by a *mayate*, everyone would start thinking La Eme was getting soft, that they could be taken.

That couldn't happen.

Zuniga was more pissed at Harrison than he was at DuPont, because DuPont didn't know any better, but Harrison rejecting Zuniga's peace offer was a piece of studied disrespect, *jefe* to *jefe*. If the *mesa* let that stand, he was done.

So he started planning the riot.

Word went to all of La Eme to get out their *pedazos* and move them to secure hiding places on the yard. Then Zuniga held a strategy meeting with his top guys, among whom Eddie was included.

Eddie watched DuPont walk up for his one-on-one with Herrera. And he was walking cocky, because he knew the skinny Mexican was no match for him.

Plus he had ten brothers hiding in the back, ready to jump in.

Which would have been good, except Herrera had sixty Mexicans.

With shanks.

And they weren't waiting. They charged.

Shanks came out of shirt fronts, jackets, pant legs; hell, shanks came out of assholes. Eddie had his *pedazo*, a sweet sharp blade fashioned from tin can lids filched from the kitchen, taped to his leg.

Sixty crazy beaners ran at full speed, sunshine glinting off the blades raised above their heads. Shit, it could have been the Alamo with black guys instead of peckerwood Texans, and the blacks didn't even have a wall to shield them.

They bolted.

So many black guys were sprinting it looked like the NFL combine, Eddie thought, but there was nowhere for them to run, and the fence, rather than protect them, trapped them. More blacks came running across the yard, but then so did more Mexicans, from three sides, just as planned, and it only took a few seconds before the blacks were backs to the wall. Well, backs to the *fence*, and it was clear that the COs were going to do exactly shit because the sole uniting factor in Victimville was a shared hatred for the blacks.

Eddie had heard the saying that love brings people together, but he knew that hate is the stronger bond.

Hate is the Krazy Glue of social emotions.

The monkeys went all see-no-evil-hear-no-evil as a wave of Mexicans slammed the blacks against the fence and *muchachos* started punching, slashing and stabbing.

Blood was being, as they say, spilled.

DuPont, being a tall motherfucker and a focus of attention to begin with, was one of the first to go down, because a prison riot is not the best place to be a tall motherfucker and a focus of attention.

One of the Mexicans swung a sock with a padlock tied inside and caught DuPont in the side of the head. DuPont fell to his knees, which was another bad idea in a riot because the Mexicans started stomping him like they were trying to plant him into the hard-packed dirt. Other blacks tried to fight their way to him, but Eddie saw that wasn't going to happen.

The blacks in front punched, slashed, and stabbed back, but the ones in back started climbing the fence. These motherfuckers were so desperate they were throwing themselves on the coils of razor wire that topped the fence, then tried to free themselves from the barbs to drop into the next yard.

Most got hung up and were stretched out up there screaming, but Eddie saw that one of the few who made it over the top was Darius Darnell, who reached up and helped his cellie, an older guy named Jackson, down the fence.

Eddie didn't hesitate.

He dug his foot into the chain-link fence and climbed.

Reaching the razor wire, Eddie took a deep breath and then launched himself onto it, slicing his arms and legs. He ripped himself off, screamed, dropped to the ground and started running after the fleeing blacks like he was just crazed with outrage.

Darius looked like he had some quick to him, but he didn't use it. He stuck with the older, slower Jackson, which was a balls-to-the-wall, hard-core loyal thing to do because about a dozen other Mexicans followed Eddie's example, scaled the wall, and chased the blacks along the fence.

But Eddie took the lesson—Darnell was a stand-up guy.

Darnell was running for a fenced-off segregation exercise yard, a rectangle about twenty by twenty feet. A CO stood at the open gate, waving him toward it, and Eddie saw he meant to lock Darnell and Jackson safely inside.

But the others didn't make it.

One deliberately fell back to fight a holding action and was swarmed by five *vatos*. Jackson tried to go back to help him, but Darnell grabbed him by the shirt and shoved him toward the seg yard, yelling, "Move it, man. You can't do him no good!"

The CO reached out, grabbed Jackson and pulled him through the gate. Darnell followed him.

Eddie was just behind, just reached it as the CO, a young Mexican, went to swing it shut.

Instead, he smiled and said, "*Adelante, 'mano.*"

Be my guest, brother.

Eddie stepped in.

The gate locked behind him and the guard walked away.

Then Eddie saw six *vatos* come out into the yard from the inside, smiles on their faces and shanks in their hands.

Darnell and Jackson were dead *mayates*.

One of the *vatos* told them so. "What happened? Did you think you were safe? We're going to slice you up."

Except Eddie stepped in between. "*Suficiente.*"

"Who are you to say when it's enough?" the lead *vato* asked Eddie.

Eddie recognized him as Fernando Cruz, a thick, mean motherfucker close to Zuniga. But not that close, and Eddie could tell he was a little unsure of himself as he said, "You a *mayate* now, Ruiz?"

"We're done. The point has been made."

"*My* point ain't been made," Cruz said. "My blade ain't been wet. Get out of my way, you don't want me to wet it on you."

"You don't want to shed brown blood," Ruiz said.

"You ain't La Eme. You just a *camarada*."

"I ride in the car, though," Eddie said. "In the *front* seat."

Reminding Cruz that he and the shot caller do *business* together.

"You think because you're some kind of big *chiva* slinger you can give me orders?" Cruz asked. "I said step out the way. Or if you want to be a *mayate*, we can treat you like one."

Eddie ripped the shank taped to his leg. It would have hurt like crazy if he weren't too afraid to feel much of anything.

He brought the blade up waist high.

"There are six of us," Cruz said, "and one of you."

"But it's *your* throat I'll slice," Eddie said.

"To protect two *mayates*?" Cruz shook his head. "Benny Z isn't going to like this."

"I'll talk to him."

"So will I." But Cruz backed off. Looked around Eddie at Darnell and Jackson and said, "You're lucky Ruiz here has a thing for black cock. You better fuck him real nice tonight."

Eddie thought about opening up Cruz's face for him but decided against it. Cruz stink-eyed him but took his boys back inside.

"Why'd you do that?" Darnell asked.

Eddie got his first real look at him.

Darius Darnell was about six one, not skinny but on the lean side and jacked from prison iron. Hair cut short, had him a mustache and a small goat. Dark-skinned, a *black* man.

Now he repeated, "I asked you why you did that."

"Because you and me," Eddie said, "are going to make millions together."

. . .

Cruz was right—Zuniga wasn't happy about what Eddie did.

But Eddie had to get this message through a kite because the COs put the whole place on lockdown following the race riot. A slip of paper came in on a fishing line with a message that the shot caller wanted to see him as soon as the lockdown was over.

The word was out that Eddie was in the hat.

"They ain't gonna do nothing," Eddie told Julio.

"How do you know?" Julio asked. He was scared of Eddie getting assaulted, scared that he might be included, scared that Eddie no longer being in good standing with La Eme would fuck up his own status, keep him on the bumper or worse.

"Because I know," Eddie said.

His relationship with Caro would protect him.

He hoped.

Eddie was more concerned about the lockdown because it was a pain in the ass. Trapped in that goddamn cell 24/7 with a shower once a week. And the food was terrible—peanut-butter-and-jelly sandwiches, a Kool-Aid and a small bag of potato chips.

For lunch and dinner every day for the month they were locked down.

It sucked.

What sucked worse was he had no access to Crystal.

Which meant no pussy, no outside information, and he knew she would have heard about what happened with him and Darius Darnell and started putting two and two together and coming up with four. Which he didn't want her to do—it was important that when she started putting two and two together he could sell her that it was three or five, anything but four.

And now he couldn't do that.

Frustrating.

Frustrating also that he couldn't continue his conversation with Darnell. After Eddie tossed his line about "making millions," Darnell had given him what could best be described as a "dark look."

"The fuck stupid shit you talking about?" Darnell asked.

"I have a business proposition for you," Eddie said, "when you gate out."

"Not interested."

"You haven't heard it."

"Don't need to," Darnell said.

"I just saved your fucking life," Eddie said. "Put my own ass on the line, and you won't as much as give me a listen?"

"I ain't ask you to step in," Darnell said. "I ain't owe you shit."

Yeah you do, Eddie thought. And you know you do. Behind all the fronting, you know that without me you're lying on the ground bleeding out, so subconsciously, at least, you're in my debt. But he said, "Cool. I'll make some other nigger rich."

Darnell looked at him for a few long moments, making up his mind whether to dance or listen. Then he said, "What you got?"

"Heroin," Eddie said. "A pipeline to Mexico—deep, long and strong. An exclusive New York metropolitan area dealership—Mets and Yankees, Giants and Jets, Knicks and Nets. Right now the Mexicans are selling to the Dominicans, cutting the blacks out. You could be the only major black distributor in New York. You have the network, you have the troops, all you need is the product."

"I won't sell poison to my people," Darnell said.

"Don't," Eddie said. "Sell it to white. They gobble this shit up. Remember meth? We made a fortune selling it to albino hillbillies. Now we have an urban market, a suburban market—sky's the limit."

"So why you need me?"

"The Mexicans are cutting me out, too," Eddie said. "Old grudges, that kind of shit. But now I have some serious backing on the product and transport side, what I need is a retail partner. I can't go to brown, so I'm coming to black. Call it 'diversity.' A multicultural narco revolution."

"And you gonna run this from the Ville?"

"I'm two years out from my EPRD," Eddie said. "But, yeah, in the meantime I can take care of business from here."

Darnell was quiet for a second, then he said, "Maybe on the bricks I want to be clean."

"How's that going to work?" Eddie asked. "What kind of 'you want fries with that' job are they going to give, with your sheet? One year, two at the tops, working with me, you can walk away, get you a house in, what do you call it, Westchester, or someplace, join the country club, play golf, your old lady can be in the Junior League. Look, I'm not going to sell you. You want this, great; you don't, okay, forget about what happened today, it's on the house, my treat."

"Your people going to give you trouble?"

"That's my problem, don't worry about it." But he wanted Darnell to worry about it. He wanted Darnell to feel guiltier than shit.

"You have a problem," Darnell said, "you can reach out."

"Brother, I just did."

"Let me think on it," Darnell said.

Then the COs came and hauled them out and Eddie realized he was bleeding from the razor wire so they took him to the infirmary and patched him up before they put him back in the cell and on lockdown.

Finally, the warden brought all the shot callers into his office for a come-to-Jesus and they all promised to make nice and all Kumbaya and shit because they were all tired of PB&J, and the lockdown ended.

And Eddie got summoned to the birdbath.

"Are you going to go?" Julio asked.

"Do I have a choice?"

"I guess not."

"Then what the fuck stupid kind of question was that?" Eddie asked. "What you need to do is cook up some clear and get us back to making money, let me handle La Mariposa, okay?"

He went down to Zuniga's cell.

The *mesa* had four of his baddest guys there, including Cruz, so Eddie knew it was trouble.

Zuniga got right to it. "You forget who you are, Eddie? Maybe you think you're black instead of brown now?"

It was no time to take a step back. "No, I'm pretty sure I'm brown."

"You're pretty sure?" Zuniga asked.

"It was a figure of speech."

"You broke the *reglas*," Zuniga said. "You went against your own people. You're in the bad. Cruz here wants me to hold a trial on you."

"You can't hold a trial on me," Eddie said. "I'm not La Eme. And if Cruz here wants me dead, why don't he just do it himself?"

He looked at Cruz and smiled.

Zuniga said, "That's not how it works."

Eddie knew he had no choice but to jump into the deep end, with both feet. If he pulled it off, he was free and clear. If he didn't, Zuniga would green-light him and give the ticket to one of his *vatos*—probably Cruz—who would do the job in the shower, on the yard, someplace, but he'd get it done or he'd be on the list himself.

So Eddie said, "*Here's* how it works—you reach out to Rafael Caro, who will tell you I was acting on his instructions, and that's all he'll tell you because the 'why' of it is above your pay grade. He will tell you to let me do my fucking business and offer me any and all assistance. That's how it works."

"It will take time to get to Caro."

"What else we got," Eddie said, "but time?"

Eddie walked out of the cell all tough but felt like he wanted to piss his pants. He was pretty sure Caro would give the right answers, but then again the old man had been in Florence so long he might have forgotten all about what he said, what he ordered.

But it bought him a hall pass for at least a week. Nobody was going to touch him while they waited for Caro's response.

Next on Eddie's agenda was Crystal.

She had a night shift and they got together in the storeroom.

A month was a long time to go without getting laid and the first thing on Eddie's mind was to get her pants down, but it wasn't the first thing on hers.

"You used me," she said.

No shit, Eddie thought. "Baby, I've missed you."

She slapped his hands away. "I heard about you and Darnell. What have you gotten me into?"

"Come on, baby, I know you've missed me, too."

He put her hand on his cock.

She took it off. "I'm done, Eddie. I can't do this anymore."

"Yeah, you can," he said. He didn't want to go here yet, but she wasn't leaving him any choice. "You're going to do what I want you to do."

"You can't make me."

"Listen to me, you dumb whore," Eddie said. "If I go to the warden . . . no, be quiet now and listen . . . and tell him you fuck me, I'll go to SHU, but you'll go to jail. If I tell him you brought me paper, you'll do eight to fifteen. Federal time. In max."

She started to cry. "I thought you loved me."

"I love my wife," Eddie said. "I love my kids. There's a chocolate Labrador retriever down in Acapulco I *might* love, but you? No. I love *fucking* you, though. If that's any consolation. So here's what you're going to do, Crystal. You're going to keep giving me information. And right now you're going to get down on your knees and suck my dick, and if you do a good job, I might fuck you. And if you don't do those things, *mamacita*, you'll get to see what *tortilleras* do to a former CO in prison."

As he pressed gently down on her shoulders, she asked, "Are we still going to Paris?"

"Jesus, Crystal," Eddie said. "Just suck."

"You're not thinking about doing this, are you?" Arthur Jackson asked.

He was on his bunk in his cell, looking at Darius Darnell.

"I don't know," Darnell said, looking back across the cell at the older man. "Maybe."

"What's drugs ever got us," Jackson asked, "but misery?"

Serving a triple life sentence, Jackson knew something about misery. He was a twenty-year-old college student in Arkansas when he introduced a friend to a crack dealer and took a fifteen-hundred-dollar finder's fee for his trouble.

They got busted.

Jackson refused to rat.

His friend didn't have such scruples.

The friend got probation, the crack dealer seven years. Arthur Jackson took the full hit. He never posted bond, never got to meet with the prosecutor, didn't know how the system worked because he'd never been in trouble before.

His friend and the dealer lied on the stand. Laid it all on Arthur.

The jury found him guilty on all counts of conspiracy to distribute cocaine. The jurors didn't get to hear about the sentencing he faced.

Three life sentences for making a phone call.

Arthur Jackson watched big-time traffickers walk out of this place. He watched rapists, gangbangers, child molesters, and murderers walk out of this place while he rots.

His plea for commutation was denied by President Bush.

Obama was Jackson's last chance, but he already rejected thousands of applications and anyway the days were winding down on his administration, and with them the clock on Arthur Jackson's hopes.

And yet Arthur kept his hope that a brother would see the injustice in his case and free him.

Darius loved Arthur.

He thought that Arthur Jackson might be the best, kindest person he'd ever known. Arthur had done twenty years in this hellhole without ever hurting a single other human being, but Darius thought his friend was wrong about Obama.

The president was a brother, but he was a Harvard brother, a brother who went to private schools, a brother who had to worry about being a black president and so who wasn't going to be in a hurry to be seen letting black drug slingers out of jail. The crazy thing was that Arthur might have had a better chance with a white president who didn't have to worry about looking soft on black crime.

The hard truth—although Darius loved Arthur too much to tell him the hard truth—was that Jackson was forty-one years old now, had spent his best years in prison and would probably die in prison.

And yet every day, every day, Arthur waited for that letter from Pennsylvania Avenue.

He had a "Clemency Calendar" of the Obama administration on the wall, and he crossed off a day at a time. There were far more squares crossed off than empty.

Darnell didn't know how Arthur did it, how he didn't go stark screaming crazy, how he didn't just rip his veins out with his own teeth, or kill someone, knowing that his whole life had been thrown away for *one fucking phone call.*

But Arthur stayed calm, Arthur stayed kind.

Arthur read his Bible and played his chess and helped other inmates write letters and their own appeals.

Arthur made peace when others wanted to fight.

And now he tried to talk Darius out of something Darius already knew he was going to do. "What have drugs ever brought us but misery?"

Money, Darnell thought.

Plain and simple.

Money.

Darius was no kid himself. He was thirty-six now, his kid was in middle school, and what were his prospects, really? Ruiz was right about that—maybe he gets a minimum-wage job. Maybe. As opposed to—

Millions?

Ruiz is right about this, too, Darius thought—you have the network, you have the people, and when you get back on the street those people are going to have certain expectations, and those expectations don't include you putting on some paper hat.

They expect you to get back in the game.

And you expect that, too.

But he told Arthur, "Nothing but misery, brother."

"That's right," Arthur said. "And if you get busted again, you come back for life. Do you want to be like me?"

"I could do a lot worse."

"You can do a lot better," Arthur said.

Yeah, how? Darius thought. How I'm going to do that?

Arthur asked, "So what are you going to tell Ruiz?"

"Going to tell him no," Darius said.

He didn't like lying to Arthur, but he didn't like hurting him, either. Jackson has had a lot of disappointment in his life, he has more disappointment coming up, and Darius didn't want to be another one.

Sometimes he heard Arthur crying at night.

Now Eddie sees Cruz bring the shank up.

Eddie balls his fist—his only chance is to get in first and smash Cruz in the face, maybe make him miss with his first stab. It ain't a good option, but it's the only option.

Then Cruz stops.

Hands Eddie the shank and says, "Cut me."

"What?"

"Zuniga says you can cut me." Cruz literally turns the other cheek, offering it to Eddie. "For the insult."

So Caro got back to them.

With the word that Eddie was untouchable.

"No, forget it," Eddie says.

"You have to."

"Didn't you guys get the word?" Eddie hands him back the shank. "I don't have to do anything."

He moves around Cruz and walks.

Surprised he's still alive.

Darius Darnell is gated out.

A happy occasion except for saying goodbye to Arthur.

"You be good, you hear?" Arthur says to him.

"You too."

Arthur laughs. "I got no choice."

"It going to happen for you," Darius says, even though he doesn't believe it. "You'll see."

"Don't you go writing no letters on my behalf," Arthur says. "They'd keep me in here forever."

"I'll send packages."

"I'll look forward to that."

The two men hug. They've spent seven years together in a space six feet by thirteen and never had a single cross word.

Then the CO walks Darnell off the tier.

Brother convicts cheer and yell.

An hour or so of paperwork and he's out.

A little over nine hundred miles away, another convict steps out of the gate.

Rafael Caro stands there for a moment and lets the sun hit his face.

A free man.

He's done 80 percent of his hitch, and with time off for good behavior, this model prisoner has been released.

Deported, of course, immediately.

A condition of his release.

This is fine with Caro, he can't wait to leave El Norte and never come back.

A limousine is waiting for him. A man gets out, walks over, embraces him, and kisses him on both cheeks. "El Señor."

He opens the back door and Caro gets in.

An open bottle of Modelo sweats in a bucket of ice.

Caro lets the cold beer sluice down his throat and it feels marvelous.

Like life.

The car takes him to a private airstrip outside Pueblo, where a jet awaits. A beautiful young flight attendant hands him a new suit of clothes and shows him where he can change.

When he comes out, she wraps a towel around his neck, cuts his hair, shaves him, and holds a hand mirror to his face. "All right?"

Caro nods and thanks her.

"Is there anything else I can do for you?" she asks.

"No, thank you."

"Are you sure?"

He nods again.

The plane takes off.

A few minutes later she comes back with a tray covered in white linen that holds a plate with thinly sliced steak, rice and asparagus tips.

Another Modelo.

He eats and drifts off.

She wakes him up just before the plane lands in Culiacán.

Keller watches the television screen as Caro walks through the press of reporters.

The old narco is frail, with that prison pallor and that convict shuffle, like he still has ankle bracelets.

Hugo explodes. "He helped to torture and murder my father and now he's out?! He got twenty-five to life and he's out in twenty?!"

"I know."

Keller had petitioned the BOP, phoned Justice, written official letters to object to the early release of Rafael Caro, reminded them of what he had done, but to no avail. Now he has to sit and watch one of Ernie's torturers go free.

It brings it all back.

He sees Caro stop and speak into one of the microphones pressed to his face. "I'm an old man. I made mistakes in my past and I've paid for them. Now I just want to live my life out in peace."

"Fuck him," Hugo says.

"Don't do anything stupid," Keller says. "I don't want to hear about you taking any trips to Mexico."

"You won't."

Keller looks at him. "I won't hear about them or you won't go?"

"Both."

Turning back to the television, Keller watches Caro's people usher him into the back seat of a town car.

So Caro's out of prison, he thinks. Jesus, when do I get out? Or am I serving life, with no time off for good behavior? And something hits him from his other war, his first, Vietnam. Something Ho Chi Minh had written:

"When the prison doors are opened, the real dragon will fly out."

4

The Bus

Jesus wept.
—John 11:35

Culiacán, Mexico
September 2014

At first Damien Tapia is shocked, disappointed by the little house in which Rafael Caro lives, the plain clothes that the man wears. The house, built back in the '80s, is modest—a single-level one-bedroom with a bathroom, small living room and smaller kitchen. The furniture is old, like you'd find at a yard sale.

This is Rafael Caro, one of the founders of the Federación—he should be living in a mansion and wearing Armani, not an old denim shirt and wrinkled khaki trousers. He should be dining at the best restaurants, not scraping leftover *frijoles* from a pan.

Damien feels cheated.

But then he sits with the old man and sees that what he thought was degradation is in fact simplicity, that the man hadn't fallen but is above it all, that his years in solitary confinement have turned him not into a madman but into a monk.

A sage.

So he sits and listens as Caro says, "Adán Barrera was your father's enemy. He was mine, too. He sent your father into death and me into a living hell. He was the devil."

"Yes."

"I didn't know your father," Caro says. "I was already in prison. But I have heard he was a great man."

"He was."

"And you want to avenge him."

"I want to restore my family to its proper place," Damien says.

"I heard you came into possession of a large amount of heroin," Caro says.

It's true. Damien and his boys hit a Núñez lab in Guerrero and took fifteen kilos. But how does the old man know?

"But you have no way to move it and no American market," Caro says.

"I have docks in Acapulco," Damien says.

But he knows what the old man is getting at. The docks are useful for bringing chemicals in, but less valuable for exporting drugs. The Pacific port only gives him access to the American West Coast; the trip is slow, unwieldy and risky. You can move marijuana by sea, dropping bales of it in the ocean off California where boats will come out and get it, but there's no profit in weed anymore.

He needs the heroin trade to take on Sinaloa, and Caro is right—they've locked him out of the transport and market infrastructure.

"Some of your father's old friends are moving Sinaloa heroin on buses out of Tristeza," Caro says.

Damien knows. Guerreros Unidos has become a client of Sinaloa. He can't blame them, they have to survive, they have to eat.

"What if they moved product for you, too?" Caro asks.

"They won't," Damien says. "The Rentería brothers are under Núñez's thumb."

"Maybe they want to get out from under."

Damien shakes his head. "I've approached them."

The Renterías were his father's old friends, worked for him for years, fought for him against Adán. After Diego's death, they went with Eddie Ruiz. Damien's known them since he was a kid. But when he tried to feel them out about helping him, they blew him off.

"It's one thing if *you* approach them," Caro says. "It's another thing if *I* do."

The city of Tristeza sits on Route 95 near the northern edge of Guerrero State where it borders Michoacán and Morelos. An old city, founded in 1347, it has a history. It was here that the Mexican War of Independence officially ended, here where the first flag of Mexico was raised.

It's a pretty town, known for its tamarind trees, its neoclassical churches and the lake just outside the city.

Damien follows a car along Bandera Nacional, then left onto Calle Álvarez.

"Where are we going?" Fausto asks.

"I don't know," Damien says. "El Tilde just said follow him."

"I don't like it."

"Just keep the gun ready."

Tilde pulls over opposite the Central de Autobuses.

"The bus station?" Fausto asks.

"I guess," Damien says, getting out of the car. He jams a black baseball cap onto his head because the sun is hot. He's wearing a black shirt over jeans and Nikes, a Sig Sauer .380 bulging slightly under the shirt. Fausto, he isn't fucking around with a small piece, but takes a MAC-10 out of the back seat, even though this is supposed to be a friendly meeting.

El Tilde steps out of his car, a big smile on his face, his arms outstretched in welcome, "*¡Bienvenidos, todos!* It's been too long!"

Cleotilde "El Tilde" Rentería was another one of Damien's father's bodyguards who then went with Eddie. The story about Tilde is that he killed twenty tourists one time in Acapulco, thinking they were rival gang members. They weren't, but Tilde's response was something along the lines of "better safe than sorry."

After Eddie left, Tilde and a few others of the old Tapia and Ruiz organizations formed their own thing—Guerreros Unidos—and now Tilde's two brothers, Moisés and Zeferino, run the organization with him.

Tilde wears a striped blue-and-yellow polo shirt over khakis, Damien notices, a throwback to Eddie's old rules that his people dress sharp. Now he walks up and throws his arms around first Damien and then Fausto.

"It's a beautiful thing," Tilde says. "From here, these buses go everywhere. Guadalajara, Culiacán, Mexico City. How much are we talking here?"

"Fifteen keys now," Damien says. "Maybe more later. I have the product, I just have to move it out of Guerrero. I came to you first out of respect."

Tilde doesn't want to know where Damien laid his hands on fifteen bricks of heroin paste, although he has a pretty good idea. One of Ricardo Núñez's packagers in Guerrero was hit a week ago by ten hooded men with AK-47s—fifteen keys were taken—and Núñez is not happy about it. He has his people all over the state looking for his property and the men who took it.

If Núñez knew, he would shit bricks sideways.

Then he'd start killing.

Better he doesn't know.

And better I don't know, he thinks as he looks at Damien. So he doesn't ask. It's better to maintain deniability, although he has strongly hinted to Núñez that Los Rojos were behind the raid.

Fuck Núñez.

Fuck Sinaloa.

Although they're doing a pretty good job of fucking themselves, he thinks. The Esparza and Sánchez wings are going at it hard up in Baja—leaving bodies hanging from bridges or scattered in pieces on the streets.

Núñez can't stay neutral forever.

"We'll move it for you," he says.

"You're not afraid of Sinaloa?" Damien asks.

"What Sinaloa doesn't know, it doesn't know," Tilde says. "Fuck those assholes. This stays between us, yes?"

"Absolutely."

"You're a good kid," Tilde says.

Your father's son.

"Look at your boys, Ric," Belinda Vatos says. "Luis is the head of his own thing, Iván the same. Even Damien has his own outfit now."

"What are you saying?" Ric asks.

He's back from Guerrero, in her apartment in La Paz.

"None of them are Adán Barrera's godson," Belinda says. "It's all there for you. And you sit around jerking off."

"What do you want me to do?" Ric asks.

"Be a soldier," she says. "Become your father's general. Then when he retires, the big chair is yours. It's what he wants, too."

"I know."

"You know, but you don't do shit," she says. "Your father needs you."

"Who am I right now—Michael Corleone?"

"You gotta get your dick wet, Ric," she says. "You gotta fuck the Skinny Lady."

"Yeah, I've never . . ."

"Duh. Don't worry, I'll help you pop your cherry."

All of Baja is in freaking chaos. Not so much over the border crossings but the domestic drug sales and the extortion rackets. But to control the border you need soldiers, and to pay the soldiers, you have to give them neighborhood franchises where they can sling dope and shake down the bars, the restaurants, the grocery stores.

It used to be well organized under the Sinaloa monopoly, but now it's all in play—from one block to another, one day to another—in La Paz, Cabo, Tijuana, anywhere—you don't know if it's Sánchez or Esparza, Núñez or *piraterías*—independents taking advantage of the chaos to get by without paying taxes to Sinaloa. The corner slingers don't know who they're working for, the business owners don't know who to pay.

Belinda's going to tell them.

So Ric piles into a car with Belinda, Gaby, and a couple of her boys, Calderón and Pedro, and they drive down to the Wonder Bar on Antonio Navarro, not far from the marina. He follows Belinda to the bar, where she walks into the office and fronts the owner, a young guy named Martín.

"Your payment's due," Belinda says.

"I already paid," Martín says.

"Who?" Belinda asks. "Who did you pay?"

"Monte Velázquez. He said he'd take the money now."

"Monte's not with us," Belinda says.

"He said—"

"What, Adán Barrera's dead so everyone can do their own thing now?" Belinda says. She points to Ric. "Do you know who this is?"

"No. I'm sorry, I don't—"

"This is Ric Núñez."

Now Martín looks scared.

"Ric," Belinda says, "does Monte Velázquez work with us?"

"No."

"But he said—"

"Are you going to tell Ric," Belinda asks, "that he doesn't know who works with his father?"

"No, I—"

"And are you going to tell us," Belinda asks, "that Monte told you he was with Sinaloa? Really, Martín?"

"I'm sorry, I just—"

"Don't be sorry," Belinda says, "just pay us our money."

"I already paid!"

"Yeah, the wrong guy," Belinda says. "Look, Martín, if you made a mistake, it's your mistake, not ours. You still owe us our money."

"I don't have it."

"You don't have it?" Belinda asks. "What's in the safe, there, Martín?"

"I can't afford to pay twice."

"So pay us and don't pay Velázquez."

"He said he'd burn the place down," Martín says. "He said he'd kill me, my employees, my family . . ."

Then Ric sees that Martín has bigger balls than he thought.

"I pay you protection," Martín says, "to *protect* me. Where the hell are you when Velázquez and his guys come around?"

Ric expects Belinda to shoot Martín in the face, but she surprises him, too. "You make a point. We should have been here, we weren't. That stops tonight. You see Ric Núñez, Adán Barrera's godson, standing right here to give you assurances. Isn't that right, Ric?"

"That's right."

"That's right," Belinda says. "What you're going to do, Martín, is you're going to go into that safe and give us our money. In return, you have Ric Núñez's personal guarantee that nobody else will hassle you. That includes that *lambioso* Monte."

Martín looks up at Ric.

Ric nods.

Martín gets up, opens the safe, counts out the money and goes to hand it to Ric.

"To me, not to him," Belinda says. "Señor Núñez doesn't touch money."

"Of course, I'm sorry."

"Pedro here is going to come around every week for our payment," Belinda says. "If you hand anyone else any money, we will chop those hands off and nail them to the front door. Don't make Señor Núñez and me come back and do that, okay?"

They leave the club and drive past one of the corners to a vacant lot that Velázquez's people have taken over. Two *malandros* are standing out there, clearly slinging crack and heroin. They're freaking kids, really, Ric thinks. Can't be out of their teens, wearing hoodies and skinny jeans and basketball shoes.

"They're *piraterías*," Belinda says. She reaches into the back and hands Ric a MAC-10. "It's pretty easy. Put the stock into your shoulder, slide this back and pull the trigger."

She hands him the little machine gun, pulls out one of her own. Ric sees that Gaby, Pedro and Calderón are all doing the same. Pedro, driving, pushes down the button opening all the car windows.

"Time to party," Belinda says.

"Shouldn't we warn them first?" Ric asks. "Like we did the club owner?"

"These little fucks don't pay us money," Belinda says. "They cost us money. Your money, Ric. And lessons must be taught. Just stick it out the window and let loose. You're going to love it—it's like fucking, only you get off every time."

Gaby laughs.

"Let's do this," Belinda says.

Pedro turns the car around, heads back for the corner. Guns stick out the windows like porcupine quills.

Belinda yells, "Now!"

Ric points his gun at one of the kids, then tilts the gun high and pulls the trigger. The gun chatters like a speed freak on a riff. Ric sees the kid's body jerk and then stagger and then fall and he hears Belinda and the rest laughing.

People on the street run away.

Pedro turns the car around again.

"What are we doing?" Ric asks.

"Marking your turf," Belinda says.

The car stops in front of the bodies, crumpled up like trash. Gaby pulls a big sheet of cardboard out of the back, Belinda takes a can of red spray paint.

"Come on," she says to Ric.

Ric gets out, follows them to the two bodies.

Looking down at one of the kids, he's surprised the blood looks more black than red; then he looks over and sees Gaby going at the other body with a machete, chopping off its arms. After that she lays the cardboard on the mutilated body. Belinda bends over and sprays the message: *You lose the hands you sling with. This is Sinaloa turf. —Mini-Ric, El Ahijado.*

The Godson.

"The job isn't finished," Belinda says, "until the paperwork is done."

"Jesus Christ, Belinda!"

"It's not evidence," Belinda says. "*Tranquilo.*"

They get back in the car and drive away.

Down to another club by the marina, where Belinda orders a bottle of Dom, pours a glass for everyone and toasts, "To Ric popping his cherry."

Ric drinks.

She leans over and whispers, "Tomorrow, you'll be famous. You'll be somebody. Your name will be in the papers, in the blogs, on Twitter . . ."

"Okay."

"Come on, baby," she says. "Say the truth—it was good, wasn't it? It felt good, huh? I fucking came."

"So now what happens?"

"Now we get Monte Velázquez."

The arrogant motherfucker is living on a motor yacht docked at a slip in the marina.

"He likes to fish," Belinda says. "He also likes pussy."

"Who doesn't?" Gaby asks.

"What fishing and fucking have in common," Belinda says, pointing at Gaby, "is bait."

Ric has to admit Gaby looks hot. Halter top, miniskirt, heels, her black hair shimmering, full lips glossy—a narco's wet dream. She totters down the dock like a tipsy party girl, stops and takes off her heels, then keeps walking toward Monte's boat.

When she gets to the slip she calls, "'Jandro?! Baby?! 'Jandro?"

A few seconds later, Monte comes out on the deck, his fat belly pouring over his jockey shorts. "It's late, *chica*. You're going to wake people up."

"I'm looking for Alejandro," Gaby says.

"Lucky man, Alejandro," Monte says. "But this isn't his boat."

"Whose boat is it?"

"Mine. You like it?"

"I like it."

"This Alejandro," Monte says, "he your boyfriend?"

"Just a friend," Gaby says. "With benefits. I'm horny."

"I can give you benefits."

"You have vodka?" Gaby asks.

"Sure."

"*Good* vodka?"

"The best," Monte says.

"How about coke?"

"Enough to cover my entire dick," Monte says.

"You have a *big* dick?"

"Plenty big for you, *mamacita*," Monte says. "Come on up, see."

"Okay."

It's that easy, Ric thinks.

The guy doesn't even hear them step into the stateroom, he's that focused on fucking Gaby. Belinda walks over and jabs a needle into his neck.

When Monte comes to, he's tied to a chair, his feet set in a dishpan.

Belinda sits in front of him. "You been telling people you're with Sinaloa."

"I am with Sinaloa," Monte says.

"With who specifically?" Belinda asks. "Give me a name."

"Ric Núñez."

Belinda laughs. "I have bad news for you, motherfucker. Guess who this is. Ric, is this guy with you?"

"I've never seen him before."

"Telling people you're with us when you're not is a very bad thing to do," Belinda says. "You've been stealing our money and our name. You have to pay for that."

"I'll give you the money back. I swear."

"Yeah, you will," Belinda says. "But that's not good enough, Monte. You have to hurt first."

Gaby comes in from the galley with a bottle.

What the fuck? Ric wonders.

"Acid," Belinda says. "Hydrochloric or something like that? I don't know. I just know it really fucks you up."

"Oh, God."

Ric thinks he might throw up.

"It's going to burn your feet off, Monte," Belinda says. "You're going to hurt. But you're going to live. So every time someone sees you hopping around on crutches, they'll know better than to say they're with Sinaloa when they're not."

"Please," Monte says. "No, please."

"Don't worry," Belinda says, "we'll drop you off outside the emergency room."

She nods to Gaby.

Gaby pours the acid.

Ric turns his face away.

But he hears the scream—shrill, impossibly loud, something inhuman, a sound that couldn't be coming from a human being. He can hear the chair hopping on the wooden floor, then the vomit rises in his throat, he hunches over and pukes.

When he looks up, Monte's neck is arched as if it might snap, his face is red, eyes bulging.

Then he stops screaming and his head drops.

"Shit," Belinda says. "He tapped out."

"Carbs," Gaby says. "And all that alcohol."

"Now what?" Belinda asks.

"Shark chum?" Gaby asks.

Belinda has a better idea.

In the morning, the other people docked at the marina wake up to a sight.

A naked Monte Velázquez hangs by a rope from the mast, with a big sign around his neck that reads:

SAIL AWAY, PIRATERÍAS —EL AHIJADO.

The video goes viral.

Ric gets a rep and a name.

El Ahijado.

The Godson.

The bus sits in the maintenance bay a block away from the station in Tristeza.

Damien watches the mechanic carefully place the brick of heroin paste, the last of fifteen, wrapped tightly in cloth, into the false bottom of the luggage compartment. Then he lays the cover on top and, using a power tool, screws it down tightly.

If you didn't know the difference, Damien thinks, you wouldn't know the difference.

Satisfied, he leaves the station and walks across the street.

Tilde waits in a car. "You good?"

"Yeah."

Because of his friendship with Damien's father, Eddie Ruiz is paying him on both ends—he buys the heroin paste at a good price and is cutting him in for two points on the New York sales of the finished product.

It's good of Eddie, Damien thinks, he doesn't have to do that.

He's a good friend.

As he was to my father.

Eddie Ruiz was one of the last people to have seen Diego Tapia alive. Left the apartment complex where he was hiding out just a few minutes before the marine raid. Tried to fight his way back to die with him but couldn't make it through the military cordon.

Even after Damien's father's death, Eddie kept the faith. Organized his own thing out of Acapulco and kept up the fight against the Barreras until the *federales* got him and the Mexican government extradited him to the US.

And now he's going to continue the fight from there.

Even from prison, Damien thinks.

With fifteen kilos of heroin on its way to New York, they can finally put up a real fight.

Jesús "Chuy" Barajos is looking to brawl.

Nineteen years old, he has known little else in his life. He fought for the Zetas, La Familia, and the Zetas again, but now he's back on his own searching for the only thing he knows.

In a better world, the movies that play on the inside of his eyelids would be features, the product of a screenwriter's imagination and a director's style, but in Chuy's world they are documentaries; memories, you could call them, except they don't flow like remembrance but are choppy cuts, flashes of surrealism that are all too real.

They are of flayed bodies and severed heads.

Dead children.

Corpses mutilated, others burned in fifty-five-gallon drums, and the memories reside in his nose as well as his eyes. And in his ears, as he can still hear—can't stop hearing, really—the screams, the pleas for mercy, the shrill taunting laughter that was sometimes his own.

He was the perpetrator of some of these horrors, a mere witness to others, although he barely knows the difference anymore—he stopped taking his meds months ago and now the psychosis is pouring back over him like a red tide, deepening, unstoppable, impenetrable.

This is a boy who once carefully carved off the face of a man who had tortured him, sewed it to a soccer ball, and kicked it back and forth against a wall.

Cruelly, he has just enough self-awareness to know that he's a monster, but not enough to escape his monster's cage.

His body reflects his mind's agony—his movements are jerky, awkward, his legs seemingly disconnected from the rest of his body. Always slight, he now looks emaciated, forgetting to eat or gobbling junk food in ravenous bursts.

He wanders the country, a Don Quixote without even a windmill to tilt at. Causeless, purposeless, aimless, he falls in with the other lost, travels for a while with a pack until he senses—correctly—that they can no longer tolerate his insanity, his mooching and petty thieving, his incipient violence, and then he wanders off again.

Now he's in Guerrero.

In the town of Tixtla, on the campus of the Ayotzinapa Rural Teachers' College, where the students are spoiling for a fight.

Chuy doesn't know what they're fighting about, just knows that they're gathering to head for the capital to protest something and they have weed and they have beer and they have pretty girls and they have an air of youthful normalcy about them that he desperately wants at the same time he knows it is unattainable.

He's drawn to conflict—it's a homing beacon, a tractor beam that he can no more escape than he can fly, so he stands alongside scores of "other students," chants slogans and listens excitedly to the plan for that night. The students have no transportation to Mexico City but they do have a tradition, tolerated by the police, of "hijacking" a public bus for the night.

The bus station is in nearby Tristeza.

The mayor of Tristeza is also in a belligerent mood.

Ariela Palomas is hosting a conference of mayors that weekend and is not about to have herself or her city embarrassed.

If the students—notoriously leftist to the point of being communist or anarchist—come to Tristeza to commit their depredations, she is going to teach them a lesson they won't learn at university from the pinko professors who coddle the little darlings.

Someone has to stand up for law and order, she tells the chief of the local federal police. Someone has to stand up for property rights, she tells the commander of the nearby army post, and if the weaklings who own the bus company are too limp-dicked to do it, she will do it for them.

She gives firm, clear orders to the municipal police: if students hijack buses, they are to be treated as the criminals they are.

A new sheriff is in town.

Ariela Palomas is not going to tolerate lawlessness.

Keller sits at the dining room table looking at the phone, willing it to ring.

He's heard from Orduña that there's been a new sighting of Chuy and that his people are moving in.

"They'll get him," Marisol says.

"I hope so," Keller says.

He has good reason for hope. Orduña's people are the best Mexico has to offer, and very damn good. The admiral dispatched a squad in plainclothes to go to the campus and look for Chuy. Pick him up, hold him and call their boss, who will call Keller.

And then what? Keller thinks.

What do we do with him once we have him?

Can't leave him in Mexico, he'll just take off again. So do we bring him up here? He is an American citizen, so that wouldn't be the problem. The problem is . . . well, the problems are . . . daunting, maybe insurmountable.

What do you do with a nineteen-year-old schizophrenic? One who has murdered, tortured, mutilated? A human so damaged that he's beyond repair. Keller knows what his old friend Father Juan would have said. "He's a human, not an automobile. He might be beyond repair but not beyond redemption."

But is redemption for this life or the next one? Keller wonders.

It's this life we have to deal with, and what do you do with a Chuy Barajos in this life?

"Maybe he can get the care he needs here," Marisol says.

"Maybe," Keller says.

But first we have to find him.

Ring, God damn it.

Chuy is having a blast.

High on weed and beer, he joins the crowd of about a hundred students in an assault on the Tristeza bus station. A ball cap shoved down over his long hair, a red bandanna covering his face, he picks up the chant and advances on a bus.

The driver opens the door and lets the students on.

He's annoyed but not scared. This happens not infrequently—the students commandeer the vehicle and the driver to their destination, protest for a few hours, and then make the return trip. While it's a pain in the ass, neither the buses nor the drivers are ever harmed, and the company has told them to just cooperate and put up with it. It's easier, cheaper and safer than fighting it, and the students will usually buy the drivers dinner and a few beers.

Chuy gets on and takes a seat next to a pretty girl.

Like him she wears a ball cap and a bandanna, but her eyes are beautiful, her long hair shiny, her teeth white as she chants the slogans that Chuy doesn't understand but chants anyway.

The students hijack five buses; two of them take the southern route out of town. Chuy's bus is the first in a line of three that takes the northern route.

It's all good.

A road trip, a field trip.

The kids joke and laugh and sing and chant, pass around a joint or two, a little beer, a little wine.

Chuy's loving it.

He never made it as far as high school.

He was a killer by the time he was eleven.

Now's his chance to make up for all the fun he missed.

Tilde gets the phone call from one of his brothers.

"I'm downtown," Zeferino says. "There's a problem."

"There always is," Tilde says. "What's it this time?"

"Some students took the bus."

Tilde wonders why his brother thinks it's a problem that students took a bus and says so.

"No," Zeferino says, "they took *that* bus."

"Shit," Tilde says. "Why didn't you stop them?"

"There were a hundred of them," Zeferino says. "What was I supposed to do, run in there waving my arms and say, 'You can't take that bus, it's full of *chiva*!'?"

"You should have done something," Tilde says.

Because it is a problem.

A big fucking problem.

A bunch of students have a bus that is not only filled with heroin, it's filled with Sinaloa heroin, Ricardo Núñez's missing heroin, and he's going to wonder what the hell it's doing on a GU bus.

And Ariela is going to snort blood.

"What do you want me to do?" Zeferino asks.

I don't know, Tilde thinks. What do you do when something is stolen?

You call the cops.

The phone finally rings.

Marisol looks startled.

"Yeah?" Keller says.

"We lost him," Orduña says. He explains that a bunch of students hijacked buses in Tristeza and that Barajos is probably on a bus with them.

Keller doesn't get it. "Hijacking buses?"

"It's almost a tradition," Orduña says. "They do it all the time to get to protests. This one's in Mexico City."

"Jesus."

"It's a schoolboy prank," Orduña says. "They'll go, they'll have fun protesting and they'll come back. My people will be at the station, we'll pick him up then."

"Okay."

Orduña hears the concern. "Look, don't worry. This is—how do you say it—'business as usual.'"

At first the students think it's firecrackers.

Some kind of celebration, or party noisemakers.

Chuy knows better.

He knows the sound of gunfire.

The little convoy of three buses has just turned onto the northern beltway leading out of town. Chuy looks out the back window and sees the cop cars chasing them.

More popping sounds.

The girl beside him—her name is Clara, she's told him—screams.

"Don't be scared," Chuy tells her. "They're shooting into the air."

The driver wants to pull over, but a student named Eric, one of the leaders, a real firebrand, tells him to keep going. *Let them shoot into the air, it's just for show, to save face.*

The kids start to sing louder to drown out the noise.

Then Chuy hears the dull *thwack* of metal striking metal—bullets hitting the bus. He looks out the front window and sees a cop car blocking the road.

The convoy stops.

Damien thinks he might puke.

"How could you let that happen?" he asks over the phone. "How the fuck could you let that happen?!"

"We'll get it back," Tilde says.

"How?"

"Don't worry," Tilde says. "We're taking care of it now."

"Don't let them stop us!" Eric yells.

Chuy follows him out of the bus. He and ten others rush the cop car and try to lift it from behind to pull it out of the way.

A cop gets out of the car.

Chuy crawls up behind him, reaches up and tries to take his gun. The cop whirls and fires.

The bullet goes through Chuy's arm.

He feels the pain but it's disconnected, just another movie as he rolls under the car to take cover because cops on the side of the road open up on them now with rifles.

Eric drops to the ground, crawls into the bushes.

Chuy pushes himself up and dashes back to the bus. A kid running in front of him is shot in the head and topples to the ground. Another kid comes out of the bus to try to help him but is shot in the hand and kneels, numbly looking at his three shorn fingers.

Chuy runs past them into the bus.

Kids are screaming now.

They've never been shot at before.

Chuy has.

"Down!" he yells. "Get down!"

He crawls to Clara, pushes her to the floor and lies on top of her. A kid squats on the floor, talks into a cell phone, calling for an ambulance.

"We have to get out of here," Chuy says.

Clara doesn't hear him—she's screaming and screaming. Bubbles of foam come out of her pretty mouth. Chuy crawls off her, grabs her by the hand and pulls her, slithering, across the floor now slick with blood to the back door. He opens it and pulls her out; they topple to the ground and, using the bus as cover, Chuy pulls her to the side of the road and lies flat on her again.

Puts his hand over her mouth to stop her screaming.

Hears her whimper.

Then he hears the ambulance whine.

Ariela's cell phone keeps buzzing in her purse but she ignores it.

Her dinner has been a triumph, her guests sated on the gourmet food and the fine wine, and now they are just into the dessert course before coffee and brandy.

The evening will make her a political star.

The phone stops and then starts again.

Several cycles of this before she excuses herself from the table and walks out into the corridor.

It's Tilde, and she's annoyed. "What?"

. . .

The cops stop the two buses on the southern route.

Smash in the windshields and toss in tear gas to force the students out. Some run away, the cops scoop up the rest and haul them into police cars.

Chuy hears the footsteps but doesn't look up, hoping the black cap will hide him from view.

But then the flashlight shines in his eyes.

"Up," the cop says, grabbing him by the elbow, hauling him to his feet.

Another cop grabs Clara.

Chuy looks around. Cops are combing the side of the road, grabbing kids—beating them, kicking them, pulling them into cars. But at least the shooting has stopped and an ambulance is parked by the first bus, its red lights flashing on Chuy's face as EMTs take out the wounded kids.

The officer smacks him.

"I didn't do anything," Chuy says.

"You got blood on me, *pinche pendejo*." He pushes Chuy to his car and into the back seat.

Clara is shoved in beside him.

Six police cars drive the students to the Tristeza police station.

"It's going to be okay," Chuy tells Clara.

The police don't kill you in the station.

Ariela goes to her office to handle the crisis.

What is known now is that there's been an "incident" involving students hijacking buses and that shots have been fired. Several people have been taken to an emergency clinic.

She speaks with her chief of police, who confirms that his officers fired at the students "after provocations." Most of the students escaped, but around forty—he can't be sure as yet—are in custody.

Ariela gets on the phone to Tilde.

"We can't get near the bus," he says. "It's still out on the road. Some of the students have come back. Teachers from the college. Journalists."

"You have to get to that bus."

"I know."

"And journalists?" she asks. "That can't happen."

She won't have it—she can't—sympathetic stories about idealistic college students brutalized in her city. And if snooping journalists find the heroin on the bus, it's a whole different thing. And that's just on the public level—if

Sinaloa connects them to the heroin shipment, there will be a war before she's ready.

So, two stories, she thinks—one for the public, another for the narco world. One, radical students hijack buses and then attack police officers trying to do their jobs. The police defended themselves—unfortunately, some students were hurt. But the fault lies with the students and not the police.

The second story goes out to Núñez: some of the students were allied with—or at least being used by—Los Rojos and took the buses on the mistaken idea that a Sinaloa shipment was on the buses that night.

That's the story she tells Núñez.

The story she tells her own people.

Keller has turned the phone on vibrate so that it doesn't wake Mari, although he doubts she's asleep. He keeps the phone by his hand so he'll hear it as he sits in the easy chair and tries to read commutation requests.

He reflects that he and Althea were divorced by the time their kids were teenagers, she and the kids living mostly in the States, he in Mexico, so he never sat up like this waiting to hear a car pull into the driveway, the door open, the footsteps walk into the house.

Or sat and waited for the phone to ring, hoping that it's going to be his kid saying he or she is okay, giving a frantic explanation, an excuse, hoping to avoid a scolding or punishment, not realizing that what you're mostly feeling isn't anger but relief. Just praying that the phone call won't be from the police.

All that fell on Althea.

I should call her and apologize, he thinks. I should call her and apologize for a lot of things.

No, he tells himself, who you should apologize to are your kids, both adults now. The hard truth is that you gave more care to Chuy Barajos than you did to them, and it's no wonder they're virtually strangers. And it's no good to tell yourself that they're fine—they're fine in spite of, not because of you.

The phone vibrates on the side table.

Keller picks it up and hears Orduña say, "Something has happened."

The police car pulls into the Tristeza station parking lot.

A cop comes out and Chuy hears him say, "You can't bring them here."

"Why not?"

"The boss says. Take them to Loma Chica."

"Why Loma Chica?"

"I don't know, just take them there."

The cars pull out again and head for the Loma Chica substation on the northeast edge of the city.

Tilde's car, a white Land Rover, cruises slowly past the bus. There have to be a hundred people out there now—students, teachers, reporters—milling around, taking pictures, examining the bullet holes in the bus.

"We can't get near it," Tilde says.

"If you think I'm going to let a million dollars in heroin get away from us, you're crazy," Fausto says. "Turn around."

"What are you going to do?"

"Get them the fuck away from that bus," Fausto says. "Stop the car."

Tilde pulls over and Fausto gets out. "Come on."

Two other guys get out of the back seat.

They stand outside the car, level their AKs, and open fire. Two students fall dead, others are wounded.

The crowd around the bus runs.

"Let's go," Fausto says.

He trots to the bus. While the two others fire into the air, he unscrews the sheet over the luggage compartment and pulls out the bricks of heroin paste.

A few minutes later, Tilde phones Damien. "We've got it. It will be on another bus leaving in the morning."

Then he calls Ariela and tells her.

"What about the students?" she asks.

"What about them?"

"Who knows what they saw on that bus?" she asks. "Who knows what stories they'll tell?"

"They're just kids," Tilde says. "Students."

"They're not just kids," Ariela says. "They're Los Rojos."

"Bullshit."

"It's the truth," Ariela says. "Los Rojos are using the students to get at us. We can't let that happen."

"What are you saying?"

"I'm saying that this is your mess, Tilde. Clean it up."

She clicks off.

Keller sets down the phone.

"Orduña says the police picked up some of the kids and took them to the police station," he tells Mari. "His people went to the Tristeza station but they weren't there. They heard they were taking some of them to Loma Chica—"

"What's that?"

"A nearby town," Keller says. "Orduña's people are going there."

"Do they think Chuy is—"

"They don't know," Keller says. "They don't know much of anything. Apparently the Tristeza police stopped the buses, there were shots fired, kids were taken off the buses . . ."

"How many kids?"

"They don't know," Keller says. "Forty? Fifty?"

"My God. And were any shot?"

"Mari, they don't know," Keller says. "Look, Orduña's people are very good. When they get to Loma Chica, they'll take over, the local cops won't stand them down. They'll round the students up, keep them safe."

The vehicle stops.

A cop walks out waving his arms. "Not here! Go to Pueblo Viejo."

"That's out in the middle of fucking nowhere!" the driver yells back.

"Orders."

The convoy pulls out again, along Route 51 that skirts the northern edge of town, then northeast up Del Jardín toward the isolated little village of Pueblo Viejo in the foothills.

Chuy presses his face against the window.

It starts to rain.

A drop hits the glass and slides down.

Chuy goes to wipe it off as if it's on his own cheek.

Some teachers take the wounded students from the second bus attack to an emergency clinic, but no doctors are on duty.

They phone for help, but no one comes.

A teacher walks outside and shouts to soldiers standing across the street, but none of them move.

The bodies of the two dead students lie out in the rain.

The car door opens and a cop pulls Chuy out.

Then Clara.

He stands there and looks around him as cops take students out of their cars and make them stand in the rain.

Trucks pull up.

Not police vehicles, but delivery trucks, panel trucks, a weird assortment of vehicles.

A man gets out of a white Land Rover and walks over to two other men.

They talk for a minute, then the man shouts some orders and the cops start pushing the kids into the backs of the trucks.

Chuy is shoved into a delivery truck and there's barely room to stand, much less sit. He holds on to Clara as more and more students are pressed together in the back of the truck, tighter than cattle. Some are shouting, others crying, others stunned and shocked into silence.

The doors shut.

Utter darkness.

Moist, hot air.

He hears a kid yell, "I can't breathe!"

Others pound on the door.

Chuy feels dizzy. He'd collapse but there's no room as the other bodies hold him up.

A kid pukes.

Chuy has to piss so bad it hurts.

He lurches as the truck starts.

"Where do we take them?" Zeferino asks.

"Where do you take garbage?" Tilde asks back.

The EMTs take an hour to get to the clinic.

By that time, two more students have bled out.

"They weren't there," Keller says.

"What do you mean?"

"They weren't at Loma Chica," Keller says.

"Where are they?"

"No one knows," Keller says. "Orduña says his people are looking, but . . ."

The students have all gone missing.

Chuy lets his bladder go. Ashamed to do it in front of Clara but she's beyond noticing as he feels her slumped against him, unconscious.

And it doesn't matter.

The smell of urine, shit, sweat and fear fills the truck.

That and darkness, and now he doesn't have to close his eyes to see his movies, they fill his brain as he struggles to breathe, his thin chest tightening, his lungs demanding oxygen that isn't there.

They're in this dark, this hell, seemingly forever until finally the doors open and air comes in. Of the twenty-two kids in that truck, eleven are already dead of suffocation.

Clara is one of them.

They toss her lifeless body out like a sack of flour.

The bricks of heroin paste are carefully repacked in three duffel bags. Fausto and his two guys get on the bus and keep the bags at their feet.

This time there will be no mistakes.

Eric's body is found in some bushes near the attack—the flesh torn off his face, his eyes gouged out, skull fractured, internal organs ruptured.

He had been tortured and beaten to death.

On all fours like an animal, Chuy gasps for air.

Tilde kicks him in the stomach again. "Los Rojos!"

Chuy doesn't know what he's talking about.

"Tell the truth!" Tilde yells. "You're with Los Rojos!"

Chuy doesn't answer. Why should he? All his life he's been one thing or another and it's always been the wrong thing.

This is no different.

He looks up and sees that he's at a dump, beside a huge pile of garbage, some of it smoldering even in the rain.

Dead students, asphyxiated in the trucks, have been tossed on it like trash.

The living kneel or lie fetal.

Some sob, a few pray.

Most are quiet.

A few try to run and are gunned down; most stay passive, unbelieving as the men walk behind them and shoot them in the backs of their heads.

They topple forward into the dirt.

Chuy patiently waits his turn. When the man steps behind him, Chuy turns, looks up and smiles.

Hoping that this is, finally, the end of his movies.

But when he sees the gun barrel and the finger tightening on the trigger, he cries, "Mami!"

He doesn't hear the shot that kills him.

The silence, Keller knows, is ominous.

Either Orduña doesn't know anything, or he doesn't want to say what he does know.

The phone sits dead and inanimate.

Mari is upstairs, working her own connections back in Mexico, and what she has learned so far is that six people are dead and twenty-five more are wounded. Forty-three young people, probably including Chuy, are simply missing.

How can forty-three people simply vanish? Mari asks.

Keller knows all too well. He has seen mass graves in Mexico before, left by the Zetas, the Barreras and others. More than twenty thousand people have gone missing in Mexico in the past ten years, these are just the last forty-three.

When will it ever end?

He has already called Blair and his other department heads and told them that he wants every resource directed toward locating the missing kids, even as he knows that what they're probably looking for are corpses.

"The police just shot them!" Mari said, her outrage fresh. "They just stopped the buses and opened fire! How could they do that?! Why?!"

He didn't have an answer.

"And where are the missing kids?" Mari asked.

Again, he had no answer.

Just the certain knowledge that the tortured psyche of Chuy Barajos is now truly beyond repair, and that the only hope is for redemption.

The Rentería brothers—Tilde, Zeferino and Moisés—throw the forty-three bodies onto the garbage heap. Then they douse them with gasoline and diesel, cover them with wood, plastic and rubber tires, and set it all on fire.

Bodies are hard to burn.

It takes the rest of the night and most of the next day.

Even as the bodies smolder, a crowd gathers in Tristeza at the attorney general's office. Some are survivors of the attack, some are faculty, others are journalists or concerned citizens.

Some are parents. Some cry and hug their children in relief.

Others aren't so lucky—their children are dead or missing, and the parents of the latter desperately demand or plead for answers.

Forty-three kids are missing.

Where can they be?

Ariela Palomas holds a press conference.

"These students are violent radicals," she says, "and some, I am sorry to relate, are nothing more than gangsters, in league with organized crime that has been terrorizing this state. It is, of course, a tragedy when any young person is killed, but they broke the law, resisted arrest, and attacked the police."

"'They had it coming'?" a reporter asks.

"Those are your words, not mine," Ariela says. When asked, she has no idea where the missing forty-three might be. "They are fugitives. Probably hiding out."

The Renterías scoop the remains into eight plastic garbage bags and throw them in the river.

A few hours later, the fifteen bricks of paste arrive safely in Guadalajara. There they are processed into cinnamon, repackaged and shipped to Juárez, where the heroin is loaded into a tractor-trailer truck driven across the border.

A few weeks later SEIDO agents find charred remains in the garbage dump and plastic bags in the river, but can't positively identify them as the students'. Later that week, masked protesters set fires to government buildings in the Guerrero state capital, Chilpancingo. Two days later, fifty thousand people march in Mexico City. There are demonstrations in Paris, London, Buenos Aires and Vienna. Students at the University of Texas, El Paso, hold a vigil and read the names of the missing students out loud.

In Tristeza, protesters burn down city hall.

The speculation is that Ariela Palomas ordered the attack on the students because she didn't want her tourism conference disrupted by protesters and that, when it got out of hand, she brought in associates in GU to clean things up.

No mention is made of heroin on the buses.

Under immense public pressure, the governor of Guerrero asks for and receives a leave of absence. The next week, Palomas is arrested in Mexico City and held in Altiplano maximum-security prison. She says that she has no information about the missing students. How could she know anything? Ariela asks. She was at a dinner party.

The president of Mexico sends nine hundred *federales* and thirty-five hundred troops into Guerrero to maintain order.

The protests continue.

The heroin from the bus arrives at a mill in New York, where Darius Darnell breaks it down into dime bags. Some of it ends up in the arm of Jacqui Davis.

On both sides of the border, grieving parents wonder what has happened to their children.

BOOK THREE

Los Retornados

Shall I, who have destroyed my Preservers, return home?

—Alexander the Great

1

The Holidays

Christmas is over and Business is Business.
—Franklin Pierce Adams

Washington, DC
December 2014

The thought that Keller can't escape is that the Tristeza Massacre wouldn't have happened if Adán Barrera had still been alive.

It's not that Barrera would have refrained from killing those kids out of some moral compunction, it's that he was too smart to set off that kind of public firestorm. And Sinaloa was dominant, so whatever Barrera said was law.

Now there's no law.

You killed the wolf, Keller thinks, and now the coyotes are loose.

In November, a forensics team from a German university went to the dump site and identified the bones of a charred body as one of the missing students. So the truth of the Tristeza Massacre, as it's now being called, is coming to light—forty-three kids were taken to a dump, shot, and their bodies burned on top of the garbage. Some of them were doubtless still living when the gasoline was poured and matches tossed on them.

Keller walks through the winter slush into Second Story Books on P Street, looking for a volume of Leonora Carrington's paintings, a particular favorite of Marisol's. It's a hard-to-find volume; he could get it on Amazon but he'd rather shop locally, and sometimes Second Story has books other stores don't.

Ariela Palomas's story that she was trying to stop student radicals and it got out of hand is obviously bullshit. The students at that college had been staging protests for years and she never cared. Nor does the story that she didn't want to be embarrassed at her big conference hold water—the conference site was far from the bus station and none of the participants even knew about the protest, which, anyway, was being held eighty miles away in Mexico City.

No, Palomas is covering up for something or someone so powerful she's willing to spend the rest of her life in prison.

And, so far, the Mexican government is willing to buy her story.

The Mexican people aren't. The people, the media, the families are all crying cover-up, and Keller doesn't blame them.

One of the people who won't accept it is, of course, Marisol.

In November, she insisted on going to Mexico City for a demonstration.

They argued about it.

"It isn't safe, Mari," Keller said.

"The last time there was a demonstration in the capital," Mari answered, "you marched with me. Maybe you don't remember."

Keller remembered.

It was early in their relationship, and mass demonstrations had broken out over what many Mexicans saw as a fixed presidential election. Keller had marched with her, slept with her wrapped in a sleeping bag on the Zócalo. He'd also marched with her in Juárez—maybe she didn't remember that, but . . . "I do remember, but that was before—"

"I became a cripple?"

"I didn't say you were a cripple."

"Then don't treat me like one."

"But be realistic," Keller said. "Your mobility is limited. There could be violence at this thing and—"

"I'll hobble out of the way," she said. "But if you're concerned, you could come with me."

"You know I can't do that."

The headlines would be brutal, the diplomatic backlash worse. Like it or not, he has to work with the current administration in Mexico City.

"The old you would have," Marisol said.

"That's not fair."

"What's not fair," she said, starting to bristle, "is that forty-three students are missing, probably dead, six others were killed, and the government doesn't give a damn."

"I'm not the enemy, Mari."

She softened. "No, of course you're not. And you're right, I'm not being fair. I'm sorry. Will my going cause you problems?"

"Probably." Marisol is a celebrity in Mexico, the cameras would find her, the American media, particularly the alt-right, would pick it up. "But it's your safety I'm concerned about."

"I have to be there."

Over his objections, she went.

Thousands of people—families of the missing students, social activists, concerned citizens—marched on the capitol building, and for the most part it was peaceful. Then several hundred broke off from the main demonstration and marched to the National Palace.

Mari was with them.

So was Ana Villanueva.

Of course, Keller thought when Marisol called to say that he shouldn't worry because she had an escort, that the journalist had come down from Valverde to join in the protest. In front of the National Palace some of the more radical protesters donned masks and threw bottles and firecrackers at the gates. The police drove them back with water cannons and both Mari and Ana were blasted off their feet. Seeing it on television, Keller was simultaneously furious and terrified. Over the phone he asked Marisol, "Are you okay?"

"A bit wet, but otherwise fine."

"It's not funny," Keller said.

"It was *water*, Arturo."

"You could have been seriously hurt."

"But I wasn't."

He sighed. "I'll be glad when you're home."

"Actually, I'm going to Tristeza."

"What?!"

"Did you not hear me," Mari asked, "or did you not understand?"

"I don't understand because it's incomprehensible," Keller said. "What do you think you're going to accomplish there?"

"Find the bodies."

Keller just went off. How the hell, he asked, did she think that a group of untrained protesters were going to do what the government couldn't, the police couldn't, international forensic teams couldn't, his own people couldn't? And what did she think, that one student was taken to the dump and shot and others were . . . where? In a secret prison somewhere? In the basement of the National Palace? On Mars? The students' remains, he told her, are in the dump and the river, are in ashes, and are never going to be found.

"Are you finished?" she asked when he took a breath.

"For the moment."

"We are going to Tristeza," she said, "to keep the missing students in the public awareness and to force the government to conduct a real investigation. And . . ."

"God. What?"

Marisol said, "There's information that the army is holding the students on a base outside of town."

"You can't believe that."

"Can you tell me it's not true?"

"Logic and rationality can tell you it's not true," Keller said. "You're just stirring the pot."

"It needs stirring," she said. "What are you saying? 'Let the professionals handle it'?"

"Okay, yes."

"But they're *not* handling it."

"We're doing everything we can," Keller said.

"I meant here in Mexico," Marisol said. "Why are we fighting, Arturo? I thought we were on the same side."

"We are," Keller said. "I just don't want you to go to Tristeza. Mexico City is one thing. Guerrero is a war zone."

"Ana's going with me."

She was with you when you were shot to pieces outside Valverde, Keller thought. She'll be as helpless to protect you now as she was then. "I'll have Orduña pick *both* of you up and put you on a plane."

"I don't think even the head of DEA is allowed to kidnap people," Mari said. "And if you're all of a sudden going to transform into some sort of paternalistic—"

"Come off it."

"—overly protective—"

"Are you *kidding* me right now?"

"You cannot tell me what to do or not to do," she said.

Marisol went to Tristeza, looked into a television camera and said, "We are doing the job authorities refuse to do," and went off to look for mass graves.

It had gone beyond even the Tristeza Massacre now. Ana, writing once again for the national page of the Juárez newspaper *El Periódico,* reported that there might be as many as five hundred bodies buried in the area in the past year and a half.

Keller got to watch Marisol's statement on the Breitbart website, the headline of which read, DEA BOSS'S WIFE LEADS LEFT-WING PROTEST. It ran not only the clip of Mari's statement in Tristeza, but also a still of her carrying a sign that read, YA ME CANSÉ ("I've Had Enough") and a vid-clip of her being blasted off her feet outside the National Palace with the chyron RED MARI IS ALL WET.

A separate photo of Keller made it seem as if he were looking at his wife and smiling.

The *New York Times, Washington Post* and CNN were more restrained, but still ran stories about the DEA director's wife joining the protests. The

Guardian practically beatified her. Fox News ran footage of the hooded protesters throwing bottles and fireworks as Sean Hannity asked whether Art
Keller supported his wife's radical activities.

Keller was forced to issue a statement. "While this is an internal Mexican
matter, DEA is fully cooperating with the Mexican government to discover
the truth as to what happened in Tristeza. Our thoughts and prayers are with
the missing students, their families and loved ones."

Reluctantly, Keller went on CNN and watched as Brooke Baldwin showed
video of the protests. To her raised eyebrow, he responded, "My wife is obviously her own person."

"But do you support what she's doing?"

"I support *her*," Keller said. "Marisol is a Mexican citizen with every
right to protest."

"Violently?"

"I think if we look at all the footage," Keller said, "we'll see that she was
not participating in the violence."

"But she was there."

"She was definitely there."

John Dennison jumped in, tweeting, "Red Mari" embarrasses her husband. Sad.

He got a call from O'Brien. "Can't you control your wife?"

"I'm going to do you a favor, Ben," Keller said, "and not even tell her you
said that. But, as a matter of fact, I have no interest in 'controlling' my wife.
She's a woman, not a Weimaraner."

"Hey, I'm on your side, remember?" O'Brien said.

If you decide to run for president, Keller thought, you'll drop me like a
bad blind date. "So are you going to announce, Ben?"

"Right now I'm just focused on serving the people of my state," O'Brien
said. "But, hey, if the beautiful doctor could refrain from maybe, I don't
know, joining ISIS—"

"Have a nice day, Ben."

When Mari came home, she said, "I saw you on CNN. Thank you."

"We're not going to become one of those Washington power couples who
communicate with each other on cable news, are we?" Keller asked.

"No."

"What did you find out in Tristeza?"

"What you thought," Marisol said. "Nothing. Don't gloat."

"There's nothing to gloat about."

It's an understatement. Forty-nine young people dead—forty-three of them "missing," six killed at the scene—among them probably Chuy Bara-jos. Keller isn't gloating.

Marisol had more bad news. "Ana's going to pick up the investigation. She's convinced the federal government is covering something up and she's going to write an exposé. She got Óscar to credential her."

"Óscar should know better."

"He could never say no to her," Marisol said. "I'm worried, Arturo. Can you do something to help her?"

"I can call Roberto," Keller said, "ask him to keep an eye out."

It won't do much good, Keller thought. The marine special forces have other things to do than babysit a reporter, especially one as independent and stubborn as Ana. But he would put in the call.

Then Ana called him. "What can you tell me about the Palomases?"

"Ana . . ."

"Come on," Ana said, "you know this story is *mamadas*. My sources tell me the Palomas family is hooked up with Sinaloa."

Her sources were right, Keller thought. The Palomases have been hooked up with Sinaloa via the Tapia faction for generations. When the Tapias went to war with the Barreras, the Palomases stayed loyal, but when they lost the war, they bent the knee to Adán, who issued absolution and licensed them to operate in Guerrero.

"Ana, are you in Guerrero?" Keller asked.

"Where else would I be?"

"I don't know. Safe at home?"

"I've been safe at home too long," Ana said. "I want your help on this, Arturo. The whispers here are that Guerreros Unidos were involved. Can you confirm that? Off the record, of course. Deep background."

"We have sources that say the same thing."

"Why would the Mexican government cover up for GU?" Ana asked. "They're small-time players."

You already know, he thought.

The morning after the massacre, Keller had directed his Intelligence Department to give him a full briefing on Guerrero. What he had learned was that the Sinaloa cartel was investing heavily in Guerrero as a new source of opium and that Los Guerreros Unidos and Los Rojos—both shards from the shattered Tapia jar—were competing to supply the cartel. Where Sinaloa was involved, elements of the government would be in there trying to cover things up.

"People here are saying the Tristeza police turned the students over to narcos," Ana said. "Can you confirm that?"

"I can confirm people are saying it." He knew it was true. Blair had obtained transcripts of the Tristeza police interrogations, and several admitted they'd handed the kids over to people associated with GU.

Because Palomas told them to.

But who gave her the order? Keller wonders now. A small-town mayor doesn't order the murders of forty-nine kids on her own.

Cartel bosses do that.

But which?

Who?

No one even knows who's in charge of GU now.

Maybe the Rentería brothers, maybe not.

Or did it go higher?

To Sinaloa.

Ricardo Núñez is at least nominally in control of the Sinaloa cartel. He appears to be grooming his son, Adán's godson, to take over. Mini-Ric has a reputation as a useless playboy, a classic Hijo, but lately there have been indications that he is starting to involve himself in the business on a serious level.

Núñez Senior isn't known as a particularly violent or rash man. If anything, he's probably more conservative than Adán was. For him to order or even sanction a massacre like this would be uncharacteristic. Maybe his kid is more bloodthirsty, but he doesn't have the power to have ordered this.

Two other Sinaloa factions are taking heroin out of Guerrero.

Elena Sánchez is reported to be in deep mourning, but nevertheless fighting a bloody proxy war against Iván Esparza, using street dealers as pawns. Her sole surviving son, Luis, is the titular head of the Sánchez wing, but he's an engineer, not a killer.

Iván Esparza, on the other hand, is a killer.

Stupid, hotheaded and vicious enough to order or okay something like the Tristeza Massacre.

But so far there's nothing connecting him to it.

For that matter, nothing connects any of them to it.

Maybe, Keller considers, it wasn't Sinaloa at all.

Intelligence reports also indicate that the New Jalisco cartel is moving into Guerrero.

Tito Ascensión grew up poor in the Michoacán avocado fields. He did hard time in the violent cauldron of San Quentin. He's killed innocents before—thirty-five on one instance in Veracruz when he mistook them for Zetas. He wouldn't blink at killing those students if they got in his way.

But how?

How would a few dozen college kids on a lark get in the way?

And why would the government want to cover it up?

This was what both he and Ana were trying to solve.

Then Ana asked him a very interesting question. "The GU are old Tapia people. Would any of them feel any residual loyalty to Damien Tapia?"

That was out of left field, Keller thought.

What had Ana heard, what did she know?

"Why do you ask that?"

"Just tossing it around, Arturo."

Speaking of bullshit, Keller thought. Ana is a veteran journalist, once feared by everyone from narcos to cabinet officials, even presidents. She never wasted something as valuable as a question. "What makes you think Damien Tapia had something to do with this?"

"I don't necessarily think that," Ana said. "It's just that Damien has been seen around Tristeza."

"By whom?"

"When you start telling me your sources," Ana said, "I'll start telling you mine."

"No, you won't."

"No, I won't." Ana laughed. "But what do you know about Damien?"

What you probably know, Keller told her. Diego's son carries a grudge against Sinaloa for his father's death and his family's ruination. He's sworn revenge but so far done nothing but cut a few YouTube videos and write a few bad songs.

Sinaloa would probably have killed him already except that he was a good childhood friend of the Esparza brothers and Ric Núñez. He was also close to Tito's son, Rubén. The youngest of Los Hijos, he was sort of a pet, a mascot, so he was tolerated. And, if they were being honest, the powers that be in Sinaloa would admit they felt guilty about what they did to the Tapias.

"Ana, be careful," Keller said, and then clicked off.

Then he arranged for Eddie Ruiz to be taken out of his cell to a special phone.

"What do you know about Tristeza?" Keller asked.

"Nothing," Ruiz said.

"There's talk Guerreros Unidos was involved."

"So?"

"They're your old boys," Keller said. "And Damien Tapia was your friend."

"I don't know about 'friend,'" Eddie said. "I sort of babysat him when his old man was too coked up to look after him."

"Have you been in touch with him lately?"

"Yeah, Keller," Eddie said. "He comes here every Thursday and we play *Pokémon*. What do you think?"

"What can you give me on Tristeza?" Keller asked.

"Even if I did know something, which I don't," Ruiz said, "you think I'd give you information that would implicate me? I'm close to the door, Keller. I'm not going to do anything to fuck that up."

"Maybe a little bus therapy would jog your memory," Keller said. Eddie was comfortable in Victorville, safe. His family was nearby, where they could visit. Moving to a new facility would be a major hassle, maybe a dangerous one. He'd have to seek the favor of a new Eme shot caller, build new alliances. Until Keller would have him transferred again, and again . . .

"The fuck, Keller," Eddie says. "You come with all stick, no carrot? What is that?"

"What do you want?"

"Look, man," Eddie said. "It's been three years since I turned myself in. Two years since we took our little field trip down south—"

"You can't keep playing that card."

"My knowledge is worth something," Eddie said. "Maybe a few months trimmed off the back end?"

"That would be up to federal prosecutors and a judge."

"Like none of them owe you," Eddie said.

He's right, Keller thought. It would take one phone call, two tops, to get Ruiz's release date moved up. "What do I get for it?"

"Look for the Rentería brothers," Eddie said.

"The Renterías are midlevel players," Keller said. "Who gave the order?"

"I gave you what I can," Eddie said.

So whoever it was, Keller thought, is so powerful even Eddie won't dime him. But Ruiz knows he can throw the Renterías under the bus, as it were. "If this checks out, I'll get you a new EPDR."

Earliest possible release date.

"It will," Eddie said.

"It doesn't," Keller said, "I'll bounce you around the system like a pinball on crack."

"You ever get tired of being a dick?" Ruiz asked.

"No."

"I didn't think so," Eddie said.

Keller got on the horn to Orduña and the FES started to turn hell inside out looking for the Renterías. They raided homes, storehouses, tore the countryside up looking for opium farms, became a major disruption to the heroin trade in Guerrero.

But they didn't find the brothers.

Keller pondered the possible relationship between GU and Damien Tapia. What kind was it and who had the power to order the Tristeza murders? He directed his agency to put extreme pressure on all sources, defendants, and federal inmates to produce intelligence about Tristeza. Deals were to be offered, threats were to be made, arrests, searches and seizures pressed to the legal limits. All CIs were asked about Tristeza and pressed to get information.

Personnel in every field office quickly got the message—the boss is on a crusade. Pick up the banner and march with him or expect your career to stall out like a four-hundred-dollar used car.

Keller reached out to ICE and the Border Patrol—if you stop a car with as much as an ounce of marijuana, please interview about Tristeza. He called in chips with city and state police departments with the same request—ask everyone about Tristeza and if you come up with even a possible "positive" pass it along to us.

But so far, no results.

Now Keller finds the book he's looking for—*Leonora Carrington: Paintings, Drawings and Sculpture, 1940–1949.* Marisol will be pleased. He goes to the counter and pays for it, then steps back on the street.

Someone killed those students.

Keller is going to find out who it was and he's going to take them down.

Because it's on me, he thinks.

You destroyed one monster, Keller tells himself.

Now you have to destroy the next one.

There has always been philosophical speculation on the question, *What if there were no God?* Keller thinks as he walks through the slush. But no one has really asked, much less answered, the question, *What if there were no Satan?*

The answer to the former is that there would be chaos in heaven and on earth. But the answer to the latter is that there would be chaos in hell—all the lesser demons would be set loose in an amoral struggle to become the new Prince of Darkness.

The fight for heaven is one thing.

The fight for hell . . .

If God is dead, and so is Satan, well . . .

Merry Christmas.

Hugo Hidalgo has a present for him.

He comes into the office with a cat-licking-cream smile on his face and says, "Claiborne might finally be paying rent. Have you heard of Park Tower?"

"Sounds like a show on PBS."

Park Tower, Hidalgo explains, is a high-rise building of offices, shops and condominiums in lower Manhattan. Something called the Terra Company bought it back in 2007, during a real estate boom, putting fifty million dollars down on an almost two-billion-dollar purchase price.

"That's just two and a half percent," Keller says.

Hidalgo says, "The rest was in high-interest loans, due in a bubble payment in eighteen months."

The problem, Hidalgo says, is that the building has been a bust. Terra hasn't been able to find enough tenants to service even the interest, never mind the principal. And the building needs major remodeling and construction to become competitive.

Enter Berkeley, the hedge fund Claiborne works for.

Berkeley created a syndicate to refinance Park Tower and pay off the loan. In exchange they would receive a 20 percent share in the new building. Claiborne put together seventeen lenders from banks in the US and overseas—Germany, China, the Emirates.

"So what's the problem?" Keller asks.

"Deutsche Bank just pulled out," Hidalgo says. "Now Claiborne is racing the clock to hold the rest together, and he's $285 million short. It's a tough sell, because Terra's credit is for shit. So Claiborne is looking for what he calls a 'lender of last resort.'"

"That's quite a euphemism," Keller says.

"Claiborne only brought this to me because I threatened to pull the plug on him," Hidalgo says. "But when they've had similar problems in the past, they've gone to HBMX."

Keller recognizes the name. HBMX is a private investment bank that's a major money launderer for the Sinaloa cartel.

All major drug-trafficking organizations face the same problem, and it's the opposite of what most businesses face.

DTOs don't have too *little* money, they have too *much*.

And most of it comes in cash.

Cartels are credit-to-cash businesses: they front the drugs to middlemen, who pay when they convert the drugs to a retailer. It's not unusual for a cartel to advance millions of dollars in drugs on good faith, which is pretty much assured by the lives of the borrowers and their families.

It's not that risky for either party, because drugs are almost a sure sell. The only bad thing that can happen is that the drugs get busted by a law enforcement agency before they can be sold, in which case the middleman provides proof to the cartel, usually in the form of a police report, that the drugs were, indeed, seized by a governmental agency. Then they work out an extension of the debt or even, in the case of a steady customer, forgiveness.

There's that much money to go around.

But that's the problem: the business generates massive amounts of cash that has to be laundered, passed through legitimate businesses so that it can be used and spent.

A decade or so ago, the cartels cleaned the money electronically, sending it around the world on multiple digital transfers until it came back clean. But Interpol and other agencies got too good at electronic surveillance, so the cartels went old school—started physically shipping the cash back to Mexico, where it was deposited in tame banks.

Good as far as it went, but the Mexican banks couldn't handle all the cash, and the prime investment opportunities were in the United States, so they started transferring the money from Mexican to American banks. The problem was that American banks have far stricter reporting rules—they aren't supposed to accept cash deposits of more than ten thousand dollars without filing an SAR—Suspicious Activity Report—and they're supposed to file a report on any large deposits, no matter how much, the origins of which are, well, suspicious.

A couple of banks in the US and UK got caught moving drug money without filing SARs and were fined a couple of billion, which sounds like a lot of money except you're talking about $670 billion in wire transfers, and the banks' profits that year were over $22 billion.

It pays to play.

But the money can't sit in the banks and do a lot of good, or generate a return on the investment, so one of the best things you can do with it is invest in real estate.

Because real estate is expensive.

Construction is expensive.

Labor is expensive.

And all your money can be cleaned through loans, skimming on materials, paying labor that didn't labor . . . it goes on and on.

With a project like Park Tower, the possibilities are endless.

And when a company like Terra is halfway across a wide, fast-moving river like a Park Tower project, runs out of money, and can't get more credit, it's going to take whatever assistance it can get to make it to the other shore.

If drug money is the only lifeline, they'll grab it.

"Have they reached out to HBMX?" Keller asks.

"They won't," Hidalgo says, "until they've exhausted all other options."

Hence the expression *lender of last resort,* Keller thinks.

Hidalgo has a weird look on his face.

"What?" Keller asks.

"Do you know who the principal partner in Terra is?"

"No."

"Jason Lerner," Hidalgo says.

"Who's that?"

"John Dennison's son-in-law," Hidalgo says. "Are you sure you're good with going there?"

Because it's fraught, Keller thinks.

Dennison's been attacking me, so it could be perceived as payback, or political, or both. If Dennison does run for president, it could open up a nasty can of worms.

We have to be careful.

Immaculate.

"In no way," Keller says, "can you positively assert or even suggest to Claiborne that he approach HBMX or any other entity. You can only require that he provides you with intelligence about meetings that were to happen anyway."

It's a tissue-thin distinction, Keller knows, likely to tear apart anyway, but they have to maintain it.

"Have Intelligence pull whatever we have on HBMX, Terra and Berkeley," he says. "But put up flak—bury it in requests on other institutions. Strictly limited access. You bring this to me and only to me."

If Howard gets a sniff of this, he'll run straight to Dennison and then it's over before it's started.

"What about Mullen?" Hidalgo asks.

"I'll keep him in the loop," Keller says. "We owe him that. But no one else."

"Southern District?" Hidalgo asks.

"It's premature," Keller says. A money-laundering case involving Terra and Berkeley would come under the jurisdiction of the US Attorney for the Southern District of New York, and they should be involved, but there's no real evidence yet, just a suggestion of a crime that may or may not happen.

And they also could leak, which could endanger not only the operation but Claiborne himself, maybe even the call girl who's at the center of the underlying charge that makes him a snitch.

"Where's the call girl now?" Keller asks.

Hidalgo shrugs.

"I'll ask Mullen to pick her up, get her out of town," Keller says.

He doesn't think Claiborne is capable of killing the girl; he knows that the cartels are.

Marisol is prowling the Latin American shelf at Politics and Prose when she hears—"Excuse me. Dr. Cisneros?"

She turns to see an attractive middle-aged woman with ash-blond hair. "Yes, that's me."

"Althea Richardson," the woman says. "Before that I was Althea Keller."

"Oh. *Encantada.*"

They both laugh over the awkward moment of a man's ex-wife meeting his current one.

"I recognized you from the magazine photos," Althea says, "but they don't do you justice."

"You're very kind," Marisol says, "and even more beautiful than Arturo described."

"I'm sure Art never said any such thing," Althea says, smiling. "He can be clueless, but not so clueless he'd say something like that to his wife."

"Perhaps we weren't yet married," Marisol says.

"Listen, this is a little weird," Althea says, "but do you want to grab a cup of coffee or something?"

"Okay, why not?"

Marisol finds that she likes Arturo's former wife very much. It's not a surprise, really; he always spoke very well of her and put the blame for their divorce squarely on his own shoulders. What surprises Marisol is how funny Althea is, funny and sharp, mischievous and self-deprecating.

The two women are quickly laughing over Art Keller stories and finding they have a lot in common.

Not just about Art.

Their political views are closely aligned, their ideas about women's roles are simpatico, and after only a few minutes Marisol thinks that she might have found a real friend in this city.

"The attacks on you have been disgraceful," Althea says.

Marisol shrugs. "The right wing is the same in every country, no? They don't like women getting, how do you say, 'uppity.'"

"What will you do if . . ." Althea stops.

"Arturo gets fired?"

"I'm sorry," Althea says. "That was really rude."

"No, it's reality," Marisol says.

"Would you stay in Washington?"

"I think so," Marisol says. "But tell me about you."

"Not much to tell," Althea says. "I teach poli-sci at American. Recently widowed—"

"I'm so sorry."

"Bob and I had that academic couple life," Althea says. "It was nice—sitting in the living room together listening to NPR, taking day hikes in our L.L.Bean gear. Wine-tasting weekends, summer vacations on Martha's Vineyard or the Maryland coast. Then he got sick; the last year wasn't so nice."

"Again, I'm sorry."

"I'm really doing all right," Althea says. "It's just odd, you know, waking up in the morning and rolling over and that side of the bed is empty. And I can't quite get the knack of cooking for one. A lot of times I just don't bother, I get takeout. I'm a lousy cook anyway, maybe Art told you."

"No."

"The poor guy used to cook out of self-defense."

"I'm sure that's not true."

"It's sad," Althea says. "They know me by my first name at Mr. Chen's. Otherwise I spend my time haunting bookstores, accosting my ex-husband's wives."

"I'm glad you did."

"Me too."

When Keller gets home that night, Marisol says, "Guess who I ran into this afternoon? Althea." It amuses her that he looks absolutely flummoxed. "She came up to me and introduced herself. We had coffee."

"Did you talk about me?"

"What an ego," Marisol says. "At first, of course. Then, believe it or not, we found other topics of conversation."

"I'll bet," Keller says.

Marisol says, "I can see why you love her."

"Loved."

"Nonsense," Marisol says. "You can't be married to someone like that for so long, have children together, and not love her. I'm not jealous, Arturo. What, am I supposed to dislike Althea just because you used to be married to her? Excuse me if I don't care to be a cliché."

"Stereotype."

"Excuse me?"

"A cliché," Keller says, "is a trite verbal expression. A stereotype is a—"

She freezes him with a look. "Really? You're going to correct my English now?"

"No. I'm not."

"Good choice," Marisol says.

"Well, if you run into her again—"

"Oh, I will," Marisol says. "So will you, actually, she's coming over for Nochebuena. Oh, Arturo, let's do a *Mexican* Christmas this year. Let's have people in. We've had so much death. It would be good for us to have some life."

"Sure, *that's* fine, but—"

"What?" Her face is a portrait of feigned innocence.

"Althea. You might have asked me first."

"But you would have said no."

"That's right."

"So why would I do that?" Marisol asks. "She was going to be alone, and that's not right. And I really do like her, very much. Ana's coming, too, by the way. You're going to be an island in a sea of estrogen."

"Great."

"What's Hugo doing?"

"I don't know."

"Ask him."

Keller knows what she's doing, even if she doesn't. He's a loner, comfortable with solitude, but Mari is a social creature, her happiest days spent in a circle of close friends for whom a new poem was sufficient occasion for a party. He was present at a few of those gatherings—the drinking, the passionate debates, the singing, the laughter. Too many of those friends are gone now—murdered in the drug war—and she is, perhaps unconsciously, trying to re-create the warmth of that embrace, their arms wrapped around her, her arms wrapped around them. He knows that she's lonely in this cold country, so he tells himself not to be an asshole and object to her Christmas plans.

Hugo Hidalgo laughs in Keller's face. "I want to make sure I don't have this twisted—you want me to come over and have dinner with you, your wife and your *ex*-wife? No. Let me rephrase that—*hell* no."

"What *are* you doing for Christmas?"

"Not that."

"You're smarter than you look," Keller says.

"Not hard, boss."

Keller plays his trump card. "Mari would love for you to be there."

"*Damn* it."

"You should have made prior plans," Keller says. "Failing to prepare is preparing to fail."

. . .

Ana arrives on Christmas Eve.

It's striking, Keller thinks, how she resembles a bird more each passing year, with her little beaked nose and a fragile frame that looks as if it's supported only by hollow bones. Her pageboy hairstyle is white now.

Ana stands on their steps in her cloth coat, clutching her suitcase like a middle-aged orphan. Keller opens the door and she busses him on the cheek.

She smells of alcohol.

"Your room's all made up," Keller says.

"Oh, and I was thinking manger."

"I can throw some straw in there if you'd like," Marisol says.

She just might have some, Keller thinks. Mari has been in a frenzy of preparation, decorating the house with the traditional red poinsettias, laying out a *nacimiento*, a nativity scene, and buying special food like salted cod for the *bacalao*. Now she moves between the kitchen and the dining room, setting plates and glasses, stirring food, sipping wine all the time and chatting with Ana.

Then she and Ana head out for the midnight Mass.

"Althea is meeting us there," Marisol says to Keller. "Are you sure you don't want to come?"

"I'll take a pass."

"No cheating and getting into the *ponche* before we get back," she says.

"I won't." Although it smells great—the pulped fruit, cinnamon and rum simmering on the stove. That and the turkey and the ham in the oven. Marisol has gone all out; they'll be eating leftovers until Groundhog Day.

"You won't forget to baste the turkey, will you?" she asks. "We'll say hello to the baby Jesus for you."

He hits the *ponche* two seconds after they're out the door.

It hits back a little, it's as good as it smelled.

Keller is just sitting down to watch *It's a Wonderful Life* when the doorbell rings and it's Hidalgo.

"Damn," Hidalgo says.

"What?"

"I forgot my bulletproof vest."

"Won't matter," Keller says, "women shoot for the head. You want some *ponche*?"

"I want a lot of *ponche*," Hidalgo says. "Jesus, it smells good in here."

"Mari's been making tamales all week."

"Isn't it past your bedtime, boss?" Keller is a famously early riser, equally famous for being one of the first in the office every morning.

"As a matter of fact."

"Hey, if you want to take a nap, I'll maintain the surveillance."

Smart-ass.

"What's on TV?" Hidalgo asks. He grabs a glass of punch and sits down. "Oh, yeah. I like this one. So where are the sister wives?"

"Mass. Get all the jokes out of your system now, Hugo."

"Do we have that much time?" Hidalgo says.

"Another thing," Keller says. "No shop talk tonight."

"You got it," Hidalgo says. "But before the shop talk ban goes into effect, we've been running down the intel on Damien Tapia."

"And?"

"The reporter lady is right," Hidalgo says. "Tapia's been seen around Tristeza. He was spotted there that night with the Renterías. The word is GU was moving smack both for Sinaloa and Damien."

"You think they had the balls to fuck Sinaloa?"

"There's old grudges, right?" Hidalgo asks. "Weren't you there when Damien's father got killed?"

"You pull my file, Hugo?"

"Agency lore, boss," Hidalgo says. "So maybe the Renterías have rediscovered their old Tapia roots and are working with the kid."

"Maybe," Keller says. "But I don't like him for the student killings. Damien Tapia doesn't have the weight to do that on his own. Someone else gave the word."

"Who?" Hidalgo asks. "As far as we know the Young Wolf is unassociated."

"I don't know," Keller says. "Keep working it. Only not tonight. And don't say anything to this reporter."

"I thought she was your friend."

"She is." And I wish to hell she'd stay out of this.

He's already lost too many friends.

The women come back singing.

They stand on the steps like carolers and sing *villancicos*. Or at least try to, between gulps of laughter.

Althea looks lovely.

Has aged, as they say, gracefully. Her ash-blond hair is cut short, her blue eyes shine behind glasses tilted low on her long aquiline nose. Keller had forgotten how beautiful she is, and only now remembers, as he watches her sing, that she had been determined to become fluent in Spanish when they lived in Mexico.

She looks up at him and smiles.

The song ends and the three women start into the Spanish version of "Silent Night."

Noche de paz, noche de amor,
Todo duerme en derredor . . .

It's soft and beautiful and it takes Keller back to a Christmas, God, thirty years ago, the last Christmas Eve he spent with his family, back when things were good, just before Ernie was killed, and it was on that Christmas Eve that Althea took the kids and left him in Guadalajara because she was scared for them and for herself.

Entre sus astros que esparcen su luz,
Bella anunciando al niñito Jesús . . .

There were children singing *villancicos* in the street outside their house that night, when he'd kissed Althea and put her and their kids in a cab to the airport, thinking they'd be together again soon, either in Mexico or back in the States. And he'd spent Christmas Day with the Hidalgos and watched little Hugo open his presents, and it was just a few days later that Ernie was kidnapped and tortured and murdered and the world grew dark and Keller never got back with Althea, never got back to his family.

Brilla la estrella de paz,
Brilla la estrella de paz.

The song ends and there's a moment of perfect silence.
Perfect stillness.
Timelessness.
Then Keller says, "Come on in."

Other guests arrive.
It turns out that Marisol has invited everyone she knows and anyone she has seen over the past few weeks, so there are people from her charities and boards, people from the Mexican embassy, waiters from their favorite restaurants, bookstore clerks, the dry cleaners, neighbors . . .
Keller recognizes most, but not all, of the guests in his home.
Essentially a loner, he's surprised to find that he doesn't hate it and is actually having sort of a good time.
The food is fantastic.

When most Americans think of Mexican food, they think about burritos and tacos filled with chicken, beef or pork, smothered in cheese and refried beans, but Keller knows that Mexican cooking is far more varied, sophisticated and subtle.

The turkey in mole sauce is delicious, but Keller really digs into the *romeritos en revoltijo*—shrimp, potatoes and *nopales* with rosemary cooked in a sauce of ancho, mulato and pasilla chiles, almonds, cinnamon, onions and garlic.

The *bacalao* is a traditional Christmas dish. Marisol had soaked the salted cod for an entire day, then peeled the skin and deboned the fish; deseeded and peeled the ancho chiles and blended them with fresh tomatoes. Then she'd filled the house with a tantalizing aroma as she simmered the sauce with bay leaf, cinnamon, red peppers, olives, and capers. Then she added potatoes and topped it all with *chiles güeros*.

But Christmas isn't Christmas without tamales.

Marisol has stuffed the corn husks with pork, beef and chicken ("Only dark meat, please, Arturo, the breasts get too dry"), but she has also made some in the Oaxacan style, wrapping plantain leaves around chicken and onions, poblano peppers and chocolate.

If that weren't enough, a big pot of pozole sits simmering on the stovetop and there's a large bowl of *ensalada de Nochebuena*—lettuce, beets, apples, carrots, orange slices, pineapple chunks, jicama, pecan, peanuts and pomegranate seeds.

For dessert, Marisol has made stacks of *buñuelos* sprinkled with sugar, but as most of the guests are Mexican, and no Mexican would arrive at someone's door empty-handed, there are also *roscas de reyes,* rice pudding, *tres leches* cakes, *polvorones de canela* and flan.

Certainly no one goes hungry, and no one is thirsty, either.

There's steaming apple cider and hot chocolate for the nondrinkers, and *rompope*—rum-laced eggnog—and the *ponche navideño* for the imbibers. Marisol went to a lot of trouble to find *atole champurrado* ("It goes so well with tamales") and Noche Buena beer, but only the brand brewed by Cuauhtémoc Moctezuma (Keller didn't have the heart to tell her the brewery had been acquired by Heineken).

Standing back a little, forcing himself out of his admittedly dour self, Keller sees that Marisol is in her glory. Her home is full of people, food, drink, talk, laughter. One guest has brought a *bajo sexto* and has found a quiet corner to provide an unobtrusive norteño twelve-string guitar background. Keller notices that his wife is unconsciously swaying to the music even as she's making a point to introduce Hugo to a very pretty young woman Keller thinks he recognizes from Busboys and Poets.

"Matchmaking?" he asks Marisol when she's completed her mission.

"They're perfect for each other," she says. "And it would be nice for him to have someone. Have you talked with Althea?"

"Well, that was seamless. Not yet."

"But you will."

"Yes, Mari, I will."

He bumps into Althea a few minutes later in the hallway as she's coming out of the bathroom.

"Like old times, Art," she says. "It's good to see you."

"You too. I'm sorry about Bob."

"Thank you. He was a good guy."

They stand there in expected awkwardness until Keller asks, "What do you hear from the kids?"

The kids aren't kids, Keller reminds himself—Cassie is thirty-five; Michael, thirty-three—and he missed most of their growing up.

Chasing Adán Barrera.

"Well," Althea says, "Cassie has a guy. Finally. I think this one is serious— she actually takes a little time off from work."

Cassie is a fanatic special-ed elementary-school teacher in the Bay Area. Both the social concern and the fanaticism, Keller thinks, she comes by honestly.

"I don't want to get ahead of myself," Althea says, "but you might be getting a 'save the date' card sometime soon."

"You think she'd want me there?" Keller asks.

Keller had remained as good a father as he could—he supported his kids, put them through college, saw them when he could and when they wanted, but they drifted apart from one another and now they're virtually strangers. A phone call now and then, an email, that's about it. If they've been interested in seeing him, they haven't expressed it.

"Of course," Althea says. "She'll want her father to walk her down the aisle. And we should probably offer to help with the expenses."

"Glad to. Michael?"

"Is being Michael," Althea says. "He's in New York now, or maybe you knew."

"No."

"It's film this time," Althea says. "He's trying to get into a program at NYU, in the meantime he's working as a freelance 'PA,' whatever that is."

"Where's he living?"

"With some friends in Brooklyn," Althea says. "It's all on his Facebook page."

"I'm not communicating with my kids via social media," Keller says.

"It's better than not communicating with them at all," Althea says. "Call him, then."

"I don't have his number."

"Give me your phone."

Keller hands her his phone and she punches a bunch of keys. "Now you do. Call him, he'd love to hear from you."

"No, he wouldn't, Althie."

"He was hurt," she says. "You just disappeared into that place you go. He was left with this distant, hero father who was off doing noble things, so he didn't even have the comfort of resenting his abandonment without feeling guilty."

"I thought it was better if I didn't come in and out of your lives."

"Maybe it was," Althea says. "Call the kids, make inconsequential small talk, that sort of thing."

"Yeah."

"You did good with Marisol," Althea says. "She's wonderful."

"I married up."

"Twice now."

"That's true," Keller says.

"No, I'm happy for you, Art."

"Thank you."

"And try to *be* happy, would you?" Althea says. "Not all the world's problems are your fault."

"How about you? Are you happy?"

"Right now some *tres leches* cake would make me happy," she says, and then squeezes past him. "Call the kids."

It's around three in the morning when Marisol hands out the sparklers and leads the remaining guests out into the street in a relatively drunken little parade.

"The neighbors are going to call the cops," Keller says.

"Most of the neighbors are here," Marisol says, "and so are the cops. I invited at least three of them."

"Smart."

"This is *not* my first Nochebuena. And look." She juts her chin to where Hugo is standing with his arm around the young woman from the bookstore. "Do I know what I'm doing or no?"

"They're not walking down the aisle quite yet."

"You wait."

Althea comes over and hugs Marisol. "I'm going to head out. Thank you for the best night I've had in quite some time."

"It wouldn't have been half as nice without you."

"She's a keeper, Art," Althea says. "Try to keep her, huh?"

Keller watches her walk down the street, twirling a sparkler.

The sun is almost up when the last of the guests totter away. Marisol stands in the living room and says, "Maybe we could just burn the place down?"

"Let's burn it down in the morning," Keller says.

"It *is* morning," says Ana.

"Regardless, I'm going to bed," Marisol says. "Good night, my loved ones."

Keller tries to sleep in but it doesn't work. Mari is completely out when he gets up, goes into his study and picks up the phone.

He calls Cassie first.

She was always the softer one, the more forgiving. "Cassie Keller."

"Cassie, it's Dad."

"Is Mom okay?"

"Everyone's fine," Keller says. "I just called to say hello. Merry Christmas."

A brief silence, then, "Well, hello and Merry Christmas back."

"I know it's been too long."

She tries to wait him out, but then says, "So how are you?"

"Good, I'm good," Keller says. "So Mom told me you're serious about some guy."

"Don't start going all 'Dad' on me now."

"But is it true?"

"Yeah, I guess it's pretty true," Cassie says.

"Well, that's nice," Keller says. "Does he have a name?"

"David."

"What does David do?"

"He teaches."

"At your school?" Keller asks.

"Yup."

"Well, that's nice."

"Are you going to keep saying that?" Cassie asks. "'That's nice'?"

"I guess I don't know what else to say. Sorry."

"No, it's 'nice,'" Cassie says. "You should meet him sometime."

"I'd like that."

"Me too."

They talk for a couple more minutes—inconsequential small talk—and then agree that he'll call her next week. Keller has several sips of coffee before he hits Michael's number.

It goes to voice mail. "*It's Michael. You know what to do.*"

"Michael, it's your dad. Don't worry, everything is fine. I just called to say Merry Christmas. Call me back if you want."

Ten minutes later his phone rings.

It's Michael.

Keller can picture him sitting there trying to decide what to do. He's glad he decided to call back and tells him so.

"Yeah, well, I hesitated," Michael says.

"I can understand that."

"I mean, at first I thought maybe it's my birthday or something," Michael says, "and then I realized that it wasn't, it was Jesus's."

I deserve that, Keller thinks.

He keeps his mouth shut.

"So what's up?" Michael says.

"Just what I said. I wanted to say hello, see how you are."

"I'm good," Michael says. "How are you?"

"Yeah, good."

Silence.

Keller knows Michael is waiting for him to make the next move and that he's perfectly capable of waiting forever, the stubbornness also being part of his DNA. So Keller says, "Listen, the next day or so, I could hop on the Acela and be up there in three hours."

Silence, then—

"Look, no offense," Michael says, "but I'm pretty busy right now. I'm on a shoot. It's just an industrial, but work is work, and I can't afford to blow off this connection."

"No, of course not."

Michael's soft side gets the better of him. "You're okay, though, right?"

"Yeah, I'm good."

"Okay. Well . . ."

"Next time," Keller says, "I'll call, give you more notice."

"That'd be great."

It's a start, Keller thinks, clicking off. He gets that his son is too proud to make peace on the first offer. But it's a start.

Marisol comes down a couple of hours later looking the worse for wear. "If you really loved me, you'd shoot me. Oops, I suppose that was in bad taste, I take it back. Merry Christmas, Arturo."

"Merry Christmas," Keller says. "I called Cassie and Michael."

"How did that go?"

"Cassie good, Michael not so much," Keller says. He tells her about his spurned offer to go up to New York. "I got what I deserved. He's a proud kid, he handed me my head. You know what? Good for him."

"It's going to take a little time," she says. "But he'll come back to you, you'll see."

Wrong holiday anyway, Keller thinks, that's Easter.

Not everything comes back.

He's seen the end-of-year statistics—28,647 people died from heroin and opioid overdoses in 2014.

Forty-nine kids in Mexico on buses.

In the US, 28,647 from dope.

None of them are coming back.

And you're failing in your job.

"I love you but I'm going back to bed," Marisol says.

"Yeah, actually I'm going into the office."

"It's Christmas Day."

"Then it will be good and quiet," Keller says. "I'll be back before you're up."

He drives himself over to Arlington, goes into the office and pores over the intelligence gathered about Tristeza.

Because he knows they're missing something.

He goes back through history—the last time innocent people were taken off a bus and murdered was in 2010 when the Zetas stopped a bus coming up Highway 1 and killed everyone on board in the mistaken belief that they were recruits for the Gulf cartel.

Could that have happened in Tristeza?

If it was Guerreros Unidos, could they have thought that the students were Los Rojos? Maybe, but how could they have made that mistake? Veteran traffickers like GU couldn't possibly have thought that a bunch of vaguely lefty kids on a spree were nascent narcos.

Or could there be some reality to it? Could a few of the students have been involved with Los Rojos and GU killed them all to make sure they got the "guilty" ones?

Back it up, Keller thinks.

GU and Los Rojos are fighting over who supplies heroin to Sinaloa. Damien Tapia may be involved with GU. Tapia was seen with the Renterías in the vicinity of the Tristeza bus station, so . . .

Jesus Christ, he thinks, we've been focused on the wrong thing.

We've been focusing on the students, when . . .

He calls Hugo.

"Jesus, boss, it's Christmas."

"It's not about the students," Keller says. "It's about the buses."

There was heroin on the buses.

Three days after Christmas, on the Día de los Santos Inocentes, Rafael Caro makes his own breakfast in the kitchen of his home in Badiraguato.

The stove, fueled by propane, has four burners. A pot with the pozole sits on one, a pan for his mornings eggs on another, an old coffeepot on the third. Caro sits at the folding kitchen table in his denim shirt and an old pair of khakis, a blue baseball cap jammed on his head even though he's indoors. He eats his eggs and thinks about Arturo Keller.

Keller, the same man who put him in hell for twenty years, is causing him hell again, putting enormous pressure on everyone because of this Tristeza thing. At a moment when the business is on the edge of chaos, Caro thinks, when we most need to be left in quiet to work things out, Keller is all over us again.

Will the man ever just die?

He's provoked a major investigation, and who knows where that will lead? Already, it's led Caro to a tough decision—he has to shut down the GU heroin pipeline to Ruiz. At least the fifteen kilos got through and reached their connection in New York. That's good, but it's too dangerous now to continue.

They'll have to make other arrangements. Ariela Palomas has to keep her stupid fucking mouth shut, and the Rentería brothers . . . How could they be so stupid as to let a bunch of students . . . kids . . . hijack a bus full of *chiva*?

"Bring Tilde in," Caro says to the young man sitting at the kitchen table. The young man, Caro's sole employee, who drives him around on an old Indian motorcycle and goes to the *tienda* for beans, tortillas, meat, eggs and beer, goes out and returns a moment later with Tilde Rentería.

Caro juts his chin at the empty wooden chair.

Tilde sits down.

"You were careless," Caro says.

"I'm sorry."

"You're 'sorry'?" Caro says. "I had to order the deaths of forty-nine young people—children—and you're 'sorry'?"

"You gave the order," Tilde says, "but I did the killing."

"What would happen," Caro asks, "if Ricardo Núñez found out that you moved heroin stolen from him? That you're allied with Damien? That you're in business in El Norte with Eddie Ruiz? What would happen?"

"A war."

"You're not ready for a war with Sinaloa," Caro says. "You cannot win a war with Sinaloa, but that's not the main point. The main point is that wars are *bad for business*."

And not part of his plan, which is to destroy the Sinaloa cartel without ever fighting it. To make it destroy itself.

"Here's what's going to happen now," Caro says. "The federal police will get an anonymous tip where you are and they will stage a raid. You and your brothers will surrender. Then, under interrogation, you will confess to the murders of those students."

"Is this a joke?" Tilde asks.

Today is the Day of the Innocents, which memorializes Herod's slaughter of the newborn babies in Bethlehem and has become Mexico's version of April Fool's Day, replete with practical jokes.

"Am I laughing?" Caro asks.

"That's a life sentence!"

"It's better than a death sentence, no?" Caro asks. He had thought of simply killing the Renterías—it would be simple enough to have the *federales* shoot them during the raid—but it would destroy relationships with the old Tapia organization. "You confess, and you tell your Los Rojos story and shut down this investigation. You get life, you serve twenty years, when you get out you're still a relatively young man."

"I can't do twenty years."

"I did," Caro says.

And I was a lot older when I got out than you'll be, Caro thinks.

"With all respect," Tilde says, "you aren't the boss. You're, what shall we say . . . a revered uncle who gives us the benefit of his advice."

"And as your revered uncle," Caro says, "I strongly suggest that you take my advice. I'm loaning you your life, Rentería. Take it today and I can never take it back."

Another Día de los Santos Inocentes tradition—you don't have to return anything someone loans you on this day.

"We can wait until after the holidays if you want," Caro says.

He stares Tilde down.

Tilde gets the message and leaves.

Fuck him, Caro thinks.

He's nothing.

And fuck Art Keller.

He gave me twenty years in a freezing hell.

I'll have to find a gift for him.

One he can't return.

The bells rings and Marisol pops the last grape into her mouth.

It's a New Year's Eve tradition—you pop twelve grapes, *las doce uvas de la suerte*, in your mouth—one for each chime of the bells—and it brings you good luck for the upcoming year.

So now Ana rings the bell and Marisol swallows grapes. Then she holds a spoon of lentils out for Keller. "Come on."

"I don't like lentils."

"It's for luck. You have to!"

Keller swallows the lentils.

Marisol's gone almost as nuts for New Year's Eve as she did for Christmas. As befits Mexican tradition, every light in the house is on; she did a thorough cleaning, making sure to sweep from the inside out; and the place still smells of cinnamon from her heating the spice in water and then mopping with the scented mixture. Then they went upstairs, opened the bathroom window and tossed a bucket of water out into the street.

In all of this, Ana has been her enthusiastic confederate, insisting with her that they all write down their "negative thoughts"—everything bad that has happened over the past year—on a piece of paper that they will burn to ensure that the bad things don't follow them into the new year.

I wish it were that easy, Keller thinks, but he did write down the numbers 49 and 28,647, *Denton Howard, John Dennison, Guatemala,* and *Tristeza,* and now he sets a match to the paper and burns it.

"What did you write?" he asks Mari.

"I can't tell!" she says, burning her own paper.

New Year's Eve, Ric thinks, is always an occasion for wretched bacchanalian excess among Los Hijos.

But Iván has really maxed it out this year.

He's bought out the entire rooftop Skybar at Splash, the newest and most exclusive strip club in Cabo. His security team—and Ric's—are there in full force in case Elena wants to balance the books before the end of the fiscal year.

Splash's "butlers," long-legged, gorgeous women clad only in G-strings, give them private service, bottles of Dom and Cristal and the club's custom cocktails broken up into "sensory elements"—Dirty, Smoky, Sweet, Smooth, Salty, and Spicy.

Ric goes with Smoky, something built on scotch, and sucks on one of the Arturo Fuente Opus X cigars that Iván passed around at $30,000 a box. Bowls of coke—not lines, *bowls*—are set on each table as well as rows of joints—Loud Dream hybrid weed, which goes for about $800 an ounce.

On the stage, six incredibly beautiful women writhe to throbbing techno, each dressed in lingerie that Iván specifically mandated for New Year's Eve, and now he narrates his little pageant, "Okay, each girl has a color—red for passion, yellow for prosperity, green for health, pink for friendship, orange for luck, and white for peace."

None of them are dressed in black.

Black is bad luck for New Year's.

Which is why, of course, Belinda is wearing a slinky black dress, a defiant *fuck you* to tradition and fear. She's the only woman invited to the party; wives and mistresses—other than La Fósfora—have been banned, and Ric's wife, Karin, is not happy that he's chosen to spend New Year's Eve with Los Hijos instead of her.

The fuck does she want? Ric thinks. Earlier that night, Iván had paid a multiple-Grammy-winning recording artist and his band to give a private concert for all the families over dinner at Casiano. Karin got her picture taken with the singer and everything. Then Ric dropped a gold necklace into her champagne glass over dessert. He'd seen the midnight in with her, even gulping down the twelve dumb grapes. And now she's sitting it out in a suite with a balcony overlooking the ocean, so what the fuck more does the bitch want?

"It's work," he told her.

"Work?" Karin asked. "Are you kidding me right now?"

No, he wasn't.

The New Year's Eve party was Iván reaching out to him. Things had been tense between them since Ric's dad took over and then awarded Baja to Elena. So this was Iván saying he wanted to put that aside and pick up the friendship again. So, yeah, it was personal, but it was business, too, mending fences, serving as his father's ambassador to an important wing of the cartel.

"So you're the *jefe* of La Paz now, huh?" Iván asked Ric when he called to invite him.

"Come on, man."

"No, I think it's good," Iván said. "You staked out a claim and backed it up. Laid-back Mini-Ric, getting all intense. Except they don't call you Mini-Ric anymore, do they? It's 'El Ahijado.'"

"Yeah, that's me," Ric said, trying to make light of it.

"Your father's grooming you for bigger things," Iván said.

"My father," Ric said, "thinks I'm a waste of space."

"Not anymore he doesn't," Iván says. "Not after what you did in La Paz."

"That was more Belinda."

"You still fucking that crazy bitch?" Iván asked. "Be careful, 'mano, I've heard you can catch crazy through your dick. No, you're a big deal now, Ric. A rock star."

"I'm just trying to help my father," Ric said. "That's all."

"The godson doesn't want to be the godfather?" Iván asked. "What kind of shitty movie is that?"

"Actually, that *was* the movie."

"And look how it turned out."

"It was a *movie*, Iván." First Belinda, now Iván, Ric thought. Why is everyone trying to push me into a chair I don't want?

So when Karin got all twisted about him "dumping" her on New Year's Eve, Ric said, "I have to make things up with Iván. If I spurn his invitation, he'll be offended."

"But it doesn't matter if I'm offended."

"It's business, baby," Ric said.

"It's an excuse to get high and fuck whores."

Yeah, pretty much, Ric thinks as he watches the girls dance. He's higher than shit from the blow, the weed, the booze—even the cigar—and he's reasonably sure they're going to end up fucking some whores. What do you want for New Year's, he asks himself—passion, prosperity, health, friendship, luck, or peace?

Iván is going to leave it to fate. Holding up a fedora hat he says, "There's six pieces of paper in here. Each one with a color that matches a girl. You draw the paper out of the hat, and that's who you get."

The girls take it up a level. Shedding the lingerie tops, they start writhing against each other, kissing and feeling each other up.

"This is heaven," Belinda says.

Ric laughs—she's sitting there with a cigar jammed into her mouth, ogling the dancers like some horny guy. It's her and Iván, Oviedo, Alfredo, and Rubén—just six of them, one for each girl.

An empty place, replete with a bottle of Dom and a cigar, has been set for Sal.

Ric turns to Belinda. "Are you going to get jealous if I have another girl?"

"Are you going to get jealous if *I* do?"

Ric shakes his head. "Gaby will be pissed."

"You see her here?"

"No."

"Neither do I," Belinda says, clasping her hands together.

"What are you doing?" Ric asks.

"Praying for peace."

Ric doesn't blame her—the chick in white is hot. Long, shiny black hair that flows down to a bubble butt. Himself, he's kind of hoping he pulls green—health is always a good thing and the blonde has full, blow-job lips and a rack he could lie down and die on.

"Ladies first," Iván says, standing in front of Belinda. She reaches up, puts her hand in the hat and comes out with a white slip of paper. "Yes!"

Oviedo pulls pink.

Alfredo gets yellow.

Rubén, damn it, pulls the green slip.

"*Awww*," Belinda says to Ric. "*Pobrecito.*"

Ric reaches in and gets red.

"Passion," Belinda says.

His girl is certainly sexy enough, Ric thinks. The same thick black hair as Belinda's, long legs and beautiful tits.

"I get lucky!" Iván announces as he pulls the orange paper.

The girls come down from the stage in a line and then kneel in front of their respective clients.

"Passion" kneels in front of Ric and unzips his fly. Her mouth feels incredible on him. He glances over to see Belinda's head thrown back and her hands on the back of her girl's head, pressing her face into her crotch. Then her hands fly to the sides of the chair and grip the arms, her knuckles white.

Iván . . . well, Iván's gotten lucky.

He climaxes with a shout. "*¡Madre de Dios!* That was so good, I'm going to give you my car, *mamacita*!"

The party goes on.

The blow, the weed, the booze, the women.

At some point, Ric passes out.

Wakes up to gunfire.

Next to him, Belinda laps at one of the dancers like a kitten with a bowl of warm milk. Rubén is unconscious, his left arm dangling off the side of a chair, lightly resting on a beer bottle. The Esparza brothers are standing at the edge of the roof, firing AKs into the air.

There's no Rudolfo to ask them to stop.

Ric doesn't really give a fuck and tries to go back to sleep but the gunfire won't let him. Then he opens his eyes to see Lucky, dressed now in a black T-shirt over jeans and high heels, walk over to Iván.

"Can I have the car?" she asks.

Iván lowers his rifle. "What?"

"You said you'd give me your car."

Iván laughs. "You seriously think I'm going to give you a seventy-five-thousand-dollar Porsche for a blow job?"

"It's what you said."

Shit, Ric thinks. He tumbles off the couch, gets up and walks over.

"Get the fuck out of here, *conchuda estúpida*," Iván says. He raises the AK to his shoulder again and fires a clip into the air.

But Lucky is stubborn. She stands there looking at him.

"Are you still here?" Iván asks, lowering the rifle. "What about 'get the fuck out of here' don't you understand?"

"You said a car."

"Do you believe this gash?" Iván asks Ric. Then he looks at the girl. "Let me ask you something. We know you can suck, but can you suck the bullets out of a gun before I can pull the trigger? Come on, let's see."

He puts the rifle barrel to her mouth and pushes. "Open, bitch."

Ric says, "Come on, man."

Iván is coked out of his mind. "Stay out of this."

"You're high, Iván," Ric says. "You don't want to do this."

"Don't tell me what I want to do."

The woman is terrified. She's shaking as she opens her mouth around the barrel and Iván pushes it down, forcing her to her knees. "Suck the bullets out, *puta,* before I pull the trigger."

Ric sees a stream of urine run down her legs.

Oviedo laughs. "She's pissing herself!"

Everyone is looking now, stunned. But no one moves.

"You still want my car?" Iván asks.

She shakes her head and says no.

"I can't understand you with your mouth full," Iván says.

"Enough, Iván," Ric says.

"Fuck you." Iván looks back down at the woman. "I'm not sure what you said, but I think you said, 'I'm a stupid, worthless whore, so please do me a favor and put me out of my misery.' Is that right?"

He moves the rifle barrel up and down so it forces the woman to nod.

"See?" Iván says. "She wants to die."

Ric doesn't know how it happens but suddenly his pistol is out and pointed at Iván's head. "Enough."

Oviedo and Alfredo point their guns at Ric.

Iván's gunmen start to move in.

So do Ric's.

Iván looks at Ric and smiles. "So it's like that, El Ahijado? Over a fucking whore?"

"Let her go, man."

"You're a tough guy now?"

Ric can feel all the guns pointed at him. In a fraction of a second, any one of these guys could decide to pull the trigger to save his boss. There could be a bloodbath here any moment. "I'll take you with me, Iván."

Iván stares at him, his eyes looking through him.

Then he slowly pulls the rifle barrel from the woman's mouth, lowers his gun, reaches out and pulls Ric into an embrace. "Together forever, then, huh? *¡Los Hijos siempre! ¡Feliz Año Nuevo a todos!*"

Iván pulls Ric closer and whispers into his ear, "Who thought you had the balls? But you ever pull a gun on me again, *'mano,* and I will kill you."

He lets Ric go.

Ric watches Lucky struggle to her feet and walk toward the elevator on shaky legs. No one goes near her; none of the other women go up to her.

She's a leper.

He follows her. "Hey."

She turns around. Her eyes are scared and angry, her hair disheveled; the lipstick smeared around her mouth makes her look like a clown.

Ric digs into the pocket of his jeans, pulls out a set of keys and tosses them to her. "It's an Audi, not a Porsche, but it's a good car. Only thirty thousand miles on it."

She stares at him, unsure what to do.

"Take it," Ric says. "Take the car."

The elevator opens and she gets in.

Ric walks back to the party.

Iván saw what he did.

He shakes his head, smirks, and says, "You're a sucker, Ric."

Maybe so, Ric thinks.

Anyway, happy New Year.

Damien Tapia sits in the lead car of a convoy that snakes through the mountain switchbacks of backcountry Sinaloa.

Ten vehicles with fifty heavily armed men, funded by the fifteen keys of heroin he sent to Eddie Ruiz. Like Damien, all the men are dressed in black—black shirts or sweatshirts, black jeans, black shoes—boots or sneakers. Some are already wearing black hoods, others have them in their laps.

Damien tightens the scarf around his neck against the predawn chill. The sky is just changing from pitch black to slate gray but he hasn't allowed the drivers to turn on headlights even though the roads carved out of the mountain face are narrow and a slip of the wheel could send a vehicle plummeting a hundred feet straight down.

It's essential that the convoy isn't spotted, that the raid is a total surprise.

Which it should be, on New Year's Eve.

Damien is about to announce his presence in a major way. The Young Wolf is on the hunt and about to howl for everyone to hear.

You have to harden your heart, Damien has discovered. When he first found out that Palomas ordered the killing of those kids to cover up his heroin shipment, Damien was dismayed. He couldn't eat or sleep, his stomach hurt. His imagination tortured him with vivid pictures of the dead students, of bodies smoldering on the garbage pile. He thought about turning himself in and confessing. He even thought about killing himself, putting a gun to his head and pulling the trigger.

"Is that what your father would want?" Tío Rafael asked him.

Damien had gone to the old man's house to get his advice. He didn't know where else to go—his father was dead, his friends were no longer his friends—he couldn't very well talk to Iván or Ric or even Rubén.

"You're safe," Caro said. "No one can connect you to what happened at Tristeza."

"But I'm tortured by it."

"You feel guilty."

"Yes, Tío."

"Let me ask you," Caro said, "did you kill those students?"

"No."

"No," Caro said. "All you did, *sobrino*, was put some product on that bus. You put your trust in the Renterías and they let you down. But you are not responsible for the deaths of those young people."

To his shame, Damien broke down and cried.

Wept in front of Rafael Caro.

But Caro just sat there and waited for Damien to quiet.

"This business of ours," Caro said, "gives much and demands much. It offers great rewards and terrible losses. It allows us to do wonderful things but at times it forces us to do terrible things. If we accept one, we have to accept the other. Let me ask you, do you have enough money to live?"

"Yes."

"Your mother, your sisters, they have money to live?"

"Yes."

"Then perhaps you should leave this alone," Caro said. "Let the dead bury the dead and live your life."

"I can't."

"Then know," Caro said, "that you have to accept both sides of this thing. Enjoy the rewards, accept the losses, do the terrible things you sometimes have to do. Never shed blood you don't have to, but when you have to, harden your heart and do it."

Now Damien sees the narrow valley below and the hacienda almost hidden beneath the opposite ridge. The house is more modest than he'd expected, smaller than he remembered from the times he came here as a boy. The walls of the single-story building have been freshly painted pink, the roof recently redone with terra-cotta tiles. Several outbuildings sit on the valley floor below—a servants' cottage, Damien thinks, a garage, and a tin-roofed barracks for the guards.

A little farther down the valley, Damien knows, is a thin airstrip and a hangar for a small plane.

Looking through a nightscope, Damien sees that only one guard is on duty, standing by a small charcoal fire and stamping his feet against the cold. His rifle is slung over the shoulder of his fatigue jacket, and he wears a wool knit cap pulled low over his head.

Damien forces himself not to wonder if the man has a wife, a family. Children. Forces himself not to think that this man has a life that he's about to take.

The Young Wolf has never killed before.

Elena pulls the old quilt up over her shoulders and tries to go back to sleep.

The rooster won't let her.

A longtime urbanite now, Elena has grown unused to country sounds— the braying donkeys, the rasping crows, the incessant braggadocio of this goddamn rooster. How anyone can sleep through this cacophony is a mystery to her, and indeed, she hears her mother shuffling in the hallway, noisily trying to be quiet.

How many times has Elena tried to convince her to move to a more comfortable situation in the city, to one of the many condos or houses the family owns in Culiacán, Badiraguato, Tijuana, even Cabo? But the stubborn old lady steadfastly refuses to leave the only home she's known for her entire life. She will come for visits (albeit with less frequency now; she just changed her mind and decided she wouldn't come up to Tijuana for the holidays, forcing Elena to make the tiresome trip all the way out here) and she will make annual pilgrimages to her sons' tombs, but she insists on living out here, saying simply, "*Yo soy una campesina.*"

Elena has never quite believed her mother's I'm-just-a-peasant act. Surely she must be aware that the family has billions of dollars, that her late sons were the lords of a vast drug empire. She must have some notion why she is a "*campesina*" with a platoon of armed guards, a "peasant" with her own private airstrip.

But she never speaks of it, dresses in a black frock, shawl, and veil and refuses all entreaties to have the house enlarged, remodeled, made more comfortable. It was a struggle to get her to accept the badly needed paint job (and then she insisted on this hideous pink) and the new roof, even when water was running down into the living room during the rainy season and Elena had to give her a stern lecture on the dangers of mold, especially to old lungs.

And now she is up, always before dawn, as if she had breakfast to cook for a farmer husband, and at times Elena wants to scream at her, *Yes, your family were farmers, they grew poppies.*

And now she and her mother have something terrible in common.

They both mourn sons.

And, Elena thinks as she gets out of bed (What's the point of lying awake?), that weak, smarmy lawyer bastard Núñez scolds me for retaliating. He hasn't *seen* retaliation. She pulls on her robe. She's going to destroy them and all their families. Burn their homes, their farms, their ranches, their bones, and scatter the ashes to the cold north wind.

The thought warms her.

Then she hears gunfire.

Damien squeezes the trigger.

The guard falls into the fire, raising a small cloud of smoke and dust.

Pulling the hood over his head, Damien gives a hand signal and the vehicles roar down into the valley and race toward the hacienda as guards tumble out of the barracks and open fire. But his men—well-paid, highly trained veterans—return fire from the vehicles and the guards run back into the shelter of the barracks.

Pumped, Damien hops out of the car and walks to the front door of the hacienda. He's surprised that it's unlocked, but then again, if you're Adán Barrera's mother you probably don't have to think about locking your door.

A maid, maybe a cook, stands looking shocked. Then she fumbles in her apron and takes out a cell phone. Damien rips it out of her hand and shoves her against a wall. She screams, "*¡Señora! ¡Señora!* Run away!"

Señora? Damien thinks as he puts his hand around the maid's mouth and drags her back into the kitchen. Barrera's mother wasn't supposed to be here, she was supposed to be visiting family in Tijuana. The plan was to burn down Adán Barrera's childhood home, not to hurt his mother. Men have already come in behind him, torching window curtains.

"Wait!" Damien yells, letting go of the cook. "Stop! The old lady is here!" It's too late.

Flames crawl up the curtains into the ceiling. Out the window, Damien sees the servants' quarters going up, the barracks. His men are driving cars and motorcycles out of the garage as its roof is engulfed in fire.

He turns back and sees an old woman in black staring at him.

"Get out," she yells. "Get out of my house!"

A younger woman comes up behind her, takes her by the shoulders and moves her out of the way. "If you hurt my mother, if there is as much as a bruise on her body . . . Do you know who I am? Do you know whose house this is?"

Damien remembers her from when he was a kid.

Tía Elena.

"You weren't supposed to be here," Damien says, feeling stupid.

"Elena, make them go!" the old woman yells.

Smoke starts to fill the room.

"You have to get out," Damien says. "Now."

"Brave men," Elena spits in his face. "Burning an old woman out of her home."

Damien hears one of his men say, "Shoot the bitches!"

"Go!" Damien yells. He grabs Elena by the shoulder of her robe and pulls her toward the door. She won't let go of her mother and they make an awkward knot as Damien pivots behind them and pushes them out the door.

Elena wraps her arm around her mother to try to protect her from the wind and the chilly morning air.

But her mother fights her, tries to go back. "My house! My house!"

"We have to go, Mami!"

Elena doesn't know if her mother can even hear her over the noise—the wind, the men shouting, the servants screaming as they run across the open ground, the *pop-pop-pop* of gunfire and the crackle of flames. Crazily, she thinks, she hears the chickens. Not the rooster—it's finally stopped crowing—but the frantic cackling of the hens as they run around like . . . well, chickens. "Mami, can you walk?!"

"Yes!"

Elena keeps one arm around her mother's thin shoulders, the other hand gently pushing her head down as scant protection against the bullets zipping past, and then she hears one of their men holler, "Stop shooting! Cease fire! *¡Las señoras!*"

A *sicario* runs out of the barracks toward her, but a burst of gunfire cuts him and he falls in the dirt a few yards from her feet, arches his neck up and yells, "*Señora*, go!"

The scene around her, lit red by fire, is insanity. Men in flames, human torches, stagger, scream and fall.

The airstrip is too far, Elena thinks. Her mother can't make it. And who knows if these bastards have already taken it, and the plane, if the pilot is in his quarters or even alive. But she knows she can't stay here—she doesn't know who these men are. They could just be incredibly stupid robbers, or they could be Iván's.

But she can't stay to find out.

To be kidnapped and held for ransom.

Or raped.

Or murdered.

Or just accidentally shot in this chaos.

The airstrip is her best chance.

She lowers her head and keeps moving.

Fausto sees her.

Damien's right-hand man spots Elena Sánchez, dressed only in a robe, walking a woman who can only be Adán Barrera's mother away from the burning compound. He guns the Jeep through the circus of motorcycle riders and pulls up alongside the two women. "Get in!"

"Leave us alone!" Elena says.

Fausto aims his pistol at her chest. "I said get into the fucking Jeep!"

Elena helps her mother up and then gets in herself. And, of course, Fausto thinks, plays the do-you-know-who–I-am card.

"Yeah, I know who you are!" Fausto says. He hits the gas and races toward the airstrip.

The plane's propeller is already spinning, the plane taxiing to get the fuck out of there. Fausto pulls in front to block it, raises his AK, aims it at the windscreen and yells, "Not so fast, *cabrón*! You have passengers!"

The plane stops.

Fausto gets out, steps around and helps Elena and her mother down. Then he walks them to the plane, opens the door and says to the pilot, "You were just going to leave them? What kind of coward are you?"

He helps them climb into the plane.

"Why are you doing this?" Elena asks.

Because I'm not a fucking moron, Fausto thinks. Damien can survive—even thrive—from burning down Barrera's home. But hurting Adán Barrera's

sister and mother? That would turn the whole country against him and start
a vendetta that could only end in the kid's death.

And mine.

"Take off!" he yells to the pilot.

For the next two days, Damien's men rampage through the valley, burning
houses and outbuildings, stealing vehicles and generally terrifying the population in an area that had once been perhaps the safest in the world.

It stops only when the federal government sends in troops, but by that
time, Damien's force—now christened Los Lobos in the media—has faded
back into the mountains.

The raid shocks the country.

A little-known upstart attacked *the home of Adán Barrera's mother,* sending her running into the dark.

Maybe the Sinaloa cartel isn't as powerful as everyone thought.

Most people see it for what it is—

Damien Tapia's declaration of war.

The New Year will bring war.

"I'm so glad you're safe," Núñez says over the phone. "And your mother,
she's all right?"

He looks at Ric and rolls his eyes. He has the phone on speaker so Ric and
Belinda can hear Elena say, "She's tranquilized, so she's sleeping now. Yes,
we're here in Ensenada."

"It's outrageous, Elena," Núñez says over the phone. "Totally outrageous."

"Are you 'outraged,' Ricardo? Because I blame you."

"Me?!" Núñez asks, his voice a perfect parody of hurt innocence. "I assure you, I had nothing to do with this! It was all that young Tapia animal.
My God, Elena, he's crowing about it on social media."

"You had everything to do with it," Elena says. "You let someone murder
my son and did nothing; why shouldn't people think that's it all right to
attack us? Your weakness has signaled that it's now possible to commit an
outrage against Sinaloa."

"We don't know who was behind Rudolfo's murder."

"Your son was partying with his killers just last night," Elena says. "Do
you think I don't hear about these things? No, you've left my family on an
island, and now you have the nerve to ring up to express your outrage? Please
forgive if I'm not touched. Or mollified."

"We will do everything in our power to punish Damien Tapia."

"Our power is exactly the issue," Elena says. "People are going to rightly ask, 'If Sinaloa can't protect Adán Barrera's mother, who can it protect? Can it protect us?' If Adán were alive, this young punk's head would be on a spike already. Then again, if Adán were still alive, this young punk would never have had the nerve to do this."

"We're hunting him down."

"The army?" Elena asks. "The army couldn't catch a fish in a bowl. No, thank you, Ricardo—I am admittedly aging but not yet entirely toothless. Our family will deal with young Tapia on our own."

"Don't play into these people's hands," Núñez says. "This is just what they want—to divide us."

"You did that already," Elena says. "Call me when you're ready to act like a real *patrón*. Until then—"

She clicks off.

"You were at a party with Iván last night?" Núñez asks Ric.

"With all the Esparzas," Ric says, not backing down. "And Rubén Ascensión."

"Was that wise, do you think?"

"I'm trying to maintain the relationship."

"By giving your car to a whore?" Núñez asks. "Were you trying to maintain a relationship with her, too?"

He hears about everything, Ric thinks. All my bodyguards double as snitches. "Is that what you wanted to see in the media today, 'Sinaloa Cartel Figure Murders Call Girl'?"

Núñez stares at him for a second, then says, "No, you did the right thing."

Jesus Christ, Ric thinks, that's new.

"You know this Damien," Núñez says.

So do you, Ric thinks. You've known "this Damien" since he was a kid.

"What makes him tick?" Núñez asks. "Why would he do such a terrible thing? Alienated youth? A rebel without a cause?"

No, Ric thinks, I'm pretty sure he has a cause.

"I know that he's your friend," Núñez says. "But you know I have to do something."

Ric does know that his father is in a tough position. The whole Sinaloa organization is furious about the affront to Adán's memory, the insult to the women in the royal family. If the head of the cartel doesn't do something about it, they're going to think that he's weak, maybe not strong enough to be the boss.

But . . .

"I get it," Ric says. "Everyone's running hot right now. But let's remember that Damien didn't kill them. Shit, he had them flown out of there."

"After he burned down the house, killed five of their men and vandalized an entire community that looks to us for security," Núñez says. "I appreciate your loyalty to your friend but—"

"He's probably done now," Ric says. "I know Damien, he's holed up somewhere, as freaked out about what he did as anyone. Let me reach out, bring him in, see if we can work out a way back."

"What are you suggesting?" Núñez asks. "A time-out?"

I don't know what I'm suggesting, Ric thinks. "Maybe a fine, restitution? He apologizes, he rebuilds what he burned down—"

"With what?" Núñez asks. "Where is he going to get that kind of money?"

Well, Ric thinks, he had enough money to recruit a small army. "I'm just saying that people have done worse things and gotten a pass."

"I'm not without feeling," Núñez says, "for this young man's past. But his father was a hotheaded madman addled by drug addiction, and he had to go. Now the son has displayed the same sort of erratic, dangerous behavior. Yielding to pity would be a self-indulgent abdication of our responsibilities."

"Which is your way of saying that you want him dead."

Núñez turns to Belinda, and now Ric gets why she's there.

Dead isn't good enough.

Ric starts the engine. "I'm not doing it."

"Doing what?"

"Torturing a friend, I'm not doing it." He pulls out of the driveway. "And you're not, either."

"You don't tell me what to do," Belinda says. "I take my orders from your father."

Those orders are to find Damien, kill him slowly and painfully, and video it. A lesson must be taught, the world had to be shown that El Abogado is anything but weak.

"And you'll enjoy it, right?" Ric asks.

"It's my job," Belinda says. "What, you think you can save him? If we don't do it, someone else will. What do you think Elena's people will do if they find him first?"

"If I find him first," Ric says, "I'm putting two quick ones in the back of his head."

"Listen to you, the experienced killer all of a sudden," Belinda says. "I mean, are you kidding me right now? We're going to do what the boss says."

Ric pulls the car over, turns and looks at her. "Here's what we're going to do. We're going to look for Damien every place he isn't. We're going to turn over every rock and stone where he's not at. And guess what, Belinda—we're not going to find him."

"You do you," she says, "I'll do me."

Ric does him.

The new version of him, anyway—the engaged, focused, take-charge son-of-the-boss guy who starts running his father's people like they're his own. He sends planes with two hundred *sicarios* to Sinaloa to hunt down Damien and tells them—go find Damien Tapia, and when you do, bring him to *me*.

Intact.

I want to deal with him personally.

Most of them misinterpret this in exactly the way he wants—they think he wants to take Damien apart himself to avenge the insult against his godfather, and they respect him for it.

El Ahijado's stature grows.

Núñez comes on Three Kings Day.

It was only a matter of time, Caro thinks, before one of them showed up. They all will eventually, he knows, it's just a question of who is the first.

Caro meets him in the living room. The sofa is old and overstuffed, the upholstered easy chair one of those Barcaloungers that tilts backward to let an old man nod off to the television.

Núñez resists the impulse to brush off the sofa before he sits down.

The news is on the television. Caro has a small TV in every room—he likes to watch baseball.

Núñez arrived with a *rosca* and set the cake on the kitchen table as if it were a gift of great price—incense, frankincense or myrrh. Caro wonders if it's a message—inside the cake is hidden a little figure of the baby Jesus. Whoever gets that slice has to pay for the food and drink on Candlemas.

"You heard what Damien Tapia did?" Núñez asks.

"Who hasn't?"

"It's outrageous," Núñez says. "I don't want to hurt him, but—"

"But you might have to."

"If I do, I have your blessing?"

"You don't need my blessing," Núñez says. "I'm retired."

"But you still have our respect, Don Rafael," Núñez says. "It's out of respect that I came. You may know that Adán appointed me as his successor. But now I face challenges from Iván Esparza and Elena Sánchez. Not to mention young Damien."

"What do you want from me?" Caro asks. "As you can see, I am a poor old man. I have no power."

"But you have influence," Núñez says. "You are one of a great generation. One of the men who founded our organization. Your name still means something, your approval still means something, your advice and counsel . . . I would very much appreciate your support."

"What support can I give you?" Caro asks. "Did you see *sicarios* outside? Vehicles? Airplanes? Fields of poppies? Labs? You have those things, Núñez, not me."

"If Rafael Caro were to endorse my leadership," Núñez says, "it would carry a lot of weight."

"All you want is my name," Caro says. "Which is all I have left."

"Of course I didn't come empty-handed."

"Besides the *rosca*?" Caro asks. "You brought groceries? *Frijoles*? Rice?"

"You're mocking me," Núñez says. "I know my manner makes me susceptible to ridicule, but I am serious. Adán took everything from you. Perhaps I can restore what he took."

"You can give me twenty years?" Caro asks.

"Of course not," Núñez says. "I didn't mean to presume. What I should have said is that perhaps I could offer partial restitution. Make your remaining years . . . comfortable."

"A new chair?"

"Again, you mock."

"Then stop talking around the subject," Caro says. "If you think I'm for sale, make me an offer."

"A million dollars."

You're more desperate than I thought, Caro thinks. If you'd offered half that, I might have said yes. But a million makes me think that you're losing, and how can I endorse the power of someone who's losing?

"You said you valued my advice," Caro says. "Let me give you some: You're straddling the fence between Iván and Elena. That doesn't make either one loyal to you, it just makes you seem weak. Neither side respects you, neither side fears you. And the Damiens and Ascensiones see that and move on your territory. And you do nothing."

"Ascensión's not moving on my territory."

"He will," Caro says. "He's declared his independence—what does he call his organization? The New Jalisco cartel?"

"Something like that." The Cartel Jalisco Nuevo, CJN.

"He'll become your competitor," Caro says. "If he can do it, what's to stop everyone else? I won't take your money, Núñez, and I won't lend you my name. Here's what I will do for you—I won't endorse anyone else. Unlike you, I can afford to stay neutral, provide an arbitrator if needed. But you, Ricardo, you need to get strong, make them fear you. If you do that, maybe we have more to talk about."

Caro gets up from his chair. "I have to piss now."

It's the Día de los Reyes, Caro thinks as he stands and waits for his water to come, and now there are, indeed, three kings of the Sinaloa cartel. Núñez thinks he's the sole king, but there's also Iván Esparza, and the queen mother, Elena, would make a king of her sole surviving son.

Tito Ascensión, the faithful old servant, might think he can be king now, whether he admits it to himself or not.

Young Damien, too.

Who just thumbed his nose at the crown.

Núñez is in a terrible position. He has to lash out at someone, but he can't attack Elena Sánchez or Iván Esparza, and he won't be able to find Damien.

That leaves one choice.

A bad one, Caro thinks as his piss finally comes and he chuckles, thinking of the *rosca* sitting on the kitchen counter.

There's a king hidden in the cake.

The baby Jesus stares wide-eyed at Tito Ascensión.

Freshly repainted, dressed in fine silk robes, it lies on the counter of the doll shop and looks up.

Most people don't like to make eye contact with El Mastín, but Jesus has no such problem.

Tito's wife dispatched him to pick up the Niño Dios from the restoration shop and deliver it to church for the Día de la Candelaria before the family feast of tamales and *atole* that celebrates the last day of Christmas.

It's funny, he thinks as he waits for the owner to tot up the bill, you're the boss of your own organization, you give orders to hundreds of men, but when the wife gives you a honey-do list, you do it yourself. You don't delegate something as important as picking up Jesus.

The shop owner's little boy also sneaks peeks at Tito. Pretending to be busy dusting the shelf behind the counter, he glances under his arm at the renowned drug lord who controls the city. Even a ten-year-old boy knows who El Mastín is.

Tito sticks out his tongue and waggles his fingers by his ears.

The boy smiles.

The owner steps over and hands Tito the bill—on it is written *0*, and he says, "Happy Candlemas, Señor."

"No, Ortiz, I couldn't," Tito says.

He hands the man two hundred dollars.

They each know their obligations.

"Thank you. Thank you, Señor."

Tito takes the doll and walks out to where his new Mercedes SUV is parked in front of the shop. His bodyguard sits in the passenger seat with a MAC-10 sticking out the window.

"Get in back," Tito says. "Jesus gets the front seat."

The bodyguard gets out and Tito buckles Jesus in.

Most guys in Tito's position have drivers, but he prefers to be behind the wheel. Tito loves driving and now he drives through Guadalajara past graffiti that reads, ADÁN VIVE.

Tito doubts it.

Dead is dead.

He should know. He's killed maybe hundreds of people—he's lost count—and not one of them has ever come back.

The car is the second in a convoy of three.

The Explorer in front and the Ford 150 pickup behind are full of Tito's gunmen, even though this part of Guadalajara, like most of Jalisco state, is safe territory. The Jalisco cartel isn't at war with anyone, it's allied with Sinaloa, and most of the state police and local *federales* are on Tito's payroll.

But it never hurts to be safe.

In a world where people feel free to burn down Adán Barrera's home . . .

Jesus, what could that kid have been thinking?

Then again, maybe Sinaloa isn't Sinaloa anymore.

Before going to the doll shop, Tito had spoken by phone with Rafael Caro.

"Who is Iván Esparza to tell you what you can or can't do?" Caro asked him.

They were talking about Iván's refusal to let Tito take his organization into heroin.

"I owe Esparza everything."

"No disrespect," Caro said. "But Nacho is gone. If he were alive, I would never suggest this. But the son is not the father."

"I still owe him my loyalty," Tito said, remembering the day of Nacho's funeral, when he had gone up to the widow to ask if there was anything he could do. She had taken both his hands in hers and said, "Take care of my sons."

He swore he would.

"Loyalty is a two-way street," Caro said. "Are they loyal to you? Are they letting you into the heroin business—billions of dollars a year? Have they offered you Michoacán, your home? You've done everything for Sinaloa—killed for them, bled for them. What do they do for you? Pat you on the head like a good dog? Toss a few bones to their loyal, faithful 'El Mastín'? You deserve more than that."

"I'm happy with what I have."

"Billions of dollars in heroin money?" Caro asked. "A ready-made American market? It would be almost business malpractice not to take advantage of that. You already have the coke labs, the meth labs. They can be easily converted to heroin."

"Sinaloa would never let me use their plazas," Tito said. "Or they'd charge me a premium."

"Ah, listen," Caro said. "We're just talking, right? Shooting the shit."

But it is serious, Tito thinks now as he drives. Taking on the Sinaloa cartel is very fucking serious. Between Núñez, Sánchez and the Esparzas, they have hundreds, if not thousands, of *sicarios*. They have most of the federal police, the army and the politicians.

And taking Baja? Tijuana?

You have a family, he reminds himself.

You have a son.

What do you owe Rubén?

If you get into a war with Sinaloa you could get killed. Shit, *he* could get killed. His inheritance could be an early grave. Or a prison cell, the fate of a lot of others who went up against Sinaloa and found they were fighting the police, the military and the federal government, too. The cemeteries and the prisons are full of Sinaloa's enemies.

Rubén wouldn't survive prison.

He's short and slight.

Brave, a little tiger, but that wouldn't help him against a gang of muscled convicts. In some prisons you can extend your power to protect him, but in others you can't, especially if you're at war with Sinaloa.

The prisons they don't control, the Zetas do, and Tito trembles to think what would happen if the Z Company found out that Tito Ascensión's son was in one of their lockups. They'd gang-rape him every night until they got tired of the fun and then they'd kill him.

And take days to do it.

But the plus side?

Wealth beyond measure.

If you won, Rubén would inherit an empire worth not millions, but billions. The kind of wealth that changes families forever, that makes gentlemen out of peasants. That buys farms, estates, ranches, haciendas. The kind of wealth that would mean Rubén's sons would never have to dirty their hands.

They would own the avocado orchards.

And how do you want Rubén to see you?

As Iván Esparza's dog?

Or do you want your son to see his father as El Patrón, El Señor, the Lord of the Skies?

Rubén was three years old when Tito went to prison.

A little kid who cried every time he saw his *papi* and cried every time he left. Tito would stand there in his orange jumpsuit watching his *hijo*, his *vida*, his *life* being carried out howling, reaching back for him, and it would break his heart.

Couldn't show it, though.

You showed that, you showed *any* weakness in San Quentin, the wolves would sniff it out and rip you to shreds. Fuck you in your ass, your mouth—shit, if those wore out, they'd cut new holes to fuck you in.

No, you had to have a heart of stone and a face to match.

That was way back in 1993, when Adán Barrera was going fifteen rounds with Güero Méndez for the El Patrón title. Tito had been in the joint a year when he got word that Rafael Caro had been arrested and extradited to the US on a twenty-five-to-life sentence, most likely for the sin of being in Méndez's corner.

Tito, he just got four years.

It was enough.

One thousand, four hundred and sixty days behind the walls of "La Pinta" was plenty, because prison is the worst place in the world.

Four years pretending your right hand was pussy. Four years lifting weights on the yards so other men couldn't make *you* pussy. Four years eating garbage, taking crap from the COs. Four years of seeing your wife and son once every month or so in a "visiting room."

He saw a lot of guys lose it in La Pinta. Strong guys, tough guys who fell down and cried like babies. Or got hooked on the heroin that was easily available and turned themselves into ghosts. He saw men become women—start wearing wigs and makeup, tape their junk up between their legs, start taking it up the ass. Or guys would do time in the *hoyo* and lose their minds—come out babbling fools.

La Pinta was designed to break you, but it didn't break Tito, mostly because of La Eme.

He followed the rules and reported every day for *la máquina*, Eme's mandatory daily exercise sessions held to keep its men in fighting shape.

He did the calisthenics, the push-ups, the sit-ups, the pull-ups, and he jerked iron. Already strong from the avocado groves, he yoked up like a bull.

Now he feels the scar that runs down his right cheek and remembers. It sucks, he thinks, that it came not from the *mayates* or the *güeros*, but from his own people. And it happened, appropriately enough, in "Blood Alley."

The *llavero*—the Eme shot caller—had warned him not to go down to that section of the yard, at least not alone—but Tito knew he had to prove he wasn't afraid if he didn't want to spend the next four years fighting off the *norteños*, who were at war with Eme.

He wanted to get it over with, so the very next day he took a stroll down Blood Alley and the *norteños* didn't waste any time, either. He saw one of them coming, heard the other behind him.

Tito turned and swung. Put all his two-fifty behind the punch and shattered the farmer's jaw. Then he turned but was a little slow—the *pedazo* sliced down his cheek. Tito didn't feel the pain. He grabbed the knife hand and crushed it like a bag of potato chips.

The man screamed and dropped the shank.

Tito held on to the shattered hand and used his left to pound the guy into the dirt. He would have kept pounding but he didn't want the murder charge that would keep him in there the rest of his life so he stopped, let the COs Mace him and knock him to the ground with their sticks and carry him to the infirmary, where they stitched his face like a mailbag.

Then they tossed him into the *hoyo*.

Tito did ninety days in the hole, but heard that the farmer lost his fucking hand. Even better, the State of California decided that he had acted in self-defense and didn't stack any more charges on him.

Tito did his time.

Did it with strength, dignity and respect.

Like a convict, not an inmate.

He hurt on the inside.

Missed his wife, his son.

When he got out and they deported him, he swore he was never going back—to the US or to prison.

He's never going to be separated from his son again.

But can you betray Nacho, who made you? he thinks now. Can you throw the dice, risking your life and your son's?

No, Tito thinks.

You can't.

Life has given you more than you ever thought you'd have; don't tempt life to take it all away.

Then he hears the helicopter.

The Explorer in front jams on its brakes and his *sicarios* pile out.

Tito cranks the wheel. "What's going on?"

"An army checkpoint on the next block," the driver says.

Looking into the rearview mirror, Tito sees military vehicles racing up. The Ford pickup swings sideways to block the street. His men get out and take cover behind the truck. Tito hears the popping of gunfire as he turns right down a side street. Looks out the window and up and sees the helicopter bank and hover over him.

Fuck them, he thinks.

I'm not going back.

They can kill me but they're not taking me back to prison.

"¡Jefe!"

Tito sees the armored car blocking the street ahead. He throws the car into reverse and floors it.

The bodyguard shouts out the window. "The *jefe* is here! They're trying to get the *jefe!*"

Men come running out of bars and bodegas. Some of them are his *sicarios*, others are just neighborhood guys who know what's best for them. They start to throw anything they can find into the street between Tito and the army vehicle—chairs, tables, a parking sign. Others run up to the roofs and throw down bricks, lengths of pipe, shingles.

A group of five men move a car into the street and then tip it over. Then another and another, making a barricade.

Tito backs out onto the main street and drives ahead, away from the pickup, where his guys have started to pour heavy fire onto the soldiers moving up. He finds an alley off to his left and pulls in there.

Behind him, his *sicarios* walk up and down the street, open gas tanks, stick in rags and light them.

Cars go up in flames.

Thick black smoke coils skyward.

Tito speeds through the alley, not stopping when he comes to a cross street. He dodges a bus and swerves into the next alley, scraping the passenger side of his new car against the wall.

The chopper is still with him.

He hears the Klaxon horns of army vehicles ahead of him.

The chopper is directing the hunt.

He throws it back into reverse.

But he knows they have him trapped. Neither his men nor the improvised barricades can stop armored cars for very long.

Then he sees a door open from a building. A man steps out, waves his hand. "¡Jefe!"

Tito stops, flings the door open and gets out. Then he reaches back, unbuckles the baby Jesus and grabs it. His wife will make his life insufferable if he doesn't deliver the doll safely to the church.

The man pulls him inside. "*Jefe*, come with me."

They're in the back of a movie theater.

Behind the screen.

Tito can hear the action from the movie—explosions, gunfire—a livelier version than the muffled sounds of the real thing outside. He follows the man across the width of the screen to the top of a set of metal stairs, then down the steps into a basement.

Boxes of candy, cans of soda, cartons of napkins and paper cups.

The man opens a steel door and motions for Tito to go through.

He has to trust this man, he has no choice.

Tito walks through the door, the man steps in after him and closes the door behind. Flips on a light switch, and now Tito knows where he is.

"What's your name?" he asks.

"Fernando Montoya."

"Fernando Montoya, you're a rich man now."

They walk down a hallway into a room that resembles a cantina. Round tables, cane chairs, a bar made from a sheet of plywood set on barrels, a flat-screen television mounted high on the wall. A half-dozen men sit drinking beers, watching a *fútbol* match. All stand up when they see Tito.

Guadalajara cops, they all know who he is.

He used to be one of them. Used to come to this same coop to hang out, make a shift go by a little easier.

Now the cops look nervous.

"What are you waiting for?" Tito asks. "Are you going to give me a beer, or what?"

He has to play it cool, *macho*, give them a story to tell, but inside he's seething. And he can admit it to himself, scared. There have been warrants out for him for ten years, from Mexico and the US, but nobody has ever tried to execute one.

Not in Jalisco.

Now it's the army.

And if Fernando Montoya hadn't opened the side door to a theater, they would have had him.

Tito sits there sipping a beer as two of the cops say they'll go up and see what's going on, let him know—he should sit tight until things cool out, then they'll take him wherever he wants to go.

They know there'll be extra envelopes for them, fat ones, too.

Why now, Tito wonders. Why now and why the army?

But he thinks he knows.

Sinaloa has the army. Somehow the cartel got wind that he's thinking of busting into the heroin market and decided to make a preemptive strike.

It's prison mentality—get them before they get you.

Tito pulls his phone out of his pocket.

No reception down here. So he gives the number to Montoya. "Hey, call my kid, tell him I'm okay. Tell him I said get out of his house, go somewhere until he hears from me."

Montoya leaves.

Comes back fifteen minutes later, tells him the call went straight to voice mail.

Now Tito starts to worry.

It's an hour and a half before the cops come back, tell him it's clear. There was a riot in the streets—trash cans set on fire, cars, a bus. The army finally pulled out. Give it a few more minutes, we'll take you out.

Then the news comes on the television and Tito sees it.

Rubén being led out of his house in handcuffs.

Fucking soldiers with their hands on him. Push his head down and shove him into the back of an armored car.

"I want to go now," Tito says. "I have to make some calls."

In the back of the cop car, the first person he calls is Caro. "They have Rubén."

"I saw," Caro says. "They're saying they found him with thirty rifles and five hundred thousand in cash. No judge can release him off that. It's going to take time."

"How much time?"

"I don't know," Caro says. "Tito, you have to calm down."

Tito is furious.

And terrified for his son. The Zetas don't own any of the lockups in Jalisco, but Sinaloa does.

"It was Sinaloa," Tito says.

"But which Sinaloa? Elena? Núñez? Iván?"

Tito doesn't have an answer to that. "It doesn't matter. Fuck all of them."

"Does that mean you're in with the heroin?" Caro asks. "Even though it means a war with Sinaloa?"

"Sinaloa started a war with me," Tito says. "Fuck it, yes, I'm in."

Tito clicks off.

If anything happens to my son, he thinks, certain people are going to die. And they're going to stay dead.

He grabs the baby Jesus and gets out at the church.

. . .

Ric stands in the throng of people as they make way for the devotees carrying the Virgen de la Candelaria into the church of Nuestra Señora de Quila.

This ritual has been held every Candlemas for three hundred years and the streets of the small town on the outskirts of Culiacán are jammed with tens of thousands of people enjoying the festival with its food stands, games and wandering bands. Now the crowd presses forward to try to touch, or at least see, the Virgin, encased in acrylic, dressed in an aqua-blue silk robe trimmed with gold.

While he's here at the behest of his father—it's important that the cartel be represented, that someone from the family be *seen* here, and there have been whispers at the sighting of El Ahijado—Ric actually enjoys the quaint festival in Quila for reasons he can't really articulate. Most of the people here are *indios*, farmers, and Ric finds something touching in their simple if naive faith in the Virgin. They will ask her for blessings, favors—health for a loved one, the cure for a chronic illness, the redemption of a wayward child. Some stand on the route thanking and praising her for miracles already granted. Ric hears a man whose arthritic hip was suddenly made well, a woman who couldn't conceive but just had her first child, an old woman whose sight was miraculously restored after successful cataract surgery.

Go figure, Ric thinks.

The doctors get no cred, it goes to a doll encased in plastic. It reminds him of those geeky toy collectors who buy an "action figure" and won't take it out of the packaging because once you do, it loses value.

Still, he's moved by it all.

Karin is with him today, and their daughter, Valeria, two now, excited out of her mind by all the noise and the color, not to mention the sugar she's consumed at the various stands. Her pretty white holiday dress is smeared with chocolate, powdered sugar and something Ric can't identify, and now she dangles from his hand trying to pick something up from the street. We're terrible parents, Ric thinks, although he's looking forward to the sugar crash that will plunge her into a nap in the stroller.

"Do you want to go into the church?" Karin asks when the Virgin has gone by.

"Pass," Ric says. Valeria will just go nuts in the church and they'll have to take her out anyway, and—

He sees trouble.

Belinda pushing her way through the crowd toward him. It's not right, Ric thinks. A holiday like this is reserved for wives, not girlfriends, and Belinda knows that.

Karin sees her, too. "What does *she* want?"

"I don't know," Ric says, alarmed by the serious look on Belinda's face. This would normally be the occasion for a sneer and a snarky remark about how she'd be a virgin, too, if they kept her in acrylic, but she looks positively grim.

"It's your father," Belinda says before Ric can even ask. "He's been shot."

"Is he—"

"We don't know yet."

Ric hands his daughter off to Karin and follows Belinda to a waiting car.

It's weird, Ric thinks as the car races toward the hospital, the intensity of emotion he's feeling. Here's this father who he certainly doesn't love, maybe even doesn't like, and yet the fear is pulsing through him like a continuous electric jolt along with the prayer *Please don't let him die, please don't let him die . . . Please don't let him be already dead before I can . . .*

Before you can what? Ric asks himself.

Say goodbye?

Ask for forgiveness?

Forgive *him*?

Belinda works the phone, trying to figure out what happened. All they know now is that Núñez was leaving the house to go to a Candelaria service at his church in Eldorado. His was the third car in a convoy, and as they were pulling out of the mansion's curved driveway a truck sped past the first two from the opposite direction and sprayed Núñez's Mercedes with bullets.

"My mother," Ric says.

"She's all right, she wasn't hit."

Thank God, Ric thinks.

"Do we know who did it yet?" Ric asks, thinking, Don't let it be Iván.

And don't let it be Damien.

"No, they got away," Belinda says. She looks down at a text message. "Jesus . . ."

"What?"

She doesn't answer.

"What?"

"The word's out on the street already," she says, "that your father is dead."

Don't let it be true, Ric thinks.

"Jesus, Ric, that means you're—"

"Shut the fuck up."

It feels like it takes forever, but they finally make it to the small hospital in Eldorado. Ric hops out of the car before it even stops and runs into the waiting room. His mother gets up from a chair and bursts into tears when she sees him.

He brushes glass off her dress.

"The doctors say they don't know," she says. "They don't know."

The heavy car door probably saved his life, the doctor tells Ric. Slowed the round that went into his stomach and might otherwise have gone through and pierced his liver. They removed the bullet and stopped the internal bleeding, but there's still the real possibility of sepsis. "Resting comfortably" is the cliché the doctor uses.

Ric gets his mother a cup of tea from the hospital cafeteria and then finds Belinda in the car outside.

"I want to know how the fuck this could have happened," Ric says. "I want to know who's behind it, and I want retaliation before the sun comes up tomorrow."

"I've moved my own people in," Belinda says. "All his guards are being questioned—"

"Whatever it takes, Belinda."

"Of course," she says. "As to who's behind it, no one has taken credit yet. They're probably waiting to find out if he's alive or not. But you have to know that the leading candidate is your good buddy Damien."

He ignores the gibe. "Get it out on Twitter that my father is dying. Arrange for his parish priest to come, make a show of it. Then let's see who steps up to take responsibility. Get people over to Damien's mother's house. If it was him, he'll try to move his family out. Explain to them we don't want to hurt them, but they need to stay where they are."

"What if they try to leave?"

"Kill them."

But Damien Tapia is only one possibility, Ric thinks.

Elena Sánchez is another.

She's unhappy that my father hasn't taken action against Iván for Rudolfo's murder. She's questioned my father's leadership, said that he was weakening the cartel. Maybe she decided to act on her opinions.

But she's smarter than that, Ric thinks. She knows that she can't hold Baja against a combined attack from our wing and Iván's, which would certainly happen. Her organization is already short on manpower, and she's not stupid enough to let herself be isolated.

You have to consider the possibility that it was Iván.

He's still smarting over having to surrender Baja, still thinks that he should be the head of the cartel. Maybe he thinks the Esparza wing is strong enough to fight the Núñez wing and Elena; and face it, maybe he thinks he can win if it's you, not your father, who has to lead.

And he's probably right, Ric thinks.

He's a better war leader than you; he's a better leader, period.

Belinda hands him the phone and mouths, *Elena.*

"I just heard," Elena says. "I'm so sorry. How is he?"

"We don't know yet."

A silence and then she says, "I know what you're thinking."

"Really? What am I thinking, Elena?"

"I had my disagreements with your father," Elena says, "but I would never do something like this."

"Good to know."

"Give my love to your mother. Tell her that I'm praying for him, for all of you."

Ric thanks her and clicks off. Wonders if Elena was calling out of real concern, or to demonstrate that it wasn't her who had given the order, or to cover up the fact that it was. He turns to Belinda. "Who was driving my father today?"

"López."

Gabriel López, a former Sinaloa state policeman, had been his father's driver for as long as Ric can remember. Always neatly dressed with a knotted tie, punctual, professional, discreet. Unmarried, devoted to his aging mother, who suffers from Alzheimer's.

"Is he alive?" Ric asks.

"He wasn't hurt."

"Where is he now?"

"I didn't pick him up," Belinda says. "I never thought—"

"Get him."

López doesn't answer his phone.

Straight to voice mail.

Ric doesn't leave a message.

"It was him," Ric says.

"But who bought him?" Belinda asks.

"We won't know that until we talk to him," Ric says.

"He's gone," Belinda says. "We can't reach him."

We have to, Ric thinks. Whoever tried to kill my father will try again. We have to find out who it was.

Ric takes a vid of López's mother and texts it to his father's old driver. Seconds later, Ric's phone rings.

It's López.

"You need to come talk to me," Ric says.

"If I come, you'll kill me."

But I can't be the old Ric anymore. I have family of my own to protect. "If you don't come here," Ric says, "I'll kill her."

López is betting on me being the old Ric, Ric thinks. The nice, easygoing guy who wouldn't think about hurting someone's family, never mind a helpless, demented old lady who has little, if any, idea what's going on.

Christ, she thought I was her Gabriel when I came in.

Sure enough, López says, "You wouldn't do that."

Ric takes out his pistol and holds it to the old lady's head. With the other hand, he holds up his phone. "Watch me."

He pulls the hammer back.

"No!" López yells. "I'll come!"

"Thirty minutes," Ric says. "Come alone."

He's there in twenty-eight.

Belinda pats him down and takes his Glock from him.

López kisses his mother on the cheek. "Mami, are you all right? Did they hurt you?"

"Gabriel?"

"*Sí*, Mami."

"Did you bring my *chilindrinas*?"

"Not this time, Mami," López says.

She scowls and looks down at the floor.

"Where can we talk?" Ric asks.

"My study," López says.

They go into the little room, every bit as neat and tidy as López. Ric gestures for López to sit down. Belinda stands blocking the door, a gun in her hand.

"It wasn't me," López says.

"Don't lie to me, Gabriel," Ric says. "It makes me angry. I don't have time to force the truth out of you. If you don't tell me right now, I'll shoot that old lady in front of you. Tell me the truth and I'll see that she gets the finest care in Culiacán. Who bought you?"

Please, Ric thinks, don't let him say Iván.

"Tito," López says. "Ascensión."

"Why?"

"Your father went after him," López says. "He didn't get him. Do you have a silencer? I don't want her scared."

Ric looks at Belinda, who nods and says, "I'll do it."

"No," Ric says. "It has to be me."

If I don't do it, people will think I'm weak.

And they'll be right.

It has to be done and it has to be me.

"You sure?" Belinda asks. "I mean, I know you faked it in Baja."

"I'm sure."

Belinda fastens the silencer to her pistol and hands it to Ric. His heart is racing and he feels like he's going to throw up. He says to López, "Turn around. Look out the window."

López turns around. Says, "My papers are in the top left drawer. Everything is in order. I bring her *chilindrinas* every Thursday."

"I'll give standing orders." Ric tries to keep his voice from quivering.

He lifts the pistol.

Belinda said it was easy—point and shoot.

It isn't easy.

He lays the sight down at the base of López's skull.

This is it, he thinks, if you pull the trigger there's no going back. You're a killer. But if you don't pull the trigger and the people you deal with think you're weak, they'll tear your family to shreds.

They'll kill your father in his hospital bed.

If, that is, he's not dead already.

Ric's hand shakes.

He puts a second hand on the gun to steady it.

He hears López crying.

Ric pulls the trigger.

His father looks gray.

His voice is hoarse as he says, "I need to speak with you . . . We need to find out . . ."

"It was Tito," Ric says. "He bought López to set you up. Don't worry. I took care of it."

Núñez nods.

"Why?" Ric asks. "Why go after Tito?"

Núñez shakes his head again, as if to dismiss the question, and the effort seems to cost him. "A preemptive strike. Now he'll come after you, too. You have to go somewhere safe, go—"

He's unconscious.

Buzzers go off.

A nurse rushes in, shoves Ric out of the way and checks monitors.

She yells something and more nurses come in, then a doctor, and they wheel Núñez out into the hallway toward the operating room. Ric doesn't catch everything that's said, only enough to know that his father's blood pressure has dropped and that they have to "go in" again to stop the bleeding.

Ric sits in the waiting room with his mother.

He's terrified for his father but tells himself that he can't afford feeling right now; his responsibility is to be cold-blooded and think.

We're at war with Tito Ascensión and the New Jalisco cartel.

CJN controls not only Jalisco, but most of Michoacán and areas of Guerrero. It has operations in Mexico City and an available port in Puerto Vallarta. Now Tito will move on Baja, Juárez and Laredo, and the ports in Manzanillo and Mazatlán.

Tito is a fighter—an experienced, proven field general and a ruthless killer. He's already won wars. People are, rightly, afraid of him, and they'll be afraid to go against him; some of Sinaloa's people will switch to his side out of that fear, or just because they think he'll win.

Worse, and Ric hates thinking this, Tito has old and strong ties to Iván. He was Nacho Esparza's faithful guard, the head of his security and his armed wing. He fought the Gulf cartel for the Esparzas, the Juárez cartel for the Esparzas, the Zetas for the Esparzas, and he beat them all.

His most natural next move will be to go to Iván and propose an alliance against us and Elena. And if he does that, and Iván accepts, we're done.

We can't win.

The math simply doesn't add up.

We can't match the combined men, money and material of the CJN and the Esparza wing. They'll form a new cartel and destroy us.

There's only one move to make.

He knows he should get his father's advice and approval—it's really his father's decision to make—but the hard truth is that he's not capable of making it right now and Ric doesn't have the time to wait.

Ric walks outside and gets on the phone.

Driving to the meeting, Ric knows that if he's miscalculated—if Iván and Tito have already made a deal—he's dead.

They'll kill him the second he shows up.

It was stupid not to bring security, but Ric was afraid that he'd cause the very thing he's trying to prevent—a war with Iván. The guy is already paranoid, afraid of being blamed for the attempt on Núñez, and if Ric shows up with an armed force, Iván will think he's been ambushed.

Ric takes the chance.

He has a 9 mm Glock tucked into the waistband of his jeans under a To-materos baseball jacket.

"It has no safety, so don't blow your ass off," Belinda said, jacking a round into the chamber. "Just point and click."

"I hope I don't need to."

"You shouldn't be doing this," she said as he got into the car. "I shouldn't let you be doing this."

"It's not your call."

She smiled. "Hey, Ric? You're Michael now."

Iván set the meeting at a Pemex station off Highway 15 on the south edge of Eldorado and as he pulls in Ric wishes he hadn't agreed to the spot. The station sits in the middle of a large parking lot, mostly empty this late at night, with just a few tractor-trailer trucks parked at the edge.

Any one of which, he thinks, might be full of Esparza gunmen.

Or CJN gunmen.

Or both.

He gets out of the car and walks to the station. It's a long walk—he can feel guns on his back.

Iván sits in a booth by the coffee machine, a microwave, and a rack of shelves filled with junk food.

Ric slides in across from him.

"It wasn't me," Iván says.

"I didn't think it was."

"But you had your suspicions," Iván says.

"Yeah, okay, I had suspicions."

"I don't blame you," Iván says. "It would be the smart move. If he wasn't your dad . . ."

"It was Tito," Ric says, looking for signs of surprise on Iván's face. He does look surprised, but maybe he's faking it.

"See, I would have thought Damien," Iván says.

"Tito," Ric says. "My dad took a run at him."

"Bad mistake," Iván says, "to take a run at Tito Ascensión and miss. But throwing Rubén in jail? That makes you a target now, too."

"Believe me, I'm feeling it."

"So why are we here?"

"I need you on our side," Ric says.

"I know you do," Iván says. "But—and remembering a month ago you had a gun pointed at my face—why should I?"

"Baja," Ric says. "We'll give it back to you."

Iván takes this in, and then says, "So would Tito."

"He doesn't have it to give."

"Neither do you," Iván says. "Elena does."

"I'll tell her otherwise."

Iván smirks. "*You* will?"

"Yeah."

"Then she'll go over to Tito," Iván says.

"See?" Ric says. "It will work out perfectly."

"We'd have to fight her for it."

"But sided with us, you'd win," Ric says.

"Sided with Tito, I'd win."

"Maybe."

"Hey, Ric," Iván says, "whoever I go with wins."

"I guess that's why I'm here."

Iván looks around the station, then out the window. Then he turns back to Ric and says, "I could sell you to Tito right now. He'd pay a lot. Then he could trade you for Rubén."

"But you won't," Ric says, although he's not so sure.

Iván takes a long time to answer, then he says, "No, I won't. So Baja, huh?"

"You get the border crossings and most of the domestic market. All I want are the neighborhoods we already have in La Paz and Cabo."

"What about Mazatlán?"

"Yours."

"No offense," Iván says, "but did your dad approve this?"

"Not yet."

"Wow," Iván says. "Look at you, all grown up."

"Do we have a deal?"

"As far as it goes," Iván says. "But—again, no offense—what happens if your dad doesn't make it? That makes you the *patrón*. I know you're El Ahijado and all that, but I don't know if I can handle that."

"What do you want?"

"I'm next in line," Iván says, "after your old man, of course."

"Like I've told you," Ric says, "I don't want it, but . . ."

"What?"

"If I agree to that," Ric says, "it gives you motivation to kill my father."

Iván studies him for a few seconds. "*All* grown up. Then, no, no deal, El Ahijado. Tito will give me the big chair."

It's all coming apart, Ric thinks, and I can't get up from this table without a deal. My father will hate me for this, but—

"I'll tell you what I *will* do," Ric says. "If my father dies peacefully, in bed, or retires, I'll step down for you. But if he's murdered—by anyone—I keep the job."

"I'd fight you for it."

"Let's hope it never comes to that," Ric says. He puts his hand out. "Deal?"

Iván shakes his hand.

"One more thing," Ric says. "My father never knows about our arrangement."

"Give your father my best," Iván says. "Tell him that I wish him a full and speedy recovery."

Ric walks back to the car knowing that he has the deal he needed so badly and fully aware that he just gave Iván motivation to kill his father *and* him.

He gets on the phone to see if his father is still alive.

By the night of Candlemas, even Marisol's enthusiasm for the holidays has waned.

She didn't go to church, doesn't drink *atole,* certainly doesn't acquire a figure of the baby Jesus.

"I'm celebrated out," she tells Keller. One thing she does is attempt to understand his explanation of Groundhog Day.

"A groundhog comes out of his hole," she says.

"Yes."

"And if it sees its shadow . . . what happens again?"

"There are six more weeks of winter."

"And if he doesn't," she says. "It's spring?"

"Yes."

"What does one have to do with the other?" she asks. "How does a groundhog not seeing its shadow somehow trigger the start of spring?"

"It's just a tradition."

"A dumb one."

"True," Keller says. "It doesn't have the internal logic of swallowing grapes or dumping dirty water out the window."

He doesn't even attempt to explain the current pop-culture meaning of Groundhog Day—the endless cycle of repetition of the same day—but it's been that for him.

First there was the failed Mexican attempt at capturing a drug lord, this time Tito Ascensión of the New Jalisco cartel. Now there's the attempted assassination of the head of the Sinaloa cartel, Ricardo Núñez.

In between, Roberto Orduña had a success. Acting on a tip, his FES raided a house in Zihuantanejo and captured all three Rentería brothers.

Orduña called Keller and told him the Renterías had confessed to killing the students.

"What did they say as to motive?" Keller asked.

"They thought the kids were recruits for Los Rojos," Orduña said. "Sad, isn't it?"

Keller doesn't buy the Renterías' Los Rojos story, just like he doesn't buy the improbable event of Orduña getting lucky and finding them all in the same place at the same time. It was Eddie Ruiz who gave up their names. Did he give up their location, too?

And who gave him the order?

If Ruiz is running something, it must mean that someone is running Ruiz.

"We think there was a shipment of heroin on that bus," Keller said.

"Do you have intelligence to back that up?" Orduña asked.

"Working on it."

"Whose heroin?"

"Sinaloa's?" Keller suggested. "Ricardo Núñez?"

"Well, he's fucked up."

"Is he going to make it?"

"Looks like it," Orduña said. "And now the two biggest cartels in Mexico are going to slug it out."

Groundhog Day, Keller thinks.

Another war.

More deaths.

The holidays, such as they ever were, are over.

2

Coyotes

Coyote is always out there waiting . . . and Coyote is always hungry.
—Navajo saying

Bahia de los Piratas, Costa Rica
March 2015

Sean Callan wrenches out the spark plug on the outboard motor of his *panga* and replaces it with a new one.

The boat, a seven-year-old Yamaha, is twenty-two feet long with a five-foot, six-inch beam and is still in good shape because Callan is almost religious in its maintenance. He uses the boat to take guests out pole or spear fishing, snorkeling, or just for sunset cruises, so Callan keeps it in good order.

He has a love-hate relationship with the motor, a two-stroke, forty-five-horsepower E-Arrow he bought from one of the commercial fishermen in Playa Carrillo. The motor demands more attention than one of the rich women guests who come down from LA in search of the primitive without sacrificing the luxuries of civilization, a conflicting need that Callan and Nora are always struggling to meet.

Nora, Callan thinks, with more grace than me.

They've had the little "guest house"—four bungalows and a main house tucked into the trees above the beach—for a little more than ten years now and Nora has turned it into a success. They make a decent living and it's a quiet life, especially in the off-season when they have the place pretty much to themselves.

Callan loves it here.

Bahia de los Piratas is home to him now and he'd never leave. For living in a quiet, out-of-the-way place, just enough removed from the larger resort of Tamarindo and the little town of Matapalo, Callan is remarkably busy. There's always something that needs doing.

If he's not fixing the motor or maintaining the boat, he's taking customers out on the water. Or piling them into the old Land Rover (speaking of fixing and maintaining) and hauling them up to Rincón de la Vieja to go horseback riding or hiking, or taking them to Palo Verde Park to see the crocodiles, the peccaries and the jaguarundis. Or babysitting the bird-watching groups that Nora insists on booking.

Or he's shuttling the guests to the bars and clubs in Tamarindo (taking them in mostly sober, bringing them back mostly drunk), or to surf sessions, or to one of the bigger charter sports-fishing boats to go after marlin or sailfish.

If he's not tending to the customers, he's looking after the hotel itself. There's always something that needs fixing, patching, mending. If it's not new thatch for a roof, it's stucco, or a leaky pipe. In the off-season, he goes into heavy maintenance mode, resurfacing walls, sanding floors, painting ceilings.

Or he's working on the main house, originally built back in the '20s and fallen into sad disrepair when they bought it for a song. Now he lovingly restores the woodwork—the banisters, the railings, the floors, the broad deck that looks out over the Pacific.

In the shop he built far behind the house, he's making a dining room table from repurposed Spanish cedar. It's a birthday surprise for Nora, and he works at it in his odd spare time.

Callan used to be a carpenter back in New York, a fine craftsman, so he loves this work. In fact, he loves all the work—loves being outside in the parks, up in the tropical forest, along the banks of the Tempisque, out on the ocean.

It's a good life.

Nora takes care of most of the daily details of the place, although Callan helps out, and their days have taken on a pleasant routine. They live upstairs in the main house and get up before dawn to start breakfast downstairs in the kitchen.

Their helper, María, is usually in the kitchen by the time they get down, and she and Nora make platters of *gallo pinto* with eggs, sour cream and cheese. Set it out with bowls of papaya, mango and tamarind. Pots of strong coffee and tea, along with pitchers of *horchata*, the cornmeal and cinnamon drink they serve here in Guanacaste Province.

Callan usually bolts down a quick cup of coffee and, while the guests are eating, makes sure the Land Rover is working or that the boat is in order for whatever activity is on for the morning. If it's a longer trip, Nora and María will make pack lunches; if not, they clear the table, clean up from breakfast and start making lunch, which usually consists of a *casado*—rice and beans served with chicken, pork or fish.

After lunch, Nora usually goes back upstairs for a siesta—her "beauty rest," as she calls it, although Callan thinks she hardly needs that—while a small staff made up mostly of María's extended female family changes sheets and towels and gets rooms ready for incoming guests.

Callan generally doesn't have time to grab a siesta, although occasionally he can get one in, and these are some of his favorite times, lying with Nora on the sheets that have been sprinkled with cool water.

Dinners are usually small, with only a couple of the guests because most of them like to go to one of the restaurants in Playa Grande or Tamarindo. But Nora and María will lay out *boquitas* of *patacones* and *arracaches* and then small plates of ceviche or *chicharrón* before a full meal of grilled fish—depending on what fresh catch Nora can find in Playa Carrillo—or *olla de carne,* the local stew made of beef and cassava. Or sometimes Nora will get creative and go French on them—making *steak frites* or *coq au vin* or something.

Dessert is usually a fruit salad, or if Nora wants to go heavier, a *tres leches* cake, followed by coffee and brandy served on the deck, where they can sit and listen to the music of the beach in front and the tropical forest behind.

They usually turn in early, unless Callan has to make a "town run" to pick up guests, and start early again the next morning.

That's in the busy season—the dry season—from about December through April. Then the rains come, inaugurating the green season, although in Guanacaste that usually means just daily showers in the late afternoon and early evening. But it keeps the tourists away, and Callan and Nora catch up on the maintenance and also just have more time to walk the beach, take the boat out by themselves, have long, loving siestas and quiet, private dinners, make love to the sound of the rain hitting the metal roof.

The *turistas* come back in July.

Now the high season is tailing off, it's March, and Callan has the *panga* pulled up on the beach to replace the spark plugs, because sometimes he anchors out by a reef and the last thing he wants is to be a thousand yards out and have the motor quit on him.

It's hot now at noon, in the nineties, but Callan keeps his shirt on. It's a joke among the female guests, how much they'd like to see their handsome, muscled host *without* his shirt on, but for such a laid-back guy he's shy and says that it just isn't "proper." So now he wears an oversize faded denim shirt over a pair of old khaki shorts, huaraches and a tattered baseball cap. Twisting the wrench, he barks his knuckle and utters a short, sharp curse.

Then he hears a laugh behind him.

It's Carlos.

Callan has known María's son since he was a kid and has to remind himself that Carlos isn't a kid anymore but a full-grown man with a wife and two kids of his own. Whom he works like a mule to support. Carlos decks on the charter sports boats and crews on the commercial fishing boats and by working his ass off has saved enough money to put a down payment on a thirty-two-foot 1989 Topaz convertible with twin 735-horsepower diesel engines, tower release outriggers, a fighting chair and a forward cabin with a full galley so he can go into business for himself.

Callan's been helping him fix the boat up, just like Carlos helps him out when he needs an extra hand, someone to take the tourists out on the water or run them to one of the parks, or when he needs a second pair of hands fixing a roof.

Now Carlos laughs and asks, "The motor fighting back?"

"And winning," Callan says.

"You're getting old," Carlos says.

Callan is fifty-four and agrees. His shoulder-length hair is getting some silver in it. "And you look like shit."

"Out all night."

"With Bustamente?"

"Yeah."

Callan asks, "Catch anything?"

"Some yellowfin," Carlos says. "You want me to get that plug out for you?"

"No, I got it." Callan gives the wrench another crank and the plug comes out. "You eaten? They got lunch on up at the house and we're light."

Just four guests—two middle-aged birders and a hippie couple.

"I'm good," Carlos says, patting his stomach.

Or what there is of it. As María says, "If Carlos is carrying any fat, it's in his head." No, he's lean, taut-muscled and killer handsome. If he weren't such a faithful husband to Elisa, he'd be up all night banging tourist women.

Now he helps Callan swap out the spark plugs, and they make a date to work on the Topaz—Carlos wants to lay a wooden deck in the forward cabin. They talk for a few more minutes—the weather, fishing, baseball, the usual bullshit—and Carlos heads off to work a charter that's going out for marlin.

Callan goes up to the house to see if the guests want to go out snorkeling.

Nora is in the kitchen, chopping some vegetables.

They've been together—with a few interruptions—for sixteen years now and she still stops his heart.

Nora Hayden is a startlingly beautiful woman.

Hair that can only be described as golden, cut shorter the past few years for life in the tropics.

Blue eyes as clear and warm as the Pacific.

At fifty-two, Callan thinks, she's never been lovelier. Trim from the swimming and the yoga, and the age lines around her eyes and mouth just make her more interesting.

And that's just the package.

What's inside the package, Callan knows, is pure gold.

Nora is smart, a lot smarter than he is, a great businesswoman, and she has the heart of a lioness.

He loves her more than life.

Now he comes up behind her, wraps his arm around her waist and says, "How's your day?"

She arches her neck back and kisses him on the cheek. "Good. Yours?"

"Good," Callan says. "What are you doing for dinner tonight?"

"I don't know," Nora says. "Depends on what I can find."

"Carlos says they have yellowtail."

"Who does?"

"Bustamente."

Nora shakes her head. "No, he doesn't. María went by this morning, he doesn't have anything."

"That's weird," Callan says. "Carlos said they went out last night."

Nora shrugs. "What can I tell you? The boat ready?"

"Yup."

He takes the guests out snorkeling, brings back as many people as he went out with—which is the bottom-line requirement—grabs a shower and then drives them into town for dinner.

Comes back to eat with Nora.

With no guests, she's made them a simple dish of rice and beans, which Callan eats like a horse.

"Are you looking forward to the quiet season?" Nora asks.

"A little."

A lot, Nora thinks. She knows her man. He's a private person, a quiet person, and while he's good at the socializing that comes with their business—he's quite charming when he wants to be—she knows that it doesn't come naturally to him and that he prefers solitude.

Would rather be alone with his work, and her.

Nora's looking forward to it, too.

She likes the business, likes hosting, likes most of the guests, many of whom are repeat customers, but it will be nice to have some downtime and some time alone with Sean. Take their sunset walks on the beach, which they rarely have time for when the house is full.

Nora is happy with her life.

With the rhythms of their days and nights, their seasons.

She never thought she'd be happy, but she is.

After dinner and coffee, Callan drives back to Tamarindo to pick up the guests. He meets them at the Crazy Monkey. The birders are finishing up dessert, the hippies are dancing in the disco, so he has time to kill and sits down for a beer.

From the bar, Callan can see the Mexicans in the disco. They stick out, in their *norteño* cowboy garb.

It's a fairly recent development here in Guanacaste, groups of a dozen or more Mexicans, mostly men, occasionally with girlfriends. He sees them at the Crazy Monkey, the Pacífico, in Sharkey's watching *fútbol* or a boxing match.

Callan doesn't like it.

It's not that he has anything against Mexicans. He doesn't—he just has something against *these* Mexicans.

"Rains are coming," the bartender says, handing him a Rancho Humo and shaking his head when Callan reaches for his wallet.

Callan lays a tip that's more than the cost of the beer. "You gonna hang out?"

"No," the bartender says, "I'm going to go back to San José, see family."

"That's nice."

He turns back and sees Carlos.

In the disco, talking with one of the Mexicans. Thick, burly guy in his thirties, has that A-male, leader-of-the-pack look about him. Just a little better dressed than the rest, a little better groomed.

The *jefe*, Callan thinks. He's seen him around Tamarindo with two other men. Now he sees Carlos nod and then shake the *jefe*'s hand.

Callan finishes his beer, picks up the guests and drives them home.

Has a hard time sleeping.

Callan is strictly a "mind your own business" guy, and he knows that's what he should do now.

But it's María's kid.

And he likes Carlos.

So despite himself, the next morning he finds Carlos working on the Topaz and hops on board.

"I thought we said Saturday," Carlos says.

"We did," Callan says. "I wanted to talk with you."

"What about?"

"What you're doing."

Carlos looks uneasy. "What am I doing?"

"Come on, man," Callan says.

"I don't know what you're talking about."

"The coke runs you're doing with Bustamente," Callan says.

Why the Mexicans are here. They fly the cocaine up from South America, put it on small boats here that go out and meet larger boats for the run up to Mexico or even California.

They pay the local fishermen to make these runs.

Callan gets it; the fishing is bad, and even if it were good, it's nothing compared to the money you can make—a month's pay or more in a single night—running out the coke.

"I'm not—"

"Don't insult me."

Carlos gets pissed. "It's none of your business."

"Look, I get it," Callan says. "A few of these runs, you can pay off the boat and you're in business for yourself. That's the dream, right? But I know these people. Believe me, you don't want to be in business with them. You get the cash for a boat, you think you can just quit the other stuff. But they won't let you, Carlos. They'll want you to run dope on *your* boat."

"I'll say no."

"You don't say no to these people."

"How do you know so much about this?" Carlos asks.

"I just know," Callan says. "This isn't for you."

"No?" Carlos asks. "What's for me, Callan? Be your cute Tico boat boy the rest of my life?"

"You buy your own boat, you start your own charter business."

"That could be years away."

Callan shrugs.

"Easy for you," Carlos says. "You have your own business."

True enough, Callan thinks. But he says, "Just being your friend, man."

"Then *be* my friend," Carlos says. "And don't you say anything to my mom."

"I won't," Callan says. "But how is she going to feel when they throw your ass in prison?"

Carlos smiles. "They have to catch my ass first."

"You read the papers, Carlos?" Callan asks. "Watch the news? The Costa Rican government just renewed a deal with the US. The fucking US Coast Guard is out there patrolling. With the DEA."

This won't end well.

It's just the next afternoon, Callan's in the boat scrubbing out the salt water, when the *jefe* comes up on him.

"Nice boat," he says, a smarmy fucking smile on his grill.

"Thanks."

"You Donovan?"

"Yeah." It's the name Callan uses here.

"Carlos's friend."

"Right again," Callan says. There's no sense putting it off. "What do you want?"

The smile comes off. "I want you to mind your own fucking business."

"How do you know," Callan asks, "what my fucking business is or isn't?"

"I know *my* business isn't your business," the *jefe* says.

"Look," Callan says, "you can get all the boats and fishermen you want. All I'm saying is, why don't you just leave this one guy alone?"

"You know how it goes," the *jefe* says. "You make an exception for one person, you have to make it for everybody. Then it's not an exception no more."

"One guy, all I'm saying."

"We don't need no fucking *yanquis*," the *jefe* says, "coming down here to tell us what to do, not to do."

"Don't need no fucking Mexicans, either."

"You don't like Mexicans?"

"I don't like *you*," Callan says.

"Do you know who we are?"

"Pretty much."

"We're Sinaloa," the *jefe* says. "You don't fuck with us. And you let Carlos do what he has to do."

"He's a grown man," Callan says. "He can do what he wants."

"That's right."

"That is right," Callan says.

"Don't fuck with us."

"Yeah, you said that."

The *jefe* gives him a Bobby Badass staredown and then walks away. Callan watches him go.

I should have minded my own damn business, he thinks.

The next few weeks go by quietly. The rains come and the tourists leave, except for a few adventurous types looking for an experience and a bargain. Callan sees the *jefe* a couple more times, once at the Crazy Monkey, another time at the Pacífico. He even sees him again with Carlos, but Callan looks away as the *jefe* smirks at him.

Callan doesn't bring it up again with Carlos. They work on his boat, work on the guest cottage roofs and talk about anything but. I tried once, Callan thinks. Carlos is a grown man, and it would be insulting to bring it up again.

Life settles back into its routine.

Callan spends most of this time on repairs, sneaking away to his shop in the afternoons to work on the dining room table. Just before sunset, he and

Nora meet and go walk the beach, even if it's raining, because the rain is warm and they don't mind getting wet.

They have quiet dinners, make love under the tin roof.

It's May when he wakes up one morning, it's still dark, and he hears a commotion downstairs.

It's María and she's crying.

When he gets down to the kitchen, Nora has María in her arms.

"They have Carlos!" María is sobbing. "They have Carlos!"

They calm her down to get details. What she knows, anyway. There was a "seizure," an arrest out in the water. They say it was cocaine. Eleven Ticos have been arrested.

Carlos is one of them.

Callan drives into town to get details.

The local police chief talks to him.

It's not good. It's the largest cocaine bust ever in Costa Rica. Four tons of the shit. On Bustamente's boat and one other. Eleven people in custody, all of them young, not one of them with a prior criminal record.

They're all fishermen, Callan knows.

Tempted by the money.

Now they're fucked.

Two tons of coke? Whether Costa Rica tries them or the US does, they're looking at decades behind bars.

Callan drives back and he and Nora try to calm María. They'll get Carlos a lawyer, maybe he can make some kind of deal . . .

But Callan knows that isn't going to work.

If Carlos makes a deal, agrees to name names or testify, he's a dead man. They'll get to him in the jail.

They might anyway, just to be sure.

It's that night the *jefe* comes back.

He has two guys with him.

They stand off to the back and the side.

Callan's tarping the *panga* in expectation of a heavy storm that's supposed to be moving in. He hops down from the boat as the *jefe* walks up.

"You heard what happened?" the *jefe* asks.

"I heard."

"I'm wondering if you had something to do with it."

"I didn't."

"I don't know," the *jefe* says. "But you'd better talk to your boy, tell him to keep his mouth shut."

"He probably knows that already."

"Just in case he don't," the *jefe* says. "If he talks, I'll kill him, his mother, you, and that pretty wife of—"

The gun comes up from Callan's shirt in a smooth motion.

Before the *jefe*'s eyes can widen, Callan puts two bullets between them.

One of the *jefe*'s guys goes for his gun but he's way too slow and Callan puts two bullets in his face, then swings and does the same to the other guy.

Three dead in as many seconds.

Sean Callan, aka John Donovan, was known in another life as "Billy the Kid" Callan.

Hit man for the Irish mob.

Hit man for the Italian mob.

Hit man for Adán Barrera.

That was a different life, but some skills don't die.

Callan loads the three bodies into the *panga* and takes them way out. He shoves some divers' weights into their clothes and hefts them over the side. Then he tosses his pistol, a 9 mm Sig he's had for a long time and will miss.

It's raining hard now and Nora is curious when he comes in soaked. He tells her exactly what happened, because they don't lie to each other and after all she's been through, there's nothing that's going to shake her.

But it makes her uneasy, the Sinaloans being as close as Tamarindo. It was a long time ago, and most of the people she knew then are dead or in prison, but she had been Adán Barrera's legendary mistress. He was the Lord of the Skies and she was his lady, and there might still be people who could recognize her, remember her.

She hopes not, she's been happy here, finally at peace here, and she doesn't want to go on the run again. But if she has to . . .

They have money, safely stored in numbered accounts in the Caymans, Switzerland, the Cook Islands. They try to live on just the proceeds from the guest house, but if they need cash to disappear, it's there.

"Call María," Callan says. "Tell her it's okay for Carlos to name names."

"Are you sure?"

"The names he'd name are dead," Callan says. "If Carlos can make a deal, he should. All eleven of them should—the cartel could give a shit if they flip on dead men."

"What if the cartel sends more men down here?" Nora asks.

"They won't have to," Callan says.

He's going to the cartel.

. . .

Callan hasn't been in Mexico in twenty-one years.

He left after a shoot-out at the Guadalajara airport that killed the finest man he ever knew and never went back.

Father Juan Parada was his best friend.

Nora's as well.

Adán Barrera set him up to be killed.

Callan left it all after that—it was the mercy of God that he and Nora found each other, and sometimes Callan thinks it was Father Juan looking out for the two of them.

But now Callan's back in TJ.

So's Nora.

She wouldn't let him go by himself and finally talked him into it. He had to admit it was safer for her to be with him than by herself in Costa Rica.

He knows that if he's going to save their lives, it's going to be here.

They rent a car at the airport.

"Does it bring back memories?" Nora asks as they drive through Tijuana.

"A different life."

"Apparently not."

They drive to the Marriott in Chapultepec and check in as Mr. and Mrs. Mark Adamson, passports that Art Keller had arranged for them years ago. The room is bright and cheerful—white linens and pillows, white curtains, clean to the point of antiseptic.

Callan already misses Bahia.

He showers and carefully shaves, combs his hair and puts on a clean white guayabera and jeans.

"Stay in the hotel," he tells Nora.

"Yes, sir."

Callan smiles ruefully. "*Please* stay in the hotel."

"I will."

"I'd still feel better if you were in San Diego."

The border is barely two miles away.

"But I wouldn't," Nora says. "I'll be fine. How are you going to find her?"

"I'm not," Callan says. "I'm going to let them find me. I expect to be back in a few hours. If I'm not, you take your passport, you cross the bridge, you get in touch with Keller. He'll know what to do."

"I haven't spoken to Keller in sixteen years."

"I think he'll remember you." He kisses her. "I love you."

"I love you, too."

The valet brings the car up and Callan drives all the way out to Rosarito. The Club Bombay sits along the beach. It used to be one of their hangouts in Baja.

He takes a seat at the bar and orders a Tecate.

Asks the bartender, "Do the Barreras still own this place?"

The bartender doesn't like the question. He shrugs and asks, "Are you a reporter?"

"No," Callan says. "I worked for Adán back in the day."

"I don't think I know you." The bartender gives him a closer look.

"I haven't been here in a long time," Callan says.

The bartender nods and walks into the kitchen. Callan knows he's going to make a phone call.

It takes twenty minutes for the cop to get there.

A Baja state cop, not a local, in plainclothes.

He walks up to Callan, gets right to the point. "Let's you and me go for a walk."

"I was enjoying my beer."

"You'll enjoy it even more in the sunshine," the cop says. "Don't worry, no one will write you a ticket."

They walk out onto Avenida Eucalipto.

"American?" the cop asks.

"Once upon a time."

"New York," the cop says.

"How did you know?"

"It's a tourist town," the cop says. "I know accents. What brings you here, asking about the Barreras?"

"Old times."

"What did you do for El Señor?"

Callan looks straight at the cop. "I killed people for him."

The cop doesn't blink. "Is that what you're here for now?"

"It's what I'm here trying to avoid now."

The cop walks him toward a car parked at the edge of the beach. "Get in."

"First rule of a *yanqui* wanting to survive in Mexico," Callan says, "'Don't get in the cop car.'"

"I wasn't *asking*, Mr. . . ."

"Callan. Sean Callan."

The cop's pistol is out in a second. Pointed at Callan's head. "Get in the fucking car, Señor Callan."

Callan gets in the car.

. . .

Eighteen years and the legend still lives about "Billy the Kid" Callan. The American who was one of Adán Barrera's key gunmen in the war against Güero Méndez. How Callan saved Adán's life in an assassination attempt in Puerto Vallarta, fought alongside Raúl at the famous "Sinaloa Swap Meet" gun battle on Avenida Revolución in Tijuana, was there at the airport shoot-out when Cardinal Parada was killed.

They sing songs about Billy the Kid Callan, and now he sits in the back of an unmarked police car while the cop makes calls trying to figure out what to do with him.

Callan speaks pretty good Spanish by now so he knows what the cop is saying, picks up the phrase "Do you want us to just kill him?," among others. There are a whole bunch of phone calls, so it must be some discussion, and finally the cop rings off and starts the car.

"Where are we going?" Callan asks.

"You'll see."

Cops are cops, Callan thinks. Doesn't matter what nationality, they like to ask the questions, not answer them. He sits back in the seat and gives up on any further conversation as the car makes a long drive down the coast on Route 1 through Puerto Nuevo and La Misión. The car pulls off at the cloverleaf junction where Route 1 becomes Route 3.

A van sits by the side of the road.

Three men, armed with MAC-10s, get out and hold guns on Callan as the cop takes him out of the car and hands him over. One of the guards pats Callan down.

"You think I wouldn't know if he had a gun?" the cop asks, irritated.

"Just making sure."

The cop shakes his head, gets back in his car and drives off. The guard ushers Callan into the back of the van.

Another guy, maybe in his forties, Callan thinks, starts in as the van pulls south onto the road, toward El Sauzal. "What do you want? What are you doing here?"

He's not Mexican, and from his accent Callan makes him to be Israeli. It doesn't surprise him—the Barreras used to use a lot of former Israeli military as security.

"I want to speak with Señora Sánchez."

"Why? What for?" the Israeli asks.

"There's a problem."

"What? What kind of problem?" the Israeli asks. "Did Iván send you?"

"Who's Iván?"

"Who sent you?"

"No one," Callan says. "I came on my own."

"Why?"

"We going to keep doing this?" Callan asks.

"We don't have to," the Israeli says. "We could just shoot you and dump your body out on the road."

"You could," Callan says, "but that would make your boss unhappy."

"Why is that?"

"Because I saved her brother's life once," Callan says.

"I've heard the songs," the Israeli says. "They say a lot of things in songs that aren't true. 'I'll love you forever,' 'You're my everything' . . ."

"'Santa Claus is coming to town' . . ."

"This is what I mean." He yells for the van to pull over. It stops, and they jerk Callan out of the van and haul him into a vacant lot that was a baseball field and is now just gravel and dust. They start beating him. Punches and kicks rain down on him, but they're all to the body, not to the face or head, and Callan does his best to cover up and stay on his feet as the Israeli lectures him. "You do *not* come down here asking questions about the Barreras. You do *not* come down here without being asked. Do you think we'd allow a known gunman to just traipse around our territory? Why are you really here? What do you really want? Tell me and this can stop."

"I told you."

"I'm done with this," the Israeli says.

The guards shove Callan to his knees. The Israeli points a pistol at Callan's head. "Iván sent you!"

"No."

"Tell the truth! Iván sent you!"

"No!"

"Then who did?!"

"No one!"

"Liar!"

"I'm telling the truth!"

The Israeli pulls the trigger.

The sound is horrific, deafening. The muzzle flash scorches Callan's ear. He slumps face-first into the dust. The guards turn him over and he looks up at the Israeli's face. He can't hear a thing except the loud buzz in his ears, but he can read the man's lips as he says, "Last chance—tell me the truth."

"I am. I have."

They pick him up.

"Bring him back to the car."

They sit him in the van, give him a bottle of water, and Callan drinks as he watches the Israeli talk on the phone.

The van pulls out on the road and heads south.

"You're telling the truth," the Israeli says.

"I already knew that."

"What do you want to discuss with Señora Sánchez?"

"None of your fucking business."

The Israeli smiles.

Sometimes what they sing in songs is true.

Nora lies out by the pool and it reminds her of her youth.

The California Girl, the Golden Girl, the Laguna Beach babe that all her friends' fathers hit on. It was lying by a pool in Cabo, she reflects now, that she met Haley, who turned her out, put her into the life.

And all that followed.

Adán.

She was the mistress of the world's biggest dope dealer.

Then she became Keller's most valued informant.

Then Callan saved her life.

In so many ways, Sean has saved her life and made it worth living.

And she his.

They've built a life together, a life worth living, but then the past comes creeping out of its ooze, like old sins for which there's no redemption, only the delay of punishment, a suspension of the sentence, and now here they are back in Mexico.

As if Adán had reached out from the grave to pull them both back.

He loved her, she knows that. Maybe she even loved him once, before she knew what he really was. Art Keller told her, Art Keller taught her what Adán really was, and then Keller used her, like all the other men in her life used her.

Until Sean.

But you used them, too, she thinks. If you're honest with yourself—and what's the point otherwise—you used them, too.

So don't play the victim.

You're better than that.

Stronger.

Callan told her if he doesn't come back to walk across the bridge, but she isn't going to do that. If he doesn't come back, she's going to find him, bring him back or bring his body back or at the very least find out what happened to him, and now she's angry at herself that she let him go alone.

I should have gone with him, she thinks, forced him to "let" me. I could talk to Elena at least as well, if not better.

After all, I knew her.

Dined together, shopped together, shared family gatherings. She knew her brother loved me, she knew that I was good to him.

Up to a point.

She never knew that I betrayed him.

If she did . . .

But I should have gone.

The house sits on a point north of Ensenada.

The van stops at a security gate—the guard waves them through—then goes up a gravel driveway.

Callan doesn't go inside. The Israeli leads him around to an expanse of manicured green lawn overlooking the ocean and the black rocks below. A stand of tall palm trees wave in the breeze on the north side, a huge stretch of beach runs to the south, then there's a marina with sailboats. The house, Callan thinks, must cost millions. White stucco, enormous picture windows—tinted—generous decks and patios, several outbuildings.

The Israeli sits him in a white wrought-iron chair by a table and walks away—out of earshot, Callan notes, but within eyesight. A young woman clad all in black comes out and asks him if he'd like anything to drink or eat. A beer, perhaps, some iced tea, maybe a little fruit?

Callan declines.

A few minutes later, Elena Sánchez walks out of the house.

She's wearing a long, loose white dress; her black hair is tied back. She sits across from Callan, inspects him for a few moments, and then says, "I apologize for the rough treatment. You understand that my people had to be sure. I believe that you performed similar services for my brother. If story and song are to be believed, you saved his life once."

"More than once."

"Which is why I agreed to see you," Elena says. "Lev said there was some kind of problem?"

Callan gets right to it. "I killed three of your people."

"Oh."

Callan tells her what happened in Bahia, and then says, "I came to make things right."

"Sit for a few minutes, please," Elena says. "I'll be just back."

Callan watches her walk back to the house. Then he sits and looks at the ocean. The adrenaline is wearing off and his body is starting to hurt. Lev's guys are professionals—no bones are broken—but the bruises are deep.

And he's feeling his age.

Fifteen minutes later Elena comes back out.

A young man is with her.

"This is my son, Luis," Elena says. "He is actually in charge of the business now, so I thought he should be present."

If he were really in charge of the business, Callan thinks, *you* wouldn't be present, but he nods to Luis. "*Mucho gusto.*"

"*Mucho gusto.*"

It takes only a second glance at Luis to know that he doesn't want to be in charge of the family business, that he'd rather be anywhere in the world but in this discussion. Callan has known a lot of narcos—Luis isn't one of them.

"The three men you killed were independent contractors," Elena says, "but under our protection."

And paying a percentage of their profits for the privilege, Callan thinks. "I'm willing to pay restitution, even protection, if that's what it takes."

"You can't possibly pay what they were," Elena says. "I'm at war, Mr. Callan, and as I'm sure you remember, wars are expensive. I need all the income I can get. I need the money that was coming out of Costa Rica."

"I only want for my wife to be safe," Callan says. "So would Adán."

Elena looks surprised. "Why is that?"

"He loved her," Callan says.

It's rare, but Elena actually shows surprise. "You're married to Nora Hayden?"

"Yes."

"Extraordinary," Elena says. "I was always envious, such a beauty. Actually, I liked her very much. Do give her my best. All the legends coming back. First Rafael Caro, now you and Nora—"

There's a burst of noise as three children run out onto the south end of the lawn, giggling, yelling, chased by a nanny as another woman looks on.

"My grandchildren. The young are so resilient." She sees Callan's uncomprehending look and adds, "Their father was killed not too long ago. Murdered, actually. In front of them. Iván Esparza ordered his hit."

Which explains the war, Callan thinks. And my rough reception. *Iván sent you!*

She leans back in her chair and looks out at the ocean. "Beautiful, isn't it?"

It is if you haven't seen Bahia, Callan thinks.

"All this beauty, all this wealth," Elena says, "and we have to slaughter each other like animals. What is wrong with us, Mr. Callan?"

Callan assumes it's a rhetorical question.

"Perhaps we can come to some kind of arrangement," Elena says. "I give you amnesty for my three people, I leave your little village alone, not to mention the beauteous Nora . . ."

"In exchange for what?"

"Iván Esparza," she says. "Kill him for me."

As Lev drives him back to Rosarito, Callan thinks about Elena's offer.

Fight for me, fight for Luis. Help us take the cartel and if we win, I will give you everything you want.

Absolution.

Safety.

Your wife, your home.

Your life.

He knows he has no choice.

He's back in the war now.

Keller sits beside Marisol and watches the evening news.

Specifically, John Dennison announcing his candidacy for the presidency of the United States. *"I'm going to build a great wall along the Mexican border, and nobody builds walls better than me. I'll build a great, great wall down there, and you know who's going to pay for that wall? Mexico. Mark my words."*

"'Mark my words,'" Marisol says. "How is he going to get Mexico to pay for this damn wall?"

"Our country," Dennison goes on, *"has become a dumping ground. When Mexico sends its people, they're not sending their best. The people they send bring drugs, they bring guns, they bring crime. They're thieves, they're murderers and they're rapists."*

"It's an expensive TV," Keller says. "Please don't throw your glass through it."

"'Rapists'?!" Marisol says. "He calls us murderers and *rapists*?!"

"I don't think he meant you personally."

"How can you joke?" Marisol asks.

"Because it *is* a joke," Keller says. "This guy is a joke."

The Republicans might win the next election and I'll be out of a job, Keller thinks, but it won't be this guy handing me the pink slip, even though he's famous for firing people.

Dennison goes on, "*So many are in the room, so many friends—and they told me that the biggest problem they have up here is heroin. How is that possible with all these beautiful lakes and trees? The drugs are pouring across our southern border and when I say I'm going to build a wall—we're gonna have a real wall. We are going to build the wall, but we're going to stop the poison from pouring in and destroying our youth and plenty of other people. And we're going to work on those people that got addicted and are addicted.*"

The next morning the *Washington Post* asks Keller about Dennison's promise to build a wall.

"In terms of stopping drugs," Keller says, "a wall won't do a thing."

"Why not?"

"It's simple," Keller says. "The wall would still have gates. The three biggest are called San Diego, El Paso and Laredo—the busiest commercial border crossings in the world. A tractor-trailer truck comes through El Paso every fifteen seconds. Seventy-five percent of illegal drugs that come up from Mexico come through these legal crossings, most of them in trailer trucks, some in cars. There's no way we can stop and thoroughly search even a small portion of those trucks without completely shutting down commerce. There's no point in building a wall when the gates are open twenty-four/seven."

He knows he should let it go at that but he doesn't.

"You had to shoot your mouth off about the wall," O'Brien says.

"It's a stupid idea," Keller says. "It's worse than stupid, it's a cynical political ploy—to tell grieving parents in New Hampshire that you're going to stop the flow of heroin by building a wall."

"I agree," O'Brien says. "I just don't go to the *Post* and say it."

"Maybe you should," Keller says.

"It's the optics," O'Brien says. "The head of DEA comes out against something that might stop the flow of drugs from Mexico—"

"Again, it won't."

"—and he has a Mexican wife."

"I mean this with all respect and affection, Ben," Keller says. "Go fuck yourself."

"Dennison isn't going to win," O'Brien says. "His wall isn't going to get built. Leave it alone, let the silly season pass. Why pick a fight with this asshole?"

Because, Keller thinks, among other things, Dennison's son-in-law is neck deep in drug money.

Terra has gone to the well at least three times before, borrowing millions from HBMX for building projects in Hamburg, London and Kiev.

Claiborne was the syndication broker on the first two. The Kiev deal went through Sberbank, a Russian institution now under US sanction.

HBMX has its own problems. In 2012, its US affiliate was fined $2 billion for "failure to stop criminals using its banking systems to launder money." The investigation was a slow burn; over a five-year period HBMX in Mexico sent more than $15 billion in cash or suspicious bulk traveler's checks to its US branches. The bank was also sanctioned for "a resistance to closing accounts linked to suspicious activity"—it had over seventeen thousand unreviewed SARs.

No wonder, Keller thinks, it's a "lender of last resort."

But now Claiborne reports that Lerner is desperate.

He hasn't found a replacement for the Deutsche Bank money, the clock is running down on his balloon payment for Park Tower, and the building is hemorrhaging cash.

"Jason wants me to go to Russia," Claiborne told Hidalgo, "or Mexico."

Either way it's dirty money, Keller thinks, but he doesn't care if Claiborne goes to Russia. He cares very much if he goes to Mexico.

Things are going on down there.

The biggest development is the rapid rise of Tito Ascensión and the New Jalisco cartel. The CJN has aggressively moved into heroin and fentanyl, challenging Sinaloa's dominance. Ascensión's organization is moving product through the Baja crossings, has a strong presence in not only Jalisco, but also in Michoacán and Guerrero. It's also challenging the Zetas in Veracruz.

The battle isn't just about drug exports. Mexico now has a strong domestic drug market and the competition for local corners has turned cities like Tijuana, La Paz and a dozen others into battlegrounds. The killing has reached peaks not seen since the "bad old days" of 2010 and 2011.

The foreign and domestic sales are inextricably connected—the cartels pay their soldiers by giving them domestic turf—so the domestic markets pay for the manpower they need to control the border crossings.

It isn't just drugs—the local gangs that ally themselves with one or the other cartel make a lot of their money through extortion, forcing payoffs from bars, restaurants, hotels, virtually any businesses inside their territories.

It's a relatively new development—the old, dominant Sinaloa cartel never allowed extortion on the belief that it would alienate an otherwise neutral citizenry and force the government to take action.

The CJN has no such scruples. It's extorting businesses right in Mexico City, under the federal government's nose, and daring the ruling PRI party to do something about it.

The Mexican government has tried.

Back in January, the *federales* tried to capture Ascensión but botched it. They did, however, arrest his son, Rubén.

Ascensión retaliated, ambushing a convoy of *federales* in Ocotlán with machine guns and rockets launchers and killing five of them.

The government struck back, hitting Ascensión's ranch in rural Jalisco in a predawn raid.

Two French-made, Mexican air force EC-725 Caracals—"Super Cougars"—swooped in low over the trees. Pairs of 7.62 mm machine guns peeked out the left and right front windows, and each craft was loaded with twenty *federales* or elite army paratroopers with orders to kill or capture Tito Ascensión.

The idea was to catch him sleeping at one of his many ranches and put him to sleep for good.

Except Tito was wide awake.

On a burn phone in the reinforced bedroom of the hacienda, he watched the choppers come and waited until the lead helicopter started to hover and he saw the paratroopers start to rappel down on a rope like lollipops on a stick.

And just as helpless, dangling in the air.

Five armored trucks, hidden under camouflage netting, roared out of the trees. His household guard—also elites, trained by former Israeli special forces, wore uniforms, and each truck was stenciled CJN SPECIAL FORCES HIGH COMMAND.

They opened fire with AKs.

Lollipops dropped from the sky.

A CJN gunman fired a rocket at the second helicopter, hitting it in the rear rotor. The chopper spun, crashed to the ground and burst into flames.

The "surprise" raid was over.

Nine soldiers were dead, others hideously burned.

Over the next two days, CJN gunmen ran riot all over Jalisco, hijacking and burning cars and buses, torching gas stations and even banks, even in the resort town of Puerto Vallarta. The government had to send in ten thousand troops, at enormous expense, to restore a vestige of order.

Three weeks later a group of *federales* spotted a convoy of cars with armed men leaving a ranch in Michoacán near the Jalisco border. They'd had intelligence that Tito Ascensión was possibly hiding at Rancho del Sol, so they tried to pull the cars over.

The men in the cars opened fire and raced back to the ranch.

The *federales* called in reinforcements.

First forty more *federales*, then sixty more, then a Black Hawk helicopter poured more than two thousand rounds into the ranch buildings, killing six CJN gunmen and capturing three.

Two of the CJN dead were Jalisco state police officers.

One *federal* was killed.

But Tito Ascensión was not among the dead or the captured.

Mexico City decided it just wouldn't do.

They needed a victory.

Better headlines.

The *federales* drove around the area and picked up thirty-three more suspects, men who were known or reputed to be on CJN's payroll. They brought them to the ranch and shot them in the back of the head. Then they scattered the bodies around the ranch, placed assault rifles and rocket launchers in their hands and announced that they killed forty-two CJN gunmen in the course of a vicious, three-hour firefight.

It got headlines, all right.

The Mexican media—including Ana—jumped on it, and mostly published stories that the "gun battle" was a sham and that the *federales* had basically executed forty-two men who probably had no connection to the CJN.

"Forty-nine in Tristeza," Ana wrote, "now forty-two in Jalisco. Is the federal government simply murdering its opponents?"

Or is the government simply murdering Sinaloa's opponents? Keller thinks. There's a precedent, and he was involved in it, providing US intelligence to Orduña and the FES to take down the Zetas, Adán Barrera's enemies.

And there is no question that Sinaloa and CJN are at war.

All DEA's sources report that Ascensión blames Sinaloa for the attacks on him and his son's imprisonment. The consensus is that he was behind the failed assassination attempt on Ricardo Núñez, although a minority believes that it was Iván Esparza.

That seems unlikely, Keller thinks, given the reports that Núñez reversed his previous decision and granted the Baja plaza back to the Esparzas. If true, it was the smart move, even if it alienated Elena Sánchez and drove her into Ascensión's arms, as it were. Núñez needs the Esparzas' manpower to fight his war against Ascensión.

But it has thrown Baja into absolute chaos, a multisided war as the reunited Núñez and Esparza forces fight it out with the rebel Sánchez organization and its CJN ally. So far, none of the leaders have gone at each other directly—since the attack on Núñez—but are fighting it out on the street level, slaughtering each other's corner dealers and shakedown thugs.

The "street" is suffering.

Dealers, soldiers, bar owners barely know from day to day who's in control, who they're supposed to pay, to whom they owe their loyalties. Any mistake is lethal, and they're blind pawns in a game of 3-D chess, and they're getting knocked off the board with increasing frequency.

And brutality.

Bodies are hung from bridges and overpasses, burned, decapitated, chopped up and the pieces strewn along the sidewalks. One Sinaloa operative—the chief of the Núñez armed forces, a psychotic little number named La Fósfora—has taken to spray-painting the corpses green, proclaiming it Sinaloa's color, and that "Baja is green."

What Baja is, Keller thinks, is an *abattoir*.

If it were just the only one.

Sinaloa and CJN are also fighting for port cities, not only for the drug sales and extortion but for the critical ability to control the shipping from China that provides both fentanyl and the base chemical for methamphetamine.

But port cities also tend to be resort towns, and now famous vacation destinations like Acapulco, Puerto Vallarta and Cabo San Lucas have experienced heretofore unheard-of violence, driving away critical tourist dollars.

The more prosaic ports like Lázaro Cárdenas, Manzanillo, Veracruz and Altamira have become battlegrounds, Veracruz in a three-way fight between Sinaloa, CJN and the Zetas. In Acapulco, the Sinaloa versus CJN struggle is complicated by the presence of Damien Tapia and the old remnants of the Eddie Ruiz organization.

Only two supercartels exist now, Keller thinks—Sinaloa and CJN. But there are a handful of second-tier organizations: the "New Tijuana" cartel headed by the Sánchez family; the Zetas, who are resurgent in Tamaulipas and parts of Chihuahua; and Guerreros Unidos, who seem to be allied with the old Tapia organization under Damien Tapia. Then there are the remnants of the Knights Templar and Familia Michoacán. Those are the major players, but there are now more than eighty identifiable DTOs in Mexico.

If Keller had to handicap it, he'd pick CJN, albeit narrowly. They've made large gains in heroin profits, and Tito is the more experienced war leader. There's no question that Núñez is personally weakened, still recovering from his wounds, and that the Núñez wing is being led by his son, Ric. On the other hand, Mini-Ric seems to be growing in the role, he has an alliance with Iván Esparza, who is a strong wartime leader, and Ascensión is somewhat constrained in his actions because his son is in federal custody. But if pushed, Keller would have to say that CJN is the most powerful cartel in Mexico now.

Which is a tectonic shift in the power structure.

But the Mexican federal government is going after Tito hammer-and-tongs, so he hasn't leveraged his new power into political influence.

Mexico City is still hanging on to Ricardo Núñez and Sinaloa.

John Dennison is running for president.

And his son-in-law is digging for drug money.

He's one of Los Hijos, Keller thinks.

The party is in full swing.

For Oviedo's birthday, Iván has taken over a whole restaurant in Puerto Vallarta and invited all Los Hijos and their wives.

No *segunderas* allowed.

Girlfriends and mistresses are for the after party, which Ric knows will be a drug- and booze-fueled orgy, but the dinner at the posh restaurant is a pretty grown-up affair—the guys all cleaned up, the wives dressed to the nines. All in black, as per the invitation, because the restaurant is all white—white walls, white furniture, white tablecloths.

Elegant, adult.

The food is also very adult—beef tartare, shrimp *aguachile* to start, then pork shoulder, seafood ravioli and duck ragout, polished off with chocolate crème brûlée and banana bread pudding.

Ric sips on a cucumber martini—new one on him—and talks with his wife, also a relatively new one on him but it's something he's been doing more and more, spending most of his nights at home with Karin and the baby.

The weird thing, even Ric has to admit, is that his father's wounding, and the long recovery, has forced Ric to become the guy people think he is, that his father wants him to be. And he starts to enjoy it, discovers that when he stops the partying, the boozing, the drugging, that he likes taking care of the business—the strategizing, the allocation of resources and personnel, even fighting the war against Elena and Tito.

Ric and Iván sit down regularly to coordinate their activities vis-à-vis the Cartel Baja Nuevo Generación, the CBNG. It's complicated—street dealers on some corners had to be shifted from Núñez to Esparza and vice versa; likewise, their respective gunmen, spies and cops have to be given clear divisions of responsibilities and territories so they're not tripping over each other's feet.

It's detailed, painstaking work, the kind of thing Ric would have run away from just a few months ago but now diligently tackles. They pore over Google Maps, discuss reports from *halcones,* even standardize the money they pay to police so that the cops don't try to play one against the other.

"The New Baja Generation Cartel," Ric had said at one of their meetings, "is just Luis's way of letting everyone know that he's in charge now."

"It's going to take more than that," Iván said. "Everyone knows that Mami still calls the shots. Luis is an engineer. What does he know about running an organization or fighting a war?"

What do *we* know?, Ric thought, but he didn't say it. We're all new to this, even Iván. None of us were serious about this shit until recently, and now it's all on-the-job-training. Luis might not know dick about fighting a war, but Tito Ascensión knows plenty; Tito's forgotten more than we ever knew.

Iván asked about Damien. "How are you doing on the great Young Wolf hunt?"

"Nothing," Ric said. "You?"

"The kid has disappeared," Iván said. "Probably a good idea. That was fucked up, what he did."

"No question, but . . ."

"But?" Iván asked.

"I don't know," Ric said, "was it really that bad? End of the day, no one that matters got hurt."

"That's not the point," Iván said. "He disrespected us."

"He attacked Elena," Ric said. "The woman we're at war with right now?"

Like, maybe we should be allies with Damien?

"Doesn't matter," Iván said. "He attacked Adán Barrera's mother. Your godfather's mother. We let someone get away with that, we might as well just bend over and let everyone fuck us up the ass. No, Damien's gotta go."

"Okay, but there's 'going' and there's 'going,'" Ric said. "You know what I mean?"

"He has to go hard, Ric."

"Okay."

"Ric . . ."

"I heard you," Ric said. It was worth a shot. He changed the subject. "Hey, speaking of disrespect, did you see where that fucking *yanqui* said he'd kick our asses?"

"Who?" Iván asked. "Dennison? The one running for president? The one who's going to build this wall?"

"He said if he gets elected, he's going to 'kick the Sinaloa cartel's collective ass,'" Ric said. "He put it out on Twitter."

Iván got that Iván look on his face, the one that usually meant trouble. "Let's fuck with him."

"What do you mean?"

"Guy likes to tweet, right?" Iván took out his phone. "So let's tweet."

"This isn't smart."

"Oh, come on," Iván said. "We've been too good lately. All work and no play. We need to have a little fun, too."

He typed into his phone and showed it to Ric.

If you keep pissing us off, we're going to make you eat your words, you Ronald McDonald, Cheeto-headed, fat bastard. —the Sinaloa Cartel

"Jesus Christ, Iván, don't hit send."

"Too late, just did," Iván said. "He'll piss his pants."

"I think I just pissed mine," Ric said.

But he was laughing.

Iván was laughing, too. "We're the fucking Sinaloa cartel, *'mano*! We got more money than this guy, we got more men than this guy, more guns than this guy, more brains, bigger balls! We'll see who kicks whose ass. Fuck him. *¡Los Hijos siempre!*"

Los Hijos forever, Ric thought.

He left the meeting and went back to looking for Damien where he wasn't. Which didn't mean, however, that he knew where Damien was.

Belinda kept doing Belinda.

Her people found out that the head of operations for the CBNG hung out at a *palenque* in Ensenada.

The man liked his cockfighting.

She hit it and killed four CBs but the guy got away.

Not for long.

Two weeks later, he was going home from a meeting at four in the morning on Highway 1 when La Fósfora and her people pulled up alongside his Navigator on motorcycles and ventilated it, him, the driver and his bodyguard.

Belinda and Gaby dismounted and spray-painted the bodies green.

"I've decided that's our color," Belinda explained. "Sinaloa in Baja is green. I'm calling it the 'green sky.' It's optics."

"Optics."

"Optics are important," Belinda said. "I watch CNN."

Optics are important but so are words, which explained why she also left a placard on the bodies that read: *The sky is green, CB motherfuckers. We are here and we will always be here —Sinaloa in Baja.*

A month later, she found another CB operative at a strip club in TJ's

Zona Río and left his (green) pieces in a black plastic bag with the message: *Just another reminder that we're still here and will always be here. You don't even exist. The sky will always be green, even for strippers and CB/Jalisco dollies.*

"What do you have against strippers?" Ric asked.

"Nothing," she said. "I like strippers. I like strippers a lot. But if they're going to strip, they're going to strip for us, not those CB traitors and their Jalisco buddies."

"Yeah, but 'dollies'?"

Belinda looked concerned. "You think that's sexist? Because I'm a feminist, I'm all about women's empowerment. I mean, I'm the first female head of security for a major cartel, right? And I don't want people thinking—"

"No, you're good."

"You still on your search-and-avoid mission?" she asked.

"We really can't find Damien," Ric said. "What we hear is that he's buried deep somewhere in Guerrero."

"You want me to send some of my people?"

"Focus on Baja."

"The fuck you think I've been doing?" she asked.

Yeah, *green sky,* Ric thought.

"This is delicious," Karin says now, holding up a spoon of pudding. "Have you tried it?"

"It's great."

"How old is Oviedo anyway?" Karin asks.

"Twenty-five going on thirteen," Ric says.

Technically, Oviedo is the plaza boss for Baja, but Ric finds it easier to work around him and meet with Iván, who's having a hard time letting go of control anyway. Oviedo is a nice kid, but he's still a kid, not serious, and Ric finds it tough to get anything done with him.

Iván walks over to the table. "I have to make a call. You got this?"

Ric nods.

"Where's he really going?" Karin asks.

"There's sort of a party after the party," Ric says. "He's probably taking care of a few details."

Coke, hookers . . . coke.

"Are you going to that?" Karin asks.

"No, I'm going back to the hotel with you."

"Are you sorry you're not going?"

"No," Ric says. "No, I'm not."

About five minutes later the restaurant door opens and Ric looks over, expecting to see Iván, but instead sees a guy dressed in black with a hood over his head and an AK-47 pointing in front of him.

Putting his hands on Karin's shoulders, Ric pushes her under the table. "Stay there."

More men come through the door.

Ric sees Oviedo reach for a gun at his waist that isn't there. None of them are carrying, this being a fancy dinner in Jalisco where Tito Ascensión has personally guaranteed the Esparza brothers' security. So they're totally fucking helpless as the gunmen—there are about fifteen of them—start to sort the women from the men.

Karin screams as a man reaches under the table and grabs her wrist.

"It's okay, babe," Ric says to her. To the gunman, he says, "You hurt her, I'll kill you."

The gunman who came in first starts shouting orders. "Women on this wall! Men on that wall! Move!"

Ric knows the voice.

Damien.

Ric steps over to the wall and lines up alongside Oviedo, Alfredo and six other men. He looks across the dining room at Karin, who's crying and looks terrified.

He smiles at her.

The floor is littered with handbags, purses and high-heeled shoes.

"Go!" Damien yells.

His people start down the line of men and one by one turn them against the wall, secure their wrists behind their backs with plastic ties, and walk them out the door.

Ric's the last one.

"Not him!" Damien yells. "Leave him!"

He walks up to Ric. "Where's Iván?"

"I don't know, man." Ric shrugs.

Damien leans back and points the AK barrel at Ric's face. "Where the fuck is he?!"

Ric feels dizzy, like he's going to pass out. Feels like he could shit his pants but he forces his voice to stay level as he says, "I told you, I don't know."

He can see Damien's eyes through the slits in the hood.

They're blazing with adrenaline.

"We'll wait for him," Damien says.

"You don't have time for that, D," Ric says with a calm he didn't know he had. "We have people just down the street. They'll be here any second. If I were you, I'd go before you have to shoot your way out."

"I heard you've been sticking up for me," Damien says.

"Now I'm sorry I did."

"Don't be," Damien says. "It's the only reason I'm not taking you with the rest of them."

Then Damien backs off and yells, "Okay! Let's go! We got what we came for!"

Well, two out of three brothers, anyway, Ric thinks.

The gunmen go out, and Damien is the last through the door.

Ric goes and grabs Karin. Wraps his arms around her and says, "It's okay, it's okay. It's all good now."

Except he knows it's not.

Keller sits with Marisol on the little deck outside the second floor, trying to get some relief from the sweltering August night. Summers in DC are what he calls "three-shirt weather"—if you go out more than once, you have to change your shirt twice.

Marisol has made a pitcher of sangria, though, and they drink it over ice, like *yanqui* barbarians, and she's instructing him that the way to deal with the heat is to sit completely still when his phone rings.

It's Hidalgo. "Someone grabbed up the Esparza brothers. Well, two of them anyway."

"Which two?"

"It's unclear right now," Hidalgo says. "Univision has had it three ways so far. Check this out—a group of gunmen waltzed into a restaurant in PV where they were having some kind of party, grabbed all the men and took them outside into a van. They let everyone go except for the Esparzas."

"Who has the balls to do that?"

"I don't know," Hidalgo says. "Says something about Sinaloa, though, doesn't it?"

Yeah, Art thinks—people aren't afraid of them anymore.

Although they did kick up a short-lived media scare when they threatened "the candidate," as Keller has come to call him.

Now he says, "I'll meet you at the office."

"So much for remaining completely still," Marisol says.

"I will when I'm dead."

Plenty of time for that then, he thinks.

. . .

Iván is apoplectic. "He has my brothers! He has my brothers!"

"Calm down," Ric says.

"*You* fucking calm down!" Iván yells. "He has my brothers! He could have killed them already, for all I know!"

It's been forty-five minutes, Ric thinks.

If Damien had dropped their bodies somewhere, they'd probably have heard about it by now. And he and Iván have men out all over Puerto Vallarta, cruising the streets, the back roads, searching the beaches. They're talking to cabdrivers, street people, even tourists, asking if anyone has seen anything.

So far nothing.

And no phone call.

No ransom demand.

What the fuck is Damien doing? Ric wonders. If he wanted to kill the Esparzas, he could have just done it at the restaurant. But now he has hostages. For what? Ransom money? Something else?

"Why did he leave you behind?" Iván asks.

"So he would have someone to negotiate with," Ric says. "Someone he trusts."

"That better be the reason," Iván says.

"What are you saying?" Ric asks.

"I don't know," Iván says. "I'm out of my fucking head right now. I swear to God, I'll take Damien's sisters, I'll take his mother—"

"Don't do anything rash," Ric says. "Don't do anything that makes the situation worse. We will work this out. Let's go back to Culiacán. We can't do anything here."

"Don't tell me what to do," Iván says. "This is the guy you wanted to show mercy to, right? This is the guy who didn't do anything all that bad . . . When I find him, and I will find him, I'm going to carve him up like a chicken, then I'm going to slice all the skin off him, then I'm going to start getting serious."

"If he was going to kill your brothers, he would have done it already."

"How do you know he hasn't?"

"Because he can't," Ric says. "He's just figured it out. He went for the home run swing, to take out the Esparza brothers. But he missed the most important one—you. He swung and missed, Iván. Now he has to deal with you."

"Then why hasn't he?"

Damien has to make his strikeout look like a hit, Ric thinks. He can do that in the media, pretend this was an exercise to show the world that the Sinaloa cartel isn't what it used to be, that he can stick it to them, he's not afraid and no one else should be, either. So he'll let the media have a field day with this, just like they did after the raid on the Barrera hacienda. Maybe, hopefully, humiliating the Esparzas is enough for him.

"He'll hold them until the story loses legs," Ric says. "Then he'll let them go. Unless you get stupid here, Iván."

If Iván goes Iván, gets all crazy and grabs the Tapia women, then Oviedo and Alfredo will probably end up facedown in a ditch somewhere.

And that, Ric thinks, will launch a war that won't *ever* end.

His father doesn't meet him in the office, but in the living room.

Núñez sits in a big easy chair, the cane he needs less and less now leaning on the arm of the chair.

He still looks weak, Ric thinks.

Better, out of danger now, but still weak. He hasn't gained back much weight, and his face is drawn, his skin pale.

And he speaks softly, as if it's an effort. "However this works out, I'll be blamed. They'll say I'm too passive, too vacillating, so weak that the Young Wolf felt emboldened to walk in and kidnap two of the Sinaloa royal family. And if the Esparza boys are dead, Iván will break away from the cartel and go out on a blood-soaked vendetta against the Tapia organization that will further inflame the country. The government will be forced to respond and will wonder why I can't keep control. They'll look for someone who can. Perhaps Tito."

"Tito was in on this," Ric says. "He had to give at least his tacit permission for this to have happened in Jalisco."

"That's right," Núñez says. "Tito holds the key, but we can hardly reach out to him."

So, Ric thinks, we have to reach out to someone who can.

Rafael Caro tilts his chair back.

Ric sees the soles of the old man's shoes.

The left one has a hole in it.

"Don Rafael," Núñez Sr. says, "thank you for hosting this meeting. As a venerated, respected elder statesman, the éminence grise, as it were—"

"What's he talking about?" Caro asks.

"I think he means you have gray hair," Tito says.

"It's white," Caro says. "I'm an old man, retired, no longer connected to the business. I don't have a dog in this fight. But if that lets me be an objective mediator, I'm happy to do what I can to help settle this problem."

He might be the only one who can, Ric thinks. The only neutral party with prestige enough to make everyone come to the room, and to accept whatever comes out of it.

When he first got there, Ric was shocked at the famous Rafael Caro's shabby living conditions. Now they all sit, crowded into the small, stuffy living room as an old TV drones on low volume. There is no table, none of the usual feast that typically accompanies a meeting. Caro's gofer had just offered each person a glass of water—no ice—and Ric sits on a footstool sipping his from an old jelly jar.

Outside, it's a different story.

The security is immense.

His father's people are there, so are Iván's, and so are Tito's—all standing by their vehicles, fully armed, waiting for the slightest spark to set this off. Farther off, state police have set up a cordon to keep curious public or, God forbid, media far away.

Not to mention the army or the *federales*.

Ric knows that's not going to happen. The government has as much interest in this meeting going well as anyone here. They don't want this blowing up.

"Why isn't Damien here?" Iván asks.

"I can speak for him," Tito says.

"And why is that?"

"Because he knows he'd be killed if he came," Tito says. "And, as I said—and I won't say it again—I can speak for him and guarantee he'll accept whatever decisions are reached here."

"So that means he's with you," Iván says, jumping to his feet. "That means you were in on this with him."

"Sit down," Caro says. "Sit down, young man."

Amazingly, Ric thinks, Iván sits.

He glares at Tito, but the Mastiff doesn't grace him with a look back. Instead, he addresses Caro. "Some people in this room have tried to have me killed. The same people in this room had my son put in jail, where he remains because these people have told their judges not to set him free. But . . . out of my respect for Ignacio Esparza, I am here as a go-between to try to free *his* sons."

"Can you guarantee the Esparza brothers' safety?" Caro asks him.

"They're safe and comfortable," Tito says.

"I want them released!" Iván says.

"Everyone wants them released," Caro says. "That's why we're all here, am I correct? So, Tito, why don't you tell us what that's going to take. What does the Young Wolf want?"

"First of all, he wants an apology for murdering his father."

Iván says, "We didn't—"

"Your father was part of that decision," Tito says. "So were other people in this room."

"As were you," Núñez says. "I seem to recall that you were particularly effective in fighting the Tapias."

Tito looks to Caro. "Tell that person not to speak to me."

"Don't speak to him," Caro says. "So?"

"I imagine," Núñez says, "that we can find some forum to express . . . regret . . . about what happened to the Tapia family."

Caro looks at Tito. "What else?"

"He wants forgiveness for the attack on the Barrera home," Tito says.

"He wants a pass for that?!" Iván says. "That's not right!"

"It's not a matter of right or wrong," Caro says. "It's a matter of power. Tapia has your two brothers and that gives him the power to make demands."

"But there are standards," Iván says. "There are rules. You don't touch families."

"I'm old enough to remember when Adán Barrera beheaded my old friend's wife and threw his two children off a bridge," Caro says. "So let's not talk about 'rules.'"

"I can only speak for our organization," Núñez says, his voice tired. "I can't speak for Elena. Maybe you can, Tito. But as for us, we are willing to forget the attack on the Barreras. Is there anything else?"

"If Damien releases his hostages," Tito says, "he wants a guarantee that there will be no recriminations against him."

"He's out of his fucking mind," Iván says. "I'll kill him, I'll kill his family—"

"Shut up, Iván," Ric says.

Iván glares at him.

But he shuts up.

Núñez says, "Young Damien can't expect to kidnap major figures in the cartel, hold us all up to ridicule in the media, and get away with it. What will people think? We'd lose respect, make ourselves targets."

"You can't expect the boy to negotiate his life away," Tito says. "If he's going to be killed anyway, he has nothing to lose by killing the Esparzas first."

"We're at loggerheads here," Núñez says.

"I'm tired." Caro pulls a phone out of his pants pocket and punches in some numbers. While it's connecting he says, "Sinaloa will issue an apology and forgive the attack on the Barrera home. There will, however, be no amnesty for this kidnapping."

Tito looks at Iván. "Then your brothers are dead."

"You swore to protect them," Iván says.

Caro holds up the phone.

Ric leans forward and sees Rubén, Tito's son, standing in an office, surrounded by prison guards. His old friend looks scared.

He should.

One of the guards has a knife to his neck.

"The Esparzas will be released," Caro says to Tito, "or your son's throat will be cut while you watch. But once they are released, a judge will find that there were no grounds for the charges against your son, that the raid on his house was illegal, and will order him released."

After all, Ric thinks, it's not about right or wrong, is it?

It's about power.

"Do we have an agreement, Tito?" Caro asks.

"Yes." He looks at Núñez and Iván. "This is just a truce, not a peace."

"Good," Iván says.

Núñez just nods.

"You had better call young Damien," Caro says to Tito. "When we hear that the Esparzas are free, the arrangements to free your son will go forward."

"I need more detail than that."

"You need more than my word?" Caro asks, staring him down.

Tito doesn't answer.

"Good," says Caro. He struggles up from the chair. "Now I'm going for a nap. When I get up, I don't want to see any of you, and I don't want to hear that you've killed each other. I was at the table when M-1 put this thing together. I was in prison when all of you let it fall apart."

He walks into his bedroom and shuts the door.

On the drive back Ric asks his father, "You knew about Rubén and the prison before we went in the room, didn't you? You knew Caro had that kind of influence with the government."

"Or I wouldn't have gone in the room," Núñez says.

"Let me ask you something," Ric says. "If Tito hadn't caved, would you have let them kill Rubén?"

"It wasn't up to me," Núñez says. "But Caro would have, you can be sure. It was a pretty safe bet that Tito would back down—it's the rare man willing to be Abraham."

"What does that mean?"

"That it's a rare man who will sacrifice his own son."

Ric smiles. "Which begs the question . . ."

"Of course not," Núñez says. "I'm shocked you would ask. You're my son and I love you, Ric. And I'm proud of you. What you've done lately . . ."

"So we won."

"No," Núñez says. "The world knows Damien felt safe enough to do what he did. That's a blow to our prestige. I want you to put it out on social media what we did with Rubén. That will help, it will show we're ruthless. Still potent. Put it out through one of our bloggers so it can't be tracked back to us. If anyone asks if it really happened, deny it—that will make them believe it even more."

"So Damien's allied with Tito now," Ric says. "What does Elena think about that?"

"What choice does she have?" Núñez says. "She doesn't like it, but she has to accept it. With Tito and Damien on her side, she thinks she can beat us. And she might not be wrong. Because Caro might be with her now, too."

"He just sided with us!"

"Did he?" Núñez asks. "Think about it. Tito got what he really wanted. His son is going to be released. At no cost except making Damien let the Esparzas go. I wouldn't be surprised if Caro okayed their kidnapping. I wouldn't be surprised if Caro was behind the whole thing."

"Why would he do that?"

"To make us come to him," Núñez says. "Now we owe him, Tito owes him, Damien owes him. And he just showed the world that he's the only one who can make a deal. Now he'll sit back and see who's winning. Then he'll make his real move."

Núñez lays his head back on the seat and closes his eyes.

"Caro," he says, "wants to be El Patrón."

La Bestia

Suffer the little children,
and forbid them not . . .
—Matthew 19:14

Guatemala City
September 2015

For all of his ten years, Nico Ramírez has known nothing but El Basurero. The garbage dump is his world.

He's a *guajero,* one of the thousands who scrape out a scant living scavenging garbage in the city dump.

Nico is very good at what he does.

A small scrawny kid dressed in torn jeans, holey sneakers and his one treasure—a Barcelona *fútbol* shirt with the name of his hero, Lionel Messi, number 10, on the back—he is a master at eluding the guards at the big green gates into the dump. Kids aren't supposed to go in—although Nico is one of the thousands who do—and he doesn't have one of the precious ID cards that would gain him entrance as an "employee," so he has to pick his spots.

That's where being small helps, and now, clutching a black plastic bag in his right hand, he ducks down behind an adult woman and waits for the guard to turn his head. When the guard does, Nico dashes in.

The dump occupies forty acres in a deep ravine, and Nico looks up to see the parade of yellow city dump trucks wind its way down the switchback, delivering over five hundred tons of garbage every day. Each truck has numbers and letters painted on the side and Nico, although he can barely read or write, knows the meanings of these numbers and letters as well as he knows the alleys and warrens of the shantytown he lives in just outside the dump. The codes refer to the neighborhood from which the truck collects, and Nico has his eye peeled for the trucks that come from the rich parts of the city, because that's where the best trash comes from.

Rich people throw away a lot of food.

Nico is hungry.

He's always hungry.

He throws away nothing.

The boy's hair and skin are white from the perpetual cloud of smoke and dust that hangs over the dump and permeates every aspect of the *basureros'* lives—their clothes, their skin, their eyes, their mouths, their lungs. His eyes are bloodshot, his cough chronic. The smell of smoldering garbage— sour, fetid, acid—is in his nostrils, but he knows nothing different.

No one in El Basurero does.

Nico wipes his nose with his sleeve—his nose is always running—and peers through the smog at the line of trucks winding down into the ravine.

Then he spots it—NC–3510A.

Playa Cayalá, a rich neighborhood all the way out in Zone 10.

Those people, they throw away treasures.

Moving deeper into the dump, he tries to gauge where the Cayalá truck will stop. He knows other *basureros* have spotted it, too, and the competition will be fierce. Some people say that there are five thousand dump pickers, others say it's more like seven thousand, but it's always crowded and it's always a fight for the good stuff.

His mother is among them somewhere, but Nico is too intent on tracking the Cayalá truck to look for her. He'll see her at home later, hopefully with money in his hand from collecting a full bag.

He does spot La Buitra.

The Vulture.

Thousands of *real* vultures circle overhead, waiting to land and fight the human *guajeros* for the choice scraps, but La Buitra—Nico doesn't know her real name—has the keenest eye of them all. The middle-aged woman has sharp eyes and long sharp fingernails that she's not afraid to use. She'll claw, scratch, kick, bite—anything to get at the best pickings.

Then there's her stick—a short piece of wood with a sharp metal spike she uses to stab bits of garbage and put them in the bag. Or she uses it to poke people out of her way.

Or worse.

One time Nico saw her plunge the spike into Flor's hand. Flor is his friend, about his age, and one time she stooped under La Buitra to grab a sandwich wrapped in yellow paper and La Buitra jammed the spike right into the back of her hand.

It got infected and her hand still isn't right.

There's a hole in it just the size of La Buitra's spike and it's all red around it and sometimes yellow stuff oozes out the hole and Flor can't close her hand the whole way.

That's what La Buitra will do.

But Nico's not afraid of her—at least, that's what he tells himself.

I'm faster, Nico thinks, and smarter. I can duck under her claws, jump away from her kicks. She can't catch me—no one in El Basurero can.

Nico wins every race, even against the older kids. Nico Rápido, they call him, "Fast Nicky," and on the rare occasions when they can find something resembling a *fútbol,* Nico is the star—quick, shifty, clever, skilled with his feet.

Now he sees that La Buitra has spotted the Cayalá truck.

Nico can't let her get to it first.

He needs the money that truck might bring, needs it desperately because he and his mother already owe the *mara* a week's payment, and if they fall another week behind, the gang's retribution will be terrible.

A good *guajero* can make as much as five dollars a day, and of that, they owe the *mara* two dollars and fifty cents, or half of anything they make. Everyone in El Basurero, everyone in every barrio, pays the *mara*—either MS-13 or 18th Street—half of what they make.

Nico has seen what happens to people who don't make their payments—he's seen them beaten with sticks and electric cords, seen the gangsters pour boiling water over their children, seen them drag the mother of the family to the ground and rape her.

He and his mother have been saving every *quetzal*—the money that might otherwise have gone to breakfast this morning is in a tin can buried in their dirt floor—but they are still behind, and Calle 18 will be by to collect tonight.

A *marero* came last night to tell them so.

His name is "Pulga." They call him the Flea because he bites and bites and bites, sucking blood out of everyone in the neighborhood. Nico is terrified of him—the Flea's face is covered with tattoos: the Roman numerals *XVIII* cross his forehead, the letters *UNO* run down the right side of his nose, the letters *OCHO* down the other. Mayan designs are inked on the rest of his face so that not a square inch of flesh shows.

Pulga looked down at Nico's mother, who sat on the dirt floor with her knees folded under her. "Where's my money, *puta?*"

"I don't have it."

"You 'don't have it'?" Pulga asked. "You'd better get it."

"I will." Her voice was shaking.

Pulga squatted in front of her. Skinny, his muscles taut, he took her chin between his fingers and lifted it, forcing her to look at him. "*Puta,* you have my money tomorrow or I will take it out of your pussy, your ass, your mouth."

He saw the flash of anger in Nico's eyes.

"What, little faggot?" Pulga asked. "What are you going to do? Stop me? Maybe I make you suck my cock, get it good and hard for your *mami*."

Nico was ashamed, but he pressed himself back against the wall, a section of an old movie billboard they'd found in the dump.

Pulga said, "You want your *mami* to have a good time, don't you?"

Nico looked down.

"Answer me, *hijo*," Pulga said. "Don't you want your *mami* to have a good time fucking me?"

"No."

"No?" Pulga said. "What limp dick did she fuck to make you? She didn't have a good time then, did she?"

The insult hurts Nico's heart. He was four when his *papi* died, and they buried him in the Muro de Lágrimas, the Wall of Tears—tiny crypts built into the cliff above the dump like little apartment buildings, one on top of the other. Nico and his mother have to come up with twenty dollars a year to keep his remains there. If you don't pay, or can't afford to be put there in the first place, they toss your body down into the ravine below the wall.

Nico can't let his *papi* be thrown into the Canyon of the Dead.

It's the worst place in the world.

Nico remembers his *papi* and loved him, and now the *mara* was saying terrible things.

"I asked you a question," Pulga said.

"I don't know."

Pulga laughed. "Nico Rápido they call you, right? Because you're fast?"

"Yes."

"Okay, Fast Nicky," Pulga said, "I'll be back tomorrow, and you better have my fucking money."

Then he left.

Nico shuffled from the wall and hugged his mother. She's young and pretty, he knows Pulga wants her, sees the way the *mareros* look at her.

He knows what they want.

Like he knows his mother's story.

She was four years old when the PAC came into her village, deep in the Mayan country, looking for Communist insurgents that they didn't find. En-raged, they grabbed the villagers, heated wires on open flames and shoved the red-hot wires down the villagers' throats. They made the women cook them breakfast and forced them to watch as they ordered fathers to kill their sons and sons to kill their fathers. Those who refused, they doused with gasoline and set on fire. Then they raped the women. When they ran out of women, they started in on the little girls.

Nico's mother was one of them.

Six soldiers raped her into catatonia, and she was one of the lucky ones. Others they raped, then hanged from trees, slashed with machetes, or dashed their heads against stones. She watched them cut pregnant women open and rip the babies from their wombs.

These PAC were civilian militia, almost children themselves, raised in the same Mayan villages and then brutalized and drugged into becoming animals by the Kaibiles, special forces trained by the US in its global war against communism. After the Guatemalan Civil War, some went to the United States, where they encountered racism, unemployment, isolation and no help for the psychosis they brought with them. Some went to prison and formed gangs like Mara Salvatrucha and Calle 18.

The vicious *maras* were conceived in an American-backed war and born in American prisons.

When the PAC left the village, Nico's mother was one of twelve left alive.

Twelve out of six hundred.

Like thousands of other Mayans, she migrated into the city.

Now Nico has to beat La Buitra to the Cayalá truck. No, he thinks, don't get in front of her where she can see you. Stay behind her, watch what she sees, then swoop in at the last second and grab it.

If she's the vulture, he thinks, you're the hawk.

La Buitra, meet Nico Rápido, El Halcón.

Bending low to become even smaller, he squeezes through the crowd, peering between legs and around arms to keep his eye on La Buitra as she shoves her way to the Cayalá truck.

The truck stops, its carriage tilts up and the hydraulics groan like a giant mechanical mule as it dumps its trash. La Buitra moves in, her hips swinging resolutely, her elbows flying, bumping people out of her way.

Other trucks are dumping their trash, *guajeros* poring over their contents like ants swarming on a hill. Nico doesn't look at their finds, he just focuses on La Buitra's stubby legs. His excitement is intense—what could have come out of the Cayalá truck? Clothes, paper, food? He stays low behind her, keeping two other *guajeros* between them.

She beats everyone to the Cayalá truck and then Nico sees it.

A treasure.

Strips of aluminum.

He can get forty cents a pound for aluminum. Just three pounds—a dollar twenty—would be enough to pay off the *pandilleros*.

La Buitra sees it, too, of course. Unable to stab it, she clutches her stick under her arm, reaches down to pick up the aluminum.

Nico makes his move.

Moving out from his human screen, he dashes in under La Buitra's outstretched arm and grabs the strips.

She screams like a bird.

Grabs her stick and swings at him, but he's Nico Rápido, El Halcón, and dodges easily out of her way. She swings a backhand, just missing his head, and she raises the stick to stab him, but he scrambles away, clutching the precious strips of metal to his stomach.

He doesn't stop to put more trash in his bag. He has to go to the *vendedor* to sell the aluminum. Then he can come back and pick more trash. But first he has to get out and get his money.

His money, he thinks.

The phrase sings in his head—*my money*.

The smile won't leave his face as he pictures himself walking into their shack, pulling the bills out of his pocket and saying, "Here, Mami. Don't worry about anything. I took care of things."

I'm the man of the family.

Maybe, he thinks, I'll find Pulga myself, step up to him and say, "Here's your fucking money, you limp-dick *pendejo*."

He knows he won't, but it's a happy thought and it makes him laugh. He puts his head down and trots toward the gate and then he sees—

a McDonald's wrapper—

white—

a hamburger—

untouched.

God, Nico wants that burger.

God, he wants it.

He's so hungry and it smells wonderful and it looks beautiful with red catsup and yellow mustard leaking out from the bun. A McDonald's— something he's heard about but never had. He wants to shove it in his mouth and bolt it down but . . .

Nico knows he should sell it to one of the meat vendors in El Basurero, who will put it in a stew. He can probably get as much as ten cents for it, five of which will belong to Pulga and Calle 18.

But the other five cents he should share with his mother.

He sticks the burger into his pocket.

Out of sight, out of mind is his idea.

But it isn't.

Out of his mind.

It lingers there like a tantalizing dream. He can smell the burger even over the stink of the dump, the acrid smoke, the smell of seven thousand human beings scavenging garbage to survive.

Mami would never know, he thinks as he gets to the gate.

Calle 18, Pulga, would never know.

But you'd know, he thinks.

And God would know.

Jesus would see you eat the burger and he would cry.

No, he thinks, sell the burger and take so much money home to Mami that she will cry with joy.

Nico's thinking this happy thought when the stick hits him in the face.

Knocks him off his feet and stuns him. Through teary eyes he sees La Buitra reach down and snatch the aluminum strips.

"*¡Ladrón!*" she yells at him. "Thief!" La Buitra swings the stick again, hitting him in the shoulder and knocking him onto his back.

He lies there and looks up at the sky.

Or what there is of it.

A cloud of smoke.

Vultures.

Nico reaches up and feels the blood on his face. His nose hurts like crazy and he can feel it already swelling.

He starts to cry.

He's lost the money.

And Pulga will come tonight.

Nico lies there for several minutes, a little boy on a pile of garbage. He wants to lie there forever, give up, just die. He's so tired and they say death is like sleep and it would be good to sleep.

It would be good to just die.

But if you do, he thinks, you leave Mami alone to face Pulga.

He makes himself sit up.

Then he pushes himself up with one hand and gets to his feet. He still has the burger and that will bring a little money. Then he can come back to the dump and maybe get some more.

Maybe enough to pay their debt to the *mara*.

He trudges out to find the meat man.

The meat man takes the burger and sniffs the wrapper. "It's no good."

"It's not spoiled," Nico says, thinking the man is trying to cheat him.

"No, it's not spoiled," the man says, "but the McDonald's sprays oil on their garbage so it can't be eaten. I can't sell this—it will make people sick. Now go away, go find something I can sell."

Nico walks away. Why would they do that? he wonders. If they're not going to eat it, what's the harm of letting other people have it? Because they can't pay? It doesn't make any sense.

Hungry, tired and discouraged, he sneaks back into the dump. His face hurts like fire, the blood on his face sticky and mixed with soot. The trucks from the rich neighborhoods will have been picked through by now, so Nico searches through the piles of garbage picking out anything that he can sell—a pair of old socks, trash paper, anything.

Finding a jar of jam, he smells it first, then runs his finger inside and licks some jam off. It tastes good, sweet, but only stimulates his hunger. He drops the jar into his plastic bag—he might get a few cents for it.

His stomach aches from hunger, but more from anxiety.

Time is running out, he hasn't found enough to pay the *mareros*, and he knows that he won't.

"What are you going to do?" Flor asks. She tears the tortilla and hands him half.

Nico shoves it into his mouth. "I don't know."

"I wish I had some money, I'd give it to you." She's nine years old and looks much smaller. But not younger—undernourished with a chronic low-grade infection, the little girl has sallow skin and dark circles under her eyes. "Pulga will do what he says."

"I know." Pulga will, because he has to collect a certain amount of money every week and has to pass it up not only to his bosses in the *mara* but to the police as well. If he doesn't do either, he's done—dead or in jail.

And Pulga has to prove himself—he's not even a full-fledged Calle 18 member, but a *paro*—an associate. He has to make money to pass up the ranks to a *sicario*, who passes up to a *llavero*, who passes up to the *ranflero*, the boss of the *clica*, the local cell of Calle 18. And the *ranflero*, Nico thinks, probably passes up to his bosses, who also have to pay the police to stay in business.

It's the way of the world, Nico thinks. Everyone passes up to someone. Maybe somewhere at the very top, there are men who just collect and collect, but he has no idea who those people are.

"Pulga will hurt you, too," Flor says. She already knows what men do to women, what some men do to kids.

"I know," Nico says.

"I can borrow a knife," Flor says, "and go kill La Buitra."

"She's already sold the metal."

"Then I'll kill Pulga."

"No," Nico says. "You get me the knife, and I will. It's a man's job."

But they both know that neither of them is going to kill the gangster, even if they could. More *mareros* would only come, and the punishment would be worse.

"There's one other thing you can do," Flor says.

Nico knows.

And he's terrified.

"It's okay." Flor reaches out and takes his hand. "I'll go with you."

Waiting until the sun is low in the hazy sky, the two children go down into the Canyon of the Dead.

Getting down is dangerous in itself.

The path is narrow, steep and muddy, alongside a sheer cliff that falls a straight hundred feet into the canyon. Nico doesn't want to look down—it makes him dizzy and sick to his stomach. He's heard people joke about falling off the trail—"Well, at least you land where you belong"—but he doesn't think it's funny now. And his feet slip inside his shoes—an old pair of Nikes he got from the Cayalá truck a year ago. They're way too big for him and the soles are worn away to almost nothing, and now as he makes his way down the slope, his toes press painfully against the shoes.

When he gets down into the canyon, Nico gags.

His eyes, already teary, water even more from the horrible stench, and he fights to keep down what little food is in his stomach.

Some of the bodies are old—just skeletons, empty rib cages, skulls with vacant eye sockets. Others are fairly fresh, fully clothed, and Nico tries to tell himself that they're only sleeping. The worst are the bodies that have been there for a few days—bloated with gases, rotting, foul.

Hungry dogs flank Nico and Flor warily, waiting for a chance to dash in and grab a meal. A vulture lands on a dead man, pecks a hole in his stomach and flies away with his intestines in its beak.

Nico hunches over and vomits.

Wants to run away but makes himself stay.

He has to do this, has to stay and find something with which to pay the *mareros*. So he steps over rotting corpses and skeletons looking for valuables someone else might have missed. The footing is tricky, and he trips and stumbles, sometimes falling down on a body, other times on the hard ground.

But he picks himself up and keeps looking. Makes himself touch the dead bodies, go through their shirts and their pockets looking for loose change, handkerchiefs, anything that other looters haven't already found and taken.

He trips again, falls and lands with a blinding pain. He's nose to nose with a dead man's face. The eyes stare at him accusingly. Then he hears Flor yell, "Nico!" and looks over to where his friend kneels by a man's bloated body.

"Look!" She's smiling as she holds up a chain.

It's thin, delicate, but it looks like gold and it holds a medal at the end.

"Saint Teresa," Flor says.

They make their way up out of the canyon.

Some thirty thousand people are crammed into the ravine around the dump. Their shacks and shanties are made of old crates, signs, sheets of plastic, odd bits of wood—the lucky have some corrugated tin for roofs, the unlucky sleep in the open.

The streets—muddy dirt paths with rivulets of open sewage—wind in a maze of warrens that Nico and Flor navigate easily as they run to find a junkman who will buy the chain. It's dark now and El Basurero is lit by fires in trash cans and charcoal stoves. Here and there an electrical light glows, illegally wired into the power lines that run above the barrio.

Gonsalves is still in his "shop"—a half of a C-container set on its side and lit with a jerry-rigged power line. He sees the children come in and says, "I'm closed."

"Please," Nico says. "Just one thing."

"What?"

Flor holds up the chain. "It's gold."

"I doubt it." But Gonsalves takes the chain and holds it up to the naked bulb. "No, this is fake."

Nico knows the old man is lying. Gonsalves has made a living cheating everyone—buying cheap and selling dear.

"Because I am a kind man," Gonsalves says, "I'll give you eight quetzals."

Nico is crushed. He needs twelve q to pay Pulga.

"Give it back," Flor says. "Herrera will give us twenty."

"Then take it to Herrera."

"I will," Flor says. She holds out her hand.

But Gonsalves doesn't give the chain back. He peruses it carefully. "I suppose I could do ten."

"I suppose," Flor says, "you could do fifteen."

No, Flor, no, Nico thinks. Don't drive too hard a bargain—I only need twelve quetzal.

"You said Herrera would give you twenty," Gonsalves says.

"It's a long walk over there."

"Well, if one more q would save you a walk . . ."

"Three," Flor says. "Thirteen and it's yours."

"You're a mean little girl," Gonsalves says. "Very hard."

"Herrera loves me."

"I'll bet he does," Gonsalves says.

"Well?"

"I'll give you twelve."

Take it, Nico thinks. Flor, *take it.*

"Twelve," Flor says, looking past Gonsalves to a counter made of a two-by-four stretched over sawhorses, "and that chocolate bar."

"That's worth a whole q."

"Are we going to argue all night," Flor says, "or will you just throw in that chocolate bar?"

"If I cheat myself like that," Gonsalves asks, "will you promise to sell to Herrera from now on and never come in here again?"

"With pleasure," Flor says as Gonsalves counts out twelve quetzals and hands it to her. "The chocolate?"

Gonsalves takes the candy off the shelf and gives it to her. "You're never going to find a husband."

"Promise?" Flor asks.

"We have to run," Nico says when they get outside.

As they trot through the barrio, Flor tears the wrapper off the chocolate and hands Nico half. He shoves it down as he runs and it tastes wonderful.

When he gets home, Pulga is already there.

His mother, sitting on the floor, is crying.

"I have your money," Nico says. He hands Pulga what they owe him. "Now we're caught up."

"Until next week," Pulga says, shoving the money into his pocket. "Then I'll be back."

"I'll be here," Nico says, summoning up his courage.

The man of the family.

Pulga looks at him closely. "How old are you now?"

"Ten," Nico says. "Almost eleven."

"That's old enough to sign up," Pulga says. "You want to protect *mi barrio,* don't you? I could use a fast kid to deliver packages."

Drugs.

Crack cocaine. Heroin.

Pulga says, "It's time you did your duty to the *mara,* Fast Nicky. Time you became Calle 18."

Nico doesn't know what to say.

He doesn't want to be a *marero*.

"Sit down," Pulga says. He pulls out a knife. "I said, sit down."

Nico sits.

"Stick out your legs."

Nico sticks his legs out in front of him.

Pulga holds the blade to the charcoal brazier until it's red hot. Then he squats over Nico, grabs his left leg and presses the blade into the flesh above his ankle.

Nico screams.

"Be quiet, be a man," Pulga says. "You scream like a girl, I'll treat you like a girl, you understand?"

Nico nods. Tears stream down his face but he keeps his jaws clamped shut as Pulga burns the *XV* and the *III* into his ankle.

The smell of burned flesh fills the shack.

"I'll be back," Pulga says, getting up. "To beat you in. Don't look so scared, Fast Nicky, it's just eighteen seconds. A tough kid like you can take that, can't you? You took this, you can take that, can't you?"

Nico doesn't answer. He swallows back a scream.

"I'll be back," Pulga says. He smiles at Nico's mother, makes a kissing sound, and leaves.

Nico falls to his side, grabs his ankle, and sobs.

"He'll be back," Nico's mother says. "He'll make you join them. If the Numbers don't, the Letters will."

The "Numbers" are Calle 18, the "Letters" are Mara Salvatrucha.

Nico knows she's right but he doesn't want to leave. He cries. "I don't want to leave you."

What will she do without him?

To keep her company, to wake her up when she screams in her sleep, to go to the dump and find the things that give them money to eat?

"You have to leave," she says.

"I don't have anywhere to go." He's ten years old and has never been out of El Basurero.

"You have an uncle and aunt in New York," his mother says.

Nico is stunned.

New York?

El Norte?

It's thousands of miles away, through Guatemala, all the way across Mexico, and still hundreds of miles into the United States.

"No, Mami, please."

"Nico—"

"*Please* don't send me away," Nico says. "I promise I'll be good, I'll be better. I'll work harder, find more things—"

"Nico, you have to go."

His mother knows the facts.

Most of the *mareros* die violently before they reach the age of twenty. She wants what any mother wants—she wants her child to live. And for that she is willing to give him up forever.

"First thing in the morning," she says, "you will go."

There is only one way to go.

On the train they call La Bestia.

The Beast.

Nico lies in the weeds by the track.

He's not alone; a dozen others hide in the dark and wait for the train to come. Trembling—maybe from cold, maybe from fear—he tries not to cry as he thinks about his mother, about Flor.

He went to see her last night.

To say goodbye.

"Where are you going?" she asked.

"*El Norte.*"

She looked terrified. "On La Bestia?"

He shrugged—how else?

"Oh, Nico, I've heard things."

They all have. Everyone knows someone who has tried to ride the train north through Mexico to the United States. The train has many names: El Tren Devorador—"The Train That Devours"; El Tren de Desconocidos—"The Train of the Unknowns"; El Tren de la Muerte—"The Train of Death."

Most people don't make it.

They get caught by the Mexican *migra* and sent back on El Bus de Lágrimas—"The Bus of Tears." But they're the lucky ones—both Nico and Flor know people who fell under the train and had both their legs cut off; they roll around now, pushing little carts with their hands.

Some die.

Or at least that's what the kids guess, because they never hear from those people again. And yet the kids know people who have tried to make the trip five, six, ten times.

A few have made it to El Norte.

Most never do.

Flor wrapped her arms around him and hugged him tight. "Please don't go."

"I have to."

"I'll miss you."

"I'll miss you, too."

"You're my best friend," Flor said. "My only friend."

Sitting on the dirt floor of her shack, they held each other for a long time. Nico felt the wet of her tears on his neck. Finally, he pulled himself away and said that he had to go.

"Please, Nico!" Flor said. "Don't leave me!"

He could hear her crying as he walked out in the street.

Now he lies in the weeds, turns his head and looks at the boy lying beside him. The boy is older, maybe fourteen or fifteen, tall and skinny, with a white pullover shirt, jeans and a New York Yankees baseball cap pulled down low on his head.

"This is your first time," the boy says.

"Yes," Nico says.

The boy just laughs. "You have to run fast. They speed up so we can't climb on. Go for a ladder at the front of the car, so if you miss, you can maybe catch the one at the rear."

"Okay."

"If you fall," the boy says, "push as hard as you can so your legs don't fall under the train, or—"

He makes a slicing motion across his legs.

"Okay."

"My name is Paolo," the boy says.

"I'm Nico."

He hears the train coming, rattling along the tracks. People start to stir, rise up from the wet grass. Some carry satchels, others plastic bags; some have nothing at all. Nico has a plastic grocery bag—inside is a bottle of water, a banana, a toothbrush, a T-shirt and a sliver of soap. He's wearing an old jacket, his Messi shirt, his holey sneakers.

"Tie that bag through your belt," Paolo tells him. "You'll need both hands. And tie your jacket around your waist."

Nico does what he says.

"Okay," Paolo says, getting to his feet in a low crouch, "follow me."

The train is here—a long freight train with maybe twenty boxcars and hoppers. The engine belches black smoke as it speeds up.

"Come on!" Paolo yells.

He breaks into a sprint.

Nico has a hard time keeping up with the long-legged, athletic boy but he does his best, telling himself, *You're fast. You're Nico Rápido, you can do this.*

You can catch the train. Everywhere around him, people are running for the train. Most of them are teenage boys, but there are some grown-up men, and a few women. Some families, with little girls and boys.

He runs up the embankment to the track and is scared by the whoosh of hard metal flashing past him. Paolo jumps and grabs a ladder at the front of a boxcar and pulls himself up as Nico runs and tries to keep up and isn't going to make it, but Paolo reaches a hand down.

Nico grabs it. Paolo hauls him onto the ladder.

"Hold on!" Paolo yells.

Looking back, Nico sees an older man trip and fall.

Some people have made it onto the train while others fall behind, give up and stop.

But I made it, Nico thinks. Nothing can stop Nico Rápido.

Paolo starts to climb up the ladder toward the roof of the car. "Come on!"

Nico starts to follow but then he sees—

Flor.

Running for the car.

She's yelling, her arm is stretched out.

In a glimpse, Paolo takes it all in. "Leave her!"

"I can't! She's my friend!"

He starts back down the ladder.

Flor runs toward him, but she's out of breath and losing ground.

"Come on!" Nico yells, holding out his hand.

She grabs for it.

Misses.

Nico goes down to the last rung and leans out, his body just a foot from the tracks that rush past faster and faster. His grip on the ladder is loosening as he reaches out again with his other hand. "I'll catch you!"

Flor lunges.

He feels her fingertips, slides his hand down and grabs her wrist as she jumps.

For a second she's suspended in the air, just above the crushing wheels.

Nico can't hold on.

Either to her or the ladder.

He starts to fall but he holds on to her hand, then—

Nico feels himself being pulled up.

Both of them being pulled up.

Paolo is immensely strong, with taut muscles like wire, and he pulls them both onto the ladder and yells, "Now come on!"

They follow him to the top of the car, fourteen feet above the ground.

It's crowded up there.

People sit and squat, hold on where they can. Paolo pushes a space for them to sit, then says to Nico, "I told you to leave her. Girls are worthless. Only trouble. Does she have food? Money?"

"I have two mangoes," Flor says, "three tortillas and twenty q."

"That's something, I guess," Paolo says. "Give me a tortilla, for saving your life."

She pulls a tortilla out of her bag and hands it to him.

He wolfs it down and says, "I've made this trip four times. Last time I got all the way into the United States."

"What happened?" Nico asks.

"They caught me and sent me back," Paolo says. "My mother is in California. She works for a rich lady. This time I'll make it."

"So will we," Nico says.

Paolo looks them over. "I doubt it."

Because to get to the United States, they have to go through Mexico.

The tracks head west through the Guatemalan mountains and then take a sharp turn north toward the border.

Nico doesn't really comprehend this, his knowledge of geography basically stops at the edge of El Basurero. He's never been out in the countryside before, never seen the greenery, the little villages, the small farms. For him so far this is a grand adventure as he sits atop the club car with Flor and Paolo.

He's hungry, but he's used to that.

The thirst is something different, but people pass around what water they have, usually in old soda bottles, and once, when the train stops for a few minutes near a village, Paolo hops down and begs water from some farmers.

"It'll be different in Mexico," he tells them when he climbs back up. "They don't like us there."

"Why not?" Flor asks.

"They just don't," Paolo says.

There's nothing much to do on the top of the train but look at the scenery and talk, and hold on when the track dips one way or the other, or duck when branches are coming up. Nico begins to like the ritual of shouting "¡Rama!" when they see a branch—it's like a game.

Paolo does most of the talking, taking on himself the role of a grizzled veteran.

"First thing to know," he says, "is don't trust anyone."

"We're trusting you," Flor says.

"I'm different," Paolo says, a little miffed. "Don't trust the men, they'll do things to little girls, do you know what I mean? Don't go inside the boxcars, especially with the men. Sometimes the *migra* come along and lock people inside."

Paolo is a font of information.

They'll have to get off the train when they get to the border because the Mexican police will be waiting at the checkpoint. There's a river between Guatemala and Mexico and they'll need money to pay someone to take them across on a raft.

"I don't have any money," Nico says.

"You better get some."

"How?" Nico asks.

"Beg." Paolo shrugs. "Steal. You know how to pick pockets?"

"No," Nico says.

Paolo looks at Flor. "Sometimes they'll let a girl pay them by tugging their cocks but I wouldn't do that if I were you."

"Don't worry, I won't."

But you don't want to spend too much time getting across the river, Paolo tells them, because the town you have to wait in is full of bad people—thieves, gangsters, drug dealers, perverts. Some of them are people who tried to ride La Bestia but just gave up—victims once themselves, now they hang around the town and prey on other people.

"You're just trying to scare us," Flor says.

Paolo shrugs again. "I'm just telling you how it is. Do what you want."

Nico is scared, but the sunset is beautiful.

He's never seen a dusk unobscured by the city's smog or the dump's smoke. Now he looks at the brilliant reds and oranges and wonders if this is what the world looks like. It's so beautiful.

When it gets black, he sees the stars.

For the first time in his life Nico sees the stars.

Flor shares a tortilla and a mango with him, and he starts to feel drowsy. But he's afraid to fall asleep. The roof of the boxcar slopes toward either side and it would be easy to slide off. Then he hears singing. "El Rey Quiché" starts a few cars back but then spreads forward up the train as the migrants sing to keep each other awake.

Nico joins in.

Then Flor.

They sing and clap and laugh and it's the happiest that they've been all day, maybe the happiest they've been in their lives. When the song ends, someone starts "El Grito," and after that "Luna Xelajú," and then the singing fades away and Nico feels himself swaying, about to drop off.

"Lean against me," Paolo says. "I won't fall asleep."

Nico dozes off. He doesn't know how long he's been asleep when Paolo nudges him and says, "The border. We have to get off."

Drowsy, Nico takes Flor's hand and they follow Paolo down the ladder. Most of the migrants climb off the train, like ice melting off a metal roof, and flow into the brush along the tracks.

The area is a migrants' hovel—remnants of plastic sheets, pieces of cardboard, torn socks, underwear, punctured bottles.

It smells of urine and shit.

Nico and Flor find a piece of cardboard and lie down on it. Snuggle with each other to stay warm. Exhausted, they fall asleep quickly but only for a little while because they have to get money to buy passage across the river.

But when they get up, Paolo is gone.

"Where is he?" Nico asks.

"I don't know," Flor says. "He left us."

Walking into the little town, they see whores standing in doorways, other children leaning against walls with begging bowls in their laps, men who watch them like hungry coyotes.

Music comes from an open cantina and they walk in.

The bartender, an old woman with her hair dyed red, sees them and yells, "Get out, you little cunts! No begging here!"

They run out.

Walk farther down the street.

An old man sits on a cane chair in an alley. He smokes a cigarette, has a beer in his other hand, and openly stares at Flor. Then he unzips his fly, takes his dick out, and shows it to her.

"I'll kick his ass," Nico says.

"No, I have an idea," Flor says. She looks back at the old man and smiles.

"What are you doing?" Nico asks.

"You just be ready," she says.

She leaves him standing there and walks over to the old man. "You want me to touch it?"

"How much?"

"Five q," she says.

"All right."

"Give me the money."

"Touch it first," the old man says.

His cheeks are white stubbled, his eyes rheumy.

He's drunk.

"Okay," Flor says. "Pull down your pants."

He weaves to his feet, loosens his belt, looks around and tugs his dirty khaki trousers down to his knees.

Quicker than a flash, Nicky Rápido swoops in, reaches into the old man's pocket and pulls out money. Bills.

"Run!" Nico yells.

He grabs Flor's hand and they take off down the street. The old man yells and tries to go after them, but trips and falls.

People watch.

No one tries to catch them.

Nico and Flor laugh as they run out of town into some trees.

"How much did we get?" she asks.

"Twelve q!" Nico says.

"That's enough!"

It isn't hard to find the river crossing; they just follow the flow of migrants. Some walk, others sit in carts pulled by kids pedaling tricycles. Nico and Flor walk because they don't want to spend the money.

Paolo is on the shore.

"Did you get money?" he asks.

"Yes," Flor says.

"How?"

He looks at them funny when they both crack up laughing. "Never mind. Come on, we need to get going. Give me your money."

"Why should we give you our money?" Flor asks.

"Because they'll cheat you," Paolo says. "They won't cheat me."

They give him the money and he walks off to talk to a group of men standing by a raft made of planks strapped onto old inner tubes. They watch as he negotiates, waving his arms, shaking his head, showing money and then snatching it back. Finally, he gives some of the money and walks back.

"It's all set," Paolo says. "They'll take the three of us."

"Why are we paying for you?" Flor asks.

Nico frowns at her. "He's helping us."

"I don't trust him."

But Paolo's already walking away and they follow him to the water's edge, then wade in up to their knees and climb onto the raft, which bobs under them until they get their balance. One of the men gets on last and rows them across the river.

They get off the raft and set foot into Mexico.

"Now we walk," Paolo says. "We can get on a train again outside of Tapachula."

"What's Tapachula?" Nico asks.

"A town. You'll see."

It's a six-mile walk on a single-lane paved road that runs through fields and orchards. The local people just stare at them, or shout out insults and call them names.

Nico trudges along the road.

Hungry, thirsty, tired.

Paolo walks them right past the train depot, where Nico sees other migrants stopping.

"Why aren't we going there?" he asks.

"Too many gangsters," Paolo says. "Mara 13 runs this whole area."

He walks them to a cemetery.

It's close to the tracks and a good place to hide.

The train comes early.

Nico's legs feel like wood. His mind is wooly, his mouth dry.

He and Flor slept last night behind the cover of a headstone. Nico had dreams about the Canyon of the Dead, about bodies reaching out from the grave he was lying on to grab him for stealing that man's gold chain.

The cemetery is crowded with the living. They rise from the graveyard in the silver mist of morning, shove what few things they own into bags or pockets, and march out toward the tracks like an army of the lost.

Trudging sleepily toward the tracks, they use stepping-stones to get across a sewage canal, then up the embankment, where they crouch and wait for a train they hope will take them to a home where they've never been.

The train speeds up as it comes toward the cemetery.

The rush starts.

Nico pushes Flor between him and Paolo. The older boy gets to the ladder first and reaches down to help her up. Nico scrambles up behind, they create a little space for themselves on top of the boxcar, and settle in for the ride.

It doesn't last long.

Just a few minutes later, the train slows to a near stop and the *maras* get on.

They climb up the train three cars behind Nico's. He looks back and sees the commotion, hears the shouts and screams.

"Where are you from?" Paolo asks Nico.

"Guatemala City."

"I know that, dummy," Paolo says. "Where?"

"El Basurero."

"That's 18th Street turf," Paolo says. "You have a tat?"

Nico rolls up his pants leg, shows him the *XVIII* scarred into his skin.

"If Mara 13 thinks you're connected with 18th Street," Paolo says, "they'll kill you. You better run."

"Where?"

Paolo points toward the front of the train.

It's moving again. The engineer had slowed down just to let the *maras* get on and now he speeds up to trap the migrants on top. Nico looks—the gangsters are just on the next car and moving up.

"Go!" Paolo yells.

Nico stands up.

So does Flor.

"Not you," Paolo says. "You'll slow him down. Nico, go!"

Nico runs.

Fourteen feet up, on a train moving forty miles an hour, the ten-year-old runs to the forward end of the car and jumps the four-foot gap onto the next boxcar. He lands hard, falls on all fours, then gets up and trips over a man's legs. The man curses him, but Nico gets to his feet, looks back and sees the *maras* coming after him.

Like dogs that will chase something that runs.

Nico keeps going, stepping over feet, legs, toes. Two *maras* leap onto his car and come after him. He jumps to the next car and then the next and then—

The next car isn't a boxcar, but a tanker.

The top is convex, curving sharply to the sides.

And the jump isn't four feet—it's nine.

Nico looks back over his shoulder and sees the *maras* coming. Grinning, laughing, knowing that he's trapped. They're close enough now that he can see the tattoos on their faces and necks.

If he stays, he's in for a bad beating, maybe they kill him.

But if he tries to jump and doesn't make the nine feet, he'll fall between the cars and get crushed under the train's wheels. Even if he makes it, he could slide off the curving surface and land on the tracks.

There's no more time to think.

Nico takes a few steps back, runs as hard as he can, and then launches himself into the air.

"Why did that boy run?" the *mara* asks Paolo.

"I don't know. I don't know him."

The *mara* looks down at Flor. "You? You know him?"

"No."

"Don't lie."

"I'm not."

"Is he 18th Street?" the *mara* asks.

"No!" Flor says.

"I thought you said you didn't know him," the *mara* says, glaring at her.

Flor glares back at him. "I know MS-13, I know 18th Street. That boy, he wasn't either."

Around them, the *maras* systematically work their way through the migrants, stealing cash, taking clothing, demanding phone numbers of relatives who can send more money. They interrogate the boys and the young men—"Where are you from? Are you cliqued up? With who? Us? Eighteenth Street?" The *maras* strip them to check for tattoos. Wrong ink fetches a beating or a slashing before they toss the unlucky kid from the train.

"Do you have money?" the *mara* asks Flor. "Give it."

"Please, I need it."

"Maybe you need a good fucking more, *niña*."

She hands him the few coins she has. The *mara* thinks about fucking her anyway, decides she's too small, then slaps Paolo a few times in the face, takes his Yankees cap, and moves on.

Nico lands hard.

His fingers grab at the slick metal but he slips down the side of the tanker like a fried egg sliding out of a hot pan.

Falls with a thud onto a railing that lines the bottom of the car.

It drives the air from his lungs but he hangs on. Facedown, he sees the rails zipping past, hears the iron singing, knows that he's inches away from being crushed or cut in half. A strut connects the railing to the car and he risks reaching out and grabbing it, then pulls himself along until he reaches a ladder in the center.

He clutches it, catches his breath, and holds on, panting from exertion, fear, pain and adrenaline. Afraid to move his legs for fear of falling off, he makes himself do it. Pulls his feet under him, stretches his right leg out and gets a foot on a rung.

The train slows down to allow the *maras* to get off, so Nico stays pinned to the side of the tanker, hoping they won't spot him or at least won't care. When the train starts to pick up speed again, he climbs slowly, achingly, up the ladder. A railing wraps around the fuel bay at the top and he holds on to that.

. . .

The single-track train moves north along the Pacific Coast of Chiapas.

Nico has never seen the ocean before and, with the resiliency of childhood, finds it thrilling and beautiful. The green mountains to his right and the blue sea to his left, he feels like he's in a different world.

Light-headed from hunger and heat—the temperature is 105 and the sun beats down on the tops of the train cars, turning their metal into a stove top—Nico exists in a semihallucinogenic state, taking in the sight of plantain trees and coffee bushes as if they were strange imagery in a dream.

His body aches.

The fall from the train bruised and maybe cracked his ribs, the right side of his face is swollen from where it hit the rail. Still, he'd had enough presence of mind to climb down from the fuel car when he saw others getting off the train before it got to a government checkpoint at La Arrocera.

Flor and Paolo found him lying in the bushes beside the track, helped him walk around the checkpoint and waited with him until the next freight train came, then helped him get on board.

Now he sits atop the train and looks out at a wave breaking like a white pencil being drawn across a blue piece of paper.

Flor tears a tortilla in half and hands him a piece. "Can you chew?"

Nico puts the tortilla in his mouth and tries to chew. It hurts, but he's hungry and it tastes good. "Do I look funny?"

"Kind of funny," she says. "You're talking funny."

He smiles, and that hurts a little, too. "Funny how?"

"Like your mouth's always full," she says.

He looks around. "It's pretty here."

"Very pretty."

"Maybe someday we can live in the country," Nico says.

"That would be nice."

They talk for a few minutes about getting a farm, having chickens and goats and planting things, although they don't know what.

"Flowers," Flor says.

"You can't eat flowers," says Paolo.

"But you can look at them," Flor says. "You can smell them."

Paolo snorts in disgust.

Nico thinks he looks weird without his Yankees cap. His hair is short and chopped, like it was cut with a knife or something, and he holds a piece of a cardboard box over his head to protect it from the sun.

"We could grow corn," Nico says. "And tomatillos, and oranges."

Paolo shakes his head. "I'm going to own a restaurant. Then I can eat anything I want whenever I want it. Chicken, potatoes, steak . . ."

"I'm eating one now," Nico says. He mimes cutting a piece of steak and sticking it in his mouth. "*Mmmmm*. Delicious."

He's never tasted steak, but his imagination makes him purse his lips and roll his eyes back in delight.

Even Paolo laughs.

The train runs past a series of large lakes that separate the mainland from a thin strand, then turns north away from the coast, through farms and past villages.

Nico is sorry to leave the ocean.

He thinks New York is by an ocean, but he's not sure.

That night, they get off the train to go into a small town for something to eat, even though they have no money to buy food. And it's dangerous— *madrinas*, local civilians who help the *migra*, patrol the areas around the tracks, looking for migrants. Sometimes they turn them in to the police, who demand a hefty bribe to let them go. Those are the lucky ones; the *madrinas* are known to beat, rape and murder others.

Paolo explains all of this to them. "There's a safe house near a church. If we can get there, they'll give us food, a place to sleep."

Under a quarter moon, he leads them down a creek bed away from the tracks.

Nico can see flashlights in the distance, *madrina* patrols looking for victims. He keeps his head down and follows Flor, keeping his hand on her back, trying not to trip and make noise. They walk out of the creek bed to the outskirts of town, where Nico sees a small church, and beside it, a one-story cinder-block building.

"This is it," Paolo says, sounding relieved. "It's run by a priest, Father Gregorio. The *madrinas* won't go in because they're afraid of him. He threatens them with hell."

They go inside.

A few bunk beds line the wall and mattresses are spread across the open floor. Pots of stew and beans simmer on a small kitchen stove. Tortillas are stacked on a side table. A dozen or so migrants are either sleeping or eating.

Father Gregorio is a tall silver-haired man with a long jaw and a hook nose. He stands by the stove with a ladle in his hand. "Come in. You must be hungry."

Nico nods.

"You look hurt," Father Gregorio says to him.

"I'm all right."

Father Gregorio steps up to him and looks at his swollen face. "I think you need a doctor. I can walk you to the clinic. No one will bother you, I promise."

"Just some food, please," Nico says.

"Eat first, then we can talk about it," Father Gregorio says. He ladles out bowls of soup, pours beans over the top and gives them tortillas.

Squatting on the floor, Nico starts to eat.

"Cross yourself first," Flor whispers. "You'll make the priest mad."

Nico crosses himself.

The food is hot and delicious. Even though it hurts to eat, Nico wolfs it down. Then Father Gregorio walks over and asks, "What about that doctor?"

Seeing Paolo slightly shake his head, Nico says, "I'm okay."

"I'm not so sure," Father Gregorio says, "but all right. All the beds and mattresses are full, you'll have to sleep on the bare floor. There's a shower out back if you want to wash up."

After eating, Nico goes outside and finds the shower, a spigot that comes out of the wall behind a wooden slat door. The water, more of a trickle, is un-heated but tepid in the summer heat. He stands under it and uses the sliver of soap on a plastic tray to wash himself, then uses a communal towel, damp from other users, to dry off as best he can.

He touches his right side and winces—it's a massive bruise—and he struggles to raise his arm and get his shirt back on. Then he climbs back into his jeans and steps outside.

Paolo is waiting to use the shower.

"It's good you're not going to the clinic," Paolo says. "The *migra* watch it like hawks, swoop in as soon as Father Gregorio leaves."

"Thanks for warning me."

"You'd never make it without me."

"I know." Nico steps aside and lets Paolo get into the shower. But instead of going back in, he sits on a small patch of grass to enjoy the air and the stars. But then through the slats, he sees something amazing—Paolo un-wrapping tape from around his chest.

Nico sees Paolo's breasts.

Paolo, he realizes, is a girl.

When the water stops running, Nico sees Paolo—he guesses now it's really Paola—carefully wrap the tape tightly around her chest, hiding her breasts under her shirt. When Paola gets out, she sees Nico sitting there and looks startled.

"What are you doing?" Paola asks.

"Just sitting here."

"Spying on me?"

"I won't tell, I promise," Nico says.

"You won't tell what?" Paola asks, advancing on him. "You won't tell *what*?!"

"Nothing!" Nico says. He gets up and runs into the house.

But lying next to Flor later he whispers in her ear, "Paolo is a girl."

"What? That's silly."

"No, I saw—"

"What?"

"You know." He cups his hands over his chest. "Why would—"

"Don't be so stupid."

"Well, why?"

"Because of what men do to girls," Flor says.

"Don't tell I told you."

"Go to sleep."

"Don't."

"I *won't*," Flor says. "Now go to sleep."

Suddenly he's asleep and just as suddenly it's morning.

It's hard to get up. Nico's ribs burn as he pushes himself first to his knees and then to his feet. Father Gregorio gives them each a tortilla, two slices of mango and a glass of water. As Nico chews his tortilla, he glances at Paola, who glares at him and then looks away.

A few moments later, Paola says, "We have to go. Come on."

Nico is sad to leave but doesn't really know why.

He can't realize that it's one of the few places he's ever received kindness.

Kids on bikes suddenly appear on the dirt roads that run through the corn-fields and then start pedaling beside the railroad tracks.

They smile and wave and call out hellos.

Nico waves and hollers back, then the bikes speed ahead and he loses sight of them. A minute later he looks toward the front of the train, where a copse of trees stands beside the track. There's something odd in the trees, some-thing he can't quite make out.

Are those balloons in the trees? White balloons?

Or are they piñatas?

No, he thinks, they're too big for that.

The train starts to slow down.

What's going on? Nico wonders. He looks at the trees again and then re-alizes that what he's been seeing are mattresses.

Mattresses balanced on the tree limbs.

He doesn't understand.

Then he sees the kids on bikes under the trees, yelling and pointing back at the train. Men lift up off the mattresses and start to drop from the trees like heavy fruit. Then the train stops under the trees and the men, holding machetes and wooden clubs, are all around them. They're not *maras*—no tattoos, no gang colors, they just look like farmers—but they're bandits, sleeping in the trees until the local kids told them the train was on the way.

Paola yells, "Run!"

She pushes her way through other migrants and scrambles down the ladder, jumping from the fifth rung. A bandit grabs Nico by the front of the shirt but he twists away, grabs Flor's hand and pulls her to the ladder.

They climb down and run into the cornfields.

The corn is taller than they are and they can barely see around them, but Nico thinks he catches a glimpse of Paola running through the stalks.

Maybe it's Paola, but Nico can't really see.

Screams of pain and fear come from the train.

Out of breath, they stop and crouch, hiding in the cornstalks.

Nico feels his heart pounding, is afraid the bandits will hear it. He hears feet crashing through the stalks toward them and puts his hands over his ears. They get closer and closer and he can't decide whether to run or stay still and hope they don't see him.

He's frozen with fear.

Then he hears shouts. *"Got one! Come here! I've got one!"*

"Leave me alone! Get your hands off me!"

It's Paola.

Nico thinks he should go try to help her but he can't make himself move. Can only sit and hear the struggle, the voices . . . there are four of them, maybe five—shouting and laughing, and then one says, "Look! It's a girl! You think you can fool us, you little whore?!"

Go help, Nico tells himself.

You are Nico Rápido.

Nico the Fast.

Nico the Brave.

Go fight them.

But he can't move. He's a ten-year-old boy and he can't make his legs move when he hears Paola scream as they rip the tape off her chest. Can't move as he hears them yell, "Hold her down!," as he hears her scream and struggle, and then as her voice is muffled under a man's hand.

Nico is from El Basurero.

He knows the sounds of sex, knows the sounds of men fucking women, the grunts, the moans, the dirty curses, and now he hears all of that and he also hears laughter and shouts and muffled cries and sobs as they take turns on her, use her in all the ways he knows from a childhood spent in a garbage dump.

The boy wants to be a hero, wants to help his friend, wants to knock the men off her and kill them and save her, but his legs won't move.

All he can do is crouch and listen.

He's ashamed.

And then it's quiet.

For just a moment, and then Nico hears the men walk away, and he's ashamed that he's glad that they're walking away and haven't found him, and he sits and listens to Paola whimpering and her feet kicking in the dirt.

A few minutes later he hears the train engine.

Flor moves first.

She crawls through the stalks toward Paola.

Nico sits for a few more seconds and then follows her.

Paola stands in a small clearing, the cornstalks flattened where they laid her down. She's pulling on her jeans, and Nico sees blood trickling down her legs. She bends over and picks up her shirt, puts it on and starts to button it. Then she sees them and says, "Go away. Leave me alone."

She starts to walk toward the railroad track.

When they follow her, she looks back over her shoulder and yells, "I said leave me alone! I'm fine! You think it's the first time?!"

The train is gone and there's nobody by the tracks except two bodies— one's head is crushed, the other has been chopped up by machete blows. Garbage—plastic bags and empty water bottles—is strewn around, but everything of value has been taken.

The children sit by the track and wait.

A few hours later, another train comes and they get back on the Beast.

The train heads north, through Oaxaca and toward Veracruz.

Paola sits alone, silent.

She won't look at them or speak.

The train descends into Veracruz and they pass through fields of pineapple and sugar cane. The people get warmer, too—some even wait by the track and toss food up to them.

Paola won't eat, even when Flor tries to give her some of the food.

The train crosses more mountains in the Pica de Orizaba.

As it passes through the mountains, the scorching weather turns to cold, and Nico and Flor huddle together, shivering. At night, the danger of freez-

ing to death is very real; when dawn comes, the faint sun is barely enough
to warm them.

It's outside of Puebla, as the train heads toward Mexico City, that Paola
finally talks to them. She stands up, looks toward the front of the train, then
turns back to Nico and says, "It wasn't your fault."

Then Nico spots the high-tension wire ahead and yells, "Get down! Paola,
get down."

She doesn't.

Paola turns to the front again and flings her arms out. The wire hits her in
the chest and she becomes a flash of lightning on a sunny day.

Nico puts his arm over his eyes.

When he takes it away, she's gone, leaving only a faint trace of burned
flesh that quickly blows away in the cold northern wind.

The train comes to a stop on the outskirts of Mexico City.

More gangs are waiting.

As patient and sure as vultures, they jump on the migrants as soon as they
get off the train, and make them pay to walk the twelve miles to the shelter
in Huehuetoca.

"We don't have any money," Nico says.

"That's your problem, not mine," the gangster says. He runs his eyes
over Flor.

"I have this shirt," Nico says.

"'Messi,' huh?" the gangster says. "Okay, Number Ten, give it to me. It's
probably worth more than the girl."

Nico strips the shirt off, hands it to the gangster.

Then he and Flor trudge to the shelter.

The volunteers there find a T-shirt for him. It's way too big and hangs
down close to his knees, but he's glad to have it.

In the morning, he and Flor walk back to the train tracks. Nico knows
from talking to veteran migrants at the shelter that a number of tracks run
north from the terminal. The Ruta Occidente goes up to Tijuana, the Ruta
Centro to Juárez, the Ruta Golfo to Reynosa. He wants the last one, because
it's the farthest east, the closest to New York.

The tracks outside the terminal are a confusing puzzle, but finally he finds
the one he thinks is the Ruta Golfo, and they walk along the tracks until they
find a safe place to jump on board, and wait for the train.

It's been raining off and on, but now it's stopped, and the sky is a pearl gray.

"What will we do when we get to the border?" Flor asks.

Nico shrugs. "Cross the river."

Although he doesn't know how they're going to. He's heard the stories by now—about people drowning, "coyotes" demanding money to get them across, about the American *migra* waiting on the other side.

He doesn't know yet how they're going to cross, he just knows they will, and there's no point in worrying about it yet, because first they have to make it there.

Five hundred more miles on La Bestia.

"Then what?" Flor asks.

"I'll call my aunt and uncle," he says. The phone number is written on the waistband of his underwear. "They'll tell us what to do. Maybe they'll send us tickets, we can ride on the inside of a train."

She sits quietly for a moment and then asks, "What if they don't want me?"

"They will."

"But what if they don't?"

"Then we'll go someplace else," Nico says. If my aunt and uncle don't want her, they don't want me, he thinks. They don't own New York, we'll find a place somewhere.

It's America.

There's a place for everybody, right?

He sees the train coming.

There are fewer migrants here and the trains are different. They carry less produce and more industrial goods, like refrigerators and cars.

"You ready?" Nico asks.

Flor gets up. "I miss Paola."

"Me too."

They start to run alongside the train.

The rain has made the creosote on the wooden rails slick and it's hard to gain footing, but they've gotten good at this with practice. Nico is still a little slowed from his injured ribs and Flor gets ahead of him to grab the ladder and help him up.

She gains the car, reaches for the front ladder and holds her hand out for Nico.

He reaches for it and slips on the creosote.

Falls on his face.

Picks himself up and tries again but now her hand is yards away and the train starts to pick up speed.

"Nico, hurry!" Flor yells.

He keeps running but the train is faster.

"Nico!"

She hangs from the ladder, thinking about jumping down, but the train is too fast now and she'll get hurt and he waves for her to go ahead.

"I'll get the next one!" he yells. "I'll meet you in . . ."

But she's farther away now, getting smaller, her voice fading as she screams, "*Nicooooooo . . . !*"

For the first time in his life, the boy is alone.

Nico rides the train alone, keeps to himself, trusts no one, speaks little, and when he does, it's to ask about Flor. When he gets off the train to look for food, he asks about her. She's not at the first stop or the next. He asks about her at the shelters, the clinics. He has no photo of her, he can only describe her, but no one has seen her, or at least they're not saying.

He gets back on the train and rides north.

Lonely, sad, afraid.

He makes no friends, doesn't try, because he can't trust anyone and besides, friends just disappear—in a flash of lightning or on a train fading into the distance.

Finally, the Beast stops.

Nico knows that he's in Reynosa, but little more than that. Paola had told him about a shelter where he could spend the night before trying to cross the river, and he finds his way to the Casa del Migrante, run by the priests.

There he gets a simple meal and news about Flor.

She was arrested, a woman tells him. Yes, a little girl matching that description was taken away by the Reynosa Police just by the train.

"You saw this?" Nico asks.

"I saw," the woman says.

"What do they do with them?" Nico asks. "The people they arrest?"

The people who have no money to pay bribes.

"Send them back," the woman says.

So Flor is on El Bus de Lágrimas, heading all the way back to Guatemala City and El Basurero.

At least she's alive, Nico thinks, at least she's safe.

He falls asleep on the concrete floor.

The river, the Río Bravo that the Americans call the Rio Grande, is wide and brown. With swirls and eddies.

Nico stands at the edge.

He can't swim.

He's come a thousand miles to get here and now he doesn't know how to get across the last hundred yards. The coyotes charge a hundred dollars or more to get someone over, and Nico doesn't even have one.

Now he watches as coyotes take groups of people across on inflatable rafts and drop them in the brush on the other side. The people get out of the boat and run before the American *migra* come and find them.

Nico finds a spot in the mesquite brush and waits for sundown.

When it finally comes, when the water turns black, he walks a quarter mile upstream, away from the rest of the migrants waiting to cross, and crouches by the riverbank. He's been watching this spot all day and it looks shallow—he's seen people cross by foot with poles to balance them.

Nico has a small branch.

As it gets darker, when the figures crossing upstream are just silhouettes, he walks down to the water's edge and looks across. He doesn't see the head-lights of the *migra*'s cars, doesn't hear engine noises. It's a quiet part of the river, a narrower part on a curve, and he's sure he can make it across, scramble up the steep bank, and hide in the mesquite on the other side.

Crouching, he waits for darkness, then steps into the black water.

It's cold, much colder than he thought, but he makes himself keep going, feeling the rocky bottom with his feet, trying not to trip over stones and sunken branches. Twice he almost falls, but leans on his stick and stays upright.

The water gets deeper.

First to his knees, then to his waist, and it's only then he figures out that the people he had watched fording the river were grown men and not ten-year-old boys.

The water comes up to his chest and he feels the current pulling at him, trying to claw him downstream.

He pushes hard with his legs but then the water is up to his chin, and then his mouth and then his nose, and he has to walk on his tiptoes to breathe but he knows the deepest part of the river is in the middle and that it will get better.

Then he plunges into a hole.

The water is over his head, the whirling eddy strips the stick from his hand and he starts to lose his feet, they're slipping out from under him and the water is all around him and he holds his breath because if he gasps for the air that his lungs are screaming for, he'll swallow water and drown.

Feeling the bottom, he pushes as hard as he can with his toes and he comes up, inhales a breath of air and then falls forward, splashing face-first into the water. He flails his arms as the current carries him downstream, a whirlpool spinning him around and around until he doesn't know where the shore is; there's only darkness as the water pulls him along and he sinks again and swallows water and then comes up again coughing and gasping and he's so tired now his arms won't even flail and his legs feel like heavy stone and refuse to kick and his body wants to go to sleep in the water that is no longer cold but very warm and then the current carries him to the shore.

A jagged branch snags his T-shirt. Nico reaches out, grabs it, and pulls himself up onto the sand.

He lies there, gasping, coughing, exhausted, and then he feels light on his face.

A flashlight.

Nico hears a voice. "Jesus, it's a kid."

Hands grab Nico by the arms and pick him up.

He blinks and sees a badge.

It's the American *migra*.

Which Darius **Darnell** apparently could, based on the weight that Cozzo
and Andrea started to spread around the city.

Cirello knew this personally because he's graduated to pulling security for
the heroin deliveries, making sure that Narcotics Division doesn't have any
of the locations up and that none of the shipments are ripped by local gangs,
hijackers, or even cops who are truly dirty.

The work is excruciating, goes against everything Cirello ever believed or
did in his past life as a legit drug cop. He helps those assholes move smack,
millions of dollars' worth, any one of which deliveries would have been a
major case. They could have had Cozzo and Andrea any time they wanted,
but Mullen said no.

"It's fifteen pounds, boss," Cirello said. "You know what that will do on
the streets?"

"I do know," Mullen said, "but it's not what we're in this for. We're not in
this to win a battle, we're in it to win a war."

Then he went off on some World War II analogy about some city that
Churchill let the Germans bomb even though he was forewarned they were
going to bomb it.

"It would have tipped the Germans that we had their code," Mullen said,
"which might have lost the war. So Churchill had to let thousands of innocent people get killed in order to win the war."

Cirello doesn't know about the war, he just knew that addicts all over the
East Coast were going to die because he let these shipments go through.

It kills him.

He asked out.

"I'll do parking violations in Far Rockaway," he told Mullen.

"Hang in there, Bobby," Mullen said. "I know what this is costing you,
but hang in there. You're the best. You know how I know that? Because,
before you, I was the best."

Yeah, yeah, Cirello thought, that's Mullen tugging on my cock.

"I need you to climb the ladder," Mullen said. "Create a relationship with
Darnell."

"How'm I going to do that?"

White cop, black drug dealer.

Forget about it.

"Be patient," Mullen said. "Whatever you do, don't push. Wait until he
comes to you."

Which is never going to happen, Cirello thought.

But two weeks later, just like the boss said, Andrea comes to him and says,
"Darnell wants to meet you."

4

This Upside-Down World

If you gaze long enough into an abyss, the abyss will gaze b
into you.

—Friedrich Nietzsch

Beyond Good and Ev

Cirello hates his job.

He's tired of cuddling up to drug slingers, taking their mon
tending to be as filthy as they are. A half-dozen times now he
Mullen to be reassigned—to freakin' *anything*—but the boss has sai

"We're just getting somewhere," Mullen said. "It's no time to quit

Problem is, Cirello thinks, and "just the facts, ma'am," I'm too g
what I do.

He's played Mike Andrea and Johnny "Jay" Cozzo like twin pianos a
of those annoying bars people go to on their birthdays. They thought
were playing him—had him doing favors to square his gambling jones—
it was checking out license plates to see if they belonged to cops, then it
running checks on potential partners to see if they were under scrutiny.

Things really took off when he gave Darius Darnell a clean bill of heal

"Guy did a stint in Victorville," Cirello told Andrea, "but he was a stand-t
convict. NYPD doesn't have him up."

"You guarantee that?"

"One hundred per," Cirello said.

"What about DEA?"

"They don't care about him," Cirello said. It had been an easy get—he
took Cozzo's fifty K to "buy" a DEA contact, then went to Mullen, who went
to God knows who, who brought back word that if the DEA ever had its eye
on Darnell, its eye was now off. "But, seriously, you guys are working with
moolies now?"

"We're woke," Cozzo said.

"You're what?"

"Woke," Cozzo said. "It means we're postracial."

"It means we work with moolies," Andrea said, "if those moolies can get
us grade A heroin."

Pull back, Cirello thinks. Go the other way, don't look eager. "What for?"

"We have a big piece of business coming in," Andrea says, "and before it does, Darnell wants to meet you personally. Something about 'looking you in the eye.'"

"What, he doesn't trust me?"

"It's what the man wants."

"You taking orders from moolies now?" Cirello says. "I don't want to meet him."

"The fuck not?"

"Because the more people I'm exposed to," Cirello says, "the more I'm exposed."

"He already knows your name."

"Who gave him that?" Cirello asks.

"I did."

"Fuck you, Mike."

"You're coming to meet him."

"Says who?"

"Says the Lakers when they don't make a three-point spread," Andrea says. "You think I don't know about that?"

So they go and do a meet-and-greet with Darius Darnell.

Cirello figures he'll tell Mullen about it after it happens so the boss doesn't fuck it up by sending in the whole bureau as backup. He just gets in a car with Andrea and they drive out to the Linden Houses in East New York.

"We might be the only white people here," Cirello says as they get out of the car.

"You white?" Andrea asks. "I'm Italian, you're Greek. We ain't white."

A small delegation of G-Stone Crips is waiting for them at the entrance to the project and walks them into one of the buildings, into the elevator to the top floor, then up some stairs to the roof.

A tall black man stands on the edge, looking out at the city.

"There he is!" Andrea says. "The king surveying his kingdom!"

Just like Andrea, always kissing ass, Cirello thinks.

Darnell turns around.

He's wearing a Yankees jacket and designer jeans. Not the usual high-top basketball shoes Cirello expects from black drug slingers, but a pair of work boots.

"I spent a lot of years inside," Darnell says, "I like to be outside when I can."

"Beautiful day," Andrea says.

Darnell ignores this and looks Cirello up and down. "You must be the police these guys keep talking about."

"Bobby Cirello."

"I know your name," Darnell says. "You know what I learned in prison, Bobby Cirello?"

"Probably a lot of things."

"Probably a lot of things," Darnell says. He steps up close, just inches from Cirello's face. "One of them was I learned to know a snitch when I saw one, and you know what, Bobby Cirello, I think you're a snitch. I think you're UC, and I think the only question is whether we shoot you or throw you off the roof."

Cirello is scared shitless.

Should have told Mullen.

Should have got backup.

Too late now.

He goes the other way with it. "Or shoot me and *then* throw me off the roof. Or, if you really want to get crazy with it, throw me off the roof and *then* shoot me. So there are options. But here's the thing, you ain't going to take any of these options, because no drug-slinging smoke is going to murder a white New York City gold shield, so why don't we knock off the shit."

One of those long silences.

Then Darnell says, "If he was wired up, the black-and-whites would already be rolling in to save they boy's life. He clean."

"Good," Cirello says. "Can we go now? I hate fresh air."

"I got a meeting tonight," Darnell says. "With a person I don't trust so much. I want you to come as security."

"The G Boys here aren't good enough for you?"

"They good," Darnell says. "But like you say, ain't nobody going to mess with a gold shield. Nine o'clock, meet you at Gateway, in front of Red Lobster. Make sure your car clean, you driving."

"Who are we meeting?"

"You find out."

Cirello goes and gets his car detailed. At nine o'clock on the dot he pulls up outside Red Lobster.

Darnell is already there and gets in the passenger seat.

"What is it with white boys and Mustangs?" he asks.

"It's a Steve McQueen thing," Cirello says. "*Bullitt.*"

"This ain't the *Bullitt* car."

"No, I couldn't afford that," Cirello says. "You gotta tell me where we're going here because I don't know."

He's impressed that Darnell came alone, no entourage.

Unusual for a slinger.

"Take the Belt south," Darnell says. "Brighton Beach."

"You dealing to Russians now?"

"What are you carrying?" Darnell asks.

"My service weapon," Cirello says. "A Glock nine. You?"

"You know better," says Darnell. "Ex-con with a piece, we get stopped I go back to V-Ville."

"We get stopped," Cirello says, "I show my badge and we go on our merry way."

"Nice life for white."

"Ain't the white, it's the blue," Cirello says. "You don't like white people much, do you?"

"Don't like white people at all."

"Good to know where I stand."

Cirello takes the Belt all the way down to Ocean Parkway.

"This person I'm meeting," Darnell says, "him and me have boundary issues."

"He's got no boundaries?"

"They just not as big as he thinks," Darnell says. "That's what we got to work out, who can sell to who down here. I give him his boundaries if he buys from me exclusive."

"Sounds like a plan."

"I'm introduce you as a NYPD detective," Darnell says. "I won't say your name."

"I gotta show him my shield?"

"No, fuck that. Just look like a cop."

"I'll do my best," Cirello says. "Where do you want me to turn?"

"I'm looking at my phone."

"Google Maps?"

"That snooty bitch tell you where to turn," Darnell says. "I shut the sound off."

"I know, I hate her."

"Right on Surf Avenue, left on Ruby Jacobs."

"That's not Brighton Beach," Cirello says. "That's Coney Island. That's by that roller coaster, the what-do-you-call-it, the Thunderbolt."

"I don't ride no roller coaster," Darnell says. "My life a roller coaster."

"Okay."

"There's a Mexican place end of the street."

"I don't know about this," Cirello says.

"What you don't know?"

"Like why here?" Cirello asks, looking around. "All this empty space. Parking lot, a construction site . . ."

"You scared, white?"

"I'm not white, I'm Greek," Cirello says. "You see that movie, *300*? Those were Greeks."

"Didn't show that at V-Ville. Too gay."

Cirello pulls into a parking spot in the middle of Ruby Jacobs. It's the last space available, still a half block from the restaurant, which he doesn't like at all. You have to walk down something called Polar Bear Club Walk to get there.

"Polar Bear Club?" Darnell asks.

"New Year's Day," Cirello says. "Guys jump in the ocean."

"Black people ain't so foolish."

They're just at the edge of the parking lot when Cirello sees it. Movement from the corner of his left eye.

He tackles Darnell, drives him to the pavement.

The bullets zip over their heads.

Cirello looks up, sees guys running.

In the car, Cirello says, "I told you, I fucking told you it wasn't good!"

"Should have listened."

Cirello realizes that he's racing back up the Belt and he takes his foot off the gas. His head is spinning. I acted like a skel, he thinks, not a cop. I should have acted like the cop I am—stayed on the scene, called it in, waited for the uniforms and then the detectives. Instead of running like the dirtbag I'm pretending to be.

He thinks about turning around and going back, but he doesn't.

There'd be no way to explain it, no way to explain why he left the scene that wouldn't destroy his career. And it would shut down the investigation— all that work, all those months of climbing into bed with criminals wasted.

He keeps driving.

Knowing that what he should do is call Mullen. Drop Darnell off and call Mullen. Go sit in his kitchen and tell him everything, let the boss decide what to do.

Cirello drives Darnell back to Red Lobster.

"You saved my life," Darnell says.

"That was my job," Cirello says. That's what I'm supposed to do, that's what a cop is supposed to do, save people's lives. Even a piece of shit like you, who sells poison to kids.

"You could have just dove out of the way," Darnell says. "You didn't."

Maybe I should have, Cirello thinks.

"You don't work for the Italians no more," Darnell says. "I'm picking up your tab."

"You don't have to do that."

"I thought I had to, I wouldn't," Darnell says.

"They're not going to be happy."

"Ain't up to me to make them happy," Darnell says. "Up to them to make *me* happy. I ain't they nigger, they mine. They don't like it, I cut them out, find me other niggers. Call me when you feel better, we work it out."

"What are you going to do about the Russians?" Cirello asks.

"I'll deal with them."

Cirello drives home.

Goes into the bathroom and throws up.

When Libby comes home she asks him how his day was and he says it was fine. Later, she reaches out for him to have sex, but he pretends he's asleep. He isn't, he barely sleeps all night, and she's gone to class when he finally gets up.

That's how Bobby Cirello becomes Darius Darnell's chief driver and bodyguard, pulling security on major deliveries, watching the radar to make sure Darnell's light isn't blinking. And the Italians don't like it, although they don't say shit about it to Darnell.

Cirello, they say shit to.

"You've come up in the world," Andrea says to Cirello. "Chauffeur to a *ditzune*? Geez, Bobby, my back hurts a little where you stepped on your way up."

"I didn't ask for this."

"Yeah, but you got it, anyway, huh?"

Mullen is a little more enthusiastic. "How did this come about?"

"I don't know, you said get close, I got close."

He comes clean about the rooftop meeting.

"You shouldn't have gone up there without backup," Mullen says.

"Probably not," Cirello admits.

"But now you're in, Bobby, you're in," Mullen says. "The next step is to find out where Darnell is getting his heroin."

The next step, Cirello thinks. There's always a next step.

When's it going to stop?

Crazy thing is, Mike Andrea comes to him a few weeks later and makes the exact same request.

"You like working for Darnell?" he asks.

"It pays."

"It could pay better," Andrea says. "Darnell thinks he's the king of New York, but when you really look at it, all he is, he's just a middleman. If we could make a direct connection to his supplier, we could buy direct without his markup."

"Okay."

"You know who his supplier is?"

"No."

"But you could find out," Andrea says. "You make that connection for us, Bobby, there'd be something in it for you. Cut Darnell out, cut you in."

Cirello has to acknowledge the humor of it, two mob guys and the head of the NYPD's Narcotics Division wanting him to do the same thing. The fact that this makes sense is just part and parcel of the bizarre life he's living, which has its own internal logic. In this world, you don't bust heroin dealers, you assist them; you don't resist corruption, you embrace it; the worse you are, the better you are.

It's like one of those old Greek plays where they talked about "cloud-cuckoo land."

He knows he can't maintain it forever.

Then again, he won't have to, because it's fundamentally an unsustainable situation, a matter of time before one wall or the other closes in on him. In his police life, the word is already out on Bobby Cirello. Nobody says anything, but that's the point. Other cops avoid him, cut him out of the intelligence loop, don't want to be seen hanging with him. One night he walks into a bar near One Police and every cop in the place suddenly finds a reason to look into their drink.

There's this sense out there that Cirello, "Mullen's pet," just isn't right. Police precincts are hothouses and One Police Plaza is that times ten. Rumors spread faster than head colds, and Cirello's name just keeps coming up—Cirello has a gambling problem, Cirello's in deep to loan sharks, hey, plainclothes guys in the One Four saw Bobby Cirello hanging out with Mike Andrea in a bar on Staten Island.

He knows that IAB will come sniffing around, because the Internal Affairs guys are like dogs in a park, they just can't keep their noses out of the shit. If they aren't on him already, they will be.

And there's always the chance that someone, one of the Italians, one of the blacks, will get busted and, looking at serious drug time, will try to sell him. He almost hopes it happens, because then Mullen will have to step in and shut the thing down.

But it isn't just IAB or NYPD Cirello has to worry about. There's the

New York State Police and there's DEA. The feds have a major, generational hard-on for the Cozzos; what if they have Jay Cozzo up? Shit, the New York families have more rats than an abandoned pier; what if Andrea or even Cozzo is already a cooperating witness?

Mullen tries to reassure him. "We have federal protection on this operation, from the highest level."

Yeah, that's great, Cirello thinks. What about the midlevels, the lower levels? Did they get a hands-off order on him? And if they did, it would only take one actually dirty fed to slip a word to the Italians or to Darnell to get him killed.

Because that was the other wall moving in on him. Again, just a matter of time before he fucks up, or someone fucks up, and blows his cover. A matter of time before Darnell asks him to do something he just can't do and then will want to know why he won't do it. It keeps Cirello up at night . . . well, a lot of things keep him up at night . . . that Darnell would want him to reveal an undercover, name a snitch, and get someone killed.

Or even worse, that Darnell would tell him to do it.

Darnell hinted at it one time. "You double-oh-seven."

"What does that mean?"

"You got a license to kill," Darnell said.

Yeah, Darnell is the one with the license.

Cirello knows this because he's the guy who drives back down to Brighton Beach, where this Russian wiseguy hands a duffel bag to Cirello and says, "There's a hundred thousand in there. Please tell Mr. Darnell that we're sorry, it was a mistake, and the people responsible have been punished."

Someone scared the living shit out of the Russians, someone got the word to them that Darius Darnell was not to be fucked with, and Cirello figures that it has to be certain people in Mexico who had the weight to do that.

He delivers the bag to Darnell at one of his co-ops in East New York. Darnell opens the bag, looks inside, and then hands Cirello a wrapped stack of hundred-dollar bills as a "service charge."

That's the way it works. Cirello's on Darnell's payroll, but it's not like he gets a weekly check and a 401(k) contribution. How it works is he does a job for Darnell and the man gives him a random amount of cash.

Which Cirello brings to Mullen, and they carefully log and document all the money, which goes into a safe.

Well, most of it.

Some of it he has to spend to sell himself as a dirty cop. He buys some clothes, for instance, he takes Libby out for some expensive dinners, he makes a few bets. Has to, otherwise Darnell would get suspicious. The dealer even asks him one time, straight up, "What you do with the money I give you?" Cirello explains that he puts most of it away, saving it for when he pulls the pin, because if he starts spending like a Kardashian now, it would attract attention from IAB, who look for cops living above their pay grade.

Darnell buys that, it makes sense.

But undercover operations are never sales, they're always rentals. The whole idea is to eventually get out and move on and Cirello can't wait to do that. But to do that, he has to get the name of Darnell's suppliers.

The same people who could tell the Russians they had to get on their knees and suck Darnell's dick.

Those are heavy people.

The people killing kids on Staten Island.

So Cirello hangs in there.

It plays hell on his relationship with Libby. Normal police work is hard enough on relationships, but undercover work is sheer murder. He does his nine-to-five at One Police—but he's on call, having to bop out whenever Darnell needs him. Tough to explain to Libby why his phone rings at one in the morning, he has to go out, and he can't tell her where he's going or why.

"It's the job," he says one time.

"I know that."

"It's not another woman," he says.

"I know that, too."

Yeah, she probably does, Cirello thinks. She knows she's beautiful, she's smart, any man would be lucky to have her and wouldn't even think about looking for something on the side.

No, she knows it's the job, she just hates the job.

Hates that he can't share that part of his life with her.

And she sees the changes in him—the Zegna suits, the Battistoni shirts, Gucci ties and Ferragamo shoes. "What is this, wiseguy chic?"

"You don't like it?"

"I don't dislike it," she says. "It's just, you know, different."

And she wonders where the money comes from. The Bobby Cirello she knew was frugal, knew where every dollar was. He always dressed well, but always looked at the price tag. And now he's dropping thousands on his *wardrobe*? It doesn't seem like him.

It isn't just externals like clothes.

Bobby is changing.

It seems like he's tense all the time. Will get up at night and go into another room; she can hear the television on low volume. He's drinking more—he doesn't get drunk, but he's definitely drinking more.

And talking less—long periods of almost sullen silence.

Then there are the times he just goes away somewhere. Leaves without explanation, comes back without explanation, usually geared up, angry, spoiling for a fight she won't give him.

Libby loves Bobby, she's *in* love with Bobby, but this can't go on.

She's close to leaving him.

He knows it.

Libby doesn't say anything, doesn't make threats or issue ultimatums, but he knows she has one foot out the door.

Cirello can't blame her.

Shit, *I'd* leave me if I had a choice, he thinks.

He thinks he loves her, he thinks he's in love with her, but until he gets out from under he's not even going to think about shopping for a ring. In his upside-down world, he's growing distant from Libby and closer to Darnell. That's a well-known danger to undercover work; everyone knows that you tend to start identifying with your targets—it's almost a prerequisite for success—but Cirello finds that he's actually starting to like Darius Darnell.

Which doesn't make sense, because he fucking hates Darnell.

But they're starting to get tight.

One night they're driving down from Inwood, past Grant's Tomb, and Darnell says, "I read a book about him in V-Ville."

"Oh yeah?"

"That man won the war."

Turns out Darnell read a lot of books in the joint, probably more books than Cirello has ever read, and is pretty knowledgeable about American history.

And opinionated.

"Ain't no white man," he says one time, "in the history of this country ever did anything for a black man except there was something in it for him."

I saved your life, motherfucker, Cirello thinks, but he says, "What about your man Grant?"

"Made him president."

"Okay, how about Lincoln?" Cirello asks.

"Racist."

"He freed the slaves."

"Just to save the Union," Darnell says.

"You a hard man, Darius."

"You know it."

Another time Darnell opens up about his time in prison. "You know what the criminal justice system is, Bobby Cirello? Niggers in cages."

"There are white guys in prison," Cirello says.

"*Po'* white guys," Darnell says. "Po' black guys, po' brown guys. They'd be po' yellow guys except there ain't no such thing."

"So the issue isn't race," Cirello says. "It's class."

They're standing on the roof up at Linden, sipping beer and watching the sunset. Darnell says, "No, it's race. You got a white man running for president admits to grabbing women by they pussies. What you think happen if Obama said he grab a white woman by the pussy? They bring back lynching."

"Probably."

"Ain't no probably about it," Darnell says. "They lynch him and then they lynch half the brothers in DC just to make sure. You ain't never heard of Emmett Till?"

"Who's that?"

"He was fourteen years old," Darnell says, "and they lynched that boy because a white woman say he whistled at her. *Fourteen years old*, Bobby Cirello."

Cirello looks over and thinks he sees a tear roll down Darnell's cheek.

"You crying, Darius?"

"I ain't cry since the doctor slap my black ass."

"Okay."

"I *heard* men cry, though," Darnell says. "I heard men cry at night in they cells."

"I'll bet."

Darnell laughs. "That's what you shouldn't do, Bobby Cirello. You shouldn't bet. On *nothin'*. That's how you got in this mess the first place. How you doin' with that?"

"I've dialed it down."

"That's good," Darnell says. "You go to meetings? Like some of the addicts go?"

"I'm not much of a meeting guy."

Another time Cirello is taking him home and Darnell tells him to turn down Ninety-First Street.

"Where are we going?" Cirello asks.

"Pick up my kid."

"I didn't know you had a kid."

"He at that school, right over there."

Cirello knows Trinity, a private school with a hefty annual tuition. Darnell's son is standing outside in his school blazer and gray slacks, a book bag over his back, and holding a lacrosse stick.

Cute kid, about thirteen years old.

"DeVon," Darnell says, "say hello to Mr. Cirello."

"Bobby," Cirello says.

"No, Mr. Cirello," Darnell says. "The boy has manners."

The boy is shy. "Hello."

"How was practice?" Darnell asks.

"I scored a goal."

"Good for you."

They drive him to his mother's place on 123rd and Amsterdam. Cirello waits while Darnell walks his son inside.

"Nice kid," Cirello says when Darnell gets back in the car.

"That's his mama," Darnell says. "I was gone most of his growing up."

"Hey, now he's in Trinity, right?"

"Then he goin' to college. You got kids?"

"No," Cirello says.

"You missin' out."

"I figure I got time."

"We all figure we got time," Darnell says. "Ain't true. Time got us. Time undefeated, man. You never beat it. You wanna know about time, ask a convict. We experts on the subject of time."

It was after that Cirello takes a theory to Mullen. They sit at his breakfast table when Cirello lays it out. "Darius Darnell did eight years in federal lockup. Prior to going in, he was a low- to midlevel Brooklyn coke slinger. Within six months of getting out, he's moving major weights of high-grade heroin. What does that tell you? He made his connection in Victorville."

"Black and brown don't mix in the joint."

"But we know he's slinging Mexican smack," Cirello says, "so they mixed somewhere. Look, we know that the Mexicans usually do their East Coast deals through their own, or other Latinos—Dominicans and Puerto Ricans. That's their MO. But this supplier deals with black, which means there's a new player in the game who either doesn't care about tradition or who couldn't go through the normal channels."

"A Mexican outlier."

"It's a theory."

Yeah, okay, Cirello thinks, a "Mexican outlier."

He knows a little something about being an outlier.

Eddie Ruiz stayed in the witness protection program for about thirty-seven minutes.

Which is about the time it took him to scope out St. George, Utah, and say, "I don't think so."

It was an open question of whether his relocation to St. George, in the heart of Mormon polygamist country, was the DOJ's sly joke on Eddie's ambiguous marital status—his having one family by a woman he married in the US as a teenager, and another he married in Mexico somewhat later—but the Department of Justice only recognized his first family and therefore was only willing to move them.

The first wife, Teresa, a former Texas high school cheerleader, was not thrilled with the privilege. "There's nothing here."

The two kids dutifully echoed the sentiment. "There's nothing here."

But Eddie was playing the deep game. "What do you mean? They have everything here. Costco, Target, McDonald's, Yogurt Barn . . ."

"It's all Mormons," Teresa said.

"Mormons."

Eddie, having been away, didn't know when his fifteen-year-old girl and twelve-year-old boy had turned into Donnie and Marie (speaking of Mormons), but he quickly changed the subject. "This is where the government assigned Daddy to, you know, do his secret work."

Eddie Jr., having only recently abandoned Santa, still believed this "Daddy is a secret agent" story, but Angela was too internet hip and had read all about her daddy having been a big-time drug dealer. She also knew that if the government was moving them somewhere, it was because her dad ratted someone out.

"Where did you learn about that?" Eddie asked when she confronted him about it.

"*Mob Wives*," Angela said. "It's a TV show. One of the wives' father is Sonny Gravanno, and he went into the witness protection program because he was a rat."

"I'm not a rat."

"Whatever," she said. "But why did they have to call us 'Martin'? We're Hispanic, we don't look like Martins."

"Ricky Martin is Hispanic, and his name is Martin," Eddie said, savoring this small victory because even small victories are few and far between with fifteen-year-old daughters.

When Eddie was in the joint, he heard countless guys endlessly moan, "I just want to be back with my kids, I just want to be back with my kids." In all fairness, he did pretty much the same, but now that he was back with his kids he realized that it wasn't all it was cracked up to be.

His son was a walking orthodontist bill, always at the dentist when he wasn't locked in his room jerking off, and his daughter was resentful about having to leave her friends back in Glendora, mostly a boy named Travis who Eddie was pretty sure she was blowing.

"Oral sex isn't sex," Angela said one night on the drive up to Utah. "A president said so."

"Then why do they call it sex?" Teresa asked.

"I'll bet you saw lots of oral sex in prison," she said to Eddie.

"Prison?" Eddie Jr. asked.

"Daddy was undercover in a prison for a while," Eddie said.

"Wow."

Eddie was a little sad that his son and namesake was a moron.

"She was blowing him," Teresa said in bed that night. "I know it."

"Well, she won't be blowing boys in Utah."

"How do you know?"

"Because those are Mormon boys," Eddie said, "and blow jobs are big sins. Plus, they wear that underwear."

"What are you talking about?"

"They wear this underwear," Eddie said, tired from the drive and listening to his kids whine. "It's hard to get off."

"Leave it to you to know about getting men's underwear off."

"Nice," Eddie said. "See, this is where she gets it."

Anyway, Eddie got Family Number One settled into the nice three-bedroom at the end of a cul-de-sac in suburban St. George and reported to his job as an assistant manager at a NAPA Auto Parts Store, which is where the thirty-seven minutes came in.

He managed to stay in the job for thirty-six minutes, and it was just after his new boss, Dennis, asked him and the family over that night for a rousing game or two of Uno and his special ice cream sundaes ("Walnuts are the key") that Eddie walked down the street, paid cash for a Chevy Camaro and drove south on the 15 to Las Vegas.

Eddie checked into the Mandalay Bay, ordered a fifth of vodka and a call girl and finally celebrated his release from Victorville. He celebrated for three days, then got back in the car and drove all the way to San Diego, where he had stored Family Number Two.

Priscilla was *pissed*. "You've been out a week and *now* you come see us?"

"Baby, I had business."

"You didn't miss me?" Priscilla asked. "You didn't miss your daughter, your son?"

"Of course I did."

Yeah, in reality not so much. His little girl was five and a half now and the boy was three and a half and they were already certified brats. Spoiled because Priscilla gave them everything and was unapologetic about it. *Well, they didn't have a daddy, did they?*

Eddie never ceased to be amazed that his wives could cheerfully take his drug money and then self-righteously bitch about him spending time in prison. He knew guys who did thirty years and their wives kept their mouths shut about it.

And their thighs, too.

He had a deep suspicion that Priscilla was fucking some guy while he was away because she always seemed happier than she should have. When Teresa came to visit, she looked properly frustrated and miserable, but Priscilla usually had this fresh I-just-got-laid look about her.

Eddie asked her about it the first night in San Diego, after they had finally bribed the kids into going to bed.

"Let me ask you something," he said, "did you fuck other guys while I was away?"

"*No.*" She'd already developed a California accent, so it came out "*No-wah.*"

"Okay," Eddie said. You lying bitch. "So what did you do for sex?"

Priscilla reached into the side-table drawer and came out with a vibrator. "Just me and the rabbit, baby. You think you can compete with this?"

She turned it on and he checked it out. "Well, I can't make my dick twirl."

"C'mere, baby. I'll make it twirl-uh."

Pretty much she did, and Eddie was, like, *out* when his phone went off the next morning and he saw it was Teresa. He threw on some jeans and hustled outside to take the call. "Hey, baby."

"'Hey, baby,' my ass. Where the fuck have you been?"

"Business trip."

"That guy Dennis has been calling, all worried and shit," Teresa said. "He says he's going to have to fire you."

Oh no, Eddie thought. "Look, Teresa, I am not going to be an auto parts salesman in Utah."

"So you're just going to leave us here?"

"No, baby," Eddie said. "Let me just get settled, and I'll send for you."

"Settled where? Where are you?"

"California."

"California? Why?"

Because that's where the business is, Eddie thought. "Really, T? Do I really have to lay this out for you?"

"What are the feds going to say?"

"Who gives a shit?" Eddie said. "I'm not on parole, I can leave protection anytime I want to. Look, tell Eddie Jr. I'm on a mission, tell Angela, I don't know, whatever, and then chill. I'll call you."

He clicked off and tried to go back to bed.

Nothing doing.

"Who were you on the phone with?" Priscilla asked.

"What?"

"Outside, where I couldn't hear," she said. "Who was on the phone?"

"It was business."

"Pussy business."

"Do you want me to make you a witness, is that what you want?" Eddie asked. "I was protecting you. Jesus Christ."

He got out of bed and went downstairs to make some coffee and get something for breakfast. The kids were already in the kitchen, splashing Cheerios and milk all over the place.

"Priscilla!" he yelled. "Will you get in here and take care of your kids?!"

"They're your kids, too!"

The kids were staring at him.

"What?" Eddie asked.

The little girl, Brittany, asked, "Are you our daddy?"

"Is there someone else you call Daddy?"

Brittany kept staring at him.

Eddie reached into his jeans and came out with a crumpled bill. "You want twenty dollars, Brittany?"

"Yes."

"I want twenty dollars," Justin said.

I'm pure Mexican, Eddie thought, Priscilla is pure Mexican, and we have kids named Brittany and Justin. "Okay, who wants the twenty? Is there someone else you call Daddy?"

Priscilla walked into the room. "Twenty, Eddie? Cheap."

"I'm going to Starbucks."

"Go."

Eddie went.

Found himself a hotel on the beach up in Carlsbad and chilled out for a couple of days.

Now he gets on the horn and calls Darnell. "I'm out."

"Welcome back to the world, my brother."

"Thanks. You got my money?"

"Is all here for you. Every cent."

Eddie's been fronting Darnell on the heroin until he got out. Something like three mil now.

"I trust you. Can you get it to me?" Eddie needs the money to pay Caro. The way it works, Caro fronts the dope to Eddie, Eddie fronts to Darnell, Darnell fronts to retailers. The retailers sell to the users and then the money backwashes up the same route. "Do you have a mule you can trust with that kind of cash?"

"Yeah, I think so," Darnell says. Then he says, "Eddie, there's a problem."

Of course, Eddie thinks—there's always a fucking problem.

The particular problem, Darnell tells Eddie, is that they have competition. Sinaloa has been sending people to New York like pharmaceutical reps, going to the retailers and offering to front them heroin. They mostly go to Dominicans in Upper Manhattan and the Bronx, but more and more they're seeking out Darnell's customers in Brooklyn and Staten Island.

The Dominican gangs are a problem, too, selling the Sinaloa product up the Hudson, in New England and down in Baltimore and DC, territory that Darnell wants. Used to be that Chicago was Sinaloa's major hub, from which it distributed cocaine across the country. But now that the cartel is into heroin, it wants New York, too. And it ain't just Sinaloa. Darnell's running into slingers who are buying from some firm out of Jalisco.

"It ain't right, Eddie," Darnell says. "You gotta straighten this shit out."

Eddie's not so sure he can. Back in the day when the Sinaloa cartel was one organization, Adán Barrera and Nacho Esparza could simply issue a ruling dividing up retail turf in the States. But now the Sinaloa cartel is at least three cartels—Núñez, Esparza and Sánchez, aka the CBNG—and Eddie doesn't want to clue Darnell in that his supplier is actually an old Sinaloa outlier—Damien Tapia. And then there's Tito Ascensión and the New Jalisco Cartel. And of course, everyone wants to sell in New York.

It gets worse.

The competition's product is better, Darnell tells him.

They're undercutting him on price and quality.

"It's this fentanyl shit," Darnell says. "Cinnamon ain't good enough anymore. We gotta catch up with that shit."

"I hear you."

"Can you get fentanyl?"

Why not? Eddie thinks. Fentanyl comes in from China on boats, and his old crew still controls Acapulco and its port, so it shouldn't be a problem. "Yeah, we can work this two ways, D. We can lace H with the fentanyl, and then we can also sell the fentanyl straight up. Give the customers a choice."

"In small doses, though," Darnell says. "We ain't want to kill off our customer base. Gotta move on this, Eddie. I'm losing turf and money. And you get these Sinaloa motherfuckers off my turf or I will."

"Easy, D," Eddie says. "We don't want a war."

"No, but I ain't gonna let them just take over, you know what I'm sayin'."

"Don't do anything rash, I'm all over it," Eddie says.

He works the phone.

Cirello's double life is about to end.

With an enormous bust.

Twenty kilos of fentanyl are on their way to Darius Darnell. A panel truck with twenty keys of the deadly drug, fifty times the strength of heroin, is en route. Darnell will take it to a mill in Upper Manhattan and turn it into pills and dime bags of "fire"—fentanyl-laced heroin.

And Cirello is pulling security for the delivery.

It's the bust they've been working at for almost two years now—a gimme-putt arrest of Darnell and enough fentanyl to kill literally millions of people.

Cirello knows the math, and it's staggering. A kilo of fentanyl costs about $3,000 to $4,000 to make. Darnell is going to pay $60,000 for that key, so a cool $1.2 million for this shipment. But if he laces it into heroin, each kilo of fentanyl will make about twenty keys of retail product, worth over a million a key. If he turns it into pure fentanyl, in the form of pills, the numbers get crazy—the pills are less than two milligrams (anything more would just kill the user) so each kilo will produce 650,000 doses, which sell for $20 to $30 each.

So this shipment could put *thirteen million* pills out on the street.

Thirteen million doses of fentanyl that will go up and down the East Coast like a plague, killing addicts in New York, Boston, Baltimore and DC. That will devastate small towns in New England, Pennsylvania, Ohio and West Virginia.

Except it won't, Cirello thinks.

Because we're going to stop it.

Now Cirello is on his way to Mullen's kitchen to deliver the good news. Make plans for the bust—what personnel (Narcotics and SWAT), how it's going to go down, how they'll communicate. He doesn't know the exact location of the delivery yet—as soon as he does, he'll have to find a way to communicate it to Mullen. The troops will have to be ready to roll in a heartbeat.

It's complicated but exhilarating.

The bust will save a lot of lives.

Including mine, Cirello thinks.

He's losing it. Can't live with the stress anymore, the isolation, the pretending to be the opposite of what he is.

Or maybe it isn't, he thinks as he drives to Mullen's. Maybe it's just a different part of me, a part that likes the easy money, the crazy nights, the nice clothes, the gambling, the drinking, the adrenaline rush of risk. And if that *is* the case, Cirello thinks, it's an even better thing that this is coming to an end, before I really become what I'm pretending to be.

Mullen meets him at the front door. "Come in, come in. What's up?"

They go into the kitchen. Mrs. Mullen says a quick hello, kisses Cirello on the cheek, and makes herself scarce.

Cirello tells Mullen about the upcoming fentanyl delivery.

Waits for his boss to jump out of his chair and start fist-pumping.

It doesn't happen.

Mullen takes it in and just sits there, frowning, thinking.

"What?" Cirello asks.

"We let it go through," Mullen says.

"What?!"

"We let it go," Mullen says. "Think it through, Bobby. If we make this bust, we keep twenty keys of fentanyl from hitting the streets. That just means that hundreds more kilos, thousands, will come in. We don't want to bust the drugs, we want to bust the people."

"We'll get Darnell."

"We want the people *supplying* Darnell," Mullen says.

"You're not listening to me," Cirello says. "It's a delivery. The suppliers will be there."

"Some midlevel sales reps will be there," Mullen says. "They're expendable. If we bust them, there are dozens of others. If we bust Darnell, the supplier will just find another Darnell."

Cirello doesn't say anything.

He doesn't know what to say.

The disappointment is crushing.

"I want to talk with someone about this," Mullen says.

"I'll go." Cirello gets up.

"No, stay. You should be in on this."

Mullen picks up the phone. Twenty minutes later he's on with Art Keller. Cirello listens to him tell the DEA boss what's going on, and then ask, "What do you think? Is it time to pull the trigger?"

Cirello hears the long silence, then, "No."

"I concur," Mullen says. "But, Art, you realize that people are going to die as a result of this decision."

Another silence. "Yeah. I do."

"Okay. I'll get back to you with details." He clicks off. "Bobby—"

"Don't say it," Cirello says. "Please don't say it, sir. I don't want to hear how important this is, how we need to look at the big picture, I don't want to hear about the bombing of Coventry—"

"I know I'm asking a lot—"

"There'll be *dead kids*."

"God damn it, I know that!"

They sit quietly for a minute, then Mullen says, "I know you're at the end of your tether. I know what this is costing you . . ."

No, you don't, Cirello thinks.

"If there were a choice, I'd take you out," Mullen says. "But you're the only one who has a relationship with Darnell, you're higher up the ladder than anyone we've ever had, and if we have to start over again . . ."

More kids will die, Cirello thinks.

"Bobby," Mullen says, "can you hang in a little longer? If you can't, you can't; tell me and I'll pull you out now."

He's offering you the out, Cirello thinks, take it.

He's offering you your life back, take it.

"No," Cirello says. "I'm good."

In this upside-down world, I'm good.

When he gets home, Mike Andrea is parked out in the street. Cirello gets to the car before Andrea can get out. He leans against the door, signals Andrea to roll down the window.

"The fuck you doing here?" Cirello asks.

"You haven't been around much lately, Bobby," Andrea says.

"Don't come around my house."

"Yeah, I saw her when she went in," Andrea says. "I don't blame you, wanting your privacy. No, we thought we'd have heard from you by now, Bobby. That thing we talked about? Where Darnell gets his dope?"

"I told you I don't know."

"But he has a big shipment coming in, doesn't he?" Andrea asks.

"Who said that?"

"He did," Andrea says. "Like that guy used to say on TV, 'I'm also a customer.' He's selling us a piece. You'll be there, Bobby, making sure everything is copacetic, right? Meeting new people, making new friends . . . Just don't forget about your old friends, huh? Your old friends are the people who keep you safe, make sure that pretty girl is safe—"

Cirello grabs him by the lapels, hauls him halfway out the window. "You keep her out of your filthy mouth, and you stay away from her. Or I'll kill you, Mike. You got me? First I'll turn your brains into a paint gun and then I'll kill your idiot boss."

He pushes Andrea back into his seat.

Andrea smooths his lapels down. "You'd better watch yourself . . . putting hands on me . . . threatening people . . ."

"You just remember what I said."

"And you remember who the fuck you are," Andrea says. "We want to hear from you, Cirello."

He rolls up the window and pulls out.

Cirello goes into his place.

Libby takes one look at him and says, "Bobby, what is it? You're shaking."

"I am?"

"Yes. Come here." She wraps her arms around him.

"Yeah," he says, "maybe I'm coming down with something."

Cirello drives Darnell to the meet.

"You sure?" Darnell asks.

"I told you, it's clear," Cirello says. "You're off the radar."

"Feds, too?"

"Like I told you."

"Better be," Darnell says. "Cost me enough."

It's not about the money, Cirello knows, it's just him grousing to cover up his nerves. He has a lot at stake here—tens of millions of dollars and a position in what has become kind of an arms race between drug slingers as to who can sell the strongest dope. Darnell's under a lot of pressure from the competition—the Dominicans and Puerto Ricans, the Chinese—and he needs this shipment to get ahead or just stay even.

And there's too much that could go wrong—a sting, a bust, a hijacking. Another vehicle—a van—trails behind them with four of Darnell's Brooklyn boys, armed with ARs. Another team is waiting in the vicinity of the delivery site—scoping it out, standing guard, ready to move in if something goes down. A third crew is waiting by the mill, for the same reason.

If necessary, Darnell is going to slug it out.

Cirello has his nine at his waist and another weapon, a .380 throwaway, strapped to his ankle, and a Mossberg 590 shotgun under a coat in the back seat.

He's ready to slug it out, too.

He just doesn't know who with.

There are just too many people involved with this now—Mullen, DEA, the Italians, IAB sniffing around, God knows who else.

He drives up the West Side Highway.

"Take the GW," Darnell says.

"We going to Jersey?" Cirello asks.

"What it look like?"

"I don't have jurisdiction in Jersey," Cirello says. "If Jersey has you up, I wouldn't know about it."

"Then you better hope they don't."

It's classic drug dealer technique, Cirello thinks, to cross jurisdictions, making it harder for the cops to make busts. Transfer drugs in New Jersey, take them to New York. It works on the micro level, too, why low-level street slingers will stand on the border between two precincts and just cross the street when cops from one show up, knowing those cops don't want to do the cross-precinct paperwork.

Cirello pulls onto the bridge.

"Stay on Ninety-Five, then get off on Four North," Darnell says. Just a couple of minutes into New Jersey, he says, "Pull over here."

"The Holiday Inn?" Cirello asks.

"Not good enough for you?" Darnell asks.

It's convenient, Cirello thinks. Just off the 95. The Mexicans can turn over the dope and get right back on the highway. He sees the trailing van park three slots away and a couple of Darnell's people get out and check the parking lot.

"Gotta wait for the geek," Darnell says.

"Huh?"

"Computer geek in the van," Darnell says. "Encrypted software. He talking to the Mexicans, let them know we here."

Darnell gets a call and says, "Let's go do this. Room 104."

They get out, walk through the lobby and turn right down a hallway. When Darnell goes to knock on the door, Cirello moves him aside. "Don't stand in front of the fucking door. Someone in there wants you dead, they shoot through it."

He stands to the side and raps on the door with the backs of his knuckles.

"*¿Quién es?*"

"It's Darnell."

The door opens a crack, then the chain slides off and it opens all the way. Cirello holds his left arm straight out, holding Darnell back, keeps his right hand on the butt of his gun, and goes in.

The man at the door is in his forties and looks more like a low-level salesman than a drug mule. Which I guess is the idea, Cirello thinks, because this is the kind of place a sales rep would stay. Or a tourist couple looking for a cheap place within reach of Manhattan, because the woman sitting in the chair is also in her forties, a little frumpy, carrying an extra twenty pounds or so.

No desk clerk would take a second look at them.

The television is turned on to a Spanish-language channel, the volume low. An open MacBook Pro sits on the small desk.

Two nondescript used suitcases sit on the floor under the window.

"I'm going to pat you down, okay?" Cirello asks the man.

The man shrugs his acceptance.

Cirello frisks him, doesn't feel a weapon or a wire and then says, "Her too."

The woman gets out of the chair, turns around and puts her arms up, shoulder level, and Cirello knows this isn't her first lap around the pool. He pats her down and she's clean.

Cirello waves Darnell in.

It isn't like it is in the movies, in some warehouse with squads of guys with machine guns on catwalks. It's mundane—a dull-looking couple in a cheap motel room. They don't carry guns because they're not going to shoot it out with cops. They're not going to shoot it out with hijackers, either. If that happens, they'll give up the dope and the cartel will track the thieves down when they try to lay it off and deal with it then.

With prejudice.

No, they just load the dope into a car or a truck and drive from California, and the cartel trusts them not to steal it themselves because usually they have a close family member left in Mexico as hostage to their good behavior. There isn't a parent in the world who's going to run away with a million dollars in dope if they know it means their kid is going to be tortured to death. Even if there were—and Cirello really hopes there isn't—where would they sell it?

What will happen is that Darnell will communicate to his supplier that he has the product, the hostage will be released from what is probably a luxury hotel suite somewhere, and these two will pick up a nice piece of change.

The woman says to Darnell, "Your friend sends his regards."

"Send them back."

Then she looks at Cirello. "I'm going to open a suitcase. Is that all right?"

"Just don't put your hands inside."

She bends down, opens one of the suitcases, and Cirello sees bricks tightly wrapped in plastic with supporting bands of heavy tape. Straightening back up, she says, "I'm not going to open one."

Darnell shakes his head. "I trust my friend."

Anyway, it's too dangerous, Cirello knows. Cops and EMTs have been killed just coming into contact with fentanyl. If you have an open cut, or if you accidentally inhale some, it's lights out.

"Two bags," she says. "Ten kilos each. Do you want to weigh it?"

"Like I said, I trust my friend."

She closes the suitcase.

What happens next that surprises Cirello is what doesn't happen next.

No money is exchanged. Not a cent.

Darnell just picks up one of the bags, gestures for Cirello to pick up the other, and they leave.

They put the bags in the trunk of Cirello's car.

Darnell gets on the phone. "Tell them we have it."

Then back across the GW, north on Riverside Drive, a right on Plaza Lafayette and then a left on Cabrini Boulevard to Castle Village, a complex of five four-wing high-rise apartment and co-op buildings overlooking the Hudson.

A small two-bedroom goes in the high six figures.

Not the kind of place you'd expect to find a heroin mill, but again, Cirello thinks, that's the idea.

Location, location, location.

A quiet, upper-middle-class neighborhood with easy access to Route 95, Route 9, and 181st Street going over to the bridge toward the Bronx, Queens, Brooklyn and Staten Island.

Cirello pulls into the garage.

He and Darnell get out of the car, grab the bags full of dope and take the elevator to the top floor of the northernmost building.

Darnell bought all three apartments in the wing.

An armed guard meets them at the elevator and walks them to the door of an apartment. Cirello sees it's sort of an office waiting room—a couple of chairs, a sofa, a television and racks of hazmat suits along a wall.

"Put one on," Darnell says.

Cirello feels stupid, but he climbs into one of the white suits.

Darnell does the same and hands him plastic gloves.

A guarded door leads to the next apartment. The guard opens it and Cirello walks into the heroin mill.

Five women in hazmat suits are waiting like workers ready for their shift to start.

Which I guess they are, Cirello thinks.

He sets his bag next to Darnell's on a folding table. One of the women walks up to Cirello and hands him a mask to go over his nose and mouth. Then slips a mask on her own face, opens one of the suitcases, takes out a brick and slices it open with a mat knife.

"Debbie has her a master's in chemistry from NYU," Darnell says. "I hired her away from Pfizer."

Debbie carefully uses a swab to remove a small amount of the powder and move it into a test tube. Then she puts a test strip into the tube and removes it a few seconds later. "Eighty point five. Excellent."

The women go to work, laying the bricks of fentanyl out on tables and cutting it into pans of heroin, then distributing the fire into the small glassine bags that will go out on the street.

Debbie takes the second suitcase and leads Cirello and Darnell into a third room. Tables are set up with several immaculate stainless-steel machines.

"RTP 9's," Debbie says. "Rotary tablet presses. State of the art. We can crank out sixteen thousand pills an hour with these."

"Where did you get them?" Cirello asks.

"The internet," Debbie says. "They're made in the UK, but we get them from the Texas rep in Fort Worth."

"You know how to use these?" Darnell asks.

"A child could do it," Debbie says. "You pour the powder in here, it comes down to this rotary, is forced into these channels and comes out as pills. You want to watch?"

It's as simple as she said.

Cirello has seen microwaves more complicated and he stands and watches as the machine starts spitting out pills like bullets from a machine gun.

They'll be wrapped and out on the street tomorrow.

And tomorrow, someone will probably die.

The last room is a security station, for lack of a better expression. At the end of their shift, each employee has to come here, strip naked and stand for a cavity search. Then another guard runs a gloved finger inside their mouths to make sure that they haven't "cheeked" anything.

"I know it all from V-Ville," Darnell says.

"What do you do when you catch someone?" Cirello asks.

"Don't know yet," Darnell says. "It ain't happened because they know they gonna be searched, and I pay well. Prevention always better than cure."

"Hey, Darius?" Cirello says. "No one sticks their finger up my ass unless I ask them to, and I never ask."

"Thought you was Greek."

"That's a racist stereotype."

"Black man can't *be* racist," Darnell says.

Darnell leans out over the roof railing and looks out at the lights of Manhattan across the river.

"Took my boy to the zoo other day," he says.

"The zoo?" Cirello asks.

"Bronx Zoo," Darnell says. "He doing a paper on gorillas, so we go to the 'Congo Gorilla Forest,' look at the gorillas. The boy, he taking notes, there this little crowd around, looking at the gorillas, but me, I'm standing there and I realize I'm not relating to the other people, I'm relating to the gorilla. I mean, I know just what that gorilla thinking, looking out from inside a cage."

"Yeah, but it's not a cage, right? It's one of those 'environments.'"

"That's the thing," Darnell says. "It don't look like a cage, but it still a cage. Those gorillas, they can't leave, they got to be in there, let people stare at them. When I was in V-Ville, I knew it was a cage because I'm looking out through bars. Now I'm out, it don't look like a cage, but it still a cage. I'm still the gorilla. Black man in this country, he always in a cage."

Then, suddenly, he asks, "How I know I can trust you?"

Cirello's stomach flips. Darnell sounds serious, not like he's just goofing. "Shit, I saved your life, didn't I?"

"How I know that wasn't your game," Darnell asks, "you ain't on some undercover?"

"You want to pat me down, go ahead."

"You too smart to wear a wire," Darnell says. "Maybe I need you to do something you can't do you're 'UC.' You UC, you can't do no felony, can you?"

"What do you have in mind, D?"

"They's this old joke about shootin' cans," Darnell says. "Africans, Puerto Ricans, Mexicans. Maybe I need you to shoot a Mexican."

"I didn't sign up for that."

Darnell says, "This Mexican moving in on my turf, stealing my customers. I have to defend myself. Figure I kill two birds with one stone, defend my turf, find out if I can trust you."

"I thought you already trusted me."

"Got something big in mind for you," Darnell says. "Need to know first."

Darnell is showing me the open door, Cirello thinks. The way out of this fucking assignment. Just walk away and don't come back. No one could blame you. Even Mullen won't sanction a murder.

Even what's-his-name, Art freaking Keller in DC, won't okay a murder.

Walk toward the light, Bobby, he thinks.

Walk toward the light.

"I'm not down for murder, Darnell. Sorry."

"You ain't got kids," Darnell says, "but you might someday. And they gonna be smart like you, they goin' to college. You want them to graduate with all that debt on they backs or you want them to start they life debt free? I ain't talkin' about Fordham money, John Jay money. Kind of money I'm talkin' about Harvard money, Yale money. Sleep on it, Bobby Cirello, get back to me."

Cirello doesn't sleep at all.

He lies there thinking.

He just put twenty kilos of fentanyl on the streets he swore to protect, and now he's being asked to commit murder.

"What is it, Bobby?" Libby asks.

"I'm thinking of pulling the pin," he says suddenly, surprising himself.

"I thought you loved being a cop."

"I do," Cirello says.

I did, anyway.

At least I think I did.

Hard to remember now.

The next night he stands outside the Word Enlightenment House of Jesus Christ next to the Umbrella Hotel in the Bronx.

Where Efraín Aguilar is staying.

Darnell was pleased when Cirello told him that he'd changed his mind. "Now you thinkin', Bobby Cirello."

Efraín Aguilar is basically a pharmaceutical sales rep from a competing cartel selling fentanyl; he's undercut Darnell with three of his retailers in Brooklyn, and Darnell wants a message sent.

Cirello's been on the motherfucker all day and now is waiting for him to come back from shopping at the Nine West Outlet across Third Avenue. Must be getting presents for the family or the girlfriend or something before heading back to Mexico with his order sheets filled.

Thought about taking him on Third but decided it was too busy. Besides, there's a kids' clothing store and a pet shop there and Cirello doesn't want to take a chance on any kids getting hurt.

He feels bad about what he's about to do but then decides fuck it. How many lives has Aguilar taken with his product? It's like that old song, "God Damn the Pusher Man," and there's a special place in hell for the shit that slings this stuff.

Now he sees Aguilar coming up the street.

Yup, shopping bags in hand.

Cirello walks toward him.

Aguilar isn't on his game, should see it coming, but doesn't. Cirello's on top of him before he notices, lets him pass, and then turns around and sticks the gun into his back and says, "See the white van parked up there, mother-fucker? Walk to it and get in."

"Please don't shoot me."

"Walk."

Aguilar walks to the van. When he gets beside it, the door slides open and Cirello shoves him inside, gets in after him and shuts the door.

Hugo Hidalgo pulls the van out.

Cirello pushes Aguilar to the floor, jams a rag in Aguilar's mouth and a hood over his head. Hidalgo drives to St. Mary's Park, the two of them haul Aguilar out of the car and walk him along a footpath to an isolated patch of grass behind some trees, where Cirello pushes Aguilar to his knees, rips the hood off and presses the pistol barrel against his forehead. "Say good night now."

"Please," Aguilar says.

His eyes are red from crying, his nose is running, and he's pissed his pants.

"You got one chance," Cirello says.

"Anything."

"Lie back." Cirello pushes Aguilar onto his back, holsters his pistol, then takes a Roller Pen and inks a neat hole in the middle of his forehead. "Open your eyes wide and open your mouth."

Aguilar does it.

Cirello takes his phone and snaps a photo.

He sends it to Darnell.

"Back to the van," Cirello says. "You're dead now. You tell anyone any different, we'll find you and kill you for real. ¿Comprende?"

"I understand."

"It's better than you deserve, piece of shit."

Hidalgo drives Cirello back to his car and then takes off with Aguilar handcuffed in the back.

"What did you do with him?" Darnell asks.

"You don't mind if I don't make you a potential witness against me, do you?" Cirello asks. Actually, D, Aguilar is on his way to some fort somewhere as a protected federal witness and is probably doing his best Freddie Mercury imitation for DEA right now. "Suffice to say you don't have to worry about him anymore, and the message has been sent."

"I ever get busted again I'm looking at life anyway," Darnell says, "so the first name I give is yours, and the first story I tell is this."

"Yeah, I get that," Cirello says. "So what's my big reward? Where's my Harvard money coming from?"

"You going to Vegas."

"That's it?"

"To deliver money," Darnell says.

To his supplier.

Maybe he feels guilty.

Maybe Cirello feels he owes them something, but he leaves Darnell, goes to see Mullen, and then drives out to the Starbucks on Staten Island.

Jacqui isn't happy to see him.

"Can you take a break?" he asks.

"If I want to lose my job."

"When is your shift over?"

"You said you'd go away," Jacqui says.

"I lied," Cirello says. "That's what cops do. When is your shift over?"

"Four o'clock."

"Travis picking you up?" When she nods, he says, "I'll meet you both at four. Don't make me come looking for you."

He goes out and sits in his car.

At five past four, Travis's van pulls up, Jacqui comes out and gets in. Cirello walks over and pounds on the door. When Jacqui opens it, he says, "There's a Sonic on the next block. I'll buy you a meal."

"We have to go score."

"A fucking burger. Ten minutes."

They meet him at Sonic. He buys them burgers, milkshakes and fries and they sit down at a booth. He can see they're both jonesing.

He and Mullen debated this. The chief was against it. "Why do you think you owe these kids?"

"I don't," Cirello said. "I just want to give them a chance."

"You're a cop, not a social worker."

"They blur."

"They shouldn't," Mullen said. "We need to keep a clear bright line."

"With all respect, sir, there's no such thing," Cirello said. "What are we doing all this for, unless it's to keep the needles out of their arms?"

"We do that by interdicting the supply."

"And they gave me information to do just that."

"Because you jammed them up," Mullen said. "There are thousands of addicts out there, Bobby, we can't put all of them into a program."

"I'm not asking all of them," Cirello said. "Just these two."

"We are not budgeted to—"

"I have cash coming in all the time," Cirello said.

"That money needs to be vouchered."

"Or not," Cirello said. "You have to love the irony, boss, you have to love the symmetry—using heroin money to treat heroin addicts."

Cirello waited him out. He knows his boss, knows his heart. The man is a steel cupcake. Sure enough, after a long silence, Mullen said, "Okay, make the offer."

So now Cirello sits across a table from the two addicts and makes his pitch. "I have a one-time, take-it-or-leave-it offer for you. If you want to kick, I can get you into a program. Both of you."

"What is this, like an intervention?" Jacqui asks.

"Yeah, okay."

"We don't have insurance," Jacqui says.

"There's a fund for this kind of thing," Cirello says. Well, there is *now.* "It's a place in Brooklyn, it's not some Malibu, sit-by-the-ocean-and-do-yoga spa. But if you want it, I can get you beds tonight."

"Why are you doing this?" Travis asks.

"You want it or not?" Cirello asks.

"How long would we be gone?" Jacqui asks.

"I don't know how long," Cirello says. "I don't know what color the walls are, I don't know if they have basic cable . . . I do know they get results. You can detox in a bed instead of a cell, you can get clean."

"I don't know," Jacqui says.

"What's there not to know?" Cirello asks. "You're junkies living in a van. You're sitting in Sonic jonesing. You don't know where your next fix is going to come from. I'm not sure what you think you're giving up here."

"Heroin," Jacqui says.

"Look," Travis says, "maybe it wouldn't hurt us to get clean for a while."

Cirello hears the temporizing but doesn't care. If they get these kids for a few days, they might be able to hold on to them. At least they have a chance.

Jacqui doesn't see it that way.

"You chickening out on me?" Jacqui asks her boyfriend. "Going pussy? But, hey, if you want to go . . ."

"Not without you."

Touching, Cirello thinks.

Junkie love.

But maybe it works, maybe they guilt each other into it. Whatever it takes, he doesn't give a shit.

"Okay," Jacqui says. "I'll go."

Travis nods.

"I'll make the calls," Cirello says. "Get your shit, such as it is, together,

and I'll meet you here at six, take you over there. You have anyone you need
to inform?"

"No," Travis says.

"I guess I should tell my mom," Jacqui says.

"Yeah, do that," Cirello says. "Six o'clock. Hang in until then, things are
going to get better."

One last fix, Jacqui thinks.

She's sicker than shit.

"You don't want to go into detox too sick," she tells Travis.

"How do you know?"

"I know people who've detoxed," she says. "Shit, Shawna did it five times.
She told me."

"We don't even know where to score."

"It's Heroin Island," she says. "Just drive."

"I dunno."

"Come on, baby," Jacqui says. "One last high. One last party before we go
all twelve-step and shit."

They cruise Tottenville.

Down Hylan, along Craig, across Main.

They don't see anyone.

It's the problem with scoring on the Island. It's all invisible, you don't see
it. It's behind doors, in back rooms, behind stores. If you didn't know there
was a heroin problem on Staten Island, you wouldn't know.

They find it, appropriately enough, in an alley behind a drugstore off Arthur Kill—a van parked where it has no business being, the side door open
and two black guys standing there like they're open for business.

They are.

Jacqui gets out of the van and walks over.

"What you looking for, mama?"

"What you got?"

"What you need."

She gives him a twenty. He reaches back into the van and comes out with
two envelopes.

"It looks funny," Jacqui says.

"It's new shit."

"What's that?"

"The future," he says. "You do this, you never go back."

She takes the envelopes and gets back into the van. Travis drives up to
South Bridge Street and pulls over into a parking lot by a body shop.

"Come on," Jacqui says. "We don't have a lot of time."

They have to meet the pushy do-gooder cop in forty-five minutes.

She cooks up.

So does Travis. "What is this shit?"

"Something new. Supposed to be great."

"I hope so," Travis says. "For the last ride."

Jacqui is shaking so bad she's having trouble holding her needle in the cooker.

"Hold on," Travis says. "Let me fix and I'll shoot you up."

He stretches out his long white arm, puts the needle into his vein and pushes the plunger. Then he takes the needle out and dips it into her mix.

"The fuck you doing, man?" she asks.

"I'm bigger than you," Travis says. "I need more."

He pops again.

Smiles at her.

Then his head snaps back, his body begins to tremble and then shake and then jerk around like he's being electrocuted.

"Travis!" Jacqui grabs him by the shoulders. Tries to hold him but he's jerking like a live wire and she can't. The back of his head hits the floor of the van. "Travis! Baby! No!"

Then he's quiet.

Limp.

His chest heaves.

Bubbles froth from his mouth as he gasps.

His empty eyes look at her.

"Travis!!!!! Noooooooooo!!!!!!"

Cirello sits waiting outside the Sonic.

I should have known, he thinks, they wouldn't show up. Mullen tried to tell me, I wouldn't listen.

Bleeding-heart liberal asshole.

Then he hears the call come across the radio. Squad car calling for the EMT and he knows it, just knows it. He puts the flasher on the roof, pulls out and races toward South Bridge Road. Jacqui's sitting on the ground outside the van, her arms around herself, rocking back and forth, moaning.

The EMTs are already there.

Cirello shows his badge to the uniform. "What do we have?"

"White male, twenties, OD," he says. "They administered Narcan, but too late. Waiting for the ME now."

"What about the girl?"

"Possession."

"You write it yet?"

"No."

"Do me a favor?" Cirello asks. "Cut her loose?"

"You got it, Detective."

Cirello makes a note of the patrolman's name and badge number, then walks over to Jacqui and squats in front of her. "I'm sorry for your loss."

"It was going to be our last high," she says. "We were going to kick."

"Sit tight."

He goes into the van. Travis's body is sprawled on the floor.

Fentanyl, Cirello thinks.

Maybe the same shit I helped deliver.

The kid didn't know.

Cirello goes back out, says to Jacqui, "Get in the car."

She shakes her head. "It's too late."

"For him, not for you."

"It's the same thing."

"Don't do this Romeo and Juliet shit," Cirello says. "Save yourself. If it's any comfort, he'd have wanted you to. Now get in the car."

"No."

"What do I have to do," Cirello says, "cuff you?"

"I don't care what you do."

"Okay." He hauls her to her feet, turns her around and cuffs her behind her back. Walks her to his car, opens the door, presses her head down, and pushes her inside. Then he drives her to Brooklyn while she pukes all over the front of his car.

Cirello walks her into the rehab, where the admitting nurse says, "I thought you were bringing two."

"One didn't make it." He uncuffs Jacqui. "She's coming in on her own."

"Got it."

"Good luck, Jacqui."

She's out of it but manages, "Fuck you."

"Yeah, fuck me," Cirello says as he walks out. He takes his car to a self-wash, vacuums the interior, wipes it down and sprays it until it smells like vanilla puke instead of just puke.

5

Banking

My house shall be a house of prayer
But you have made it a den of thieves.
—Luke 19:46

Washington, DC
July 2016

Keller meets O'Brien at the bar at the Hamilton.

O'Brien asks, "You want a beer, or something stronger?"

"Just coffee," Keller says. "It's a school day."

The bartender overhears and sets a mug of coffee down in front of him. The bartenders and waiters hear everything in this town, Keller thinks. The cabbies—although it's more Uber drivers now—see everything.

"Jesus Christ, who thought that asshole could win the nomination?" O'Brien asks.

"You should have run," Keller says.

"That clown car was already too crowded," O'Brien says. "And I'm one of those evil 'professional politicians.' It's the amateur hour now. And let's face it—guys like you and me, the Vietnam generation, we're dinosaurs."

"Dennison is from the same generation."

"But he didn't serve," O'Brien says. "He didn't go. You and I did."

"Are you going to support him now?" Keller asks. "After all the shit you said about him? All the shit he said about you?"

"It's shit under the bridge," O'Brien says.

"And 'the wall'?"

"A lot of my constituents like that wall," O'Brien says.

"If you want to throw me under the bus, it's okay, I get it," Keller says. "No hard feelings, *vaya con Dios.*"

"I might have to," O'Brien says. "You haven't made any friends with that wing of the party."

"I haven't tried to make any friends," Keller says, "with any wing of any party. If it comes to that, whoever is president, I'll go peacefully."

"What will you do?" O'Brien asks.

"I have a decent pension," Keller says. "We could live well somewhere. Maybe not DC . . ."

"You're not thinking about going back to Mexico, are you?" O'Brien asks.

"No," Keller says. "Maybe Costa Rica? I don't know, Ben, we haven't really thought it out."

They haven't even discussed it.

Keller goes back to the office.

There's a lot to do before he leaves this desk, including a stack—that's a mild word for it, he thinks—of literally thousands of drug-related pardon or commutation requests that the White House sent over for his recommendations. If a Republican administration takes over, it will shitcan the requests. They've already said they'll instruct federal prosecutors to push for maximum sentences on all drug cases.

Back to the bad old days, Keller thinks.

He's in a race to approve pleas that he thinks are worthy, a race to protect his people inside the agency, to reassign them to postings they want, a race to move Operation Agitator forward.

His receptionist buzzes. "Agent Hidalgo to see you."

"Send him in."

"Claiborne set up a meeting with the Mexicans," Hidalgo says.

"When and where?"

"New York," Hidalgo says. "Tomorrow."

"Will Lerner be there?"

"No," Hidalgo says.

So Claiborne is the cutout, Keller thinks.

Okay.

One step at a time.

"Do you want to go out tonight or stay in?" Keller asks Marisol.

"I'd love to stay in," she says. "Do you mind?"

"No," Keller says. "Chinese, Indian, or pizza?"

"Indian?"

"Sure."

Keller pours himself a strong scotch and sits down in a chair by the window.

Getting a warrant to wire Claiborne for the meeting is a problem.

The federal jurisdiction would be the Southern District of New York, and while Dennison doesn't have a lot of friends there, the prosecutor might be reluctant to request a warrant with Terra and Jason Lerner as its target. It could be seen as too political during a presidential campaign.

It also puts Mullen in a tough position. How long he can keep the investigation from his superiors is doubtful, and the potential blowback is worrisome. The nominee has a lot of allies in NYPD, New York is his base, as it is the Berkeley Group's. It would take only one cop, one lawyer—hell, one secretary—to tip Berkeley off. And Lerner could exert enormous pressure to shut the investigation down completely.

The warrant is also a problem just on substance, Keller has to admit. We don't have a compelling argument, just a statement from an informant that Berkeley *might* take a meeting with a financial institution that *might* have a connection with a Mexican drug cartel. Even the most independent, disinterested judge might reject that as a predicate for a wire.

Keller thinks, It's the same old vicious circle that we always face when trying to get a surveillance warrant—without underlying evidence we can't get the wire, and without the wire we can't get underlying evidence.

"Where did you go?" Marisol asks.

"I'm sorry?"

"Just now, where did you go?" she asks. "Do you want me to call for the food, or do you want to?"

"No, I'll do it. The usual?"

She nods. "I've become a sad creature of habit."

What's sad, Keller thinks as he picks up the phone, is that I have a delivery service on speed dial. He orders Marisol's usual chicken tikka masala and himself a lamb vindaloo and gets the standard answer that it will be about forty minutes. It's been Keller's experience that no matter what you order, whether it's a pepperoni pizza or pheasant under glass, the response is always that it will be about forty minutes.

They eat in front of the television, watching the convention in Cleveland and a schlumpy, profusely sweating politician leading the crowd in a chant of "Lock her up! Lock her up!"

"This is what it's come to," Marisol says. "That could be your new boss. They say he's going to be the new attorney general."

"Who is he?"

"The governor of New Jersey."

"I thought it was Fred Flintstone."

"Or Hermann Goering," Marisol says. "Tell me they can't win."

"They can't win."

"You don't sound convinced."

"I'm not," Keller says. "Have you given any thought to what you want to do next?"

"I don't know," Marisol says. "Are you ready to retire?"

"Maybe."

"And do what?" she asks.

"Read books," Keller says. "Go for long walks. We could travel."

"I'm not going on a cruise," she says.

Keller laughs. "Who said anything about a cruise?"

"I'm just saying."

"Okay, no cruises," Keller says. "I feel bad, Mari. I took you from your life, your work, and I brought you up here with the expectations of a certain kind of life. And you've been . . . great. You've helped me fight every goddamn battle, usually better than I have, and I don't know what life I can give you now."

"You don't have to 'give' me anything," Mari says. "I made my choices, I'm very happy with them."

"Are you?"

"Yes!" she says. "How can you ask that? I love you, Arturo, I love our life here. I've loved the work I've been doing."

"So you'd like to stay in Washington," Keller says.

"If we could, yes," Marisol says. "I'm not ready to play golf yet, or go mall-walking, or whatever retired Americans do. Neither are you, if you're being honest."

There are things I could do in DC, Keller thinks. He's been dodging calls from half a dozen think tanks, all of which would love to bring on a former administrator of DEA. On his call-back list are messages from Georgetown and American University. And he's had feelers from two television news networks about being an on-call expert about drug issues.

But do I want to be involved with "drug issues" on any level? he asks himself. I've walked away from that world twice now, and it's always drawn me back in. Wouldn't it be great to walk away for good this time?

And what's best for Mari? "Aren't you tired of being attacked?"

"The attacks will stop," she says. "I won't be relevant anymore. And really, Arturo, Breitbart? Fox News? Amateurs in the attack business. I eat chunky little boys like Sean Hannity for lunch."

True enough, Keller thinks. This woman faced down the goddamn Zetas. "We can make a comfortable living in DC. If you really want to stay here, given . . ."

"That it might be the new locus of fascism in North America?" Marisol asks.

"A tad overstated, but okay."

"It's not overstated," Mari says. "The man is a fascist, his ideas are fascist."

"And you'd want to stay in his capital."

"What better place to join the resistance?" Marisol asks. "Anyway, it's not going to happen."

Your lips to God's ears, Keller thinks.

He doesn't tell her what he fears—that this crew could win the election and come into power owing the Mexican cartels.

The phone rings.

It's Mullen. "The meeting is set. The Pierre."

"Why not the Berkeley offices?"

"Awareness of guilt?" Mullen asks. "They don't want the HBMX people seen walking through the door. I'm surprised the Mexicans are okay with that."

"We have to get a wire," Keller says.

"What's the predicate?" Mullen asks. "We have bankers and real estate people meeting about a loan. It's not like we have reason to believe they're making a drug deal."

"They *are* making a drug deal," Keller says. "Two kids pass twenty bucks' worth of weed on a corner, I can wire them. These guys are moving hundreds of millions and get a pass because it's going down at the Pierre?"

"We're on the same team here," Mullen says. "What I'm saying is that I don't think a judge is going to agree. What if we weren't wiring Claiborne to tap the meeting, but so we could monitor his personal safety? A CI going into a high-risk meeting . . ."

"We can't sell that," Keller says. "Fear for Claiborne's safety? In the Pierre, with bankers and real estate developers? What are we afraid of, he chokes on the foie gras? We can bust in and give him the Heimlich? We have to have something we can bring to a judge and not get laughed out of chambers."

"Maybe not," Mullen says. "Suppose Claiborne keeps his phone in his pocket and records the meeting for his own purposes? There would be an evidentiary problem if you wanted to use it in court later—it would get tossed on an exclusionary ruling—but if we're just looking for intelligence, that doesn't matter."

"Remind me never to screw with you," Keller says.

"Will Claiborne do it?" Mullen asks.

He's going to have to, Keller thinks.

Claiborne is as nervous as a whore in church.

Hidalgo's afraid the guy is going to blow it, go in there and throw up or break down into tears or something.

"What if they tell us to turn phones off?" Claiborne asks.

"Then you make like you turn it off, but you don't," Hidalgo says.

Jesus.

"What if they confiscate phones before the meeting?"

"You've been in meetings like that?" Hidalgo asks. "Because I'd like to hear about those meetings."

"No, I haven't."

"Then chill," Hidalgo says. "Remember, we want names. Descriptions. If you take notes, we want those notes. If there are documents, we want copies of those documents."

"I don't know if I can get you those."

"You'd better get us those," Hidalgo says. "Your free ride on the merry-go-round is over, Chandler. You need to grab the fucking ring."

"I don't know . . ."

"Do everything you normally do," Hidalgo says. "Just be your normal asshole self. Don't worry about saying anything incriminating because we'll cut you a new deal anyway. One more thing, if there are more meetings, you make sure you're included."

"How am I going to do that?"

"Fuck if I know," Hidalgo says. "Am I an investment banker? You got where you are by insinuating yourself upward, right? Make yourself necessary, essential. Kiss ass, suck cock, whatever."

"How long do I have to keep doing this?" Claiborne asks.

"Until," Hidalgo says.

"Until when?"

"Until we say stop," Hidalgo says. After we've squeezed every last drop of juice out of you, he thinks, or until you give us someone bigger, whichever comes first.

But you're a smart little fuck, you've figured that out already.

When a phone rings at four in the morning it's usually bad news.

Keller rolls over and picks it up. "Keller."

"I've always believed," Mullen says, "it's better to be lucky than good. Are you ready for this?"

"What?"

"We need linkage between Terra and the cartels, right?" Mullen says. "I think we just got it."

That wakes Keller up. "Jesus. How?"

"My UC? Cirello?" Mullen says. "Darius Darnell just told him to provide security for the meeting at the Pierre."

Keller waits in the office.

And uses the time to read commutation files. One is from a Florida inmate serving life for dealing fifty dollars' worth of coke, but it was his third conviction. Another is a three-time loser sentenced to life without parole for selling a small amount of meth. The next one is a convict, a first offender named Arthur Jackson, who's doing three life sentences for making a phone call to set up a low-level cocaine deal.

It goes on and on.

Bobby Cirello is living large.

What else would you call hanging out in the Pierre, he thinks, drinking a ten-dollar cup of coffee and munching on a twenty-buck cheese Danish while you check the suite for hidden microphones?

He's looking tight—black Zegna suit, pearl-gray Battistoni shirt, red Gucci tie with matching pocket square, black Ferragamo shoes. Like his ya-ya used to say about some of the wiseguys who'd come in for the dollar breakfast special, "He has more money on his back than in his bank."

Darnell told him to dress sharp.

This meeting is with bankers and real estate heavyweights and "special guests" up from Mexico, so he was told to look tight, keep his eyes and ears open and his mouth shut, make sure the suite is clean, and be a "presence," letting the guests know that they're safe and secure because one of New York's finest is on the job.

"What's your interest in this?" Cirello asked.

"What's that to you?"

"Like to know what I'm walking into," Cirello said.

"Need to know the meeting room ain't wired," Darnell said. "And our visitors need to know they're meeting with serious people. Just go there, look like a cop."

I'll do my best, Cirello thinks now as he steps out into the hallway. "Special guests," my aching ass. Real estate developers, bankers—just a higher level of dirtbag, as far as he's concerned. The kind of people who kill people—like that poor kid Travis.

The elevator doors open and a man gets out. A real Brooks Brothers type, Cirello thinks, probably wears L.L.Bean on his weekends in Connecticut.

The guy looks shit scared.

"Chandler Claiborne?" the guy asks, like he's not sure he knows his own name. "I'm here for the meeting."

"You're the first to arrive," Cirello says.

"And you would be . . ."

"Security," Cirello says. "Go on in. There's coffee and things. I'm sure the rest will be here any minute."

"Did you sweep the room?" Claiborne asks.

"I'm sorry?"

"Sweep the room," Claiborne says. "You know, for bugs, that sort of thing."

"Oh yeah, the room is totally swept."

Jesus Christ.

Claiborne goes in.

The Mexicans, three of them, arrive about five minutes later. One looks to Cirello to be about fifty, the other two maybe in their mid- to late thirties. Expensively dressed, chilled out—these people are used to meetings where there's security at the door.

"Mr. Claiborne is inside," Cirello says.

The fiftyish guy says, "Then we're all here. Please see that no one else comes in."

"Yes, sir."

They close the door behind them.

Cirello waits in the hallway for an hour and a half before they come out.

Keller gets the call.

"Claiborne's out," Hidalgo says.

"And?"

"He got it all," Hidalgo says. "I'm sending you the audio file now."

"How's Claiborne?"

"Shaken," Hidalgo says. He chuckles. "You know how UC work is."

"Sit on him for a while," Keller says. "Make sure he doesn't go crying to his bosses to confess."

"We're having martinis as we speak," Hidalgo says.

"Hugo? Good work."

"Thanks, boss."

There's a lot to do.

Keller starts by listening to the audio file.

Most of it is mumbo jumbo to him, financial discussions that he doesn't understand. What's clear from the meeting, though, is that Claiborne is pressing the Mexicans for a quick decision on the loan, offering to "move up their position" on the syndicate pyramid, and reassuring them that Park Tower is a viable investment.

"Why has it lost money for nine years, then?" one of the Mexicans asks.

"A declining real estate market," Claiborne says. *"But that's changing now. We're moving into a seller's market, and Park Tower will be a prime location."*

"Then why did Deutsche Bank pull out of the syndicate?"

"Some people have the guts to make money," Claiborne says. *"Others don't. The question is, do you?"*

"No, Chandler, the question is, how are you going to guarantee our money?"

"Haven't we always?" Claiborne says. *"When has Terra, or Berkeley for that matter, defaulted on you?"*

"No, that's true. But Terra is about to default now."

"Which is why we're here," Claiborne says. *"Look, let's get real. We each have needs. We need cash, and you need to place some. We can help each other. It's a symbiotic relationship."*

Keller hits the pause button again. *We need cash, and you need to place some.* Does that indicate awareness of guilt? That they know the $285 million they're seeking is drug money? He starts the file again and hears one of the Mexicans ask, *"Why aren't people from Terra here?"*

"Well, I'm the syndicate broker."

"That's not an answer. Why should we invest hundreds of millions with people who won't sit down with us?"

"This is just a preliminary meeting," Claiborne says. *"Just exploratory to ascertain your interest. If you want to sit down with Terra—"*

"Not just with Terra. With Jason."

"If I could tell him you're on for the whole two-eighty-five—"

"The amount isn't the problem. We're concerned about the relationship."

Claiborne says, *"If we can come to a preliminary agreement here, I'm sure Jason would love to sit down with you."*

"With that understanding," the Mexican says, *"we're willing to look at the numbers."*

Forty minutes of numbers ensue, as Keller prays, Push for the next meeting. Push for the next meeting. God must be listening, because the Mexican boss wraps up the session with *"We're willing to close. But only with Jason personally."*

"I'll see if I can set that up for tomorrow," Claiborne says. *"Can I arrange some entertainment in the meantime?"*

"That's very kind, Chandler, but we can arrange our own entertainment."

"Of course."

The meeting ends. Goodbyes. Shuffling of shoes, closing of doors.

The next step is to ID the Mexican bankers, Keller thinks. He gets on the horn with Mullen.

"Two of my best people picked them up outside the Pierre," Mullen says. "We have them under surveillance. They're staying at the Peninsula. We're working on getting the registration."

"They'll use false names anyway," Keller says. "Did your guys get photos?"

"Yeah, but they're not great," Mullen says. "They didn't want to get too close and spook them."

"No, that's right," Keller says. "Send them anyway, we'll run them. How about Cirello? Can he give us descriptions?"

"Got them already."

Keller tells Mullen about tomorrow's meeting with Jason Lerner. "Look, these guys aren't virgins, they've been in bed with these people before. I'll send you the audio file, you'll hear it."

"Can it get us a warrant?"

"I don't know," Keller says. "Depends on who 'these people' are."

"We'll send you the photos now."

"To me directly. I'll scramble for a warrant," Keller says. "We'll want it as evidence. We have to work Claiborne into pushing these guys into an admission of awareness. Hopefully Darnell will put Cirello on security again. Can he work the Darnell side?"

"He can't push too hard."

"Yeah, I don't want to get him jammed up." I already got one undercover killed, Keller thinks. Hugo's dad. I don't want another on my conscience. "Tell him to be careful. But if we can link Darnell to the money people . . ."

"Jesus Christ, huh, Art?"

"Yeah, talk to him, too."

The photos come in a few minutes later.

Mullen was right, they're not great. A little fuzzy, shot from across the street. Three men leaving the Pierre. Same three men checking into the Peninsula. Keller doesn't recognize any of them.

He looks at the individual shots.

The one he labels "Mexican Banker 1" looks to be in his fifties—gray hair, gray goatee. About five ten.

"MB 2" is younger, late thirties or early forties, black hair, pushing six feet. "MB 3" is in his early thirties, Keller guesses.

He'd run them through the DEA database but there are people in the agency who are giving anything he does straight to Denton Howard.

Howard can't know about this yet.

Maybe ever.

Keller calls Orduña in Mexico. "Can you run some photos for me?"

"You have better resources than I do."

"But I can't use them," Keller says.

There's a long silence. "*¿Así es?*"

So it's like that?

"*Así es,*" Keller says.

I can't trust my own people.

"Send them."

"Can you put a rush on them?"

"You're a pain in the ass, Art."

"Famous for it," Keller says. "Roberto, you know how you're always bitching that the US doesn't take responsibility for its ownership in the drug problem? This is me taking responsibility. At the highest level."

"Is this you getting yourself in worse trouble?" Orduña asks. "Your days might be numbered."

"That's why I need it now."

"There's always a job for you here," Orduña says.

Keller sends the photos and then waits three endless hours before Orduña calls back. "In ascending order, MB 3 is Fernando Obregón. He's an investment banker with HBMX. MB 2 is Davido Carrancistas, a lending officer with the same bank. MB 1 is your winner—León Echeverría. He's an independent player."

"Name is familiar."

"Actually, you have him in your database," Orduña says. "Check your photo file on the Adán and Eva royal wedding. He was a guest. Same with Adán's wake and funeral. We've had him under watch for years, decades. But . . . Arturo, I don't know what you're getting into up there, but here? Echeverría is connected, not just to Sinaloa, but to certain people very high up in Mexico City."

As high as it gets, Orduña explains. Echeverría is a major contributor to PRI on all levels. He has business interests alongside the current administration, in fact, helps them with their own investments.

"He's *intocable,*" Orduña says.

Untouchable.

Keller meets with Judge Antonelli in the bar of the Hay-Adams Hotel on Sixteenth Street, joining him in one of the red banquettes beneath an old caricature of Tip O'Neill.

"Why the spy versus spy, Art?" Antonelli asks. "We both have perfectly functional offices."

"I need a warrant."

"You have a battalion of lawyers to do that."

Keller tells him who the warrant is on.

"You're asking me to commit career suicide if they win," Antonelli says.

"If they win, they're going to replace you anyway."

"Maybe not," Antonelli says. "I might fly under the radar. Unless I do this. If I give you this warrant, it could get labeled a political witch hunt. An attempt to throw the election to the Democrats."

"It's not," Keller says. He shows Antonelli some of the photos that Orduña sent—Echeverría dancing at Adán Barrera's wedding, Echeverría at his wake, at the funeral. Echeverría with Elena Sánchez, with Iván Esparza, with Ricardo Núñez, Tito Ascensión, even a photo of a younger Echeverría with Rafael Caro.

"I'm assuming all these people are cartel figures," Antonelli says.

"That's right."

"So what?"

"There's enough here to justify reasonable suspicion of a crime," Keller says.

"A bank lending money?"

"HBMX has been caught with its fingers in the cookie jar before," Keller says. "In 2010, it funneled drug money through Wachovia Bank, in 2011 it was HSBC, 2012 it was Bank of America. These are all on judicial record. The banks concerned reached settlements with Justice and paid fines."

"Why hasn't Mexico prosecuted?"

"I guess because they're no cleaner than us," Keller says.

Antonelli drums his fingers on the table. "You have no clear connection between this meeting and drug traffickers."

"A heroin trafficker named Darius Darnell arranged security for the meeting."

"How do you know that?" Antonelli asks.

"Bill . . ."

"You're asking me to lay my ass on the line here."

"We have an undercover close to Darnell," Keller says.

"Get me a sworn affidavit."

"If that leaked," Keller says, "it could get this guy killed."

More drumming. "Can you put this person on the phone?"

It takes twenty minutes. Keller calls Mullen, he calls Cirello, Cirello calls Keller. Keller says, "Do not identify yourself. I'm about to hand the phone to a federal judge who is going to ask you some questions."

"Okay."

Keller hands Antonelli the phone.

"This is Justice William Antonelli," he says. "I need you to understand that this conversation has the same force and function as if you were appearing in my office and were under oath. Do you understand that?"

"Yes, Your Honor."

"Good," Antonelli says. "Do you have a relationship with a Darius Darnell, and, if so, what is the nature of that relationship?"

"I work for him in my capacity as an undercover police officer," Cirello says.

"To your direct knowledge," Antonelli says, "is he involved in drug trafficking?"

"To my direct knowledge, Darnell traffics in heroin."

"And do you perform security functions for him?"

"In my capacity as an undercover police officer," Cirello says, "I do perform certain security functions for Darius Darnell."

"And did Mr. Darnell ask you to provide security for a meeting at the Pierre Hotel between a representative of Terra Realty Trust and certain Mexican banking institutions?"

"He asked me two days ago," Cirello says, "but he did not tell me who would be attending that meeting."

"Did you later learn the identities of those individuals?"

"Yes, I did."

"From Mr. Darnell?"

"No."

"Is it your understanding," Antonelli asks, "that this meeting was connected to Mr. Darnell's drug trafficking?"

Keller holds his breath. This is *the* question. If Cirello answers that he doesn't know—which is probably the accurate response—the warrant is most likely shot.

Then he hears Cirello say, "That's my understanding."

"Based on what?" Antonelli asks.

Keller hears Cirello lie. "He told me so."

"Thank you." Antonelli clicks off. "I don't know."

"Bill," Keller says, "I need this warrant. I need you to do the right thing here."

"If only it were that easy to know what the right thing is," Antonelli says.

"You know what the right thing is," Keller says.

"You did the right thing," Mullen says.

Lying to a federal judge? Cirello thinks. Then again, it's part of my bizarro world—the wrong thing is the right thing.

"You did the right thing," Mullen repeats. "We got the warrant."

And that's what matters, Cirello thinks.

Mullen says, "Now we just have to hope Darnell sends you to the meeting again."

"No reason he shouldn't," Cirello says.

. . .

Chandler Claiborne is freaking out.

"I'm not doing it again," he says.

"You don't have to," Hidalgo says. "The room will be wired."

"Jason's my friend," Claiborne says. "We've made millions together. I won't walk him into a trap."

"What are you saying?"

"I'm calling off this meeting," Claiborne says. "I'll go somewhere else for the money."

"How are you going to explain that to Lerner?"

"I'll tell him the Mexicans pulled out."

"You do that," Hidalgo says, "and I'll call up Jason Lerner and play him the tape. I'll tell him you're a cooperating witness. What do you think happens to you then?"

Chandler stares at him. "You people are evil. You are truly evil."

"Why don't you and I get in my car," Hidalgo says. "We'll go to the morgue, I'll show you a heroin overdose."

"I don't stick the needles in their arms."

"You think Lerner is a stand-up guy?" Hidalgo asks. "That he'd eat it for you? Tell you what, we'll bring Lerner in, and we'll see who flips first. And let me tell you how that works—the first guy who flips walks, everyone else gets the bus to the federal lockup. Listen, I'm done debating. What's it going to be? Do you give us complete cooperation, or do we play Immunity Family Feud?"

Claiborne chooses door number one.

"This meeting," Darnell says, "you might see someone you recognize. I'm counting on your discretion."

"Who am I going to tell?" Cirello asks.

"That true."

Cirello decides to nudge it forward. "What's going on? What are these meetings? I mean, no offense, but these aren't exactly your kind of people."

"They ain't." He pauses for a second, then chuckles. "Even though my son go to school with they sons."

"So . . ."

"A black man only make it so far in this country on his own," Darnell says. "Then he need white men."

"For what?"

"I ain't goin' back to prison," Darnell says. "No matter what happen, I ain't goin' back there."

Cirello doesn't push it any further.

Because he has his answer. Darius Darnell figures if he gets busted again, his partners at Terra and Berkeley will get him out.

Or he'll take them with him.

And what Cirello thinks is, Good for you, Darnell.

Good for fucking you.

Because you know what the difference between a syndicate and a cartel is? Danish.

Cirello "sweeps" the room by carefully placing several microphones—in a vase, behind a painting, beneath the sofa—and then starts humming to himself.

Keller, in his office, hears it perfectly.

Now it's a matter of hoping that nothing goes wrong at the last second, that all the participants in the meeting show up.

The Mexicans did manage to entertain themselves last night. According to Mullen's people, they dined at Le Bernardin and then migrated to an exclusive brothel on the Upper East Side, not returning to the Peninsula until after 2 a.m.

Good, Keller thinks, anything that makes them less alert.

Cirello steps out into the hallway and waits.

Claiborne is the first to arrive again. "Good morning."

"Good morning, sir." And fuck you.

A few minutes later it's Jason Lerner. Darnell was right—Cirello does recognize the man, because he's on Page Six of the *Daily News* every other day, usually with his gorgeous wife on his arm, at some charity event or another. And for the few minutes that Cirello watched the convention, Lerner was standing at the podium.

Cirello keeps his smile deep down inside himself, but it's there. When Darnell gets him a white boy, he gets him a good one. He nods to Lerner and says, "One of your colleagues is already here."

Lerner nods back. "Thank you."

Oh, don't thank me, Cirello thinks.

Asshole.

The Mexicans are there five minutes later.

So now, Cirello thinks, the party can start.

Keller listens to Claiborne chair the proceedings.

"I trust everyone had a good evening."

Clown, Keller thinks.

"We've prepared a detailed offer sheet," Claiborne says, *"and if you find its terms acceptable, we have the contracts ready to sign. So, please, look it over, take your time, and if there are any questions, we'd be happy to answer them."*

The sound is good, Keller thinks. The usual clink of coffee cups and ice in water glasses, but the voices are clear. And Cirello will be able to testify as to the identities of the people in the room.

Shuffling of papers.

A few muted comments about detail points.

Claiborne asks if he can refill coffee cups.

Then someone—by the sound of the voice Keller thinks it's the older Echeverría—says, *"Jason, it's good to see you again."*

"Good to see you."

"How long has it been?"

These people are so arrogant, Keller thinks. They're walking right into it.

"Cabo," Lerner says. *"Two New Years ago, I think."*

"That sounds about right."

The tension is palpable, Keller thinks. Echeverría is still annoyed that Lerner didn't come to the first meeting. This is him letting Lerner know that it was an insult.

Claiborne picks up the ball. *"So you've had a chance to look at the deal points. If you need more time—"*

"The deal points are acceptable," Echeverría says. *"We just want to look Jason in the eye and ask him if our money is safe with him."*

"It was safe on Bladen Square, wasn't it, León?" Lerner asks. *"It was safe on the Halterplatz project. It's safe with Park Tower."*

Lerner's not quite ready to eat shit, Keller thinks. Maybe it's his new status. But, Jesus, the guy just gave us an entire history of his business relationship with Echeverría.

Echeverría isn't ready to make nice, either. *"But unlike those other projects, Park Tower has been losing money. You want to sell us a piece of a losing entity, and I'm wondering if that's how old friends treat each other."*

"León, if you think I'm using you just to reduce my liability—"

"If I thought that, I wouldn't be sitting here."

"So . . ."

"Gentlemen," Claiborne says, singing for his supper, *"this is a unique situation—"*

"How so?" Echeverría asks.

"As we discussed yesterday," Claiborne says, *"you need to place your money, and your options are, shall we say, not unlimited."*

"Our money isn't clean enough for you?" Echeverría asks.

You're close, Claiborne, Keller thinks. Come on, keep pushing.

But Lerner steps in. *"Your money is as good as anyone else's, of course. If we didn't think that, we wouldn't be sitting here. León, you're right, we're old friends, and if I've done anything to damage that friendship, I apologize. I'm sorry. Between old friends, I need you. If you don't step in, I go into foreclosure and I'll lose this property."*

Keller sits through the long silence. Then he hears Echeverría say, *"We're ready to sign."*

"That's great," Claiborne says.

Keller hears papers shuffle. Then he hears Lerner say, *"Actually, León, we could do it this way, or we could just dispense with contracts."*

"Jason, I—" Claiborne says.

He's clearly surprised.

But Lerner says, *"I'm sure you understand that we're under increased scrutiny these days. It's like living in a fishbowl with a spotlight on it. No offense in the world, gentlemen, but HBMX's name on a syndicate might attract attention that we don't want at this particular moment. If there were a way we could . . ."*

"You're suggesting we do $285 million on a handshake?" Echeverría asks.

"As you said, we're old friends."

Claiborne says, *"Jason, this is highly—"*

"Thanks, Chandler. I have this."

Yes, shut the hell up, Chandler, Keller thinks.

"How would you account for the monies?" Echeverría asks.

"As you observed," Lerner says, *"we have empty space in the tower. Maybe you have shell companies who could lease some of that space, and the money would appear as income. Other funds could go into construction overcharges . . . I mean, there are a hundred ways."*

Echeverría chuckles. *"Jason, I am trying to clean money here, not make it dirtier."*

Bingo, Keller thinks.

"I understand that," Lerner says, *"but if we could come to a . . . less formal . . . arrangement, we'd be willing to give you an extra two points, which would move you up to third place in the syndicate. I promise you, León, Park Tower is going to be a winner. Your backers are going to make a lot of money. Clean money."*

Jesus Christ, Keller thinks. Lerner just confessed to a bagful of felonies. He hasn't incriminated himself on laundering drug money, but to massive fraud and violations of dozens of federal statutes.

But he has balls, Keller has to admit.

Two hundred and eighty-five mil with no paper.

And therefore no collateral.

But that's common for drug cartels. They rarely get collateral because they don't need it. The borrowers' lives, their families' lives, are the collateral. Lerner has to know this, but maybe he feels so powerful now, so connected, he thinks he's above it.

He's *intocable*.

But will Echeverría go for it? Cartels commonly front a million, two, maybe even five in drugs, but $285 million?

"I need to make a call," Echeverría says.

"We'll give you privacy," says Lerner.

"No, I'll just step out into the hallway."

No, Keller thinks. No, God damn it, no.

But Echeverría steps out, and all Keller hears for the next ten minutes are the feet of people getting up and down, liquids being poured, low-volume small talk about the fucking weather, sports, the best fucking route to get out to JFK . . .

Finally Echeverría comes back in. *"Three points, Jason."*

That's all? Keller wonders. He negotiates a one-point bump, and that's it? No.

"And," Echeverría says, *"as you noted, you're under increased scrutiny these days because of your close connections. I would hope, if we did this favor for you, as an old friend you would make some of these connections available to us if we need an ear to listen to our point of view."*

As much as Keller despises them, as much as he wants to put this whole crew away, he's almost rooting for Lerner to turn the man down flat.

"I can't promise," Lerner says, *"that our connections would or would not take any specific actions—"*

"Of course not," Echeverría says.

Okay, Keller thinks.

"But you will always find an ear," Lerner says.

My God, Keller thinks.

My God.

If John Dennison wins the election—

The cartel has bought the White House.

We've crossed the border now.

BOOK FOUR

Inauguration

And thus I clothe my naked villainy
With odd old ends stolen out of Holy Writ . . .
—Shakespeare
Richard III, act I, scene 3

Foreign Lands

Anaxagoras said to a man who was grieving because he was dying in a foreign land, "The descent to Hades is the same from every place."

—Diogenes

Washington, DC
November 2016

Keller wakes up the morning after the election thinking that he doesn't know his own country anymore.

We're not, he thinks, who I thought we were.

Not who I thought we were at all.

He goes through the early morning motions mechanically. Stands in the shower as if the hot spray will wash the depression off him (it doesn't), shaves, dresses, and then goes downstairs and heats water for coffee.

What depresses him is loss of an ideal, an identity, an image of what this country is.

Or was.

That his country would vote for a racist, a fascist, a gangster, a preening, crowing narcissist, a fraud. A man who boasts about assaulting women, mocks a disabled man, cozies up with dictators.

A demonstrated liar.

It's worse than that, of course.

Keller watched last night as John Dennison mounted the stage, and right behind him was Jason Lerner, a man in bed with, and in debt to, the cartel. Lerner had already been named as a "special adviser" to the new president, and as such he'll have national security clearance, access to all top-secret briefings.

Which means that the White House, the DEA and the national intelligence apparatus have all been penetrated by the cartel.

And you have two months, Keller thinks, to stop it.

He takes a cup of coffee upstairs, where Marisol has the blankets pulled over her head.

"You have to get up sooner or later," he says, setting the cup on the side table.

"Not necessarily."

"Are you going to spend the rest of your life with the covers pulled over you?" Keller asks.

"Possibly." Her face pokes out from under the blanket. "Arturo, how could this happen?"

"I don't know."

"Will you resign?"

"I would have either way," Keller says. "It's SOP."

"But she wouldn't have accepted it."

Keller shrugs. "You don't know. The new president has a right to his own person in the job."

"Stop being so stoic," Marisol says.

"It's not stoicism," Keller says. "It's existential despair. I'm going into the office."

"Seriously?"

"It's a working day."

The loan goes through.

Claiborne dutifully turns over all the paperwork.

It's immense.

Some of it comes in the form of rental contracts, as shell companies get money from HBMX and take space in Park Tower. And they're *literally* shell companies, Keller thinks; the offices are empty, there's nothing inside them.

Some of the money goes on an around-the-world tour, transferred from HBMX to Costa Rica to the Caymans, then over to Russia, from where it's distributed to different banks there and in the Netherlands and Germany. The money then goes to shell companies in the United States, to law firms and hedge funds, before finally making its way to Terra.

Then there are purchase orders for improvements on the building— windows, drywall, plumbing, carpet, cleaning supplies—items that are purchased but, as Claiborne explains, never actually materialize.

Through one form or another, HBMX transfers $285 million to Terra.

Terra meets its bubble payment.

Berkeley gets ten mil in commissions.

Claiborne's bonus is a million.

Keller reviews his potential case.

He already has Lerner, Terra and Berkeley on possibly two federal money-laundering statutes. Lerner has incriminated himself on tape about avoiding reporting requirements, it involves a monetary transaction over $10,000 (no shit), and there's a financial institution involved.

But 18 USC 1957 is the lesser of the two charges, with a maximum sentence of ten years. The big bell is 18 USC 1956, which doubles the sentence and calls for a fine equal to twice the money laundered. But 1956 requires that the defendant know that money is dirty. Lerner, Claiborne and the rest had to *know* that the $285 million came from drugs.

We don't have that yet, Keller thinks.

We're close, but a good defense attorney—and these guys will have the best—would rip right through what we have.

Or rather, what we don't.

We don't have Lerner acknowledging that he knows Echeverría is representing drug money.

They have to send Claiborne in again.

Hidalgo sits in a van parked off Bay View Drive in Jamestown, Rhode Island, and listens on a headset.

Claiborne has gone into Lerner's summer "cottage" across Narragansett Bay from Newport. Lerner also has a place in the Hamptons but thinks that it's gotten "too cliché."

Hidalgo hears glasses clink.

"This shit is older than our fathers," Lerner says. *"I've been saving it for an occasion."*

"I'm honored."

"No, listen," Lerner says, *"you pulled us out of a deep hole, and I'm grateful."*

"It's my job."

"Above and beyond," Lerner says. *"Cheers."*

"Cheers," Claiborne says. *"And thanks for sending the chopper."*

"The Ninety-Five is a pain in the ass on a Friday," Lerner says. *"I wouldn't put you through that."*

Silence.

"So why are we here?" Lerner asks. *"It sounded urgent."*

"I'm worried."

"You look worried. What about?"

Come on, Chandler, Hidalgo thinks. Get it done. It's freezing out here.

"You know the provenance of the HBMX money, right?" Claiborne asks.

"I've done deals with Echeverría before."

Cagey bastard, Hidalgo thinks. Stay with it, Chandler.

"So you know it's drug money," Claiborne says.

My man.

"*I don't know that for a fact,*" Lerner says. "*Neither do you.*"

"*Come on, Jason.*"

"*Come on yourself, Chandler,*" Lerner says. "*You put the syndicate together. If some of its provenance is problematic, that's your responsibility, not mine.*"

Balls, Hidalgo thinks. Whatever you have to say about Lerner, the guy has stones. You gotta push him, Chandler.

"*If I go down,*" Claiborne says, "*I'm not going down alone.*"

"*Meaning what?*"

"*Meaning I'm telling you it's drug money,*" Claiborne says.

"*Jesus Christ, are you wearing a wire?*"

Fuck. Don't freak, Chandler. Sack up.

"*Don't be an asshole.*"

"*Are you?!*"

"*No!*"

"*Because if you are—*"

"*You think I'd cross these people?*" Claiborne asks. "*You know who they are, you know what they do.*"

Good job, my man. You're getting good at this. Brought it right back around.

"*Yes, I do. Do you?*"

An implied threat. Inherent guilty knowledge.

"*They'd kill me and my whole family,*" Claiborne says.

"*Yes, that's right.*"

"*I'm scared, Jason. I'm thinking of maybe going to the police.*"

Here we go.

"*Don't do that,*" Lerner says. "*That's the* last *thing you want to do.*"

"*If this goes south—*"

"*We're covered,*" Lerner says. "*Don't you get that? If it's drug money, if it's Russian money, whatever, we can have any investigation shut down. We're golden now. We're untouchable.*"

Maybe not, J, Hidalgo thinks. Maybe not after you put yourself on record saying that.

"*I don't know . . .*"

"*Chandler, I needed this fucking loan,*" Lerner says. "*My father-in-law needed this fucking loan. Do you know what I'm getting at here?*"

Holy shit, Hidalgo thinks. Holy fucking shit.

Silence.

"*Drink your scotch and sack up,*" Lerner says. "*It's going to be fine.*"

"*I hope so.*"

"I know so," Lerner says. *"I'll have the chopper take you back."*

"Okay. Thanks."

Hugo Hidalgo puts his headset down.

Okay, he thinks.

Thanks.

"You did good," Hidalgo says. He takes the microrecorder out from under Claiborne's collar, plugs it into a USB port, and downloads the contents onto his laptop.

"What if he had patted me down?"

"He wouldn't have found this."

"What if he had?"

"Then I guess you would have had one of those prep school bitch-slapping matches until one of you swooned," Hidalgo says. "The point is he *didn't* find it and now we have his balls in a 1956."

"I think he's suspicious."

"Of course he's suspicious," Hidalgo says. "Everyone's suspicious."

"What happens now?"

"We'll let you know," Hidalgo says. "You go on living your life until we get hold of you. Play squash, sip martinis, go sailing, whatever you people do when you're not busy sticking it to the rest of us. We'll reach out for you when we need you."

"I'm sure you will."

"Nice to know there are some certainties in life, isn't it?"

Keller listens to the recording.

"Chandler, I needed this fucking loan. My father-in-law needed this fucking loan. Do you know what I'm getting at here?"

Yeah, I think I do, Keller thinks.

Dennison has an interest in Terra. One that he hasn't revealed in any financial disclosure form.

But does he know about the Park Tower loan?

Keller honestly hopes that he doesn't, but that's a step away. The thing now is to prosecute Lerner.

The problem with getting an indictment against Jason Lerner, Keller knows, is finding an assistant US attorney—a federal prosecutor—who will take the case.

Like him, US attorneys are appointed by the White House and generally "turn over" with each new administration. Some keep their jobs, quite a few don't. But the actual prosecutions of cases are run by assistant US attorneys—AUSAs—appointed by, and serving at the pleasure of, the United States attorney general.

The incoming AG won't find it a pleasure to prosecute Jason Lerner.

Or Terra.

Lerner said it himself—*"We're golden now. We're untouchable."*

The arrogant prick might just be right.

An AUSA will be afraid to touch the case—career suicide—and if I even go to a federal prosecutor with what I know, Keller thinks, he or she might run right to Lerner and spill it all.

The irony is brutal—the same attorney general who is going to press for maximum sentences for marijuana possession will block prosecution of people laundering the biggest dope money in the world.

Because they're rich, white and connected.

Have a ten-dollar bill change hands in the projects, you go to jail. Change three hundred million on Wall Street, you go to dinner at the White House.

"We're golden now. We're untouchable."

Maybe not, motherfucker.

Maybe not.

The approach has to be made carefully, delicately, because he'll only get one shot at it.

And if I'm wrong on my hunch, Keller thinks, it's over. He leaves the office early on Friday, takes the Acela up to New York and checks into the Park Lane.

The room has a beautiful view of Central Park.

The doorbell rings.

The attorney general of the State of New York reaches out his hand. He's tall, thin, with black hair streaked with silver. "Drew Goodwin."

"Art Keller. Come in."

Goodwin comes in and checks out the view.

"You want a drink?" Keller asks.

"Bourbon if you have it," Goodwin says. "But the suspense is killing me—the head of the NYPD Narcotics Division asks if I'll take a secret meeting with the top guy in DEA. In his hotel room. People will be thinking I'm having an illicit affair."

Keller pours him a Wild Turkey from the minibar. Goodwin takes the drink and sits down on the sofa.

"I need your word," Keller says, "that what we say in this room stays in this room."

"We're in Vegas now?"

"You're no friend of the incoming administration."

"Hardly a secret," Goodwin says. "I'm your basic liberal, Democrat New York Jew."

"You've pushed for sentencing reform on drug sentences."

"So have you."

"And you sued Dennison for fraud."

"His so-called university *was* a fraud," Goodwin says. "I didn't come here to get a Wiki on me. What are you getting at?"

"I need someone who isn't afraid of the new administration," Keller says. "Someone who doesn't owe them, someone who doesn't need them to keep his job. You check those boxes. But you have New York City ties. You get campaign donations from New York business interests."

"I'm not going to audition for you, Keller," Goodwin says. "Mullen tells me you're the real deal, but show me your cards or I have better things to do."

"I need a prosecutor."

"You have thousands of prosecutors," Goodwin says. "It's called the DOJ."

"None of them would take this case."

"And you think I will," Goodwin says.

"All the predicate actions occurred in New York."

Goodwin shrugs. "Pitch me."

Keller plays him the tapes.

Goodwin listens to—

"It was safe on Bladen Square, wasn't it, León? It was safe on the Halter-platz project. It's safe with Park Tower. . . ."

"Your money is as good as anyone else's, of course. If we didn't think that, we wouldn't be sitting here. León, you're right, we're old friends, and if I've done anything to damage that friendship, I apologize. I'm sorry. Between old friends, I need you. If you don't step in, I go into foreclosure and I'll lose this property. . . ."

". . . if we could come to a . . . less formal . . . arrangement, we'd be willing to give you an extra two points, which would move you up to third place in the syndicate. I promise you, León, Park Tower is going to be a winner. Your backers are going to make a lot of money. Clean money. . . ."

"And as you noted, you're under increased scrutiny these days because of your close connections. I would hope, if we did this favor for you, as an old friend you would make some of these connections available to us if we need an ear to listen to our point of view."

"I can't promise that our connections would or would not take any specific actions . . . but you will always find an ear."

"Who am I listening to here?" Goodwin asks.

"Jason Lerner."

"Jesus Christ."

"He's talking to León Echeverría," Keller says, "a major player in Mexican financial and political circles. Echeverría has put together a syndicate from several drug cartels and runs it through a bank called HBMX."

"You don't have Lerner's awareness."

Keller plays more tapes.

"If I go down, I'm not going down alone."

"Meaning what?"

Goodwin stops the tape. "Who's talking here?"

"Chandler Claiborne."

"I know the guy."

Keller starts the tape again.

"Meaning I'm telling you it's drug money."

"Jesus Christ, are you wearing a wire?"

"Don't be an asshole."

"Are you?!"

"No!"

"Because if you are—"

"You think I'd cross these people? You know who they are, you know what they do."

"Yes, I do. Do you?"

"They'd kill me and my whole family."

"Yes, that's right."

"I'm scared, Jason. I'm thinking of maybe going to the police."

"Don't do that. That's the last *thing you want to do."*

"If this goes south—"

"We're covered. Don't you get that? If it's drug money, if it's Russian money, whatever, we can have any investigation shut down. We're golden now. We're untouchable."

"I don't know . . ."

"Chandler, I needed this fucking loan. My father-in-law needed this fucking loan. Do you know what I'm getting at here?"

Keller shuts off the tape.

"I think I need another drink," Goodwin says.

Keller pours him one.

Goodwin says, "You know what you have here, right? What this could lead to? No wonder you can't get a federal prosecutor to take the case."

"You can take it on a 47:20," Keller says. New York State has its own money-laundering statute, a Class B felony with up to twenty-five years in prison and a million-dollar fine, doubled with an enhancement for drug involvement.

"Nice end run, Keller," Goodwin says.

"You're an elected New York State official," Keller says. "The administration can't touch you."

"The optics are fucking terrible," Goodwin says. "Dennison's been on your ass since you took the job. It's going to look like revenge. Same with me, I'm already on record saying our new president is a crook. Who else knows about this?"

"Mullen," Keller says. "One of my guys, me. That's it."

"You want me to move on some of the most powerful people in New York," Goodwin says. "I'm in clubs with people from Terra, Berkeley. They've contributed to my campaigns, their kids go to school with mine."

"You have kids dying all over this state," Keller says. "Your club buddies are laundering heroin money and they know it."

"Don't get sanctimonious with me." He stares out the window, then asks, "Have you given me everything you have?"

"When your forensic accountants look into Park Tower," Keller says, "they'll find shell companies, cost overruns, paper-only purchases . . ."

"I have no doubt," Goodwin says. "What's in this for you, Keller? You're on your way out. You do this, they're going to *hang* you."

"They'll try."

"So why?"

"Does it matter?"

"Yeah, it does," Goodwin says. "If I go into this fight, I'd like to know the guy beside me. Do you have a hard-on for Lerner, or our new president, or do you just want to make a bang on your way out the door?"

"You're going to laugh at my answer."

"Try me."

"I'm a patriot."

Goodwin stares at him. "I'm not laughing. My grandfather came here from Poland. If I got in bed with these pricks, he'd curse me from his grave."

"What would he say if you let these pricks skate?" Keller asks. "Because now you can never say you didn't know."

"I'll need Claiborne," Goodwin says. "To validate the tapes."

Goodwin sets his glass down and stands up. A clear signal that he considers the meeting over and that everything that needed to be said has been said.

He nods politely to Keller and goes out the door.

. . .

"You don't think I'm testifying," Claiborne says.

"You don't think you're not?" Hidalgo asks. "We have to go to a grand jury to get an indictment, and we can't get that without your testimony."

"You have the tapes!"

"We need you to certify the validity of the tapes."

"I'm not testifying," Claiborne says.

"Then you go to jail."

"You told me," Claiborne says, "you promised. I was just on, what, 'background,' just to provide intelligence. You didn't say anything about testifying."

Hidalgo shrugs. "Look at your agreement. In exchange for immunity you agreed to do whatever we need you to do. If you bail on that, New York will proceed with the prosecution and we'll file on money-laundering charges. So let's say you do five in New York; *after* you get out, you'll start serving your federal time. By the way, just so you know, federal time means you serve a minimum of eighty-five percent of your sentence. So say you get twenty, which is not unreasonable, you serve . . . well, you're a numbers guy, do the math."

"You don't understand," Claiborne says. "You don't know these people."

I don't *know* these people? Hidalgo thinks. *These people* tortured my father to death.

"I'd rather go to prison," Claiborne says. "I'll take prison."

He gets up.

"Sit down, Chandler," Hidalgo says. Keller coached him exactly how to play this moment. "I said sit down."

Chandler sits back down.

Hidalgo waits until he has Claiborne's full attention. Keller schooled him, *Get him in the habit of obeying you, even in the small things.* "Let me explain this to you. You don't have choices. *We* have choices. We choose for you. If you walk away, here's what happens—we leak it back to Lerner that you're a rat. Lerner runs to Echeverría, Echeverría turns to his friends in the cartel."

Claiborne looks terrified. "You'd do that."

"That would be on you," Hidalgo says. Jesus, Keller was dead-on. What I'd say, what Claiborne would say.

He stares Claiborne down.

Now Claiborne has nothing to say.

"But if you stay," Hidalgo says, "if you work with us, we'll work with you. We'll provide protection, a new identity, a new life."

"How do I know I can trust you?"

"You don't," Hidalgo says. "But who else do you have to trust? Run down the list of candidates for me, Chandler—your close personal friends at Terra? Lerner? Echeverría? Or the person who is sitting with you right now, looking you in the eye, promising you that he will pull your family out of the jackpot that *you* put them in. Run the numbers—not a single person who has ever entered the Federal Witness Protection Program and stayed with the program has been killed. Guys who took the prison option, though . . . happens all the time. And if you take that option, your family's on their own."

"You wouldn't protect them?"

"*I* would," Hidalgo says, "if it was up to me. But how am I going to go to my bosses and justify an unlimited expenditure on a guy who just fucked us? They'd laugh me out of the room. Your family is nothing to them."

"You're the worst people in the world."

"Yeah, we're terrible," Hidalgo says. And you didn't give a flying fuck about the families of people who've ODed on the smack you launder. You take money from the people who broke my father's legs, stripped the skin from his body and kept him alive with drugs so he'd feel the pain.

Fuck you.

Fuck your house in the Hamptons.

Fuck your family.

"So what's it going to be?" Hidalgo asks. "My train's coming, I don't want to miss it. I have a dinner date."

He already knows what it's going to be.

Just like Keller told him—give people a choice between a bad option and a worse option and they'll take the bad option. They'll twist, they'll squeal, they'll protest, they'll yell, but it's like those old stages of grief—eventually they'll accept.

"You don't give me any choice," Claiborne says.

"I'll be in touch," Hidalgo says.

He gets up and walks to the door that leads to his train.

Keller's not dead yet but they're already cutting up his corpse.

In the hallways in Arlington, out in the field offices, people are scrambling to adjust to the new situation, jockeying for position to save their jobs or find better ones, shifting their philosophies to align more closely to the incoming administration.

Keller can't blame them, survival is a natural reaction.

It starts with Blair. He comes into the office with a face like a rainy day.

"What?" Keller asks.

Blair looks at the floor.

"If you have something to say," Keller says, "say it."

"You're leaving, Art," Blair says. "I have to stay. I have one kid in college, another in her junior year in high school . . ."

"And you don't want to be transferred to East Mongolia."

"I need to put some distance between you and me," Blair says, "between now and when the new guy takes over."

"It's going to be Howard."

"Is that the word?"

"That's the word." And you know it's the word, Tom. Otherwise you wouldn't be here.

"I hope there are no hard feelings," Blair says.

"Of course not," Keller says. "So what do you want to do? Have a fistfight in the hallway? I accuse you of taking my sandwich from the office fridge . . ."

"You might have some things going on," Blair says, "I just don't want to have anything to do with."

"What have you told Howard?"

"Nothing."

"What are you *going* to tell him?" Keller asks.

It's what the cartels do with their people who've been busted, Keller thinks. They tell them it's all right to give up information, just tell us what you're going to say so that we can make adjustments.

"That you're looking at Lerner?" Blair says.

"Are you asking me or telling me?"

"I guess I'm asking permission," Blair says.

"You want my permission to fuck me?" Keller asks. "Okay, but just put the tip in. Give Howard a heads-up that he might want to look out for his buddies, but you don't know details. Can you live with that?"

"Can *you* live with that?"

"I'll have to, won't I?" Keller stands up and Blair takes the signal that the meeting is over. "Thank you for all your great work and support, Tom. I truly appreciate it."

"I'm sorry, Art."

"Don't be."

That's why they build life rafts, Keller thinks. Only the captain is expected to go down with the ship.

Keller gets Hidalgo in.

"Blair is going to the dark side," Keller says. "He's going to tip Howard to Agitator."

"That's it, then."

Keller shakes his head. "We'll use it to our advantage. If Howard wants to stick his head in a noose, we'll let him."

"What do you mean?"

"Let's see who he tells," Keller says. "If this gets to Lerner, it will tell us a lot about how wide this thing is. We inject the dye, see where it goes through the bloodstream."

"If Howard leaks this, it's obstruction of justice."

"Vacuum up all the Agitator intel," Keller says. "Clean it off computers, take the physical files. I want them out of the building."

"Speaking of obstruction."

"If you're not up for this—"

"I'm up for it."

"From now on we run Agitator off premises," Keller says. "Who do we have in Intelligence that's still loyal?"

Hidalgo runs out some names. "McEneaney, Rolofson, Olson, Woodley, Flores, Salerno . . ."

"Have them create a ton of meaningless intel as chaff," Keller says, "and route that through Blair. Anything of any importance bypasses him and goes directly to you and from you to me. Will they do that?"

"Those guys would walk through hell for you," Hidalgo says. "There are a lot of people who would—"

"We don't need a lot of people," Keller says, "just the brave, the few, the career suicidal. They need to understand I can't offer any protection as of January 17."

"A lot of people are already packing," Hidalgo says.

"Develop some false information," Keller says, "and feed it to Blair."

An echo test.

It doesn't take long.

Howard is in Keller's office that afternoon.

"Measuring for curtains?" Keller asks.

"Are you keeping an investigation from me?" Howard asks.

Blair made his deal.

"I don't trust you," Keller says. "You use intelligence you receive to undermine me."

"You have created private fiefdoms inside this organization," Howard says, "in direct violation of our policies of transparency, in order to advance a personal, politically motivated agenda that is in conflict with our mandated purpose."

"Who wrote that for you?"

"Creating a false-flag operation inside the agency might even be a crime," Howard says.

"You're the lawyer."

"You don't know what you're messing with."

"Anytime you want to tell me, Denton," Keller says. "I'll be happy to take your sworn affidavit."

"For this witch hunt?"

"We keep talking around this," Keller says. "You want to be specific about what you're concerned about here? Put a name to it?"

Howard doesn't answer.

"Is that a no?" Keller asks. "Then what do we have to talk about?"

"I want those files."

"And I want a pony."

"If I detect," Howard says, "any effort on your part to sanitize or remove files before your departure, my hand to God, I'll see you criminally charged."

"Get out," Keller says. "Before I get myself criminally charged with assault."

"True to form," Howard says. "What is it they call you? 'Killer Keller'?"

"You might want to remember that," Keller says.

They meet by the Washington Monument.

Inconspicuous among the tourists.

It's cold; Keller has his coat collar turned up and wishes he had worn a hat.

"I'll get right to it," O'Brien says. "Are you investigating Jason Lerner?"

"You're flirting with obstruction of justice," Keller says.

"Have you informed the attorney general of this investigation?" O'Brien asks.

He wants to know who knows what about Lerner, Keller thinks. How far a potential investigation has gone, to what level he has to go to cut it off. "Let me ask you, what do *you* know about Lerner? What prompts these questions? Has Denton Howard been to see you? Did he send you?"

"I'm not Howard's errand boy."

"Or did Lerner come himself?" Keller asks. "Or was it your president-elect?"

"If Howard came to me," O'Brien says, "it was in my role on the Intelligence Committee and therefore perfectly legitimate."

They stare at each other.

Then O'Brien says, "If you have an investigation going on Lerner or Terra, you need to drop it. Now."

"I'm not confirming that I do or I don't," Keller says. "I'm going to do what I'd do on any investigation. I'll pursue it wherever it takes me, and if that leads to a potential criminal charge, I'll turn it over to the appropriate prosecutors. It's not political."

"*Everything* is political," O'Brien says. "Especially these days."

"You don't know what you're talking about, Ben." At least I hope to God you don't, Keller thinks. "You don't know what you're asking here."

"I'm the chair of the Senate Intelligence Committee," O'Brien says. "If the head of DEA is investigating a potential connection between Terra and drug traffickers, I should know about it."

"Apparently you already do."

"I need details," O'Brien says. "I need to know what you have."

"Then subpoena me for a closed hearing and I'll testify under oath," Keller says. O'Brien doesn't answer. He won't bring me in on the record, Keller thinks, even if it's sealed. Because there'll be other senators in the room, some of them Democrats. "You don't want to do that?"

"I thought we had a relationship."

"I thought so, too." But you've flipped. You brought me here to stop the heroin epidemic, and now you've sold yourself to the people who launder its money.

I don't know you anymore, Ben.

"Leave office gracefully and live your life," O'Brien says. "If it's money, Art, we can arrange a soft place to land. There are think tanks, foundations, you could name your number."

"I don't have a number," Keller says.

"Everyone has a number."

"What was yours?"

"Fuck you," O'Brien says. "Fuck you and your sanctimonious, holier-than-thou, lapsed-Catholic bullshit."

"Yeah, okay."

"What, you're a virgin now?" O'Brien asks. "When did your cherry grow back? You've played this game dirtier than about anyone I've ever known. You've made plenty of deals in your life, some of them with me. You know there are all kinds of coin."

"Tax cuts? Immigration? The wall?"

"I don't like this son of a bitch Dennison any more than you do," O'Brien says. "But he's not wrong about everything. And you don't want these people as enemies."

"I've had Adán Barrera, the Sinaloa cartel, and the Zetas as enemies," Keller says. "You think I'm afraid of 'these people'?"

"They will escort you out of your office, under guard, with a cardboard box in your hands."

First the bribe and then the threat, Keller thinks.

I feel like I'm back in Mexico.

"You're in no position to be lobbing shots from the moral high ground," O'Brien says. "Your own feet are in a swamp."

"What if I told you," Keller says, "that there's a real concern that drug cartels are purchasing influence at the highest levels of the United States government?"

"*Are* you telling me that?"

"Do I need to?" Keller asks. "Jesus Christ, Ben, you brought me here to win this war—"

O'Brien says, "Do you seriously believe anyone really wants to win this war? No one has an interest in winning this war; they have an interest in keeping it going. You can't be that naive—tens of billions of dollars a year in law enforcement, equipment, prisons . . . it's *business*. The war on drugs is *big business*. And that's 'purchasing influence at the highest levels of the United States government' and always has been. And you think you're going to stop that? Grow up. As your friend, I'm begging you, let this one go."

"Or what?"

"They'll destroy you."

"You mean 'we'll.'"

"Okay," O'Brien says, "*we'll* destroy you."

O'Brien starts to walk away, then turns around. "The good things in this world aren't done by saints. They're done by compromised people doing the best they can."

They walk off in opposite directions.

"He's a smart man," O'Brien says. "He'll do the smart thing."

"Can we take that risk?" Rollins asks. "Keller has been a loose cannon his entire career."

O'Brien doesn't like Rollins.

The man has been around the game for a long time; former special forces, former CIA, and now one of those intelligence veterans generally known as "operatives," Rollins has worked for a host of consulting firms, renting himself out to foreign governments, corporations and political parties.

He's a fixer.

Now he's "fixing" for Berkeley.

"What are our options?" O'Brien asks.

"The man spent time tending bees at a monastery, for Chrissakes,"

Lerner says. "He's unstable. He has a prejudice against POTUS—his foreign wife is a well-known left-wing radical."

"Art Keller is an American hero," O'Brien says. "He has devoted his life to fighting for this country."

"We don't even know that Keller's an American citizen," Lerner says. "His mother was a Mexican national, wasn't she?"

"That's your response to this?" O'Brien asks. "A birther controversy? Look, you can discredit Keller all you want. But evidence speaks for itself independent of the source. Does he have evidence, Jason? Is that possible?"

"I don't see how."

"What I'm asking," O'Brien says, "is whether there's basis for a DEA investigation into your business dealings."

"I put together a loan package from a Mexican bank," Lerner says.

"With ties to drug traffickers?" O'Brien asks.

"I didn't ask where their money came from."

"Shut it down. Now."

"The loan has already come through," Lerner says. "It's a done deal."

"God damn it."

"He has me talking to Mexican bankers," Lerner says. "So what?"

"What conversations did you have with Claiborne?" Rollins asks.

"A lot of conversations."

"We have to assume Claiborne was wired," Rollins says. "Did you ever say anything about drug money?"

"Maybe."

"That puts you in the crosshairs."

"What does Keller have?" Lerner asks.

"That's the problem," Rollins says. "We don't know. He hasn't brought anything to the AG's office."

"Can't we get to the AG," Lerner asks, "have her instruct Keller to turn over his investigation data to her?"

O'Brien asks, "You think the current AG wants to do us any favors? It would have to wait until the inauguration, and then the new AG could make that demand."

"Which Keller would have to obey."

"Knowing him," O'Brien says, "he'd probably tell the AG to go fuck himself."

"Then we could fire him," Lerner says.

"And what good would that do?" O'Brien asks. "He goes to the media."

"Then we charge him with malfeasance."

"So goddamn what?" O'Brien asks. "Keller's in a cell next to you?"

"Take care of it," Lerner says.

He walks out of the room.

The bribe, the threat.

In Mexico they phrased it *plato o plomo*.

The silver or the lead.

They come with more silver the same afternoon.

Howard calls to ask for a few minutes in his office.

"Art," Howard starts. "You and I have had our differences, both personally and in terms of policy, but now I think we're suffering under a mutual misunderstanding."

"What have we misunderstood?"

"That I want your job," Howard says.

"You don't?"

Howard smiles a politician's smile, as sincere and heartfelt as a twenty-dollar hooker, but without the warmth. "I've talked with the president-elect. He expressed a willingness for you to continue in office."

"Is that right?"

"He knows your record," Howard says. "He's actually a fan. He thinks you're the same kind of straight shooter from the hip that he is."

"Uh-huh."

"He thinks that with his ideas about border security and your passion to interdict drugs," Howard says, "you could do great things together."

"When did he have this epiphany?"

"President Dennison would be willing to give serious consideration to some of your policy ideas regarding marijuana legalization, sentencing reform and resources for treatment," Howard says.

When the devil comes, Keller thinks, it's with full hands. Offering you choice of a "greater good" so you can rationalize the bad. And I've made that deal, more than once. And it's ingenious, it is tempting—think of all the good you could do if you just let the Lerner thing go.

"And I assume with this fresh attitude," Keller says, "the right-wing attacks in the media would recede?"

"I think I'm safe in making that representation," Howard says. Now his smile is the smirk of a salesman who's sure he's closed.

"What's the *quid*?" Keller asks.

"I'm sorry?"

"In the *pro quo*," Keller says. "I'm guessing you're not offering me this in exchange for nothing."

Howard's face goes to stone. "I think you know."

"I think I do, too."

"I'm not going to waltz into an obstruction trap here, Keller."

"Then waltz out."

Howard stands up. "I've never liked you, Keller. I've always thought you were a hypocrite, maybe even a criminal. But I never thought you were stupid. Until now. Think about our offer—you're not going to get a better one."

There's the silver, Keller thinks. Where's the lead?

It doesn't take long.

"When you leave this office," Howard says, "and I take over, I'll launch an investigation of my own, about certain things that happened in Guatemala. You know what I'm talking about, and you know it will land you behind bars."

Bang.

The bullet.

The night lasts forty years.

A sleepless recounting of forty years fighting this war.

Four decades ago, the night told him, you were burning poppies in Sinaloa. You were saving Adán Barrera's young life, God help you. Fast-forward, as fast as an endless night goes, five years, you and Ernie Hidalgo were trying to tell the world that the Mexicans were running Colombian cocaine through Guadalajara, but no one would listen.

More late-night movies—you busting Adán in San Diego, his pregnant wife falls trying to run, his daughter is born with a birth defect. He blames you. You and Ernie uncover the Mexican Trampoline—small planeloads of coke bouncing from Colombia to Central America to Mexico and the United States, fueling the crack epidemic. M-1 threatens your family—Althea takes your kids and leaves. Ernie is going to transfer out but Adán grabs him first—tortures him to find out who his source is but there is no source—you made it up to cover an illegal wiretap.

Ernie dies for your sins.

You swear to bring down the Barreras.

You arrest M-1.

Turns out he was funding an NSA op against the contras in Nicaragua. Part of something called Red Mist—an overall, ongoing operation to slaughter Communists in Central America. You could have blown the whistle, you didn't. You made a deal instead—like O'Brien said—you lied to Congress about Red Mist in exchange for a license to go after the Barreras.

You got them.

Not before Adán killed Father Juan, the best man you ever knew. Not before you used Adán's mistress Nora to betray him.

You did something filthy to lure him across the border—told him his daughter was dying. Put him in cuffs outside the hospital.

The cartel had Nora.

You were going to trade Nora for him.

More movies—the meeting on the bridge.

Sean Callan was supposed to put a bullet in you. He didn't. He loved Nora, she loved him.

You put a bullet into M-1.

Then put Adán behind bars.

You should have killed him right then.

Try to sleep now.

Go ahead.

The movie won't let you, the movie goes on.

You try to find some peace in a monastery.

But they let Adán go back to Mexico to serve his sentence.

You know what's going to happen. It does. He escapes. He launches a war to take all of Mexico back.

A hundred thousand people die in that war.

You go back down there to find him.

Worse devils rise—the Zetas.

Beheadings, disembowelments, burnings.

Mass slaughters, mass graves.

You meet Marisol. You fall in love with Marisol. The Zetas gun her down, cripple her. You side with Barrera to destroy the Zetas, protect her.

More blood, more killings, more atrocities.

Adán sets up the Zetas.

You go into Guatemala.

You kill the Zetas.

You're supposed to bring Adán out with you.

You kill him instead.

Payback for Ernie, for all the dead.

Forty years.

Fighting that war, doing wrong for the greater good, making deals, playing God, close-dancing with the devil.

The sun comes up.

Cheerless winter sky.

It comes up on junkies, men in prison, grieving families, the strung out, the jammed up, a country that doesn't know itself anymore.

Sleep won't come in daylight any more than in the dark.

You have a choice to make.

A decision.

Make another deal, give them what they want.

Let Lerner slide.

You're being an asshole, and a selfish one, to boot. Think of what you could do with what they're offering you—the addicts who will get treatment, the people who will get out of prison. You could do a monumental amount of good, but you're going to flush all that just to put some slimy asshole like Lerner behind bars for a few years? Even assuming you could do it, which is a very long shot.

Take the money to treat addicts, empty some of those cells.

Or.

Fight.

Keep fighting.

You'll go down but you'll take them with you.

Maybe. If you can.

Maybe keep them from stealing the country.

If they haven't already.

O'Brien calls Keller. "People are getting edgy. Impatient. I need to know what to tell them."

"Tell them," Keller says, "to go fuck themselves."

Claiborne opens the door to the call girl he called to relieve his stress.

She comes in, three men come in behind her.

One of them slams a pistol butt into the back of his head. He wakes up tied to the bed, a ball gag in his mouth.

Rollins sits in a chair in the corner and explains things to him. "When I remove the gag, Mr. Claiborne, you are going to tell me everything you revealed. You are going to be thorough. If you do anything else, I am going to kill you, your wife, and your two little girls. Nod if you understand."

Claiborne nods.

Rollins gets up and takes out the gag. "Talk."

Claiborne talks.

Through sobs, tells them everything.

Rollins puts a needle into his arm. "Your family's going to be fine."

He pushes the plunger.

Claiborne's death makes the *Times* and the *Daily News*.

REAL ESTATE BANKER DEAD OF APPARENT OVERDOSE.

His body was found in a suite at the Four Seasons, on the floor where he toppled from the bed, the needle still in his arm.

The ME rules the cause of death as an overdose of heroin laced with fentanyl. He attributes the bruise on the side of Claiborne's head to his striking the corner of the bedside table when he fell.

Hotel staff tell police that Claiborne was a frequent guest and that he often had "company," although none of them on duty remember a woman going up to his suite. Colleagues at Terra express no knowledge of Claiborne's drug use, although a couple of them eventually admit to police they had seen him use cocaine.

The obituary notes that the deceased is survived by a wife and two children.

Cirello figures the best defense is a good offense. Darnell is going to blame him for that asshole Claiborne being wired—it's smarter to get off first. So he yells at Darnell, "Did you motherfuckers kill that guy?!"

"Who you m-effing, motherfucker?!" Darnell yells back. "You was supposed to make sure the room wasn't wired!"

"If you wanted me to pat down your bankers," Cirello says, "you should have told me that's what you wanted! It's on you! And I didn't sign up for murder!"

"You want out, you out."

"Yeah," Cirello says, "I go out the door with an accessory tag on my back. Fuck you."

They're in one of Darnell's cribs in Harlem.

Sugar Hill.

Darnell isn't happy. "They ain't tell me neither, they was going to kill him. They just did it. Don't tell the nigger nothin'."

Cirello accepts it as a peace offering. "Your name come up on the tapes?"

"Man didn't know my name."

"Well, that's good," Cirello says. They're quiet for a minute, then he says, "Claiborne had two kids."

"He was in the game, man."

"Did he *know* he was in the game?" Cirello asks.

"He didn't, he should have," Darnell says.

"So what's next?" Cirello asks.

"Back to business is all," Darnell says. "You going to deliver some money for me. To my supplier."

"You fucking kidding?" Cirello asks. "The DEA is onto the loan, the syndicate . . . they're going to shut it down, put people in jail."

"They ain't going to do shit," Darnell says. "Bunch of cops against the White House? White House wins."

Uh-huh, Darnell thinks.

White always win.

It's possible he overdosed.

No, it isn't, Keller tells himself. Don't kid yourself.

They killed him.

But not before he told them everything. They'd have drained him of all information first, hit him on the head and then popped him the fatal shot. And they know that the tape of him and Lerner is problematic in front of a grand jury without Claiborne there to verify it.

Goodwin knew it, too. Called Keller and said, "Your key witness killed himself?"

"Quite a coincidence, huh?"

"Come on," Goodwin said. "The Lerner people are a lot of things, but they're not murderers."

"You can still get a grand jury to indict," Keller said.

"Maybe," Goodwin said. "But then a trial judge tosses the tape without a verification of its provenance. Even if he doesn't, the defense asks the jury if they're going to take the word of a drug addict."

"You're not going to take the case."

"There's no case to take," Goodwin said.

"How about the Claiborne murder case?!"

"The ME has it down as a suicide!" Goodwin said. "Do you know how hard it is to reverse a—"

Keller clicked off.

Lerner's people—who aren't, of course, murderers—got the job done, Keller thinks.

They made a mistake, though.

Killed the one man who could identify Hugo Hidalgo.

Hidalgo is torn up.

Keller knows the feeling—the first time you lose a guy you've been handling, it rips you apart.

It doesn't get much better with the next or the next.

He wants to tell Hidalgo that it isn't his fault but he knows the kid won't buy it. All he can do is channel Hidalgo's anger.

And try to keep him safe.

"Did I get Claiborne killed?" Hidalgo asks.

"You can't think like that," Keller says. "*They* killed him."

"They wouldn't have if—"

"Don't eat yourself up," Keller says. "Claiborne never cared about any of the people he hurt."

"What about his kids?" Hidalgo asks. "They didn't do anything."

"No, they didn't," Keller says. "You're done here; I'm sending you out west."

"Why out west?"

"Because that's where Darnell's supplier is," Keller says. "If they think I'm going to let all this just slide, they're out of their goddamn minds. The thing now is to work the drug angle back up, find out who provides Darnell with his dope. Whoever that is also told him to get security for the Park Tower meetings."

We can work it back that way, Keller thinks.

It's money and drugs.

If you can't work the money, work the drugs.

Because money and drugs are like two magnets—eventually, they'll come back together.

Cirello is the only passenger on a Citation Excel jet that could seat seven. There's no flight attendant, but he can make himself drinks or a light lunch in the small galley. And there's plenty of room for his carry-on luggage, which is the point.

Cirello has two suitcases filled with $3.4 million that Darius Darnell owes his supplier. Other than the cash, he has enough clothes to do Vegas for three days, and some presents for a friend of Darnell's.

"After you handle business, do me a favor," Darnell said. "Drive to V-Ville, see this friend of mine, bring him a few things for me."

"I'm not delivering dope to a federal prison facility," Cirello said.

"Ain't dope," Darnell said. "This guy don't do dope. It's some books and some banana bread."

"Banana bread?"

"Man like banana bread. That okay with you?"

"Did you make it?" Cirello asked.

"Why that a surprise?" Darnell asked. "Three-hour drive from Vegas to Victorville. I already got you on the visitor list."

The jet cruises at 500 per, so it's a five-hour flight. Cirello settles in with a Bloody Mary and thinks about things.

It's been a wild few months.

First he's in a hotel suite with billionaire real estate developers connected to the potential next president. Now he's on a private jet flying to Vegas with a few million dollars in cash at his feet. They chose Vegas because a gambler like Cirello would go there, although he gets the sense that the supplier isn't based in Vegas but somewhere within easy striking distance.

The supplier doesn't want the courier to know where he's based.

Cirello has his instructions.

Take a cab, not an Uber, from the airport, Darnell said. Pay cash. Check in at the Mandalay Bay, carry your own bags, no bellboys. Stay in your room. Don't be callin' no hookers because it would be bad if one of them walked out the room with one of them suitcases while you was taking a piss. Just chill and watch TV. Someone will call you.

After you pass the money, you stay a day or so and you gamble. Win, lose, don't matter. Get laid if you want. Take in Blue Man Group. Don't be conspicuous but don't be snaky, either. Just a cop on a little Vegas vacay.

Fly commercial home.

"Commercial?" Cirello asked.

"It don't matter what TSA find in your bag coming home," Darnell said. "What, you spoiled already? You think you Jay-Z now, you can't fly commercial?"

"Okay, but first class, right?"

"Coach."

"Come on."

"You win big, upgrade," Darnell said. "Otherwise, ain't no reason a cop fly first class. Cops cheap. Look at your shoes."

"What's wrong with my shoes?"

"If you don't know . . ."

Cirello falls asleep on the flight. Wakes up, makes himself a roast beef sandwich, cracks open a beer and watches some DirecTV.

The trip's putting more strain on his relationship with Libby.

"If you can wait until Sunday," she said, "I could come with you. We're dark Sunday and Monday."

"Has to be Saturday, babe."

"Okay," she said. "I could join you on Sunday. I'd like to see Vegas."

"I have to do this alone, Lib."

"So it's work," she said.

"You know I can't talk about that."

"What work does a New York cop have in Las Vegas?"

"The kind of work he can't talk about," Cirello said. "Jesus, cut me some slack, would you?"

"Hey, Bobby? I'll cut you all the slack you want."

Meaning, Cirello thinks now, she'll cut me loose. That's her telling me she doesn't have a hook in my mouth. I want to swim away, swim away.

A couple of hours later he's in Vegas.

Gets a cab, checks into his room.

Nice room overlooking the Strip.

It would be nice to get out there but he has to stay and wait for the phone to ring. Knows it's going to take a while because the supplier is going to perform his due diligence. Going to make sure Cirello came alone, going to make sure the adjacent rooms aren't loaded with feds or Vegas PD, going to have an eye on everyone coming in and out of the hotel lobby.

So he stays put.

Grabs a Coke and some Toblerone from the minibar, turns on the television and finds some college football.

Tight game, USC v. UCLA.

Five minutes left in the fourth, of course, that's when the phone rings.

Eddie Ruiz is a big believer in multitasking.

Arranges to get his money in Vegas so he can then run two hours up the 15 and see the family in St. George.

Lay some of the cash on Teresa to keep her sweet. A green poultice on the low-grade infection of her resentment at being stuck in Utah. See the kids, listen to them bitch, take everyone out to dinner and some shopping, then hit the road back to Dago to mollify *that* family.

Plus, he didn't want the courier knowing he lives in San Diego.

Guy doesn't need to know that yet, maybe ever.

Besides, Eddie likes Vegas.

Who doesn't?

If you have money, and Eddie has money, Las Vegas is heaven. He goes a couple of days early. Gets himself a suite at the Wynn, gets on Eros.com and books an unbelievable blonde named Nicole and takes her to Carnevino for a *riserva* steak, aged for eight months, that's priced by the inch.

He don't know what Nicole's priced by, but it's worth every dollar when they get back to the suite, and he tips her an extra G when she leaves. Gets himself a good night's sleep, calls down for a masseuse and, relaxed, goes downstairs and blows forty G's at blackjack. That night he hits Mizumi with an Asian chick named Michelle and then sleeps in until Osvaldo calls to tell him his money has arrived.

Eddie showers, gets some breakfast and a pot of coffee sent up, and by the time he's jammed that, Osvaldo has made good and sure that the courier, an actual cop, is alone and clean.

"So go get my money," Eddie says.

. . .

The doorbell rings.

Cirello gets up, goes to the door and looks through the peephole. Sees a young Hispanic guy standing there alone and opens the door a crack.

"Cirello?" the guy asks.

"Yeah." Cirello opens the door.

The guy walks in and looks around. "You mind if I check the bathroom?"

Cirello gestures *Help yourself.* The guy walks into the bathroom and then comes back in, apparently satisfied they're alone. "You got something for me."

"I need to hear a series of numbers."

"5-8-3-1-0-9-7."

"Bingo." Cirello goes into the closet, takes out the bags and sets them on the floor by the guy's feet. "I'll need a receipt."

"Huh?"

"Joking."

"Yeah," the guy says, not especially amused. "My man says to give your boss love and respect."

"Back at him," Cirello says, even though Darnell said no such thing.

The guy picks up the bags. "Nice meeting you."

"You too." Cirello opens the door and the guy walks out.

Just like that.

It makes sense, Cirello thinks. A guy leaving a hotel with a couple of suitcases is going to attract zero attention.

Hidalgo is looking for the suitcases, not the guy.

Sitting at the lobby bar, he sees the guy get off the elevator with the cases in his hands and talks into his collar mike. "Coming out now, Hispanic male, five eleven, pink polo shirt, khakis."

"Got him."

The woman outside, Erica, is gorgeous enough to be a Vegas showgirl except she's an LVPD plainclothes. Keller called in a chip with the local department because he's not using any DEA personnel on this except Hidalgo.

Hidalgo would ask her out except this is business and he's dating the woman back in DC. Anyway, Erica has a visual on the guy and she's good. In seconds, she sends a photo of him waiting for the valet to bring his car up.

Hidalgo forwards the photo to Keller.

Then he hears her relaying the make and license of the guy's rental car. Two LVPD Narcotics guys wait in a car to tail the guy.

Hidalgo orders another beer and waits. It's all he can do now. Then Erica calls. "They're on him."

He listens as she relays news from the two narco cops. The subject goes north up Las Vegas Boulevard, the Strip, past the Luxor, the Tropicana, the MGM Grand. Then Caesars Palace, the Mirage and Treasure Island. He crosses Sands Avenue and turns into the Wynn, takes the suitcases out, flips the keys to the parking valet and goes in.

Eddie, wrapped in a white terry-cloth robe, opens the door and lets Osvaldo in. He eyeballs the suitcases. "What's the guy like?"

"Like a cop."

"Nervous?"

"He made a dumb joke."

"About what?" Eddie asks.

"Getting a receipt."

"That's kind of funny, actually," Eddie says. He opens a suitcase, takes out a stack of bills and hands it to Osvaldo.

Osvaldo leaves.

Eddie doesn't count the money—Darnell is too good a businessman to short him.

What Eddie does is get back into bed and take a nap.

I must be getting old, he thinks.

I'm fucked out.

Hidalgo gets the word that the guy left the Wynn without the suitcases.

"Get up there," Hidalgo tells Erica. "Pull your guys off and watch the place. I'm on my way."

He calls Keller. "The guy who went to meet Cirello is probably a gofer. He went to the Wynn and dropped the money. Do we have an ID yet?"

"Not yet," Keller says.

Hidalgo hustles up to the Wynn. Erica is in her car on the street that leads from the Strip to the hotel.

"Is there any other way out?" he asks.

"By car, this is it."

Keller calls. "We have a name: Osvaldo Curiel. A Salvadoran, former special forces. Worked for Diego Tapia and then Eddie Ruiz."

"Boss, Eddie Ruiz was in Victorville, wasn't he?"

"Same time as Darius Darnell."

"Jesus Christ."

"Stay on him, Hugo."

"You got it." He turns to Erica. "Can you get a look at the guest register?"

"Without a warrant?"

"No paper on this."

She thinks about it for a second. "The hotels are usually willing to play with us. I'll give it a shot. What am I looking for?"

"An Eddie Ruiz," Hidalgo says. "Although it's a long shot he registered under his own name. But if you see any cute version of it . . ."

He knows Ruiz will have fake ID and credit cards to match. But sometimes these guys don't like to get too far away from their own names or initials.

Hidalgo digs in to wait.

Keller sends him the most recent image of Ruiz, his induction photo into Victorville.

Erica's gone for forty-five minutes. When she gets back in the car she says, "There's no Eddie Ruiz."

"I didn't think so."

"But . . . no, it's probably nothing."

"Tell me."

"Wasn't Ruiz some kind of high school football hotshot in Texas?" she asks. "A linebacker?"

"Yeah, I think."

"There was an 'L. R. Jordan' registered, checked into a suite two nights ago," Erica says. "He's been spanking the AmEx card."

Hidalgo starts to hit Google.

"I did that already," Erica says. "Lee Roy Jordan was a famous Dallas Cowboys linebacker."

"Did you get a—"

"Room 1410," Erica says. "If he calls down for anything, the desk is going to text me."

Hidalgo stares at her. "Oh, you're good."

"Don't tell *me*, I already know," she says. "Tell my boss."

"You got it."

They sit there for an hour and a half. Then she gets a text—Mr. Jordan just called for a cheeseburger and fries.

"You ever been a server?" Erica asks Hidalgo.

"No. You?"

"Put myself through college at Hooters," she says, "which is enough to put you off men the rest of your life."

"Did it?"

"No."

"You think they'd let you—"

"When a hotel in this town needs a cop, it needs a cop," Erica says. "Sometimes they need a cop and they don't want it to show up on the books, and if we can do that, we do that. So, yes, I think they'll let me."

She's back in forty-five minutes. "It's your boy, Ruiz."

"Did he hit on you?"

"Hugo . . . it's Hugo, isn't it?"

Hidalgo is crushed. "Yeah."

"They *all* hit on me." She hands him a parking stub. "And I got you this. It's not a rental. He drove here. I have the parking slot."

"Erica . . ."

"Hugo, you go do what you have to do," she says. "But leave me out of it. I've bent enough laws today. I'll be in the lobby if you need me."

Hidalgo gets on the phone to Keller.

Keller takes the call and hears—"Darnell's supplier is Eddie Ruiz."

The best trap, Keller reflects, is one of your own making.

I've crafted this one for myself and there's no way out.

No good way.

If I pursue prosecution against Lerner and the rest, it brings in Eddie Ruiz, and if I take Ruiz down, he takes me down with him.

But if I don't, the cartel could buy its way into the government of the United States. It's not just a matter of influence, of having an "ear" in the administration—that's bad enough—but it's a matter of blackmail. The cartel could wield a virtual sword of Damocles over the administration's head they could drop anytime they wanted.

It only makes sense, he thinks, that people whose only loyalty is to money would find each other.

Shit seeks its own level.

So now we have a cartel in Mexico, and a cartel here at home, and they're coming together.

Into one cartel.

The smart thing, Keller thinks, is to walk away. Hell, you don't even have to walk, they're going to boot you out. Go, take your pension, take a consulting job, live your life.

You've earned it.

Read books, travel with Mari, sip some wine, watch the sunsets together.

The alternative is ending your life behind bars.

And what difference does it make? Stop this deal from going through and there'll just be other deals. Stop this source of drugs and there'll just be other sources. You'd be sacrificing yourself for absolutely nothing.

It's one thing to give your life for something, another thing to give it for nothing. I'm on my way out, he thinks. A few weeks, a few months tops. But I've given my whole damn life to fighting drugs.

Ernie Hidalgo gave his life.

And I'll be goddamned if, after all that, I'm going to let a bunch of pushers and traitors steal my country.

It wasn't the best burger Eddie's ever had but it sure as shit was the best waitress, a black chick so hot Eddie wanted to call Darius up and tell him, *I get it now, brother, I get it, I get it.* Next time he comes to Vegas, an AA woman is going to be on his menu. He calls down to have his car ready and waiting, throws his shit in his bag and takes the suitcases full of cash.

Twenty minutes later he's on 15 North, headed for St. George and his ration of domestic drama.

Keller follows Ruiz's progress from Washington.

The little light from the tracking device Hidalgo put under the rear bumper—illegal as hell without a warrant—blinks its way up the map on I-15.

Keller has to chuckle.

Eddie's headed to see his Utah family.

But the ramifications are anything but funny, Keller thinks.

We now have a direct connection between fentanyl-laced heroin in New York, Darius Darnell, and Eddie Ruiz. And there's a financial connection between Darnell, Ruiz, and the Terra Company, the Berkeley Group, Lerner, and Echeverría.

Echeverría connects the dots to high-ranking people in the Mexican administration and finance.

Lerner does the same in the United States.

It all somehow leads back to Tristeza.

And Eddie Ruiz, he thinks, leads back to you.

Cirello drives the other way on the 15—south and west toward California.

He stayed at the Mandalay, dropped five K on craps, then rented a car and headed out. You live in New York, you don't do this kind of distance driving, but he finds that he likes it. The desert should be monotonous, but he's never seen desert before so he enjoys it.

The highway runs straight to Victorville and he checks into a Comfort Inn.

Motels in the vicinity of big prisons tend to be sad places. Most of the guests are families or defense lawyers with clients who have already lost, so none of them are very happy. The kids come out of cars in the parking lot with eyes swollen from crying, the women look exhausted, the lawyers emerge with briefcases full of no-hope appeals.

There's a swimming pool that the kids get in while the mothers sit around and compare cases. The lawyers mostly head to the nearest bars or gun it straight south to LA and try to forget about their day in Victorville—which they have dubbed, inevitably, "Loserville."

If the motel is depressing, it's Disneyland compared to the prison itself.

A prison is one of the saddest places on the face of the earth, Cirello thinks as he rolls up to Victorville Federal Penitentiary. It's not just the walls and the wire—Cirello is often struck by how much jails and prisons resemble any warehouse you'd see on the backstreets of Queens, Brooklyn or the Bronx. Things are stored there. It's the palpable feeling of hopelessness, waste, loss and pain.

Prisons are palaces of pain.

If the walls could talk, they'd howl.

Cirello's no bleeding-heart liberal. He's put a lot of guys in prison and is content that most of them belong there. Like most cops, he sees the victims of crime, he knows their pain as well, he's seen it firsthand on the street, in the E-rooms and the morgues. He knows the people who bear the scars of beatings, the women who live with their rapes. He's been the one who's had to go to a victim's family to tell them that their loved one is never coming home.

Talk about pain.

No, Cirello has little sympathy for the assholes suffering behind these walls, but he knows . . .

Some of them don't belong here.

It's not just the innocent, the cases that the system gets wrong; it's the system itself. As a narcotics cop, he's sent scores of drug offenders to the joint, and fuck most of them, they dealt death for money.

But then there are the others.

The addicts who sell to pay for their own habits, the losers who got popped slinging a small amount of weed, the idiots who broke into a drugstore looking for pills, or the bigger idiots who robbed a gas station to buy meth.

Hey, if they shot someone, hurt someone, killed someone getting money for their dope, let them rot in here, it's where they belong. But for a nonviolent crime? Filling up the prisons with losers who didn't hurt anyone but themselves?

What's the point?

Just to add to the general level of pain?

Cirello's on the BOP list of approved visitors for Jackson, but uses his NY gold shield instead, letting the admitting guards know right away he's not a lawyer—COs hate lawyers—but a cop who needs an interview room to talk with a convict.

"You brought presents?" the guard asks.

"I need this guy to talk to me," Cirello says. "Is there a problem?"

"We'll need to search through it."

"Sure."

They set him up with a room.

A few minutes later they bring in Arthur Jackson, shackled at the wrists and ankles.

Cirello had a look at Jackson's PSI. The guy is doing life-times-three from a crack beef in Arkansas.

Life wasn't enough? Cirello wonders. What the guy did was so bad he has to serve three lifetimes in the pain palace? I've busted killers who were back on the street in five years. And Jackson doesn't look like a killer. He looks more like a worship leader in some country church.

Jackson sits down and smiles. "Thank you for coming."

"Sure."

"How's Darius doing?"

"Yeah, fine."

"He behaving himself?" Jackson asks. "No drugs?"

"He's behaving himself."

"That's good," Jackson says. "He found a job?"

Something evil in Cirello's soul wants to answer, *Yeah, in pharmaceuticals,* but he says, "He's hanging drywall. Doing well. He asked me to bring you this stuff."

Jackson looks immensely pleased. Two of the books are on chess strategy, another is an exegesis on the Book of Matthew. "And banana bread? Darius used to make banana bread here!"

"No shit?"

"Straight up," Jackson says. "Well, thank you for taking the trouble."

"Anything for Darius."

"How do you know him?" Jackson asks.

"He drywalled my apartment," Cirello says. "We got to be friends. When I said I was coming out near here, he asked me to stop by."

"Darius becoming friends with a police." Jackson shakes his head. "How about that?"

"I'll bring another care package the next time I come out."

"That's nice," Jackson says. "But I won't be here."

Say what? "Mr. Jackson, I thought . . ."

Jackson smiles. "I'm getting a presidential commutation."

"The president commuted your sentence?"

"Not yet," Jackson says. "But he will."

Cirello thinks the sound in his chest might be his heart cracking. He doesn't know the president, but he's pretty sure that Barack Obama has never heard of Arthur Jackson. He's had eight years in office to commute Jackson's sentence. A child could tell you it ain't gonna happen. Arthur Jackson is going to spend the rest of his life—and the next two—right here in this prison.

He's not dead yet, but he's already buried.

"I know what you're thinking," Jackson says. "But I have faith. Without faith, Mr. Cirello, there's nothing in this life. Or the next one."

Cirello gets up. "It's been great meeting you."

"The pleasure is mine," Jackson says. "Although, and please don't take offense, I hope I don't meet you again."

"I hope so, too, Mr. Jackson."

Cirello's maybe thirty miles down the highway, headed for Vegas, when suddenly he's pounding the dashboard with his fist. When he gets back to town, he gets reasonably drunk, drops ten more on the craps tables and gets on a flight to New York.

He doesn't upgrade.

Eddie Ruiz is so happy to be back on the highway he could get out and kiss the asphalt.

"Pain in the ass" doesn't start to describe Teresa and the St. George family. Teresa and the fam were prison love. Not that Eddie ever experienced ass rape in the joint, but he heard enough of it to know it was similar to having to put up with his wife and kids.

"I don't take care of you?" Eddie asked during one of his several fights with Teresa. "I don't provide?! I just gave you two hundred K!"

"We never see you!" she said. "And we're in Utah!"

"There are worse places."

"Name one!"

Eddie could name two, Florence and Victorville, but he thought that a reference to his years in prison might not be the way to go. "I promise, as soon as I have things set up, I'll send for you, we'll all be back in California."

"*Where* in California?" Teresa asked. "Not some shithole."

"No. La Jolla." Eddie was making this shit up as he went along.

Angela wanted a car.

And not just any car. A Beamer.

"You're fifteen," Eddie said.

"I'll be getting my license soon."

Right, Eddie thought. Kids in Utah get their licenses when they're, like, eleven. But a BMW? No fucking way. "I'll *maybe* get you a used Camry."

"Fuck that!"

"Hey!"

"What do I look like, Dad?" Angela asked. "Some stringy-haired blond Mormon girl engaged to her cousin?"

Eddie didn't know what to say to that.

He didn't know what to say to Eddie Jr., either.

Eddie didn't remember dropping him on his head or letting him munch on paint chips or anything like that, but the kid is dumb. And passive as a Barcalounger, except a Barcalounger will sit up if you push the right buttons.

Not Eddie Jr.

Supine is his default position.

So Eddie is happy to be driving back to Dago.

He thought about stopping back in Vegas to fuck a black woman but decided it was too risky with three million in the trunk. He just called Osvaldo, gave him his location, and the boy has fallen in behind him to guard his six.

Osvaldo watches the car when Eddie pulls off in Primm to take a piss, and then Eddie gets back in and drives straight through to San Diego.

But not back to Priscilla.

Eddie's had enough family drama for a while.

So he goes to his place in Solana Beach.

Eddie's rented a condo on the bluff right over the beach. It's small—one-bedroom—but the floor-to-ceiling window in the living room provides what the Realtor calls a "whitewater view," because he can see the waves coming in on the sand and the whole ocean stretch out in front of him.

The kitchen is minuscule but Eddie doesn't care, he's not going to do a lot of cooking anyway. There's a place a couple of blocks away that serves a very decent breakfast burrito and you can't swing a dead cat in Solana Beach or Del Mar without hitting a good restaurant.

Or a yoga studio.

Doesn't matter where you are, 360 degrees around you, hot women and yummy-mummies are strutting out of their yoga classes in Lululemon pants with their downward-facing-dog asses.

Eddie is happy here.

And anonymous.

He took the place under a different name, paid twelve grand in cash for three months' rent, and no one asked a single question. Southern California's famous self-absorption works well if you're trying to disappear, because no one gives a shit about anyone else.

It's perfect.

Eddie feels safe here.

He's thinking about taking up surfing.

Hidalgo gives Eddie a polite nod.

One of those guy-to-guy stranger acknowledgments.

They're sitting outside at a little coffee shop in Solana Beach where Eddie is scarfing down a burrito.

Hidalgo goes back to looking at his phone.

Knows better than to make any extended contact with Ruiz.

They know where he lives now, in one of those condos that absentee owners rent to tourists on a weekly or monthly basis when they're not using it themselves. Highly mobile population, people in and out all the time, no one draws attention. A subterranean garage where Ruiz can park his Porsche.

They could pop Eddie right now, he's in possession of three million dollars in cash they can track back directly to Darius Darnell. Even if they can't connect Eddie to the heroin shipments, it puts him in violation of his sentencing agreement. They could put him away for a thirty bit.

Under that threat, they could squeeze Eddie to give up his Mexican source. Ruiz has a history of snitching, so it shouldn't be that hard to get him to go now.

But Keller nixed it.

"If we bust Eddie, we have Eddie," the boss said. "If he gives us his Mexican source, we may or may not be able to get him. I want it all—Eddie, his source, the bankers, the real estate developers, everybody. If we don't do that, what are we doing?"

I don't know, boss, Hidalgo thinks, but I know we're running out of clock in this game. It's football, not baseball; we're not guaranteed to get up to the plate for our swings before the new guy gets in and blows the whistle. We have to make our move now.

But he gets it. There's something to Keller's argument.

The warrant issue is another story.

Hidalgo wants to wire Eddie's crib.

They turn it into Muscle Shoals, they might get Crazy Eddie on the phone, talking to his people south of the border. They'd get all kinds of useful shit. Yeah, they'd want a warrant, but why can't Keller get it from the same federal judge he got the Pierre warrant from? They have more predicate on this than they had on the big banker meeting.

Except the boss won't go there.

"Too risky."

What's the risk? Hidalgo wonders. That it will leak? That the opposition inside DEA will get wind of it? Or that it gets back to our banker buddies and they shut down their deal? But if that were the case, the judge would have blown them already.

So why won't Keller do it?

He wants to "think about it."

Hidalgo even took a chance and bumped it to the next level. Like, okay, boss, if you don't want to go for a warrant, let's do it off the books. He even said he'd risk breaking into Eddie's place and setting the wire, monitor it himself. Hell, they went cowboy on the tracking device, what's the difference?

Keller said no again. Or at least he said "not yet."

Again, he wanted to think about it.

What's there to think about?

Keller isn't exactly Mr. By-the-Book. The stories about him are legend, and those stories aren't about his slavish adherence to proper procedure.

So has he just lost his nerve? His drive? Or . . .

What's he afraid of?

It's worrisome. Hidalgo knows that Keller and Ruiz go way back, that Ruiz was a source of his back in Mexico, that Eddie gave up Diego Tapia, and in return Keller brokered Eddie's sweet sentencing deal.

So is he still protecting Eddie?

And if so, why?

Hidalgo makes sure he doesn't look up from his phone as he sees Eddie get up, toss his burrito wrapper into the garbage can and walk away.

Where are you going, motherfucker?

To the bank.

Well, banks, plural.

First Eddie drives two hours all the way east to Calexico, a town that, as the name indicates, straddles the California-Mexico border. There are four small banks in the town and he uses small banks because they need money and they don't get the attention from the government that the big banks get.

Eddie already knows which ones play.

That is, which banks will take multiple $9,500 deposits of cash in a few days from the same people and not file a Suspicious Activity Report. Under

$10K it's at the bank's discretion, but by law, if they get suspicious deposits under the ten, they're supposed to file an SAR.

Some banks are less suspicious than others.

Eddie doesn't go to Wells Fargo.

Too big, too much supervision.

He picks two smaller banks and deposits $9,500 at each.

Then he works his way back west, stopping in little towns like El Centro, Brawley, Borrego Springs, Julian and Ramona, making deposits in each like Johnny Moneyseed. Then he hits the suburbs, Poway, Rancho Bernardo, then small cities like Escondido and Alpine. Back in San Diego metro, he works the outskirts and hits banks in El Cajon, National City and Chula Vista.

It takes several days, but by the time he's done, he's dumped a mil.

The other two he gives to Osvaldo to drive down to Mexico and take to Caro.

Eddie's buying into the syndicate.

He's a proud investor in Park Tower.

Vegas, baby.

A suite at the Four Seasons.

Cirello settles in and waits for Ruiz's courier.

Funny what you get used to and how quick, he thinks, looking out the window at the Strip below. Private jets, hotel suites, room service, blue-ribbon booze on the bar . . . it's all the norm now, business as usual, what he expects.

Except things are going to change now.

If he can make the big play.

The next step up the ladder. First it was DeStefano, then Andrea, then Cozzo. Then the move up to Darnell.

Next.

The doorbell rings.

It's Osvaldo. "You have my package?"

"Come on in."

Osvaldo looks hesitant.

"We need to talk," Cirello says.

"You breaking up with me?" Osvaldo asks. But he steps in. "What?"

"I have to meet your guy," Cirello says. He hands him the bags.

"Is there a problem?"

"Every problem is an opportunity, right?" Cirello asks. He lays it out the way Mullen told him to. "You know I've been kicking to a guy in DEA. Now the guy is getting hinky—and he wants a bigger taste. That's the bad news. The good news is he has some ideas."

"What kind of ideas?" Osvaldo asks.

"Growing the business."

"I'll take it to my guy," Osvaldo says.

"No, *I'll* take it to your guy," Cirello says. He knows it's the moment, make or break. They buy or they don't. They don't, they bitch to Darnell, and he's back on duty at One Police. He's not sure how he wants this to go. "Here's the thing. I don't know you. All I know, I could be delivering cash to a cop, earning myself thirty-to-life. My DEA guy has the same concerns. We need to know who we're dealing with here."

"Ask Darnell."

"Darnell's got nothing to do with this."

"It's his money in those bags."

"No, it's your guy's money in those bags," Cirello says. "And I need to know that he exists, and then I need to eyeball him."

"How's that going to help?"

"Because I'll know," Cirello says. "And I'll present your boss with an opportunity that, believe me, he doesn't want to miss."

Osvaldo thinks it over, then, "I'll ask."

"I'll wait."

For two long hours.

Then the phone rings. "Five minutes. Lobby. You sit at the bar."

Cirello goes downstairs and sits at the bar. Lets whoever wants to look at him look at him, make sure he's alone. Maybe they're on the phone to Darnell, in which case he's fucked. His phone rings. "Rent a car. Right now. Drive to the Speedway and park."

Pain in the ass, Cirello thinks.

But he goes to the desk, rents a Camaro and drives north on the 15 to Las Vegas Speedway and pulls into the enormous parking lot. Maybe twenty other cars and trucks are spread out over the lot. Cirello knows they're in one of the vehicles, watching him.

He sits there for twenty minutes. Is about to leave—fuck 'em—when a Shelby Mustang pulls up on the driver's side.

Eddie Ruiz is behind the wheel. "Get in."

Cirello gets out of the Camaro and gets into the Shelby. If they're going to pop him, it's going to be right now. But there's no one in the back seat.

Ruiz leans over and pats him down.

Feels the gun but no wire.

Because there isn't one.

"What are you carrying?" Ruiz asks.

"A Sig nine."

"I like the Glock," Ruiz says. "No safety to deal with."

"I like the safety."

"You wanted to look me in the eye," Ruiz says. "Look me in the eye."

Cirello does.

"So now you seen me," Eddie says. "What do you want?"

"To do some business."

"We *are* doing business," Eddie says.

"You and Darnell are doing business," Cirello says. "I'm just a gofer."

"I know who you are," Eddie says. "Does Darius know you're trying to do a separate deal?"

"Not unless you told him," Cirello says.

"What happens in Vegas . . ."

"So you're interested."

"Let's go have some fun."

Eddie has rented time on the track. Fifty bucks a lap, what does he care? They put on helmets and all that happy shit, roll out onto the track and Eddie hits the gas. Eighty, ninety, a hundred, they slide into a banked turn and Cirello feels like he's going to puke.

Next lap Eddie kicks it up to a buck twenty. He's hooting, hollering, giving it one of those shitkicker Texas whoops, and Cirello imagines what it's going to be like smashing into the wall, flipping over it, spinning in the air, crashing in a ball of flame.

They hit the straightaway, Eddie yells over the roar of the engine, "Talk!"

"The fed I kick to!" Cirello says. "He wants to sit down with you!"

"This guy have a name?!"

"Meet him, you can find out!"

The curve comes up so fast. Eddie shuts up and concentrates—even he's a little scared. The car drifts up and out, but Eddie doesn't hit the brakes, he hits the gas, powers through the curve, lets the car do the work.

Cirello's stomach is coming through his mouth.

One thirty . . . forty . . . fifty . . .

Next fucking curve. Jesus Christ.

"You scared?!" Eddie asks.

"Yes!"

Eddie laughs.

Speeds up.

One sixty, one sixty-five going into the next curve. Cirello's pretty sure he's going to die. But the car sails through the curve and makes it out the other side. On the straightaway Eddie yells, "They say this thing can hit two hundred!"

"You ever done this before?!"

"No!"

Great, Cirello thinks. "Can we stop dicking around, get down to business?!"

"This is only our first date!" Eddie says. "Don't push me into a threesome already! Besides, life is short, man. You have to get your fun when you can. Aren't you having fun?!"

No, Cirello thinks. And he can't let Eddie jerk him like this, it sets a bad precedent for the power relationship. "You don't meet this guy, I'm out! Too risky having him as an enemy!"

"You threatening me?!"

"I'm just telling you how it is!"

"I can buy another New York cop!" Eddie says.

"You want referrals?!"

Eddie bails at one eighty, lets up on the pedal, eases into the pit. "That was a *rush*. Holy shit. I mean, when you were a kid, did you ever think you'd be doing a buck eighty-five in a primo car on a private track?!"

"Didn't occur to me, no."

"Okay, I'll meet your guy," Eddie says. "But it better be worth my fucking time."

Nobu Hotel at Caesars Palace.

Osvaldo opens the door and lets them in. Pats them down—guns are okay, wires verboten.

A suite, natch.

It's bigger than Cirello's apartment. A bar, of course, a "media room" with a flat-screen LED, even a pool table. Cirello knows Ruiz has had it swept upside down and backward, and neither he nor Hidalgo is wired up.

Too risky and no need.

He only hopes Hidalgo is as good as his rep. The guy did fine in the bag job back in New York, but undercover is a different gig. Hidalgo is smart and tough, no question, but this is a big play to pull off.

Hidalgo looks the part, though, rocking a slate-gray Armani that cost more than his pay grade should allow. Open white custom shirt, Gucci loafers. A young wolf on the make. It's in the playbook Keller gave them—Ruiz pays a lot of attention to clothes. Today he's in his trademark polo shirt—sky blue—and khaki trousers.

Hidalgo makes his play straight off.

It's ballsy.

"I'm going to pat you down, too," Hidalgo says. "Both of you."

Could have queered the meet right there, but Eddie smiles and lifts his arms. Hidalgo pats him down for a wire, does the same with Osvaldo. Then he takes a sweeper, runs it around the room.

"I did that already," Osvaldo says.

"You did it for you," Hidalgo says. "I'm doing this for me."

He doesn't find a bug.

"Happy now?" Eddie asks. "Sit down, have a drink."

Osvaldo bartends—a Dos Equis for Cirello, a vodka and tonic for Hidalgo. Eddie has an iced tea, Osvaldo doesn't drink.

"Eddie," Cirello says, "this is Agent Fuentes."

"Tony," Hidalgo says.

Keller has created a whole identity for him. If anyone checks, they'll find his file at DEA. Came up through Fort Worth PD, caught on with DEA, did UC in California, then at the Seattle office, then came into DEA Central.

Career on a bullet.

Divorced, no kids.

Condo in Silver Springs.

"Hello, Tony," Eddie says. "You Mexican?"

"Mexican American."

"A fellow *pocho*."

"I know who you are," Hidalgo says.

"The price of fame," Eddie says. "Look, if you want more money, you should be talking to Darnell, not me."

"Darnell is a field hand," Hidalgo says. "I want to deal with the plantation owner."

He has balls, Cirello thinks.

Clanging.

Eddie looks at Cirello. "Have you told Darnell he's a cotton picker?"

"I probably left that out," Cirello says. "Let me put this another way. I'm a New York guy, I can give you New York. Fuentes is at DEA headquarters, the Intelligence Division. He sees everything."

"You're jacking me up for a raise?" Eddie asks Hidalgo. "Okay, what are we talking? Give me a number."

"I don't want an employer," Hidalgo says. "I want a partner."

"Then buy a Souplantation."

Push it, Cirello thinks. You have to push him now or lose him.

"You're looking at this wrong," Hidalgo says.

"I am?"

"Yeah," Hidalgo says. "Right now you have one outlet for your product—Darius Darnell. That gives you certain markets in New York, and if that's all you want, fine, we'll have a drink and I'll find someone more ambitious, no hard feelings. But you have all your eggs in one black basket, and it's a small basket. Anything happens to Darnell, you're out of business. In the meantime, your competitors south of the border are moving in on New York in bigger ways, working with Hispanics. It's only a matter of time before they drive Darnell out of the market. And then, once again, you're out of business."

"And how are you going to prevent that?"

"How did Adán Barrera rise to the top?" Hidalgo asks. "You know, you were there."

"Why don't you tell me anyway?"

Cirello sees Eddie is starting to get angry.

"The Mexican government helped him kill off his competition," Hidalgo says. "The rest had no choice but to come in with him. With my access, we can do the same for you here in the United States."

Dead fucking silence.

"Don't just think defensively," Hidalgo says. "Don't just think, 'This fed can tell me whether or not I'm on the radar.' Think *offensively*—'This fed can steer DEA operations against my competitors.' It can work the other way, too—you get information on your competitors, you give it to us, we can act on it. Just like Barrera."

"How do I know you have that kind of stroke?"

"Log on to the papers tomorrow," Hidalgo says. "Because tonight, DEA is going to hit a Núñez heroin mill in the Bronx for fifteen kilos. My gift to you, call it proof of concept."

Eddie looks at Cirello. "You'd fuck your boy Darnell like this?"

"No one is talking about fucking Darnell over," Cirello says. "We're talking about expanding. He can ride the elevator with you, that's your choice. But he can't know about Fuentes."

"Why not?"

"Because he's a black ex-con," Hidalgo says. "I can't trust him. Eddie, you want to be a small-market team, that's fine. I get it. It's good money, it's a good life, every few years you make the playoffs. But if you want to be the Yankees, the Dodgers, the Cubs, we can help you get there. We can get you into Washington, Baltimore, Chicago, LA."

"Vegas, for that matter," Cirello says.

"We can help you move your money," Hidalgo says. "Tell you what banks are safe, what loans, what syndicates . . . We'll even set you up with people."

Cirello watches Ruiz thinking.

Ruiz is a survivor.

He came out of a small gang in Laredo and made himself the head hit man for the Sinaloa cartel.

Then he went with Diego Tapia.

Flipped on him when it was a matter of saving his own skin.

Eddie Ruiz's loyalty is to Eddie Ruiz.

"And what do you get for all this?" Eddie asks.

"Points," Hidalgo says. "I eat when you eat."

"How much of my dinner do you want?"

"My mother always told me, 'Eat like a horse, not like a pig,'" Hidalgo says. "So five percent."

"You're out of your fucking mind."

"Make me a counter, then."

"Two."

"Thanks for the drink," Hidalgo says. He looks at Cirello like, *Let's get up.* "I don't get out of bed for two."

"Can you set your alarm for three?"

"Maybe four."

"Three and a half," Eddie says. "If you check out, if you do what you say you can do."

"I will," Hidalgo says, "and watch the news tomorrow. No offense, but are you the decision maker, Eddie? Or do you need to talk to someone else?"

"I'll need to run this past some people."

"I'll be in town for the weekend," Hidalgo says. "You can reach me through Cirello here. He'll be the go-between, the bagman."

"I'll be in touch."

Hidalgo goes for the close. "Eddie, we can really do something here."

Eddie throws him a curve. "Why? Other than money, why are you doing this?"

Hidalgo is quick.

"Because I'm sick of fighting a war we're never going to win," he says. "Because I'm sick of watching other people get rich. And because you guys are going to start slugging it out over turf, I don't want to see this become Mexico. So we pick a winner early and get peace."

The Mexican scenario.

The Pax Sinaloa.

Now a thing of the past.

"And just let us sling dope?" Eddie asks.

"Junkies are junkies," Hidalgo says. "They're going to get it somewhere. Fuck them, I want the streets safe for people who aren't shooting poison into their arms."

"I'll be in touch," Eddie says.

"I look forward to it."

"You guys need reservations or anything?" Eddie asks. "I can get you a table at Nobu."

Hidalgo laughs. "We probably shouldn't be seen dining at Nobu."

"More like Denny's," Cirello says.

"Got it," Eddie says. "But I mean, you want some women or something, Osvaldo will set it up. World-class *chocha*, on me."

"I appreciate it," Hidalgo says, "but I like the hunt, you know what I mean? And Vegas is a target-rich environment."

Eddie looks at Cirello.

"I'm going to hit the tables," Cirello says.

"Ozzie, give the guys some chips, let them play on us."

Osvaldo gives them some chips.

They get downstairs, Hidalgo takes a deep breath. "Jesus Christ."

"You were great, man," Cirello says. "Very impressive."

"You think so?" Hidalgo asks. "You think we made the sale?"

"I think so, but who knows?" Cirello says. "He's gonna get on the phone now, kick this up. Then we'll see. In the meantime . . ."

Hidalgo goes out to call Keller.

Cirello hits the blackjack table.

Plays with the cartel's money.

Keller waits for the call.

Already regretting he sent Hugo.

A hundred things could go wrong, the least of which is Ruiz rejecting the overture, sniffing out the trap. Ruiz could drive Hugo out into the desert, put a bullet in his head, and into Cirello's. No, he wouldn't do that, he's too smart. Still . . .

The downside is horrific.

But the upside . . .

A chance to turn the cartel inside out.

The phone finally rings. "Are you out?"

"Yeah, I'm fine."

"And?"

"I think he bit," Hidalgo says. "He's going to kick it up."

"Did he say who he needs to talk to?"

Because whomever he talks to is running things. The real connection to Echeverría and the syndicate.

"No," Hidalgo says, "and I didn't want to push it."

"That was the right call," Keller says. "You're sure you're okay?"

"I'm great."

He sounds jacked up, Keller thinks. Coming off an adrenaline high. "Okay. Lay low. Check in."

It takes Eddie forty-five long minutes to decide to take this upstairs. The number he calls is in Sinaloa and the call lasts for almost an hour. Orduña's people run it down for Keller—the closest cell-phone tower is near Rafael Caro's house in Culiacán.

Rafael Caro, Keller thinks.

Everything old is new again. The past comes back.

Follow the drugs, follow the money.

Caro connects to Ruiz and Darnell.

Caro connects to Damien Tapia, who connects to Ruiz and Darnell.

Damien Tapia moved heroin with Caro.

It was Caro who gave the order to kill the Tristeza students.

Caro connects Echeverría to Claiborne to Lerner.

In effect, Caro to Lerner.

Okay.

Keller is going to pull the whole wall down.

Right on top of himself, if necessary.

2

Death Will Be the Proof

Death will be the proof that we lived.
—Castellanos

Sinaloa, Mexico
December 2016

His father looks old.

I guess, Ric thinks, getting shot will age you.

But his thick hair is now more silver than black—prematurely—and there seems to be a constant grimace of fatigue (or is it pain?) on his face. The bullets didn't kill him, but they certainly diminished him. He's as bright as he always was, and every bit as analytical, but his energy is quickly depleted.

Ric knows what they're saying about his dad now: *If you want to talk with El Abogado, do it before lunch, before his daily siesta. After that, he's not so sharp.* To be sure, more and more, they're not going to see him at all, they're going to Ric.

Clearly, his father's life is attenuated, from his reduced energies to his limited diet, no alcohol—maybe a Sunday sip of sherry—and bland meals that won't irritate his repaired stomach lining. Ricardo Núñez Sr. was never exactly the life of the party, but he was always a gracious host—now the gatherings at the house are few and truncated and guests know to leave when they see the dark circles appear under Núñez's eyes.

In the movies, people get shot and either die or completely recover. Ric's learned that the reality is somewhat different.

Now he sits with his father in the back seat of a car on the way to a meeting. He hadn't wanted his father to come at all, or at least to hold the meeting at home, but Núñez Sr. wanted to dispel the notion that he's an invalid.

"The *patrón* has to be seen," he said. "Otherwise they start thinking there's nothing behind the curtain."

"Huh?"

"*The Wizard of Oz.* You never saw it?"

"I don't think so."

"This powerful wizard runs a kingdom, just with his voice, from behind a curtain," Núñez said. "But when they pull the curtain back, they discover that he's just a man."

But you *are* just a man, Ric thought.

The meeting is with the leaders of a group called La Oficina, one of the splinter groups from the old Tapia organization.

At Ric's last count, twenty-six separate groups—sometimes cooperating, sometimes fighting each other—have sprung from the Tapias. Some are autonomous, others claim allegiance to Damien, others still pledge loyalty to Eddie Ruiz. And they're spread all over the country now—most, like GU and Los Rojos, in Guerrero and Durango, but others in Sinaloa, Jalisco, Michoacán, Morelos, Acapulco, Tamaulipas, even all the way down in Chiapas. A few of the groups exist right in Mexico City. What they have in common is they're all causing problems.

Throw in the *autodefensas*—the volunteer militias that claim to be fighting to defend civilians against the cartels. Some legitimately try to do that; others started that way and have evolved into just more examples of corruption and coercion.

It's a clusterfuck.

Chaos everywhere.

The biggest mistake Adán Barrera ever made was betraying his old friend Diego Tapia and touching off a civil war inside the Sinaloa cartel. While he was alive, Ric thinks, he could rein in the results; now he's left my father to try to pour the spilled wine back into the bottle.

It's impossible.

But today's meeting is an effort.

La Oficina has made overtures that they want to come back into the Sinaloa fold. It's worth a try, Ric thinks—we could use allies.

The war with Tito isn't going well.

For one thing, we're losing Baja.

The Sánchez-Jalisco alliance has taken Tecate, the smaller but still important border crossing into San Diego. That means it can ship its coke, meth and heroin directly into the US, breaking what had been a Sinaloa monopoly. And it's lending the Tecate border crossing to Damien and other Tapia splinter groups, further fueling and funding the insurgency against Sinaloa in Guerrero, Durango and Michoacán.

From his stronghold deep in the Guerrero mountains, Damien is raising sheer hell. Far from backing down after kidnapping the Esparza brothers, he's become more aggressive, conducting ambushes on Sinaloa drug couriers and army and police patrols. He recently killed three Guerrero state police in a four-hour gun battle near an opium farm. A week later, he ambushed an army convoy and killed five soldiers.

He's becoming freaking Che Guevara.

It's not just in the countryside.

Acapulco has become a nightmare.

The seaside resort town, once peaceful territory, is now a battlefield where Sinaloa, New Jalisco, and Damien are fighting it out for the valuable port, so necessary for bringing in the base chemicals for meth and fentanyl.

Eddie Ruiz used to run it, and Ric has to admit that he did a good job. But since Ruiz's departure from the scene, his organization has splintered into competing factions that act independently or make ever-shifting alliances with one or more of the major players.

The butcher's bill has been high.

And grotesque—one group of former Ruiz guys likes to flay the faces off its victims and leave them on their car seats. Another favors the now commonplace tactic of hanging bodies from bridges or scattering limbs along the sidewalks. GU and Los Rojos are fighting in the city, and the only Sinaloa ally right now is a group known as the "Sweeper Truck," which does, indeed, sweep some of its enemies off the street.

Acapulco is up for grabs.

So is Mazatlán.

Our major port, Ric thinks, and we might lose it.

Another Tapia splinter group, Los Mazateclos, fought Sinaloa during the civil war, faded out when it lost, but now is back after Barrera's death.

With a vengeance.

Literally.

We're holding on there, Ric thinks, but the plaza is definitely heating up, and with Tito helping to fund the old Tapia groups, it will only get worse. Baja, Guerrero, Durango, Michoacán, Morelo—*everywhere*—the little groups are springing up like mushrooms after a wet winter.

And old plants, thought dead or dying, are starting to rise again from the old soil.

In Juárez, the busiest and most valuable border crossing, the bloodiest battleground of Barrera's war, fought for and won by Sinaloa at tremendous cost, the defeated Juárez cartel is coming back.

In Chihuahua, the moribund Gulf cartel is rising from the dead. Its old boss, Osiel Contreras, will soon finish his sentence in an American prison and come home, one of *los retornados*. Who knows what Contreras will want?

And in Tamaulipas and Veracruz, the Zetas—the most violent, sadistic and psychopathic of the cartels—the enemy put down by an unholy alliance of Sinaloa, the Mexican federal government and the American DEA, the people who killed Barrera and Esparza in Guatemala—are coming back.

The murder rate rises.

Ric has studied the numbers.

In October 2015, Mexico had 15,466 murders.

In October 2016, the number is almost 19,000.

More than a 20 percent bounce, a level not seen since the bad old days of 2011, when Barrera was fighting the Tapias, the Gulf, Juárez and the Zetas.

The government can't stop it.

The government is panicking.

Looking to *us* to stop it.

If we don't, Ric knows, they're going to find someone else.

Maybe they already have.

Earlier on the drive, his father gave him alarming news. "Rafael Caro has put together a syndicate."

"What you mean? What kind of syndicate?"

"A loan fund," Núñez said. "He's working with bankers, government people and some people in our business to loan $285 million to an American real estate group owned by the son-in-law of the new president. The syndicate has basically bought the American government for a paltry three hundred million. It's the bargain of the century."

Ric spun through the ramifications—

The people in the syndicate would not only have influence in Mexico City, but in Washington, DC, as well. They could potentially impact the DEA—gleaning intelligence, using it to act against enemies . . .

. . . like us.

The loan gives the syndicate a voice in the highest business circles in the United States, especially in New York, where Sinaloa is struggling to gain a foothold.

The upside is unlimited.

But so is the downside of being excluded.

"How did you find out about this?" Ric asked.

"We still have friends in Mexico City," Núñez said. "They assumed we were in on it. I didn't disabuse them."

"Which people in our business?"

Núñez dropped it like a bomb on his son's head. "Iván Esparza, among others."

"They went to Iván and not to us," Ric said, his head whirling.

"It would seem that way."

"And Iván didn't tell us."

"The point is," Núñez said, "we've been frozen out. With the complicity of your good friend Iván."

Ric didn't take the bait. He hasn't told his father about his succession deal with Iván. It wouldn't be accepted. But this is Iván jumping the gun, Ric thinks now. Making a play to buy that kind of influence without sharing it with us. It feels like a violation of their friendship, not to mention their business relationship.

It feels like a betrayal.

There's been tension between them.

Ric holds Iván responsible for the problems in Baja. They argued over it at their most recent sit-down, this time at a seaside bar out in Puesta del Sol.

Iván didn't want to hear the truth that Tito and Elena now had Tecate.

"Not just Tecate," Ric said. "La Presa, El Florido, Cañadas, Terrazas, Villa del Campo . . ."

One by one, territories in Baja are falling to Tito and Elena. The only places where Sinaloa is still strong are the places that Ric and Belinda have— Cabo and La Paz. Belinda is active in Tijuana, but it's a battlefield, very much in play, with tit-for-tat killings.

"What else is on your mind, young Ric?" Iván asked.

"It's your brother."

"Oviedo?" Iván asked, bristling. "What about him?"

"He's fucking up," Ric said. "Since you made him the Baja plaza boss . . . I mean, he's not doing the job. You can't get him on the phone, he's high half the time, he's trying to fuck other people's women—"

"He'll settle in."

"When?" Ric asked. "We're under fire, Iván. And Oviedo is screwing around. You can't get a decision made, it's whoever talks to him last."

"With all due respect," Iván said, "you run certain neighborhoods in La Paz and Cabo, but the rest of Baja is my business, not yours."

Then take care of your business, Ric thought. "What happens in Baja affects all of us. Tito and Elena having the Tecate plaza hurts all of us. If they get the Tijuana crossing—"

"They won't."

"They just killed Benny Vallejos."

Benny Vallejos was one of Iván's main shooters in Tijuana. They found his bullet-riddled body on a lonely stretch of highway with a sign on his torso that read, *Greetings from Your Fathers in the New Jalisco Cartel.*

"We'll pay them back," Iván said.

"It's not a matter of payback," Ric said. "It's a matter of controlling territory."

"Listen to you," Iván said. "Mr. All-Serious right now. I remember you used to be a party guy yourself."

"Maybe I grew up," Ric said, starting to get pissed. "Maybe Oviedo should too."

"Shut up about my brother, Ric."

"Iván—"

"I said shut the fuck up."

Ric shut the fuck up. But it bothered him, Iván's unwillingness to listen. And now he's really bothered that Iván has gone behind his back to make a serious play.

"We have to sit down with the Esparza brothers," Núñez says. "I want an explanation. They have to let us buy into this syndicate."

"I agree."

"Set it up," Núñez says. "As soon as possible."

He sits back and closes his eyes.

Ric looks out the window at the countryside flanking Route 30 as the little convoy makes its way west toward El Vergel. The meeting is set at a farmhouse south of town, among the endless flat fields of bell peppers.

He hears his father snore.

Looks at his watch and confirms that it's siesta time.

The convoy—armed uniformed guards are in SUVs in front of and behind them—drives through El Vergel and then turns south on a two-lane road through Colonia Paradiso and then out of town to a cluster of trees along the river.

The farmhouse, a typical stucco with a red tile roof and a broad porch, is set among the trees.

Ric walks around the car, opens the passenger door and helps his father out. Núñez gets up slowly and is unsteady as he sets his feet down. They walk into the house. Guards go in first, others set up outside.

The Oficina people—someone named Callarto and another called García—are already sitting at the kitchen table. The place is rustic, the table wooden and painted white, old plates on wall shelves, broad plank floors.

They stand when Núñez comes in, a good sign.

Núñez gestures for them to sit back down.

Ric takes a chair beside his father.

"It's good to see you again," Núñez says. "It's been too long."

Classic, Ric thinks—his father's lawyerly way of reminding them that they've been disloyal while also suggesting that it's water under the bridge. At the same time, everyone in the room is aware that La Oficina are small players, that a year ago—shit, six months ago—Ricardo Núñez wouldn't have bothered to sit down with them personally at all.

Ric hopes they didn't come with an inflated view of their importance.

They're still small players.

But the 2016 reality is that the big players will have to put together coalitions of a lot of small players. La Oficina operates in Aguascaliente, in the Federal District. As Tito has created a presence in Mexico City, it would be good to have an ally perched on his flank to worry him. Good but not essential, Ric thinks, and he hopes that his father doesn't give away too much for what might be a slight advantage.

Then again, the alliance is as much preventive as aggressive. Tito would like to consolidate his power in the District by securing his flank, and an agreement here with La Oficina would prevent that.

"I am painfully aware," Núñez says, "of the long-standing tensions between the Tapia wing of the organization and ourselves. Bitterness and mistrust remain. But we have apologized for what we now recognize as mistakes . . . injustices, really . . . in our past treatment of the Tapia brothers. You have suffered some of those injustices. But the past is the past, and all we can do now is sit down together and inquire how we can move forward."

"Cut the shit," Callarto says. "We need an outlet for our product. Can you help us or not?"

"Did Tito turn you down?"

"We haven't gone to him. Yet."

García says, "We thought we'd come to old friends first."

"What do we get in return?"

"Loyalty," Callarto says.

"Loyalty is a concept," Núñez says. "I was hoping for something more concrete."

"What do you want?"

Núñez smiles. "I don't bid against myself."

"If you need action against Jalisco in the District," Callarto says, "we'll jump in."

"With both feet?" Ric asks. "Into the deep end?"

"Within reason," Callarto says.

Within reason, Ric thinks. That translates as "as long as we think you're winning." They think my father is weak, they think they can take advantage of it. He says, "We don't need any fair-weather friends."

Núñez puts his hand up. "Ric—"

"No, these guys are playing us," Ric says. "They'll take our routes and leave us in the lurch when we need them."

He can see it in Callarto's eyes.

"I'm not asking for your loyalty," Ric says. "I'm demanding it. You get back on board or we'll crush you like the bugs you are."

"You're a pretty confident kid," Callarto says.

"I'm not a kid," Ric says.

"Maybe Tito will offer us a better deal."

"He will," Ric says. "But he can't deliver on it."

"He can deliver the Tecate crossing to us," Callarto says.

"We'll take it back," Ric says. "We're winning in Baja. We're winning in Acapulco, all of Guerrero. Mazatlán's a done deal. You pick the wrong side of this and we'll bury you."

"Let me ask you something," Callarto says. "Who the fuck are you to talk to us like that?"

"I'm the Godson," Ric says. "Now let me ask *you* something: How many men do *you* have outside?"

Callarto glares at him. Then says, "I *heard* you grew up. I guess I heard right. Okay, we'll—"

Blood splatters Ric's face.

Callarto's mouth is gone, a gaping maw.

He slides from his seat.

Ric lunges at his father and pulls him to the floor. Bullets zip over them, smack into the walls, shatter china. García snakes across the floor toward the back door. Blood pools beneath Callarto's head, his dead eyes stare at the ceiling.

Ric crawls to the window, risks a look out.

Four SUVs and a canopied flatbed truck form an arc in front of the house. All the vehicles are marked CJN. *Sicarios* shoot from behind car doors. His own men are scrambling for cover—some return fire from behind the trees, others from the cars, others lie on the ground, dead or wounded.

Ric pulls his Sig 9, shatters the window with the butt and fires out.

He lets loose five shots and then a round jams in the chamber. Pulling out, he leans his back against the wall and tries to clear it. Belinda has shown him how to do it a dozen times, but he can't seem to get it done as bullets come through the window.

"Fuck, fuck, fuck, fuck."

He has to get out of there.

Has to get his father out of there.

Ric looks back out the window. Three of his vehicles are there, but one is gone. Either they took off or they're coming around the back of the house. Some of his guys stand with their hands over their heads. CJN *sicarios* pull them toward the truck and shove them in.

Crawling back to the table, he grabs his father by the elbow. "Stay low."

They crawl out of the kitchen through the small living room, past the old sofa, a coffee table, an ancient television set.

Ric sees the back door.

Open where García went through.

He gets his dad into the doorway and looks out.

One *sicario* stands outside.

Ric makes himself breathe.

Makes himself get calm and then clears the jam in the pistol and jacks another round into the chamber.

He has to make the shot good. Aligning the sight center mass, Ric holds the gun in both hands and squeezes the trigger.

The *sicario* falls back, dropping his gun.

Three of Ric's people roar up in an SUV. The passenger door flies open. Ric pushes his father ahead, jams him into the passenger seat and then hops in himself.

The car takes off.

If there's no back road out, they're dead.

The car smashes through a fence into a pepper field.

They four-wheel through the deep dry dirt, down a gentle slope, and then hit the river. No choice but to try it. The driver sets it in the water and eases his way across. Up to another field until they hit a dirt road. Find their way onto the highway back to Culiacán.

Ric feels blood flow down his face.

Wonders if he was hit, then feels up to his hairline and realizes it's slivers of glass. Pulls down the sunshade, looks into the mirror and pulls them out.

"You okay?" he asks his father.

Núñez nods. "Who was it?"

"Tito."

"Now he has the nerve to hit us in Sinaloa," Núñez says.

Yeah, it's not good, Ric thinks.

Not good.

He blinks the blood out of his eyes.

"The *fuck*, man?" Iván asks over the phone. "In El Vergel? Tito has some fucking balls on him. Is your old man okay?"

"He's a little shaken up," Ric says, "but he's okay. We had two of our people killed and another four taken away. I don't know what's happened to them."

"Well, either they've changed uniforms," Iván says, "or you'll find them on the side of a road somewhere."

"I suppose," Ric says. "Iván, we need to sit down."

"Sounds serious."

"It is," Ric says. He tells Iván about his father wanting to meet with all the brothers, to clear the air.

"Clear the air about what?"

"Don't jerk me around right now."

"I don't know—"

"Your investment?" Ric says. "With Rafael Caro? You fucked us, Iván."

"Hey, not everyone is invited to every party."

"We have to be invited to this one," Ric says. "You and I had a deal—my father runs the cartel until he retires or passes—*then* you take the big chair. You can't go off on your own. We're still one thing."

Long sigh. "When do you want to sit down?"

"As soon as possible. Tomorrow, the day after . . ."

"Neutral territory, though," Iván says. "It can't look like I've been summoned to the principal's office."

"Yeah, whatever."

"And I want someone to guarantee my safety."

"You don't trust me now?"

"I don't trust your old man," Iván says. "He'll find a way to blame this attack on me."

"That's pretty paranoid."

"I'm paranoid?" Iván says. "He's paranoid. I want Caro. If he arranges the meeting, we'll be there."

Ric says he'll get back to him and goes upstairs to his father's room. Núñez is in bed but awake, sitting up. Ric sits at the foot of the bed. "How are you?"

"I'm fine," Núñez says. "I wouldn't be without you. You got us out of there."

Ric doesn't answer.

"What I'm saying is that I'm grateful."

"Okay."

"Did you speak with Iván?"

"I did."

"And?"

"He was evasive," Ric says. "Defensive. He knows he's in the wrong."

"He has to make it right," Núñez says. "We need to be in that syndicate, more than ever now. We need the leverage it would bring over Tito. Without that . . . All three brothers are coming, yes?"

"Yeah, but why do you—"

"They all need to listen," Núñez says. "They need to understand that while we gave them Baja, they are still part of the cartel, and I am the head of that cartel."

"Iván wants it on neutral ground," Ric says. "And he wants Caro there to guarantee his safety."

"Did he know about the Oficina meeting?" Núñez asks. "Did you tell him?"

"I might have said something."

"If you and I are both dead," Núñez says, "the cartel goes to Iván."

"I don't believe he'd do that."

"He froze us out of the syndicate," Núñez says.

"Caro froze us out."

"And Iván went along with it," Núñez says. "You know he wants to be boss, you know he's always resented us."

"He's my friend." But Ric feels sick. Because he realizes that he has doubts. You made the deal with Iván, he tells himself. You gave him the motive to kill us and not to wait. Iván Esparza isn't exactly known for his patience. "He wouldn't do that."

"If you say so," Núñez says. "But I'll know at the meeting. I'll know when I look him in the eyes. His father could mask his thoughts; the sons, not so much. Also, I want to talk to you about Belinda Vatos."

"What about her?"

"My old head of security, Manuel Aleja, is getting out of prison," Núñez says. "I want him to take his old job back. I'm sure Belinda will understand."

Ric's pretty sure she won't. Her entire identity is tied up with being the chief of security. "It's not fair."

"Neither is it fair that Aleja spent five years in prison for us," Núñez says. "He deserves to have his old position. He's earned it."

"So has she."

"She's young," Núñez says. "She'll have plenty of opportunities. Please thank her for her service. Give her some kind of bonus—some more territory in La Paz for drug sales or something."

Yeah, she's not going to be happy with a tip, Ric thinks. It'll only make her angrier. "She already has that."

"Then give her more."

"This is a mistake," Ric says. "We're in the middle of a war and she's one of our best fighters."

"She's too flamboyant," Núñez says. "Frankly, I think she's a little crazy, maybe even psychotic. Her killings are . . . grisly . . . macabre. We don't want to be associated with that kind of thing."

"We want, what, clean killings?"

"She's small potatoes," Núñez says. "You need to stay focused on the big picture. Right now that's the Park Tower syndicate. And New York. Ultimately, we'll beat Tito by gaining influence in Washington and by winning New York and the East Coast market."

Ric knows his father is right about New York. Their representatives are killing it there with the fentanyl-enhanced heroin. It's a page from Barrera's old playbook—boost production, raise quality, cut prices and drive the competition out of the market.

And the profits coming back from the New York hub are truly phenomenal, Ric thinks.

But his father is wrong about Belinda.

"First things first," Núñez says. "Let's set up the meeting with the Esparzas."

Ana Villanueva looks at the old man.

He looks harmless and bland. A long-sleeved blue checked shirt buttoned to the neck, pressed denim jeans, a blue baseball cap. A cheap watch with a black plastic band, a medallion of the Virgen de San Juan de Lagos around his neck.

Rafael Caro could be anyone's grandfather, she thinks.

"Ask me anything," he says. "I have nothing to hide."

"You spent twenty years in an American prison," Ana says, "for the torture-murder of an American agent."

"Thirty-one years ago I was a marijuana grower," Caro says. "But I didn't kill Hidalgo. I had nothing to do with it."

"So the governments of Mexico and the United States were misinformed."

"Badly misinformed," Caro says. "I spent twenty years in prison for growing marijuana. Now it is mostly legal."

He shrugs fatalistically.

"You knew Adán Barrera," Ana says.

"We were friends once," Caro says. "Then we were enemies. That was a long time ago. Why are you asking me questions about things that happened in another lifetime?"

"Okay, let's talk about now," Ana says. "There are rumors that you are supporting the old Tapia people in their war against the Sinaloa cartel. Is there any truth to that?"

Caro chuckles. "None. Why, after twenty years in prison, would I want more trouble? I don't want war, only peace. Peace. Besides, wars cost money. Look around you, do I look like I have money? I have nothing."

"Some people say you want power."

Caro says, "All I want is peace. I apologize to the family of Hidalgo, to the DEA and to the Mexican people for any mistakes I made."

"Have people been to see you?" Ana asks. "Seeking your support?"

"What people?"

"Ricardo Núñez," Ana says. "Iván Esparza . . . Tito Ascensión . . ."

"They have all been to see me," Caro says. "To pay their respects. I told them all the same thing I told you. I'm an old man. I'm done with the business. I want no part of this."

"And that was all right with them?"

"Yes," Caro says. "They have their lives, I have mine."

Ana is quiet for a moment.

Caro sits in perfect stillness.

Serene as a Buddha.

Then Ana says, "Tristeza."

Caro shakes his head. "A shame what happened to those young people. A tragedy."

"Do you know anything about it?"

"Only what I read in the newspapers," Caro says. "What you people write."

Ana takes a risk. "Would you like to know what I've heard?"

"If you'd like to tell me."

"I heard," Ana says, "that there was heroin on that bus. Heroin that Damien Tapia stole from Ricardo Núñez."

"Oh."

"And I've heard that Damien Tapia has been to see you," Ana says.

The slightest stir. The slightest edge to the eyes. "I don't know the Young Wolf."

"But Eddie Ruiz does," Ana says. "And you know him."

"No, I don't think so."

"His cell was right above yours at Florence."

"Is that right?"

"Help me out here, Señor Caro," Ana says. "I don't think Palomas could have made the decision to have those kids killed all on her own. Certainly, the Rentería brothers didn't have the authority. So who gave the order, do you think?"

"As I told you, I know nothing about it." He lifts his arm and looks at his watch.

"Do you have an appointment?" Ana asks.

"My urologist," Caro says. "Don't get old—it's a mistake."

He stands up slowly. The interview is over.

"Thank you for seeing me," Ana says.

"Thank you," Caro says. "I just want people to know the truth. Please write the truth, young lady."

"I will."

Caro has no doubt of that.

The phone rings.

It's Ricardo Núñez.

The meeting is set deep in the mountains, far to the north of Culiacán, at an old camp along a curve of the Humaya River.

Caro's caution is appropriate, Ric thinks—the entire leadership of the Sinaloa cartel will be gathered in the same place at the same time. A single strike from Tito, Elena or Damien could destroy them. But the trip is arduous, a jarring drive up a bumpy single-lane road. Ric notices his father wince when the car bounces.

Ric knows that the meeting has to go well.

So much weighs on it.

They have to reestablish unity with the Esparzas. Tito is too strong to fight if they're at all fractured, if there's mistrust between them. Besides, Ric misses his friendship with Iván, hates the tension that's come over them lately.

But the Núñez wing has to be allowed into the syndicate. Without that, they become second-rate players, and his father has made it clear that is unacceptable for Adán Barrera's rightful heirs.

So Ric hopes that Iván is in a conciliatory mood and that Caro will be reasonable.

And that his father is on his game.

He wasn't in the meeting with the Oficina people, Ric thinks, and neither Iván or Caro will tolerate me stepping into the lead position in my father's place.

The convoy pulls off onto an even smaller, bumpier road, through a thick stand of trees and then onto a low bridge across the river to the eastern bank. The dirt track parallels the river for a couple of wooded miles, then veers into the clearing where the meeting will be held. The ground is open, sloping down to the river; on the other side are thick brush and trees, beyond that, steep wooded mountains.

The Sierra Madre Occidental—prime opium country.

Caro set strict rules—three vehicles per party, a total of ten armed guards for each group. Ric sees that they've arrived first.

Núñez looks at his watch.

Ric's father reveres promptness.

And they're sitting out in the open. An ambush from the trees could annihilate them in an instant.

Ric is a city boy; the quiet makes him uneasy.

Then he hears engines, the sound of vehicles coming up the road toward them. Leaning out the window, he sees the lead car and recognizes one of Iván's people behind the wheel. The Esparza boys will be in the second car, with a trailing vehicle behind.

There's a gap and then three more SUVs.

That will be Caro, Ric thinks.

The lead Esparza car comes into the clearing.

Now Ric sees Iván in the second car, his brothers in the back seat behind him. It's odd meeting like this, Ric thinks; we should be just sitting down over a beer. Iván's bodyguards get out of the lead car.

Rifle shots come from the trees, cutting the bodyguards down.

Then the fire shifts to Iván's car.

It rattles like a junkie.

Iván tries to pull his gun but he's hit and spins in his seat.

Oviedo's head snaps back.

Alfredo drops.

Their car goes madly into reverse, slams into the car behind it. *Sicarios* pile out of that car, shooting toward the trees, but they are quickly cut down.

Caro's cars reverse, speeding backward up the road.

Iván's car lurches forward, disengaging, then turns and races away. Ric sees blood streaming from the driver's arm like a red pennant. Iván slumps forward against the dashboard, his head bouncing back and forth like a broken doll's.

The shooting stops.

Ric whirls on his father. "What did you do?! What did you do?!"

"What you wouldn't," Núñez says.

It was Iván all the time, Núñez explains on the endless drive to a house out in the country south of Culiacán. Iván who set up the Candlemas attempt on his life, Iván who tipped Tito to the Oficina meeting.

"I don't believe that," Ric says.

"Which is why I had to act without telling you," Núñez says.

"Caro is going to go crazy," Ric says. "He'll keep us out of the syndicate, ostracize us, maybe even move against us."

"He will at first," Núñez says. "But he's a practical man. With the Esparzas dead, he has to come to us. He has nowhere else to go."

"Elena. Tito."

"At the end of the day Caro's a Sinaloan," Núñez says. "He won't go with an outsider over his own people. When I explain to him that Iván tried to have us killed, he'll come around. I'm sorry, I know you thought Iván was your friend."

"He was."

"He was using you," Núñez says. "Ric, you would never become *el patrón* with Iván alive. He would never have allowed it."

"I don't care about that. I never wanted it."

"It's your legacy. Your godfather wanted it for you."

"You killed my friend!"

"And you know the truth," Núñez says. "When you're ready to admit it to yourself, you'll thank me."

Thank you? Ric thinks.

You've destroyed us.

You've killed us.

Iván isn't dead.

Neither is Oviedo or Alfredo.

They're wounded, they're shot up, but they're alive. Their driver made it to a side road, up to a village where the people are loyal to the Esparzas and gave them shelter. Sent for a doctor who patched them up.

This is the story that reached Caro.

That Ricardo Núñez swung for the fences and missed.

Exactly as Caro knew he would.

There's an old joke about prison:

A white-collar criminal—and that's what Núñez is, still just a lawyer at heart, not a real narco—is confronted by his enormous *mayate* cellmate, who says, "We have a game here. We play house. Now, do you want to be the husband or the wife?"

The white-collar criminal thinks through the choices, both of them bad but one of them worse, and says, "I'll be the husband." The *mayate* nods and says, "Okay, husband—now get down on your knees and suck your wife's cock."

This is the position Caro put Núñez in. Whichever choice he made, he'd lose. If he let Iván Esparza cut him out of the syndicate, he lost. If he took violent action against Iván, he lost. Now Caro can go to Núñez's political friends and say, "Look, he's out of control. I guaranteed everyone's safety and he violated that. We can't trust him."

It was a no-lose scenario for Caro—if the Esparzas prevailed, he would ally with them, if Núñez won, he'd make do with the lawyer. Either way, half of the potential rivals in the Sinaloa cartel would be eliminated.

And Núñez had managed to procure the worst possible outcome—he had violated the security agreement but not killed the Esparzas. Now his enemies are still in place and they hold the moral high ground.

Núñez has dug himself into a deep hole.

Now all that's left is to shovel dirt on him.

There's only one loose thread hanging.

Tristeza.

That bitch reporter knows something. Even if she doesn't, even if she's just fishing, throwing lines in the water to see if he'd bite, she can't be allowed to spew her lies in the newspapers.

She especially can't be allowed to tell the truth.

Caro puts out the order.

The indictment was sealed, but it was leaked to Núñez.

Ric reads it.

IN THE UNITED STATES DISTRICT COURT FOR THE
EASTERN DISTRICT OF VIRGINIA—Alexandria Division—
UNITED STATES OF AMERICA
v.
RICARDO NÚÑEZ
Also known as "El Abogado"
Count 1: 21 U.S.C. 959, 960, 963
(conspiracy to distribute five kilograms or more of cocaine for
    importation into the United States).
Count 2: U.S.C. Code 952
(conspiracy to distribute five kilograms or more of heroin for
    importation into the United States).
Count 3: 18 U.S.C. 1956(h) 3238
(conspiracy to commit money laundering).

"The DEA will be coming after me now," Núñez says.

"The government will protect us," Ric says.

"We might have lost our friends in the government," Núñez says. "In any case, we can't take the chance. I'm going into the wind. I suggest you take your family and do the same."

"Am I indicted?"

"I don't know," Núñez says. "I haven't seen an indictment—but that doesn't mean it doesn't exist. Go. Go now. If we've lost our friends in the government, it could mean that the police, the army, maybe the marines, are coming. If you're captured and extradited, that would be the end. The thing now is to survive until we can straighten this out."

Straighten this out? Ric asks himself. How the fuck are we going to "straighten this out"?! It's been ten days since the ambush on the Humaya, and the world seems to be turning against them.

Allies won't take calls. Cops, prosecutors, politicians and reporters who have taken our money, attended our parties, shown up dutifully at weddings, baptisms and funerals don't know our names anymore.

Cell leaders in Sinaloa, *sicarios* in Baja, growers in Durango and Guerrero have openly announced their allegiance to the Esparzas. Others haven't been so brazen, but they're wavering under intense pressure.

Just two days ago, a thirty-truck convoy full of Esparza gunmen rolled into a Núñez-controlled town, kidnapped four of our people and burned buildings and vehicles. Announced that it was a warning for all towns and villages that supported the "criminal Núñez faction."

But we haven't responded, Ric thinks, haven't retaliated, haven't shown the strength that could reassure our people. Part of the reason is that Núñez has been in a funk, almost a depression, keeping to his room. The other reason is that the gunmen we'd use to carry out a retaliation aren't answering their phones.

And Iván has been all over social media—Twitter, Snapchat, all of it—denouncing the "chickenshit, sneaky ambush." He's attacked Ric personally—"My *cuate*, my good friend, my old pal Mini-Ric tried to kill me. While he was talking peace and brotherhood out of one side of his mouth, the little bitch was ordering my murder with the other. He's just like his old man—the douche doesn't fall far from the bag."

He added an audio clip from Tupac:

Who shot me? But you punks didn't finish
Now you're going to face the wrath of the menace . . .

Damien weighed in—"I guess Barrera's godson takes his legacy seriously. He betrays his best friends just like his godfather did."

There've been thousands of posts responding, almost all of them supporting the Esparzas and banging on the Núñezes.

Iván's now the righteous victim.

We're the turncoats, the sleazy cowards, Ric thinks.

Iván is cool, I'm a bitch.

His father doesn't get it, but Ric takes it seriously, knows that losing the social media war could mean losing the actual war.

And now we're at war with Iván.

Not just tensions, a shooting war.

We're at war with Iván, we're at war with Elena, we're at war with Damien, we're at war with Tito. We can't go to Caro to broker peace. As far as joining the syndicate is concerned, well, forget that.

And now the Americans are coming after us.

"We still have resources," Núñez is saying, "we still have friends and allies. It's a matter of keeping our heads down for a while until we can consolidate our support."

Okay, Ric thinks.

Take your family and go.

Yeah, except his family doesn't want to go.

"I'm not indicted," Karin says when Ric goes home and tells her to pack. "There are no charges against *me*. *I* didn't try to kill Iván. Why should *I* go on the run?"

"To be with your husband?"

"How can you hide with a wife and kid in tow?" Karin asks. "You can't move quickly, you can't move fast. You'd be worried about protecting us."

"You'd just be more comfortable at home."

"Of course I would," she says. "So would your daughter."

"*Así es.*"

"Don't put this on me," Karin says. "You made your choices."

"You didn't mind the money, did you?" Ric asks. "You took the houses, the cars, the jewelry, the meals, the suites, the prestige . . ."

"Are you done?"

"Oh, yeah," Ric says. "I'm done."

He throws a few things in a bag and takes off.

The Young Wolf isn't going to be an old wolf.

Chained to a chair set on a concrete floor in some basement, he's been around the life long enough to know there's only one way this ends.

He feels stupid.

First for coming to Baja, thinking he could stage a daring raid on the enemy's home turf. Then for meeting this hot chick, going home with her, accepting a drink. Next thing he knows he wakes up in this chair.

No, I shouldn't have come here, he thinks.

Because I'm never leaving.

Now the hot chick comes in and smiles down on him.

"You're really cute, Damien, you know that?" she says. "It's too bad what I have to do to you. I'm with Sinaloa, and they said I have to hurt you, really bad, for a long time."

Now he knows who she is.

He's heard about La Fósfora.

She's psycho.

"You're still groggy," she says, "so we have to wait for the dope to wear off. I mean the point is that it hurts, right? Sorry, it's just, you know, my job."

Ric runs to La Paz.

Belinda doesn't tell him who she has down in the basement.

He'd object.

"I'm going off the radar for a while," Ric says. He tells her about the indictment, about the pressure on them since the Esparza ambush.

"I'll set up security for you," Belinda says.

"About that . . ."

"What?"

"My father wants his old guy back, Aleja."

"Are you fucking kidding me right now?" she asks.

"We can give you more territory."

"You're going to give me what I can just take?" she asks. "La Paz is mine because it's mine."

"Don't be this way."

"Fuck you."

"Look, I have to go."

"Go."

Damien watches the girl come back down the stairs.

Tries to keep his shit together because he knows it's going to start now. He's heard the stories about her—acid baths, chopping off people's arms . . . He wants to go out like a man, not disgrace his name, but he's scared, really scared.

He just wants his mother.

La Fósfora smiles down at him again.

"It's your lucky day, Young Wolf," she says. "I just got off the phone with Tito Ascensión."

"I thought you were with Sinaloa."

"I thought so, too," she says. "I guess we were both wrong. Anyway, you get a pass, Damien. You can thank your uncle Tito."

She unshackles him.

He gets the fuck out of La Paz.

So does Ric.

He runs.

The Owl blinks.

Legendary editor Óscar Herrera, the dean of Mexican newspapermen, sits with his stiff leg propped up on his desk at *El Periódico*. The Barreras tried to kill him years ago but didn't finish the job. Three bullets in his leg and hip left him with a limp and a cane.

Now he stares at Ana and blinks.

Ana doesn't blink. She's worked for Óscar for coming on twenty years and she knows the secret to pitching him a story is to show no doubt or hesitation. He got his nickname because he sees everything, in light or in darkness.

So she doesn't back down when he says, "Your story is pure conjecture."

"Nothing is pure," Ana says. "And it's not a story yet. That's why I want the time to develop it."

"You were just supposed to interview Caro."

"I did," Ana says. "Print it."

"You went fishing on Tristeza," Óscar says, "and came up with an empty hook."

"He was lying," Ana says. "I could see it in his eyes."

"Certainly you don't expect me to print a story based on your psychic abilities," Óscar says.

"No, I expect you to let me go out and get the evidence," Ana says. "The Tristeza story is bullshit."

A small-town mayor orders narcos to murder forty-nine students over a protest? she thinks. Doesn't pass the smell test. The "rival gang" theory stinks, too. Guerreros Unidos are stone-cold narcos, but they're not the Zetas. They wouldn't pull the missing forty-three kids—boys and *girls*—off a bus and kill them because they thought a few of them might be aligned with Los Rojos.

It's classic government cover-up—put out competing, contradictory explanations to obfuscate the real story.

Which, Ana is convinced, is about heroin.

She's plumbed all her sources on this, interviewed survivors, other students, teachers. She's talked to city cops, state cops, *federales* and soldiers, met secretly with narcos from GU, Los Rojos, Sinaloa and the old Tapia group.

No one has the whole story, but start to put their pieces together and a picture starts to emerge:

Damien Tapia stole heroin from Ricardo Núñez.

GU and the Rentería brothers put the heroin on the buses they've been using to move drugs out of Guerrero.

The students unluckily hijacked one of the heroin-laden buses.

Palomas was hooked up with GU.

She gave the orders—get the dope back and kill the students.

That's where it falls apart, Ana thinks. If the recovery of the heroin was the motive for stopping the buses, why not just take the drugs back? Why kill all those kids? Why take them away to shoot them and burn their bodies? Why do the police take the kids to three police stations before turning them over to GU?

Because it was an evolving situation, Ana thinks. Because the cops were getting different orders as events ensued. And the kids were killed, she thinks, not to get the heroin back, but to protect the transportation system. The Renterías, Palomas and GU didn't want Núñez to find out they were moving his stolen heroin for Damien Tapia.

Maybe, she thinks.

That was part of it.

Or maybe it was to protect the people behind the transportation system.

Nothing has come out about any further investigation into the mass murder. Damien Tapia is a relatively small player, only one step up from the Rentería brothers. He doesn't have serious political influence.

So who does?

Who's covering it up?

It's not Núñez—he has the political weight, but no motive for covering up Tristeza. For the same reason, it isn't Iván Esparza or Elena Sánchez. And Tito Ascensión has nothing to do with it.

The rumor among the old Tapia people is that Damien was moving his heroin up to Eddie Ruiz. Even if it's true, it's a dead end, because Ruiz has no political influence in Mexico and no sway with anyone who matters here.

Except Eddie was in prison with Rafael Caro.

The only reaction she got from Caro during their entire interview was when she mentioned Eddie. And the old man, who remembers everything, feigned that he didn't even know that Eddie was in the cell above him.

Is that what they thought they were protecting by killing the students? The connection to Caro?

She lays the theory out to Óscar.

"A man who's been in solitary confinement for twenty years?" Óscar asks.

"He's an icon."

"*I'm* an icon," Óscar says, "and I have no power whatsoever. Caro's ancient history, he has no organization behind him."

"Maybe that's the point," Ana says. "He's neutral, he can provide good offices. Rumor has it that he negotiated the release of the Esparza brothers."

"Being an éminence grise is not equivalent to political influence."

No, Ana thinks, but money is.

Money and politics are rice and beans.

And yesterday she got a call from Victoria Mora, Pablo's widow, now a financial reporter for *El Nacional*. Victoria is a conservative, a no-nonsense, by-the-numbers business analyst who relayed a story that she didn't want to investigate herself. She said that there's talk in banking circles about HBMX forming a syndicate to lend $300 million to an American real estate concern.

"Why are you calling *me*?" Ana asked.

Victoria has never particularly liked Ana. Not only because she's a flaming leftie, but also because she slept with her late husband, albeit after they were divorced.

"You know," Victoria said, stiff and cold as ever.

"No, I don't."

"This bank is notorious for laundering drug money," Victoria said. "León Echeverría runs in narco circles."

"Is there a reason you're not doing the story yourself?" Ana asked, her radar screens up.

"There are a hundred reasons," Victoria said. "I rely on these bankers and certain government officials to do my job. If I were to come out with this, or even look into it . . ."

"They'd cut you off."

"I'd be ostracized."

"So why are you . . ."

"Ana," Victoria said, "it's bad. I'm actually, well, dating a man from HBMX and he's very upset. He heard a name of someone who's involved . . ."

"What name?" Ana asked, her stomach sinking.

"Rafael Caro," Victoria said. "What my friend heard was that Echeverría went to Caro to help put narco investors together because he can talk to all of them. My friend is concerned that this could expose HBMX to investigation from the DEA, Interpol . . . If there were to be an article, HBMX might back out before it's too late."

"Well, thank you for coming to me, Victoria."

"Pablo always said you were the best."

"I miss him," Ana says. "How is Mateo?"

Pablo's little boy, who must be what now, twelve?

Mateo was with Ana when Pablo was murdered.

"He's fine, thanks for asking," Victoria said. "Growing like a weed."

"I'd love to see him."

"Absolutely," Victoria said. "We don't get back to Juárez very often, but when we do, I'll be sure to look you up."

Ana knows it will never happen.

And now she doesn't share Victoria's lead with Óscar. It's premature. He would only quiz her about sources and then tell her to work one story at a time. But it might be one story, Ana thinks.

It might be the same story.

If the Tristeza students were murdered to protect the Caro connection, that connection might go a lot farther up the ladder.

If Caro is using heroin money to invest with big banks . . .

And big banks and the government are the same . . .

It would explain why the government is covering up the real story of Tristeza.

"Let me see if Palomas will talk to me," she says. "And let me go see if I can get an interview with Damien Tapia."

"Ana . . ."

"What?"

"It's too dangerous," Óscar says.

She sees the sorrow in his eyes. He's already lost two reporters—Pablo and the photographer Giorgio. For all his curmudgeonly veneer, El Búho is softhearted—he still aches for those losses. And the danger is real: more than 150 Mexican reporters have been murdered covering the drug wars. At the height of the violence, Óscar had even forbidden them from covering the drug situation.

Ana had responded to the prohibition by creating an anonymous blog to report the narco news.

The Zetas put out an order to shut it down.

Poor Pablo, poor sweet Pablo, had figured out it was her and took the responsibility. Sent her across the border with Mateo and wrote a final blog before they found him, tortured him, cut him to pieces and scattered his parts around the Plaza del Periodista.

By the statue of a newsboy.

It was my fault, Ana thinks.

Pablo paid for my arrogance.

She quit after that. Always a social drinker, she became an *anti*social drinker, pouring alcohol on her guilt and grief, hiding from everyone, especially herself. Marisol wouldn't let her disappear, though, bullied her into coming to live with her in the little town, cajoling her to go work in the clinic.

Little by little, her life came back.

But it was Tristeza that woke her from her sleep, kindled a fire of outrage that she thought had long since expired to cold ash. She had once been a respected, even feared, journalist; it was what she knew how to do.

Now she's doing it again.

If Óscar will let her.

When she first came back, he put her on "safe" stories, "women's" stories—charity benefits, arts assignments, human interest angles that were far away from the crime, narco and political beat that she'd inhabited. She was an investigative journalist but he wouldn't let her investigate anything deeper than a society snub (such as any existed in a backwater like Juárez) or a leaking sewer pipe.

She investigated Tristeza on her own time and her own money.

And still will, if Óscar won't authorize it.

Forty-nine dead kids.

Forty-nine grieving families.

And everyone seems to have forgotten.

Just another tragedy in Mexico.

"We're journalists," Ana says. "If we're not going to cover the important stories, why do we even exist?"

"It was always my conceit," Óscar says, "that my reporters would come to *my* funeral and say embarrassingly laudatory things about me. Not the other way around."

Óscar's eulogy for Pablo was beautiful.

Ana read it in the paper. She hadn't been able to make herself attend the funeral. She stayed home, drank and cried.

Ana says, "Óscar, you know this is what we should be doing."

Óscar closes his eyes, as if consulting something in the past. Then he opens them, blinks, and says, "Be careful."

Ana calls the Bureau of Prisons and gets paperwork to request an interview with Palomas.

Then she gets on the phone to Art Keller.

"Let's play a game," she says. "I tell you the first part of a story and you finish it for me."

Ana runs down her theory and then tells him about the HBMX deal and its possible connection to Rafael Caro. She guesses Keller already knows about this, and then she says, "Here's where *you* start playing. Who is the HBMX loan going to? Who is the 'real estate concern'?"

"Even if I knew that," Keller says, "I couldn't tell you."

"Couldn't or wouldn't?"

"They're the same thing," Keller says.

"But you know."

"I can't confirm or deny—"

"Oh, stop, Arturo," Ana says. "This is on deep background. You know I'd never reveal the identity of a source."

"That's not the point," Keller says. "I wish you'd drop this, Ana."

"In your capacity as a government official," Ana says, "or a friend?"

"A friend."

"If you're my friend, help me."

"I'm trying," Keller says. "Look, why don't you come to the United States and work on your story. If you think it has an American element . . ."

"I will," Ana says. "But I have lines of inquiry here first."

"Who gave you Caro's name?" Keller asks.

"Oh, you'll ask questions but not answer them? I just told you that I don't reveal sources." But now she knows she's onto something. Questions often reveal as much as answers, and Keller just revealed that Caro is a person of interest. She decides to push it. "Do *you* think Caro is connected to Tapia, Art? Do *you* think he's involved with HBMX?"

"Come up here," Keller says.

That's a yes, Ana thinks. "How's Mari?"

"Busy being Mari," Keller says. "Ana, be careful, huh?"

"I will."

The prison official gets Ana's request and calls Tito.

Tito calls Caro.

Caro tells him what needs to happen and makes his own request.

Tito relays it to his people.

Ana goes home.

A one-bedroom apartment on Bosques Amazonas in Las Misiones.

A quiet place in a quiet neighborhood.

Some nights it doesn't occur to Ana to drink, other nights it seems as if there's no other option. She supposes she's what they call a "functioning alcoholic," although she's functioning better than she did a year or so ago.

But some nights the ghosts visit and they arrive demanding libation.

This is one of those nights.

Ana has a bottle of vodka shoved in a kitchen cabinet for ghost nights; now she takes it out, sits down at the table and pours some into a squat water glass. She's not intending to get drunk, just sodden, just a little numb to take the edge off.

Some people find memories comforting. They remember the good times with departed loved ones and it makes them feel better. The good-time memories make Ana feel worse. It's the contrast, she guesses, the fact that she misses the happy-drunken nights, the laughs, the songs, the arguments, the work. The good memories are painful, sharp reminders of things she'll never have again.

Sweet, shaggy, unshaven, overweight Pablo.

Drunken, undisciplined, underperforming, wonderful Pablo, dizzy with love for his child, for (hopelessly) his ex-wife, for his beloved, shattered city. Pablo wasn't so much a Mexican as he was a Juarense; his world began and ended within the limits of the border town, on the edge of both Mexico and the United States, its location simultaneously its reason for being and the reason for its destruction. Pablo loved every dirty, tawdry inch and resented every improvement the way an old girlfriend resents the newer, younger, prettier version.

He loved Juárez for its flaws, not in spite of them, just as Ana loved him for his shortcomings—his stained, wrinkled sport coats, his stubble as perpetual as his hangover, his self-destructive, career-stunting predilection for the weird, offbeat, quirky stories that relegated him to the back pages of the paper and the lower rungs of the salary ladder.

Pablo was always broke, always cadging money and drinks, always struggling to pay child support; he ate fast food in his car, the floor of the old vehicle strewn with paper wrappers and cardboard cups. Now Ana is crying.

Pathetically crying into my booze, she thinks.

The first drink calms.

The second drink numbs.

The third makes you question yourself.

Why am I really doing this? she wonders. Because I believe that the truth is important, or that some good will come out of it? Because I believe those kids should get justice, the justice that Pablo, Giorgio, Jimena and thousands of others didn't get? Why do I think anything will happen, even if I find the truth?

What difference does the truth make?

We all know it, anyway.

The truth of the Tristeza Massacre comes down to just more details in a long story. What difference do they make?

Same story, different facts.

Ana knows she should eat, gets a frozen dinner—chicken and rice—out of the freezer and sticks it in the microwave. She's eating, without taste or appetite, when her phone rings. She wouldn't answer but sees that it's Marisol. "Hello?"

"Just calling to say hello, catch up."

"Arturo told you he was worried."

When Marisol doesn't answer, Ana says, "And yes, I'm a little drunk. One of *those* nights."

"Ana, why don't you come up for a visit?"

"Don't patronize me," Ana says. "Or would that be 'matronize'?"

"You're witty when you're in your cups."

"Famous for it," Ana says. "Pablo used to say I was nicer when I was a little drunk."

"So you'll come?"

Relentless Marisol, Ana thinks. Always so sure that she knows what's right and so relentless about making it happen. Self-assured, self-righteous Marisol—martyr and secular saint, perfect wife, perfect hostess, perfect pain in the ass. "When I've finished my work. Very busy right now, Mari."

"Yes, Art said you were working on a story."

"I think we're working on the same story," Ana says. "We're competitors. Your husband is trying to scoop me."

"Hardly. Ana—"

"'Ana, be careful. Ana, don't drink so much. Ana, take your vitamins.'"

"Why don't I call you tomorrow?" Marisol asks.

"When I'm sober, you mean."

"All right, yes."

Ana asks, "Do you remember when we were happy, Mari?"

"I'm happy now."

"Goody for you."

"I'm sorry, that was cruel," Marisol says. "Yes, I remember . . . before all the killing started. We shouted poetry into the night . . ."

"'We have to laugh,'" Ana quotes. "'Because laughter, we already know, is the first evidence of freedom.'"

"Castellanos," Marisol says. "'I am the daughter of myself. My dream was born. My dream sustains me.'"

"'Death will be the proof that we lived.'"

"Come visit me," Marisol says. "I have no one to quote poetry with."

"Soon."

Ana clicks off and goes back to dinner, such as it is. Debates whether to have another drink, but she already knows who the winner of that argument is. She takes her next vodka into the bathroom and gets into the shower, stepping out of the spray to sip the drink.

Dries off and drops into bed.

When Ana wakes up, the bottle is by the side of the bed.

Her head is splitting, she feels like shit. She brushes her teeth, rinses her mouth out with Listerine and squeezes Visine into her bloodshot eyes. A shower seems like too much effort, so she throws on some clothes—a blouse, sweater, jeans—puts on her shoes and heads out to go to work.

They take her in the driveway.

She sees the two men in front of her but not the two behind, who scoop her feet from under her and lift her as the other two grab her shoulders. One puts his hand over her mouth and they shove her in the back of the van before she really knows what's happened.

A very professional snatch job.

A rag is stuffed in her mouth, a hood pulled over her head, plastic ties are fastened on her wrists, twisted behind her back.

Hands push her to the floor of the van, feet keep her pressed down.

Ana is terrified.

She tries to keep her head, tries to estimate the minutes that she's in the van before it stops, tries to listen to sounds that might give her a clue where she is. She's written about kidnappings, about abductions, she's interviewed police, knows what she's supposed to do.

Can't.

It's all she can do to breathe.

The van stops.

She hears the door slide open. Hands grab her, lift her.

Hands on her elbows walk her inside.

Slam her ungently onto a chair. Cuff her to the chair legs.

"Tell us what you know," a man's voice says.

"About what?"

The slap knocks her head to the side, hurts her neck, makes her ears ring. She's never been hit before, it's shockingly painful.

"Tristeza," the man says. "Tell us the story you believe."

She tells him.

Runs down her whole theory—

Núñez's heroin.

Damien's theft.

Heroin on the bus.

Students killed to protect the information.

Killed to protect—

"Who?" the man asks.

"I don't know."

A closed fist this time. She's a small woman, slight. The chair falls over with her. Her head hits the concrete floor. Kicks come into her ankles, her legs, her hips, her stomach. They hurt. Her face is on fire, her cheekbone broken.

The man asks, "Guess. Who do you think?"

"Damien Tapia," Ana says, crying. "Eddie Ruiz."

"Who else?"

"Rafael Caro?"

Most people think they'd resist. That they'd suffer torture, hold out.

Most people are wrong.

The body won't allow it. The body overrules the mind, the soul.

Ana tells him.

Gives up every name.

Survivors, other students, teachers. City cops, state cops, *federales*, soldiers, narcos from GU, Los Rojos, Sinaloa, the old Tapia group, Jalisco. Gives them anything and anyone so they won't start again.

Orwell was right.

"Do it to Julia."

It does her no good.

"HBMX," the man says. "What do you know about that? What were you going to write?"

"Caro. Collecting drug money for a loan. American. Real estate."

"What American?"

She sobs. "I don't know."

"Tell me and this can stop."

"I don't know. I swear."

"Who told you about the loan?"

She gives him Victoria's name.

"Who else?"

"That's all."

"Who have you told this to?"

"No one. Nobody. I swear, I swear, please . . ."

"I believe you." The man asks, "Are you religious? Do you believe in God?"

"No."

"Then you don't want to pray."

"No."

"Face the wall. This won't hurt."

Ana twists her body to face the wall.

"My dream was born. My dream sustains me."

The man shoots her in the back of the head.

Death will be the proof that she lived.

Keller hears Marisol scream.

He runs upstairs.

She's clutching a phone. Her eyes are wide. She looks as if she might fall. He grabs her and holds her up, she wraps her arms around him.

"They killed her," Marisol says. "They killed Ana."

Her body was found in a roadside ditch in Anapra, just over the border. She'd been tortured.

Lessons must be taught.

Examples set.

Dedos—informers—who talk to the police, the military, the press must be silenced but first punished.

In a way that teaches lessons, sets examples so the rest aren't tempted to talk out of turn.

Manuel Ceresco sits tied to a chair in the countryside outside Guadalajara. Sticks of dynamite are strapped to his chest. Thirty yards away, his twelve-year-old son, also Manuel, is also tied to a chair with sticks of dynamite stacked beneath it.

Tito knows that killing Manuel Sr.—boss of a small cell who spoke with the woman reporter—would scare people but not terrify them.

This story will get out and people will be terrified.

He shouts to Manuel, "See what you did with your big mouth?! See what you did to your own son?!"

"No! Please!"

Manuel Sr. begs Tito to spare his son. "Do what you want with me, but don't hurt my boy. He's innocent, he's done nothing." When he sees it's futile, he begs for them to kill him first. But one of Tito's men walks behind Manuel Sr., and with his thumbs and forefingers holds his eyes open. "Watch."

The boy yells, "Papi!"

Tito gives the signal.

Another one of his men pushes the plunger.

The boy explodes.

Tito's guys laugh. It's funny. Like a cartoon.

Manuel Sr. screams and yells. Tito's man walks away from him. When he's far enough, Tito gives the signal again.

Manuel Sr. explodes.

More laughter.

As kids they blew up frogs with M-80s.

Now they can blow up people.

The video clip is out on social media within an hour.

It goes viral.

Victoria Mora leaves her house in the Roma neighborhood of Mexico City. She gets into her BMW and sets her briefcase down on the passenger seat. She's reaching over to pull down the seat belt when the truck roars up behind her, trapping her car in the driveway.

A man gets out of the truck, walks up beside the BMW on the driver's side, and rakes it with AR-15 fire.

The bullets chop Victoria to pieces.

The man gets back in the truck and it drives off.

A woman out walking her dog screams.

The girl is ten years old.

Her father, an accountant who spoke with Ana, is handcuffed to a heating pipe in the warehouse. A man holds his head and makes him watch while seven of Tito's men take turns on his little girl.

When they're finished, they cut her throat.

They let her father absorb this for twenty minutes, then they take baseball bats and beat him to death.

Óscar Herrera is the last one in the office of *El Periódico*.

He sent everyone else home.

Now he writes his last article, announcing that the paper will cease publication after this issue. He cannot allow any more reporters to be murdered. Óscar finishes the column, gets up, grabs his cane and shuts off the lights.

Keller knows it was Caro.

Who ordered Ana's murder.

Keller and Marisol flew to El Paso and then drove over to Juárez—both American and Mexican officials going nuts that the head of the DEA was coming without the proper security preparation.

"I'm going," Keller said.

In that tone that let people know not to argue with him.

Federales, Chihuahua state police and Juárez city cops met them at the

crossing and insisted that they leave their rental car and get in the motor-
cade. Keller assented and Marisol didn't care at all.

Her heart was broken.

And her mind set on justice.

"Who did this?" she'd asked Keller when the shock had worn off a little.

"We don't know," Keller said. "She was digging into the Tristeza matter.
She interviewed Rafael Caro."

"Is there a connection?"

"Look, Mari . . ."

He told her about the syndicate and the loan to Terra, and then that Ana
had told him about an anonymous source that connected it all to Caro.

Mari isn't stupid. She got it right away. "Victoria Mora."

Killed just hours after Ana. And now Mateo is an orphan, both parents
murdered by the cartels.

"Probably," Keller said. He didn't add the obvious, that Ana had given her
torturers Victoria's name.

Ana's funeral was brutal.

Pathetic in the true sense of the word.

The autumn north wind swirled dust and garbage around their ankles
at the Panteón del Tepeyac cemetery. The gathering was small: a couple of
reporters, a few people who had come down from Valverde, and it occurred
to Keller that many of the people who would otherwise have been there—
journalists and activists—were already in graves.

Giorgio would have been there, but Giorgio was dead.

Jimena would have been there, but Jimena was dead.

Pablo would have been there, but Pablo was dead.

Óscar Herrera was there.

Leaning on his cane, looking old and frail, as if the *norteño* might blow
him away. He said little, only brief muttered greetings, and declined to speak,
just shaking his head, when the opportunity arose to eulogize Ana.

Marisol stood and recited from one of Ana's favorite poets, Pita Amor—

*"I'm vain, a tyrant, blasphemous, prideful, haughty, ungrateful, disdainful /
But I keep the complexion of a rose."*

Marisol broke down, then recovered. "And I say, in the words of Susana
Chávez Castillo—also a daughter of Juárez, also murdered in this city for her
social activism in the cause of murdered women—'Not one more.'"

A priest said some words.

A guitarist sang "Guantanamera."

The coffin was lowered into the ground.

That was it.

There was a little talk about gathering somewhere afterward to share memories but it didn't come together. The police escorted Keller and Marisol back to the border and they drove to the airport.

Now Keller watches the president-elect on television.

"We must end the illegal flow of drugs, cash, guns and people across the border that is fueling the crisis, end sanctuary cities that provide a haven for drug traffickers, and put the cartels out of business once and for all."

Except, Keller thinks, you're in business *with* them.

"I'm transferring you," Keller says to Hidalgo back in the office. "Any spot you want except Mexico, but as far away from me as possible. When I get blown up, I don't want you to catch the shrapnel."

"Too late," Hidalgo says. "I'm linked with you. The new administration will send me to Bucharest. Howard would send me to the moon if we had an office there."

"Then take the new assignment while you have the chance."

"I want to see this case through."

"No."

"Why?" Hidalgo asks. "Because it's leading to Caro? Because you think I can't control myself? I can."

"There are other reasons I don't want to put you any closer to Caro," Keller says. Caro was one of the people who killed Hugo's dad and Keller is scared to death of putting the kid in the same situation.

"Don't punish me for your guilt," Hidalgo says. "I know my father was two weeks from transferring out of Guadalajara when he was killed. But it wasn't your fault."

"Yes, it was."

"Okay, it was, whatever," Hidalgo says. "Carry your goddamn cross around but don't drop it on me. I want to finish what my dad started."

"You're putting me in a tough position here, Hugo."

"Boo fucking hoo," Hidalgo says. He looks at the floor for a second, then looks back up and asks, "I mean, you are going to pursue this, aren't you?"

"What do you mean?"

Hidalgo looks right at him. Reminds Keller of his old man. "You and Ruiz."

Keller holds his stare. "Yeah? What about me and Ruiz?"

"Come on, boss."

"You brought it up, not me."

"Ruiz was a source of yours in Mexico," Hidalgo says. "And there are stories that the two of you were together on some covert mission in Guatemala."

Keller doesn't react.

Hidalgo says, "Then you have Ruiz's PSI power washed."

"You been digging around?" Keller asks. "I have *you* up my ass now?"

"I'm on your side," Hugo says. "I just want to know where the lines are."

"What do you want to ask me, Hugo?"

"Does Ruiz have something on you?"

"If you're wired up," Keller says, "it will break my heart."

"How can you ask me that?"

"The times we live in," Keller says.

"I'm not wired," Hidalgo says. "Jesus, I'd lie to protect you."

"That's what I don't want," Keller says. "We will arrest Eddie Ruiz when he's taken us to the top of the pyramid, and when we do, he will threaten me with something he knows. And I will not yield to that threat."

"And you'll take Caro down with you."

"If I can."

"I want in on that," Hidalgo says.

"It will destroy your career."

"I can catch on with some PD somewhere," Hidalgo says. "You owe this to me."

"How do you figure?"

"For my dad."

"You fight dirty, Hugo."

"It's a dirty fight," Hidalgo says.

"All right," Keller says. "I'll keep you on this. Ruiz and Caro are eating what we serve them now. So we poison the food, feed them bad information. We'll do that through you."

Hidalgo stands up. "I'm not saying that you killed Adán Barrera. But if you did . . . thank you."

He leaves.

You're welcome, Keller thinks.

Now it's time to take down Caro, Ruiz, Darnell, and Lerner, and, yes, Dennison if it comes to that.

All those sons of bitches who killed forty-nine kids—

who killed Ana—

to cover up their dirty money deal.

3

Bad Hombres

Some bad hombres have come in here and we're going to get them out.
—John Dennison

America is heaven.

This was Nico's first thought, over a year ago now, when the *migra* picked him up, wrapped him in a blanket, put him in their car and cranked the heat up. Then they gave him a hamburger and a chocolate bar, which Nico wolfed down like he hadn't eaten in days, which he hadn't.

This is El Norte, Nico thought.

Everything he'd heard was true—it was wonderful. He'd never had an entire hamburger before.

The *migra* smiled at him, asked him questions in Spanish—*What's your name? How old are you? Where are you from?* Nico told the truth about his name and his age, but told them he was from Mexico because he'd heard that was better.

"Don't lie to us, *hijo*," one of the *migra* said. "You're not Mexican."

"Yes, I am."

"Listen to me," the *migra* said. "We're trying to help you. If you're from Mexico, you're going straight back on the next bus. You're a Guaty, I can tell from your accent. Now tell the truth."

Nico nodded. "I'm from Guatemala."

"Where are your parents?"

"My father is dead," Nico said. "My mother is in El Basurero."

"You came alone?"

Nico nodded.

"All the way from Guat City?"

Nico nodded again.

"On what? The train? La Bestia?"

"Yes."

"Jesus Christ."

They took him to a building and put him in a cell. It was really cold—the air-conditioning was blasting—and Nico heard one of the *migra* say, "The kid is still wet, he's going to freeze in there."

Another man said, "I'll find him something."

Nico was amazed because a few minutes later the man came back with some clothes. They were old and too big, but they were clean—a sweatshirt and some sweatpants. Clean white socks and a pair of sneakers.

"Get out of those wet things," the man said. "You don't want to catch cold." Nico changed into the new clothes.

There was a cot in the cell. He lay down and before he knew it fell asleep. When he woke up, they gave him another burger and a Coke, and a white plastic bag with his old clothes in it. Then they put him on a bus with a lot of other migrants, mostly women with their children.

A few were Guatemalan, others were from El Salvador or Honduras. Nico was the only kid there by himself, and he sat quietly and looked out the window at the flat, dry Texas plain and wondered where they were going.

The bus drove through a little town that looked empty, as if everyone just left. Nico saw boarded-up stores and a restaurant with a CLOSED sign. A larger sign showed a slice of watermelon and said DILLEY.

A few minutes later he saw a long wire fence with some low white buildings behind it. The buildings looked new. The bus stopped at the gate, where a guard talked with the driver for a second, and then drove in.

The gate swung closed behind them.

Nico saw that the buildings were really big trailers.

Everyone started to get off the bus so he got off, too, and followed them into one of the trailers and sat down on a bench. A guard behind a wooden desk sat and called out names, and those people would go into another room.

Finally, he heard his name.

The guard led him into a little room and told him to sit down in a chair in front of a desk. The woman behind the desk had brown skin and big brown eyes and black hair, talked to him in Spanish. "Nico Ramírez. My name is Donna, Nico. I'm your case manager. I'll bet you don't know what that is."

Nico shook his head.

"That means I'm going to look after you until we can get you where you belong, okay? So first I have to ask you some questions. Do you have any identification, Nico?"

"No."

"But that's your real name? You're not telling me stories?"

"No. I mean, yes. That's my name."

She said, "And your mother is still in Guatemala City?"

"Yes."

"You made this whole trip alone?"

"No," Nico said. "I was with a girl named Flor and a girl named Paola."

"Where are they now?"

"I don't know where Flor is," Nico said. "Paola died."

"I'm sorry," Donna said. "How did she die?"

"She got hit by a wire."

Donna shook her head. "Do you have any family in the United States, Nico?"

Nico didn't answer.

"Nico," Donna said, "if you have family here and you're not saying because you don't want to get them in trouble, I don't care if they're here legally or not. Do you understand? That isn't part of my job."

Nico thought for a little while. Then he said, "I have an uncle and an aunt."

"Where?"

"In New York."

"City?"

"I think so."

"Do you know how to get hold of them?" Donna asked. "Do you have their phone number?"

"Yes." He gave her the number.

"And what are their names?" she asked.

"My uncle is Javier and my aunt is Consuelo," Nico said. "López."

"Okay," Donna said. "I'm going to try to call them. Maybe tomorrow I can put you on the phone and you can talk with them. Would you like that?"

Nico nodded.

"Now," Donna said, "would you like to talk to your mother, tell her you're safe? I'll bet she's worried about you. Shall we call her?"

"She doesn't have a phone."

"Okay," Donna said. "Maybe she'll call your aunt and uncle and they can tell her and we'll figure out how to get hold of her. Now, by law I have to tell you certain things. You're not going to understand a lot of it, but I still have to tell you, okay?"

"Okay."

"You're what we call an 'unaccompanied alien minor,'" she said. "That means you aren't in this country legally, so we're going to detain you. That means we're going to keep you here. But we're going to keep you here for as short a time as we can, and then maybe we can let you go stay with your aunt and uncle. Do you understand?"

"Yes."

"I'm going to ask you a very hard question now," Donna said. "Do you know what sexual abuse is?"

Nico shook his head.

"It means when someone touches your private areas," Donna said. "Has anyone touched you like that?"

"No."

"And how are you feeling?" she asked. "Are you hurt anywhere? Do you feel sick?"

Nico didn't know how to tell her that he hurt everywhere, that his whole body was bruised, cut, sunburned, frozen, hungry and parched. He didn't have the words to express his sheer exhaustion.

So he said, "I'm okay."

"I'm going to take you to a doctor anyway," Donna said. "Just to be sure. He's going to give you a shot called a 'vaccination'—don't be afraid, it won't hurt. And he's going to test you for tuberculosis, which sometimes happens when you cough a lot. Do you cough a lot, Nico?"

Nico coughed all the time—he coughed from the smoke of the train, the cold, the dust that got into his nose and mouth and lungs.

"But first we're going to get you some clothes," Donna said. "The ones you have are in pretty tough shape."

Donna led him out of the office and down a hallway, and then into a room where there were shelves and shelves of new clothes. Nico couldn't believe it when she took a shirt and a pair of pants down and then grabbed a pair of socks and a pair of brand-new sneakers and said, "These look about your size. But you don't want to put them on until you've had a shower. Come on."

She took him into a large room where there was a shower. "This dial is hot water, this one is cold. There's soap and shampoo, and there's a towel. I'll wait outside, unless you want me to help you."

"No."

When she left, Nico stripped out of his clothes and walked into the shower stall. It was so clean but it smelled like bleach. He turned the hot dial first and jumped back when the water came out in a hard spray. Stepping around the water, he reached in and turned the cold dial and stuck his finger into the spray until it felt hot but not scalding.

Then he stepped under the spray.

He'd never had a shower like this. The few he'd ever had were cold trickles from old, rusty pipes. This water smelled like boiled eggs, but Nico didn't care—it was wonderful.

This was El Norte.

This was America.

The *champú* bothered him, though. The lady told him the word, but he didn't know what it was and was afraid to open the little plastic bottle. He soaped his hair down, though, until it was clean, and let the hot water run down his body.

He got out, toweled himself dry and then put on his new clothes. It was still unbelievable, this place where they give you clothes and shoes.

Donna was waiting for him in the hallway and took him to the doctor.

The doctor made him take his shirt off, then had him cough and ran a cold metal thing over his back and his chest. He made Nico open his mouth and put a stick in it, told him to make a noise. He had Nico step on a scale and then lowered a little metal bar onto his head.

"Four foot six," the doctor said. "Fifty-three pounds. His growth is stunted and he's extremely undernourished. Residual contusions on his chest and rib cage. Does he report having been beaten?"

Donna asked the boy about the bruises.

"I fell off the train," Nico said.

"Does he report sexual abuse?" the doctor asked.

"No."

"Should I do a rectal exam?" the doctor asked.

"I don't think that's necessary right now," Donna said. "If he opens up about something later, maybe."

"He can put his shirt back on," the doctor said. "He shows symptoms of respiratory distress, probably from breathing in dust and smoke. Same cause for what looks like a chronic eye infection, but some eye drops should clear it up. He's also displaying sinusitis, but I think a nasal wash instead of antibiotics and we'll see how it goes. Mostly, this kid needs food and rest. Donna, could I have a word with you alone?"

Donna walked Nico out of the examination room to a bench in the hallway and went back in.

"The kid has a gang tattoo burned into his ankle," the doctor said. "Calle 18."

"Could you leave that out of the report?"

"You know I can't."

"Didn't hurt to ask."

Back out in the hallway, Donna asked Nico, "Do you know what a cafeteria is?"

"No."

"It's sort of like a restaurant."

Nico was worried. "I don't have any money."

"That's okay. The food is free."

Nico couldn't believe his ears. Then his eyes. They walked into this big room where some migrants were sitting at long tables, eating, while others were in line with trays and people behind the counter were heaping rice and beans and meat onto their plates.

"Take a tray and a plate," Donna said. "And there are the forks, knives and napkins. Then get in line."

"They'll just give me food?"

"They'll just give you food," Donna said. "But say thank you."

Nico said *gracias* again and again as the people behind the counter put rice and beans and meat on his plate. At the end of the counter there were glasses with juice, punch or water. Nico looked at Donna.

"Take one," she said.

He took a glass of punch and sat down at a table with her.

Then he couldn't believe his ears again because he heard people complaining about the food—the rice was undercooked, the beans were overcooked, the meat was stringy, there wasn't enough.

It's *free food*, Nico thought.

They *give* you food.

He started to shovel his down before they changed their minds.

"Slow down," Donna said, smiling. "Nobody's going to take it away from you, *m'ijo*."

Nico wasn't so sure. He ate ravenously with his right hand, his left wrapped protectively around the plate.

"I have some more things I have to tell you," Donna said while she watched him tear into the food. "Because you're an unaccompanied minor, we can't house you in a dormitory with adults who aren't related to you. So we have to put you in a room by yourself."

Nico had no idea what she was talking about.

He didn't care.

A room to himself? He literally couldn't imagine it.

"But hopefully by tomorrow," Donna was saying, "we can move you to a group home. It's like a regular house. There'll be like a mom and dad, and you'll have other kids to play with. And if you're there long enough, you'll go to school. Would you like that?"

Nico shrugged. How would he know?

"Now go up and get an apple and a cookie," Donna said, "and then I'll take you to your room."

The room was a small rectangle, painted in a bright blue, with murals of zebras and giraffes. A single bed was set by the wall. The window was barred.

"Here you go," Donna said. "There's a bathroom down the hall you can use if you need it. But, Nico, you know you can't leave the building, right?"

Nico nodded.

A room of his own, a bathroom, a shower, free food and drink, clean new clothes, a pair of sneakers . . .

Why would he ever want to leave heaven?

Donna went back to her office and called the number Nico gave her.

A man answered.

"Is this Señor López?" Donna asked in Spanish.

"Yes."

The voice sounded tentative, suspicious.

"Señor López," Donna said. "My name is Donna Sutton, I'm from the Office of Refugee Resettlement. Do you know a boy named Nico Ramírez?"

"Yes."

Now he sounded frightened.

"May I ask," Donna said, "what is your relationship to Nico?"

"He's my nephew," López said. "My wife's sister's son."

"We have Nico in our custody," Donna said. "We want you to know he's perfectly safe."

She heard him yell, "Consuelo!," then heard him tell her that "they" had found Nico. When he came back on the phone he was crying. "We were afraid that . . . we hadn't heard . . ."

"Are you in touch with Nico's mother?"

"She calls when she can," López said. "She doesn't have a phone."

"The next time she calls," Donna said, "will you please tell her Nico is safe and give her this number? She can call collect."

"Can we speak with Nico?"

"I'll call back tomorrow and put him on the phone," Donna said. "I hope he's asleep right now."

"What happens next?"

She walked him through the process. She would send them the Family Reunification Application, which they would have to fill out and get back to her. Then there would be an interview, and if everything checked out, Nico could be released to their custody until a deportation hearing, usually within ninety days, would determine if Nico could stay or would be returned to Guatemala.

"He can't go back," López said. "They'll kill him."

"We'll take it a step at a time," Donna said.

She got their address and told them she would call them in the morning. Then she called ICE and told them—as she had to by law—that she had a UAC with a gang tattoo on his ankle.

"We have to pick up the file," the agent said.

"I know, Cody," Donna said. "But could you step lightly on this one? He's a ten-year-old."

"You know the environment right now, Donna."

"I know."

"I'll do what I can, but . . ."

Yeah, she thought as she hung up. It's the story of our lives—Border Patrol agents, ICE, case managers with more files than we can really digest, volunteer lawyers who might get minutes with their "clients" before a hearing—we're all doing our best, but . . .

It wasn't as bad as it was back in 2014, when UACs surged from thirty thousand the year before to almost seventy thousand, overwhelming the system from top to bottom. The number of kids fleeing Central America dropped earlier in 2015, but now it was on the rise again and threatening to once again flood the system.

Her desk was overloaded—so were the case files of every child advocate and of all the pro bono attorneys who had come and volunteered their services.

Donna left the facility and drove up Highway 35 to Pearsall and pulled into Garcia's Bar and Grill.

Alma Baez was right at the bar where Donna thought she'd be, sipping a bourbon and branch water. Donna plopped down on the stool next to her and raised one finger to the bartender, signaling her usual, a scotch with two rocks.

"Has it been a day?" Alma asked.

"The usual flood of misery," Donna said. "I'm glad I found you. I have a UAC who's going to need an advocate."

Donna worked for the Office of Refugee Resettlement, which contracted with a private business, Corrections Corporation of America, to run the migrant detention center. CCA ran eight other detention centers, but its main business was prisons. It housed sixty-six thousand inmates in thirty-four state and fourteen federal prisons as well as four county jails.

As a case manager for ORR, Donna had the right—in fact, the duty—to call in an advocate for a child when she deemed it necessary.

She deemed it necessary for Nico and told Alma his story.

"Was he trafficked?" Alma asked.

"No, but I'm classifying him 'vulnerable,'" Donna said. The classification would get the boy an advocate, and he needed one. "There's a problem. I want to group-home him until we can find him a sponsor—"

"Is there one?"

"An aunt and uncle in New York."

"So what's the problem?" Alma asked. "You want to share some nachos?"

"Yeah. He has a gang tattoo," Donna said. "Calle 18."

"But he's ten, did you say?" Alma asked. "Chicken or beef?"

"Right, but they still might try to 'threat' him," Donna said. "Chicken."

In unaccompanied-minor cases, a judge holds a bond hearing as quickly as possible and 90 percent of the time releases the child to a group home. But the problem with Nico was twofold, Donna knew. Thanks mostly to the upcoming presidential election, the country was virtually hysterical about Central American gangs like MS-13 and Calle 18, and "gangbangers" coming across the border. So judges like the one who would preside at Nico's hearing were extremely reluctant to let anyone with any kind of gang affiliation out of custody.

The second issue was business.

Dollars and cents.

The Corrections Corporation of America wouldn't make any money on Nico Ramírez if he got transferred, as he should be, into a group home. But if the judge deemed Nico a "threat" because of a gang tattoo, he would be sent to a "secure facility," which would make sixty-three bucks a day on the boy.

CCA was a publicly traded company.

It had to show a profit to its stockholders. To do that, it had to fill beds and cells. CCA wasn't in the business of releasing inmates, it was in the business of retaining them.

Nico was money on the hoof.

But, hell, people have to live, and the CCA was now the biggest employer around here. Dilley was once the "Watermelon Capital of the World," but the watermelons rolled south across the border. Then "fracking" was going to be the savior, except that turned out to be a bust, too.

Prisoners were a more reliable source of money.

You never ran out of them.

But if Nico got deemed a threat and sent to a secure facility, it would be that much harder to get him reclassified and released to his aunt and uncle, assuming they passed the application process.

He could linger in the facility for months, if not years, before a final decision was made, and that decision would likely be to deport him, in effect to deliver him right back to the gang he had fled.

"We should get him a lawyer," Alma said.

"How about Brenda?"

"She has files stacked up to her eyebrows."

Brenda Solowicz had come down to Dilley for a couple of weeks at the height of the migration crisis in 2014 and stayed ever since, moving into a double-wide near the Best Western. There were a number of good lawyers working pro bono for the migrants, but in Donna's opinion, Brenda was the best.

"So what's one more?" Donna asked.

Alma sighed. "I'll call her. When can I meet this kid?"

"First thing in the morning?"

"I'll be there."

"You're the best," Donna said.

"I'll be even better when I get another drink in me," Alma said.

Donna knew what she meant—as a child advocate, Alma had orphans, little girls who'd been gang-raped, turned out on the street, kids who'd been beaten or even tortured. And she worked with the knowledge that, in most cases, the kids would be in the country for a few weeks or months and then get sent right back to where they'd come from.

And it was only going to get worse.

Donna's scotch was gone as if someone had helped her drink it.

She signaled for another one.

Nico drank his orange juice and finished his cereal as the lady named Alma talked to him.

"Listen to me very carefully now," Alma said. "You can only stay in this country if you have what we call a 'credible fear' that you will be hurt or killed if you go back to Guatemala. A judge is going to ask you questions. I can't tell you what to say or not to say, but understand that you can only stay here if you're afraid you'll be hurt if you go home."

Nico nodded.

"*Are* you afraid to go home, Nico?" Donna asked.

"Yes."

"Why?" Alma asked.

"They were going to make me join Calle 18."

"Did they threaten you?" Alma asked. "Or hurt you?"

"They said they'd hurt my mother." He didn't mention that they'd burned a tattoo into him. He'd already forgotten that pain.

But the lady named Alma brought it up. "Donna said you have a tattoo. Can I see it?"

Nico pulled up his pant leg.

Alma winced. "How did that happen? Did you get that on your own?"

Nico shook his head. "Pulga did it."

"Who's that?"

"A *marero*."

A young woman with a tangle of wild red hair strode into the room, sat down and set a briefcase on the table. "Sorry I'm late. Is this . . . Nico?"

"Yes."

"I'm Brenda, Nico," she said. "I'm going to represent you at your hearing."

"Nico was just showing us his tattoo," Donna said.

"Can I see, Nico?" Brenda asked. She looked at the tattoo then over at Alma and Donna like something was really bad. Then she said, "So, Nico, in a few minutes we're going to walk over to another building and talk to a judge. He won't be there, he'll be on, like, a television, but he can see you and hear you, okay?"

"Okay."

"I'm going to talk a little and then he's going to ask you some questions," Brenda said. "You just tell the truth, all right?"

"All right."

Brenda looked at Donna. "What are the odds on getting a cup of coffee?"

"The odds are good, the coffee is terrible."

"I'll take it."

Brenda got her coffee and they walked over to the other building. Nico sat on a bench between Brenda and Alma and watched as mostly women got up and talked into a camera, answering questions to a judge on a television screen.

It scared Nico.

The women were talking in Spanish and trying to explain why they and their children should stay in the United States.

The judge wasn't friendly.

Some of the women left crying.

He heard the judge call his name. "Nico Ramírez?"

Brenda took him to a table in front and sat him down in a metal folding chair. "Brenda Solowicz, appearing pro bono for Nico Ramírez, an unaccompanied alien minor."

The judge said, "I see that ORR requested this bond hearing?"

"That's correct, Your Honor," Brenda said. "ORR would like to place Mr. Ramírez in a group home until he can be released to a sponsor."

"Has a sponsor been identified?"

"Mr. Ramírez has an aunt and uncle willing to take him," Brenda said, "and they've started the application process."

Nico watched the judge look down as if he was reading something. Then the judge looked up and said, "Ms. Solowicz, I'm sure you're aware that there's a problem here. Is the representative from ICE present?"

"Here, Your Honor," Cody Kincaid said.

"Is ICE maintaining that Mr. Ramírez is a threat to public safety?"

"Mr. Ramírez has an apparent gang affiliation," Kincaid said.

"As per . . ."

"As per a gang tattoo," Kincaid said. "Of Calle 18."

"Do you contest this, Ms. Solowicz?"

"No, Your Honor," Brenda said. "But, Your Honor, he's a ten-year-old boy—"

"Well, that's a guess, isn't it?" the judge said. "We have no documentation of his age. He could be thirteen, fourteen . . ."

"—fifty-three pounds soaking wet—"

"Is that a bad pun, Ms. Solowicz?"

"No, Your Honor."

"Does Mr. Ramírez speak English?" the judge asked. "I suppose that's too much to hope for."

"He doesn't, Your Honor."

"Do we have a translator?"

"Your Honor? I'm Alma Baez, Mr. Ramírez's CA," Alma said. "I can translate."

"Nice to see you again, Ms. Baez," the judge said. "Let me speak to Mr. Ramírez. Good morning, Nico. There's nothing to be afraid of, Nico. I'm just going to ask you some questions, and you just answer them honestly. Are you a member of Calle 18?"

"No."

"Then why do you have a Calle 18 tattoo?"

"They made me."

"Who made you?"

Brenda said, "If I may, Your Honor—"

"No, you may not," the judge said. "I'm talking to Mr. Ramírez, and he's capable of answering."

"Pulga tattooed me."

"Why did you let him?"

"He said he'd hurt my mother."

"Why did you come to the United States?"

"So I wouldn't have to join Calle 18," Nico said.

"But aren't you afraid they'll hurt your mother because you left?" the judge asked.

"Yes."

Nico watched the judge think for a few minutes. Then the judge said, "Agent Kincaid, what are ICE's wishes in this matter?"

"We would prefer to see Mr. Ramírez sent to a secure care facility."

Brenda said, "Your Honor, as per the *Flores* decision, UAC is supposed to be held in 'the least restrictive facility possible.' That would be a group home, not a secure care facility."

"I don't need you to educate me about *Flores,*" the judge said. "Nor do I remember asking you a question."

"I apologize, Your Honor."

The judge said, "Mr. Ramírez has expressed fear that a close family member is vulnerable to a criminal gang, and therefore he might be subject to extortion or blackmail by that organization here in the United States. As such, he does represent a threat and I am going to deny the request to transfer him to a group home. Mr. Ramírez will be housed in a secure care facility pending successful application of sponsorship, at which time his status will be reviewed."

"Preserving right to file a BIA appeal, Your Honor."

"Of course you are, Ms. Solowicz. Next case?"

Outside, Brenda said, "Shit, if Jesus Christ came in with a tat these days, they'd threat him."

Nico had no idea what happened.

"Where are you going to place him?" Alma asked.

Donna had only two choices, a facility in Northern California or one in southern Virginia. "I'll try to get him on the East Coast, a little closer to his people, anyway. Maybe they can drive down to see him."

She had to get on the phone and tell Nico's uncle and aunt that the government was sending him to a juvenile detention center. "Look, hopefully he won't be there long. A month or two."

"A month?!"

"These things take time, Mr. López," Donna said. But it was time that worried her—the system is like quicksand: the longer you're in, the deeper you get, the harder it is to get out. She knew kids who'd lingered in the system for years. "Would you like to talk to him? He's just outside."

"Yes, please."

She stepped into the hallway where Nico waited on a bench. "I have your uncle on the phone."

Nico followed the woman inside her office and she handed him the phone. "Hello?"

"*Sobrino,* how are you? Are you all right?"

"Yes."

"We're trying to get hold of your mother."

"Okay."

"Be strong, Nico."

"Okay."

Nico handed her back the phone.

López had already hung up.

"Nico," she said, "in a couple of days we're going to take you to a new place to stay while we're waiting to see if you can go live with your aunt and uncle, okay?"

"Okay."

And that, Donna thought, is how you tell a ten-year-old that he's going to jail.

She got overrefreshed at Garcia's that night with Alma. Brenda was there too when Donna slammed her hand on the bar and said, "He's a *child*, for Chrissakes!"

Brenda looked over her beer bottle at her.

"Oh, Donna," she said, "there are no children here."

Now Nico sits with his back against the wall of the dayroom at the Southern Virginia Youth Detention Facility and watches other kids play checkers at the tables bolted to the floor.

Good thing it is, Nico thinks, because as soon as Fermín loses—which he's about to do—he'd tip that table over if he could.

Same with the stools, they're bolted down.

Even the checkerboard is set into the table so it can't be used as a weapon.

The table isn't going anywhere, the stools aren't going anywhere, the board isn't going anywhere, and I'm not going anywhere, Nico thinks.

He's been in here almost a year now.

At first it was fresh.

Started with his first ride on an airplane, which was amazing. He went with an escort from ORR, who let him have the window seat, and Nico looked out and saw the world from thirty thousand feet.

It was beautiful.

Except as soon as they left the airport, the escort put him in handcuffs.

Sorry, it was the rules.

But he gave Nico a "break" and cuffed his hands in front of him instead of behind and helped him get his seat belt on and they stopped at a McDonald's "drive-through" so Nico could get a Big Mac and a Coke, which he held between his legs and sipped through a straw.

When they got to "the facility" it was pretty much the same as the last time. First they took him to a nurse, who weighed him, took his temperature and looked in his mouth and his ears, and then they took him to the shower, then gave him some more clothes and showed him to his room. On the way they walked him through the dayroom, where all the other kids shut up, stopped what they were doing, and stared at him.

Fresh meat.

He walked up the stairs to the tier where his room was, put the towel they gave him on the bed and sat down.

Now Nico waits for Fermín to erupt.

Fer doesn't like to lose and he has a temper.

Takes *nothing* to set him off.

Nico has seen him blow up because they were out of apple juice, because someone changed the channel from *Property Brothers* (Fer *loves Property Brothers*) and because a kid called him a Sally because he's from El Salvador.

That's when Fer has a reason.

Sometimes he goes off for no reason at all except for what's going on inside his head, which Nico doesn't want to even know about.

At least Fer's regular afternoon meltdown is some entertainment as the guards come in, tackle him, drag him out and give him his meds until he's quiet. Sometimes they put a netted hood over his face so he can't bite anyone. It's something to look at and better than *Property Brothers* anyway, and kills some time before *People's Court,* which they all like because the judge is so pretty and she's a Latina and doesn't take any shit from anybody. Fer started banging his head into the wall when Carlos told him the judge was Cuban, not Salvadoran.

Now the head banging is going to start again because Santiago is about to jump one of Fer's pieces. Nico knows this because he sees the look in Santi's eyes and the little smirk he gets just before he's about to win at something.

Fer makes his move.

Santi jumps three of his pieces and says, "King me."

Yeah, Nico thinks, that's not going to happen.

What happens is what Nico thinks is going to happen—Fer sweeps all the pieces off the board, jumps up, walks over to the concrete wall and starts banging his head into it. Nobody tries to stop him because they've all learned that if you try to stop Fer from banging his head into the wall he's just going to bang your head into the wall, and anyway, one of their games is to see how long it takes one of the guards to come in.

Eight bangs this time, then the guard they call "Gordo" runs in and says, "Jesus, Fermín, what did that wall ever do to you?!"

Fer is too busy chanting, "I'm so stupid"—*bang*—"I'm so stupid"—*bang*—to answer, and Gordo wraps him up in a bear hug, lifts him off his feet and backs him away from the wall when two of the other guards (Chapo and Feo) come in, grab Fer by his kicking feet and carry him screaming out of the dayroom.

Santi smiles and says, "Fermín's going to get *good* drugs."

Then it's time for *People's Court* so they all sit and watch the television mounted high on the wall.

"I'm going to jerk off to her tonight," Jupiter says.

"Don't say that," Nico says.

He loves Judge Marilyn.

He has a major crush on Judge Marilyn.

"I am," Jupiter says, making a jerking motion with his hand. He's seventeen and big and doesn't give a shit what a midget like Nico says. "I'm going to jerk off thinking about fucking her mouth and her *chocha*."

All of a sudden Nico hears himself yelling, "Don't say that! No, you're not!"

"*Chúpala*, watermelon."

And everyone is shocked, really shocked, when quiet, shy, agreeable Nico launches himself at Jupiter, swinging his fists wildly, trying to reach up and connect. Jupiter doesn't care how small this kid is, he hauls back and punches Nico in the nose.

It doesn't stop him.

Blood flowing down his face, Nico keeps swinging until Jupiter grabs him, slams him to the floor and sits on top of him, punching him in the ribs and the face.

The guards run back in and pull Jupiter off him.

"Jesus," Gordo says as he picks Nico up and carries him out, "what's *with* you kids today?"

Nico hears himself yelling, "I'll kill him! I'll fucking kill him!"

"You're not going to kill *any*body. Settle down."

Gordo takes him to one of the "recovery rooms," a narrow rectangle with a bed and a door that locks.

The nurse comes in. Wiping the blood off Nico's face, she says, "What's going on with you? You're usually such a nice boy."

Nico doesn't answer.

"Your nose isn't broken. Are you hurt anywhere else, honey?"

"No."

"Okay, you'll have to talk with the counselor before you go back to gen pop," the nurse says.

The counselor, a young guy named Chris, comes in a few minutes later and sits on the bed beside Nico. "Who hit you?"

Nico shrugs.

"You don't know who hit you?"

"No." Nico has learned a few things here. One of them is that snitches get stitches. The worst thing you can be is a *dedo*.

Chris laughs. "Nico, you know there are video cameras in the dayroom. You know we have everything on tape."

"So look at it," Nico says.

"I did," Chris says. "You started the fight. Why?"

Nico is too embarrassed to repeat what Jupiter said about Judge Marilyn and too embarrassed to admit his feelings about her. So he goes the other way with it: "If you already know what happened, why are you asking me what happened?"

He knows the answer to his question—the staff has it in for Jupiter and would like a chance to write him up. Nico doesn't like Jupiter either—he's an asshole—but he also knows what side he's on, so he's not going to help them.

"I'm just giving you a chance to tell your side of the story," Chris says.

Another shrug.

"Okay," says Chris, "I think you'd better spend the night in here and let this cool off. And I'm going to consequence you with a week's playground suspension. You'll do the study room instead. If you want to challenge your consequence, you can take it up with Norma."

"Fuck that."

"Language," Chris says. "You want another day?"

Chris stares him down, forcing an answer.

"No."

"Okay," Chris says. "Do you want to see the mental health counselor?"

"No."

"You sure?"

"Yes."

Chris gets up and leaves, locking the door behind him. Nico edges up to the wall and knocks on it. "Fer? You in there?"

"Yeah."

"You okay?"

"Yeah."

His voice is dreamy. Santi was right, Fermín does get some good drugs.

"What did you do?" Fer asks.

"I punched Jup."

"Why?"

Nico tells him.

"The prick," Fer says.

"Right?"

"What did you get?" Fer asks.

"A week."

"Not bad."

It's not. Chris could have written him up. Every report goes into your file, and if you get enough write-ups, it could keep you from being released. "Chris is an okay guy."

"Canela might still write you up."

"I hope not."

"Me too."

A little while later, Gordo comes in with a tray—macaroni and cheese, bread, apple juice and an oatmeal cookie. Mac and cheese is one of Nico's favorites, but he likes the chocolate chip cookies better than the oatmeal. Anyway, it's good food.

After he eats, Nico wraps up in his blanket, lies down, and thinks about *fútbol*.

They play *fútbol* on the basketball court.

When the bad white and bad black kids aren't shooting hoops, the bad brown kids get the space to play soccer.

Nico's good at *fútbol*.

Nico Rápido makes his reappearance on the court as he cuts and slashes, dribbles around and through the opposition, makes passes and gets into open space for a shot at the goal, a space against the chain-link fence defined by orange cones.

The *fútbol* games give Nico some respect.

The shrimp is just too good, making some of the kids think that he really isn't eleven years old but maybe thirteen, fourteen, even fifteen. They all want Nico on their team, but usually the sides break down on national lines—the Central American kids versus the Mexican kids—which reflects the same situation in the dayroom. The Mexican boys look down on the Salvadorans, Hondurans and Guatemalans. Blame them for sneaking into Mexico and fucking things up on the border with El Norte.

But no one looks down on Nico when they're playing *fútbol*, and now he plays a match in his head. In his mind he flicks the ball to Fer, moves around Jupiter like he's standing still, takes the pass back from Fer, shoots and . . . *scores*.

The other boys throw their arms around him, pat him on the head, yell, "Nico is Messi!" as the Mexicans glower at him.

Then he thinks about Flor. Wonders where she is, if she's okay. He has this fantasy that she made it across the border and met this nice woman who took her in and adopted her and now she lives in a big, clean house and has nice clothes and goes to school. And that the woman is helping her find Nico because she wants to adopt him, too.

They let him out in the morning for breakfast with the rest of the boys. Jupiter is there but ignores him, and Nico returns the favor.

Then he has to go in and see Norma in her office.

The supervisor is a squat, middle-aged woman with bright red hair. The boys call her "Canela."

"Nico," she says, "you know that we have a zero-tolerance policy on violence."

Nico knows this.

They have a "zero-tolerance policy" on a lot of things—violence, bad language, "disrespect," jerking yourself off, jerking someone else off . . . drugs, unless they're the drugs *they* give you. Except for the drugs, there's a zero-tolerance policy on things that happen all the time.

"We simply won't tolerate it," Norma says.

"Okay."

"You're starting to get yourself in trouble," Norma says. "You're developing an attitude, young man. I don't want to see that."

"Then don't look," Nico says.

"Are you asking me to write you up?" Norma asks.

"No."

"I'm sorry?"

"No, ma'am."

"Go to class now," Norma says. "Come back here at recess and we'll see if we can get your aunt or uncle on the phone."

Nico wants to talk with them, but he's sick of just talking on the phone. He's been here for close to a year and they haven't come down to see him. He knows it's not really their fault—they don't own a car and it's too much money to fly. Nico thinks it's something else, too—they're afraid to come near authorities because they're "illegals" and they're afraid they'll be arrested.

They put their address on the paperwork, though, at least the lady Alma told him they did. She's still his CA, even long distance from Texas, and she says that Tío Javier and Tía Consuelo filed the application for sponsorship and "we're all still waiting" for it to be approved.

No, Nico thinks as he's walking to the classroom, *I'm* still waiting.

Like he's waiting for an appeal to get through.

Alma told him that the other lady, the lawyer Brenda, has filed three unsuccessful appeals to change his "status" as a threat, which Nico didn't really understand until Santi explained it to him.

"We're all threats, *güerito*," Santi told him, "that's why we're here."

Thirty kids, all Hispanics, live in the unit, which is separate from the rest of the facility where the kids who did bad things in Virginia are held.

"If they think you're in a gang," Santi told him, "or you're a sexual pred-ator, or you've committed crimes—"

"I haven't committed crimes," Nico said.

"That tattoo on your ankle is your crime," Santi said.

It's a real problem, Nico has to admit. Not only because it landed him here, where he's stuck, but also because there are kids in this place who really *are* gangstas, two of them who are Mara 13 and have flat out told Nico they'll kill him if they can.

"Some night when the guards aren't watching," a Salvadoran named Ro-drigo told him, "we're going to come in your room, you 18 *pisado*, make you suck our cocks, then fuck you in the ass, then cut your throat."

And I'm the "threat," Nico thinks. At least there are no Calle 18's here, because they *would* kill him for running away, like the 13's tried to kill him on La Bestia.

"They're just running their mouths," Santi told him. "They're not so tough—one of them cries every night, the other one wets his bed."

Nico knows Rodrigo isn't the only one who cries at night or wets the bed. Some of them wake up screaming, some can't stop scratching themselves or banging their heads into the wall. There's one kid who never talks.

Ever.

Mudo Juan, as he's come to be called, mostly just sits there. He eats, he goes to class, he sometimes even plays basketball, but he has nothing to say.

Ni una palabra.

Mudo Juan is huge, well over six feet and he has to go two hundred pounds. There are all kinds of stories about him, but who knows what's true, because of course he isn't saying. Some of them go he was just born that way, others go that he saw his baby sister burn up in a fire, others that he had to watch his mother get raped by a gang of *mareros*.

Mudo Juan isn't saying.

Nico has tried to get him to talk, practically has made it his mission in life to get Mudo Juan to say something. Will pull up a chair right in front of him and ask him questions, or tell him jokes, call him every dirty name he can think of, say very bad things about his mother, anything to get a reaction from him, but nothing.

"Give up," Santi told Nico.

"Never."

Once a week, every Tuesday, Mudo Juan goes and sees the "mental health professional" who comes in, but that guy hasn't made out any better than Nico.

One day, Nico just went off.

Started yelling at Mudo Juan, "Say something, Mudo! Anything! One fucking word! I'll give you anything! I'll give you all my snacks for a week, I'll suck you off if you want, just for the love of God, say something!"

Santi was rolling around on the floor he was laughing so hard.

Mudo said nothing.

Nico doesn't give up.

So sometimes it's funny in there, other times it's crazy, other times it's just sad; most of the time it's all those things at once.

More and more it's just sad.

Nico feels sad.

Sad he's in there.

Sad his aunt and uncle haven't come to see him.

Sad he talked to his mother.

It was two days ago they finally put it together, when his mother could get hold of a phone for a few minutes and they could find Nico and bring him in the office and he heard her ask, "Nico?"

Like she couldn't believe it.

"Yes, Mami, it's me."

"Nico . . ."

And then she started to cry.

And cry and cry and cry.

That was most of their phone call, her crying, between sobs asking him if he was all right, telling him that she loved him, loved him very much, loved him so much . . .

"Can I come home, Mami?"

"No, *m'ijo*."

"Please, Mami."

"You can't, *m'ijo*. They'll hurt you."

"Can you come here?"

"I'll try."

"Please, Mami."

"Be a good boy. I love you."

That was it. The phone went dead.

He handed it back to Norma.

"All done?"

"Yes."

"Already?"

"Yes."

Nico knew she couldn't come here, he knows it now, knows that she doesn't have the money and couldn't survive La Bestia. He thought talking to his mother would make him feel better, but it just made him sadder.

Now he walks to class.

ESL.

Nico thinks it's crazy they're teaching Mudo Juan to say nothing in two languages.

Waiting, waiting, waiting.

All the boys are waiting.

Waiting for their threat status to be changed, waiting for their sponsorships to be approved, or just waiting for their eighteenth birthday when, as adults, they'll be put on a plane and flown back to wherever they came from.

So they wait.

Go to classes, play checkers, play cards, play *fútbol,* watch TV, go to breakfast, lunch and dinner, talk shit, take showers, go to bed, get up, go to classes, play checkers, play cards, play *fútbol,* watch TV, go to breakfast, lunch and dinner, talk shit, take showers, go to bed.

Day after day after day.

The only change is who's doing the waiting, because the population changes. A kid gets sponsored and leaves, another one has his threat designation removed and goes to a foster home or a regular group home, another blows out a candle on his cupcake and then is taken away. A few who committed serious felonies in the United States while they were minors turn eighteen and are transferred to the big leagues—a prison in America.

Those guys look bad going out, Nico thinks. They try to look all macho, like they're happy to be going, it's no big deal, but Nico can see that they're scared.

"He *should* be scared," Santi says, watching one of them go. They'll all be lining up to jump his ass. A Mexican, he'll have to clique up to survive, which means deciding if he's *sureño* or *norteño,* and whichever he chooses, the other gang will be out to do him. "He's totally fucked."

Santi, he knows he's just killing time until his eighteenth, because there's no chance in fucking hell of getting reclassified or sponsored. He's a threat because he was sexually trafficked, and when the American doctor asked him if that made him angry and want revenge, he said hell yes on both counts.

"They thought that meant I wanted to fuck some little boy," Santi says. "I said no, it means I want to kill the people who fucked *me*."

He got a glimpse at his file and it said, *Sexual deviance with homicidal tendencies.*

"So I'm not going anywhere," Santi says, "until they ship me back. Until they do, I'm going to milk it, Nico. Most of the idiots in here don't realize what we have—a bed, food, clothes, shower . . . a clean fucking toilet? Flat-screen TV? Snacks? Come on, 'mano."

Santi gets a lot of snacks.

The reigning board game champion of the Southern Virginia Youth Detention Facility, he beats everyone at chess and checkers and wins their Skittles, their cookies, their M&Ms, their Snickers. Santi is literally getting fat in secure detention, and he uses these winnings to gamble on *anything*—the *fútbol* games on the court, *fútbol* games on TV, which way the judge is going to decide.

What Nico doesn't understand is how Santi always gets the other guys to play or bet. They almost always lose, but they do it anyway. Santi can even get Mudo Juan to play chess and to bet on the judge by pointing his finger at the plaintiff or the defendant.

"You know what I like about Mudo Juan?" Santi has asked Nico. "When he loses, he never complains."

And Santi finally explained to Nico how he sucks guys in. "It's about hope, Nico. Most of these kids hope for things they know, deep in their hearts, they're never going to get. They hope for their status to get changed, they hope for a sponsor, they hope they're going to live happily ever after in America. They know none of that is going to happen. But they always have the hope they can beat Santi. That isn't going to happen, either, but they hope. I give them hope, Nico."

Fermín is Santi's most reliable victim.

He always plays and he always loses.

Fer has an uncanny ability to pick losers, and Nico has tried to argue the logic of this with him.

"Make your pick," Nico said, "and then bet the other way."

"Why would I do that?"

"Because you always pick wrong and lose," Nico said. "So if you go the other way, you'll pick right and win."

Santi watched this conversation with condescending amusement. "Knock yourself out, Nico. It won't make a difference."

"Why not?"

"Don't you get it?" Santi asked. "He *wants* to lose. It gives him a reason to bang his head against the wall."

"Is that true, Fer?"

"No! I want to win."

"He never does," Santi said calmly. "He never will."

"Yes, I will."

"Tell you what," Santi said, "for a Snickers, without even hearing the case, you pick the plaintiff or the defendant, I'll pick the other one."

"That's just a coin toss," Nico said.

"He'd lose that, too," Santi said. "So what about it, Fer? A Snickers?"

"You're on."

"Fer!"

"Shut up, Nico," Fer said.

He picked the plaintiff.

Case dismissed. The judge found for the defendant.

Fer handed Santi his Snickers and went and started banging his head into the wall until Gordo came in and hauled him away.

"I did him a favor," Santi said. "He got everything he wanted—a good head bang, and good drugs."

It goes on like this.

Day after day.

Nico becomes an old veteran himself.

He watches kids come and watches them go.

Becomes very helpful to the *fresca*, the new meat. Walks them through the drill, clues them in on the staff—who you can get over on, who you should avoid—gives them the same dope about the other kids.

Some listen to him, some don't.

Nico doesn't care.

Santi loves new meat. "I don't see obnoxious little newbies who fuck everything up. I see Snickers."

Actually, it's Nico who comes up with what the staff comes to refer to as "Fermíngate."

Nico is sitting against the fence, taking a breather before going back into the *fútbol* game, when he says to Santi, "What if Fermín beat you at checkers?"

"What if Becky G blew you?" Santi asks.

"Think about it," Nico says. "Everybody is going to bet on you, but I put my snacks on Fermín. Think of the odds we can get. You lose and we clean up."

"Everyone will see right through that."

"Not the *fresca*."

"You realize that what you're suggesting is fraud," Santi says. "Morally and ethically reprehensible."

"Yes."

"I'm in."

It takes some setting up because everyone knows Nico and Santi are *cerotes*. So they stage a little falling-out in the dayroom. Nico is trying to get Mudo Juan to talk, saying horrible things about his mother and a goat.

"Why don't you leave him alone?" Santi asks.

"Why don't you mind your own business?" Nico says.

"It is my business," Santi says. "You're pissing me off."

The dayroom starts to take notice. Boys look up from what they're doing, or away from the television. It's something different—Nico and Santi are friends, and neither one of them is aggressive, Nico's Judge Marilyn meltdown notwithstanding.

"So what?" Nico says.

"So knock it off."

"So make me."

Santi gets up and walks over, but not so fast that Gordo can't come in and get between them. "Settle down."

"He's bothering Juan."

"Since when *doesn't* he bother Juan?" Gordo asks. "Go back to your seat. Watch TV."

Santi gives Nico a bad look, then goes back to his seat.

Nico goes back to Juan's mother and the goat.

In minutes, it's all around the facility that Santi and Nico are beefing. They play it up—stink eyes at each other in the hallway, a rougher-than-called-for bump in the *fútbol* game.

Two days later, Fermín challenges Santi to a game of checkers.

"Two Snickers," Fermín says.

When Santi accepts, Nico says, "I want a piece of that."

"A piece of the Snickers?" Santi asks.

"A piece of the *bet*," Nico says. "I'll take Fermín."

"Are you crazy?" a kid named Manuel asks. "Fermín always loses."

"You want to bet on that?" Nico asks.

"Yeah!"

"Okay, but you have to give me odds," Nico says. "Fermín has to be, what, a million-to-one long shot? Give me three-to-one."

"If Fermín wins, you get three Snickers," Manuel says. "If Santi wins, I get one."

"Yeah, that's what three-to-one means, genius."

"Okay."

It spreads quickly. By the time the game starts, Nico has covered eleven three-to-one bets on Fermín. There's only one hiccup—

Rodrigo says, "Wait a second . . ."

Nico is scared Rodrigo has sniffed out the scam.

Then—

". . . does Nico have enough Snickers to cover these bets?" Rodrigo asks.

"If I lose," Nico says.

"Oh, you'll lose," Santi says.

"Tell you what," Nico says. "I'll take a punch in the stomach for every Snickers I'm short."

"Oh, I'll take the punch," Rodrigo says.

Nico quickly does the math—if he loses, he's going to get punched in the stomach ten times. But if I win, he thinks, Santi and me share thirty-three Snickers. Which we can trade for other goods and services, or lend out at interest.

We could be rich.

It's worth the risk.

The game starts.

Everyone in the dayroom, even the nongamblers, are watching.

At first, Santi plays a risky game, making his usual sharp moves, and Fermín . . . well, Fermín makes mistakes that can only be described as "Fermínesque." It looks like the everyday Santi v. Fermín mismatch, and kids start taunting Nico, making moans as they enjoy their putative Snickers, Rodrigo punching the air with vicious digs into the belly.

Nico plays it out, his face a study of anxiety and regret.

"I'm going to hit you so hard," Rodrigo tells Nico, "your mother will feel it."

Nico lets it go.

Then the game begins to turn.

Santi moves a checker and Fermín double-jumps him. A ripple of doubt goes through the room.

Shrugging it off, Santi moves again.

Fermín jumps him again.

"What the fuck?" Rodrigo asks.

Santi sits back, looks perplexed. Then he leans forward and engages in what will doubtless be a ruthlessly efficient counterattack that will finish the game.

It's close.

Way too close, as far as Nico is concerned.

Santi comes way too close to winning twice as he struggles to offer openings that even Fermín can see, sets up traps that even Fermín can spot in advance.

It's not easy.

The usually unflappable Santi breaks out in a sweat.

So does Nico.

Then he hears Fermín say, "King me."

It's over. Fermín has won.

Dramatically, Santi sweeps the checkers off the table. "Shit!"

"Fermín, you won!" Nico yells.

Fermín can't quite believe it himself. He sits staring at the board as he hears curses rain down on him.

For winning.

"Everyone hates me," he says softly. "Everyone hates me because I'm so stupid. So fucking stupid."

He walks over to the wall.

Bang. Bang.

Nico doesn't notice, he's too busy collecting Snickers and insults. A few kids can't pay, so he lets them write IOUs. "You know there's going to be interest, though?"

"What?"

"What, *güerito*, you think Snickers are free?" Nico asks. "Time is money, man. You pay tomorrow, you owe four, the next day it's five . . ."

"How are you going to collect?" Santi asks him later.

"Huh?"

"If some kid tells you to go fuck yourself, he isn't paying," Santi says, "how are you going to make him pay? No one is afraid of you, Nico."

Santi has a point.

Nico is the smallest kid there, and his fight with Jupiter wasn't exactly impressive. He thinks about this problem for a minute, then goes over to Mudo Juan.

"Mudo," he says, "if someone gives me a problem, you take care of it, and I'll give you a Snickers. You understand? Just nod."

Mudo nods.

"So we have a deal?"

Mudo nods again.

"Okay," Nico says. "Here's a two-bar retainer. Call it good faith."

Santi watches this transaction. When Nico walks back over, he says, "If you're here long enough, you and me, we could *own* this place."

Rodrigo sees them talking.

He's pissed.

Looking blood at Santi, he says, "You threw that game."

Santi's look of hurt innocence could fool a middle-school nun. But not Rodrigo. "You two little fuckers. I want my Snickers back."

Nico smiles at him. "Tell it to Mudo."

Yeah, Rodrigo isn't saying *shit* to Mudo.

Like the rest of them, he saw Mudo, on one of the rare occasions he got mad, snap a mop handle in half with just his hands.

Not over his leg, just with his hands.

Rodrigo's eyes narrow as he looks at Nico. "I'll kill you, you little fucker. I'm not messing with you this time, either. I'm going to kill you."

But he walks away.

"Fuck him," Nico says. Rodrigo isn't so bad now that his wingman Davido has moved up to the bigs.

This is the beginning of Fermíngate.

It comes up at the next day's group meeting, when Chris says, "I sense some tension in here today. What's going on?"

Nobody says anything.

Because snitches . . .

Chris is on his game, though. "Would it have anything to do with the incredible stash of candy bars Ramírez has in his room? Have you guys been gambling? Because you know that gambling is against the rules."

Nothing.

Someone must say something, though—probably one of the *frescas*—because Canela calls Nico and Santi into her office. "You boys have something you want to tell me?"

"How pretty you are?" Santi says.

"Because if you tell me," she says, "before I find out, it would be better for you."

They don't say anything.

"Be that way," Canela says. "I'm going to interview you separately, and, I promise you, one of you will break."

She starts with Nico. "Where did you get all the candy bars?"

"Kids gave them to me."

"Why?"

"Because they're nice."

"It wouldn't have something to do with a checkers game," Canela says, "between Santi and Fermín?"

"I don't know."

"Some kids are saying you cheated."

Nico shrugs.

"Here's the deal, Nico," she says. "The first one of you who talks to me doesn't get a write-up. The other kid does. You think Santi is going to have your back?"

Nico doesn't think, he *knows*. Santi has nothing to lose no matter how many times they write him up. Santi's going nowhere, and even if he was, Santi would never give him up. Just like Fermín would never give him up, or Mudo, even if he could.

They're brothers.

Fellow *veteranos* in detention.

They hang tight, she doesn't break them.

Not for lack of trying—Canela brings in about every kid in the unit, but by that time even the *fresca* have learned that they don't talk. She brings in Rodrigo, Fermín, she even brings in Mudo, who doesn't say anything.

Canela can't make a case so she eventually gives up.

Nico and Santi parlay the scam into a small fortune of candy bars, bags of chips, sodas and all kinds of shit. They don't make their own beds anymore— a kid who's behind in his payments does that—they don't do their own laundry. They get to cut the line at mealtime, they get to pick what's on TV.

And it's a self-perpetuating deal, because the other kids will make any kind of stupid bet trying to get even.

"It's another human delusion," Santi explains to Nico. "Just like hope. People always want to get even, they think they can get even and they just get further and further behind."

Santi is so smart.

He gets the other kids betting not against him and Nico, but against each other, with Santi and Nico as the bank. The two boys pay off the winners and collect a fee from the losers. More often than not the loser can't pay, so they end up lending him the stuff at interest.

"This way," Santi says, "we make on every bet. Something my grandmother taught me—the house always wins."

Santi, as usual, is right.

They own the place.

It has to happen.

Has to happen.

You lock thirty adolescent boys into a single place, sooner or later they're going to have a pissing contest.

It could have been worse.

The original idea was a jerk-off contest.

"Won't work," Santi explained. "Who wins? The kid who comes first? Who comes last? Who comes best? How do you judge it? With pissing, we have a standard metric: distance. It's measurable."

"Who's going to be the judge?" Rodrigo asks.

"Seeing as me and Nico aren't going to compete," Santi says, "we will."

"But then you can't bet," Rodrigo says.

"Right," Nico answers.

Rodrigo is so slow.

Fermín asks, "Where are we going to do it?"

"In the showers," Santi says, "so we can wash away the evidence."

They work out the rules—each of the contestants will put down five snacks, to be banked by Santi and Nico. Winner takes all. No side bets are allowed—someone might take a dive by "short pissing." You're only allowed to bet on yourself, although the boys with bigger dicks are allowed to give odds.

"Dick size is not necessarily linked to projection power," Santi says.

"How do you know?" Nico asks.

"You think this is my first pissing contest?"

The staff is puzzled the next day when there's a run on juice and soda and kids are hitting the water fountain like camels.

Chris gets it. "Pissing contest."

"I'll break it up," Gordo says.

"No, don't," Chris says. "There are a thousand nasty things they could get up to. This is fairly benign."

"You know they're gambling."

"Takes their minds off other things," Chris says.

"Like what?"

"You kidding me?" Chris asks. Just little things like not knowing where they're going to live, or where their families are, if they're going to get sent back into the shit they risked everything to escape. Little stuff like that. "Just find somewhere else to be while they're doing it."

"We're just going to let them piss in the shower room."

"You never pissed in the shower, Gordo?" Chris asks. "Tell the truth now."

That night, thirteen contestants line up in a very crowded shower room. Some are hopping up and down in discomfort from having saved an entire evening of fluids in their bladders. Others are shifting from leg to leg.

"Ready?!" Nico yells.

They're more than ready.

"Dicks out!" he yells.

They do it.

"Piss!"

Thirteen streams of urine arc across the shower room. Santi, wearing sunglasses (splash concern) squats a few feet away.

The mass urination stops.

Santi is on all fours now. He carefully crawls over the tiles, looking down, his concentration intense.

Then he stands up.

The room is silent.

Then Santi says, "We have a tie."

It's a stunning decision.

"In lane five," Santi says, "we have Manuel, and in lane eleven, Mudo Juan! It's dead even!"

Controversy breaks out. Kids rush up to check the stains for themselves. They argue, the Mexicans taking up for their boy Manuel, the Central Americans for Mudo Juan. Santi lets them blow off steam for a minute, then talks over the roar to say, "The judge's decision is final! The question now is what do we do from here?"

Some of the kids say they should split the winnings evenly between Manuel and Mudo. Santi has a better idea. "This was winner-take-all, so there has to be a single winner and he has to take it all. There's only one thing to do—this means a piss-off, Manuel v. Mudo."

"That's right!" Nico says.

"How come you guys get to decide?" Rodrigo asks.

"Because we're the Southern Virginia Juvenile Detention Center Gambling Commission," Santi answers.

"Why you?" one of the new kids asks.

"Do you know what a gambling commission is?" Santi asks.

"No."

"That's why."

Santi outlines the new rules. In two days (giving their bladders a chance to rest) Manuel and Mudo will go head-to-head (as it were), the winner getting the existing kitty. Everyone can wager on the outcome—straight up, no odds—all bets to go through the SVJDC Gambling Commission.

"What if it's a tie again?" one of the kids asks.

Santi hadn't thought about this. He contemplates for a few seconds and gives his ruling. "Then we go to jerk-off. First to shoot wins."

"I feel like Dana White," Santi says when the group breaks up.

"Was it really a tie?" Nico asks.

"Grow up." Mudo won by a half inch, Santi explains. But now they'll get a percentage from a new round of betting, which is going to be heavy, and . . . "We need to put our whole stash down on Mudo."

"We can't bet. We're the judges."

"We go through Fermín."

"The whole thing?" Nico asks. "Are we that sure Mudo is going to win?"

"He's hung like a horse."

"But you said there was no—"

"I know what I said. That was subterfuge."

The excitement over the next two days is *intense* as the Mexican kids line up behind Manuel, the CA kids back up Mudo, the teachers notice a sudden outbreak of interest in hydro-physics among their students, and the staff monitoring internet use notice a lot of googling queries like "What liquid makes you piss the most?"

"It's all about trajectory," Santi quietly coaches Mudo. "You have to find exactly the right trajectory. Shoot too high or too low, you lose distance."

Mudo nods.

"What is the best trajectory?" Nico asks. "Do you know?"

"Yahoo puts it at forty-five degrees."

"You got that, Mudo?" Nico asks. "Forty-five degrees."

Nico is worried, his entire hard-won fortune is on Mudo getting the trajectory just right. And on the right choice of fluid.

"Water," Santi says. "No sodas—the bubbles get in your dick and slow your piss down."

"They do?" Nico asks.

"Try it. I did." Santi looks back at Mudo. "And no jerking off. Save it up in case it comes to a tiebreaker. You have someone to think about?"

"He's not going to answer you, Santi."

"That's okay. It's better if he keeps it all inside," Santi says. "Just as long as you have someone, Mudo. Think about her, rub, but don't come. That way, when the time is right—*bam,* hair trigger."

"I heard Manuel is going with Katie Barbieri," Nico says.

"That skank?" Santi says. "We've won already. But it's not going to come to that, you're going to win on piss."

"And remember," Nico says, "you have the honor of all Central America riding on you. A whole continent."

"I don't think it is," Santi says.

"Sure it is," Nico says. "North America, South America, Central America."

Canela is ready to shut the whole thing down. There's no way thirty excited adolescents are going to keep this kind of thing a secret, and it gets to her. She tells Chris to put a stop to it, pronto. "They're abusing Juan."

"That's one way of looking at it."

"Is there another way?"

"Sure," Chris says. "That we have a kid who's been basically catatonic, we haven't been able to reach him, and Nico and Santi—"

"Meyer Lansky and Lucky Luciano."

"Those were gangsters?"

"Yes."

"They have him participating in something," Chris says.

"Something disgusting."

"They're teenage boys," Chris says. "They're disgusting by definition. And this is making Juan the center of attention."

"They're using him as a figure of fun."

"That's *our* projection," Chris says. "And we know Juan isn't going to do anything he doesn't want to do. Let them do this, Norma. Let them get away with something, think they're getting over on us. These kids don't get a lot of wins."

"This isn't what they're here for."

"No," Chris says. "They're here so the county can bill ORR. They support the rest of this facility."

"That's not fair."

"I couldn't agree more," Chris says. "C'mon, Norma."

After a few seconds she asks, "Who are you betting on?"

"Juan," says Chris. "A beer with Gordo."

"Cheapskates."

Chris shrugs. "Pay us more."

"I can't."

The big day arrives. The nerves are palpable. The kids pay even less attention in class, they play the afternoon *fútbol* game perfunctorily, as a preliminary to the main event. All day, all eyes are on Manuel and Mudo Juan, assessing their condition, their readiness, their horniness if it comes to that.

Nico's a mess.

The Mexican kids are too confident, as if they know something. But all Jupiter will say is "Mexicans can piss! And if it comes to the tiebreaker? Manuel is the premature ejaculation champion of the world. He practices all the time. You guys fucked up."

Nico hopes not.

He's come to enjoy wealth.

The kids are so overexcited by dinner they can barely eat.

Except Mudo.

He eats like a pregnant hippo.

Nico wonders if this is a good thing.

"It is," Santi assures him. "A full belly puts extra pressure on the bladder."

Nico isn't so confident about Santi's knowledge of anatomy.

The evening until lights out is endless. The boys try to watch TV or play cards, but no one's heart is in it.

Mudo sits draining bottle after bottle of water.

"You're sure about this soda thing?" Nico asks Santi.

"Absolutely."

"Because Manuel's drinking Cokes."

"Good, it'll fuck him up."

Finally, finally, it's lights out and the boys dutifully troop to their rooms. Gordo makes himself missing, and the kids come out and assemble in the shower room.

Nico thinks Mudo looks nervous.

It makes *him* nervous.

Santi holds his hand up to his mouth like a microphone. "Laaadies and gentlemen . . ."

"What the fuck is he doing?" Jupiter asks.

"I have no idea," Nico says.

"For the thousands in attendance and the millions watching around the world," Santi yells, "this will be a one-round pissing contest for the heavyweight championship of the wooooorld! In the red corner, pissing out of Ciudad Juárez, Mexico . . ."

The Mexican kids cheer.

"Manuel 'El Micción' Coronado!"

More cheers.

Boos from the CA kids.

"And in the blue corner," Santi says, "pissing out of . . . well, we have no fucking idea where he's from . . . Juan 'El Mudo' Something or Other!"

Cheers and jeers.

"Gentlemen, touch hands if you want . . ."

They don't.

"I want a clean urination," Santi says. "No dribbling, no pissing behind the back of the head . . ."

"What?" Jupiter asks.

"Just go with it," Nico says.

"In charge of the ring tonight, Nico 'He's Firm but He's Fair' Ramírez!"

"All right," Nico says, then he repeats what Santi told him to say. "Let's get it on!"

Manuel and Mudo walk up to the line.

"Ready!" Nico yells. "Dicks out!"

The dicks come out.

The tension is unbearable.

"Piss!"

Nico watches Mudo's stream of urine arc up and out in a perfect forty-five-degree trajectory. It's beautiful, like water from a fire hose, and it carries Nico's hopes and dreams with it.

He almost wants to cry.

Then it lands.

Right next to Manuel's splatter.

The silence is heavy as Santi walks over, bends down, examines the stains. Then he looks at the crowd and says, quietly and solemnly, "We're going to overtime."

The crowd erupts.

The Mexican kids are jubilant—they know they have it now.

"There will be a ten-minute break," Santi says, "and then the jerk-off."

Nico and Santi huddle with Mudo during the break.

"How you feeling?" Santi asks. "Horny?"

Mudo doesn't answer.

He looks grim.

"You've *got* this, *güerito*," Santi says, squatting in front of him. "Look, you were literally *born* to do this . . . because, let's get real, you're never going to actually get laid."

No answer.

Mudo just looks scared.

This is not good, Nico thinks. He sees poverty staring him in the face in the form of Mudo's blank eyes.

He grabs Mudo's shoulders. "There comes a time in every man's life when he has to step up to the plate and *be* a man. This is that time. This is *your time*, Juan. Tune out all the noise, focus, and jerk off like the champ we know you are. Okay, let's go."

They reassemble.

"No preliminaries!" Santi announces. "At Nico's signal, each man will start giving himself *una puñeta*. The first one to shoot is the winner. Nico?"

"Dicks out," Nico says. Then, "Commence!"

Mudo is game, you have to give him that.

His eyes are closed in a tight clench, his neck is arched back, his right hand flies as fast as a big man's hand can fly.

Manuel looks like he's taking a more nonchalant, dreamier, fantasy-based approach.

"I didn't realize Manuel was left-handed," Nico says.

"Ambidextrous," says Jup.

"Will it make a difference?"

"I don't think so," Jup says. "I've seen him rub one out with his feet. No, seriously, I have."

We're fucked, Nico thinks. Being rich was nice while it lasted.

"The judge!" Nico yells. "Mudo, think of the *judge*!"

Mudo picks up the pace, jerking furiously.

Manuel glances over, like an elite sprinter who hears footsteps coming up behind him. His nonchalance disappears and he takes it up a notch.

He's not going to let himself get caught.

It's as good as over.

Nico has an inspiration.

"The judge, Mudo," he yells, "*and* Canela!"

Mudo's eyes open.

His mouth opens.

His balls open.

A moment of stunned silence, then—

"The winner," Santi yells, "and new champion of the world—*El Mu-dooooooooo!*"

The CA kids surround Mudo, slap him on the back, hug him, kiss his cheek. Shit, they'd lift him on their shoulders and carry him around the room, but that isn't going to happen. He accepts the praise and congratulations wordlessly and tucks his penis back into his pants.

The Mexican kids are cursing.

Nico is beyond ecstatic.

Snack wealthy beyond measure.

"Canela?" Santi asks him. "Where did *that* come from?"

"I don't know," Nico says. "It just came to me."

"Brilliant," Santi says. "Sick, but brilliant."

Nico goes to bed that night a rich and happy man.

The next morning, Norma listens to Chris's report and says, "Am I to understand that a young man traumatized to the point of elective muteness brought himself to climax by the image of me in a lesbian relationship with a reality television star?"

Chris smiles. "Pretty much."

"Given the options, I'm going to choose to be flattered." She holds up a document. "The gang is being broken up anyway. Ramírez's FRA was approved. His uncle is coming to get him tomorrow."

"Does Nico know?"

"Not yet. I thought you'd like to tell him."

Chris finds Nico on his way to class after breakfast. "Hey, *güerito*, pack your shit, you're getting out of here."

Nico is stunned. And scared. Are they sending him back to Guatemala?

"It's good news," Chris says. "Your sponsorship went through. Your aunt and uncle are coming to get you."

It's dizzying.

The first person Nico tells, of course, is Santi. "I'm going to live in New York. I'm going to be an American."

Santi shakes his head. "You don't know, do you?"

"Know what?"

"This doesn't mean you get to stay permanently," Santi says. "It only means you get to stay until they hold a 'deportation hearing.' Most of the time, they deport you. That's why it's not called a 'Welcome to America' hearing."

"Oh."

"But look, congratulations, *cerote*. At least you're out of here."

Then Nico feels bad. He's getting out of here and Santi isn't. He's going to miss Santi, and Fermín, even Mudo.

Nico never had brothers before.

But he's still excited.

Nico is by nature and necessity an optimist. New York is going to be great, his aunt and uncle are going to be great, and maybe—no, not maybe, probably—the judge at the deportation hearing will be nice and pretty like the judge on TV and will decide that he can stay.

He tells this to Fermín.

"Sure they'll let you stay," Fermín says. "You're a good kid, why wouldn't they let you stay?"

By lunch, Nico has convinced himself of it. Also that he'll get a job and make enough money to send for his mother, and they'll let her in, too. By that afternoon, he firmly believes that Flor will come, too, and they'll go to school together.

"That's what's going to happen," Santi says.

"But you said—"

"I say a lot of stupid shit," Santi says. "I talk out of my ass. You're going to have a great life, Nico."

Yeah, except Rodrigo disagrees.

When he hears about Nico's news, he walks up to him in front of Santi, Fermín, Mudo and a bunch of others and says, "You're never getting out of here, *culero*."

"Yeah? Why not?"

"Because I'm going to kill you first."

"Why does that guy hate me so much?" Nico says after Rodrigo walks away. "It's crazy."

"It's not," Santi says.

He explains the rationale. Rodrigo is headed for his eighteenth birthday and deportation back to El Salvador. He doesn't want to go. Slicing up Nico gets him to a prison here instead, and he goes in already on the bumper to get into the Mara Salvatrucha car by killing a Calle 18.

It makes perfect sense.

"It's just a bonus for him that he hates you," Santi says.

"But why?"

"He's jealous," Fermín says. "You're getting out."

"Fuck him," Nico says. "I can fight him."

"No, you can't," Santi says. "He has six inches and fifty pounds on you. He can beat the fuck out of you, and anyway, he has a *pedazo*, he's been making it for months. He's planning to stick you."

"Tell Chris," Fermín says.

Nico shakes his head. "I'm not a snitch."

"Fuck that," Fermín says. "The guy is a psycho. He could kill you, Nico."

"I won't snitch," Nico says.

"*I* will," Santi says. "I'm going to Chris."

"Don't," Nico says. "I'm serious, don't."

"But, Nico—"

"I can take care of myself."

"No, you can't," Santi says. "Look, it's no shame, *güerito*. You have a chance for a life. Don't throw it away by trying to be some kind of macho asshole."

"If you tell," Nico says, "I'll never forgive you."

He's scared to death, terrified, but if he snitches on Rodrigo and the word gets back to Guatemala, they could go take it out on his mother.

That evening, his supper tastes like dirt in his mouth, he's that scared.

It doesn't help that Rodrigo grins at him from another table, and when he gets up to leave, mouths, *Esta noche.*

Tonight.

Nico's legs feel like wood as he walks up the stairs to his room. He tries to focus on packing the few things he has into the plastic bags they gave him. It doesn't work; his mind stays on Rodrigo, on the blade, on what it could do.

He's seen people killed, he knows what it looks like.

He wants to cry for help, he wants to throw up, he does neither.

When Nico's finished shoving things into his bag, he lies down on his bed but doesn't close his eyes.

He waits.

And thinks about the long ride on La Bestia, about Paola, about Flor, the attack from the trees, the hunger, the cold, the heat, the thirst, the fatigue, crossing the river.

I should have known better, Nico thinks. I should have known I'd never get out.

Kids like me don't get out.

Then he hears a scream.

Then shouting, then running footsteps slamming on the concrete floor.

He hears Gordo yell, "Jesus Christ!"

Nico jumps from his bed and walks out onto the tier.

Other boys are already out there—Santi and Fermín, Mudo and others looking down over the rail.

Rodrigo lies splayed on the floor below, the *pedazo* clutched in his hand, blood pooling from the back of his head.

His neck broken like a chicken's.

Mudo turns to Nico.

Says, "You owe me a Snickers."

4

Billy the Kid

Tijuana, Mexico
December 2016

Sean Callan is on the hunt.

Like hunters over thousands of years, he's a predator for the survival of what he loves—his woman, his home. He has to track down and kill Iván Esparza to give life to what he loves.

Kill Iván and Nora is safe.

Kill Iván and Elena will make sure that your beloved village is left in peace.

But killing the head of a cartel wing isn't a matter of headhunting. Callan knows he'll never get to the head without first getting to the body. You have to chip away, work your way up, erode his base, denude his strength, his income, make the people who support him start to believe that they've backed the wrong horse in a race in which the losing bettors pay not in cash but in blood.

Mob bosses survive for as long as they're making money for other people and as long as the income stream from those people flows upward, providing them with the cash for gunmen, payoffs, safe houses and weaponry.

You don't cut a tree down from the top, you chop it at the trunk.

Olivier Piedra is one of the people making money from Iván's patronage and kicking up to him in return.

Olivier Piedra's prime profession is running whores in La Coahuila, Tijuana's red light district, but lately he's branched out into extortion and dope. This wouldn't be a bad thing, except he's doing it under the Esparza flag.

And he planted it on a Sánchez corpse.

Elena can't afford to lose another block to the Esparzas.

Olivier's gotta go.

It's chaos in Baja.

War all the time while the splintered Sinaloa cartel fights it out with it-

self. You got the Sánchez group fighting the Esparzas and now the Esparzas
fighting the Núñez people. Add the Jalisco people into the mix, it's a clusterfuck. Half the clowns on the street don't even know who they're killing for,
they only know to kill the guy who isn't them.

Some of them know, though.

Hunter-killer teams prowl TJ and the rest of Baja like homicidal summer
camp kids in a lethal flag war.

We even have colors, Callan thinks.

It was that psycho-bitch La Fósfora who started that.

"Baja is green."

Spray-painting corpses green like it was St. Patrick's Day or something.
And if Sinaloa is green, Jalisco had to pick it up and started spray-painting
in red, and even Elena, who is usually removed from that kind of nonsense,
decided they'd better have a color and picked blue.

The Young Wolf picked up the theme in Guerrero and, of course, went
for black.

Motherfucking ridiculous.

And, of course, no one can kill anyone anymore without leaving a *manta*,
a message. Used to be, you clipped a guy, that *was* the message. Sent and
received. Now you have to write a note and explain it, brag about it, threaten
the survivors. Who, of course, turn around and do the same thing, tit for
fucking tat.

The body count in Baja, which for years was relatively peaceful Sinaloa
territory, is at an all-time record high.

The summer of 2016 was brutal.

In August, La Fósfora and her crew left the body of a Sánchez loyalist in a
black bag outside a Zona Río club with the *manta: We're here and we'll never
leave. Here's a reminder that we're still giving the orders and that you don't even
exist. Not even Sánchez strippers and Jalisco dollies. The sky is green!*

Then she left another dismembered body by the Gato Bronco Bridge:
This is what bridges are for. We're still in charge. Baja is green.

Elena's people struck back the same day, shot a Núñez guy and left the
manta: Here's your fucking green sky. Go fuck yourselves. Baja is blue.

Two days later, two bodies were hanging from a bridge in Colonia
Simón Bolívar: *This is what the Sánchez-Jalisco alliance looks like. Go fuck
yourselves.*

The next day it was an Esparza-protected nightclub that burned down:
*This will happen to all businesses who align themselves with traitors. Get with
the real owners of the city and not these dirty bastards. Go red. We're strong and
united—Sánchez-Jalisco.*

The autumn was no better.

Someone threw the dismembered corpses of four Jalisco people off a pedestrian bridge with notes threatening Elena, Luis and El Mastín. One of the bodies landed on a passing car. Two weeks later, an eighteen-year-old Mexican American girl was shot to death off Vía Rápida. Her boyfriend slung dope for the Esparzas.

Callan wasn't involved in any of these killings.

They're beneath his skill level.

Callan heads up a hunter-killer team that scours Baja for enemy hunter-killer teams or high-ranking members of the opposition. They rove the territory like submarines in a wide ocean, trying to get radar pings on other submarines.

You have to have a certain standing to get whacked by Sean Callan or Lev, they're not wasting their bullets on low-level *malandros*.

And they ain't spray-painting nobody.

Olivier Piedra just made the cut.

Oviedo Esparza would be better.

Iván Esparza would be the home run.

And Callan thinks it would just be a good thing for the world to remove La Fósfora from it. In addition to running an extremely efficient crew of killers who have made La Paz her stronghold, the woman is an out-and-out sadist with no apparent limits to her depravity. She likes burning people, dousing them in acid, chopping them up and leaving the parts scattered in splashes of green paint.

Well, actually now she has a new color.

Pink.

A feminist statement.

It would be a benefit to mankind to take her off the count.

So Callan hunts.

He kills.

In between he has gone home to the haven of Costa Rica and Nora. Sometimes Nora comes up to a pad they're keeping in San Diego, but mostly she stays in Bahia and he flies down there.

Elena Sánchez has kept her word, kept her people away from Bahia, left the people there alone. It's a little haven, a refuge from the ever-expanding narco world, the irony being that it's Callan's bloody work in Mexico that keeps it peaceful.

His murders are the price of peace.

As long as Elena is winning the war. If she loses it, any of the others could come into Bahia—the Esparzas, the Núñez people, even the old Tapia group under Damien. Another reason for Callan to keep fighting—like any soldier he wants victory, he wants to win this war so he can go home and live in peace.

He needs to make the sky blue.

"She's getting old, she's getting worn. We can't get as much. Sell her. Get what you can."

Flor hears the man she knows as Olivier talking to the man she knows as Javier.

They've had her for months now.

The train took Flor to Tijuana.

Close to the American border, but she never made it because the pimps were lined up like crows waiting for grasshoppers.

Picked them off one at a time.

The one who grabbed Flor called himself Olivier. Told her that he worked for an agency that hired girls as maids and cleaners and that he could get her a job where she could save her money and earn enough to cross the border.

Flor wasn't sure she believed him but she didn't have a choice. He already had her by the wrist and put her in a car and took her into a building where he locked her in a room. An older woman came in a few minutes later, took her clothes off and jabbed at her between the legs.

Muttered, *"Virgen, valiosa,"* and then took her down the hall to a shower. Washed her, shampooed her hair and combed it, then took her back to her room.

Olivier came back in and took pictures off her.

First naked.

Made her pose.

Kneeling on the bed.

Lying on her back.

Her legs open.

Her legs crossed.

Made her smile.

Made her pout.

If she resisted, he hit her with an extension cord on the soles of her feet, where it wouldn't show in the pictures.

Then he dressed her.

In a pink little girl's dress and the woman put bows in her hair and lipstick on her lips and rouge on her cheeks.

He took more pictures.

Made her hold up a sign that read: SERÉ TU AMOR. SERÁS MI PRIMERO.

He made her smile, he made her pout.

He gave her tortillas with some chicken.

He put her pictures on the internet.

The first man who came was an American, old. He told her he had paid a thousand dollars to be her *primero*, her first. She would be his little *amor*, his sweetheart. He laid her down and raped her.

The second was Asian.

He didn't speak at all.

He cried when he finished.

The third was a woman.

After that she lost track. Every few days they'd move her to a different hotel, a different house. They showered her, shampooed her, perfumed her, fed her, gave her pills to be happy, pills to be calm, to be a little sweetheart. When she wasn't, they whipped the soles of her feet until she screamed.

This went on for weeks, then months.

Now she hears Olivier talking—"She's getting old, she's getting worn. We can't get as much. Sell her. Get what you can."

Olivier needs cash to pay for some new turf he's buying. Corners to sell girls, to sell drugs, to extort the street merchants. That would bring in more money than a worn-out little whore, and there were fresher ones coming in every day.

So a man who calls himself Javier comes in and takes her to a different building. He rapes her and leaves her on a mattress and locks the door.

Tells her he'll be back with her new owner.

She waits.

She doesn't care.

Flor knows her life is one long rape and that's all it will ever be. Sometimes she thinks about Nico and wonders what happened to him.

She thinks he's probably dead.

For his sake, she hopes so.

Javier walks down Calle Coahuila.

Tijuana's Zona Norte.

Aka "La Coahuila," a "zone of tolerance" for prostitution.

Prostitution is legal in Mexico, as long as it's in designated areas and the women are at least eighteen. But many of them are a lot younger, and men flock to Tijuana for the young, the teenagers, the "fresh meat."

Or younger.

TJ's famous for it.

The pedophiles who can't afford a flight to Bangkok come to TJ to get off. The narcos never used to tolerate it. In Barrera's day they would have strung up a guy who sold children by his dick with barbed wire; now it's just another business. Now they tolerate anything, as long as it makes money to support their troops.

There are no rules anymore.

Anything goes.

The *pirujas*—the whores—are everywhere, walking up to men, saying, "*Vamos al cuarto*"—"Let's go to a room."

Most of the men do, that's what they're here for.

Javier sees one who doesn't.

Just keeps walking, ignoring them.

He hasn't seen what he's looking for, Javier thinks. In his forties maybe, casually but well dressed. A *yanqui,* too, and he looks like money. Javier scopes him, trails him. Watches him turn down two more whores, pretty teenagers at that.

Javier makes his move.

Walks up to his side and whispers, "I have a new car. Maybe ten years old. Never been driven."

"How much?"

"Five hundred dollars to rent," the pimp says, "two thousand to buy. You take her to El Norte, friend, you can make some serious money, on the dark net. You can sell her over and over again."

"Where is she?"

"Money first."

The gringo peels out three yards. "The rest when I see her."

"To rent or to buy?"

"I won't know until I see her. Is she pretty?"

"Face like an angel. A body made for fucking."

Javier leads the gringo up a side street to the cheap hotel. Up to the second floor and opens the door.

The girl sits on the bare mattress.

"What's her name?" the gringo asks.

"Teresa." Javier shrugs. He's making it up. Like, what the fuck difference does it make? He shuts the door. "You want her or not?"

"Yeah," the gringo says. "I do."

He reaches into his shirt, takes out a silenced pistol and shoots Javier between the eyes. Then he opens the door and goes into the room. Takes the girl by the hand and lifts her off the mattress. "You're coming with me."

The girl knows.

She's done the drill before.

She's been driven.

Time and again.

Like a wooden doll, she lets him lead her down the hallway and down the stairs. A couple of *pirujas* crack open doors and look out. They either don't see or they don't care or they know a killer's eyes when they see them.

The man walks her out into the street and hands her to another man, who puts her in the front seat of a car.

No one stops him.

Two other men get out of the car.

"Stay there," the man says.

She does.

Callan kicks in a door and they go up the stairs. A guard in front of a locked steel door starts to pull the pistol from his belt, but one of the Israelis shoots him twice in the throat, then tosses him down the stairs.

Lev shotguns the lock off and they step inside.

Callan moves down the hallway and goes through a door at the end of the hall.

A woman stands to the side with a hairbrush and a tin of makeup. A tall, stout man with long hair holds a camera. He turns and sees Callan's 9 mm Glock pointed at him.

"Do you know who I am?" he asks. "I'm Olivier Piedra. I'm with—"

Callan blows the top of his head off.

The woman screams and starts to run, but Lev fires the shotgun into the back of her legs. She falls face-first, her arms splayed in front of her. Lev walks over, pulls a pistol and puts a bullet in the back of her head. "*Zonna.*"

A customer backs against the wall, throws his arm in front of his face.

Callan walks up to him. Presses the pistol against the top of his left knee-cap and fires. The man bellows and collapses.

"Crawl out of here," Callan says. "Tell them there are new rules in the Zona. You touch a kid, you die."

They go back down the stairs.

"I hate child molesters," Callan says.

"Apparently," says Lev.

"What's your name?" Callan asks the little girl.

"Flor."

"You're safe now," he says. "No one's going to hurt you anymore."

He can see that the girl doesn't believe him.

She's heard that before.

Now he needs to figure out what to do with this little girl so he can take Piedra off his honey-do list and continue the hunt for the brothers Esparza.

There's only one thing to do.

It's five minutes to the border.

The wait this late at night is only about half an hour and while he's sitting in line he gets a call from Lev telling him to go into Lane 8.

The agent there is on the Sánchez arm.

They sit there for twenty-five minutes and the girl stares straight ahead. She doesn't fidget, she doesn't cry, she doesn't say a word.

Not one.

Callan pulls up, shows his American passport.

The agent looks at the girl. "Is this your daughter?"

"Yeah."

"Welcome home, Mr. Callan."

"Thank you."

He hopes Nora feels the same.

They rent a "vacation condo" off Craigslist in the beach town of Encinitas, north of San Diego. It's a small one-bedroom, but it overlooks the ocean and Nora likes to walk on the beach. Callan pulls into the underground parking structure, gets out, takes Flor's hand, walks her up to the condo and lets himself in.

Nora is still up, watching television.

She sees the little girl.

"Nora, esta es Flor."

He can see the questions in Nora's eyes but she's too smart and too sensitive to ask in front of the child. Instead, she gets up from her chair, squats in front of the kid and says, *"Hola, Flor. Bienvenida."*

"Flor might stay with us for a little bit."

"That would be lovely," Nora says. "Are you hungry, sweetheart? Thirsty?"

Flor nods.

Nora takes her hand, walks her toward the little kitchen area. "Let's see what we have."

They have some tortillas and some cheese, some sliced turkey and an orange. She fixes the girl a plate and sits her down on a high stool at the breakfast counter. They don't have milk, but Nora pours her a glass of orange juice.

The girl eats and drinks slowly.

Afterward, Nora leads her to the sofa, where she sits watching and eventually falls asleep.

Then Nora says, "Explain?"

"They've been pimping her out."

"Where's her family?"

"Guatemala?" He's quiet for a minute, then he says, "You've always wanted a child."

"So you *bought* me one?"

"I didn't exactly buy her."

"Oh." She looks at the sleeping girl. "The life we lead now, it's not exactly the best for a kid."

"Compared to what she has?"

"We don't know what she has," Nora says. "She might have a family looking for her."

"Most of these kids come in on the train," Callan says. "They're trying to make it to the States."

"If she has family here, maybe we could find them."

"Maybe."

"Of course we'll look after her until we do," Nora says. "Just don't fall in love with her, Sean."

"She's not a puppy."

"I don't know." Nora strokes the girl's hair. "Kind of she is."

They talk to her in the morning, find out that she's from Guatemala City, that she has no surviving parents and an older sister who won't miss having another mouth to feed. No, she has no family in the United States.

"Why did you come?" Nora asks.

"My friend Nico," she says. "He was coming. I would have missed him."

"Where is he now?" Callan asks.

She doesn't know. They got separated in Mexico City. She thinks that she took the wrong train.

"What do you want to do?" Nora asks.

Flor shrugs.

No one has ever asked her what she wanted to do.

Nora sends Callan out to buy clothes. He has no clue so she writes down sizes, tells him to go to Target. She'd go herself but she doesn't want to leave Flor alone and the girl is still afraid of men.

Callan goes out with his shopping list.

Blouses, pants, underwear, socks, shoes, sweatshirts, sweaters, a bathing suit. Pajamas, a robe, blankets, sheets, a pillow. Shampoo, toothbrush, toothpaste, hairbrush. Crayons, pencils, drawing paper. And kids' food, food she might like and is used to. Rice, chicken, milk, cereal, tortillas.

Also dolls.

"What kind of dolls?"

"I don't know," Nora says. "When is the last time I bought a doll?"

When is the last time *I* did? Callan thinks, but he goes shopping and draws lines through the list. Gets back to the condo to look out from the balcony at Nora and Flor walking on the beach, hand in hand.

He drops the stuff off and drives back to Mexico to kill people.

He's summoned to a tactical meeting at Elena's.

Luis briefs them.

As war leader, Callan thinks, Luis is one hell of an engineer.

"The tactical situation has changed," Luis says. "Núñez's failed attempt on the Esparza brothers has changed the landscape. On the one hand, it's a positive, because the Núñez faction has lost support in Mexico City. On the other hand, it's a negative because it strengthens the Esparzas."

"What do we know about their condition?" Callan asks. He's never known bullet wounds to strengthen anyone.

"Not much," Luis says. "They're holed up somewhere deep in the Sinaloa mountains. The rumors are that Iván took two rounds in the shoulder, Oviedo was hit in the upper back, and that Alfredo wasn't hit at all. But we don't really know."

Elena sits with her jaw tight.

Callan knows how badly she wants Iván dead.

But her tactical choices are limited. The best move would be to reach out to Núñez and offer him an alliance against the Esparzas in exchange for Baja. Núñez would make that deal now, but Elena can't make that alliance without alienating Tito Ascensión. If she drives Ascensión into Iván's arms, she loses.

And Ascensión's beef was with Núñez, not Esparza. With the split between them, Ascensión no longer has a reason to fight Iván. In fact, Iván, with his power in Sinaloa, would be more useful to him than Elena in a fight against Núñez.

Elena's in a tough spot.

She needs a game changer.

So do I, Callan thinks.

I need out of this life.

He says, "The Esparza brothers are in the same place at the same time. They've done that to consolidate their protection, but it also makes them vulnerable."

"What are you suggesting?" Elena asks.

"If you can get the location," he says, "let me go in. Me and Lev and a handpicked team of our best guys. We go in, we terminate the Esparzas and we get out."

"It's a suicide mission," Luis says. "It can't work."

"It's *my* suicide." Callan shrugs. "Look, it's a chance to end this war, win this war, in one stroke. If we keep fighting it the way we have been fighting it, we're going to lose. You know that."

Elena considers what he's saying.

She knows that he's right.

And there are things that Callan doesn't know that make the situation even worse. Elena has heard that Rafael Caro has put together a group that is loaning money to a business concern in the United States with close connections to the new government.

Rafael didn't approach her.

If it's true, Iván will be well-nigh unstoppable.

The clock is not our friend, Elena thinks. If we don't kill Iván soon, he'll kill my last son. She looks at Callan. "How do you evaluate the chances of success?"

Callan thinks for a second, then he says, "Three to one against. But that's better than our odds of winning a protracted war."

"And you'd be willing to go," Elena says.

"I want one thing," Callan says.

Papers created.

A US passport.

The Young Wolf is getting shorn.

Damien has come in for a haircut, because he doesn't want to look like a total barbarian when he meets with Tito.

He's been in the hills a long time since his release from Baja. Growing opium, moving opium, fighting the police, the army, the marines.

Fighting Sinaloa.

And now his old friend Ric is on the run. It's funny, but it's bad, because the Esparza brothers will gain from it. But it was a wrong thing to do, and he's ashamed of Ric. There's a code, and he violated it.

Now Damien sits in the barber chair to get rid of his long hair and his beard. It feels good to be back in civilization and Tito has guaranteed his security in Guadalajara, where no one would dare fuck with the Jalisco boss. Even so, Damien has four bodyguards with him in two vehicles, all armed for a fight.

Damien has a grenade tucked under his shirt.

If it looks like they're going to take him out, the Young Wolf isn't going out alone.

The meeting with Tito might be tough.

With Ric and his dad on the run, Tito has no good reason to keep fighting the Esparzas. But Damien has to keep him in the fight. The Esparzas aren't going to forgive the kidnapping of Oviedo and Alfredo, and he doesn't have the power to go up against the brothers on his own. Not yet, even though the heroin and fentanyl money is pouring in from Eddie. There was even enough money to invest with Rafael Caro.

I'm a real estate mogul now, Damien thinks, laughing at himself.

But it's good.

Good to bring back the family fortunes.

And the money will give him the power to take Acapulco back, and when he has the port under control, it will bring a lot of the old Tapia people to him.

The meeting with Tito has to go well.

Damien pushes it out of his mind, leans back and relaxes. He knows the barber is good, Tito recommended the place. The barber massages his neck, and before he knows it, Damien falls asleep.

The shouting wakes him up.

Shouts and curses and he opens his eyes to see rifle barrels pointed at him. Black-clad marines in black hoods and masks scream at him to get down. He glances out the window—his bodyguards have their hands behind the backs of their heads, two of them are already cuffed.

He reaches into his shirt for the grenade.

"Don't!" a marine yells.

Damien hesitates.

Live or die?

You always think you'd go out a hero. A legend in a song. The Young Wolf wouldn't be taken alive. He went out with a bang.

It's different when it's real.

Fuck all that.

Damien decides to live.

He slowly raises his hands.

Two nights later, Damien Tapia gets visitors in his cell.

Three guards.

All of them huge.

He's scared. "What do you want, brothers?"

They don't answer him. Two of them grab him and throw him down on his bed. One holds his legs down, the other stretches his arms out.

"Who sent you?" Damien asks. "Was it Elena? Tell her I'm sorry. Tell her it was a mistake."

They don't answer him.

"Núñez?" Damien asks. "I'll never do it again. I'll pay him back. Please. Tell him."

The third guard takes out a homemade blade.

"Call Caro," Damien says. "He'll tell you I'm good people. He wouldn't want you to do this. Please. Call him. No, call Tito. He'll tell you. I'm with him. I'm with him. Please. Please.

"I don't want to die."

The guard slashes Damien's wrists.

"I heard he killed himself," Caro says.

"Do you believe that?" Tito asks, sitting in Caro's kitchen, watching the old man make pozole. He didn't like doing it, setting Damien up for arrest by the marines. But Caro had argued that the Young Wolf was causing too much trouble, shooting police, soldiers. That they didn't need that kind of heat.

"Why not?" Caro says. "The whole family is crazy. The father? All this killing, this violence, it's no good for anyone. Maybe it's for the best."

"And you'll take over his heroin routes," Tito says.

Caro stirs the pozole. "What can I do for you, Tito? What brings you here?"

"My thirty million dollars," Tito says. "I want to see a return."

"You already have," Caro says. "Núñez has been indicted."

"Means nothing unless the government goes after him."

"They will," Caro says. He sips the pozole, then shakes in some salt. "I've heard he's left Eldorado and is in the wind. The kid, too. Good riddance."

"I thought you were a loyal Sinaloa guy."

"They let me sit in a cell for twenty years and did nothing," Caro says. "Your thirty million dollars are in Washington, DC, working hard for you."

Caro places the lid on the pot and steps away from the stove.

"Do you know what the secret to making good pozole is?" he asks. "Let it cook slow."

Let Sinaloa kill itself.

First thing Eddie wants to know—am I on DEA's radar?

No, Hidalgo tells him, DEA hasn't tripped to him yet. As far as the feds are concerned, you're an ex-con who opted out of the witness protection program and they couldn't give a shit what happens to you.

What about Darius Darnell? Is he on the DEA radar?

No, Darnell is off the screen.

Then Eddie toe-dips on his money-laundering operation—names a few banks where he puts money. Hidalgo says he'll get back to him—waits a week and then comes back—no, the banks are safe.

Except, of course, they're not now.

At Keller's direction, Hidalgo, as Tony Fuentes, has been feeding Eddie misinformation like little morsels of poison hidden in his food.

Fuentes also brings gifts—answers to questions that Ruiz hasn't asked. Eddie, here's the DEA's intelligence on three rival organizations operating in New York. Here's surveillance info on a Núñez "sales team" reaching out to gangs in Manhattan, a Jalisco slinger moving into Brooklyn. Listen to this, Eddie—audio of a Sinaloa customer in Staten Island who's unhappy, maybe open to an approach.

Then they watch the pings.

The Núñez sales team stops making cold calls and the Staten Island retailer turns out to be open to switching jerseys. Interestingly, the Jalisco dealer in Brooklyn gets a pass.

Does that mean that Caro is getting closer to Tito Ascensión? Keller wonders.

Stay tuned.

They're careful, they're cagey, feeding Ruiz only bits and pieces so he doesn't get suspicious on the basis that if it seems to be too good to be true, it is. Eddie tests—asking Fuentes about the safety of a two-kilo shipment he has moving into Manhattan.

Ruiz can afford to lose two kilos if Fuentes is a plant.

Keller lets it go through. Makes sure NYPD lays off it, too. Lays off but stays close enough to track it to Darnell, and from Darnell out to his sales teams in Brooklyn, SI and upstate.

It had taken a few weeks for Ruiz to pop the big question—what can Fuentes tell him about a DEA investigation of money laundering in New York City?

You have to be a little more specific, Hidalgo tells him.

Banks? Real estate? Loans?

Hidalgo feeds him back what he already knows—there's a high-level DEA investigation into Berkeley and Terra regarding a loan from HBMX with possible drug money behind it.

Ruiz puts the next question to him—what's the current status of the investigation?

Stalled, Hidalgo answers after going to research it.

The chief witness overdosed.

The Park Tower investigation is going to die on the vine. In a month, Keller will be out of there and the new boss won't take it up.

You can all breathe easy.

Over the next couple of weeks Ruiz switches the emphasis to Mexico—what does the DEA know about his fields in Guerrero? His smuggling routes, his people—his traffickers, his accountants, his gunmen? What about the cops on his payroll, politicians, government officials?

The truth is they don't know much.

But this is where the process of turning the organization in on itself begins. Keller takes what little intelligence he has on the Ruiz operation, solicits more from Orduña, and uses it to inject the poison into Eddie.

Claudio Maldonado is one of Ruiz's most effective gunmen in Acapulco, Orduña tells Keller. Keller feeds it through Hidalgo that Maldonado is under SEIDO surveillance and could be arrested at any moment.

Eddie pulls him from Acapulco.

A processing lab in Guerrero is producing high-quality product. Hidalgo clues Ruiz that the marines have located it and are planning a raid. The lab is abandoned, the opium and equipment moved until a new site can be found.

The play gets darker, dirtier.

Eddie wants the identities of snitches.

Orduña provides Keller with the names of two of the most violent Tapia veterans fighting in Acapulco and in the mountains of Guerrero. Only one of them, Edgardo Valenzuela, is a *dedo*. But he's a slimy, psychotic rapist who'd been feeding Orduña's people mostly little balls of shit, so the admiral considers him expendable. The other, Abelino Costas, "El Grec," is a stone sociopath who ambushed a marine column and killed three of them.

Valenzuela and Costas are both tortured to death.

Valenzuela gives it up.

Costas spits in their faces before they hand him his guts.

It bothers Hidalgo.

"They were murderers and sadists," Keller says. "They got what was coming to them."

Giving up informers boosts Ruiz's trust in Fuentes, because DEA never gives up snitches under any circumstances.

The scope of information he wants expands.

Does DEA know where Núñez is?

Where Mini-Ric is?

Do you have a line on where the Esparza brothers are holed up?

No, no and maybe, but the last question presents a dilemma. Crypto-traffic analysis and satellite imagery have given them the location of an *estancia* deep in the Sinaloan mountains where the brothers might be.

But Ruiz wants this information for Caro, so the problem is, how far do they go in helping Rafael Caro? How far do you ever go in helping one DTO over another, and why?

The Mexican drug world is in chaos, the violence is worse than ever, and the government is turning to the old guard, *los retornados* like Caro, to try to restore order.

But is restoring order in Caro's interest?

As long as there are multiple, competing groups, the narcos need Caro as a supposedly neutral "godfather" who can mediate disputes, mete out rough justice, guarantee agreements, cease-fires and truces. A man who's not at war with any party and so can solicit money from several parties to form a syndicate?

He's valuable because he doesn't have a dog in the fight.

Paradoxically powerful for his lack of power.

But if one party—a Núñez, an Esparza, an Ascensión—wins and becomes dominant, Caro becomes unnecessary, superfluous, just another old *gomero* living out his life telling tales of past glories.

What if Caro isn't trying to hold the Sinaloa cartel together but is trying to keep it divided? He owes them nothing; they sat and let him rot in Florence for two decades.

If that's the case, Hidalgo thinks, he might be using Tito Ascensión as a stalking horse, because none of his requests or actions have been directed at Jalisco, and when we gave him the name of a Jalisco-connected dealer in Brooklyn, he let him slide.

So first Caro allied himself with the old Tapia organization, a Sinaloa enemy, then he apparently cooperates with Tito Ascensión, another Sinaloa rival. Damien Tapia is dead and Caro is still running heroin through the network that Tapia and Caro set up with Ruiz.

What if Caro has figured out that, at least for the time being, the position of godfather, the *padrino*, is a liability, that it's smarter and more profitable not to control one whole thing, but to take a piece out of a lot of things? What if he's moved on from merely running Ruiz to taking a percentage from every other organization?

Then it would be in his best interests not to subdue the confusion, but to encourage it, to nurture a perpetually unstable situation in which he's the only stability. What if he manipulates a balance of power, now supporting Ruiz, then Tito, suborning Núñez, maybe going after the Esparzas—playing one against the other when all the while he seems to the government to be the great hope for peace, the reasonable man that they can turn to?

Like they turned to Barrera.

Adán Barrera was the Lord of Rule.

Rafael Caro is the Lord of Chaos.

And he's going to let the chaos continue until it all falls apart, the other potential leaders are gone, and they have no choice but to come to him.

Now you have an in with him, Hidalgo thinks, via Ruiz, and the question is, how much do you work with him? If you believe your own theory about him perpetuating chaos, then you bring him down as fast and hard as you can.

Or do you?

Or do you help him play it out, help him damage the other organizations as much as he can, and when you think he's inflicted maximum damage, reel him into the boat?

Do you let him run his game, see where it goes inside the Mexican power structure—banking, finance, government? Hell, see where it goes inside the *American* government.

Help him climb as high as he can.

Then kick the ladder out from under him.

Because if Caro is manipulating all the other organizations, and if you can manipulate Caro . . .

You're *el padrino.*

Cirello meets Ruiz at the Palomino Club ("alcohol *and* full nudity") in North Vegas, and Cirello has to sit in a booth in the VIP room looking at T&A while he tries to brief Eddie. "You asked for a location on the brothers Esparza."

"You got one?"

Eddie's eyes don't leave a tall black dancer wearing, well, nothing.

"You know how traffic analysis works?"

"I know to avoid rush hour," Eddie says.

He's a funny motherfucker, Cirello thinks. "This comes from Fuentes. Shortly after the Esparzas were wounded in that ambush, DEA monitored unusually heavy telephonic and internet traffic in the area of La Rastra, Sinaloa, way down south near the Durango border just north of Nayarit. They intercepted some encrypted messages but our codebreakers determined that they were referring to a certain ranch. Satellite surveillance shows increased activity and an increase in vehicles and personnel at this place."

He slips Eddie a satellite photo of a few buildings in a clearing on the top of a heavily wooded ridge in the Sierra Madre between La Rastra and Plomosas.

Eddie glances at it.

"Check this out," Cirello says, pointing out a brown rectangle amid the green. "Looks like a landing strip to me."

"Speaking of landing strips—"

"Focus," Cirello says. "You want this or not?"

Eddie slips the photo into his pocket.

"The coordinates are on it," Cirello says.

"I'm thrilled," Eddie says. "You want a lap dance?"

"No."

"Are you gay?" Eddie asks.

"No."

"I mean, it's all right if you are," Eddie says. "It's just that we're in the wrong club."

"You have a good time." Cirello gets up.

The black chick is fantastic. Even better when she comes back to Eddie's suite to finish the job. After she leaves, Eddie gets on a burn phone to Culiacán. "Our guy came through."

He reads out the coordinates.

After he clicks off, he scans the photo onto his laptop and sends that.

So many ways to play this, Caro thinks.

You could reach out to Iván's people here and let them know that he's been compromised, earn his gratitude. Or you could give the location to Tito and let things take their course.

He decides.

Gets on the line to Elena Sánchez and tells her where she can find Iván Esparza.

"My gift to you," he says. "Avenge your son."

Callan pores over the satellite photo.

And Google Maps.

He looks at Lev. "It's a bitch."

One road in, one road out. Both will be heavily guarded with no way to get in undiscovered. They could hoof it, but it would be miles through steep, heavy forest and bush and there's no good staging area where they wouldn't be seen by locals who are doubtless loyal to the Esparzas.

"The smartest thing to do," Callan says, "would be to leak this intel to the FES, let the marines go in with choppers."

"But would they?" Lev asks.

The Sinaloa cartel pretty much owns the federal government, and while the marines have been aggressive against all the other organizations, they've been notably passive against Sinaloa.

"Elena wants Iván dead, not arrested," Lev says.

And what La Reina wants, La Reina gets, Callan thinks. But the complex on top of the ridge is a virtual fort, a firebase surrounded by fences topped with razor wire. It's hard to tell from the photos, but what look to be the living quarters seem to have been reinforced with metal screens and fire slits. He knows that there will be sound and motion sensors that will touch off searchlights. There might even be underground bunkers with reinforced concrete.

A B-52 might do the job, but Callan doubts that even Elena can call up a B-52.

Callan counts what look like five vehicles—four SUVs and a flatbed truck—under camouflage netting. A low concrete building outside the wire is probably a barracks and a kitchen for . . . twenty, thirty? . . . guards. Another building, prefab steel, probably houses more vehicles, equipment, maybe a plane, because there isn't one on the landing strip, at least when the photo was taken.

There's too much they don't know. They need a thorough reconnaissance, but that would be just as difficult and risky as the actual mission and risk spooking the Esparzas. And they have to move fast. The brothers are there now, but who knows if they'll still be there tomorrow or the next day?

We don't have enough intel and we don't have enough time to plan, Callan thinks. We'll be going into a fortified location we don't know and we'll be outnumbered.

Other than that, it's all good.

"First problems first," he says. "Access. How the hell do we get in there?"

"The airstrip?" Lev asks.

"I'm thinking the same thing," Callan says.

It isn't good—it isn't even close to good—but it might be the only option. Two small planes, go in at night, hope you can stick the landing. One team lays fire on the guards, pinning them down; another goes into the house to take out the Esparzas, the third holds the airstrip.

If everything goes well—which it never does—your guys hold the strip and the planes are intact when you come out of the house for the "exfil," as Lev calls it. If not, you come out of the house—*if* you come out of the house—to bodies strewn around burning airplanes, and you hump across the mountains into Durango.

Drug cartels have air fleets.

They use them to carry drugs and move people around.

Callan and Lev choose two—a Pilatus PC-12 and a Beechcraft C-12 Huron, the military version of the King Air 350. Each can hold ten people with enough fuel capacity to fly to the target from Mazatlán and back. Importantly, both have good reputations on rough airstrips and are used by various armed forces.

Good, tough little airplanes.

The next decision is personnel.

They have to be the best—not just street thugs who can loose a clip from a speeding car, but trained, disciplined paramilitary types who will do their jobs, only their jobs, and trust their teammates to do theirs.

The Barreras have been in the business a long time and have used former special forces since the nineties, bringing them in from Israel, South Africa, Britain, the US, Mexico and elsewhere.

Callan and Lev have eighteen spots to fill. Lev chooses three men from his own regular team, but he wants to leave the rest to provide security for Elena and Luis.

Four Israelis, including Lev.

They're very good.

Callan fills out the mission with two South Africans, a former Rhodesian Selous Scout, three former SAS guys, a former American marine and eight Mexican guys from the air force, army and marines. Two of the guys double as combat medics—if both are hit, well, the wounded are just fucked.

He has to be up front with them. He won't tell them where they're going until they're on the planes, but these guys aren't stupid, and experience is going to tell them that the odds of coming back aren't great. So Callan gives them the choice of opting out.

None take it.

Maybe because this war has been going on long enough for them to have lost buddies they'd like to get payback for, or they have a genuine loyalty to Elena, or they're just macho sons of bitches. More likely because Callan offers a bonus of $50,000 a man—payable in cash or coke—as well as a "death payment" of $100,000, deposited straight into offshore accounts, for the family of any man who doesn't make it back.

Then Callan has to find pilots crazy and cocky enough to make a night landing in the mountains on a rough, unknown strip, stay in the cockpit during a firefight, and then (hopefully) take off under fire. And he doesn't need just two of these guys, he needs four, he needs copilots, because about the stupidest thing in the world would be to pull this off and then die outside a perfectly good airplane because your pilot caught one in the head and you have no one to fly it.

Narco pilots are notoriously nuts. Free-spirit adrenaline junkies who have thrown away lucrative military and airline jobs for a shot at bigger money and bigger thrills. A lot of them leave the gigs but usually come back. They get hooked on the blow, the parties, the women that come with the narco lifestyle, so the "real world" becomes just too dull.

Callan needs ex-military pilots, guys with experience at going in hot, who aren't going to freak out if some rounds start zinging around them. He can't afford the excess personnel to do what narcos sometimes do—leave a guy on the plane with a gun at the pilot's head to make sure he doesn't make a premature takeoff.

Lev has one of his own guys, an Israeli Air Force veteran used to dropping in and out of Syria and Lebanon. Then they get "Buffalo Bill," an American who's been around the Mexican narco world since Barrera's time, and whose long white hair, beard, filthy old cowboy hat and omnipresent joint hanging out of his mouth could scare the shit out of you if you didn't know he could fly a piano and land it on a submarine deck. A Mexican from the Fifth Air Group, 107th Squadron, has hundreds of hours on the Pilatus; another Mexican Air Force veteran flew C-12s—both went on missions against the Zetas and the Tapia organization.

They won't bug out.

Then there's the question of arms.

Cartels have air fleets; they also have arsenals.

Short of an atomic device, you want it, you pick it.

Callan wants each guy to have an assault rifle, but lets each man choose the one he likes working with, so the teams go out with a variety of compact Galils, C-8s, Belgian FNs, an M-27, HK-33s and even a few classic AK-47s.

Two of the Israelis will carry MATADOR (Man-Portable, Anti-Tank, Anti-Door) shoulder-fired rocket launchers to rip a gap into the fence, punch through any walls, or take out an armored SUV. The marine will also take a Mossberg twelve-gauge pump for close action and blowing the locks off doors.

Callan chooses an HK MP7 with a suppressor and an Elcan reflex sight. He's also going to take a Walther P22, in case he gets in close enough to put two .22 rounds bouncing around inside Iván Esparza's skull.

They go to Elena's house in Ensenada and brief her and Luis.

"I want photos," she says, "of Iván's corpse."

"If there is one," Callan says, "and if we have time."

"There will be," Elena says. "And make time."

Callan reminds her of their deal. He does this job—success or failure, whether he comes back or he doesn't—Elena and her people leave Bahia alone. Nora . . . and now Flor, he guesses . . . get to go back there and live in peace.

Elena reaffirms their arrangement but adds, "You know it's only good as long as I'm in control. If Iván wins, he'll do what he wants. Just so you have the added motivation."

Yeah, thanks, Callan thinks. What I need is added motivation. He's leaving when Luis follows him outside.

"I want to go," Luis says. "Avenge my brother."

"Did your mother send you out here?"

"She doesn't know," Luis says. "She wouldn't allow it."

"Neither will I," Callan says. "I respect the hell out of you for asking, but you don't have the skills, and I won't have the time to babysit you. No offense, but you'd be a liability."

"I won't get in the way. I can take care of myself."

"Luis, you would be in the way," Callan says. "Every guy on the mission would know who you are and would feel obligated to keep you safe."

Despite himself, Luis looks relieved, and he looks ashamed that he looks relieved.

"We'll just say you came," Callan says. "We'll put it out you were there. They'll sing songs about you."

In the car, Lev asks, "What was that about?"

Callan tells him.

"That's all we need," Lev says.

Callan drives up to Encinitas.

Flor is asleep.

"How's she doing?" Callan asks.

"She's remarkable," Nora says. "But she's going to need a lot of care."

"Take her back to Bahia," Callan says.

Nora looks at him quizzically.

"It's safe now," Callan says. "It's taken care of."

"Where will you be?"

"Taking care of things."

"Sean—"

"We've had a good run," Callan says. "For a long time. I hope we have a long time left. But if we don't, there's an extra hundred K with your name on it in the Cook Islands."

"You think I care about that?" Nora asks.

"No."

"I won't—"

"You can give this kid a life," Callan says. "Bring her home; you and María can love her to death."

"How long before I know?"

"A day or two."

"I'll wait here," Nora says.

"Okay," Callan says. "But then go back to Bahia."

They make love to the sound of the waves crashing on the beach.

Callan sits in the C-12 and studies the sat photo of the Esparza compound.

When the plane took off from Mazatlán, he distributed a photo to each guy on the plane and went over the rough tactical plan and assignments—who will move on the house, who will fire on the guards' quarters, who will hold the airstrip. The assignments are redundant for each plane so in case one crashes, the other team can still go on with the mission.

He can smell weed from the cockpit.

"How can you fly doing weed?" he'd asked Buffalo Bill.

"Can't fly *not* doing it," Bill answered.

Bill is pretty relaxed, but the atmosphere in the back of the plane is tight. Guys sit staring straight ahead, a couple of them mumble prayers, others fidget checking gear for the three hundredth time—ammo clips, Velcro straps on their Kevlar vests, morphine ampules taped to sleeves or caps.

A few of the men wear religious medals, some have IDs taped inside their shirts. The Mexicans wear no identification of any kind—in case they're killed or captured they don't want retaliations against their families.

Callan hears Bill shout, "Five minutes, boys!"

Two of the Mexicans finish their prayers and cross themselves, kiss the tips of their fingers.

The C-12 is the lead plane, the Pilatus with Lev and the other team about ten seconds behind. It's critical that there's not more of a gap or each of the teams could be chopped up piecemeal.

An instrument landing on a mountain in the dark, but Buffalo Bill brings it in like a United flight coming into O'Hare. The wheels bounce wickedly on the rough strip, though, jarring Callan and giving him a neck ache he knows he'll have for days.

The plane rolls to a stop.

Callan unbuckles, grabs his HK and goes out the door.

He sees the Pilatus coming in behind him. It hits the landing strip, bounces once and then settles and rolls in. The door opens and Lev trots toward him to head to the house.

Then they're hit by white light.

Blinding.

Huge spotlights.

Bright as day.

They're out in the open of the landing strip as fire comes in from all sides. Callan hears the rounds ripping the air or the hollow, bass *thunk* of bullets hitting bodies as his guys start to go down.

Callan flattens on the ground and has time to think, *They knew we were coming,* when he hears the *whoosh* of an incoming rocket and the C-12 explodes in flame. Buffalo Bill staggers out, his beard on fire. He frantically slaps at his face. Then the flames ignite his hat and he twirls like a drunken clown.

The Pilatus blows up. A shard of metal spins across the strip and slices the marine in half.

Callan hears screams of pain.

Pleas to gods and mothers.

He always thought death would be quiet, but it's noisier than hell.

Another explosion and then blackness.

It's night again.

And silent.

Callan awakes, if you can call it waking, sitting with his back against a metal wall. His hands are plastic-tied behind him, his legs are stretched out in front of him, his ankles shackled.

Dried blood cakes his ears and his nose from a concussion. He feels sick to his stomach and dizzy, he can barely hear.

His head throbs.

The building is large, a warehouse . . . or maybe a hangar because a small plane sits in the center. *Sicarios* armed with machine pistols wander around. A couple sit in folding metal chairs.

Across the room he sees what must be bodies—lumps under sheets of bloodstained canvas.

Callan turns his head.

The pain of just doing that is horrific and he fights off the urge to vomit.

Lev, still unconscious, his chin dropped on his chest, sits beside Callan. Beyond him, Callan can make out a row of men—he thinks there are seven but his vision is blurry and it's hard to count—all that are left from the raid.

He tries to see who they are, who survived. There's Lev, then another one of the Israelis. The Rhodesian, he thinks, two of the Mexicans, maybe one of the Brits. Beyond them he can't see.

The effort is exhausting. He just wants to go back to sleep.

But Callan forces himself to stay awake.

He focuses on sounds—Lev's labored breathing, a man weeping, another whimpering. He looks down the row to see why—the Brit's left leg is fractured, the bone jutting through his skin.

Light comes into the hangar as the door opens.

It hurts, like being stabbed through the eyes. Callan shuts them tight to try to stop the pain.

He feels a man stand in front of him, examining him, then hears, "Look at me."

Callan opens his eyes and looks up.

From old photos, he knows it's Iván Esparza.

"You came here to kill me?" Esparza asks. "How's that working out for you?"

His voice sounds like it's fifty yards away.

Callan doesn't answer.

Esparza hauls off and hits him hard in the side of the face. Callan's head explodes with pain. He lurches over and throws up.

"How it's going to work," Esparza says, "is when I ask you a question, you answer me. Do you get that now?"

Callan nods.

"Who are you? What's your name?"

"Sean Callan."

"Who sent you?"

"What?"

"Jesus, you *are* messed up," Esparza says. "Who . . . sent . . . you? Núñez? Tito? Elena? Don't lie to me, *pendejo*, because I already know. I just want confirmation."

Callan tries to think. "What was the question?"

Esparza hits him again.

Callan throws up again.

He can barely hear Esparza say, "Listen, asshole, I have a team flying in here. All they do is hurt people. They like their job and they're very good at it. They're going to start hurting people in ways you can't imagine. I'll have them hurt my countrymen down there until they give me their names and where I can find their families—I guarantee you they'll give up their wives, their parents, their kids—and I'll have them all killed. Or—"

The Brit screams.

"Help him," Callan says.

"Sure." Esparza walks down the row, pulls a pistol, and shoots the Brit in the head. He comes back to Callan. "Anyone else you want me to help?"

"No."

"Where were we?"

"Elena Sánchez."

"Sent you."

"Yes."

"That dumb cunt," Esparza says. "Núñez swings and misses. Elena swings and misses. Would you blame me for thinking that I'm immortal? I asked you a question."

"No."

"Good answer," Esparza says. He inspects Callan for a few seconds. "Sean Callan. I've heard of you. 'Billy the Kid' Callan. You're a fucking legend. Is it true you saved Adán's life once?"

"Yes."

"I heard that story," Esparza says. "Heard the song, too. Haven't seen the movie, though. But I'm impressed. Then again, whatever you can say about Elena, you can never say she's cheap. Only the best for La Reina."

"That's right . . ." Callan loses his thought, then, "These guys . . . they're talented . . . they have skills you can use . . . they'll work for you . . ."

"How about you?" Iván asks. "Will you work for me?"

"Yeah."

"It's tempting," Esparza says. "It is. But here's the thing—*I* want to be the legend. And to be the legend, I have to break the legend."

Iván walks to the end of the row.

One of his guys walks behind him, holding up a cell to get the video.

One by one, Iván shoots each prisoner in the head. When he comes to Lev, he says, "Wake him up."

One of Iván's guys slaps Lev conscious.

Lev looks up, blinks.

"*Shalom,* motherfucker." Iván shoots him.

The blood sprays the side of Callan's face.

Now Iván stands in front of him. "See, I'm just sick of people coming to try to kill me. It really pisses me off. And YouTube loves this shit. It'll go viral."

He points the gun at Callan's forehead. "Any famous last words?"

"Yeah," Callan says. "Fuck you."

Callan wants to close his eyes but forces them to stay open and glare at Esparza.

Live tough, die tough.

Iván lowers the gun. "Never waste a good legend."

He has one of his guys hose the puke off Callan.

Callan sits soaked, shivering.

. . .

Nora waits for three days.

When she doesn't hear from Callan, she takes Flor and heads out.

She doesn't go to Costa Rica, though.

Nora goes to Mexico.

The woman is stunning.

No wonder, Elena thinks, my brother loved her. And the little girl with her is lovely, although clearly not her daughter. She looks at the darling girl. "Sweetheart, could you go with Lupe here so your mother and I can talk? She'll give you something nice."

Flor looks to Nora, who nods.

The girl goes off with the maid.

"We met years ago," Nora says.

"I remember, of course," Elena says. "My brother was the Lord of the Skies, and you were 'La Güera,' his famous lady. I was a little jealous of you, to tell the truth. And you're even more beautiful now. How is that possible?"

"Where's my husband?"

"Right to the chase," Elena says. She looks out the window. It's one of those rare rainy winter days—the Pacific is gray and rough. "To answer your question, I don't know. But if I had to hazard a guess, I'd say that he's dead."

"He went to do some kind of job for you."

"And didn't come back," Elena says. "I take it you haven't seen the video clip?"

Nora shakes her head.

"Iván Esparza was thoughtful enough to send it to me," Elena says. She walks Nora over to a desk and opens a file on the computer. "I suppose I should issue some sort of warning as to content."

"I'm all right."

Nora watches the video.

Sees Sean—wounded, hurting, dazed—look up at Iván Esparza and say, "Yeah. Fuck you."

She says, "Esparza didn't shoot him."

"Not on camera," Elena says, "but it's hard to imagine him tolerating that kind of defiance. Then again . . ."

"But we don't know Sean is dead," Nora says.

"No."

"What are you doing to get him back?"

"Nothing," Elena says. "What *can* I do?"

"Everything in your power," Nora says.

"I *have* no power," Elena says. "I'm beaten. The new powers have turned on me, set me up. As we speak, people are packing my things so that I can go somewhere. The problem with that is, I have nowhere to go."

Iván, Caro and maybe even Tito are hunting her in Mexico, indictments for her and Luis wait across the border.

She'll go to Europe, maybe.

For as long as it lasts.

"You can't just leave him there," Nora says.

"You don't understand," Elena says. "Women like you and me, our days are over. We're the defeated. We believed in some level of decency, decorum, even beauty. The loveliness that comes from order. All that's gone now. We depart the scene, leaving only chaos."

Elena sees it now.

I should have seen it before, but now it's too late, she thinks.

Tito Ascensión will take it all.

But he's only Caro's puppet.

The old man manipulated us into destroying each other so he can pick up the pieces and run Tito like the dog he's always been. Sooner rather than later, Tito will kill the Esparzas, not even knowing he's doing it at Caro's behest.

The government will back Caro, thinking he'll restore order.

But they're wrong.

The genie of anarchy is out of the bottle and they'll never get it back in. There are too many demons now for any one devil to control, and they'll viciously, mindlessly slaughter one another on the streets of Tijuana, the beaches of Cabo, the hills of Guerrero. They'll kill in Acapulco, in Juárez, in Mexico City itself.

The killing will never stop.

"Go back to Costa Rica," Elena says. "I can't protect you there, but I'm sure you can make some sort of accommodation with whoever takes over. You know these men—they're fools for beauty."

Nora leaves Elena's house in Ensenada and drives to the airport.

Five hours later, she and Flor are in Washington.

Keller watches the video.

He's seen similar ones before, too many times. It was Eddie Ruiz who started the whole vid-clip thing, years ago when he captured four Zetas sent to Acapulco to kill him. Eddie interviewed them on camera like a talk-show host, then shot each one of them and posted the clip everywhere.

It started a trend.

Now Keller watches the executions and puts the pieces together.

Through Cirello, they fed Caro the location of the Esparza haven in Sinaloa. Just days later, an airborne raid on the place is ambushed. And that's what it was—the Esparzas clearly knew the raid was coming—satellite photos show the skeletons of two charred planes on the landing strip. They were hit on landing. Most of the raiders were killed outright, some captured, the men he's looking at now being executed in what looks like a hangar.

He freeze-frames on one of them.

The face matches photos from intel files on Elena Sánchez, her alleged head of security, Lev Ben-Aharon, former IDF. Hence "*Shalom*, motherfucker." Two other recognizable faces are of a Mexican national, Benny Rodríguez, and a Rhodesian, Simon van der Kok, both in the files as Sánchez operatives.

The last man in the line is a problem. We don't see Iván shoot him. And the exchange:

"Any famous last words?"

"Yeah. Fuck you."

Sean Callan.

"Billy the Kid."

Was in his early twenties when he ran the Irish mob on New York's West Side. Made an alliance with the Cimino crime family and became one of their prime hit men. Had to leave New York after he helped assassinate the godfather, ended up as a mercenary in Central America and then a gunman for Adán Barrera. Saved Barrera's life in a gun battle but left him when the Barreras killed Father Juan.

Keller knew him.

Hell, they went on a covert raid in Baja together, to pull Nora Hayden out. That was a long time ago. Callan and Nora went away together, off the radar, Keller never knew or tried to find out where.

Let them live in peace.

But what the hell is Callan doing on a Sánchez raid to kill Iván Esparza? Is he back to his old profession?

Why?

Christ, it's all coming back.

Keller focuses on the issue at hand.

You give the Esparzas' location to Caro, he thinks.

Caro gives it to Elena.

Then tells Iván that Elena's people are coming?

Why didn't he give it to Tito, Keller wonders, who would have had a better chance of taking the Esparzas out? You answered your own question—he wanted to eliminate Elena first. Set up her best troops to get slaughtered.

So now two of the three factions of the Sinaloa cartel are crippled:

Núñez *père* and *fils* are on the run, trying to manage their operation from underground.

The Sánchez wing is damaged, probably beyond repair.

The Esparzas are what remains, but they're literally wounded, and at war with Tito's increasingly powerful Jalisco cartel.

The one constant in those developments is Rafael Caro. Keller has to hand it to him. I tried to destroy the Sinaloa cartel for decades, he thinks; Caro has done it in months.

That's the good news.

The bad news is that the Jalisco cartel is the new power.

Rafael Caro didn't do all this just to put the crown on Tito's head. If Tito is king, Caro is Richelieu, he's Wolsey, he's Warwick. He'll use Ascensión to polish off Sinaloa—let Tito take the throne and the heat that comes with it—while he rides the chaos dragon, thinking he can control it, be the real king.

But there are no kings anymore, Keller thinks.

The last one died in Guatemala.

Elena sits in the back of the Escalade.

Luis is beside her.

In her purse are two first-class tickets to Barcelona. From there, who knows? She tries not to think about the dubious future. One step at a time. First is the drive to Tijuana International. Her small convoy consists of three vehicles—any more, she decided, would engender more attention than security.

Security is an issue.

Nine phone calls to Tito, none returned.

Seven calls to Rafael, same result.

Calls out to *sicarios,* cell runners, police, politicians. No one wants to know her, old friends don't remember her name.

She had one incoming call.

From Iván.

"Did you get my video?" he asked.

"Yes, it was charming, thank you."

"You shouldn't have done that," Iván said. He sounded high. "I didn't kill your son, you know. I didn't kill Rudolfo. I never liked him very much, he was kind of a dick, but I didn't kill him."

"Then who did?"

"Núñez?" Iván said. "Caro?"

"Caro was in prison."

"Bosses have never reached out from prison?" Iván asked. "I don't know, I just know it wasn't me."

"Why are you telling me this?"

"So you'll stop hating me," Iván said.

"That matters to you?"

"Believe it or not," Iván said.

"You won, Iván," Elena said. "I'm taking Luis and leaving. You can have whatever you can take from Tito, or keep from him. And God help you."

She clicked off.

Now she sits in the back of the car and knows that Iván was telling the truth.

It was Caro.

It was always Caro.

Sitting in a cell for twenty years thinking about how to revenge himself on the people he thought betrayed him.

If I had known . . .

Too late now, though.

Now all she can do is save Luis's life.

The car drives up Route 3, past Punta Morro, La Playita, and El Sauzal. Elena never sees El Sauzal without a twinge of pain; it was here that Adán ordered the slaughter of nineteen innocent people to make sure that he killed one informer.

The convoy passes El Sauzal, then Victoria, and then the driver takes an exit onto a roundabout that continues on Route 3, which runs inland. He should merge onto Route 1, which goes up to Tijuana and the airport.

She leans forward. "What are you doing? You need to be on 1."

The lead car took the right route and went off on Route 1, so now there's no car in front of Elena's.

"Take the next roundabout," Elena says. "You can get back on 1."

The driver doesn't. He blows right past and continues east on Route 3 and then Elena hears a loud buzzing sound behind them. She turns and looks through the back windshield. There must be ten motorcycles, they come up behind her trailing car, then pull alongside it.

Flashes burst from gun barrels.

The car swerves and crashes.

The motorbikes—bizarrely, all of them are pink—come after her car. She hears the whining of more engines and turns to look in front. More bikes are coming straight at them.

The driver pulls over.

"Don't do that!" Elena yells.

The driver lies down in the front seat.

Now the bikes are circling her, like Indians in one of those bad old American westerns.

Elena sees that girl—that vulgar, vulgar girl from Adán's wake, the same one who killed Rudolfo's assassin—on one of the bikes as they circle tighter. The girl raises a machine pistol and fires. Elena gets down, but Luis panics. He opens his door and tries to run, abandoning her. She grabs at him, tries to stop him, but he's out and running.

Into a wall of bullets.

They smack into his legs, his chest, his face.

Arms akimbo, he falls on his back.

Elena crawls out of the car and kneels by her son's shredded, bleeding, mutilated body. She lifts him, holds him in her arms, looks at the skies and screams. Screams her voice out, her heart out.

A shrill, unearthly sound.

Belinda gets off her bike.

Walks over, puts a pistol to Elena's forehead, and says, "You always thought you were better than me."

She pulls the trigger.

Elena falls on her dead child.

The Barrera drug dynasty is dead.

Deader, in fact, than most people know.

The doorbell rings at Eva's house in La Jolla.

She looks through the peephole and sees a man standing there alone, dressed in a plum polo shirt and khakis. He looks harmless, so she opens the door.

"Yes?" she asks.

"You probably don't remember me, but I was at your wedding," he says. He looks behind her to where her twin sons stand shyly peeking out at him. "Who are these two little cuties? You must be Miguel and Raúl."

"Who are you?" Eva asks.

"Eddie," he says. "Eddie Ruiz."

Eva, Eva, Ev*uuuh*, Eddie thinks.

Eva Esparza Barrera.

Still as hot as gravy drippings and she's what—twenty-eight now. A MILF. Squared. Two kids and she still has an ass like an apple and tits that look just as firm as they did when Adán B. reached down and snatched her out of the cradle.

El Señor's child bride.

Married off to an old man to cement an alliance and produce heirs who would unite two wings of the cartel. Sweet demure virginal Eva, whose old man guarded her *chocha* like it was worth its weight in gold, which it sort of was.

The two little princes here—Prince Miguel and Prince Raúl. Eddie wonders which of them popped out first, because technically he'd be first in line for the crown.

Now that their *papi* is dead.

Their uncle Raúl dead.

Their great-uncle M-1 dead.

Their cousin Sal *muerto*. Okay, *I* killed Sal, Eddie thinks, but whatever. You get born a Barrera, your odds of dying of old age aren't spectacular. And little Eva here—who Eddie thought about fucking when she was walking down the aisle—is a smokin' hot widow.

With tens of millions of dollars that Eddie wouldn't mind, uh, tapping into.

"How did you find me?" Eva asks.

"Persistence," Eddie says.

And a source in the DEA.

Eva is an American citizen. Her *papi* drove her *mami* across the border to have her in Dago, so she's here perfectly legally, and while her late lamented dearly beloved was the world's biggest drug dealer, there's not a single charge pending against his grieving widow.

Eva's sheet is clean.

"What can I do for you?" Eva asks.

"Maybe the boys could go watch *Sesame Street* or something?" Eddie says.

"That hasn't been on for years," Eva says. "Where have you been?"

"Away."

"Overseas?"

"Okay."

Eva says, "I can put a movie on for them."

"That would be great."

She opens the door and lets him in. Then she walks the boys down the hall. A few minutes later she comes back, takes Eddie into the living room and gestures for him to sit on the couch.

It's a nice house, Eddie thinks.

New furniture, view of the ocean.

Seven figures, easy.

Lunch money for Adán.

Eva's wearing black—a black blouse over tight black designer jeans and sandals. Her hair is pulled back into one of those yummy-mummy ponytails like she just got home from yoga.

"Eddie Ruiz," she says. "Didn't you used to work for my husband?"

"Work for him"? Eddie thinks. Bitch, I took Nuevo Laredo for your husband. I set up Diego Tapia to get killed for your husband. I dropped into Guatemala to save your husband. And while we're at it, princess, I turned the man who killed your father into a highway torch. So let's not be talking to me like I just dropped off the dry cleaning. "That's right. Back in the day."

When your husband was on this side of the grass.

"What do you want to talk about?" she asks.

"Money."

"What about it?"

"Who handles your money now?" Eddie asks. "Your brothers?"

"That's none of your business."

"It could be, though," Eddie says. "And I wouldn't steal from you."

"You think my brothers are stealing from me?"

"How would you know?" Eddie asks. "You just take what they hand you, right? And say 'thank you'?"

"They look out for me."

"Like you were a little girl," Eddie says.

"I'm not a little girl," she says, bristling.

"Then why act like you are?"

He lays it out for her—she's owed all the money that comes from Adán's faction of the cartel. That's tens of millions a year—money that needs to be laundered and invested. Okay, so her brothers say that they do that, but do they really? Does she get every penny she's owed or do they just give what they think she deserves? Do they even send her all the money, or do they send her a monthly allowance?

He sees from the look on her face that it's the latter.

"Are you kidding me right now?" Eddie asks. "You're a grown woman with two kids."

He presses. Are they at least investing her money well, is she getting the return she should be getting? She doesn't know, does she, because she doesn't track the accounting, she doesn't ask.

"And it's your money, not theirs," Eddie says. "If you put your money with us, we'd be very aware that it's your money, not ours."

"Who's 'us'?"

Halfway home, Eddie thinks. If she wasn't interested, she would have already told him to get the fuck out, been on the phone to her brothers. "I'm part of a syndicate with some very important people whose names you may or may not know."

"Try me."

"Rafael Caro."

This is where it could crash and burn, Eddie thinks. If she's aware that Caro and Barrera fought a war with each other back when she was a rug rat. When, like, *Sesame Street was* still on.

She doesn't know.

He can see it from the blank look in her eyes.

Jesus, can she really be as dumb as they say?

"I haven't heard of him," she says, as if Caro is some musician she doesn't have on her playlist.

"He's been away," Eddie says.

"Same place as you were 'away'?"

As a matter of fact, Eddie thinks. "Caro has connections at the highest levels of both Mexican and American government and business circles. He . . . we . . . can make those connections work for you. Make you a lot more money, put you in charge of your own life."

"If I betray my brothers."

"Loyalty is a two-way street," Eddie says. "Eva, you think I don't get you, but I do. You were seventeen when your father married you off to an old man for business reasons. Now your brothers are in trouble, and they need to make peace with Tito Ascensión. Remember him, big ugly old guy, looks like a dog?"

"What are you saying?"

"You know what Iván has to offer Tito?" Eddie asks. "You."

"He wouldn't do that."

"If you're lucky, they'll marry you off to Tito's son," Eddie says. "About your age, not bad looking. But if Tito has a hard-on for you, well, stock up on chew bones, Eva, they might keep him off you for a few seconds now and then."

"You're gross."

"I thought you were a woman, you still want to be a girl. My mistake." He gets up. "Nice to see you again. Sorry I wasted your time."

"Sit down."

Eddie hesitates for a second to let her think he's reluctant, then sits down and looks at her.

"How would this work?" she asks.

He runs it down for her. She wouldn't even have to confront Iván. They already know the people who do the day-to-day with her money; they'll go to these people and explain that the arrangements have been changed, that Eva Esparza Barrera is taking control of her own life. If they go along with that, great, if they don't . . .

"I don't want any violence," Eva says.

Of course not, Eddie thinks. You married a guy who once threw two children off a bridge, but you don't want any blood on your hands. Like most of the *esposas,* you like the money and the clothes and the jewelry and the cars and the house, you just don't want to know where they come from.

"No violence," he says.

Unless necessary.

But then he sees he's losing her.

And he doesn't want to lose her. If they have the *mami* of the royal twins in the car, the vag from which emerged the spawn of Barrera, it gives them instant legitimacy. Shit, there are people in Mexico still lighting candles, saying prayers to Santo Adán.

And her money don't hurt, either.

But she's saying, "I don't know . . ."

Eddie knows what "I don't know" means to a chick. It means no. It means "I like you as a friend." It means she'll sip wine and watch Netflix with you, but she isn't going to fuck you.

But yeah, you are, Eddie thinks. You don't know it yet, Eva, but you're going to get on all fours and stick your ass up for me. I didn't want to do this, I wanted this to be a seduction, not a rough fuck, but . . .

"You want to know what *I* know?" Eddie asks. "Your former bodyguard, Miguel? You fucked him in your condo in Bosques de las Lomas back in 2010. Just about nine months before the twins were born."

"That's absurd."

"Miguel didn't want to rat you out," Eddie says. "He held out for a long time. But then it turned out he valued his balls more than you. Can you blame him?"

"He's lying."

"No, he's not," Eddie says. "Look, I don't blame you. You had to get pregnant or Adán would replace you with another pageant queen he couldn't knock up. I get it. You did what you had to do. And as long as you're with us, it's in all our best interest to pretend that the two little bastards in there watching whatever the fuck they're watching are products of the holy sperm of Adán Barrera and not some juiced-up boy toy you didn't make wear a condom.

"But if you're not going to go with us . . . what would your brothers do if they knew that? Beat you? Kill you? Cut off the money, for sure. How about the rest of the world, when they find out you're not the demure, grieving widow but a . . . I don't know . . . slut? Whore? I mean, Jesus, Eva, really? The bodyguard? It's so . . . porn."

Now he's really going to find out if she's a girl or a woman.

A girl starts crying.

A woman makes a deal.

Eddie gives her a nudge in the direction he wants her to go. "We could build an empire, Eva. Those boys in there could be kings. For the first time since you were born, you could be in charge of your own fucking life."

Eva doesn't cry.

She nods.

"Ok*aaaay*," Eddie says. He stands up again. "I'll get it working."

She walks him to the door.

Eddie asks, "You seeing anybody? You have a guy?"

She smiles. "That *is* none of your business."

No, Eddie thinks.

But it *could* be.

Rafael Caro just took over the Sinaloa cartel, Keller thinks when he gets the intel that Eddie Ruiz went to visit Eva Barrera.

Then Eddie starts dumping tons of money into his laundry banks. A lot more money than he has. It can only be Eva's money, going into banks around San Diego, going into real estate in the US and Mexico, into construction projects in both countries, in Europe and the Middle East and, yes, going into HBMX.

Going into the syndicate.

Word comes in that some of the Esparza money handlers and accountants have moved over to Ruiz, a couple of others have been found dead at the wheels of their cars.

Keller knows that a lot of the old Barrera loyalists are going to defect to the Caro-Ruiz combination when the word gets out that Eva is with them. It's only surprising that Caro didn't take Eva for himself—at least not yet.

But now Eddie will raise the Barrera flag.

Adán vive.

Barrera has the cartel again.

It has the syndicate.

The syndicate has become the cartel and the cartel has become the syndicate.

Soon the syndicate will have the White House.

One and the same.

Over my dead body, Keller thinks.

White Christmas

I heard the bells on Christmas Day
Their old, familiar carols play . . .
—Henry Wadsworth Longfellow
"Christmas Bells"

Kingston, New York
December 2016

Jacqui haunts the streets like the zombie she is.

It's not *The Night of the Living Dead*, it's *The Night and Day and Day and Night of the Living Dead.*

In her lucid moments, Jacqui has come to believe that heroin was not created for human beings, but that human beings were created for heroin as a means of perpetuating itself. It's a Darwinian thing, she thinks as she strolls along the sidewalk in search of her next fix. The survival of the fittest, and heroin is definitely fitter than people. The evidence is unassailable, herself being only Exhibit A of about a million whole alphabets.

Heroin even evolves to get fitter.

First there was Mexican black.

Then cinnamon.

Then fire, as heroin grew its opposable thumb, fentanyl. Now there are rumors of co-fentanyl, an even stronger evolutionary leap. Then there are the related subspecies—Oxy, Vicodin and the rest of the pharmaceutical products.

Yeah, heroin is taking over the world like *Homo sapiens* once took over the world.

Unstoppable.

A lot of us are dying, Jacqui thinks, but a lot of us aren't. Because, unlike people, heroin is too smart to destroy its own environment. It will keep enough addicts alive to keep itself in need, in circulation, to keep human beings growing those poppies.

And heroin is patient.

Heroin will wait for you.

Waited for Jacqui until she was done with her rehab, clean-and-sober halfway-house foolishness.

Then welcomed her back like the prodigal daughter.

All is forgiven, come on home.

Come on back, baby, into my loving arms.

Bring it on home (G7) to me (C).

Yeah, Jacqui did rehab and passed with the proverbial flying colors. At first it was a bitch, she was sicker than shit, but the nurses got her through the detox, and when she came out of that, the counselors and the other patients got her through the rest of it.

They told her she was only as sick as her secrets, so one day she told about her molestations and cried all that out and felt a lot better. They told her she had to come to terms with her grief, so she opened up about Travis dying in her arms and cried some more. They told her that to get well she had to dump her guilt, make amends, so she called her mother and said she was sorry about all the nasty shit she did, and her mother forgave her and then they told her she had to forgive herself, and she did.

She went to therapy, she went to "group," she went to the meetings and did the Steps, even the one about finding a Higher Power, which was hard because the last thing that Jacqui believed in was, like, God.

Doesn't have to be God, they told her, but it has to be something, you have to find *something* bigger than yourself to believe in because the day is going to come when there's nothing standing between you and the drug but that Higher Power. So first she used the group, then she graduated to some unspecified astral force out there, then Jacqui found Jesus.

Yup, Jesus.

Of all the fucking things, Jacqui thought at the time.

But she was ecstatic. She'd found a high that was higher than dope, higher than cinnamon, higher than freaking anything.

It was so goddamn beautiful.

Jacqui left rehab on a high.

Clean and sober and happy about it, with new friends and a new outlook and a new life, and a new look for herself with about fifteen pounds and clean, fresh skin and hair, and they told her she wasn't ready to go back into the world, and they warned her to avoid "people, places, and things," that she shouldn't go back to Staten Island where the same old environment would lead her back to the same old behavior.

It was too much of a risk, even with Jesus.

She prayed over it, and she and Jesus decided she should take their advice and go to a halfway house for six months somewhere away from Staten Island. There was a space available in a sober living house upstate in Kingston, New York, so she went there.

And it was cool, it was good.

So different from what she'd known, a small town of twenty-three thousand people on the Hudson, with old colonial houses, and old redbrick factory buildings, old churches with tall white spires, and the sober-living house was a big old Victorian in the Roundout neighborhood, which Jacqui learned had been put on the National Register of Historical Places.

And the halfway house was cool. Thirteen women lived there, all of them recovering addicts, and the woman who ran the place, Martina, was strict but nice. There were rules, curfews, and everyone had to help with the cleaning and the cooking, which Jacqui actually came to like.

After a month, they let her get a job and she found one working the drive-through window at Burger King, within walking distance of the house. The job was boring but not stressful (she was supposed to avoid stress), and she had her friends at the house, and her meetings (ninety in ninety days) and her NA friends, and they told her not to have a relationship for the first year, so she didn't do that and she was really happy.

One day she was walking home from work and a guy on the corner of West Chester and Broadway hissed to her, "Girl, I got what you need."

Like, he did, right?

Like he looked right through her skin and saw what she really needed.

And just like that, that's all it took, she just followed him around the corner behind the Valero station and bought a dime bag and some works and shot up and Jesus didn't come with her and that's when she learned that her real Higher Power—the Highest Power—was heroin.

Maybe, she thinks now as she looks for her hookup, heroin *is* God.

We sure as shit worship it, and we have all these little religious rituals that go with it: the swabbing, the cooking, the injection . . .

Muslims pray five times a day, she thinks.

I'm up to four.

They threw her out of the halfway house, of course. She got away with it for a while, held it together, bluffed her way through it, flat-out lied to Martina's face that she was getting high, lied to her roommate, but you can't get over on those bitches, they've seen it all, shit, they've done it all. The rules of the place said that Martina had the right to give her a piss test and it rang the bell so she was out on her ass.

She was out on the street.

Jacqui kept her job for almost another week, then she nodded out and didn't show up for a shift and got a warning and then she slept through another shift and didn't bother to go in just to hear that she was fired.

So now she's jobless, homeless and addicted.

The Holy Trinity, she thinks.

Actually, she has two homes.

A refrigerator box below the Washington Avenue Bridge where it crosses Esopus Creek, ironically not far from the Kingston Best Western Plus, and her "weekend place," a spot underneath the Highway 587 overpass by the old railroad tracks near Aaron Court.

When the cops chase them out of one spot, the little homeless colony migrates across town to the other.

It's a game.

Jacqui prefers her Washington Avenue home because the dumpster diving is better. Not only is there the Best Western, but Picnic Pizza is just up from the bridge, and if she crosses the river she can hit the dumpster at the Olympic Diner and maybe manage to sneak into the restroom at Larry & Gene's gas station across the street to take a piss or a shit.

Sometimes they see her and chase her away, tell her to get her skanky junkie ass out of there.

Rude.

The Aaron Court location is less convenient; all it has within easy walking distance is a Domino's Pizza, and the dumpster isn't very good because, well, Domino's delivers. But then she can walk up Broadway, where there are a lot of bars, and where there are bars there are lonely drunk guys who will give her ten bucks to go down on them in the front seats of their cars.

Don't get it twisted, she's not a prostitute.

It isn't sex, it's just oral.

Like going to the dentist—open wide, swirl, spit and rinse.

Okay, not rinse, but spit.

Her Washington Avenue domicile isn't all that far from a Baptist mission in a former Mexican restaurant where they'll let her come in and take a shower once or twice a week or even do her laundry.

She can't stay there, though, or in any of the other homeless shelters, because they all have a zero-tolerance drug and alcohol policy and will make you blow into the tube or piss-test you, which strikes Jacqui as counterproductive because most of the homeless are addicts or drunks.

Or psychotic.

Yeah, a lot of the homeless are addicts, but most addicts aren't homeless.

Jacqui has learned this on the blocks and in the parks and housing projects where she scores and shoots up. Most of the junkies out there with her have jobs—they're roofers and carpet layers, or auto mechanics, or they work at one of the few factories that survived after IBM pulled out. There are housewives shooting up because it's cheaper than the Oxy pills they got hooked on, there are high school kids, their teachers, people who drive down from even smaller towns upstate to score.

You have homeless like her who stink of body odor and you have suburban queens who smell of Mary Kay products and pay for their habits from their Amway earnings, and you have everything in between.

Welcome to Heroin Nation, 2016.

One nation, under the influence.

With liberty and justice for all.

Amen.

The problem is, as they say on the TV show, winter is coming.

Fuck that, winter is *here,* Jacqui thinks, and now the danger isn't overdosing, it's freezing to death. Well, overdosing *and* freezing to death.

Whichever comes first.

Overdosing is quicker.

But cliché, Jacqui thinks. Shit, overdosing has to be the leading cause of death among rock stars, right? Like, overdoses are a dime bag a dozen, but going Popsicle has some originality to it. Except it sounds like it really hurts.

Jacqui walks past a boarded-up house. Trash blows across the weeds that used to be a lawn.

Man, she thinks, when IBM left it ripped the heart out of this town.

She comes up on a vacant lot.

A young black guy stands there, his hands shoved in his denim jacket, stamping his feet to keep them warm. "Girl, I got what you need."

"You got fire?" Jacqui asks.

Not all the slingers do. Some just have cinnamon, and that ain't gonna cut it with Jacqui anymore. What Jacqui has heard through the junkie community network—which is about as reliable as you'd think—is that the fire comes up from the city just through a couple of gangs, one of which, Get Money Boys—the GMB—has the house on the other side of the lot.

"Girl, if you got the money, I got fire."

"I got twenty."

"It twenty-five."

"I don't have twenty-five."

"Then you have a nice day," he says.

"Come on, man."

"Move along, girlfriend," he says. "You attracting unwanted attention."

"I'll blow you."

"Girl, this a business, not a hobby. You want to get on your knees, go to church."

"I have twenty-three."

"I look like Daymond John, this *Shark Tank*, we negotiate?" he asks. "Now get the fuck out of here, 'fore I smack you."

"Okay, twenty-five." She takes a twenty and a five out of her pocket, slides them into his hand.

"You a lying whore."

"Yeah, I'm a lying whore."

"Try to talk me down," he says. "Gonna blow me for *five dollars*. Why I want a blow job from a white girl? You got no lips. Walk up the house, knock on the back door, you lyin', five-dollar, probably-give-my-dick-a-disease, lizard-lip bitch."

"'Lizard lip'? It better be good shit." Jacqui walks to the back door and knocks. It opens a sliver and a hand reaches a glassine bag out. She snatches it and shoves it into her coat pocket. Then she walks back to the Washington Avenue Bridge, gets into her sleeping bag, cooks, fixes and shoots up.

It's good shit, all right.

Fire gets you higher.

It's her Higher Power.

God and evolution aren't contradictory, she thinks as she nods out.

They're the same.

Cirello's head swivels.

"What's with you?" Darnell asks. "You look like you seen a ghost."

Sort of I did, Cirello thinks. "Nothing."

He's driven Darnell upstate. You going to cracker country, Darnell told him, it's good to have a white man at the wheel. Especially one with a badge. They drove up to Kingston so Darnell could meet with the boss of the GMB and settle him down. GMB shot a rival dealer up there and Darnell needs to straighten him out.

They drive to Motel 19 on the outskirts of the town, where Darnell houses the gang. Darnell throws everyone else out of the room except Mikey, the crew chief.

Darnell asks, "The fuck is wrong with you, child?"

"What you mean, D?"

"*Shooting* a brother."

"Some brothers need shooting," Mikey says, trying to face it out.

"You know Obama?" Darnell asks him.

"The president?"

"Yeah, *that* Obama," Darnell says. "Ain't nobody kill an Arab they don't get his say-so. I'm your Obama, Mikey. You want to pop someone, you get my say-so first. Except you ain't gonna get it."

"Why not?" Mikey's still fronting.

"Think," Darnell says. "Be smart. This a small town. A white town. They gonna let you sell dope to white trash because they trash. But they ain't gonna let you put bodies on the street, even if they black. That shit gets attention, young blood, and attention is bad for business. Bad for *my business,* you feel me?"

"Yeah."

This is Mikey climbing down, Cirello thinks.

"Don't make me replace you," Darnell says.

"I won't."

"Your cousin Kevin say hello."

"How is he?" Mikey asks.

"He good."

Cirello hears the subtext—fuck with me again and I'll not only kill you, I'll kill your little cousin.

On the drive out of town Darnell says, "Problem with this business isn't product, it's personnel. Finding people who will do what you tell them to do, don't do what you tell them don't do."

"My boss says the same thing."

"There you go," Darnell says. "Who was she?"

"Who was who?"

"That junkie we drove by," Darnell says. "You knew her."

"I might have busted her one time down in the city."

"And you thought you saved her," Darnell says. "You should know better, Bobby Cirello. You can't save junkies."

"I guess not."

"You know *why* not?"

"I know you're going to tell me."

"Because, end of the day," Darnell says, "junkies ain't lookin' to get high. They lookin' to get *gone.*"

I suppose so, Bobby thinks.

He puts the girl Jacqui out of his mind.

She had her shot; if she blew it, that's on her.

"Need you to have your head on tight," Darnell says.

"Why's that?"

Because, Darnell, tells him, the biggest shipment ever of fire is coming. Forty kilos.

"Going to be a white Christmas," Darnell says.

"They all are."

"True that."

• • •

It's time, Keller thinks.

In fact, you're running out of time. The new administration will come and shut this down because it all leads back to them.

As the man said, "Follow the money."

You have Eddie dead to rights on trafficking.

You have Darius Darnell.

You have Jason Lerner.

Ricardo Núñez is already under indictment.

You can get US indictments against Tito Ascensión and Rafael Caro for money laundering, then see if their Mexican government protectors will dump them if it gets too hot.

Keller works it.

Calls in every favor and obligation.

The US attorney in San Diego needs no urging—is more than happy to take the evidence Keller provides him on Ruiz's drug trafficking and money laundering, combine it with his own, and issue sealed indictments.

San Diego has long had indictments against the Esparzas for heroin and cocaine trafficking. Turns out that Texas and Arizona do, too, and they both have sealed indictments against Ascensión and his kid.

It's time to make raids, to make busts, nail down the coffins.

And it's time to stop the heroin.

He calls Mullen. "I'm ready to bust Darnell."

"Thank God," Mullen says. "The thought of allowing forty kilos of fire onto my streets has been killing me. Cirello is on the verge of mutiny."

"How about if you take the bust?"

"Are you kidding me?" Mullen says. "Merry Christmas."

Keller walks up to his house.

A woman stands under the tree outside.

Nora Hayden is as beautiful as ever.

There are lines and creases where there didn't used to be, Keller thinks, but somehow they only make her lovelier.

Her eyes are still sharp and radiant.

Commanding.

It's been eighteen years since he's seen her.

On a bridge in San Diego.

Then when she testified against Adán.

Nora Hayden was, until he met Marisol, the most beautiful woman he had ever seen. The most beautiful woman a lot of men had ever seen, because they paid thousands of dollars to be with her.

One of those men was Adán Barrera.

Nora became his exclusively, his full-time mistress, his legendary golden goddess when he was the Lord of the Skies.

Then she flipped on him.

Well, that's not exactly accurate, Keller thinks.

I flipped her.

They'd had a mutual friend, a priest, later a cardinal, named Juan Parada. Keller had met him in Sinaloa around the time he met Barrera and the man had been like a father to him.

Nora Hayden was even closer to the priest. She described him as a friend, and sometimes Keller wondered if they were more than that but never asked either of them.

It was none of his business.

It was his business when Barrera set Father Juan up to be killed.

His own priest, the man who had baptized his daughter.

Barrera betrayed him.

Keller used that to turn Nora, and for long months she was the highest-level informant anyone had ever placed in a cartel, literally in bed with the *jefe* of the world's largest drug-trafficking organization.

She reported only to Keller, and only Keller knew her identity.

But the cartel found her out, as they inevitably do.

Tío Barrera snatched her up.

Hence the hostage exchange on the bridge and everything that followed. Keller hasn't seen her since Barrera's trial. She just disappeared.

Keller hoped that she'd found peace and happiness.

And love.

With Sean Callan.

Nora and Sean Callan faded away, like memories.

Now, like memories, they're both back.

Keller knows why she's here. He says, "Callan's missing."

She tells him what she knows, what she learned from Elena Sánchez, what she saw on the video clip.

"I saw it," Keller says.

"You knew about the raid?" Nora asks.

I did everything but send it, Keller thinks. "It was in remote mountains in southeast Sinaloa. That's Callan's LKL."

She looks at him quizzically.

"Last known location," Keller says.

Nora is as frank as ever. "Do you think he's alive?"

"I don't know," Keller says. "Esparza didn't brag about killing him, which is uncharacteristic, and we didn't see it on the clip."

"Why would he kill all the others and not Sean?"

"Because he's Sean Callan," Keller says. "Maybe Iván thinks he's more valuable alive."

"Sean saved your life once," Nora says. "On the bridge that night. He was the shooter. He was supposed to have killed you. He killed the other people instead."

"I always wondered," Keller says.

"Now he needs you," Nora says. "I need you."

"I'll do everything I can, but . . ."

"But . . ."

"I don't have absolute power in Mexico," Keller says. "I can probably get FES to stage some raids, go out and look for him, but that might just get him killed. And here in the States, well, I'm a short-timer, a lame duck. I don't have the influence that I used to."

She takes this in, and then says, "Before I was with Sean, before I was with Adán, I had a lot of clients in Washington and New York power circles. Some of them were young men then, now they're in more powerful positions. I'll do what I have to do."

"I understand."

"Bring him back, Art," she says. "You owe him that."

I owe you that, too, Keller thinks. "Where can I reach you?"

"The Palomar."

It's just a few blocks away.

"I'll be in touch," Keller says.

When he goes inside, Marisol asks, "Who was that?"

"The past," Keller says.

She leaves it at that.

He reaches out to Orduña.

"I think your guy is dead," Orduña says. "He mouthed off to Iván, Iván had the camera turned off and then did him. Probably in some horrible fashion unsuited even for the internet. You're asking me to look for a corpse, Arturo."

"Will you look anyway?" Keller says.

"What's this guy to you?"

"An old friend."

"Really?" Orduña asks. "Because we have him as one of Adán Barrera's old *sicarios*. Which makes him an unlikely friend of yours."

"You know how it goes."

"I do," Orduña says.

He tells Keller that the Esparza brothers have abandoned the place where the raid occurred and are currently in the wind.

"You're looking for them?" Keller asks. "No offense, but I thought they were sort of untouchable."

"Yes, but less so than they used to be," Orduña says. "Don't get me wrong, they still have a lot of influence, but I'm getting drumbeats from Mexico City that some people wouldn't mind if they got touched. So you looking for a job? There's always one for you here."

"Thanks," Keller says. "Try to find Callan, would you?"

He tells his own people—well, those who still care what he tells them—to beat the bushes for the Esparza brothers. It's a natural request that screens his interest in Callan, but the fact is that if Callan is still alive, he's probably in proximity to the Esparzas.

Iván will keep his hostage close.

Until he finds the best deal or decides just to kill him.

The Esparzas have gone to ground—deep. None of the usual sources have much of a clue as to where they are—satellite runs, computer traffic analysis, phone intercepts all come up empty.

Social media is wondering about it, too. All the blogs, Twitter, Snapchat, the usual suspects are speculating as to where the leadership of the Sinaloa cartel has gone.

Well, they know where Elena and Luis have gone. The "red press" was full of lurid photos of their bodies splayed on the highway in pools of blood. So that mystery is solved, but where are the Núñezes, father and son? And where are the Esparza brothers? Rumors of a bloody raid on one of their havens, backed up by Iván's posting the execution of the raiders, are rife, but where are they now?

And, people wonder, who is the mystery man who had the stones to tell Iván Esparza "Fuck you"? Clearly he's a *yanqui*, but who? Is he alive or dead? He even picks up a nickname, El Yanqui Bally—"the Ballsy American"—and a norteño band with allegiance to Tito comes out with a *narcocorrido* about El Yanqui Bally making Iván Esparza look like an asshole.

A song like that, Keller thinks, could get Callan killed.

If he hasn't been already.

Keller contacts Nora.

Has to tell her there's no word.

Christmas is coming.

And with it, the big heroin shipment that will determine everything.

City sidewalks, busy sidewalks
Dressed in holiday style . . .

Keller thinks of this old song as he arrives in New York two days before Christmas. Marisol has decided not to come. After Ana's death, she's not in the mood to celebrate the holidays and Keller strongly hinted that there was a business element to his trip and that she might be in the way. Now he's on Fifth Avenue working his way through the crowds of last-minute shoppers.

The shipment is scheduled to come on Christmas Eve, a smart move as every law enforcement agency is stripped down to skeletal staffs. Not the NYPD Narcotics Division—Mullen will be working and he has a squad of highly trained, heavily armed officers standing by to bust Darius Darnell at whichever mill the heroin goes.

Which Cirello will tell them as soon as it's on its way from Jersey. If for some reason the heroin goes somewhere else, Cirello will tell them that, too, and they'll improvise. Hidalgo is in San Diego to arrest Eddie Ruiz as soon as the Darnell bust goes down. Others will pick up Eva Barrera on money-laundering charges.

If, if, if—it all goes well.

Bobby Cirello is tired of being a tool.

Sick of being a toy in everyone else's game.

Has a game of his own now.

He finds a parking spot on Garretson Avenue and walks into Lee's Tavern. Mike Andrea and Johnny Cozzo are already in a booth.

"About time you remembered who your friends are," Andrea says. "We was beginning to think you'd become a moolie."

"You got plans for Christmas Eve?" Cirello asks.

Keller has dinner with his son.

Doesn't sound like a big deal but it's a *big deal*. This meal is overdue by about twenty years, and it's taken him a solid year of phone calls, letters and emails to get Michael to meet him tonight.

Keller is nervous.

What do you say to a kid—a man now—whom you basically abandoned in childhood to go chasing monsters? How do you explain that you chose that over him, that he wasn't as important as bringing down a nemesis? That your need for revenge was greater than your love for him? How do you ask him to forgive the unforgivable?

You don't, Keller thinks.

You don't put that on him.

You just have dinner, is what Althea advised. Just have dinner, make small talk, ask him about his life, take it one small step at a time.

He made reservations at a trendy place called Blue Hill. It's a little too "foodie" for him but he thought Michael might like it and it's a place he probably can't afford on his own. And it's down in the Village, so easier for Michael to get to from Brooklyn. Now he sees Michael come down the stairs into the restaurant and look around for him.

Keller walks up to him. "Michael."

"Dad."

It's awkward—they don't know whether to shake hands or hug so they settle for something in between. The hostess takes them to their table and they sit down, Keller with his back to the wall.

"Thanks for coming into Manhattan," Keller says.

"Thanks for coming up from DC," Michael says.

Jesus, he looks like his mother, Keller thinks. The same blond hair, the green eyes, the lips that are always poised to break into a sardonic smile.

"Is this place all right?" Keller asks.

"Yeah, it's great."

"Farm to table," Keller says.

"Right."

The server comes over and goes into his routine. They decide to go with the tasting menu with dishes like "murasaki sweet potato" and venison in a blackberry sauce.

"How's work?"

"Yeah, it's fine," Michael says. "We've been picking up some industrials. Nothing very exciting, but it brings in some money."

"And you're editing?"

"I am," Michael says. Then he gets that slightly mischievous look on his face and asks, "How's *your* work?"

"I guess you read the papers."

"Online," Michael says. "The alt-right sure doesn't like you."

"The left's not so crazy about me either," Keller says. "But I want to know about you. Tell me about you."

"Not much to tell," Michael says. "I mean, I like the film work. I'm pretty good at it."

"I'll bet you are."

"Spoken like a dad," Michael says.

"About time, huh?"

Later, Michael studies the dessert offerings. "Okay, I think I have to try the malted triticale porridge."

"What's that?"

"'White chocolate, apple, and beer ice cream,'" Michael reads. "You game?"

"Why not?"

The malted triticale porridge is, well, interesting. Michael seems to enjoy it. Maybe aided by the wine and beer they've consumed, the dinner has been more relaxed than Keller feared.

"What are your plans for Christmas?" Keller asks.

"Going to my girlfriend's family," Michael says, rolling his eyes. "On Long Island."

"I didn't know there was one," Keller says.

"A Long Island?"

"A girlfriend."

"There is," Michael says.

Then silence.

"Does she have a name?" Keller asks.

"She does," Michael says. "Amber."

"Pretty name."

"Pretty nineties," Michael says. "How about you? For Christmas, I mean."

"Working," Keller says.

Which might have been a mistake because he sees his son stiffen up.

"Drug dealers don't take Christmas off, huh," Michael says.

"Not *these* drug dealers," Keller says, cursing himself for bringing the gun into the cell. After dessert, he pays the check while Michael taps into his phone.

"There's an Uber just four blocks away," Michael says. "A couple of minutes. You want it?"

"I'll grab a cab."

"Old school," Michael says.

"I'm old."

They go up to the sidewalk.

"Let's do this again," Keller says. "More often."

"More often than every twenty years?" Michael says.

He's Althea's son, Keller thinks. And yours. He can't help taking a shot, it's in his DNA. "Merry Christmas, Michael."

"Merry Christmas, Dad."

Keller is half a second from telling him that he loves him, but he doesn't do it. Too much, too soon, and Michael might rightfully resent it.

Michael gets into his Uber.

Keller gets to his room, showers and then tries to sleep. It's not happening. He gets up, makes himself a weak scotch from the minibar and puts the television on.

Thinks about calling Mari, but it's too late.

He'll have to wait until morning.

Tomorrow will be endless, anticipating the bust.

A sign of the times that he can't set himself up at the DEA's New York office because he doesn't know who he can trust. Would sit it out with Mullen but he can't be seen at One Police, either, because that would put Mullen in the crosshairs.

So he'll stay in his room, work things on the phone.

The truth of it is, though, there's not a lot for him to do except monitor the situation and hope. All the active parts are in other people's hands now.

So many things could go wrong.

Darnell could get hinky.

Cirello, knowing that he's finally going to be able to bust this thing, could unconsciously tip his hand—a change in behavior, in attitude, hell, just the look on his face. Same with Hidalgo. He's smart, an experienced undercover, but Ruiz is smart too, with a survival instinct like Keller has never seen.

And what if Denton Howard has found out? He's tight with Lerner, but how tight are either of them with Caro, Ruiz, or Darnell? Close enough to tip them, warn them off?

Everything has to go right and it only takes one thing going wrong.

His phone rings. It's Marisol. "I couldn't sleep. I was thinking about you."

He tells her about his dinner with Michael and she thinks it's wonderful, she's so happy for them both.

"*Te amo, Arturo.*"

"*Te amo también, Mari.*"

Darius Darnell's grandmother loves him.

Cirello can see that.

The woman is ancient—"ninety-three and going strong, honey"—and tiny, her thin hair as white as fresh snow, and her hand trembles as she heaps more sweet potatoes on Darnell's plate. "My baby don't eat enough."

Cirello feels like he's going to explode—smothered chicken, pork chops, greens, sweet potatoes, and Grandma is threatening them with pecan pie.

He had just left his meeting in Staten Island when Darnell called. "What you doin'?"

"Nothing, why?"

"We, you know, busy tomorrow night," Darnell said, "so my grandma doin' Christmas Eve dinner for me tonight. Wants me to bring a friend, thought maybe that's you."

"Me?"

"I don't wanna bring no thugs or whores to my grandma house," Darnell said. "You minimally respectable, know how to use a napkin. And we got shit to go over, you know?"

Cirello knows.

He sits there filling his face, thinking about tomorrow night.

Betrayal on top of betrayal on top of betrayal.

What he's going to do with this nice woman's baby.

Darnell bought her this house in East New York because she wouldn't leave the old neighborhood. It's still sketchy and violent, but she's as safe as a baby in a crib because nobody is going to lay a hand or a harsh word on Darius Darnell's grandma. She could walk past fiends and muggers with fifty-dollar bills hanging out from her pockets and no one would touch her because it would be a slow death sentence.

Darnell has everyone within five square blocks on the arm. His slingers on the corner look out for her, his boys walk or drive her wherever she wants to go, some uniform cops in both the Seven Five and the Seven Three get fat Christmas envelopes for looking in.

The grocer *delivers* to Darnell's grandma.

The pecan pie is insane.

Cirello helps clear the table and load the dishwasher, then Grandma opens her present, a new microwave.

"Baby, I don't need this."

"It's for your Stouffer's," Darnell says.

"I do love my Stouffer's."

"Boys be by tomorrow, install it," Darnell says.

Grandma looks at Cirello. "My baby too good to me."

"Impossible," Cirello says.

She admires the oven for a few minutes, then sits down in her chair and sips a sherry. Two minutes later she's sound asleep.

"That woman raise me," Darnell says, looking at her. "I was in V-Ville, she the only one who write me."

They go over the plans for tomorrow. The shipment is due in Jersey at eight o'clock. Cirello says they should split the shipment into two halves, two vans, twenty kilos in each. That way if, God forbid, one gets hit, Darnell can pay back the loss with the other. One goes to the mill in Castle Village, the other to a new place they've built on the top floor of a building on West 211th and Vermilyea in Inwood. At the corner, on Tenth Avenue, is a restaurant called Made in Mexico, which Darnell thinks is fairly comical.

"You take the Castle Village van," Darnell says. "I'll go with the Inwood one. Done by ten, everyone home in time to open presents."

"You going to see your kid?"

"Christmas morning," Darnell says. "You?"

"I'll hit the family in Astoria," Cirello says. "I have a ya-ya of my own."

"A 'ya-ya'?"

"A Greek grandma."

"You good to her?"

"Not as good as I should be," Cirello says.

Darnell is quiet for a long time, like he's thinking about something, trying to decide whether to tell it to Cirello or not. Finally, he says, "This my last one."

"Christmas?" Cirello asks. "You sick or something?"

"Last *shipment*," Darnell says. "I'm getting out the dope business."

"Are you serious?"

"As a broken leg," Darnell says.

How much rice can a Chinaman eat? he asks Cirello. He's fat with money and legit investments—could live off just that tower—why take any more chances? This shipment is his 401(k).

"Thought I should let you know," Darnell says, "so you could adjust for the loss of income."

"I'm good," Cirello says. "I made enough."

"Hope you put some of this away," Darnell says. "Not lose it on basket-ball, nigger clang a free throw and you broke again."

"I quit gambling," Cirello says.

"That's good."

"It's more than that, isn't it," Cirello says. "It's more than the risk."

"Tired of the thug life," Darnell says. "The hustle, the violence, the para-noia. Knowing someone always looking to take your place, can't trust no one. Got no real friends . . . You my best friend, Bobby Cirello, and I barely like you. How sad is that?"

"Pretty sad."

"No, I just wanna sit back," Darnell says, "watch my kid play lacrosse—

lacrosse, that's crazy—maybe get back with my ex, maybe not, I don't know. I just know I'm done with this. Tomorrow, it's over."

Ain't that the fat truth, Cirello thinks.

The fat, ugly truth.

He looks at Darnell's grandma asleep in the chair.

In the drug game there are no innocent bystanders.

Keller meets Mullen and Cirello by the Christmas tree in Rockefeller Center to go over the night's plans.

Cirello confirms the time and place—the heroin will come over from Jersey shortly after eight p.m. and be driven to an address on West 211th. Mullen's guys will stake the place out but lay way off until Cirello bangs anything into a text.

Then they go in heavy.

"Darnell will be there?" Mullen asks.

"Yeah," Cirello says. "This one's too big to delegate. Anyway, I'll have him on camera, receiving the drugs in Jersey."

As soon as Darnell is in cuffs, Keller will activate the arrest of Eddie Ruiz.

Ruiz will connect Lerner.

And he'll rat on me, too, Keller thinks.

Doesn't matter.

Not with what else is at stake.

"We're good to go?" Keller asks.

Cirello nods—good to go.

They split up.

Keller kills the day doing tourist things, so if Howard does have him up, surveillance will see a guy who came to New York to see his son, do some Christmas shopping, enjoy New York.

He wanders around Rockefeller Center, visits St. Pat's, goes into Bergdorf's and buys Mari a bracelet. Then he walks along Central Park to Columbus Circle and up Broadway, grabs a burger and a beer at P.J. Clarke's, then catches a movie at the Lincoln Plaza Cinemas.

"Don't fuck it up," Cirello says.

"I was pulling hijacks when you were potty training," Andrea says.

But Cirello can tell he's edgy, nervous. He should be, Cirello thinks, he has a couple of mil at stake. "If Darnell makes you for this, I'm not helping you. You're on your own."

"But you still want your taste."

"Fuck yes I do," Cirello says. "You know the risk I'm taking here?"

"Cops, you eat with both hands," Andrea says. "Don't worry, we'll lay it off in Providence, Darnell will never hook it to us."

Cirello knows he's lying, there's no way he can lay off twenty kilos of fire in a small town like Providence. They might take some of it there, but they're going to sell the rest here in New York and think Darnell's too dumb to figure it out.

He just hopes the Italians have their shit together. Andrea probably does, he's an old-school heist guy. But Cozzo? Who knows if he's ever earned his stripes or is just coasting off the family name. And Stevie DeStefano didn't impress as exactly tough when Cirello fronted him.

The other guy Cirello doesn't know. One of Cozzo's Bensonhurst crew.

Cirello hopes he's good.

Because Darnell's people are.

He goes over it again with Andrea: the parking structure in Castle Village is where Darnell's people will be most vulnerable, with the bonus of it being out of sight and hearing.

But they'll have to hit quick, hard and right, Cirello thinks.

"And keep your fucking mouths shut," Cirello says. The Italians will get made the second they say more than a word or two, and Cirello is hoping the rip will get blamed on the Dominicans or rival Mexicans. Darnell's people are going to get asked some hard questions about what they saw and heard.

"They can't say shit if they're dead," Andrea says. "That's the right way to do it, you ask me."

"I'm not asking you," Cirello says. "The rip gets Darnell's people on our ass, but they can't go to the cops. A bunch of dead bodies in a parking garage gets NYPD Homicide on us."

"They don't give a shit about dead moolies."

"They give a shit about headlines," Cirello says. He knows how it works—the mayor leans on the commissioner, who leans on the chief of D's, who leans on the Homicide guys, who have to clear the case or watch their careers spiral down the shitter. "We're going to do this my way or we're not going to do it."

"It's your play," Cozzo says.

He tells Andrea he doesn't want anyone killed unless it's absolutely life-or-death necessary, and if they do it right it shouldn't be necessary.

Cirello doesn't want anyone dead.

Not even dope slingers.

It goes smooth in Jersey.

Same couriers, same routine.

Cirello and Darnell pick up the suitcases of dope, walk out of the hotel into their separate vans with their crews and take off for Manhattan.

All good.

The vans split off when Cirello's turns off the 9 to get to Castle Village and Darnell's keeps going north to Dyckman.

Cirello's car, a black Lincoln SUV, pulls into the parking structure.

The Italians are already inside, waiting, gas masks over their faces. DeStefano guns a Ford F-150 pickup—a work car, stolen, clean—from its slot and plows into the Lincoln's driver's-side door, smashing it into a pylon.

It slams Cirello sideways into the front passenger door. He can't get it open because it's jammed into the pylon.

Darnell's guys go out the other doors.

Andrea pulls a CS grenade, jerks out the pin and tosses it. He draws his MAC-10 and moves in, yelling, "*¡Abajo! ¡Abajo!*"

Fucking idiot, Cirello thinks, trying to use Spanish.

The driver tries to jam the Lincoln into reverse, but another car, a Caddy, slides, blocking its way. Cozzo gets out of the Caddy, an AR-15 at his shoulder, covering. His guy jumps out of the Ford and does the same. Andrea moves to the driver's side, jerks the door open, and pulls the driver out. Then he tosses in another grenade.

Cirello goes down, gagging, gasping for air, his eyes burning.

Andrea leans in and grabs the case, walks back to the Caddy, tosses it into the back seat and gets in. His two other guys jump in the back.

"*¡Ándale!*" Cirello hears.

Then he hears the car roar out.

One of Darnell's guys gets up and tries to shoot, but he's not going to hit anything.

Cirello presses buttons on his phone.

Darnell is on the top floor of the apartment building on West 211th.

Lays the case full of fire on a table.

It's over for him, he thinks.

His people will lay this off to the gangs and the other retailers, he'll get his money and be gone. Place upstate maybe, up on the Hudson somewhere close enough to see his kid and his grandma, far enough away from this shit.

Maybe he'll get a boat.

He picks up his phone to call Cirello but the cop don't answer. Straight to motherfuckin' voice mail. Tries again, same result.

Darnell feels a stab of fear go straight up his spine.

Then he hears feet pounding and yelling.

"NYPD!"

A small, dull explosion and the door swings opens like it's dead.

Cops in black hoods and body armor, badges on the vests, assault rifles to their shoulders. *"On the floor! Down! Down! Down!"*

Their voices hyped. Would shoot a nigger in a heartbeat.

Darnell lies down face-first, stretches his arms out in front of him, a long way from the gun at his hip. A second later someone grabs his hands, jerks them behind him and cuffs him. Hands pat him down, take his gun.

Then he hears someone say, "Darius Darnell? Brian Mullen, NYPD. You're under arrest for possession of heroin with intent to sell."

Mullen starts reading him his rights.

Darnell doesn't listen.

I don't have no rights, he thinks.

Never did.

Cirello staggers out of the parking structure onto the street.

His eyes are red and swollen, his throat parched.

He dials Andrea.

The mobster is pumped. "We did it! We did it! Without sacrificing a single Mau!"

"Where are you?" Cirello asks. "I want my cut."

Keller answers the phone.

"Darnell's in cuffs," Mullen says.

"Congratulations."

"There's a problem," Mullen says. "We only got twenty keys."

"Where are the other twenty?" Keller asks.

"I don't know."

"What does Cirello say?"

"He's not here," Mullen says.

"Where is he?"

"I don't know," Mullen says. "I'm scared to fucking death. He's in the wind."

Keller clicks off and calls California.

Arrest Eddie Ruiz.

It's been Eddie's experience that the hottest women are the worst in bed.

Maybe, he thinks, because they feel that the bestowal of their beauty is gift enough and they don't have to put in any effort beyond the makeup and hair.

Eva Barrera is no exception.

She looks great.

A genuine California ten on the looks scale but maybe a three in the skills department. She gives Eddie the obligatory opening blow-job action, but she does it like she's sucking on a lemon; her face gets this sour look, and her tongue stays on the bench the whole time, just will not get in the game.

Eddie finally gets tired of it, flips her over and says, "I can't wait any longer, I'm dying" (of boredom) and prongs her. He's had more of an enthusiastic reaction from his right hand. Eva makes that babe in V-Ville look like Stormy Daniels, she lies there with this *aren't you lucky* look on her face, like some Mayan virgin about to be lobbed into a volcano. Which Eddie would be willing to do, if there were any handy volcanos in Solana Beach.

It pisses him off.

He takes pride in his ability to give a woman a good time, his work has received rave reviews from a wide variety of amateurs and professionals, and Eva here is acting like she's getting a mildly pleasurable pedicure.

He pulls out, deciding to show her how to give head.

"What are you doing?" Eva asks.

"What do you think?"

"No, I don't like that. It's dirty."

That's why I like it, Eddie thinks. He climbs back on top of her, intending now to finish as soon as he can, and he's working hard at that objective when the bedroom door comes in.

Eva's eyes open wide and she screams.

Sure, *now*, Eddie thinks.

"DEA! US Marshals! Down! Get down!"

Eddie rolls off her onto the floor.

Eva pulls the sheets up around her.

Eddie looks up to see Agent Fuentes.

Mother*fucker*, Eddie thinks.

Fuentes asks her, "Who are you?"

"Eva Barrera."

"Two birds," Fuentes says.

What the fuck does that mean? Eddie wonders. Then Fuentes says, "Edward Ruiz, you're under arrest for the trafficking of illegal drugs. Put your hands behind your back."

"Come on, man, let me put some clothes on," Eddie says. They hold guns on him but let him pull on a shirt and jeans. "Jesus, you couldn't have waited five minutes?"

"Five minutes?" Fuentes says. "Doesn't say much for you."

Doesn't say much for her, Eddie thinks.

They haul him out into the living room.

"Great view," Fuentes says.

"Call your boss," Eddie says. "Tell him you just busted Eddie Ruiz, see what he says."

"Who the hell you think sent us?"

Keller sent them? Eddie thinks.

He must be out of his mind.

Cirello goes home, washes his face and then calls a buddy of his, Bill Garrity, in the 101. "I know it's late."

"Isn't that the start of some bad old song?" Garrity asks.

"You might want to find a reason to hit a house at 638 Hunter."

"What's there?"

"Your career," Cirello says. "A bump to first grade, easy. But go in heavy. Bring people."

"This come out of Narcotics?"

"That's where I work."

"If it's so good," Garrity asks. "Why don't you take it?"

Cops, Cirello thinks. They won't just look a gift horse in the mouth, they'll come in it. "I have my reasons. I need distance from this."

"Can you get me a warrant?"

"Do I have to wipe your ass, too?" Cirello asks. "Maybe you heard a gunshot in there. You'll find weapons."

"Six-Three-Eight Hunter."

"You got it."

"Thanks, I guess."

"I guess you're welcome."

He clicks off.

Fuck Mullen.

Fuck Keller.

They got what they wanted, now I get what I want.

I want dope off the streets.

All the slingers and mobsters in jail.

I'm a New York City police officer.

"What the hell did you do?!" Mullen yells. "What did you do?! Did you tip Cozzo off so he could do a rip? That's a goddamn felony, Cirello!"

It's the next morning and he's waving a copy of the *Daily News* in Cirello's grill. Headline screams about HUGE HEROIN BUST NABS MOB SCION.

John "Jay" Cozzo.

And Mike Andrea.

Cirello holds his open hands in innocence. Looks at a photo of Garrity posing with the stacks of smack.

"Bill got lucky, I guess," Cirello says.

"Bill Garrity couldn't find a hooker in a whorehouse," Mullen says. "You trying to tell me he answered a gunshot call and tripped across Darnell's missing heroin shipment?"

"I'm not trying to tell you anything."

"Did you tip him?" Mullen asks.

Cirello doesn't answer.

"Did you?"

"The fuck you want from me?!"

"The truth!"

"Since when?!" Cirello says. "I've been living a lie for two years and *now* you want the truth?! I'm not sure I even know what that is anymore!"

"Well, you'd goddamn better learn!"

"You want the truth, here it is," Cirello says. "I set up the Italians for that rip, because I don't want them putting any more dope on the street!"

"And this is your way of doing it?!" Mullen says. "What if someone got killed?!"

"No one did."

"What am I supposed to do with you?!" Mullen asks. "Half the division already thinks you're dirty."

"Are you fucking kidding me right now?!"

"You don't think Andrea and Cozzo are singing your name to IAB?!"

"Then tell IAB it was an undercover," Cirello says.

"Nothing in your assignment told you to set up a rip," Mullen says. "If IAB doesn't come down on you, the department will. And Keller wants you hanged from the highest tree."

"Does this jam you up with him?"

"Fuck Keller, he's not my boss," Mullen says. "Where's Libby now?"

"St. Louis, Kansas City . . ."

"Go see her," Mullen says. "Spend some time."

"Libby thinks maybe she's spent enough time with me."

"Maybe you can fix that."

"Maybe." He doubts it.

"Go home, Bobby," Mullen says. "Don't stay there long. Just pack a few things and go somewhere. Take disability leave, go away, let things quiet down, I'll see what I can do."

"I want to see Darnell first."

"You don't have to do that, Bobby."

"I want to."

"I'd advise against it," Mullen says. "What's the point? Guilt? Masochism?"

Cirello says, "Because I'll feel like a coward if I don't."

"You just made the biggest heroin case in the department's history," Mullen says. "No one thinks you're a coward, just an asshole. Five minutes. If Darnell says the word *lawyer,* you walk away."

Darnell sits in an interview room, his hands shackled to a metal table.

He looks up when Cirello comes in. Cirello doesn't dodge his stare, figures he owes it to the man to look him in the eye.

"You ate at my grandma house," Darnell says. "You sat down and ate at my grandma house."

"I was always undercover," Cirello says. "I didn't betray you."

"You just another white man."

Cirello sits down across the table. "You can help yourself here. You can cut ten, fifteen years off your time. Maybe you can't be a father to your son, but you can be a grandfather to his."

Darnell doesn't answer.

"You once told me these rich white assholes would keep you out of jail," Cirello says. "Where are they? You see them here? You see their high-price lawyers here? Who *is* here? Me."

"You ain't asking me to *trust* you now."

"Who else you got?" Cirello asks.

He lets the silence sit for a minute.

"They're going to ask you questions," Cirello says. "The answers you give them are going to be the difference between you ever getting out of prison again and you dying in there. So when they ask you, 'Who told you to set up security for those meetings at the hotel?,' you're going to want to tell them to go fuck themselves. But that would be the wrong answer. The right answer is 'Eddie Ruiz.'"

"We was in V-Ville together," Darnell says. "He saved my life."

"He needed a black guy to sling his dope in the hood," Cirello says. "Lerner and Claiborne and all those other assholes needed a black guy to sell dope to pay for their big shiny building they'd never let you into except to scrub the toilets. You think Lerner's going to invite you to the White House? Get you a presidential pardon? You know what you are to these people? J-A-N. Just Another Nigger."

"Get outta my face."

"I'm not sorry for what I did to you," Cirello says. "You poison people, you kill people. Prison is what you deserve. I'm not sorry for your grandma, either—she knows where her groceries come from."

"Where Libby at?" Darnell asks. "Wherever she is, I can reach out."

"*There's* the real Darius Darnell. *There* he is. Thanks for making me feel better." Cirello leans in. "Now listen to me, motherfucker. I ain't no Mikey. I'm a New York City gold shield. If I hear that one of your thugs as much as says hello to Libby, I'm going to come to whatever shithole they throw you in and beat you to death. You *feel* me, *brutha?*"

Darnell stares at him.

"I came here because I thought I owed it to you to look you in the eye," Cirello says. "But I don't owe you anything. Do what you want. I'm hoping you do the smart thing, the right thing. But if you want to be just another nigger, that's your choice. I'm done with you."

He walks out the door.

He's done with Darnell.

The UC is over.

Eddie is in the San Diego federal lockup.

The former residence of Adán Barrera.

Eddie doesn't look at it as a promotion, he sees it as the potential end of life as he knows it. He knows that if he's ever going to wear anything but a jumpsuit again, he has to be very smart, he has to walk through raindrops.

He knows he can't play their game; if he plays their game, he loses, because by strictly legal standards, he's fucked. Forty kilos of H in the current environment? Back to Florence, for good this time.

So he can't let this get to court, he can't let this get close to court.

A deal has to get cut long before that. And the deal is clear—either he does business with Keller or he does it with Lerner. Either one has a get-out-of-jail-free card to hand him, and if either one thinks Eddie's going down alone, he'd better get his head out of his ass.

In the meantime, all Eddie has to say to anybody are the magic four words:

I want my lawyer.

Keller takes a call from Ben Tompkins.

"I'm representing Eddie Ruiz," Tompkins says. "Mr. Ruiz suggests, and I concur, that I should have a conversation with your lawyer."

"I don't have one."

"You're going to need the best," Tompkins says. "I'm conflicted out but I can make a recommendation."

"No, thanks," Keller says. "And you can say what you have to say directly to me."

"That's imprudent."

"Get on with it."

"Fine," Tompkins says. "Mr. Ruiz says that he can talk to the government about Jason Lerner or he can talk to the government about you."

"If Eddie's holding an auction," Keller says, "I'm not bidding."

"That's a shame because Eddie would prefer you were the highest bidder," Tompkins says. "I can't imagine why, I don't see it myself, but for some reason he likes you."

"Tell him his affections are misplaced," Keller says. "I think of him as a drug-dealing piece of shit, a punk-ass informer I had a long time ago. Tell him I think he's a bitch."

"At least let me tell you what information Eddie can—"

"I know what Eddie has on me," Keller says. "I don't care."

"You should."

"Probably," Keller says. "If you want to help your client, the call you should be making is to the New York AG. You want me to have that put through?"

"Not just yet."

"Then we have nothing to talk about," Keller says.

"Mr. Ruiz has a lot to talk about."

"Then go talk to him." Keller clicks off.

Eddie sits with Ben Tompkins.

"Darnell rolled over on you," Tompkins says. "He's going to testify about his dealings with you and about the Berkeley loan meetings."

"Did you talk to Keller?" Eddie asks.

"He basically told you to go fuck yourself," Tompkins says.

"He's bluffing," Eddie says.

"I don't think so," Tompkins says. "I've been dealing with this guy for twenty years, I've never known him to bluff."

"I can put him behind bars."

"He doesn't seem to care."

"Crazy motherfucker," Eddie says.

He's truly pissed. Why is Keller being this way? It could all be so easy, and he has to make it hard.

But okay.

"Call Lerner," Eddie says.

. . .

Like old times.

They meet upstairs at Martin's.

"Ruiz is threatening to blow up Guatemala," O'Brien says.

"I don't care."

"I do," O'Brien says. "He blows me up with you."

Keller says, "Ruiz doesn't know anything about your involvement. I don't want to take you down, Ben."

"No, just the president of the United States," O'Brien says.

"If he's guilty."

"If you do this," O'Brien says, "you are crossing a line—"

"*I'm* crossing a line?!"

"I asked you not to do this," O'Brien says. "Now I'm telling you. Walk away from this. Hand over the tapes to Howard, walk away, take Mari and live your life."

"Are you speaking for yourself?" Keller asks. "Or Dennison?"

"This comes from the highest level."

"And we point fingers at Mexico," Keller says.

"For once in your life, make the smart decision," O'Brien says. "Make a decision for the people who love you. Or—"

"Or what, Ben?"

"Are you going to make me say it?" O'Brien asks.

The senator gets up and walks away.

Arthur Jackson crosses the last square off his calendar.

Marking Barack Obama's final day in office.

And his last hope.

Now he knows that he's going to complete his three life sentences here in Victorville. Spend the rest of his life here, die here, be buried here. Do the last two life stretches in the grave.

Jackson breaks down and cries.

Sobs his heart out.

Knows for the first time the true meaning of hopelessness.

The complete loss or absence of hope.

He tries to pray, turns to his Bible—*So I am ready to give up; I am in deep despair. I remember the days gone by; I think about all that you have done, I bring to mind all your deeds. I lift up my hands to you in prayer; like dry ground my soul is thirsty for you.*

Jackson knows that giving up hope is a sin, but he's a sinner and now he can't help himself, can't help but believe that God has abandoned him in this place, that Jesus is going to leave him in this hell.

It's a guard that brings him the news. "Arthur, you have a phone call."

Leads him down to the bank of phones.

It's his volunteer lawyer, a young lady.

Arthur steels himself. "This is Arthur Jackson."

"Arthur! It was granted!"

"What?"

"Your clemency!" she shouts. "Obama pardoned seventeen offenders on his last day! You're on the list!"

Jackson drops the phone and falls to his knees.

Sobs again.

And speaks a psalm: "I waited patiently for the Lord to help me, and he turned to me and heard my cry. He lifted me out of the pit of despair, out of the mud and the mire. He set my feet on solid ground and steadied me as I walked along."

Praise God.

"You don't have it," Goodwin says.

"What don't I have?" Keller asks. "Darnell told you that Eddie Ruiz set up security for the Terra meetings with HBMX."

"And Ruiz isn't saying anything."

"Yet," Keller says. "He could give you Rafael Caro and Caro is a known associate of Echeverría."

"And there's still nothing to connect Lerner to that knowledge."

"You heard the tape!"

"And I don't have corroboration!"

"Hidalgo can testify that he wired Claiborne."

"And we can't prove that Claiborne was talking to Lerner," Goodwin says. "Keller, I'm sorry. But you got forty keys of fire off the streets. Major drug dealers. The biggest bust in history. Go out on that and be happy."

"So you'll prosecute Darnell," Keller says. "You'll prosecute Cozzo and Andrea, but you won't prosecute the money people. The usual suspects go to jail and the rich guys walk."

"I can't bring a case I don't think I can win."

"Well, there you go."

Keller sits Hidalgo down in his office.

"We're not going to get Lerner," Keller says. "We'll get Darnell, Ruiz and the mob guys, but we're not going to get Lerner."

"That's a shame."

"We're not going to get Caro, either."

"Why not?" Hidalgo asks.

"Mexico won't prosecute."

"Because the prosecutors are on Caro's payroll," Hidalgo says.

"That's part of it," Keller says. "The other part is that the government thinks they need him to try to restore the peace."

Because the Sinaloa cartel is all but dead and the new king is Tito Ascensión.

And Tito is a brutal thug.

The Mexican government is hoping that Rafael Caro will be a restraining influence.

Hidalgo takes it in. "You promised me we'd go after him."

"We did," Keller says. "We just didn't get him. I'm sorry."

"That's not good enough."

"It's going to have to be, Hugo."

"I don't accept it," Hidalgo says. "We can keep at it."

"I'm out of here tomorrow," Keller says. "The new people are not going to pursue this and we both know why. But be patient, play the long game. This administration could go down. Or change in four years."

"Nothing changes." Hidalgo gets up. "You lied to me."

"I didn't mean to."

"Yeah, you did."

"Where are you going?" Keller asks.

"I quit."

Keller watches him walk out.

He doesn't blame Hidalgo, knows exactly how he feels. Remembers when he himself was told that he couldn't go after Adán Barrera.

Inauguration Day comes cold and cloudy.

Keller doesn't attend the ceremony, he spends the morning packing the last of the few personal belongings in his office. The new president has already announced that one of the first things he's going to do after taking the oath is to fire Art Keller and appoint Denton Howard in his place.

He's also going to appoint Jason Lerner as a senior White House adviser.

Keller is heartbroken.

It breaks his heart that his country has just been mortgaged to a drug cartel.

And the drugs keep coming.

It breaks his heart that his best efforts have been futile, that heroin keeps killing Americans in greater numbers, that not only has he failed to stem the epidemic but the system that provides the drugs now has nexuses not only in Guadalajara, but in New York and, as of this morning, Washington, DC.

He glances at the speech on television.

"Together we will make America strong again. We will make America wealthy again. We will make America proud again. We will make America safe again. And, yes, together, we will make America great again."

On the other side of the country, the gates open.

Arthur Jackson walks out into the cool air of freedom.

Art Keller walks out of his office.

It's over, he thinks.

They beat you, you lost.

Let it go, it's time to fade away. Take Mari and live the rest of your lives in peace.

Your war is over.

He walks over to Arlington cemetery.

Sees row after row of headstones.

The crosses.

The Stars of David.

The crescents.

No, Keller thinks, they didn't die for this.

Not for *this*.

It's a long walk on a cold day, but Keller walks to the *Washington Post*.

BOOK FIVE

Truth

Hell is truth seen too late.
—Thomas Hobbes
Leviathan

The Most Powerful Entity on Earth

*The media's the most powerful entity on earth. They have the
power to make the innocent guilty and to make the guilty innocent.*

—Malcolm X

**Washington, DC
January 2017**

Keller never wanted to be famous.

Or infamous, depending on your point of view.

To some people, he's a heroic whistleblower, to others a subversive traitor. Some people think he's a truth teller, to others he's a liar. Some
think he's a patriot trying to save the country, others see him as a bitter ex-
employee trying to bring down a legally elected president.

But everyone thinks something.

If Keller thought that the public exposure that came with being the DEA
director was intense, it was nothing compared to the media storm that swirls
around him now after the story in the *Washington Post*.

Ex-Dea Boss Alleges Lerner Laundered Drug Money

In an exclusive interview with the Post, former DEA administrator
Art Keller alleged that White House senior adviser and presidential
son-in-law Jason Lerner knowingly accepted a loan from Mexican
banking institutions that was funded by drug-trafficking organizations, including the Sinaloa cartel and others. Keller stated that
Lerner, through his company Terra, accepted the loan to bail out his
troubled Park Tower project in order to make a "balloon payment" of
$285 million after Deutsche Bank pulled out of a financing syndicate.
The former DEA boss further stated that the money was received
extracontractually through rents paid by phony shell companies, false
purchases of construction and maintenance materials and rigged cost
overruns.

If proven, the allegations would place Lerner in jeopardy of prosecution under a number of federal and New York State money-laundering
and fraud statutes.

Keller alleged that the loans were arranged through HBMX bank by the late Chandler Claiborne, who died of a drug overdose in a Manhattan hotel room last December. Keller went on to state that he was approached by "allies" of the Dennison administration, whom he declined at this point to name, offering to allow him to continue in his job, as well as suggesting certain policy concessions, if he would cease his investigation of Lerner and Terra. Keller stated that the people told him that the offer came from the "highest levels," although he refused to specify whether they were referring to Lerner himself or to President Dennison. When he refused this offer, Keller said, the same allies threatened to "destroy" him.

Keller resigned from office on January 19, a standard practice of presidential appointees when a new administration comes into office. He said that he came to the Post with the story only because current DEA administrator Denton Howard refuses to pursue the Lerner investigation.

When challenged on his allegations, Keller stated that he has documentary evidence and alluded to the existence of recordings that "absolutely prove" his charges. Keller declined to play any portions of the alleged recordings, stating that he would turn over his evidence to the proper authorities if a "legitimate investigation is conducted by an independent entity." Keller stated that he has removed this evidence from DEA premises, fearing that it might be "destroyed, suppressed or altered," and has it in his own safekeeping. He admitted that his removal of evidence might, in fact, be a criminal offense in itself, making him susceptible to federal charges under the Espionage Act.

"I thought I had a higher duty," Keller said, "that the potential infiltration of the White House by drug cartels represents a greater threat to the security of the United States."

Keller said that he had no information to indicate that President Dennison has any financial interest in Terra or knowledge of the Park Tower loan in question.

Mr. Lerner was unavailable for comment, but anonymous sources in the White House called Keller's allegations "outrageous," "slanderous" and "criminal."

CNN called it a "bombshell."

Which was exactly Keller's intent in going to the *Post*.

To roll a grenade down the airplane aisle and blow it all up.

If a state prosecutor won't open the case, he thought, and a federal prosecutor won't open the case, maybe a special counsel will. And if the new US attorney general won't appoint a special counsel, Congress could. Congress could form its own investigative committee, but the president's party would have control, so Keller didn't think anything would come of it.

Of course, the AG is a Dennison appointee and his party controls both houses, but the allegations are so "outrageous" that public opinion might force an independent investigation.

It's Keller's last hope.

By nature, training and experience, he's an essentially private person, but now the media sits outside the house like the bivouac of an invading army. He's deluged with requests for interviews—all the networks, the cable outlets, the print media.

He turns them all down.

Because his strategy is to let other people carry the ball and move it forward. If it's just him appearing on all the shows, then he's a one-man band, a solitary voice singing the same song. He wants to put in just enough to keep the story in the news cycle.

Just now and again blow on the embers to keep the flame alive.

And now his life is public, every detail of his past and present—some factual, others fantastical—is being dug up and displayed on CNN, Fox, MSNBC, the network news, every front page.

Pundits on the talking-head shows provide "analysis" that Keller is the illegitimate son of a Mexican mother and an American father (an alt-right blog cheerfully reports KELLER REALLY IS A BASTARD).

The more rabid speculate IS KELLER AMERICAN OR MEXICAN? and generate a mini-"birther" controversy by suggesting that Keller was born in Mexico and was therefore not only disqualified from his former position but eligible for deportation.

Keller responds to this one.

"I can probably lay my hands on my birth certificate," he tells Jake Tapper, "but no one questioned my nationality when I was serving in Vietnam."

The reports go on that he grew up poor in San Diego's Barrio Logan (where his brief and mediocre Golden Gloves stint accounts for his crooked nose), went to UCLA, where he met his first wife (whose family were stalwarts in the California Democratic Party), and then to Vietnam: KELLER'S ARMY UNIT CONNECTED TO OPERATION PHOENIX—NOTORIOUS VIETNAM ASSASSINATION PROGRAM.

Well, they got that, Keller thinks when the story comes out, but they missed the real story, that he'd been recruited by the CIA. The media did get to a related story—Keller was coming out of his house when a reporter walked alongside him and said, "The early personnel of the DEA were largely drafted from CIA. Were you one of those?"

Keller doesn't answer and the story goes out as KELLER'S CIA BACKGROUND PROBED.

Also "probed" is his DEA career, that he'd been a field agent in Sinaloa in the 1970s during Operation Condor, when thousands of acres of poppy fields were burned and poisoned.

Keller watches a CNN panel discussion where an "expert" says, "This is probably where Keller first met the Barreras. One of my sources tells me that Keller actually knew the young Adán Barrera, that they were friends, that Keller actually saved him from a brutal beating by Mexican federal police."

The same expert—whom Keller doesn't know and has never met—provides "insight."

"The torture-murder of Keller's partner, Ernie Hidalgo," she says, "is really the transformative moment in Keller's life. If you track his career subsequent to that, it's really an obsessive quest to bring all the people involved to justice, especially Adán Barrera. I think Keller felt a personal sense of betrayal with Barrera, possibly because they'd once been friends."

"Back in Sinaloa," the host says.

"That's right," she says. "There's another connection—Keller and Barrera had the same priest, Father Juan Parada—later a cardinal—who was killed in a 1994 gun battle outside the Guadalajara airport. My sources say that Keller also blamed Barrera for that."

"And Keller did bring Barrera down."

"He did," she says. "In 1999, Keller arrested Barrera in San Diego—"

"What was Barrera doing there?"

"Visiting his ill daughter in the hospital," she says. "Keller arrested him and then left the DEA. But he came back in 2004 when Barrera was transferred back to Mexico."

"And then famously escaped."

"Right, and Keller was based in Mexico City for several years but never brought Barrera in," she says. "He was principally known for helping to bring down the infamous Zetas. Then Barrera was killed in Guatemala. Shortly after that, Keller became DEA director."

"Why are you watching this nonsense?" Mari asks him.

"I'm learning things about myself I never knew," Keller says.

The media keep digging, disinterring his 1992 testimony in front of the Iran-Contra committee.

The congressional committee was looking into allegations that CIA or NSC or some agency in the Reagan administration had either colluded in or at least tolerated the contras trafficking cocaine to fund their guerrilla war against the Sandinistas in Nicaragua.

Another lifetime, Keller thinks.

He lied to the committee.

Committed perjury.

They'd asked him if he had ever heard of an air-freight company called SETCO.

He'd answered, "Remotely."

A lie. The truth was that it was Keller and Ernie Hidalgo who discovered SETCO, who had tried to bring it to the attention of his then superiors in DEA.

They'd asked him if he'd ever heard of something called the "Mexican Trampoline."

No, he'd said.

Another lie.

He and Ernie had uncovered the cocaine-laden flights that bounced from Colombia to Central America to Guadalajara, Mexico.

"How about something called 'Cerberus,' Mr. Keller. Did you ever hear of that?"

"No."

"Did something called Cerberus have anything at all to do with the murder of Agent Hidalgo?"

"No."

It had everything to do with Ernie's murder, Keller thinks now. Barrera's people tortured Ernie to find out what he knew about the operation, run from the vice president's office, to illegally fund the contras by turning a blind eye to the Mexican Trampoline.

Barrera's uncle, M-1 himself, had personally funded a contra training camp, and when Keller finally ran him down in Costa Rica, CIA released him.

And Keller lied to the committee.

In exchange, he was given command of the Southwest Anti-Narcotics Task Force with a free hand to take down Adán Barrera and the people who had murdered Ernie.

Which he had done, with a vengeance.

He put away the doctor who had supervised the torture in prison. He put Rafael Caro away. It took Keller years, but he finally put Adán Barrera behind bars.

He even killed M-1—two bullets into his chest on a bridge in San Diego.

But the right-wingers, the administration's defenders, are playing a dangerous game reviving Iran-Contra. It's a gun pointed at their own heads.

It's one thing to attack me, Keller thinks as the days go by, another thing to attack Mari.

The right-wing blogs publish stories about the "radical Dr. Cisneros," "Red Mari," bringing up her history of protests against the Mexican government, her support of "left-wing activists" in the Juárez Valley; they even turn her heroism on its head by hinting that as mayor of Valverde she had been gunned down not for her *opposition* to drug cartels, but because she had "double-crossed" one of them.

Marisol blows it off.

"They're words," she says to Art, "not bullets."

But she worries that the dirt thrown at her could hit her husband and dirty him as well.

"What you have to understand," one talking head says, "is that Dr. Cisneros is as polarizing a figure in Mexico as her husband is here in the States. To the left, she's practically a secular saint, a martyr who defied both the government and the cartels. But to conservatives down there, Cisneros is a she-devil, a Communist in bed with subversive forces. You put all that together with Keller, you have quite the combination."

Another analyst "unpacks" their relationship on television. "Keller and Cisneros met in Mexico during his last assignment there. It's an absolute love story—he nursed her back to health after she'd been severely wounded by the Zeta drug cartel. Some people say that she's been a huge, liberalizing influence on him, that a lot of his positions on drug policy, prison reform and immigration come from Dr. Cisneros."

"Cisneros was back down in Mexico protesting the kidnappings and killings of those forty-nine college students, wasn't she?"

"She was," the analyst says, "along with the recently murdered Mexican journalist Ana Villanueva, a close friend of both hers and Keller's. In fact, Villanueva spent last Christmas in the Keller home here in Washington."

"And her last article before her death," the host says, "was an interview with Rafael Caro."

"The connections just keep going on and on."

So do the attacks.

Fox News and AM radio are incessant—Keller is a politically motivated liar trying to undo the election results. He's a nutjob conspiracy theorist, deranged by his guilt over getting his partner killed. He's a henpecked husband, run by his harridan wife.

"Talk to anyone at the DEA," one of the radio hosts says, "and they'll tell you that Art Keller was a terrible administrator. The agency was falling apart under his so-called leadership. And they'll tell you that he had a liberal agenda. And that's what we're seeing now."

Anything to discredit him, anything to throw shade on the story that he told to the *Washington Post*.

Then an article appears in an alt-right blog.

The Bridge to Somewhere

In the spring of 1999, former DEA director Art Keller was involved in a gunfight on Cabrillo Bridge in San Diego's Balboa Park. Keller, described then as a "hero," killed Mexican drug lord Miguel Ángel Barrera and arrested the infamous Adán Barrera, then the boss of the Mexican cartel known as the Federación. Shortly after, Keller took a "leave of absence" from the DEA and repaired to . . . wait for it . . . an isolated monastery in the desert of New Mexico, only to reemerge four years later on a renewed hunt for Barrera in Mexico, a hunt that only ended with the revelation of Barrera's death in Guatemala.

But roll the tape back. There was a second body on that bridge in 1999. Salvatore Scachi, a Green Beret officer with reputed ties to the New York Mafia as well as the CIA. What was Scachi doing on that bridge? No one, including Art Keller, has ever answered that question. And Scachi was killed, not by Keller's gun, but by a high-velocity bullet fired from a rifle. That case has never been cleared and remains in the San Diego PD cold case file.

But who was the shooter? Where was the shooter? What was the shooter's relationship to Keller? Another question whistleblower Keller has never answered, nor was he called to answer, hiding out in his New Mexico retreat at the time. No wonder the monks had a vow of silence.

Something happened on that bridge, something the American people deserve to know.

This bridge leads somewhere.

Yes, it does, Keller thinks.

As much as the right demonizes him, the left lionizes him. On MSNBC he's "principled," "heroic," "embattled." *Rolling Stone* calls him "the next Edward Snowden," a comparison that Keller doesn't find flattering.

But the liberal media are beside themselves that Keller made accusations against Jason Lerner, and therefore by extension Dennison. They can't get enough of what they inevitably label "Towergate," and as much as reporters are hounding Keller, they dog Lerner and the White House as well.

Questions come up at every White House press briefing—"What about Towergate?" "Is Lerner's job in jeopardy?" "Will Lerner be prosecuted?" "Is it true that Lerner has accepted loans from Mexican drug cartels?" "Does the president have any financial interest in Terra?" "Did the president know about this loan?" "Did President Dennison tell the attorney general to put pressure on Keller to kill his investigation?" "Did Lerner?"

Dennison responds on Twitter. Fake news. Lies. We're going to sue.

The furious denials only fan the flames. Serious journalists start to write investigative stories about Terra, the Park Tower financial situation, about Claiborne's overdose.

Keller wishes they would sue—it would force Lerner to testify under oath.

The *Times* and the *Post* lead with new angles every day—LERNER UPSIDE DOWN ON PLAZA TOWERS, GERMAN MEGA-BANK PULLED OUT OF PLAZA TOWERS LOAN, CLAIBORNE HAD NO HISTORY OF HEROIN USE.

It's the firestorm Keller had hoped to touch off when he lit the match. If he can incite enough public pressure to demand a special counsel, he has a chance to get his prosecution. Even though he knows that the fire he set is going to consume him, too, because one of the people a special counsel will want to talk to would be Eddie Ruiz, and Eddie will talk to anyone who can cut him a deal.

Keller doesn't care.

He just wants a special counsel.

Pressure builds on the AG to appoint one. Columnists call for it, Democratic senators and House representatives call for it, the all-important Sunday shows call for it.

But the AG stonewalls.

And counterattacks.

"If Mr. Keller revealed confidential information from a government investigation to the *Washington Post* or anyone else," he says, "that is a crime. If he has removed investigative materials, that is also a crime and we might seek prosecution."

How much does he know? Keller wonders. How complicit is he? Have O'Brien and the rest told him about the Claiborne tapes? This was his shot across the bow warning me not to bring them out?

"Can they really do that?" Mari asks him. "Prosecute you?"

"It's possible."

"So you could end up in prison for telling the truth," she says.

"Yup."

"Well," she says, "you wouldn't be the first."

Keller has never responded very well to threats. He'd been threatened by the old Federación, the Sinaloa cartel and the Zetas—all of which tried to kill him. He's going to knuckle under because this little cracker bastard holds a press conference?

No.

But the attorney general, David Fowler, refuses to appoint a special counsel.

Two days later, Fowler's "on the Hill" in front of an appropriations committee that's asking him about "the wall" when a Democratic senator, Julius Elmore, slips in a question about why he won't appoint a special counsel in "Towergate."

"Because there's no need," Fowler snaps, "to go outside the normal channels. If Mr. Keller thought that he had sufficient evidence to bring a case, why didn't he bring it to the last attorney general before they both left office? If he feels that he has sufficient evidence to bring a case, why doesn't he bring that evidence to me? The only time you would appoint a special counsel is when you feel there is a conflict of interest that would render the attorney general's office unable to be objective."

Elmore can barely contain a smile as he asks, "Do you have any such conflict, sir, that would not allow you to be objective in a case regarding the White House or the Terra Company?"

"No, I do not."

Gas on the fire.

The media howls with indignation. How could Fowler say he didn't have any conflicts when he was an early and chief supporter of the new president? When he campaigned for him, raised money for him, was a "surrogate" on television for him?

The answer his supporters give is that it didn't rise to the level of "conflict." If it did, few attorneys general could ever make a decision in a case involving the White House.

But a few days later the *New York Times* publishes an article that reveals that Fowler owns stock in an investment firm that lent Terra money on an overseas project. As such, he has direct, personal interest in the financial well-being of the company.

The committee calls him back in.

Elmore asks, "Sir, do you remember the answer you gave when asked if you had any potential conflict regarding Terra?"

"Yes, I do."

"You testified that you did not," Elmore says. "But that wasn't true, was it?"

"There was no attempt on my part to deceive," Fowler says. "I just didn't recall . . . I mean, no one can be aware of all the details of your portfolio . . ."

"Which is it?" Elmore asks. "You don't recall or you weren't aware?"

"Sir, I deeply resent any implication—"

"But would you say now," Elmore asks, "as you sit here today, that you do have such a conflict?"

Fowler is trapped and knows it. He admits there might possibly be "the perception of a conflict."

"Let me ask you, sir," Elmore says, "did anyone in the administration ask you to put pressure on Keller to shut down the Towergate investigation?"

"Well, sir," Fowler says, "Mr. Keller was no longer in his job when I took over."

"That's not what I asked you, sir."

"I don't recall any such conversation."

"Do you know if Mr. Howard approached Mr. Keller with that same request?" Elmore asks.

"You'd have to ask one of them."

"So you don't know?"

"I don't recall Mr. Howard telling me that."

"But if any of those conversations that you don't recall did happen," Elmore says, "that would be obstruction of justice, wouldn't it?"

The next day Fowler recuses himself from the Towergate case.

Ben O'Brien isn't happy.

"That slimy, chickenshit little bastard," he says. "All he had to do was grow a pair and gut it out."

Keller set a trap and this dumb son of a bitch walked right into it.

Rollins says, "He's afraid of a perjury charge."

"Bull*shit*," O'Brien says. "Who's going to bring it?"

It's terrible news. Not only does the AG's flip-flop have the stench of guilt about it, but now the decision to bring in a special counsel will lie with the deputy US attorney general, John Ribello, who isn't going to stop a bullet for a boss he privately detests.

It doesn't stop O'Brien from trying. He gets on the horn. "You do what you think best, of course you should do what your conscience dictates, but you know that there's nothing here. This is a witch hunt."

The answer isn't encouraging. "How do you know that, Senator? If you have information pertinent to—"

"Hell no," O'Brien says. "There *isn't* any goddamn evidence. If there was, don't you think we would have seen it by now?"

"What I'm gleaning," Ribello says, "is that Keller was reluctant to bring evidence forth because he was afraid it would be compromised or suppressed."

Is that what you're "gleaning," you smarmy Ivy League cocksucker, O'Brien thinks. He says, "No one is talking about suppressing evidence here."

"I should hope not."

They're all running scared, O'Brien thinks. This asshole is smart enough to appoint a special counsel just to get himself out of the line of fire. Dump this steaming pile off on someone else and wash his hands.

And that other smart son of a bitch Keller is sitting on those tapes. A special counsel would subpoena Keller and demand all documents and evidentiary materials.

And what will Keller do then?

What will he say?

The question now, Keller thinks as he wakes up to yet another morning of this, is what will Ribello do?

File charges against me?

Appoint a special counsel?

Both?

Nothing?

They're all options.

Even if he does appoint a special counsel, Keller thinks as he runs a razor down his cheek, who would it be? If he appoints a Republican Party hack, it will just be a whitewash—the purpose of the investigation won't be to uncover wrongdoing, but to bury it. It will be a "search-and-avoid" mission, going wherever the evidence isn't and then announcing that you didn't find any.

He finishes shaving, then gets dressed for a day of . . .

What?

Sitting around waiting?

Keller has nowhere to go—all the job possibilities are on hold until this thing is over. He could go for (yet another) walk around the neighborhood, haunting the local bookstores, but what had once been a joy has become a pain in the ass, as he can't go anywhere without being stopped and questioned, by either reporters or just people on the street who recognize him. Some of them give him a thumbs-up, others scowl, others actually come up and ask for autographs.

Marisol thinks he should get security.

"A bodyguard?" Keller asked. "I don't want that."

"You don't know who any of these people are," she said. "Some nut might want to make a name for himself."

Keller blows it off. He didn't get a bodyguard when Adán Barrera had a

$2 million bounty on his head, he's not going to get one now. I can take care of myself, thank you, he thinks. He still carries a 9 mm Sig on his waist under his jacket when he goes out.

Which is less and less.

Keller has to acknowledge that he's pretty much become a prisoner in his own home. I might as well have an ankle bracelet, he thinks.

He's pulling on a sweater when he hears Marisol yell, "Arturo, get down here!"

"What is it?!"

"Ribello's on!"

Keller hustles down the stairs.

Deputy Attorney General John Ribello is holding a press conference. "In my capacity as deputy attorney general, I have determined that it is in the public interest for me to exercise my authority and appoint a special counsel to assume responsibility in the so-called Towergate matter. This does not imply that I have reached a determination that any crimes have been committed or that any prosecution is warranted. What I have determined is that based on the unique circumstances, in order for the American public to have full confidence in the outcome, I need to place this investigation under the authority of a person who is independent of the normal chain of command."

Marisol says, "You won."

"I haven't won anything." But I haven't lost, Keller thinks. Depending, that is, on whom he appoints. He looks at the man standing behind and beside Ribello and doesn't recognize him. About my age, Keller thinks. White hair. Tall, craggy.

He steps forward as Ribello says, "Our nation is grounded on the rule of law, and the people must be assured that government officials administer the law fairly and objectively. Special Counsel Scorti will have all the appropriate resources to conduct a thorough and complete investigation, and I am confident that he will follow the facts, apply the law, and reach a just result. Mr. Scorti?"

Scorti steps to the microphone. "I don't have much to say at this point, other than that, to avoid any appearance of conflict, I am resigning my position at the law firm of Culver-Keveton. I will do my utmost to see this matter to a fair and just conclusion. Thank you."

Marisol is already googling. "He's from Boston . . . a Republican . . . graduated Dartmouth . . . served in Vietnam—Bronze Star and Purple Heart—"

"Army or marines?"

"Marines," Mari says. "Columbia Law School . . . was a US attorney . . .

then US assistant attorney general for the Criminal Division. He oversaw prosecution of Noriega—"

"That's why he's familiar."

"—the Lockerbie bombing case, and the Cimino crime family."

The past keeps coming back, Keller thinks. Sean Callan was a hit man for the Ciminos.

The phone rings. Senator Elmore. "Art, this guy's the real deal."

"Yeah?"

"He's his own man," Elmore says. "Dennison's not going to run him. That's the good news. The bad news is, neither are you."

"Okay." He clicks off. Looks out the window and sees that news trucks are already pulling up, reporters gathering outside. On the television, the reporters are peppering Ribello with questions.

"What is the scope of Mr. Scorti's investigation?" one asks. "Will he have the latitude to pursue ex-director Keller as well as Lerner?"

"Mr. Scorti will have the latitude to investigate all aspects of this matter," Ribello says.

"That includes Keller."

"I believe the word 'all' is explanatory."

"Does his scope include the death of Claiborne?"

"I don't know how else to tell you . . ."

"Will Mr. Scorti have prosecutorial powers?"

"Mr. Scorti will be able to prosecute on any federal charges he determines, as recommended by a grand jury."

"Will Scorti have the latitude to investigate President Dennison's potential financial connections with Terra?"

"Once again," Ribello says, "the special counsel will follow the evidence where it leads."

We'll see, Keller thinks.

It will take weeks, he knows, before Scorti reaches out to him. The special counsel will have to get offices, hire a staff, review documents.

"You need a lawyer," Marisol says.

"That's what Ben Tompkins said."

"Even a broken clock . . ."

"I don't want a lawyer," Keller says.

"This isn't the time to be naive or arrogant," Marisol says. "Or stubborn. Or do you want to go to jail?"

"I want to put Jason Lerner in jail."

"Great," Marisol says, "you can play volleyball together."

Keller sighs. "I don't know any defense lawyers. I mean, I do, but most of them would love to see me in a cell next to their clients."

"You know Daniella Crosby."

"Who's that?"

"One of the most prominent defense lawyers in DC," Marisol says. "We were on a literacy committee together, went to lunch a few times. She and her husband dropped by our Christmas party."

"There were so many people . . ."

"I have her on my phone."

Keller looks out the window at the gathering horde of media. "Call her."

Daniella Crosby's office is downtown, on Seventeenth and K, not far from the White House and the Hamilton Hotel.

An African American woman in her midforties, black hair cut short, oversize eyeglasses framing a strong face, she looks across her conference table at Keller and gets right to it. "I don't know if I can keep you out of jail. Did you in fact reveal details of a classified ongoing investigation to the *Washington Post*?"

"Yes."

"Did you also remove investigative materials from the DEA offices?" she asks.

"I did."

"And do you still have these materials in your possession?"

"Possibly," Keller says.

"That's a yes," she says. "Mr. Keller, you know I can't help you if you won't be truthful with me. In fact, I won't represent you."

"Ms. Crosby—"

"Reverend," she says. "If we're going to be formal, it's actually *Reverend* Crosby. I'm an ordained minister. Or shall we make it Daniella and Art?"

"Daniella," Keller says, "you're asking me to trust you, and frankly, I don't trust anyone."

"What about Marisol?"

"She's the exception."

"Make another one," Crosby says. "You've chosen to take on the president of the United States and all his cohorts, over half of Congress, several large drug cartels and now the special counsel. You really think you can do that alone?"

"I don't want you to be in possession of knowledge that could put you at risk."

"Why don't you stop patronizing me and let me decide what risks I'm willing and able to take?" she asks. "If I take your case, which as of the moment is extremely doubtful, it will be my job to protect you, not the other way around, so the sooner we get used to *that* dynamic, the better."

"I think you have the wrong emphasis here," Keller says.

"How so?"

"Your priority seems to be defending me," Keller says. "My priority is prosecuting Lerner."

"And the president."

"If that's where it leads," Keller says. "You have to understand—my entire purpose in leaking this story was to provoke a special counsel investigation. I'm not running from this, I'm running toward it."

"You run into a fire, you might get burned."

"I'm aware of that risk."

"The risk is very real."

She explains to Keller that he could be charged under three federal statutes. The first is USC 18-793—the so-called Espionage Act that was used to prosecute Edward Snowden—with a sentence of up to ten years.

"They could make that case," Crosby says, "but I would argue that 793 pertains only to information regarding the national defense, which I think would be hard for them to show."

The second statute is 18-641, the Federal Conversion Statute, which refers to the theft of government property, including records, and also has a maximum sentence of a fine and ten years.

The third is 18-1030, which figured in the Chelsea Manning case, prohibiting the transfer of information regarding national defense or foreign relations from a computer.

"If any of the information that you told to the *Post* was ever entered into a DEA computer," Crosby says, "you might be in jeopardy of a 1030 violation, another ten years."

The most probable prosecution strategy, she says, would be to throw all three of these at the wall like spaghetti and see if any of them stick.

"What's the defense?" Keller asks.

"Other than you didn't do it?" she asks.

Keller doesn't answer.

Then the best defense strategy, she explains, would be to cite the various whistleblower acts that protect federal employees from prosecution if they reasonably believed governmental officials have committed abuse, or if their actions threatened the public health and safety.

"I would certainly argue," Crosby says, "that a heroin-trafficking network purchasing influence at the highest levels of government would constitute a threat to the public health and safety. The problem is, can you prove that government officials were colluding in this or seeking to cover it up?"

"Jason Lerner is a senior White House adviser," Keller says.

"But he wasn't at the time of the offenses you allege," Crosby says. "So that might incriminate him and still not exonerate you. Do you have anything else?"

He tells her about his conversations with O'Brien asking him to quash the investigation, omitting references to the Guatemala raid.

"That's somewhat helpful," Crosby says, "but not exculpatory. O'Brien is a powerful chairman of a relevant committee but not in direct authority over you."

"Denton Howard offered me my job to shut the investigation down."

"So what?" Crosby asks. "He was your subordinate."

"He said he was acting on behalf of the then president-elect," Keller says.

"Was this conversation recorded?"

"Not by me."

"Then it's your word against his," Crosby says. "And we still have the same time frame problem. Even if Dennison did convey that offer, it's not obstruction of justice because he had no statutory authority. Did the sitting attorney general at the time ever ask you to shut down the Lerner investigation?"

"I didn't bring it to her."

"That's a problem," Crosby says. "Why not?"

Keller says, "I was in the middle of conducting not only an investigation, but an operation to bring down a major heroin-trafficking organization related to Towergate. I was concerned that any premature revelation to the AG's office might jeopardize that operation, placing not only it, but certain undercover agents in danger. My own people were already leaking to Howard, and he was passing it on to O'Brien."

"So what are you engaging me to do," Crosby asks, "defend you or help you incriminate Lerner?"

"I guess both."

"And if there comes a point when those two interests conflict with each other?"

"Would you allow a drug cartel to influence the government of the United States?" Keller asks.

"If it meant defending my client, yes."

"Then at that point," Keller says, "I'll fire you."

"Just as long as we understand each other," Crosby says. "You're not talking to the media anymore. That's what I do. I'm very good at it and you're very bad at it. Now tell me everything."

"Where do you want me to start?"

She looks at him like he's an idiot. "The beginning?"

He tells her everything.

Except about Guatemala.

Or the bridge.

Sean Callan has been moved, moved again, and then moved again.

Every time it's the same routine. They throw a hood over his head, shackle him hand and foot and toss him into the back of a vehicle, sometimes into a plane. Where the Esparza brothers go, Callan goes. Then they shove him into a warehouse, a barn, a basement, and chain him to the wall.

He gets minimal food—some tortillas, rice and beans, a bowl of pozole. Every few days they unchain him and spray him with a garden hose, maybe give some used clothes because Iván complains that otherwise he stinks.

Callan knows he smells. He hasn't brushed his teeth in weeks, his hair and beard are long and matted, he looks like a psychotic homeless man. Psychotic is about right; he knows he's losing his mind. Hour after hour of sitting against a wall—nothing to look at, nothing to read, no one to talk to.

The only exception was when Iván came to tell him a joke. "What's the difference between Jesus Christ, herpes, and Elena Sánchez? No? Elena Sánchez won't ever come back."

Callan loses track of hours, of days and nights, if someone asked him how long he's been a prisoner, he couldn't say. Weeks, months? He doesn't think it's been a year.

He misses Nora, wonders how she is, hopes she and the little girl are all right, that she's not grieving for him.

With nowhere else to go, his mind wanders to the past.

He was seventeen when he killed his first man.

Eddie "the Butcher" Friel, in the Liffey Pub back in New York, in Hell's Kitchen. Shot him in the face with a .22, gave the pistol to the Hudson.

Then it was Larry Moretti.

After that he went to work for the Cimino family, and Johnny Boy Cozzo gave him the job of taking out the boss, Paulie Calabrese, Christmas of '85. He had to leave the city after that, down to Guatemala, El Salvador, Mexico, all the garden spots where people needed people who could kill people.

He lost count of how many.

His soul was in a garbage heap until Father Juan pulled it out.

Then they killed him, too.

Adán did.

Ordered it, anyway. Adán Barrera didn't do his own killing, that's what he had people like me for, Callan thinks.

So now if I'm in hell, then I'm in hell and it's what I deserve.

He has no clue where he is the night they come in, unchain him and take him to a shower tacked to a corner wall. The water trickles, but it's warm. Then they sit him down in a chair, shave him and give him a haircut, then toss a new pair of jeans, a denim shirt and a pair of sneakers at him.

"Get dressed," one of them says. "Iván doesn't want you looking like a bum."

For what? Callan thinks. For the video when they shoot me?

He gets dressed, they slip a hood over his head and put him in the back of a car. They drive for what he guesses is about two hours, then the car stops and they take the hood off.

He knows where they are from the old days.

The border crossing at Tecate.

Two *federales* stand outside the van.

"Get out."

"Am I going to get a bullet in the back?" Callan asks.

"Not from us."

Callan gets out. The *federales* take him by the arms and walk him to the Border Patrol booth. Two men in plainclothes are waiting for him, and the *federales* hand him over.

"Sean Callan?" one of them says. "FBI. You're under arrest for suspicion of the murder of Paul Calabrese."

They turn him around and cuff him.

Take him back to America.

Crosby prepares Keller for his interview with the special counsel. They don't work every day, but most days, and for several hours. He goes to her office at nine and leaves shortly after lunch.

For the first few days, the media were camped out in front of the building, but when Keller continually declined to answer questions and Crosby gave them bland answers, they got bored and left.

Typically, Keller takes the Metro in the morning, from Dupont Circle to Farragut North. Weather permitting, he prefers to walk home up Connecticut Avenue to clear his mind after the prep session. Occasionally he stops in at Kramer Books or Second Story, but more and more often someone recognizes him and wants to talk so he usually decides not to go.

"Until we get an offer of immunity you take the Fifth," Crosby says. "After that, we give them everything they want."

"Including the tapes?"

"If they ask for them," Crosby says. "They will, in an omnibus demand for something like 'any and all materials in your possession relating to this matter.' Then you have to give them the tapes."

"What if they suppress them?" Keller asks.

"I don't make Scorti for something like that," Crosby says. "But I'll seed the field."

"What does that mean?"

"It's why you hired me," she says. "I'll go on the media and remind them of the possibility that you have materials such as recordings. Then if Scorti tries to suppress the tapes, he'll be under enormous public pressure to release them."

It's why I hired her, Keller thinks. It's smart and subtle, and I wouldn't have thought of it. And it shows she's interested in bringing Lerner down. But he's not convinced. Which is why he made copies and stored them beyond the reach of subpoena power. He notices that Crosby hasn't asked him if he's done that.

They have a working lunch in the office and go over more details. No firm date has been set for the interview.

Eddie's going crazy in the San Diego lockup.

Not metaphorically crazy, literally insane.

He thought he could do solitary again easy based on his time in Florence, but now he realizes that the supermax didn't build him up, it wore him down. The cell is twelve by six and the walls are starting to vibrate if he stares at them long enough, like they're made out of water, a sheen of water over the sand when a wave finishes washing up.

So that's not good.

He knows he shouldn't stare at the walls but there's nothing else to look at—no windows, no TV, not even a slot in the door where he could look out at the tier, and he knows that no matter how hard he stares at the walls they aren't going to wash away.

They're driving him crazy in here and Eddie thinks it's intentional, they're softening him up for the negotiations. They slide in a tray of breakfast—if you can call it that—at 6:15 *in the morning* and then come back at 7:30 a.m. to inspect the cell.

For *what*? It's twelve by six; a decent NBA player couldn't lie down in here. What do they think he's going to hide in there, a tank? The Red Hot Chili Peppers? A hot tub full of strippers?

The guards do counts at eight, ten thirty, and four, which Eddie figures is just their way of fucking with him some more. The problem Eddie is having is he's having a hard time keeping track of which count is which. The other day he thought it was the four count and it was only the eight.

The first few weeks he was religious about working out—push-ups, pull-ups, planks—because the Eme guys at V-Ville told him that was the key to keeping his spirit strong.

But now it just seems like too much work, and what he mostly does between meals (if you can call them that) is lie on his bunk and stare at the walls. Or the ceiling.

His body is going to shit.

It's all the starch they feed him.

Minimum Ben comes and tries to keep him up on things.

"What's a 'special counsel'?" Eddie asks. "Is it like the Special Olympics or something? They get trophies and shit?"

"You have to take this seriously, Eddie," Tompkins says.

"Get me the fuck out of here, Ben."

"I'm working on it."

"Work harder."

Because I'm losing my fucking mind.

They're breaking him down and he knows it. Used to be he could do something about it, he could fight it, but he's losing the fight and that's what the motherfuckers want, that's what prison is for, to destroy your mind and body and your soul until you'll do whatever the fuckers want.

Or just die.

Or worse, be one of those pathetic fuckers finger-painting with your own shit.

He realizes that he just said that out loud.

"Great," he says, "now you're talking to yourself. Well, at least you're talking to someone who's actually here, which is better than talking to someone who's not. I mean, you're not really losing it until you're talking to people who aren't here, right?"

Right?

The special counsel's offices are in a nondescript building in southwest Washington, just north of Fort McNair.

Crosby drives her BMW X5 into the parking structure and she and Keller take an elevator into the office from there, away from the eyes of the press. In the elevator Crosby says, "Scorti isn't racist, but he's a product of his generation. He and all the other Ivy League lawyers up there are going to look at an African American woman who went to Howard and think I got where I am through affirmative action. That won't last long but it will give us a temporary advantage."

The doors slide open.

Maybe for security reasons, the conference room has no windows, although Keller thinks it's more to make witnesses feel claustrophobic. He's used the same technique himself.

Scorti has fifteen lawyers on staff, each with his or her own specialty— criminal law, drug trafficking, money laundering, constitutional law. He has forensic accountants, surveillance experts and a raft of secretaries, all literally sworn to secrecy. It has been a tight ship, Keller thinks. No leaks have come out of Scorti's operation.

It's 9:00 a.m.

Scorti likes to start early and go late, he's prompt as an ex-marine, but he's not in the room when Keller and Crosby go in. Three other lawyers are there, white men in suits and ties. A secretary sits with a stenograph and small microphones are set on the table.

Introductions are passed around, Keller quickly forgets everyone's name, and everyone sits back down. One of the lawyers takes charge. "We're recording this session. It's for your protection as well as ours. We'll provide you with a transcript."

"Of course," Crosby says. "As well as a copy of the recording."

"We generally don't give those out."

"I'm not interested in what you generally do," Crosby says. "I want to make sure the transcript is accurate."

"We're not obligated to provide you with a copy," the lawyer says.

"Then it's going to be a very long day," Crosby says. "And monotonous, with me instructing my client not to answer."

"If it means that much to you." The lawyer turns to Keller. "I'm going to swear you in. Your testimony has the same effect and force as if it were in a court of law and is therefore subject to the federal statutes on perjury."

"Mr. Keller is here as a cooperative witness," Crosby says. "We didn't require a subpoena. I don't think we need to start this procedure with threats."

"I'm just stating the law."

"I'll make my client aware of the law," Crosby says. "You ask your questions. And I want some pitchers of ice water and some glasses here. Also a carafe of coffee and real cups, not cardboard. This isn't some Ansonia precinct house."

The lawyer smiles. "Is there anything else you'd like? Some Danish, croissants?"

"Do you have any?"

"No."

"Then I guess not," Crosby says. "But we will be taking regular breaks and an hour and a half for lunch, off premises. And at any time that Mr. Keller wishes to consult with me, we will do that in private."

"This doesn't have to be an adversarial proceeding, Ms. Crosby."

"I agree," Crosby says. "I'm just making sure we all know the difference between an interview and an interrogation."

An assistant brings in the water and coffee.

The lead lawyer starts with basic questions—name, DOB, occupation—which gets a small chuckle in the room when Keller says "currently unemployed." It feels odd to Keller, who's used to being the one asking the questions.

They're still playing pitch-and-catch when the door opens, Scorti comes into the room, pulls a metal folding chair against the wall and sits down, gesturing with his hand for them to keep going.

"I want to turn your attention now to the point in time when you became administrator of DEA," the lead lawyer says. "Do you have that time frame in mind?"

"Yes."

"You sort of came out of nowhere," the lawyer says.

"Is that a question?" Crosby asks.

"That *was* awkward," the lawyer says. "I guess what I'm trying to get at is how did you come to be appointed to that office?"

"I'm sure you're familiar with the process," Crosby says. "He was nominated by the president and confirmed by Congress. Please don't try to tell me that you haven't read the confirmation hearing transcripts. What's your real question?"

"What if any role did Senator O'Brien have in your getting this position?"

"Senator O'Brien came to El Paso and asked me if I'd consider accepting the position."

"You were living in Juárez, though, weren't you?" the lawyer asks.

"Just across the bridge."

"Did the senator say why he wanted you in the job?"

The interview has taken a different tack than Keller thought it would. Why is he asking about O'Brien? "He had looked at my career and thought I could do a good job."

"You're a Democrat, aren't you?" the lawyer asks. "I mean, isn't it a little odd for a Republican senator to want a Democrat in a high position?"

"Actually, I'm an independent."

"But you know what I mean."

"Not really." But now he knows what the lawyer is sniffing around at—a special relationship with O'Brien. Has Ruiz given up Guatemala? And if so, how much has he given up? Or is the lawyer just fishing? Throwing out a cast to see if I'll bite?

"I think this is a good time for a break," Crosby says. In the hallway she asks Keller, "Something you want to tell me? About Ben O'Brien?"

"No."

"Then what is this guy on about?"

"I don't know."

She looks at him. Angry. When they walk back in, Scorti gets out of his chair and offers his hand to Keller. "I'm John Scorti."

"Art Keller."

"Congratulations on the Cozzo arrest," Scorti says.

"That was NYPD," Keller says. "Brian Mullen."

"I think you had something to do with it," Scorti says. He shakes Crosby's hand. "John Scorti. I'm surprised we haven't met before. I'm familiar with your work."

They all sit back down. The lead lawyer starts to ask a question but Scorti holds up his hand and says, "Keller, you and I are old soldiers. We can go on like this or we can just cut to the chase. Vet to vet, what do you have on Jason Lerner?"

Keller looks to Crosby.

She shrugs and says, "Go."

Keller lays it out. How they had Chandler Claiborne as a CI, leveraged on a drug and sexual assault charge, how he gave them Lerner and the Terra meeting with Echeverría. How he obtained a warrant to wire the second meeting.

"Did you wire the first meeting," Scorti asks, "without a warrant?"

"No," Keller says. "Claiborne had inadvertently left his phone on 'record.'"

"You expect me to believe that?"

"Believe what you want," Keller says.

"Do you have that recording?" Scorti asks.

"Yes."

Crosby produces the recording and they all listen to it. When they're done, Scorti says, "Lerner's not in this meeting."

"Correct."

"Based on this, you acquired a 2518?"

Crosby produces the warrant and slides it across the table.

"Justice Antonelli," Scorti says. "He's solid."

"The warrant wasn't obtained solely on the Claiborne recording," Keller says. "Antonelli was persuaded by a verbal assertion from an undercover offi-cer that he was asked by a drug trafficker to provide security for the meeting."

"Can you provide the identity of that officer?"

"Robert Cirello, detective second grade, NYPD Narcotics Division."

"Where is he now?"

Keller says, "On disability leave."

"Is that a coincidence?"

"Have you ever been undercover?" Keller asks.

"Can't say that I have."

"Cirello was undercover for over two years," Keller says. "It's not a coin-cidence."

Scorti looks at one of his staff. "Track him down. We need to talk with him."

"Detective Cirello's actions were impeccable," Keller says. "He's a hero largely responsible for bringing down a major heroin network. I don't want to see him harassed or persecuted."

"You're not in charge of this investigation," Scorti says.

"But you want my cooperation," Keller says.

Crosby says, "Art—"

"Hold on," Keller says. "None of these people know what it's like on the ground. They just get to sit in their conference rooms making judgments. The guns at their heads are metaphorical. The guns pointed at Cirello were real."

"Point taken," Scorti says. "We still need to talk with Cirello. We also need to talk with Agent Hidalgo. Where is he?"

"I don't know."

"We've made numerous efforts to contact him," Scorti says. "He doesn't respond."

"I don't know where he is," Keller says.

It's the truth. Keller hasn't heard from Hidalgo since the kid left his office.

"That's kind of convenient, isn't it?" Scorti asks.

Keller shrugs.

Scorti says, "So Antonelli gives you a warrant . . ."

Keller picks up the narrative—Lerner comes to this meeting, sits down with Echeverría, who has known ties to Mexican narcos . . .

"We have photographs," Crosby says. She lays them out on the table.

"I assume you brought the recordings of this meeting," Scorti says.

They listen to that tape. Keller feels the air in the room change as they lis-ten to Lerner invite Echeverría to commit bank fraud and transmit hundreds of millions of dollars under the table.

The air gets thicker when they hear—

"And, as you noted, you're under increased scrutiny these days because of your close connections. I would hope, if we did this favor for you, as an old friend you would make some of these connections available to us if we need an ear to listen to our point of view."

"That's Echeverría?" Scorti asks.

"Correct," Keller says. "And this is Lerner—"

"I can't promise that our connections would or would not take any specific actions—"

"Of course not."

"But you will always find an ear."

The room goes silent.

Then Scorti says, "What I hear is a man offering considerations to a business partner. I don't hear anything about drugs."

"You could hear it," Keller says.

"If . . ."

"If I knew you'd use it."

"What do you have?"

"What if I had Lerner on tape acknowledging the loan came from drug money?"

"Do you?" Scorti asks.

Keller doesn't answer.

"I specifically requested all materials," Scorti says.

"Do you always get what you want?" Keller asks.

"Usually."

"My client has provided valuable information in your investigation," Crosby says, "and proven his value as a witness. I'm not going to let him offer anything further without a grant of full immunity."

"Screw that," Keller says. "I want to know what this guy is going to do about Lerner."

"I haven't decided yet," Scorti says. "I won't reach that determination until the investigation is complete."

Keller says, "I just gave you more than enough to indict Lerner."

"You're also withholding information."

"Indict Lerner," Keller says, "and I'll give you the tapes. That way I know which side you're on; I'll know you won't take the tapes and bury them."

"Who the hell do you think you are?" Scorti asks. "Who the hell do you think *I* am? I exercise the leverage here, not you. Ms. Crosby, please tell your client that I can have him put in jail until he produces those tapes."

"Not without a subpoena, you can't," Crosby says.

"I can have it this afternoon," Scorti says.

"There's no need for any of this if you'll simply grant immunity," Crosby says.

"Yeah, there is," Keller says. "No indictment, no tapes."

"Maybe I should indict *you*," Scorti says.

Keller gets up.

"We have more questions," Scorti says.

"We're done here," Keller says.

"Just one more question," Scorti says. "There have been rumors. I'm asking you now—did you kill Adán Barrera?"

Keller looks straight at him. "No."

"I'll prepare that indictment," Scorti says.

"Which one?" Keller asks. He walks to the door and turns around. "I'll be waiting to see who you are."

In the elevator, Crosby goes off. "What do you think I am, a lawn ornament? Some wall you bounce balls off? If you don't want me to represent you—"

"I told you—"

"I'm telling *you*, this man will put you behind bars."

"What do you want from me?"

"What I want is to protect you." The elevator doors open. "What do *you* want, Art?"

"I want to pull this thing down."

"Even if it's on top of you?" Crosby asks.

What Mari would call my masochistic, guilty Catholic bullshit, Keller thinks. But, yes, even if it comes down on top of me, it's coming down.

Eddie looks across the table at the fancy-ass New York lawyer.

"Eddie," Tompkins says, "we've engaged Mr. Cohn here to assist in your defense. As such, anything you say to him is privileged. Do you understand?"

"Sure." Eddie understands that Cohn here is Lerner's guy, come to make a deal.

"How can I help you?" Cohn asks.

"It's how I can help you," Eddie says. "I can peel Art Keller off your back like an old sunburn. In return, you're going to give me a plea deal that will get me out while I can still get a hard-on. Do we have a deal?"

"That depends," Cohn says, "on what you have."

They're at an impasse.

Tompkins says, "Well, someone here has to be the first to get naked."

Okay, Eddie thinks. Why not? What the fuck do I have to lose? He leans across the table, looks at Cohn, smiles, and says, "I saw Art Keller kill Adán Barrera."

Bang.

The pressure builds.

Scorti doesn't announce any indictments, doesn't take anyone into a grand jury, but he does subpoena Dennison's personal financial records.

The president goes nuts.

Tweets about "witch hunts," grumbles about firing Ribello, firing the attorney general, even firing Scorti, who has "gone beyond the scope of his investigation, crossed a red line."

The media go equally nuts.

Talking heads on split screens debate whether firing Scorti would end Dennison's presidency, if Congress would move to impeach.

Dennison doesn't do it.

He just threatens, grumbles, vents on Twitter.

Keller waits for indictments.

Lerner's.

His own.

He waits for a subpoena, a judge's order to surrender the tapes or go to jail. Nothing happens.

All that comes out of Scorti's operation is silence.

Keller reads the papers, watches the shows, sees that Scorti is interviewing witnesses, reviewing documents, poring over Dennison's financials.

But announces nothing.

Keller is tired.

He won't say it, but Marisol can tell that it's all wearing on him—the media glare, the pressure fighting the president of the United States, the worries about his future, the possibility of going to prison.

Her husband doesn't complain—she wishes he would, wishes that he'd shout, yell, throw things, but Arturo is the type who keeps everything inside and she's afraid that it's eating away at him. She knows that he's not sleeping well. Hears him get up and go downstairs, hears the television come on, or him just padding around the house.

Now he feigns interest in a hockey game on television, but she can tell that his mind is grinding away.

"So," Marisol says, "what do you want to do, when this is all over?"

"Assuming I'm not in jail?" Keller asks.

"If you are," she says, "do they have parietal visits?"

"Depends on the prison," Keller says.

"Get one that does," she says.

"When this is all over," Keller says, "and assuming I'm not in an orange jumpsuit, you want to stay in DC, right? George Washington contacted me about an adjunct faculty position."

That's good, Marisol thinks. She was half-afraid that after all this he might want to go to a monastery in New Mexico to raise bees or something. She would go with him and do whatever it is you do with bees (herd them? swarm them?), but academia sounds better.

The doorbell rings.

"I'll get it," she says.

It's Ben O'Brien. "I need to talk to Art."

"I'm not sure he needs to talk to you," Marisol says.

"Please," O'Brien says. "It's important."

She opens the door and lets him in.

Keller gets up and comes to the foyer.

"Marisol," O'Brien says, "could you give us a few minutes?"

She looks at Keller, who nods. Marisol takes a moment to give O'Brien a harsh look and then goes upstairs. Keller leads O'Brien into the living room and they sit down.

"We have Sean Callan," O'Brien says. "Name rings a bell, right? I think he saved your life one time. On a bridge in San Diego?"

Keller doesn't say anything.

"He's in tough shape, I'm told," O'Brien says. "And we got him eight ways to Sunday. We have people who will testify they saw him murder Paul Calabrese way back when. But he also just shot a couple of pimps in Tijuana, some argument over a child he was trying to buy."

"I don't believe it."

"Doesn't matter," O'Brien says. "Probably the easiest thing is to extradite him back to Mexico, let them have him for the murders. He'd get thirty in some Mexican shithole, although I doubt he'll last anywhere near that long. What do you think? Of course, the other option is we cut him loose. It's up to you."

Keller knows what's coming.

"Give us the tapes, recant your allegations, go away," O'Brien says. "You're good at that, aren't you, going away?"

O'Brien gets up. "Say ten thirty? Lobby of the Hamilton? Oh . . . and in case your gratitude to Callan isn't sufficient to pay Callan back for your life . . . Ruiz saw you kill Barrera."

"He's lying."

"He has details," O'Brien says. "It was in the jungle. Barrera asked you for water. You gave him some. Then you shot him twice in the face, dropped the gun and walked away."

That's exactly what happened, Keller thinks.

Ruiz has kept that in his pocket for a long time.

"He has the gun," O'Brien says, "in a safe deposit box. It will have your prints on it and it will match the wounds in Barrera's skull."

Yes, it will, Keller thinks. "Who did he say this to—Scorti?"

"One of Lerner's attorneys," O'Brien says. "He's prepared to testify that you killed Barrera, that you got him a sweetheart plea deal, and that you've helped him with various problems to keep him quiet."

Keller knows what he's looking at—he could be tried in the States on any number of corruption charges, including perjury. He could be extradited to Guatemala and tried for murder.

He also knows why Ruiz flipped—the White House offered him a deal, a get-out-of-jail-free card. He'll do a couple of years and then his sentence will be quietly commuted.

"Save Callan and yourself," O'Brien says. "The other option is that Ruiz testifies and you and Callan go to prison. And don't think you'll take me, or Lerner, or Dennison with you—you'll be discredited—no one will believe anything you say after Ruiz is done with you."

Keller lets him out.

Then he hears Marisol come down the stairs.

"I need to talk with you," Keller says.

They sit at the kitchen table.

Keller tells her everything.

About that night on the bridge.

And he tells her that he killed Barrera.

Marisol sits quietly while he talks, and when he's finished, she says, "You lied to me."

"I did."

"I asked you directly if you killed him," Marisol says, "and you looked me in the eye and lied to me."

"That's right."

"We promised each other," she says, "that the one thing we'd never do was lie to each other. So what are you going to do?"

"I don't know," Keller says. "What should I do?"

She gets up from her chair. It takes her a moment, it always does. She grabs her cane, leans on it and looks back at Keller. "Call Daniella. I'm not your lawyer, I'm not your shrink, I'm not your priest. I was your wife."

Keller hears her footsteps and her cane on the chair. He hears the sound of suitcases opening and closing. A little while later she asks him to carry her bags down to the door.

"Goodbye, Arturo," Marisol says. "Whatever you decide to do, I hope it's the right thing for you."

He carries her bags to the Uber outside, opens the door for her and helps her in.

Then she's gone.

Keller doesn't try to sleep.

What's the point?

It would be funny if it weren't so sad—Adán Barrera has reached up from the grave again.

Adán vive.

Keller doesn't show up in the lobby of the Hamilton.

There's no point, because at 9:00 a.m. the news comes out that Dennison's financial records showed that he had significant investments in Terra.

At 10:00, Dennison instructs Ribello to fire Scorti.

In a "Twitter-storm," the president goes on to call Keller a "pathetic liar," a "loser," a "traitor."

Ribello does fire Scorti.

By 10:30 the government of the United States is in chaos.

"It buys us time," Rollins says, "to do what we need to do."

"No," O'Brien says.

"What's the alternative?" Rollins asks. "We let this man bring down the administration and go back to eight more years of a left-wing government? Open immigration, high taxes, drug legalization? We have a unique opportunity now to turn this country around."

"Make it great again?"

"Scoff, but yes, that's right," Rollins says. "We have to clean this up. Some people have to go. You don't have to say yes, O'Brien. Just don't say anything."

O'Brien doesn't answer.

He hears the door open and then close.

Caro is reluctant.

Just a few years ago, the Zetas made the mistake of killing an American agent in Mexico. The American response, led by Art Keller, was violent and efficient. The Americans teamed with the Mexican marines on raids that were basically executions. They slaughtered the Zetas and took them off the board as major players.

But Caro doesn't need that as an example.

No one knows better than he the danger of killing an American DEA agent. After the murder of Ernesto Hidalgo, the DEA took the Federación apart. Keller himself killed Miguel Ángel Barrera, the founder, M-1. If the rumors are true, Keller killed Adán Barrera. Caro had participated in the DEA agent's murder, and for his small role, Keller had put him away for twenty-five to life.

Now he's finally free, and these men want his help in assassinating not just an American DEA agent, but Art Keller himself?

He voices his concerns to Echeverría and the American—what is his name?—yes, Rollins.

"We don't have a choice," Rollins says. "Keller hasn't come to terms yet. If he does decide to come out with these tapes, the wine is out of the bottle and we'll never be able to get it back in."

"A once-in-a-lifetime opportunity could be lost if we don't act," Echeverría says.

"And if we do, we could be destroyed," Caro says.

"This administration won't overreact," Rollins says. "You send a shooter, the shooter does the job and is killed immediately. There's noise for a few weeks, some disruption, and then it's business as usual."

Caro asks, "Why don't you use one of your own people?"

"A cartel gunman makes more sense," Rollins says. "'Mexican drug cartel murders its worst enemy.' Hell, Barrera had a two-million-dollar bounty out on Keller. Better yet, we put out flak that Keller was in bed with the cartel and double-crossed you."

Kill the man *and* his name, Caro thinks. "And you can guarantee me that there won't be repercussions?"

"These people," Echeverría says, "will be just as motivated as you to cover this up. More, actually. Of course there will be repercussions—the Americans will have to respond. But it can be arranged that they'll respond against people who are, shall we say, problematic."

Caro thinks it through—Tito won't object to it; a part of him blames Keller for Nacho Esparza's death. And Iván certainly would be all for killing the man who smashed his face in and humiliated him.

He gives the green light.

And feigns reluctance.

Can these people know, he wonders, that every night for twenty years in that frozen hell I dreamed of killing Art Keller?

. . .

Nothing is emptier than an empty house.

The vacant kitchen chair, the imprint on a sofa cushion, the pillow unsplayed with hair, absent of scent. An unspoken thought, an unshared laugh, the silence of no footsteps, no sighs, no breaths.

Marisol has called twice, both brief, once to let him know that she arrived safely in New York and was at the Beekman, another later to tell him that she had sublet a studio apartment in Murray Hill.

A spacious solitary confinement, Keller thinks as he wanders from empty room to empty room, makes a meal for one, barely eats it, listlessly sips on a beer, pays half attention to the television, which drones about a "constitutional crisis" and a "crisis of faith."

He hears an analyst say, "What this comes down to is really a mano a mano between John Dennison and Art Keller."

Keller goes upstairs to check his arsenal.

A Sig 9 for his hip, a Sig .380 for his ankle.

A Mossberg pump under the bed.

A Ka-Bar knife.

For forty years he's been at war with the Mexican cartels.

Now he's at war with his own government.

And they're the same.

The syndicate.

2

Broken

Aquí se rompió una taza.
"Here a cup got broken."
—Mexican expression meaning "the party's over"

Mexico
March 2017

Mini-Ric is becoming Micro-Ric.

I'm getting smaller every day, he thinks.

Which maybe isn't a totally bad thing, because when everyone and his dog is hunting you, it's better not to have too big a profile. And when you're constantly on the run, moving from place to place, it's better not to be carrying a lot of baggage.

I'm getting smaller, Ric thinks, because shit keeps dropping off me like excess weight. People—a wife, a daughter, bodyguards, gunmen, associates, allies, friends. Things—cars, motorcycles, boats, houses, apartments, even clothes. Power—all his life he lived in a privileged, make-it-thus world where underlings and servants and hangers-on were always around to anticipate his needs before he even expressed them. He could order an execution if he wanted; now he's lucky if he can order a pizza. Money—he never used to even think about money. It was always there and if it wasn't, he could always get more. Now money, not to put too fine a point on it, is leaking out his ass.

It takes money to run, money to hide. Money to buy clean cars, rent apartments, houses, hotel rooms; buy silence from renters, from clerks, from anyone who happens to see him and recognize him. Money to pay *halcones*, cops, soldiers. There's a lot of money flowing out and not a lot coming in because it's hard for him and his father to run their operation from underground.

How do you check on the growers when to step outside is to put yourself at risk? How do you stay in touch with your traffickers, your transport people, your soldiers, your informers when every cell phone, email or text is risky? How do you hold meetings, plan strategy when you have to come up with secret locations at the last possible moment and everyone who attends is the person who might give you up to Iván, to Tito, to the *federales*, the state police, the local police, the DEA, the army or the marines? How do you get hold of your money when accountants are scrambling to the other side, when every communication to the ones who remain is dangerous, when some of your launderers are just flat-out stealing from you because they're not afraid of you anymore?

And they're right.

The Núñez name used to scare people.

The mantle of Adán Barrera used to awe people.

Now Adán is a dead saint—people still burn candles and pray to him, but they're not necessarily going to put themselves on the line for his godson. Some do, some will—those are a lot of the people who Ric counts on now, to move him, to hide him, to make calls, run messages. These people see him as the true heir to Adán's crown and help him out of pure loyalty.

It's dangerous for them and he feels bad, because what Iván, Tito, the soldiers and the cops can't get by cajoling or bribing, they get with intimidation, beatings, burnings of houses or whole villages.

Most of them give in—Ric can't blame them. Some of the hard-core tough it out—Ric almost wishes they wouldn't. He feels worst for the people who have no information and their interrogators won't believe them. It goes hard on them and there's nothing they can do.

He keeps running.

From Eldorado to Culiacán, from Culiacán to Badiraguato, where Iván's people came within ten minutes of him getting in an apartment. He escaped to Los Mochis, but too many people there knew him, so he got a plane to fly him down to Mazatlán—and found too many of Tito's people there, fighting for the port.

Ric thought about going to Baja—La Paz was once his stronghold—but now Belinda is too powerful there and she wouldn't hesitate to sell him to the highest bidder, or just chop him up and sell him piece by piece. (There's a story making the rounds right now that she had a new boyfriend who cheated on her with a girl from his gym. Belinda kidnapped the girl and beat her to death over the course of three days. Then she got pissed when she found out that the boyfriend had fucked the girl in her new pickup, so she chopped his forearms off with a machete so he couldn't drive anymore.)

Ric made a long and dangerous car trip through Tito's base in Jalisco and Michoacán up into the hills of Guerrero and hid for weeks near one of the opium plantations. It was safe until some of the old GU people got wind of it and were trying to decide whether to turn him over to Iván or Tito, and he got out and made it to Puebla.

His father has taken a different approach.

"Movement attracts the eye," he told Ric. "It's better to sit still."

So Núñez is holed up in a condo in the upscale Anzures neighborhood of Mexico City, right under the noses of the government officials who turned on him and are now hunting him.

Ric meets him at the Pisco Grill, not far from the condo.

His father has a full beard now, and his hair is cut short. Ric is heartened to see that he's gained a little weight—his face is fleshier, although still pale.

"Are you sure this is safe?" Ric asks him.

"We still have some friends in the capital," Núñez says, "and the rest are bought and paid for."

They go over business—money transfers, routes, personnel—then Núñez moves on to strategy.

"It was Caro all along," Núñez says. "Caro who had Rudolfo Sánchez killed, Caro who tried to kill me. It was a smart strategy—he succeeded in turning us against each other."

"And Tito is the new boss."

"A dog is always a dog," Núñez says. "It never becomes a wolf. A dog craves a master and Tito will find a new one. First it was Esparza, now it's Caro."

Ric worries that his father underestimates Ascensión.

Tito is winning everywhere.

Tijuana is all but his, now that Elena's gone.

Killed by Belinda on behalf of Iván, although Ric isn't so sure that Tito didn't have a hand in murdering his supposed ally. At the very least he didn't veto it, and now he has everything she used to have. In any case, he's absorbed most of Elena's people and together they're driving Iván out of the city, and the only turf Elena and her son occupy now is a crypt in Jardines del Valle cemetery.

The Esparzas are reportedly holding their own in northern Sinaloa, but Tito has taken over the southern half and added it to his Jalisco and Michoacán territories. He's moving into Juárez, too, and points east, replicating Adán's old ambition of holding all the major border crossings—Tijuana, Juárez and Nuevo Laredo.

And you can't tell me, Ric thinks, that Tito didn't have Osiel Contreras killed, too. The old man was just out of an American prison and went down to Cancún to get a little sun after being in a cell for twelve years. Some people said he just wanted to retire, others that he had an idea of reviving his old Gulf cartel in Nuevo Laredo, but we'll never know, because he was lounging in a beach chair, sipping a drink with an umbrella in it, when someone put three bullets through his newspaper and into his face.

I guess Tito didn't want to take any chances that Contreras might want to be, as it were, top dog again.

Tito's people are also on the move in Tamaulipas and Veracruz against the Zetas, who themselves have split into factions fighting each other. He'll gobble them up one at a time.

It's only in Guerrero, Ric thinks, that Tito's not making progress, but shit, no one can make progress in that fractured, anarchistic hellhole. No one can get any traction there, not Tito, not Iván, not us. Not the army, the marines, or the dozens of citizen self-defense groups that have sprung up like mushrooms.

Poor Damien, Ric thinks. He's heard that the kid slashed his wrists in Puente Grande.

The songs are already out there—

You can't cage the Young Wolf
He set himself free
To join his father.

What a bunch of total bullshit, Ric thinks. We're a jacked-up group, Los Hijos.

Salvador Barrera dead.

Rudolfo and Luis dead.

Damien dead.

The Esparzas shot up.

Me on the run.

The only one who's doing halfway decent is Rubén Ascensión. The quiet, sensible shy one, the one who would always be cast as the solid best friend in any movie.

Ric thinks, We had the world in our hands and let it slip through our fingers.

"We still have something to offer," Núñez is saying. "We still have men, money, product. Not to mention the Barrera legacy."

His father still harbors illusions.

This is him grasping at straws, still believing that he can somehow retrieve the situation and get his power and prestige back.

Ric has more modest goals.

Keep his father and himself out of prison or the dirt.

It's not going to be easy. No one trusts us, not after what we did to the Esparzas. Worse, no one needs us. We'd go to any bargaining table as beggars. And there's only one place left for us to go.

Tito.

We could offer him gunmen in Baja to finish off Iván, Ric thinks, and *sicarios* for Juárez and Laredo. We acknowledge him as El Patrón. In exchange, he gives us protection from the police and politicians that now belong to him, Caro, and the syndicate.

It's a slim hope—Tito doesn't need our men, half of them are already going over—but it's our only hope.

But how can I even approach Tito? Ric asks himself.

He goes to his own life for the answer.

The way you always approach a father—through the son.

Jesus, Ric thinks.

Rubén is in Baja.

Rubén Ascensión isn't an easy guy to get hold of these days.

The head of security for his father in Baja now, he's insulated from the day-to-day, he's not out on the street in La Paz or Cabo, and it's not like Ric can take the risk of spending a lot of time on the streets in either of those cities. He has to keep his head down in case Iván, Belinda or even Rubén himself decides to lop it off. Or some freelancer looking to make points by taking out a Núñez.

Ric's head is on a swivel as he looks for Rubén.

In Tijuana, he leaves word at a club they used to frequent. Word and the number of a burn phone. Then he settles into a modest hotel and waits.

Two days later, Rubén calls him. "Where are you?"

"Yeah, right."

"You're the one reaching out."

"I need your help, 'mano," Ric says. "To talk to your father."

"John 4:16?"

"What?"

"Nothing," Rubén says. "You don't have to talk to my dad, you can talk to me. What are we talking about?"

"You want the Esparzas out of business as much as we do," Ric says. "Maybe we can help you with that."

Rubén gives him an address.

"Rubén, no offense," Ric says, "but I need your word that if I come there, I also leave."

"You're the ones that ambush people at sit-downs," Rubén says. "Not us."

Well, he's got me there, Ric thinks.

The address in Cabo San Lucas is a large house up in the hills on Cerro Colorado. The place looks new, the landscaping isn't even in yet. Three SUVs are parked outside, two Mercedes in the large driveway, and a number of late-model, expensive cars on the street.

Rubén is having a party, Ric thinks.

Gunmen get out of an SUV as Ric pulls up. He raises his arms and they pat him down. One leads him up to the front door and rings the bell.

Rubén answers. He reaches out and pulls Ric into a hug. "It's great to see you, brother."

They go inside.

It's a party, all right. Throbbing music, a houseful of people—narcos, musicians, your generic Cabo beautiful people, gorgeous girls.

Iván has a woman on his lap.

He looks up at Ric and says, "Party time, motherfucker."

"You're making the wrong choice," Ric says to Rubén. "My father—"

"I guess you haven't seen the news," Rubén says.

He sticks a laptop in front of Ric, who sees a photo of his father—haggard, unshaven, disheveled in a wrinkled shirt—his elbows being held by *federales*.

"Your father was arrested this morning," Rubén says. "They took him out of his condo. He's in Puente Grande."

It's a deft touch, Ric thinks, locking my dad up in the same prison where he was warden. And we're done. The government has turned its back on us. Doesn't matter, I'm dead anyway, because I'm the guest of honor at this party. He takes a shot, though. "I can give you—"

"You can't give us what you don't have," Rubén says.

"Just let me out of here," Ric says. "I'll go away, you'll never hear from me again."

"No can do," Rubén says. "You were part of the deal."

Turns out that the Esparzas don't want to be in heroin anymore. They're content to go back to the old family business—coke and meth. And they acknowledge Tito as *jefe*. Iván made the offer through Rubén, who relayed it to his dad.

Tito accepted.

There was a kicker, though.

Ric.

"You knew I'd be coming to you," Ric says.

"You didn't have a choice," Rubén says. "But Iván beat you to it."

My mistake, Ric thinks. I was betting that Iván's ego was too big for him to bend the knee to his father's former guard dog.

Well, I lost that bet.

"I'm sorry it worked out this way, nothing personal," Rubén says. Then he leaves the room.

Iván asks, "You know what really burns my ass?"

"Everything?"

"My tennis serve," Iván says. "It was coming along real good, then someone put a bullet through my ball joint. Now I can't lift my arm over my head. Did you notice the scar on Oviedo's face? No worries, I'll show it to you. Three plastic surgeries with another couple to come, and he's blind in one eye. You missed Alfredo, but the kid has nightmares, do you believe that? He pisses the bed."

Ric doesn't say that he didn't know about the ambush, that it was all his father.

It doesn't matter now.

So he doesn't say anything.

"You took us out of action for six months," Iván says, "and Tito used those six months to make himself king. I had to go suck his cock, you know how that felt, Ric?"

A worse injury than the bullet, Ric thinks.

Iván says, "You were there when Tito came to me for permission to go into heroin. Now I had to go to him and tell him I was getting out of heroin, that I was content with what we once gave him. So guess how happy I am to see you, Ric."

He lights a joint, sucks on it, then holds it up to Ric's mouth. "You're going to need this."

Ric takes a long drag and holds it deep in his lungs.

It's primo shit.

"The last party tonight, Ricky boy," Iván says. "The last stand of Los Hijos. We get drunk, we get high, we get laid, and when we're drunk out, drugged out and fucked out, you *go* out."

It's Rubén's house but Iván's party.

You have to hand it to him, Ric thinks, he has a certain sick kind of style; the motherfucker has actually had an execution *catered*. There are tables of food, and uniformed waitresses work the floor with trays of hors d'oeuvres, lines of coke and fat blunts.

A band arrives, sets up in the courtyard outside by the pool and starts banging out norteño.

Ric takes it all in—the food, the booze, the dope, the music. Why shouldn't he? There's no point in trying to run, the place is ringed with Rubén's people who would gun him down. And if he sees that as a form of quick suicide, Iván has already informed him that the *sicarios* have strict orders to shoot him in the legs.

He gets drunk, he gets high, he stuffs himself with ceviche and *camarones*, with tender strips of steak marinated in lime juice. He dances with beautiful women, he even strips down and jumps in the pool. Dives under the water and lets it play over him cool and peaceful.

When he comes up, he's face-to-face with Oviedo.

The scar is bad, a vermillion slash running from under his left eye up to his temple.

His eye stares blindly, accusingly, at Ric.

"Enjoying your party?" Oviedo asks.

"I'm sorry, O."

"You will be."

Ric gets out of the pool and wraps a towel around his waist.

Iván gets the guests' attention, has everyone's glass filled with Cristal, and calls for a toast.

Ric can tell he's jacked up on coke.

"*¡Todos!*" he shouts. "We're here tonight to celebrate old friends! Here's to Los Hijos!"

Ric tosses back his drink.

Glasses are refilled.

"Here's to absent friends!" Iván shouts. "Here's to Salvador Barrera! Rest in peace, buddy!"

They drink.

More champagne.

"To Damien Tapia!" Iván yells. "He took himself out, but we still love the fucked-up kid! Here's to Rudolfo Sánchez, who I did *not* have killed, BTW! Here's to Luis Sánchez . . . about whom . . . I can't say the same thing!"

Some nervous laughter.

Down the hatch.

"And here's to my old *cuate,* Ric," Iván says, lifting his glass to him, his voice softening. "My friend, *mi hermano . . . sangre de mi sangre . . .* whom I *loved,* who tried to kill me. This is his last party, so we have to make it a good one. This is the last party of Los Hijos . . . After this . . ."

He doesn't finish, just raises his glass and drinks.

Ric drinks.

A little while later, Iván comes over to him, sits beside him by the pool. They're both drunk and high as hell.

"We were Los Hijos," Iván says. "We had the world by the balls. What happened, man?"

"We fucked it up," Ric says.

Iván nods solemnly. "We fucked it up."

They sit quietly for a few minutes, then Iván says, "If I don't do this, people will think I'm weak."

"I get it."

It's surreal, Ric thinks, waiting for your own death. He doesn't think that anyone really believes they're going to die, even condemned men. It's just too fucking weird. But he asks Iván, "Can I call my wife, my kid? Say goodbye?"

Iván digs in his pocket, hands him a phone and steps away to give him a little privacy.

Karin answers. "It's four in the morning."

"I know. I'm sorry."

"Where are you?" Karin asks.

"Cabo," Ric says. "Could you wake Valeria up for me? I want to talk to her."

"Are you drunk?"

"A little," Ric says. "Please?"

"Ric . . ."

But she comes back on a couple of minutes later with their daughter.

"Papi?" Valeria says sleepily.

"I love you, *niña*," Ric says. "Do you know that? Papi loves you very much."

"I know," she says. "When are you coming home?"

Ric wants to cry. "Soon, honey. Put Mami back on, okay?"

"Okay."

Karin gets back on. "What's going on, Ric?"

"I'm calling to say I love you."

"You are drunk."

"And I'm sorry for everything," Ric says.

"Is this because of your father?" Karin asks. "It's been all over the news."

"If anything happens to me," Ric says, "lawyers will be in touch. You'll be taken care of."

"Okay."

"Anyway, I'm sorry."

"Get some coffee," Karin says. "Don't drive."

"All right. Good night."

He clicks off.

Now he knows what his father was trying to tell him, trying to force him to do—spend more time with his wife and kid. I'd give anything now, he thinks, for more time with them. You always think you're going to have forever, you can do it tomorrow. And now you can't.

Now it's too late.

Iván gives him a minute.

"I got a woman for you," he says. "I wouldn't send a man off without getting laid one last time."

A terminal fuck, Ric thinks.

Easy come, easier go.

Why not?

He gets to his feet and follows Iván back into the house and down a hallway to a closed door.

"She's waiting in there," Iván says. "Just so you know, there aren't any windows."

Ric goes in.

Belinda lies on the bed.

Decked out in black leather from head to toe.

"Are you going to fuck me or kill me?" Ric asks.

"First one," she says, "then the other."

"Let's skip the sex," Ric says. "You probably have razor blades up your vag."

"That would be great, wouldn't it?" Belinda says. "Shred some guy's cock? You want the fuck, Ricky. You want to delay what's next as long as you can. I've been told to hurt you, really hurt you."

"I love it when you talk dirty to me."

"You can have my mouth, my pussy, my ass, anything you want," Belinda says. "It gets me hot that after I do you, I, you know, *do* you."

"You're so sick."

"I know," she says.

She kneels in front of him and unwraps the towel. Goes down on him for what she's always called a "Belinda Special," using her lips, her tongue, her fingers, her tits. It always got him off like a burst fire hydrant, but now he can't even get hard.

"What's the matter, baby?" Belinda asks.

"You're kidding me right now."

"It's your last chance," Belinda says. "You want my *culo*?"

"No."

She shrugs and gets up.

"Why you?" Ric asks. "Why are you the one who's going to do it?"

"Because," she says with a smile, "I asked."

They find an old sweat suit and make Ric put it on, then plastic-tie his hands behind his back and walk him out.

The party is over.

Most people have left, a few are passed out on couches, chairs or the floor.

Outside, the sun is just coming up, the sky is vivid in red, purple and orange.

It's so beautiful, Ric thinks.

They put him in the back of an SUV with tinted windows.

Iván comes out and opens the door. "I thought I wanted to watch, but I changed my mind."

"Iván—"

"Don't beg, Ric," Iván says. "I want them to write songs about you. That you went out like a man."

"Just put one in my head. Please."

"You'll go out screaming like a little bitch," Iván says, suddenly hardening. "You'll go out pissing and shitting yourself, the things she has planned for you. But I'll make them cut the vid-clip before that."

"Please." Ric starts to cry.

"Jesus, Ric." Iván slams the door shut.

Belinda gets in the front passenger seat, turns around and puts a hood over Ric's head, then tells the driver to head out. Ric tries to control his terror but his right leg starts to twitch, then to spasm until it starts banging against the front seat.

They drive for what feels like three hours.

An endless three hours.

Then the car stops.

The hood is pulled off his face.

They're pulled over by a Buddhist pagoda and Ric sees that he's in Mexicali, by the border crossing.

He's sent a lot of dope across here.

Belinda gets out and opens his door. Takes out a knife and cuts the ties off his hands. "Walk to the border. DEA is waiting for you."

Ric looks at her puzzled.

"You called them earlier," Belinda says. "Told them you wanted to turn yourself in. It's not all good news, baby. They have an eleven-count indictment on you."

He gets out of the vehicle. "Are you coming?"

"I'll take my chances here," Belinda says.

"They'll kill you for this."

"Those pussies?" Belinda says. "I'll feed them their balls. Now get going, *mojado*."

She gets back in the car and it drives off.

Ric walks along Cristóbal Colón to the border crossing.

DEA agents are waiting for him. They arrest him for conspiracy to distribute methamphetamine, cocaine, and heroin, and conspiracy to launder money.

Four hours later he's in the federal lockup in San Diego.

It's the same cell his godfather, Adán, once occupied.

3

Cheap Guns

Wars and a man I sing—an exile driven on by Fate.

—Virgil

Aeneid, book 1 (Robert Fagles, trans.)

Queens, New York
March 2017

Nico stands on the roof of the building and looks out.

Jackson Heights is beautiful.

A lot of people don't think so, but Nico does.

There are nice buildings and trees and parks and food is *everywhere.* Where he lives with his uncle and aunt off Eighty-Second and Roosevelt is above La Casa del Pollo, so he can smell chicken all the time, the scent coming up through the floor. On the same block is Dunkin' Donuts, Mama Empanada and, wonder of wonders, Popeye's Louisiana Kitchen, which has opened up entire new worlds for Nico when, on Fridays, he and his uncle go while his aunt is still at work.

Or they used to, anyway.

Extra crispy, Nico thinks, might be the most beautiful words in the English language.

He started to learn English at school, just a few blocks away on Eighty-Second. To get there, Nico walked underneath the Roosevelt Avenue El, and he loved to stand there and feel the train rumble over him.

Then it was up Eighty-Second, past the Duane Reade drugstore and McDonald's (yes!), where he actually had money to eat sometimes, the Gap Outlet, where Tía Consuelo and Tío Javier bought him new clothes, then Foot Locker, Payless Shoes, and the Children's Place, which they couldn't afford. Then he'd cross Thirty-Seventh Street, a major thoroughfare about which his aunt warned him to be very careful. The next two blocks were pretty dull, not a lot on them, just "residential" (as he learned to say) apartment buildings, until he got to St. Joan of Arc Elementary, where Consuelo would like to have sent him but they couldn't afford the tuition; Nico, however, was just as glad because the kids had to wear uniforms, lame red sport jackets.

And he liked PS 212.

Of the eight hundred kids, more than half of them were Hispanic, most of the rest were Indian or Pakistani. Nico was in an ESL class with a bunch of the other Spanish speakers and did well in reading, but what he really liked was math.

Numbers are the same in both languages.

He was good with them, and every Saturday morning he sat down with his uncle and aunt and helped do the weekly budget—how much they needed for rent, for groceries, how much, if anything, they could spend going out, how much they could save.

Sometimes they went to McDonald's, KFC or one of the restaurants on Thirty-Seventh, but mostly they ate at home. A lot of rice and tortillas, but sometimes Consuelo cooked *pepián* with pork or chicken, or *pupusas,* filling the thick corn tortillas with beans and cheese or sometimes pork. When there was time and she wasn't too tired, she'd make Nico's favorite, *rellenitos,* plantains with bean paste, cinnamon and sugar. When she didn't have the time or energy, Javier usually gave him some money to go treat himself at Dunkin' Donuts.

Nico didn't see as much of his aunt or uncle as he'd have liked because they were working their asses off most of the time. Javier was a janitor at one of the condos where the rich people lived, and Consuelo cleaned people's houses. They worked as many hours as they could because they needed the money for food and rent and were saving to start their own cleaning supplies business.

Like most of the kids in his school, Nico was a "latchkey kid." He didn't think anything of it—he'd always been pretty much on his own most of the day. The only difference between being a latchkey kid in Guatemala and the United States is that in the US he actually had a key.

On Sundays they'd go to church.

Not a Catholic church, Nico was surprised to find out, but Iglesia la Luz del Mundo, because Javier and Consuelo had become "Pentecostals." Nico didn't like church very much, it was boring, the minister went on and on about Jesus and they sang really terrible music, but there was a *pupusa* stand right outside where Javier would usually spring for a few with cheese and *chipilín.*

Nico missed his mother. Every few weeks they managed to get her on the phone so he could at least say hello, but the calls were short and usually made him sad. They were trying to find a way to bring her to the United States, but between the expense and the legal complications it didn't look good. And the calls left Nico feeling a little guilty because he knew that even if he could go home to Guatemala, he wouldn't.

He was an American now. It was better here.

He didn't have to scrounge through garbage to eat, and he wasn't always sick and hungry. He had a bed behind real walls, a toilet indoors, and he went to a school where they fed him lunch, gave him an education free-for-nothing, and the teachers were nice.

One thing hadn't changed from Guatemala.

Or Virginia, for that matter.

The gangs.

Eighty-Second Street, where he lives, is Calle 18 turf.

Nico learned this one day walking home from Travers Park, where he was playing *fútbol* on the old basketball court with a few kids from school. He crossed Seventy-Eighth Street and went to cut through another ball court in back of Salem House, but a group of about five black kids stopped him.

"What you doing here, pepperbelly?"

Nico didn't know what *pepperbelly* meant, but he figured it meant him. He didn't answer.

"I ask what you doing here."

"Just going home," Nico said.

"You find some other way to go home," the kid, a big teenager, said. He was wearing a T-shirt made by the Mecca company, and Nico saw that the other four had the same gear. "This our block. You know who we are?"

Nico shook his head.

"We ABK," the kid said, and when he saw that Nico didn't understand, he clarified. "Always Banging Kings. Who you with?"

"I'm not with anyone," Nico said, struggling to say it in English.

The kid laughed. "Tell you what, I'm Not with Anyone, you run now. We give you a head start of three. If we catch you, we fuck you up. Go!"

Nico ran.

Nico Rápido ran for his life.

He'd done it before on the top of a moving train, so he was good with running across Thirty-Fourth Avenue, down Seventy-Ninth Street, through an alley to Eightieth. These *mayates* were fast and they were yelling as they chased him and he turned around to see that they were gaining on him because they were older and bigger and had longer legs.

Nico took a breath and sprinted toward Eighty-Second with the ABK right behind him and closing in.

Then Nico heard their feet stop.

He looked ahead of him and saw a group of Hispanic guys, maybe ten of them, standing on the corner.

One of them yelled, "*¡Píntale, pendejos!*"

The ABK kid who had fronted Nico yelled back, "Go home, you fucking border rat!"

But he stopped.

"I *am* home, porch monkey! This is Calle 18 turf!" The guy opened his shirt to show the butt of a gun.

The black kids threw a few more insults but backed off.

Nico said, "*Gracias*—"

The kid slapped him across the face. Hard. "What you doing over there, *pendejo*? Where you was?"

"Travers Park."

"That's all *mayates* now."

"I didn't know."

"What are you, stupid? Where you from?"

"Guatemala."

"Who you with?" the kid asked.

"No one," Nico said.

"Where you live?"

"Eighty-Second Street, over Casa del Pollo."

"Well, you belong to us, *puta*," the kid said. "You need to be cliqued up with 18."

"I don't . . ."

"You don't what?"

"I don't know."

Nico was confused as hell. These guys didn't look like Calle 18—none of them had tattoos on their faces. And they weren't dressed like gangbangers— they wore polo shirts and nice jeans or khakis.

"You don't know nothing, do you?" the kid said. "Let me tell you how this works. You got Calle 18 around here, you got Sureño 13. You wear black and blue, you're with us; you wear red, you're with them. But you don't want to be with them, *hermanito*, because every time we see you in red, we'll beat the shit out of you. You also got ABK here, and they don't care if you're black or blue or red as long as you're Spanish, they'll mess you up."

"What if I don't want to be with anyone?" Nico asked.

"Then you're a little bitch," the kid said, "and *everyone* fucks with you."

To illustrate, he slapped Nico again.

No different here, Nico thinks, than it was there.

"You think about it," the kid said. "Come find me, give me your answer. But, *hermanito*, if you don't come and find me, we'll come and find you. Understand?"

Yeah, Nico understood.

He was scared shitless that they'd see he already had the 18 tat on his ankle and they'd kill him for being disloyal and running away. And he felt stupid as shit; he comes two thousand miles to escape Calle 18 and he ends up right in the middle of them.

Nico didn't know what to do. He'd have liked to talk to Javier about it but was afraid that his uncle would tell him not to join the gang (they probably weren't too big on gangs at the Iglesia la Luz del Mundo) and then he might have to go against him, which he didn't want to do because he liked and respected Javier.

But Javier wouldn't understand, Nico thought. He probably doesn't even know what Calle 18 is.

Nico didn't sleep that night. He wanted to do the right thing, stay out of the gangs, that's what he came here for, after all; but at the end of the day, life made Nico Ramírez a realist. Life taught him that there are bad choices and worse choices, and that you have to do what you have to do to survive.

The next day was Saturday.

Nico went up to Modell's, grabbed a black Yankees cap with blue letters, shoved it under his shirt and walked out. He put it on his head and went looking for Calle 18, found them hanging in the Taco Bell on Thirty-Seventh.

The boss saw the black cap. "You're smarter than you look. What's your name?"

"Nico Ramírez."

"And you want to be Calle 18?"

"Yes."

"We'll make you a *paro*," he said.

"What's that?" Nico asked.

"You're too young to be a full member," the boss said. "You can be an associate until you prove yourself."

"Okay."

"But first you got to get beat in," the boss said. "Don't look so scared, *hermanito*, we whale on you for eighteen seconds. It's over before you know it."

"When?" Nico asked, forcing himself to not look scared at all. "Where?"

The boss looked at him with a little more respect. "Moore Playground. Tonight. Eight o'clock."

"See you there," Nico said, and walked out.

He went to the playground that night. A dozen 18's were there, nine guys and three girls. They circled around him, surrounded him, closed in.

"This is Nico," the boss said. "He's asked to get beat in."

Eighteen seconds didn't sound like a lot of time when you weren't getting shoved and punched and kicked but it was a *loooong* time when you were. Nico took it, though, and was smart enough not to go down.

"Time!" the boss yelled.

He hugged Nico. "*Bienvenido, hermano.* My name is Davido. We're brothers now."

Blood ran from Nico's nose, but it wasn't broken. His lower lip was thick and swollen and he had a black eye and bruises on his face and all over his body. His ribs hurt where one of the girls planted her pointed toe into them.

But he was in.

As a *paro*, an associate, the lowest rung on the gang ladder.

Davido and a few of the others took him to Taco Bell on Thirty-Seventh and treated him to a meal. Nico asked about the lack of tattoos.

"We don't do that anymore," Davido said. "The cops are onto it. They see that shit on you, they find a reason to arrest you and then you get deported. We pulled it back, *niño.* This shit you see is camouflage. You got to be smart."

When Nico got home that night, he tried to sneak past his aunt and uncle, but Javier was awake and saw Nico's face.

"*Sobrino*, what happened to you?"

"Nothing."

"Nothing? Look at you!"

What happened was what Nico was afraid would happen. Consuelo woke up and made a big deal of it. Washed his face with a washcloth, then put ice cubes in the cloth and made him hold it over his mouth and his eye.

While Javier interrogated him. "Who did this to you?"

"Some black kids," Nico lied. He figured it wasn't that much of a lie, because the black kids would have done this or worse if they'd caught him.

"Where?" Javier asked.

"Travers Park."

Javier was suspicious. "Why didn't they take your watch, your shoes? The blacks usually take your shoes."

"I got away from them," Nico said. "I'm fast."

"Stay away from that park," Consuelo said.

"It's right near the school."

"Find another place to play."

Javier waited until Consuelo went back to bed, then he came into Nico's room and said, "You're not getting involved with gangs, are you? Tell me you're not getting involved with the gangs."

"I'm not."

"Because I know how it is on the streets," Javier said. "I see things. I know.

You think you need boys to back you up. But you have to stay away from that stuff, Nico. It's bad. It will only get you in trouble."

"I know."

But you *don't* see things, he thought, and you *don't* know how it is.

How it is is you get cliqued up.

Or you get cliqued out.

It was good, it was sweet.

Nico sucked in another toke of the *yerba* and passed the blunt back to Davido. He held the smoke in his lungs for as long as he could and then let it go.

And giggled. "Good shit."

"No shit, good shit."

They were partying in Davido's crib on Eighty-Sixth. A dozen or so of Nico's new brothers and sisters. Big Boy and Jamsha were pounding "Donde Están Toas las Yales" on the flat-screen Sony. Nico watched the video and took another pull off the Cuervo.

On the screen, a *chica* with a big ass and big tits walked into Big Boy's crib and yelled at him. Threw his shit into a garbage bag. Big Boy got into the car with the pizza guy, Jamsha, and they started their rap as they drove through the streets looking at girls.

The girls in the video were *smokin'*.

So was the girl dancing off to the side of the TV, shaking her ass and hips like she didn't know Nico was looking.

He was looking.

Knew Dominique went to Pulitzer, was like in eighth grade.

Already had these nice tight little tits, and that ass . . . Long, shiny black hair bouncing off her ass, then brushing her tits.

"You like that, boy?" Davido asked, noticing.

Davido noticed everything.

Nico laughed. Davido handed him back the joint.

"I'm trying to educate you, *paro*," Davido said. "Pay attention. You even know what a *mara* is?"

"A gangbanger."

"Where the name came from, I mean," Davido said. "A *mara* is an ant. The kind of ant that swarms together and then kills everything in front of them. One ant is easy to crush, but an *army* of ants is unstoppable. Conquer or die, *'manito*, that's us. Like the song go, *La vida en la 18 es fatal*."

Life in 18 is fatal.

New video.

The girls from "En 20 Uñas" were twerking.

Dominique imitating.

Nico getting hard.

"Shit," Davido laughed, "there's no talking to a hard dick. It won't listen. You want some of that?"

"I don't know."

"Yeah, you know. *Dominique, venga.*"

Dominique danced over. Looked down at them and smiled.

Davido asked, "You think my boy here is cute?"

"He's okay."

"Why don't you take him into the bathroom," Davido said. "Show him you like him."

"Okay."

"I don't know," Nico said, feeling shy all of a sudden. He'd never even kissed a girl before.

"He doesn't know," Dominique said. She started to dance away.

"It's okay," Nico said.

"No, it's all good," Davido said. "You're 18 now. It works like this—you're just a *paro,* so she won't fuck you, but she'll suck your cock. Bitch, get back here!"

Dominique came back.

Davido said, "Break our boy in."

Dominque reached out her hand, led Nico into the bathroom and pushed him down on the edge of the bathtub.

Knelt in front of him.

Nico never felt anything like that.

He didn't last long.

Dominique got up, looked into the mirror, adjusted her lipstick, sprayed something into her mouth. "That was your first time, huh?"

"No."

"Yes, it was. Don't worry, *papi,* you did fine."

Nico, he was in love.

"Put yourself back in," she said.

"Oh, yeah."

She smiled into the mirror at him and walked out.

He took a second to get it together and went back out into the party. Davido grinned at him. Nico grinned back.

Pouya was on.

"South Side Suicide."

A week later Nico showed up where he was told.

The parking lot outside Burger King.

Davido walked up on him. Real close, chest to chest. Reached into his Yankees jacket, took something out and slipped it inside Nico's windbreaker. "Take this. Put it somewhere safe."

It was a gun. Nico could feel it. "I don't want it."

"Did I ask you what you want?" Davido asked. "Take it, put it under your bed or someplace your aunt won't find it."

"I won't use it."

"No shit, you won't," Davido said. "You better not. No, you keep it for me until I ask you for it, then you give it back."

"Why don't you just keep it?"

"Because you're a minor," Davido said. "If you get caught with it, you go to juvie for a few months. I get caught with it, I go upstate for years. You understand now?"

"I guess so."

"It's your job," Davido said. "As a junior. This is what comes with the weed and the alcohol and the girls. You want that, you take this."

Nico walked home hugging the gun to his chest.

Felt like everyone on the street could see it.

A cop car rolled by and he thought he might piss his pants.

Thank God no one was home when he got home, both pulling double shifts. He lifted the mattress off his bed, set the pistol between it and the box spring, then put the mattress back. Looked at it carefully to see if there was a bulge.

When he tried to go to sleep that night, he felt like the gun was poking into his stomach. But the next night it didn't feel so bad, and a couple of nights later it felt kind of good, having the gun there.

Felt powerful.

Like, come fuck with me now, see what happens.

Mess with Nico now, see what happens to you.

I'll cap your bitch ass.

Bitch.

His uncle and aunt saw it but they didn't want to see it.

They were good people, they worked hard, they were nice to Nico, they loved him, but they were making a living, busting a hump trying to get ahead in America.

So they saw the new shoes but they didn't.

Didn't want to know where they came from.

They knew new Jordans weren't from Payless. The Yankees windbreaker, the button-down long-sleeve plaid shirt, the shades, where did they come from? Where did Nico get the money for those? Where did he get the money to go to Burger King, McDonald's, Taco Bell? Where did the boy go when they were at work, when they were so tired all they could do was hit the bed and go to sleep? They knew but they didn't want to know.

They didn't want to see his grades tanking, the letter on his "attitude" going from "E" to "U"—Excellent to Unsatisfactory; they didn't want to answer the phone messages from the school asking about his absences.

They returned the calls, they went to the school, they talked to Nico, he swore he wasn't doing anything wrong; he knew he was and they knew he was, they knew what he was doing but they didn't know why.

They knew but they didn't want to know.

Nico might have been the best cell-phone booster Calle 18 ever had because he was small and he was fast. The marks didn't see him coming and they couldn't catch him going. There was money in cellies, but Nico turned all the phones right over to Davido, who hit him back with cash. So now under the mattress Nico had a gun, money and a cell phone.

Davido got more intense. Said they have to start producing more because they were moving in on ABK and that meant war and wars took money.

"Everyone pays rent," he said. "There are no guests in 18."

He put Nico on a cell-phone quota—Nico had to bring in one a week, minimum, which meant Nico had to expand his activities beyond Jackson Heights into Woodside, Elmhurst and Astoria, which was risky because other gangs worked those territories.

Didn't matter, Nico had to produce.

He was trying to figure out a way to get Dominique to suck his cock again, or go to a movie or something, when his phone rang and it was Davido. "I need that thing."

"What thing?" Nico asked.

"The thing you're holding for me."

"Oh."

"Men's room. Taco Bell. Half an hour."

Nico ran home, got the pistol, stuck it under his coat, and hustled over to Taco Bell. Davido was in the men's room already and Nico slipped him the gun.

"Be where I can find you in an hour," Davido said. "I'll call."

Nico hung out on the street for the hour and then Davido called. "Get your ass over to Roosevelt. Now."

He sounded pretty jacked.

Nico ran over to the train station.

Davido was standing on the platform. He gestured Nico close and jammed the gun into his jacket pocket. "Put it away until we need it again."

"Shouldn't I throw it in the river or something?" Nico asked.

"You don't ask questions," Davido said. "You do what you're told."

"But—"

"We're not throwing away a good gun," Davido said. "What do you think I did with it, anyway? *Go.* Get going."

Davido stepped onto a train.

Nico took the gun home and put it away.

Tried not to think about it but the next morning heard the news on television that a black kid got shot to death in Travers Park.

The *Daily News* said that he was one of the Always Banging Kings.

Davido disappeared for a couple of weeks.

Nico hung out with some other 18's, but none of them knew, anyway none of them said, where Davido went. Somewhere upstate, they guessed, until the police got tired of looking for someone who got gone, someone they'd just as soon have gone anyway.

Benedicto took over and warned everyone to have their heads on swivels, because the ABK would be looking to pay back for their boy. They wouldn't get tired, and unlike the cops, they didn't have to hunt down a specific person—they'd rather get Davido, but any 18 would do.

That's just the way it is in the thug life, Nico figured.

La vida mara.

So he kept his head up when he was out on the street now, because the ABK wouldn't be looking to put on a beating, they'd be looking to kill. It was winter and cold anyway, so a lot of the street life had gone indoors where it was warmer and safer.

The parties went on in Davido's crib, even though he wasn't around. Benedicto had a key and they went up there to blaze up and drink and Nico tried to get Dominique to give him at least a hand job, but he didn't have any luck.

"You're too young," she told him.

"I wasn't too young before," Nico argued. "And I'm older now than I was then. Come on, 'Nique."

She kept telling him no but one afternoon got loaded enough to jack him off.

"As a present," she told him.

"I don't have anything for you," Nico said.

"You got some weed?"

He gave her some weed.

. . .

The week before Christmas, Nico walked along Thirty-Seventh Avenue, happier than shit, cash in his pocket, shopping.

He got Tía Consuelo a pretty blouse and some nice bracelets, and then he found Tío Javier a nice pair of gloves and some warm socks and a new denim shirt. And he bought his mother a sweater, a pair of jeans and some of the same bracelets he got for Consuelo, so they could mail them down to Guatemala.

Nico found a silver chain for Dominique.

Then he took himself to Micky D's and grabbed a Quarter Pounder with cheese, fries and a Coke. Polished it off with an apple pie and walked home on a real high that he had the money to buy things for the people he loved.

When he opened the door Tía Consuelo was crying.

Tío Javier was standing there.

With the gun.

"What's this?" he asked.

Nico didn't know what to say.

"Nico, what *is* this?" Javier asked. In his other hand, he had the cell phone and some of Nico's money.

"It's not mine."

"It was under your mattress."

"You shouldn't have looked there," Nico said. "It's *my* bed."

Javier was a gentle man, a good man who never wanted to hurt anyone, but he stepped forward and slapped Nico across the face. Nico's head snapped back but he stayed on his feet and stared back at Javier, who looked back at him, ashamed.

"Where did you get this?" Consuelo asked. "Where did you get a gun?"

"*Maras,*" Javier said. "Isn't that right? You want to end up in prison with the other *malandros*? You want to get deported?"

I'm not a *malandro,* Nico thought. I earn my money. "I have things for you. Presents."

"Take them back," Javier said. "We don't want presents you bought with your dirty money."

Nico was crushed.

"I'm throwing this away," Javier said, holding up the gun. "I'm throwing it in the river."

"No!" Nico yelled.

"Yes."

"They'll kill me."

"Who are they?" Javier asked. "I'll go talk to them, straighten them out."

"Tell them to leave him alone," Consuelo said.

"If you talk to them," Nico said, "they'll kill *you*! Please!"

"It's going in the river."

He pushed past Nico. Nico grabbed him around the waist and tried to stop him but Javier was too big. He threw Nico off and walked out.

"They'll kill me!" Nico yelled.

Consuelo broke down sobbing.

Nico ran into his room.

They *will* kill me, he thought. The *best* he could hope for was a bad beating before they threw him out of 18. He could keep it a secret, but what would happen when Davido demanded the gun again? It would be even worse.

Nico knew he wouldn't be able to sleep because he'd just worry.

He went out the window onto the fire escape and called Davido from the street. "I have to talk to you."

"Getting laid, *'mano*." Davido was just back from his trip up north.

"I have to talk to you."

"Come on over."

Davido opened the door, Nico rushed in.

Dominique sat on the couch, pulling on her jeans. She looked at Nico like *What?*, strode past him and walked out the door.

Davido said, "What's so important?"

Nico swallowed. "I lost the gun."

"You what?"

"The gun," Nico said. "I lost it."

Davido slammed him against the wall. "How the fuck could you lose a gun?! What happened?"

"My uncle found it," Nico said. "He took it."

"Tell him to give it back," Davido said.

"I can't."

"You want *me* to tell him to give it back?"

Nico said, "He threw it in the river."

Davido let Nico go. Walked over to the table and lit a joint. Didn't offer Nico a hit. "This isn't good. You know what's going to happen to you now?"

"No."

"Neither do I," Davido said. "I have to take this to the shot callers. It could be bad, Nico. It could be real bad."

"I'll pay you back for the gun."

"How much money you got?" Davido asked.

"I got fifty."

"Give it."

Nico pulled the bills from his pocket and handed them over.

"The gun is going to be at least three hundred," Davido said. "Where are you going to get the rest?"

"I don't know," Nico said. "I will."

"I'll talk to the *llaveros*, see what I can do for you," Davido said. "You better start producing, boy. Big time. Go out, make some money, show them you're useful, you have some reason to be alive."

"Okay."

"Start with the two-fifty you owe," Davido said. "Without that, you're fucked. Now get out. Until you got that money, I don't know you. Don't come around anywhere; you see an 18, you cross the street."

Nico went home.

Javier was up, waiting for him. "I'm sorry I hit you. I shouldn't have done that."

"It's okay."

"You have your deportation hearing coming up," Javier said. "If they find out you're in a gang, they won't let you stay."

"They won't find out."

"It's not right, Nico," Javier said. "These people are garbage."

"They're my friends."

"No, they're not," Javier said. "They sell drugs, they kill people. Isn't that why you left Guatemala? Left your mother? To get away from this kind of people? To make some kind of life here?"

What kind of life do *you* have here? Nico wondered.

You work all the time, you're always tired.

Your clothes are bad.

"I bought you gloves," Nico said. "And a new shirt."

"Thank you, but I don't want them."

"Why not?!"

"You know why not, Nico," Javier said. "And you know right from wrong. You've just forgotten. You need to remember."

What I *need*, Nico thought when he went to his room, is two hundred and fifty dollars. Because you threw the gun away.

He got up early in the morning and went out to *hustle*.

Got on the S line and took the 7 train to Grand Central Station.

It was packed, mobbed with commuters rushing to work and people coming into the city to go Christmas shopping. Nico scored two phones in twenty minutes and then decided he shouldn't push his luck, so he went out onto the street.

Nico had never been to Manhattan before.

It was *amaaaazing*.

He'd seen the skyline from Queens but he never imagined *this*. The size of the buildings, their beauty, the crowded streets, people bustling everywhere, the storefronts with beautiful things in the windows.

I'm going to live here someday, he promised himself.

If I don't live here sometime in my life, I'm going to die.

He'd heard of Forty-Second Street so he walked on that until he came to Times Square, where he just stopped and stared. Even in the daytime, it was exciting, the gigantic video screens, the news crawling around the sides of buildings, the neon lights—Nico stood there and gaped. Wandered up Seventh Avenue with his neck craned, looking up, feeling smaller than he'd ever felt, more excited than he'd ever been.

This was New York.

This was *America*.

He almost forgot why he was there, but then he reminded himself, You're not here to gawk, you're here to work, you're here to steal, you're here to make money.

Three things he needed: cash, phones and credit cards.

The cash he'd use to pay off his debt, the phones and credit cards he'd give to Davido to help impress the shot callers because they make a lot of their money reselling the phones and pulling credit card fraud.

Nico picked his targets carefully.

They were easy to spot—tourists who were also awed by Times Square and were looking all around and not paying attention. He picked them out from the people who were walking fast, getting from point A to point B, obviously New Yorkers. Like any good predator, he looked and he listened—for people speaking strange languages, foreigners, tourists who weren't likely to chase him if they felt him take their wallets from their pockets.

He made his first score outside the Disney Store, a father standing there with his wife and kids looking into the window at Mickey and Goofy, his wallet poking out of his back pocket like it was asking to get away from this dork.

Nico obliged.

Grabbed it, shoved it in his jacket pocket and kept walking along with the crowd until he hit a McDonald's. Went into the men's room, into a stall and took out the wallet. It was a little disappointing cash-wise—two tens and a twenty—but it did have a Visa card. Nico shoved the loot into his jeans pocket, threw the wallet into the trash and went back onto the street.

On Forty-Seventh he crossed over to Broadway and walked south two blocks to the giant video screens, which just might be the thief's best friend, because a few hundred people were standing there looking up, pointing, smiling, taking selfies, all happy and shit.

Nico zoomed in on a group of Asian teenagers, all wearing blue kerchiefs and blue hats. Must be some kind of school group, he thought, rich kids, foreign kids. Every one of them had a cell phone and they were all taking pictures of the video screens, each other and themselves. He zeroed in on one girl holding an iPhone 7 way out to get a snap of herself and her BFF.

Bam.

He had the phone and was moving.

Heard the Asian kids yelling but there was nothing they could do because Nico Rápido was already in the middle of the crowd, cutting through, hidden in the mass of bodies. Sometimes it was good to be small.

They weren't going to catch him.

Shit, they weren't even going to see him.

One good citizen tried to grab him by the elbow but Nico shrugged him off and kept moving. Made it out to Eighth Avenue and saw another McDonald's—man, were McDonald's stores everywhere in Manhattan— and went in. Looked around to see if anyone had followed him and saw that he was safe. So he ordered a Big Mac, a Coke and fries and sat down to eat.

He was tempted to go back for another hit but then decided it was too risky. Someone might recognize him ("That's the kid!"). So he walked uptown to get into the subway and then made his way back to Queens. Under the mattress was blown as a hiding place, so he went up to the roof and jammed his stuff into an exhaust pipe.

Nico hit Manhattan for the next three days.

Ripped $327 in cash, four credit cards and three more phones.

A one-boy crime wave.

Nico called Davido. "I got the money."

"Bring it."

Six other 18's were there, including Dominique. Nico knew it wasn't good the second he walked through the door because none of them smiled at him, no greeting, no nothing. They didn't offer him a drink or a hit or anything.

Lápiz Conciente was slamming from the speakers.

Davido said, "You got the money?"

Nico handed him two-fifty.

"There were bullets in that gun," Davido said. "Bullets cost money."

Nico gave him the rest of the cash, then handed him the phones and credit cards. "I've been productive."

"Listen, I talked to the shot callers," Davido said. "They said you got to be punished, taught a lesson. They said I got to hurt you, Nico."

Two guys behind Nico blocked him from the door.

"What do you got to do?" Nico asked.

"They said to cut off a finger."

Nico felt like he was going to throw up. Maybe pass out. He thought about running, but there was nowhere to go.

"But I talked them out of it," Davido said. "So I can just break your arm instead."

"Thank you."

"Bones heal, fingers don't grow back."

"Right," Nico said. It was hard to breathe.

"Take your punishment," Davido said. "Otherwise, we're going to give you a bad beating, throw you out and you can't walk in this neighborhood anymore."

"I'll take it."

"Good." Davido picked up an aluminum baseball bat off the couch. The two guys behind Nico walked him up to the bar.

"You right-handed, Nico?" Davido asked.

"Yes."

Davido nodded at the guys and they stretched Nico's left arm between two stools.

Raising the bat over his head, Davido asked, "You ready, *paro*?"

Nico took a deep breath and nodded.

Davido brought the bat down.

It hurt like crazy. Nico felt his feet go out from under him but the two guys held him up and he didn't scream, he swallowed the pain and groaned. His eyes filled up but he didn't let the tears spill over. He felt like he was going to throw up again but held that in, too.

Through watery eyes he saw Dominique looking at him.

Nico didn't care. It hurt too much to care about anything but the pain and staying on his feet. He heard Davido say, "Take him to Elmhurst."

"I don't have insurance," Nico said.

"They have to take care of you anyway, in the emergency room," Davido said. He handed Nico a bottle of rum. "Knock some of this down. You might have to wait awhile."

Nico forced some rum down.

They took him outside, put him in the back seat of a car and drove him to Elmhurst Hospital. Pulled up in front of the E-room entrance and told him to get out. He had a hard time with the door, but managed and walked into the hospital.

He felt dizzy.

The nurse asked him what happened.

"I fell. On the stairs coming down from the train."

"Where are your parents?" she asked.

"I live with my aunt and uncle."

"Where are they?"

"At work," Nico said.

"Honey, we can't treat you without their permission."

He called his aunt. They gave him an ice pack and told him to have a seat. Half an hour later, Tío Javier got there. "Nico, what happened?"

"I fell." He could tell Javier didn't believe him.

Javier got up and talked to the nurse in Spanish. Nico heard him say that he didn't have health insurance or very much money, but please help his nephew and he'd find a way to pay over the next few months.

The nurse took Nico into an exam room.

A doctor came and they did X-rays. He showed Nico the picture. His "ulna," his forearm, was broken. It would take a few weeks but he'd be all right. The doctor set it, put Nico's arm in a cast and wrote a prescription for pain pills that Javier could get at the pharmacy.

They took a taxi home.

"Do you know the chance we take, even coming to a hospital?" Javier asked. "Don't you know they're looking to throw us out of the country, especially now?"

Nico felt bad. His aunt and uncle saved their money to open a business, and this would hurt them. "I'll pay you back."

"You're a child. It's not your responsibility."

"It's not yours, either," Nico said. "I'll get the money."

"Stealing? Selling drugs?" Javier asked. "This was because of the gun, wasn't it?"

Nico didn't answer.

"Your 'friends' hurt you. Won't you get out now?"

No.

If anything, he got in deeper.

"We have work to do," Davido told Nico earlier tonight. They were grinding at Krispy Krunchy Chicken. "Come on."

Because 18 is moving heavier into drugs. They were just slinging *yerba*, but now they're looking for the payout that comes with the *chiva*, and Davido is buying heroin and putting it out on the street.

They walked out to Ninety-Second near Northern. Davido gave him a burn phone and a boost up onto the fire escape, told him to go up to the roof. "Keep an eye out. You see anything looks like it shouldn't, hit me."

"Okay."

He climbed to the roof and looked out.

Jackson Heights is beautiful.

Nice view of Northern Playground. Nico can see Flushing Bay and planes coming in and out of LaGuardia so low they're like to hit him in the head. Then he realizes that he shouldn't be doing that, he should be looking just down at the street.

Nothing happens.

He has to pee. Stamps his feet to try to distract himself.

Then he sees a black Escalade roll up.

Black guys get out.

Nico hits Davido on the phone. "Some *mayates* are getting out of a car."

"Those are the guys we're meeting, stupid."

"Oh."

"Good looking out, though."

Nico keeps looking out. Can't be more than twenty minutes, the black guys come out, get in the car and drive away.

The phone rings. "The street clear?"

"Yeah."

Davido meets him on the street, slips him a hundy and a bag of weed.

This is how Nico gets into the drug trade.

Jacqui's giving a front seat blow job.

Because she won't give a back seat blowie.

For one thing, you'd have to open the front door, get out, open the back door, get in and close the door. The dome light comes on, goes off, comes on again. It attracts attention, too easy for cops to spot, as if they gave a shit anyway, except when the mayor's wife sees some slut giving parking lot head and tells him to tell the cops to give a shit.

Too many bad things can happen in the back seat. You get in the back, the guy usually tries to lay you down and fuck you. In the front, you bend over, you suck him off, that's that. Anything happens you can usually hit the eject button and get out the front door. Sometimes, if the guy feels sketchy, she'll blow him with one hand on the door handle anyway.

This guy is sketchy.

Cruised her in his old Camry four or five times before he pulled over.

Middle-aged white guy (go figure), big sloppy gut hanging over his belt (go figure), balding (go figure), no wedding ring (a little unusual and kind of a red flag because married guys are usually safe, they just want some head they can't get at home). She would have told him to keep moving, but it's fucking cold out and the Camry's heater works. Plus she needs the twenty to get high.

Let's face it, Jacqui thinks, some old sayings are true. Like the one that goes, "A junkie will do anything to get high." Must be true—I'm in the front seat of a shitty car sucking off a big sloppy bald guy.

Or trying to.

The asshole just won't come.

As a kid she had one of those toys where this wooden bird keeps tilting down and dipping its beak into a tube of water over and over again, and that's what she feels like now. Once you started the bird it never stopped, but she's not sure she has the stamina of a wooden bird, not to mention the economics don't work—at this pace she's getting paid about twelve cents an hour.

She sits up and sighs. "Problem?"

"You're not doing it right."

Not doing it right? Jacqui thinks. Like it's what, a cappuccino? It's a pretty simple equation there, dumbass.

It's suction, basic physics.

"What do you want me to do different?" she asks. Like be Fergie, Jennifer Lawrence, a Kardashian?

"Use your tongue more."

Jacqui sighs and goes back down. Uses her tongue more, but what does this guy want for twenty bucks—porn sex? In the front of a Camry in the middle of winter with the motor running? This is drive-through sex, asshole. It's McDonald's sex, it's not even Wendy's sex or Carl's Jr. sex. We're not going to cook it special for you—you pay your money, get your Quarter Pounder and drive away.

He presses her head down. "Deep throat me."

Deal breaker.

Jacqui forces her head back up but the guy is strong and holds her down. She starts to choke and maybe this is what the sick fuck wants (*Oh, your dick is so big, I'm choking on it, I love it*), maybe he'll get off but she doesn't care about that anymore, she just wants to breathe and then get the fuck out of there.

He won't let her up.

His hand twists into her hair and grabs. "Do it."

She bites him.

He screeches.

But he lets her go.

She pushes her head up and reaches back for the door handle, but he grabs her by the collar and pulls her back. She tries to kick the handle with her foot but it's not happening. "I'll give you your money back, just let me go."

"No, now I want it *all*, bitch."

She feels the gun barrel poke the back of her head. "No, please."

He throws the car into drive, goes up Washington and turns right on Powells Lane. There's nothing there except vacant lots and trees and he pulls over, puts it into park and pokes her with the pistol barrel. "Turn around. Pull your pants down. I'm going to fuck you, whore."

"Okay, okay." It's hard—she's terrified and it's tight in the front seat but she manages to turn around, brace her back against the door and wriggle her jeans down around her ankles. "Don't hurt me."

"You bit me, you bitch."

"I'm sorry, I'm sorry."

"I'm going to fuck the shit out of you." He crawls on top of her.

He's heavy, she can't breathe but she goes into the routine she thinks he wants. "Yeah, fuck me, fuck me, give me that big cock, you're going to make me come, Daddy." Anything, anything to save her life. "You're going to make me come, Daddy."

He groans, arches his back.

The gun loosens, slides by his waist.

By her hand.

He fumbles for it, but Jacqui grabs it first.

And pulls the trigger.

Twice.

"Oh, fuck! Oh, fuck!"

Jacqui kicks, wriggles out from under him. The door opens and she falls out on her back. She gets up, pulls up her pants and runs back up the lane, is halfway to Washington when she realizes that she still has the gun in her hand. She jams it into her coat pocket and keeps walking.

Walks all the way down to Motel 19, where she has a room with Jason.

Jason's an asshole, but she can't live under a bridge in the winter so she stays with him in the cheap motel as long as they can make the rent. Which they only can because she's out there giving blow jobs while Jason tries to figure out what kind of work he can't get.

When she gets to the room, he's high.

Skinny ass splayed out on the bed, staring at the television.

"Did you score?" she asks.

His head lolls, sort of nods at the side table.

He's an asshole but he saved her some. She cooks and fixes. It's hard, because her hands are shaking.

Straightened out, she says, "You got any money?"

"Why?"

"I gotta get out of here."

"So go."

Fuckin' asshole, Jason. "I mean out of town."

He's just awake enough he senses his meal ticket slipping away. "Why?"

"I killed a guy."

Jason laughs. "Fuck you, you didn't."

Fuck me, I did.

His jeans are on a chair. She goes through his pockets and finds six dollars and thirty-seven cents, wonders how much bus fare to New York is. Probably more than six dollars and thirty-seven cents. "This all you got?"

"I dunno."

Well then, who would, dickwad? She sits on the bed beside him. "Jason, he raped me."

"Oh."

Oh. That's it. *Oh*. What you have to remember about this world, Jacqui knows, is that at the end of the day no one gives a shit. Not at the start of the day, either. At no time during the day does anyone give a shit. "Jason—"

"What?"

"Do you have any more *money*, dude?"

"No."

This is why everyone hates junkies, Jacqui thinks.

Shit, *I* hate junkies.

The bus is a nonstarter so she walks to Route 87 and sticks her thumb out. Hitchhiking is dangerous. Some creep might pick her up and try to rape her.

Then again, she thinks, Jacqui's got a gun.

And she ain't ever gonna get raped again.

She keeps her finger on the trigger in her pocket and the barrel pointed at the guy most of the way down.

Another middle-aged guy.

This time married with a ring on his finger.

Pulled over, rolled down the window of the Subaru and said, "I don't like to see a young lady like you out here alone like this. Where are you going?"

"New York."

"I'm going as far as Nyack, if that helps you."

"I don't have gas money," Jacqui said.

"I didn't ask you for any."

Jacqui got in.

Keeps the gun pointed. It feels good in her hand.

The guy wants to make conversation. "My name is Kyle. What's yours?"

"Bethany." Like, why not?

"Are you going home or away, Bethany?"

"Huh?"

"Is New York home, or Kingston?" Kyle asks.

"I came down from Albany," Jacqui says. "My last ride dropped me off in Kingston."

"So where do you live?"

"Brooklyn."

"Got it."

You got it, Kyle? What's there to get? She takes a closer look at him and sees he's a little younger than she first thought, maybe in his early fifties. Sandy hair, starting to recede, blue eyes under glasses.

Around New Paltz he asks, "Are you hungry, Bethany? My treat."

"I could eat," she says.

He pulls off the highway and into a Dunkin' Donuts. She gets a coffee and a croissant with egg and sausage and it tastes damn good. Somewhere in the Harriman Forest she falls asleep, which she didn't mean to do, and when she wakes up Kyle is smiling at her and says, "You dropped off."

He turns onto the 287 through Nanuet.

"I can drop you off on the highway if you want," Kyle says, "or I can contact St. Ann's."

"What's that?"

"The church my wife and I attend," Kyle says. "They have a program in the winter to find places for homeless people. You're homeless, right?"

"I guess so."

"Yeah, I guess so too," Kyle says. "They can get you a bed and can find a program for you."

"What kind of program?"

"A drug program," Kyle says. "Come on. Who are you kidding?"

"What do you know about it?"

Kyle pulls off on Route 9 and heads into Nyack.

"I don't feel good leaving you on the highway." He takes two twenties out of his wallet and lays them on her lap. "I'll take you into town. Take a cab over, and that should get you to New York."

"What do I have to do for this?" she asks.

"Don't flatter yourself."

"Just drop me off in town."

Kyle pulls over and says, "Here you go. I wish you'd let me take you to St. Ann's, but it's your life. If you change your mind . . ."

He gives her his card.

"Thank you," Jacqui says. She gets out of the car.

"You got it."

Jacqui watches him drive away and then puts the card in her pocket.

She needs to score.

Junkies have an unerring radar that leads them to other junkies.

They can find each other even on strange and foreign ground.

Jacqui quickly finds another user in a little park on Main Street. Another young woman, addict emaciated.

"Hey."

"Hey."

"You know where I can score?" Jacqui asks.

"You have any money?" the woman asks. "Hook me up, too?"

"Okay."

"I'll make a call." The woman gets on her cell phone and walks away from Jacqui. A minute later she walks back and says, "Come on."

They walk down Franklin to Depew, then take a left toward the Hudson River to a group of five-story redbrick apartment buildings. They go into one of them and take the elevator to the fourth floor. The woman rings a doorbell, the door opens a crack and she says, "It's Renee."

"What you want?"

"Two bags."

Jacqui hands her a twenty. Renee slips it through the door. A few seconds later two balloons come out. The two women go out of the building to a parking lot in the back. They cook and shoot up.

"You have a place I can crash?" Jacqui asks. "Just for one night?"

"Yeah, okay."

They walk back up Depew to an old house, then upstairs to a room that Renee rents. A mattress, a microwave on the floor, an old TV. There's a bathroom—a toilet, a sink and a shower—in the hallway.

All of it stinks.

Of urine, semen, shit, and sweat.

Jacqui falls out on the floor, takes off her jacket and puts it under her head for a pillow.

Keeps her hand on the gun.

For a little guy, Nico has a big mouth.

A good thing, because he can put a lot of balloons in it.

The balloons are full of heroin.

Now Nico rides his bike east along Forty-Fifth Avenue, a cell phone strapped to the handlebar set on Google Maps and the nice lady giving him directions to the address.

He's a delivery boy.

Davido gave him the bicycle, called it a "late Christmas present."

"Thanks!"

"You're an idiot," Davido said. "This is for work."

The drug business has changed, Davido explained. It used to work like this—kids like Nico would stand out on the corner or in a park and the customers would walk or drive up and hand the kid the money. The kid would then go around the corner or into a building, get the dope from one of the older guys and slip it to the customer.

"That's how I started," Davido said. "I was one of those kids."

The system worked, he explained, because it insulated the dealers from the buyers. If one of the customers turned out to be an undercover cop, he could only bust the kid, which meant family court and maybe a stint in juvie, not hard time upstate.

That sling-from-the-corner shit still exists, Davido told him, dealers still do it, but it's stupid and risky. Why stand out there in the open when you got cell phones and texting and Snapchat and shit and the customer can contact you and you just deliver?

And this way, the white customers don't have to come to some sketchy hood filled with niggers and spics, they can stay in their nice places watching *Fixer Upper* or some *güero* shit and their high comes to them.

Which is pretty much the life that white people expect.

"You got to keep up with the times," Davido said, "to stay competitive. We live in the service age. If you're not providing service, someone else will. You heard of Blue Apron, GrubHub, DoorDash?"

"No."

"Anyway," Davido said, "we need to provide service. Deliver. That's why I got you the bike. The customer calls us, puts in his order, we deliver. I'm going to call our product Domino's—because it delivers."

Well, Nico delivers.

The same principle of using kids as couriers applies because if the kid gets popped it's no big thing. The kid takes a vacay in juvie and there are always more kids who want to make a little money and get cliqued up. What they do is they put the heroin or the coke into balloons and Nico puts the balloons in his mouth and goes out and delivers.

"What if a cop answers the door?" Nico asked.

"Then you swallow," Davido said.

"What if the balloons break in my stomach?"

"You don't have to worry about that," Davido said.

"Why not?"

"Because you'll be dead," Davido said. "But you'll be so high going out you won't know it's happening."

Maybe not, but Nico hopes they buy good balloons and not the cheap ones they sell at the ninety-nine-cent store. He really didn't want to do this—not only because he might have drugs explode in his body and kill him, but also because this is serious shit. It's one thing to boost a few cellies, another to be a lookout for a drug deal, another whole thing to actually deal the drugs.

And not just weed, the heavy stuff, heroin.

The women's NA meetings that Jacqui attends in Nyack are at the Senior Center, just a block away from the Nyack Plaza building where she scores.

It makes the decision convenient.

Clean and sober or down and dirty, within a few feet of each other.

Like a moral mall.

The food court.

Do I go for the Mrs. Fields Cookies or the salad bar? Jacqui asks herself. The junk food or the stuff that's good for you? The junk or . . .

What?

What's out there if you're not high?

Jacqui struggles with the decision every night. Shit, every day . . . shit, all the time. To get to the Senior Center she has to walk past Nyack Plaza and sometimes her feet just won't take her there. Sometimes she freezes on the sidewalk outside the Plaza, like she's paralyzed—she can't go in and she can't move past. She just stands there, feeling like an idiot, like a fool, like some weak, powerless thing, less than an animal.

Some nights the Plaza wins, other nights the Senior Center.

Sometimes it depends on whether she has money or not. If she doesn't, the decision is easier; there's no point in going into the Plaza if she can't score anyway so she walks into the meeting hoping it's enough, praying it's enough to at least temporarily fill her veins, get her through the night and into the next morning when it starts again.

There are times when she has some money and the Plaza loses—she pauses there, she stands and circles, and then walks to the meeting.

Other times the Plaza wins, she can't make it past and she goes in and scores and she might stay high for days before she forces her feet into a meeting again and sits herself down on one of those metal folding chairs and has a cup of shitty coffee and says that she had a "relapse."

Another relapse.

They always say the same thing—"Keep coming back."

It works if you work it.

They talk about shedding guilt, making amends.

Guilt? Jacqui thinks.

I killed my boyfriend with an overdose.

I shot a guy.

How do you make amends to dead people?

Some of them suggest methadone—they offer it at Nyack Hospital—but Jacqui doesn't have the health insurance to get into the program and anyway doesn't see the point of substituting one drug for another.

But little by little, almost like the erosion of water on rock, the meetings start to win. She fixes less and less, when she does it's in smaller doses, she skin-pops, she snorts. The people at the meeting wouldn't understand, they're all-or-nothing-at-all Puritans, but she thinks it's progress. The sores on her face start to heal, she gains a little weight, she looks just decent enough that she can get hours at KFC and they're so desperate for workers they forgive her sporadic availability.

She pays rent for floor space at Renee's.

It doesn't help that Renee is high all the time and hooking to get the money, but it's good when Jacqui wants to fix so she has company. But she's trying to save up enough money to get a room of her own somewhere and figures that this is about all she'll ever have in common with Virginia Woolf.

So she's clean and sober, but not a fanatic about it.

She's a fanatic about the gun, though.

Jacqui rarely lets it go, even when she's high.

The heroin and the gun aren't unrelated. Heroin, like any opioid, is a response to pain. Jacqui has some painful memories. Traumatic memories. When she's shooting up, the memories fade. But when she's not, they come roaring back.

Sometimes they are memories, movies from the past.

Other times they come as flashbacks, they're in the present, in real time, happening right now.

Her stepfather, Barry, coming into her room and fucking her when she was a girl. *This will be our secret (D), our little secret (G), I'll make you feel so good (Em).*

Travis dying, overdosing, in her arms.

The guy fucking her, raping her in the car—the gun going off.

These things aren't happening in the past, they're happening *right now* unless she fixes, gets high, gets off, gets away, that's Jacqui's horrible choice—get high and forget, stay clean and remember.

Relive this shit over and over again.

So she tries to stay clean and she clings to the gun.

The gun that protects her from new memories.

Well, sort of protects her. In some of the long nights, in the single-digit hours, she has turned the gun on herself. When the flashbacks are at their worst, when Barry is on top of her whispering in her ear, the fat guy on top of her grunting, Travis dying with his head in her lap, she's put the pistol barrel in her own mouth (like a dick? she speculates) and tried to pull the trigger.

Just to make it stop.

Make the flashbacks stop.

Make the *need* for the drugs stop.

She hears Barry say *Do it, whore,* hears her rapist say *Do it, bitch,* hears Travis say, *Do it, baby, come to me, I miss you,* hears herself say "*Do it, do it, do it, just do it.*"

But she can't.

Her hand shakes and she's afraid she'll accidentally pull the trigger while taking the barrel out of her mouth. It would be just like me, she thinks, to fuck up and kill myself while I'm trying not to. Then she sits with her memories, her flashbacks, until the pale winter sun comes through the dirty window.

Save one addict.

What Bobby Cirello is trying to do.

When he left NYC he got in his car, not even knowing where he was driving. He just drove north and pulled off in the Catskills, rented himself a cabin near Shandaken and holed up there like some kind of outlaw on the run.

Phoned in a leave of absence that no one, not even Mullen, challenged because all of One Police was pretty happy to have Bobby Cirello somewhere else.

So he sat.

All through the holidays, through the bitter-cold winter.

Went out and chopped wood for the fireplace, read some paperbacks the last tenant had left behind. Once a week or so drove to the Phoenicia Market for groceries. Otherwise lived like a hermit, like Thoreau, like the freaking Unabomber, he thought, although he shaved every day even though there was no one to care except himself.

Trying to figure out what to do now, what to do next.

Didn't come up with any answers as he watched the snow fall outside the window.

Then the snow stopped falling, started melting on the ground, and the dirt driveway up to the cabin got muddy and still Cirello didn't have a clue how to save himself, redeem himself, somehow at least try to make things right.

Then one morning he got up, made coffee and a couple of fried eggs and was packing his things before he even knew why or where he was going. Got back into his car and drove to Kingston, where he had caught a glimpse of the junkie Jacqui. He found the Kingston PD house and showed his badge.

They knew him. Well, knew *of* him.

"You're the cop that made the Get Money Boys bust," the desk sergeant said. "We're appreciative."

Five minutes later Cirello was sitting down with a detective.

"I'm looking for a Jacqui Davis," Cirello said. "She's a heroin addict. I saw her here a few months ago, before Christmas."

The detective pulled her up on the system. "Yeah, we know her. We have a warrant on her."

"Possession?"

"Attempted murder," the detective said. "She's a person of interest in a shooting. The vic said she got into his car at a red light, made him drive to an outlying area and tried to rob him. He fought her off and she shot him."

"You buy that?"

"Total bullshit," the detective said. "Your girl was hooking, we've known her for months, the guy was a john. This was strictly BGB."

Blow job Gone Bad.

"The vic is a creep," the detective said. "Still and all, we have to clear the case. The girl split town, we haven't seen her on the streets since the incident."

"Any clue where she went?"

"In the wind," the detective said. "And we don't have the budget to go chasing her. Just have to hope she gets popped somewhere and they pull the warrant. Do us a solid? If you find her, give us a shout?"

"You got it."

Dead end, Cirello thought.

He knew he should have left it there, given up, she was just another junkie among thousands.

But he didn't stop.

Couldn't even say why.

Cirello went all detective on it.

Drove back down the 87 working it out. Junkies, he knows, go where junk is. Like metal shavings to a magnet. So if Jacqui split Kingston, she probably headed south, toward the city. Maybe she's back in New York, maybe back on the island. Maybe she didn't make it that far. New Paltz has a drug scene (shit, what town doesn't?), so does Nyack.

He hit New Paltz PD.

They hadn't seen her, but they showed him where the drug drag was, and he cruised for two days. Stayed at the EconoLodge and caught naps. That is, when the feds weren't calling. Some suit from the special counsel's office kept banging his number, leaving messages for Cirello to call him.

Cirello ignored it.

Fuck them.

Fuck all of them—the special counsel, Keller, O'Brien, all of them. They could play their game without him.

He got the nod from New Paltz PD and went into Southside Terrace himself. Found an obvious addict in one of the apartment hallways and showed her his shield. No junkie is going to see the difference between an NYPD badge and a New Paltz badge or care. All they care about is not getting busted. "You seen this girl?"

"No."

"Look again, for real," Cirello said. "Or I can ask you again at the station."

The woman took a better look. "Never seen her before."

Cirello drove down to Nyack and went through the same drill. Checked in with the locals, got some information, and then went on the prowl. The biggest dope mart, Nyack Plaza, had been cleaned out with the Darius Darnell bust and the local addicts were hurting and on the prowl.

So Cirello kept looking.

Just drove around town until he saw a knot of people hanging out in a parking lot. They scattered like quail when he walked up on them but he caught up with the slowest, a woman named Renee.

"Don't know her," Renee said when Cirello showed her Jacqui's photo.

Cirello could tell she was lying.

"Here are your choices," Cirello said. "You lie to me again, you detox in a jail cell. Tell me the truth, your wake-up's on me."

"Maybe I've seen her."

"She here in Nyack?"

"Yeah."

"Don't make me pull this out of you," Cirello said. "Where is she?"

"She got her own place," Renee said. "I mean, she was staying with me—"

"Jesus Christ."

"—but she got her own place."

"Where?" Cirello asked.

"You want, like, an address?"

"Okay."

"I don't know it."

Junkies.

But she gave him the corners and a description of the house.

Cirello gave her twenty bucks.

Nature abhors a vacuum.

Which is what the arrests of the Get Money Boys in Kingston and Nyack created—a big sucking hole in the heroin business.

No vacuum in the drug world stays empty for long.

Too much money there.

So someone will rush to fill it.

Race to fill it.

Calle 18 got off the line first.

"Pack your shit," Davido told Nico. "You're going out of town."

"Where?" Nico asked.

"Nyack."

"Where is that?"

"I don't know," Davido said. "North somewhere. You and Benedicto and Flaco."

He explained that since the *mayates* got popped during the big busts, there's an opportunity in this town and the shot callers are going to take advantage of it. They'll set up at a motel and put it out on the street that you can call a certain number and get delivery.

"What do I tell my aunt and uncle?" Nico asked.

"Don't tell them nothing, just disappear," Davido said. "They'll probably be relieved."

They probably will, Nico thought.

I've just been trouble to them.

"Can I bring my bicycle?" he asked.

"How the fuck else are you going to make deliveries?" Davido asked. "Uber?"

"I have my hearing in a couple of weeks," Nico said.

"Nico, listen to me," Davido said. "You know what's going to happen at that hearing? The judge is going to have you cuffed and deported. But, *'manito,* they can't deport you if they can't find you."

Nico went home, threw a few things in a garbage bag and left before his aunt or uncle got home. Met Benny and Flaco and they took the subway to Grand Central, then a train to Tarrytown, then an Uber over the river to Nyack.

So now he hangs out in the Super 8, playing video games with Benedicto and Flaco. It's a fun life—they got money, they got weed, they got no one telling them what to do except make deliveries when the phone rings. And Nyack's got McDonald's, Burger King, Wendy's and KFC. Benny and Flaco are always bitchin' about how they miss Guatemalan food, but not Nico. He don't miss rice and beans and beans and rice as long as he can hit the Quarter Pounders.

Now he bangs the control buttons and waits for the phone to ring.

Gun in hand, Jacqui waits for her stepfather to come through the door.

This will be our secret (D), our little secret (G), I'll make you feel so good (Em).

She edges away, her back to the wall, points the gun at the door.

Of her room.

Her own room.

Jacqui's been doing well, pulling hours, paying rent for a room in a house on High Avenue, which she thinks is actually kind of funny/ironic in her more cogent moments. She's clean and sober more often than not these days, and since the Plaza closed it's easier to walk past to the meetings.

And she likes her room. On the third floor, it has a window that overlooks Gedney Street and a little park. There's a nice bakery up the street and she's talked to them about getting a few hours and maybe learning to bake.

The flashbacks, though, are killing her.

The equations are cruelly simple.

Dope = no flashbacks.

No dope = flashbacks.

So now she's clean and fucked up as hell. Barry's right outside the door, she can hear his footsteps, hear him breathing. He's going to come in, hold her down, pin her down, show her how much he cares for her.

This will be our secret (D), our little secret (G), I'll make you feel so good

(Em). She's shaking, sweating. Like she's jonesing. So what's the fucking difference?

The heroin sings to her.

This will be our secret (D), our little secret (G), I'll make you feel so good (Em).

Gun still in hand, she calls the number.

Rollins got the location on Cirello.

His Visa card showed him at the Quality Inn in Nanuet, New York, just west of Nyack. Yesterday he was in New Paltz but left before they could get someone up there. They got someone up to Nanuet. If we can find Cirello, Rollins thought, so can the special counsel. So a two-man team watched the motel from across the road and followed Cirello when he left.

Now they're on him.

Looking for the moment.

Cirello has to go.

It can be put out later that he was a dirty cop.

Cirello pulls over on High Street.

The description of the building matches.

He gets out of his car, finds the back door of the building and heads up the stairs.

Jacqui hears the knock on the door.

Points the pistol.

Thinks she can shoot through the wood before Barry comes in.

Her finger tightens on the trigger.

They get on the phone.

Rollins gives the nod.

Nico pedals furiously.

It's fun, zipping down the streets, even with a bag of heroin stuffed in his mouth like he's a chipmunk.

"Jacqui?" Cirello says. "It's Detective Cirello. You remember me?"

It brings her back to real time. "Yes."

"Can I come in? We need to talk."

Jacqui gets up, slips the pistol under her shirt and opens the door.

"Can I come in?" Cirello asks.

She lets him in. The only piece of furniture is the bed, so he sits down on that. She sits next to him.

"Jacqui," Cirello says, "do you know they're looking for you in Kingston?"

"Yeah."

"Did you shoot that guy?"

She nods.

"Tell me what happened."

Jacqui tells him.

"I want to take you back to Kingston," Cirello says. "You turn yourself in."

"No."

"Listen to me now," Cirello says. "You turn yourself in. They're going to ask you questions and you tell them exactly what you told me. They're going to ask you—because I'm going to tell them to—if you were afraid for your life, and you're going to tell them yes."

"Will I go to prison?"

"Maybe," Cirello says. "Maybe not. But if you tell them you acted in self-defense, you won't go for long."

There's a knock at the door.

Cirello hears, "Domino's!"

"Did you order pizza?" Cirello asks.

Jacqui shakes her head.

Cirello gets up and opens the door.

It's a kid.

With chipmunk cheeks.

They see Cirello's car parked on the street.

The junkie back in the park, the one they watched him talk to, told them that he was going to see another junkie.

It's perfect.

Dirty cop gets shot in a drug shakedown.

The door opens.

A hand grabs Nico by the neck and pulls him in. Then the guy turns him around and locks a thick forearm over his throat. "Don't swallow, you little prick. *Do . . . not . . . swallow.*"

Nico has no choice.

He couldn't swallow if he wanted to.

He's choking.

"Spit them out," the guy says. "Spit them out. You speak English? *Escúpalos, pequeño imbécil.*"

Nico spits out the balloon.

The guy shoves Nico against the wall. "I'm a cop. Hands behind your back. *Manos a la espalda.*"

Nico puts his hands behind his back, feels the cuffs go on.

"How old are you?" the cop asks.

"Twelve, I think."

"You think? What's your name?"

"Nico."

"Nico *what?*"

"Ramírez."

"What are you, a *paro?*" the cop asks. "With who?"

Nico knows better than to answer that one.

He shrugs.

"You think the shot callers would do a minute of time for you?" the cop asks. "They wouldn't. That's why *you're* out here instead of them. Do something to help yourself here."

Nico knows how he can help himself.

Keeping his mouth shut.

Cirello turns to Jacqui. "Did you call him?"

She looks at the floor and nods.

Ashamed, jonesing like hell, flashing like hell. The noise, the motion, the yelling . . .

It's too much.

She needs a fix.

Then she hears footsteps coming up the stairs.

Waiting outside the door.

Cirello cusses himself out for trying to rescue a junkie.

Now he has a jonesing addict to haul back up to Kingston and a dope-slinging kid to deal with.

This is what you get, he thinks, for being—

The door flies open and slams against the wall.

The guy has his gun out, shoulder high, aimed at Cirello's head.

I'm dead, Cirello thinks.

The blast is deafening.

The guy drops the gun and staggers backward out the door and then slumps against the wall.

Slides down, leaving a smear of blood behind him.

Cirello whirls around and sees Jacqui standing there.

A gun in her hand.

The barrel pressed against her head.

This will be our secret . . . our little secret . . .

"Don't," Cirello says. "Please."

Cirello takes a step toward her.

She points the gun at him.

He reaches his hand out. "You don't want to do that."

When Jacqui was little . . .
when she was little . . .
when Jacqui was a little girl.

She hands him the gun.

Nico stares up at the cop.

"What did you see?" the cop asks.

Nico doesn't answer.

"What did you see?"

"Nothing!"

"That's right," the cop says. "Now get the fuck out of here. Run!"

Nico runs.

Cirello hands Jacqui his car keys.

"Go sit in the car, I'll only be a minute," Cirello says. "Do *not* run on me. Go on, go."

Jacqui walks out.

Cirello stands over the shooter's body and puts two more rounds into his chest.

Then he calls Nyack PD.

4

The Reflecting Pool

For death remembered should be like a mirror . . .
—Shakespeare
Pericles

Washington, DC
April 2017

S pring, Keller thinks, is Washington's best season.

Famously, the cherry blossoms bloom in April, and he hopes he'll have a chance later today to walk along the Mall to see them.

Crosby is pessimistic about that; she's warned him that the hearings will probably take all day, probably more than one day, that the senators will have many questions, speeches disguised in the form of questions, and that there will be much time-consuming grandstanding.

Keller is nevertheless hopeful.

After all, spring is the hopeful season, the season of rebirth and optimism. (He recalls that grass grows up through the bones of skeletons.) He wants to be optimistic today—it could be either a beginning or an end.

For the country, spring hasn't been a time of regeneration but a season of chaos. Dennison's firing of the special counsel has triggered the "constitutional crisis" the pundits feared. The Democrats are screeching for impeachment, the Republicans shouting back that Scorti exceeded his authority and deserved to be fired. The liberal and conservative media are yelling at each other like bad, angry neighbors across a fence.

In the center of the storm is Keller.

Dennison takes every opportunity to excoriate him—Keller is a liar, a criminal, he belongs in jail, why hasn't the Department of Justice charged him and arrested him, locked him up?

"That's a real possibility," Crosby has warned Keller. "In the absence, now, of a special counsel, the attorney general's office could file against you. God knows the president is pushing him to."

Pressure also comes from the other side, the media and Democrat politicians demanding to know why Keller doesn't come forward with the evidence he claims that he has.

Crosby went on "the shows" to respond. "What mechanism is there now for Mr. Keller to release this information? The president shut down the special counsel's investigation. Is Keller supposed to turn it over to an attorney general who already, by the way, recused himself—for potential bias? Or to that AG's deputy?"

"He could turn them over to the attorney general of New York."

"We've been down that road already," Crosby said. "Unfortunately, Attorney General Goodwin did not think that the evidence was sufficiently corroborated. We think he was mistaken, and our understanding is that he is now reconsidering, in the light of recent developments."

The attempted murder of a key witness, Detective Bobby Cirello.

The story was leaked that Cirello was present at a meeting between Lerner, Claiborne, and Mexican bankers allegedly representing drug cartels. That Cirello was asked by arrested drug trafficker Darius Darnell to provide security at that meeting, but was actually working undercover and planted microphones—the source of Keller's alleged recordings.

"Scorti wanted to interview Cirello," one television correspondent reported, "and shortly before that was scheduled, someone tried to shoot him. And we're expected to believe that was a coincidence?"

The conservative media fired back. "Sources high in the NYPD tell me that Bobby Cirello was a dirty cop, he was under investigation by Internal Affairs. He has a gambling problem—he owes money to the mob—and was working those debts off by providing security for drug deals. The shooting had nothing to do with 'Towergate.' And what was Cirello doing in Nyack, far from his jurisdiction, in the company of a heroin-addicted young woman?"

But Goodwin launched an investigation into the Cirello shooting and also reopened the Claiborne death to determine if his overdose was accidental.

A witch hunt, Dennison tweeted. A disgraceful attempt to reverse the democratic decision of the election. Goodwin is weak, a dupe. Should be fired. Cirello, Keller, all of them should be locked up. Throw away the key!

"Despite Mr. Dennison's apparent belief to the contrary," the governor of New York responded, "only the people of New York can fire the attorney general of New York. That would be in an election, by the way."

But Republicans in the New York legislature started a recall action against Goodwin. Petitions were circulated around the state, supporters sitting at card tables outside supermarkets to solicit the requisite number of signatures.

"This is Watergate," Senator Elmore said to the microphones. "A sitting president has, at the very least, participated in a deliberate cover-up to subvert the workings of justice. It's a disgrace. He should resign, or failing that, should be impeached."

"There is no evidence whatsoever," O'Brien responded, "that President Dennison attempted to obstruct justice. Only that Art Keller says so. Just like there's no evidence that Jason Lerner or anyone connected to Terra—and in that I include the president—had any idea that the banks they were dealing with did business with drug cartels. If Keller had proof of that he would have brought it forward by now. He hasn't, because there isn't any. Case closed."

Which is, Keller thought, O'Brien thinking he has called my bluff, that I'm tanking to keep Ruiz from testifying.

But the case isn't closed.

All through the winter and early spring it remained an open wound on the body politic, tearing an already polarized society further apart. Protesters and counterprotesters clashed in violent outbreaks. Congress was "paralyzed," the administration "crippled" in carrying out its agenda.

Something had to happen.

Congress stepped in.

A Senate subcommittee, chaired by Ben O'Brien, was quickly formed to investigate the entire "Towergate" matter.

On the witness list—

Jason Lerner.

John Scorti.

Robert Cirello.

Attorney General David Fowler.

Denton Howard.

Art Keller.

And Eddie Ruiz.

The gun, Keller thought, at my head. O'Brien scheduled him after me as a threat.

Lerner was first.

Keller watched on television as Lerner said, "My company has done business with any number of lending institutions from all over the world, including HBMX. We can't possibly trace all the sources of their funds. We rely on the banks to police themselves and to adhere to national and international law and oversight. If the oversight was negligent in this case, I refer you to those agencies."

O'Brien asked, "So you had no knowledge that the funds you acquired in the Park Tower loan came from drug money?"

"First," Lerner said, "I still don't know that for a fact. It hasn't been demonstrated. Second, I certainly had no knowledge of that at the time."

"And if you had?" O'Brien asked.

"I wouldn't have accepted the funds," Lerner said.

"I apologize for asking this," O'Brien said, "but did you have anything to do with the death of Mr. Claiborne?"

"Of course not," Lerner said. "I liked Chandler, we were friends. I was terribly saddened by what happened."

"And the attempted murder of Detective Cirello?"

"I know nothing about that."

Elmore took the microphone next and walked Lerner through Park Tower's parlous financial condition and Lerner's indebtedness, and established that if Park Tower had been lost, Terra would have gone down with it. Then he got Lerner to admit that President Dennison had a fifteen-point equity share in the company.

"So President Dennison has a direct financial interest in the success or failure of Park Tower," Elmore said.

"I guess you could say that."

"And therefore was directly threatened by any investigation into Park Tower or Terra?" Elmore asked.

"No, I don't think he felt threatened."

Scorti went the next day.

The former marine was stone.

In his opening statement he said, "You need to understand that I can offer no definitive conclusions here, as my investigation was arbitrarily truncated. As per the Senate order, I have, under protest, produced the documents and evidence that we have developed to date, but I warn the senators to likewise draw no conclusions from these, as the products of an incomplete investigation might be misleading."

So, Keller thought, he's deliberately pissed all over any testimony he might give.

The senators tried anyway.

"Did your investigation reveal any criminal activity on the part of Mr. Keller?" O'Brien asked.

"My investigation indicated that possibility."

"But you reached no conclusion?"

"I wasn't given that opportunity."

Elmore took a whack. "Did your investigation lead you to any opinion as to criminal behavior on the part of Terra?"

"My investigation indicated that possibility."

"Did your investigation," Elmore asked, "lead you to any opinion as to criminal behavior on the part of the president—to wit, obstruction of justice?"

"My investigation indicated that possibility. Again—"

"How do you feel about your firing?" Elmore asked.

Scorti looked at him like he was an idiot. "How do I *feel?*"

"Yes."

"I don't like it."

"Do you feel that your firing is, in itself, obstruction of justice?" Elmore asked.

"I believe that is no longer my determination to make," Scorti said.

It went on like that, Scorti stubbornly refusing to give any substantive answers based on the fact that he hadn't concluded his investigation.

Attorney General Fowler testified on the same day.

"Did you offer to let Mr. Keller keep his job if he would end the Towergate investigation?" O'Brien asked.

"No, I did not."

"Did you instruct anyone to make that representation?"

"I did not."

Elmore took over. "Why did you recuse yourself?"

"There was the appearance of a conflict," Fowler said.

"The appearance or the substance?"

Denton Howard took the chair the next day.

O'Brien ran him through the same questions, and Howard denied that he had made any offer to Keller.

Keller watched the testimony in Crosby's office while preparing for his own.

"Is he lying?" Crosby asked.

"Yes."

"But you don't have tapes of that."

"I'm not Richard Nixon."

O'Brien asked, "Did the president instruct you to make an offer to Mr. Keller?"

"No."

Keller watched as Elmore asked, "Why have you refused to continue the Towergate investigation?"

"Because there's nothing to investigate," Howard said. "There's nothing to it."

By this time, the hearings had become a national obsession, with ratings higher than at any time since Watergate. Audiences were tuning in like it was a celebrity murder trial or a hit miniseries. People picked heroes and villains, they debated what was going to happen next at the office, they eagerly awaited the next installment.

Bobby Cirello was a star.

He testified that in fact, yes, Darnell had asked him to provide security for the hotel meetings, that he had, prior to the second meeting, planted microphones and had a warrant to do it.

"What did you do with those recordings?" O'Brien asked.

"I gave them to my boss."

"What did he do with them?"

"I don't know the answer to that question."

"Do we need to subpoena him?" O'Brien asked.

"I don't know the answer to that question."

Cirello has been on the witness stand many times, Keller thought.

"Do you know why," Elmore asked, "Darnell instructed you to provide security for these meetings?"

"He wanted to make sure they were safe and that there were no recording devices," Cirello said.

"I guess what I'm asking," Elmore said, "is if you know why it was a drug dealer who asked you to perform that service."

"Because another drug dealer asked him."

"That would be Eddie Ruiz?"

"That's correct."

"Do you know Mr. Ruiz?"

"I do."

"Under what circumstances?" Elmore asked.

"I muled millions of dollars to him," Cirello said, "on behalf of Mr. Darnell."

"This was drug money?"

"It was payment for heroin."

O'Brien took over. "Do you know if Mr. Lerner had any connection to Mr. Ruiz?"

"I don't know the answer to that question."

"Well, you do know the answer to that question," O'Brien said. "The answer is that you don't know that there was any connection, do you? Do you know of any connection between Mr. Ruiz and Mr. Claiborne?"

"No."

"Any connection between Mr. Darnell and either Mr. Lerner or Mr. Claiborne?" O'Brien asked.

"I don't."

"Who tried to shoot you?" O'Brien asked.

"I don't know."

"The deceased hasn't been identified yet?"

"Not to my knowledge."

"You might not even have been the intended victim, isn't that right?" O'Brien asked. "It might have been Ms. . . ."

"The gun was pointed at me," Cirello said. "I fired back."

"What were you doing there, Detective Cirello?" O'Brien asked. "Far from New York City, in the apartment of a young female?"

"I was trying to help an addict."

"Did you?"

"I don't know."

"There's sure a lot that you don't know," O'Brien said. He went on to pound Cirello. "You're a degenerate gambler, aren't you, you owe money to the Mafia, you're under investigation by your own department—how are we supposed to believe a word you say?"

Watching this, Keller got furious.

But Cirello didn't get visibly angry, certainly didn't lose his temper. He'd had a career of being attacked by defense attorneys and he let the assault wash over him before he calmly responded, "Senator, I was an undercover police officer. It's clear that you don't know what that entails, and I don't think we have the time here for me to educate you."

That clip made all the news shows.

But it doesn't change the fact, Keller thinks, that no connection has been made between Lerner and the cartels.

The next logical witness would be Hugo Hidalgo.

Hidalgo could establish the relationship between Ruiz and Caro, testify that it was Caro who instructed Ruiz to provide security for the meetings. It wouldn't establish Lerner's guilty knowledge—only the tapes could do that—but it would go a long way to link the cartel to Terra.

But Hidalgo is off the radar.

No one can find him.

Keller is worried that he's dead.

They killed Claiborne, they tried to kill Cirello, there's no reason not to believe they wouldn't have gone after Hugo, too. He's disappeared. The FBI is looking for him, the US Marshals Service is looking for him, Keller has his remaining loyalists in DEA looking for him.

Nothing.

So the next witness is Keller.

At the end of the day, it all comes down to Keller.

Because, so far, it wasn't going well, Crosby explained. Lerner held his own, so did Fowler and Howard. Cirello damaged them but couldn't make the essential link.

The president and his allies were using the hearings to make their case.

NO money laundering, Dennison tweeted. NO obstruction. Witch hunt proved. Now DOJ should do its duty—PROSECUTE KELLER.

If the hearings didn't go any better, Crosby told Keller, it would embolden the attorney general to charge him.

"In terms of Lerner and Terra," Crosby said, "it's all about the recordings. In terms of the AG, Howard and the president, it's all about credibility, now. It's your word against theirs. It just depends on who the public believes."

Crosby isn't stupid.

She saw Ruiz's name on the list, saw where it was placed, and made the right conclusions.

"What do they have on you, Art?" she asked him the day before his testimony. "What does Ruiz have on you?"

He didn't answer.

"Okay," she said. "Now you have a choice to make. I told you that I view my job as keeping you out of jail. My recommendation as your lawyer is that you take a dive. I'll advise you when to take the Fifth. I frankly doubt that, if you back down at the hearings, they'll pursue a prosecution against you. They won't want to reopen this can of worms. Let it go, Art. It's sad, it's a shame, it's not the country that either of us wants, but my advice is to let it go."

Keller heard her.

Had to admit that he'd thought the same thing.

That there was no point in making himself a kamikaze in a lost war.

At that point in time, he didn't really know what he was going to do.

Neither did the country.

Art Keller's testimony was a much-anticipated event, akin to the O.J. Simpson trial, the final episode of *The Sopranos* or the Super Bowl. Everyone was waiting to see what would happen, what he would do, what he would say.

It would be Keller against Dennison.

The showdown.

Now Keller climbs into a gray suit and knots a red tie and thinks about the phone calls he got last night.

The first was from O'Brien.

"It's your last chance," O'Brien said, "to do the right thing. Remember who we have and what we have."

The second was from Marisol.

"I just wanted to wish you good luck," she said.

"Thank you," he said. "That's kind of you."

"Oh, Arturo," she said. "What are you going to do?"

"It's okay," he said. "I know what I'm going to do."

"You do?"

Yes, he thinks as he tightens his tie.

Maybe for the first time in my life, I know what I'm doing.

I'm going to save my life.

The shooter's name is Daniel Mercado.

Army vet, Iraq vet, sniper, "illegal alien." Involuntary separation from the military due to unspecified "psychological issues." Mother and sisters still in Mexicali. On the bumper with La Eme.

Mercado is told that the request comes from the *jefe* of the Sinaloa cartel, Ricardo Núñez, on behalf of the martyred El Señor, Adán Barrera. If Mercado successfully completes the mission, $2 million will be placed in an offshore account—for him if he lives, for his mother if he doesn't. In either case, if he chooses to accept the assignment, his family will be treated like gold. On the other hand, if he decides to deny a direct request from El Patrón for a favor, well . . . who can guarantee anyone's safety these days?

Rollins knows his type—Mercado's a man with grudges—denied citizenship in the country he had fought for, thrown out of the army he loved. He desperately needs to belong to something; if it's not going to be the army, it's going to be La Eme. If he survives this job, he gets instant entry into the car. Mercado has delusions of grandeur—he wants to be a hero, a legend. The man who finally gets vengeance for Santo Adán will certainly be that.

And he can shoot.

According to Mercado's DD214, the man was an "expert" marksman, the highest level. According to his own account, which may or may not be trustworthy, he had fourteen confirmed kills in Iraq.

He is told that this is not a suicide mission.

An extraction team will be waiting at a designated place to get him out of the city and then out of the country. A backup team and location will also be in place. The chances for escape are not as slim as they appear—there will be chaos, mayhem, especially as Mercado starts to spray fire around. He has a good chance of making it to one of the two extraction points.

If you're captured, he's told, go ahead and tell them everything. We want the Americans to know that we're avenging Santo Adán. If you go to prison, La Eme will make sure that you have the best possible life—booze, drugs, women. You will be a king on the yard, a hero to *la raza*.

And Keller's shooting will have a political bonus here, Rollins thinks.

The murder of a high-ranking government official will be Pearl Harbor.

The president will be able to use it as a pretext to fund the border wall, deport illegals, take virtually any action against Mexico.

They don't tell Mercado that they're going to back him up with two other shooters who will engage if he misses. Mercado will have an AR-15, because that's what the American public will expect. The backup shooters will also use 5.56-caliber weapons.

Mercado accepts the assignment.

He's Oswald, Rollins thinks. He's Ray, he's Sirhan.

He's the perfect patsy.

You can't just walk in and see the president of the United States.

Well, maybe you can if you're Nora Hayden.

She made a call to someone who made a call to someone who made a call, and now she's in the elevator on the way to the penthouse of Dennison's building in New York. Where he probably spends more time than he does in the White House. He's certainly here on the day that Art Keller is going to testify in front of Congress, because he doesn't want to be in Washington for that.

Nora gets searched by the Secret Service guys.

She has no weapons.

That they can find, anyway.

Dennison dismisses his aides when she comes into the living room suite with its marvelous view of Central Park. He looks at Nora and says, "It's been a long time."

"Decades," she says. "But I remember it like it was last night. All the sick little games, the twists, the kinks."

"What is this, blackmail?" Dennison asks. "How much do you want? I'll give you my lawyer's number, Mr. Cohn, and you can work it out with him."

"I don't want money."

"A job?" Dennison asks, looking annoyed. "An apartment? What?"

"My husband," Nora says. "Sean Callan."

Dennison's eyes flicker. He knows.

"You'll get him released immediately," Nora says, "or I'll go to the media and make what Art Keller is doing to you look like a slap on the wrist. I'll tell every filthy thing."

"No one will believe you."

"Yes, they will," Nora says. "Look at this face, you slimy son of a bitch. I'll be a star within seconds. And everyone will believe me because I'll give them details. Then you'll deny it, I'll sue for defamation, and you'll have to give a deposition in which those details will come out. And you'll either admit them or commit perjury. So what's it going to be?"

. . .

Keller hears a child laugh.

It's discordant, odd, out of place as he walks up the steps to the Capitol. Reporters stick cameras in his face, journalists shout questions, other people want autographs signed. Some people yell, "Go get 'em, Keller!," others tell him to go to hell. Some hold up signs and placards—MAKE AMERICA GREAT AGAIN! LOCK HIM UP! THE WALL WILL BE BUILT!

He knows that he's become a polarizing figure, embodying the rift that threatens to widen and tear the country in two. He's triggered a scandal, an investigation that has spread from the poppy fields of Mexico to Wall Street to the White House itself.

Pausing for a second, Keller turns back to look down at the long stretch of the National Mall, the cherry trees in bloom, the Washington Monument in the distance. He can't see the Reflecting Pool or the Vietnam Veterans Memorial but he knows they're there—he often walks along the Wall to pay respects to old friends. He might go there later, depending on how things go inside; it might be his last chance for a long time, maybe ever. Looking back at the green lawn, the pink blossoms literally floating in the light breeze, it all seems so peaceful.

But Keller is at war—against his own DEA, the US Senate, the Mexican drug cartels, even the president of the United States.

And they're the same thing.

Some of them want to silence and imprison him, destroy him; a few, he suspects, want to kill him. He half expects to hear the crack of a rifle as he goes up the steps now to testify, so the child's laughter is a welcome relief, a needed reminder that outside his world of drugs, lies, dirty money and murder there is another life, another land where kids still laugh.

Keller can barely remember that country.

He's spent most of his life fighting a war on the other side of the border, and now he's home.

And the war has come with him.

He pushes through, into the relative safety of the Capitol, and is escorted to the hearing room. The senators are already in their places, high-backed chairs in front of wood paneling.

Keller takes his seat behind a table on the floor. It's deliberately arranged, he knows, to be intimidating, so that he has to look up at the senators. Crosby sits down beside him.

He looks around a little and sees that the gallery behind him is packed. Most of the onlookers are journalists.

But one of them is Marisol.

She nods to him and he nods back.

O'Brien raps a gavel for order, and then a bailiff swears Keller in.

He swears to tell the truth.

O'Brien starts, "Mr. Keller—"

Crosby interrupts him. "Mr. Chairman, my client would like to make a statement."

"A brief one, please," O'Brien says. "We have a lot to cover. But go ahead, Mr. Keller."

"Thank you, Mr. Chairman," Keller says. "And my thanks to the committee for hearing me out. I don't intend to answer any questions today."

There's a buzz in the room.

O'Brien raps the gavel again.

"You understand that could put you in contempt," O'Brien says. "Do you intend to take the Fifth?"

"No," Keller says. "I believe that there comes a moment where we, both as individuals and a nation, have to look at ourselves honestly and truthfully, and speak that truth. That's what I intend to do today."

The room goes quiet.

Belinda gets into the front passenger seat of the car that Tito sent to pick her up.

The new godfather wants to deliver her reward personally.

The driver says hello, Belinda says hello back and buckles her seat belt. Then she feels the pistol barrel poke into the back of her neck.

"Oh no," she says.

"I first met Adán Barrera in 1975," Keller says. "I was then a young DEA agent assigned to the field office in Sinaloa, Mexico. Barrera was, I believe, nineteen years old at the time. He introduced me to his uncle, Miguel Ángel Barrera, then a policeman. The Barreras gave me information leading to the arrest of a number of heroin traffickers. I was naive then and didn't realize that they were traffickers themselves and were using me to help eliminate competition.

"It is true that I rescued Adán Barrera from a severe beating and possible killing at the hands of Mexican federal police and American mercenary pilots. This was during Operation Condor, during which the DEA, myself included, and the Mexican military and police poisoned and burned thousands of acres of poppies, forcing thousands of *campesinos*—Mexican peasant farmers—from their fields and villages.

"The unintended consequence of Operation Condor was that it forced the Mexican opium growers to scatter across Mexico. In trying to remove a cancer, we had only metastasized it. They formed an organization, the Federación, the first true drug cartel, under the leadership of Miguel Ángel Barrera, aka 'M-1,' aka 'The Godfather.' He divided Mexico into *plazas*—territories—for the smuggling of drugs into the United States, and he ruled the Federación from his base in Guadalajara."

Keller pauses and sips from a glass of water.

"To replace the heroin trade," Keller continues, "Barrera introduced a new product—highly addictive 'crack' cocaine—which fueled a tragic epidemic that had devastating effects in urban America in the 1980s.

"At the time, DEA was concentrated on the cocaine trade from Colombia into Florida and did not fully appreciate the 'back door' of Mexico and what became known as the 'Mexican Trampoline'—that is, cocaine shipments coming in small airplanes and 'bouncing' from Colombia to various Central American locations and then to Guadalajara, from where it was distributed to the various plazas and brought into our country.

"During this period, I was the resident in charge of our Guadalajara office and tried to alert my superiors to the Mexican Trampoline. I was a voice crying in the wilderness. By this time, Adán Barrera was living in San Diego and selling cocaine for his uncle. As a result of one of our operations, Barrera had to flee his San Diego home, his then pregnant wife took a serious fall in the process of fleeing a raid, and his daughter was subsequently born with a serious, eventually fatal, birth defect.

"Barrera blamed me for his daughter's tragedy.

"At this point in time, to disguise an illegal and unwarranted wiretap that I placed in Miguel Ángel Barrera's home, I invented a fictional informant with the code name 'Source Chupar.' Enraged by the losses caused by information he believed to have come from Source Chupar, M-1 ordered Adán Barrera and others, including Rafael Caro, to kidnap my then partner Ernesto Hidalgo, to force him to divulge the identity of the informant.

"Ernie didn't have this information. I had not told him about the illegal wiretap or, obviously, given him the name of an informant who, in fact, didn't exist.

"Barrera, his brother Raúl, Rafael Caro and others tortured Ernie Hidalgo to death over the course of several days, despite a deal I had made with Adán to shut down my investigation if he released Ernie.

"In the aftermath of Agent Hidalgo's murder, Miguel Barrera fled to El Salvador, where myself and Mexican police tracked him down, arrested him, and flew him to the American consulate in Costa Rica, at which point

American intelligence personnel forcibly removed him from my custody and released him."

O'Brien raps his gavel. "I think we've heard about enough of Mr. Keller's speechifying. He was called here to answer questions, not to filibuster—and—"

"I was kidnapped," Keller says, "and taken to a training base for contra guerrillas on the Nicaraguan border, a base funded by Miguel Ángel Barrera, where a high-ranking intelligence officer named John Hobbs explained to me that the Mexican Trampoline included cocaine shipments flown by a shell company called SETCO, the money from which was being used to fund the contras in the war against the Communist government of Nicaragua.

"Let me be clear—subsequent investigative journalism made the accusation that the CIA was selling crack in American cities. This, to my knowledge, was not true. What is true is that the National Security Council ran an operation—called Cerberus—that covered up the smuggling of cocaine for the purpose of funding and arming the contras, which Congress had declined to do. I saw the drugs, I saw the planes, I saw the NSC personnel. Simply put, the war on communism trumped the war on drugs.

"In 1991, I testified in front of a congressional committee investigating this issue.

"I testified under oath that I had never heard of SETCO, or Cerberus. I also testified that I had never heard of an operation called 'Red Mist,' which was a multinational coordinated policy of assassinating Communist and left-wing leaders in Central America.

"I lied. I committed perjury."

Crosby puts her hand over the microphone. "Art—"

He gently takes her hand away and resumes. "In exchange for my assisting the cover-up, I was given control over the Southwest District of DEA, with absolute power to pursue and punish those responsible for or involved in Agent Hidalgo's murder.

"I did so, literally with a vengeance.

"It took me years to bring Adán Barrera to justice, and in the course of that pursuit I did a number of things of which I am not proud. I broke American and Mexican laws to basically kidnap suspects and bring them into American jurisdiction."

Crosby leans across, into the microphone. "Mr. Chairman, I'd like a recess. My client—"

"Is fine," Keller says. "I violated DEA procedure and numerous requirements for warrants. I used Adán Barrera's 1994 murder of liberal Cardinal

Juan Parada—an element of Red Mist—to 'flip' Barrera's mistress, an American citizen named Nora Hayden, to become my informant. Ms. Hayden was a dear friend—as was I—of Cardinal Parada's, who had also been Adán Barrera's parish priest.

"To protect Ms. Hayden's identity, I leaked false information to the Barreras that the informant was a young drug trafficker named Fabián Martínez. In response, Barrera sent a team of gunmen to slaughter Martínez and the nineteen innocent men, women and children who lived in his family compound.

"I will take the responsibility for those murders to my grave."

He pauses. The room is silent.

Old men take siestas.

And old men get up from their siestas to piss.

Caro swings his legs out of bed and puts his feet on the cold floor. He wears only an old T-shirt, a large size that hangs over his spindly legs, and they shake as he pads down the hall to the bathroom.

Getting old is a bad idea, he thinks, the stupidest thing we ever do.

So there have been setbacks.

There are always setbacks.

Overall, the situation is good.

Elena has gone to join her brother in hell.

Núñez is a spent force.

Tito is taking over more and more territory from the Esparzas and will soon put an end to them. As soon as he does, Caro thinks, I put an end to Tito. His in-laws will object, but the Valenzuelas are so rich because they value money over blood.

A year or two, maybe a little more, and I'll have what I'm owed.

And within a few hours, Art Keller will be dead.

I'm owed that, too.

He opens the bathroom door and blinks.

A young man is sitting on the toilet, a pistol pointed at him.

"What do you want?" Caro asks.

"The lady reporter," the young man says, "you had to kill her, beat her to death?"

Caro doesn't answer.

"And the forty-three kids on that bus," the young man says, "they had to die, too? You had to burn their bodies so there was nothing even left for their families to bury?"

"Who are you?" Caro asks.

"I'm an *hijo*," the young man says. "My father was Ernesto Hidalgo. Does that name mean anything to you?"

Caro's bladder empties.

Keller says, "There has been public speculation about my 1999 arrest of Adán Barrera. These are the facts: I lured Barrera across the border with false information that his daughter's death was imminent, and then arrested him in the hospital parking lot. To effect his release, American intelligence personnel kidnapped Ms. Hayden and we arranged for an exchange of hostages, as it were, on a bridge in San Diego. Miguel Ángel Barrera, John Hobbs, and an American operative named Salvatore Scachi were present.

"Their intent was not to exchange Ms. Hayden for Barrera, but to kill both her and me. In the gunfight that followed, both Hobbs and Scachi were shot by a gunman who they had engaged to shoot me. I killed Miguel Barrera and rearrested Adán Barrera.

"I can confirm the rumors that there was an additional gunman at the bridge. I later learned that he was Sean Callan, a former mercenary and onetime bodyguard for Adán Barrera who was romantically involved with Nora Hayden.

"After the incident on the bridge, I was placed under investigation and testified to a special congressional committee the truth of what I knew about the Mexican Trampoline, and Operations Cerberus and Red Mist. I believe this testimony was suppressed. To my knowledge, it has never been revealed to the public. Perhaps you can tell me what happened, Senator O'Brien, as you were a member of that committee."

O'Brien glares down at him.

"As rumor has it, I did retire to a monastery in New Mexico," Keller says. "I was trying to find some serenity and also to reflect on what I had done in my pursuit of Barrera. I remained there until Barrera issued a two-million-dollar bounty on my head, which would have put the lives of my hosts in jeopardy, and the Department of Justice agreed to transfer Barrera back to Mexico to complete his sentence. I knew that Barrera would 'escape' from Puente Grande prison. Of course, this wasn't an escape—an escape does not involve the active collusion of one's jailers. Barrera was simply released by a warden, Ricardo Núñez, who later became his chief lieutenant.

"At my request, I returned to DEA and was assigned to Mexico to aid in returning Barrera to custody. Adán Barrera re-formed his uncle's organization under the rubric of the 'Sinaloa cartel' and launched a war of conquest to eliminate various other regional cartels and seize the immensely valuable plazas of Tijuana, Nuevo Laredo and Ciudad de Juárez. Over the next ten years, the inter-cartel fighting would kill over one hundred thousand Mexican people, most of them innocents, making it the bloodiest conflict on this continent since the American Civil War, fought just across our borders. People in Texas, Arizona, New Mexico and California have literally heard the gunfire from some of these battles.

"The most violent among the competing cartels was a group known as the Zetas, which began as former Mexican special forces who deserted to serve the Gulf cartel, but eventually became a force of their own. The sheer sadism of the Zetas is almost impossible to describe or even believe—immolations, beheadings, the mass murders of women and children—all preserved and distributed on video to terrorize the population.

"I had been appalled by the murders of nineteen innocent people in 1997; by the height of the drug war in 2010 to 2012, that would have been a low daily body count barely worthy of news coverage.

"Certain elements of the Mexican government—often accused of corruption, with considerable justification—desperate to stem the carnage, made a deal with the devil. Viewing the Sinaloa cartel as the lesser of two evils when compared with the Zetas, it entered into a tacit arrangement with Adán Barrera to assist him in winning his war against the Zetas. I participated in this arrangement."

He takes another sip of water.

Callan steps out into the daylight, shields his eyes, and then sees Nora and Flor standing by a car.

He walks over and they both pull him into an embrace.

"What did this cost you?" Callan asks.

"A few bad memories," Nora says. "A distasteful encounter. It's nothing."

On the drive to the airport she says, "Flor has been talking about a little boy she traveled with. They lost track of each other. She asked me if maybe we could help find him."

"We can sure try," Callan says. "What's his name?"

"Nico," Flor says.

"Do you think he made it to the States?" Callan asks.

"I don't know."

Most of them don't, Callan thinks. Most of them get sent right back to where they came from.

If he remembers Flor's story, that was a garbage dump.

I've been luckier, he thinks.

I've been on the garbage dump more than once in my life, and someone has always pulled me off.

He looks over at Nora. "We'll start looking in Guat City."

They get on a flight to Juan Santamaría Airport in San José, Costa Rica.

María and Carlos are there to pick them up and take them home.

Keller says, "I personally met with Adán Barrera, and we agreed to suspend our conflict for the purpose of destroying the Zetas. In the interest of full disclosure, I will tell you that the Zetas had attempted to murder my now wife, Dr. Marisol Cisneros, grievously wounding her, and threatened further assaults. I am sure that this colored my judgment and informed my decision.

"In Mexico, the campaign against the Zetas was spearheaded by the FES—the special forces of the Mexican marines. The Zetas had slaughtered the family of one of their officers, and they formed a secret unit called the 'Zeta Killers.'

"I and other DEA personnel assisted in this effort by providing American intelligence resources to locate Zeta cells, training camps, and leadership. Remember that the Zetas had murdered an American DEA agent, Richard Jiménez. Not to put too fine a point on it, this was an assassination program. Far more Zetas were killed than arrested.

"Analysts of the Mexican drug situation have noted the relatively few captures, arrests, and killings of Sinaloa cartel personnel versus other cartels, including and especially the Zetas, and opined that this demonstrated governmental bias toward the Sinaloa cartel. I can affirm that this analysis is true and accurate, and that the United States participated in favoring the Sinaloa cartel as a way of bringing some kind of stability to Mexico.

"There have been rumors and reports about a covert operation in Guatemala; let me address those now.

"In October of 2012, Adán Barrera arranged a meeting with the leadership of the Zetas to discuss a peace treaty. This was to be held in a remote Guatemalan village called Dos Erres.

"It was a setup.

"I resigned my DEA position to take a job at a security company called Tidewater based in Virginia. This was actually a team of mercenaries— former SEAL and DEVGRU operatives formed to drop into Dos Erres to eliminate the Zeta leadership. It was funded by money from various oil companies—the Zetas had been attacking oil pipelines in Mexico—arranged by you, Senator O'Brien.

"I helped to lead this operation in the full knowledge that it was against both international and American law. I believed then, and believe now, that it was nevertheless morally justifiable. In another contravention of law, I obtained the temporary release of one Edward Ruiz, an American-born cartel leader and longtime informant, to accompany the raid, as he could personally identify the Zeta leadership.

"What we didn't know was the Zetas were planning to kill Barrera at this meeting. After the peace talks were completed, the Zetas ambushed the Sinaloan delegation and slaughtered them. We dropped in just as this was finishing up and succeeded in the mission of terminating the Zeta leaders, effectively destroying the organization.

"Adán Barrera's remains were only located in March of 2014, shortly after I took over at DEA. The assumption was that he had been killed during the Zeta assault.

"This is not true.

"I killed Adán Barrera."

The room erupts.

O'Brien bangs the gavel.

Keller leans closer to the microphone and says in a loud voice, "I was supposed to have located him and extracted him, if he was still alive. I did locate him. He had survived the attack and was hiding in the jungle outside his camp.

"I shot him twice in the face.

"I am fully prepared to accept responsibility for this, if the Guatemalan government chooses to extradite me, and also to accept responsibility for any crimes I might have committed under American law for participation in this raid and its subsequent cover-up."

Crosby throws her hands up, then sits back in her chair as if to say, *Go ahead, destroy yourself.*

Eddie Ruiz gets off the phone with Minimum Ben.

Who told him that he can't blow up Art Keller anymore because Keller just blew *himself* up. Copped to the whole Guatemala thing and capping Barrera, too. Took the ace right out of Eddie's hand and stuck it up his ass.

The only play I have now, Eddie thinks, is to flip on Lerner. Tell them fuck yes I set up security for Lerner's meetings. Had a dope slinger do it, because the meetings were about getting dope money.

How do I know that? he rehearsed.

Because Rafael Caro asked me to do it.

Nico finally makes it back to Manhattan.

Way downtown, in the oldest part of the city, to the Immigration Court on Federal Plaza. A long line of people stand outside, waiting to pass through security. Most of them are Latino, some are Asian. There are other kids there, some with families, a few, like Nico, alone. His aunt and uncle didn't want to come to the hearing for fear of being deported themselves.

So Nico came alone.

He makes it through security and goes up to the twelfth floor, where he finds his name and courtroom assignment on a large bulletin board. The hallway is packed, the few benches are filled, a lot of people lean against the walls or sit on the floor. Nico edges through the crowd, trying to find his volunteer lawyer, Ms. Espinosa. He finally sees her and makes his way over, and they confer in the hallway because there are no rooms provided.

She almost has to shout to make herself heard. "Nico, you're going to appear before a judge who'll decide if you can stay or be deported. Okay, we have about five minutes. Answer all the questions truthfully, and if he asks you if your life is in danger if you return to Guatemala, you say yes. Got it?"

They go into the packed courtroom and sit in the back. Nico watches the judge. He looks like an old man, with white hair and glasses. He looks mean, and Nico sits there for half an hour as the judge denies refuge to two women and a teenage boy.

Then he hears his name called.

"Let's go," Espinosa says.

She walks him to the witness stand and she says, "Marilyn Espinosa in pro bono for Nico Ramírez."

"Thank you, Ms. Espinosa. Do we need an interpreter?"

"Mr. Ramírez speaks some English," Espinosa says. "But, yes, to be on the safe side."

The judge peruses the file, then asks, "Mr. Ramírez is applying for refugee status?"

"Yes, Your Honor."

"On what basis?"

"Mr. Ramírez fled Guatemala," Espinosa says, "because a street gang, Calle 18, threatened to kill him if he didn't join. In all likelihood, they will kill him if he is returned."

The judge studies the papers some more. "But he *did* join."

"He was given a gang tattoo by force. He's a child, Your Honor."

"I have the file in front of me," the judge says. "What's the HS position?"

The lawyer from Homeland Security says, "Mr. Ramírez entered the country illegally. Recommend deportation."

"Your Honor," Espinosa says, "will you at least hear my client?"

The judge looks at Nico. "Young man, why do you want to stay in the United States?"

"Because they'll kill me if I go back," Nico says.

"Who will?"

"Pulga."

"Who?" the judge asks.

"He's the shot caller for 18 in my barrio," Nico says.

"Do you have anything else to say?" the judge asks.

Nico thinks really hard. What can he say that will make them let him stay? He's desperate.

"Because it's beautiful here," he finally says.

The judge examines the paperwork again and then looks back up. "I'm going to remand Mr. Ramírez to the custody of Homeland Security for deportation."

"Your Honor," Espinosa says, "this could be a death sentence."

"And I could be saving an American life by getting rid of a precocious criminal," the judge says. "We have enough gangbangers and drug dealers in this country already without importing them."

He looks at Nico and asks a pro forma question: "Do you waive appeal?"

Even with the translation, Nico doesn't know what he's talking about.

"No, Your Honor," Espinosa says. "We intend to appeal to BIA and request bond."

"Which in this case would just mean removal back to Southern Virginia," the judge says. "Bond denied. You have thirty days to appeal. ICE will take custody of Mr. Ramírez and proceed with deportation."

A strange man handcuffs Nico and leads him out of the courtroom. Nico looks at Espinosa, who tries to keep up beside them through the crowd.

"I'll file an appeal, Nico," she says. "And a motion to reconsider."

He understands enough to know that she's going to ask them to change their minds.

Nico knows that they're not going to change their minds.

He's going back to El Basurero.

He's garbage and he's going back to the garbage dump.

"A few months after the Guatemala operation," Keller says, "Senator O'Brien approached me about taking over at DEA. I did so because I truly thought that I could do something about the heroin epidemic afflicting the country. I thought that was why Senator O'Brien asked. I now realize that I was once again naive, that the senator put me in the position to cover up the Guatemala operation."

O'Brien says, "I think we have heard just about enough—"

"My extrajudicial execution of Adán Barrera also had the opposite effect from that which I intended," Keller says. "During the brief supremacy of his

Sinaloa cartel, Mexico experienced a period of relative peace and security. In eliminating him, I unleashed a score of lesser competitors for the throne, who have, in turn, unleashed chaos on a people who have already suffered far too much. In fact, Mexico has just experienced its most violent year, eclipsing even the horrors of 2010 to 2012.

"And the drugs keep coming in, which leads me to—finally—the matter which I have been called to testify about today."

O'Brien says, "I am going to suspend this hearing until further notice. Mr. Keller is simply making more unsubstantiated allegations—"

"I want this hearing to continue," Elmore says. "We have called Mr. Keller to testify, and he has a right to complete his testimony."

"He has no right to filibuster," O'Brien says. "I'm going to adjourn this—"

"If you do," Keller says, "I will resume it on the Capitol steps."

"You are in contempt, Mr. Keller," O'Brien says.

"You don't know the half, Senator."

"Continue," Elmore says.

Keller says, "In my role as DEA administrator, I became aware that a new heroin-smuggling network, led by Eddie Ruiz and released trafficker Rafael Caro, was sending masses of heroin and lethal fentanyl into the United States through intermediaries in New York City. I also learned that Caro had ordered the murders of forty-nine students in Mexico—some of them burned to death—and the torture-murder of journalist Ana Villanueva, who was investigating this atrocity.

"I further became aware that the Terra Company—headed by special White House adviser Jason Lerner—with the help of the hedge fund managed by Chandler Claiborne, had arranged a multimillion-dollar loan through a Mexican bank, but that the actual money had come from a syndicate of Mexican drug organizations, including the Caro-Ruiz organization that perpetrated this mass murder.

"Court-authorized wiretaps revealed that Lerner initiated bank fraud and knowingly violated anti-money-laundering statutes. Further authorized recordings of a conversation between Lerner and Claiborne conclusively show that both had knowledge that the source of the loan was drug money coming from, inter alia, Rafael Caro.

"I was in negotiations with Special Counsel Scorti to turn over the incriminating tapes and documents. Frankly, I was concerned that, if I did turn over the tapes, they might be suppressed. Accordingly, I would now like to play the relevant moments for this committee."

He lays a small tape player on the table.

"This is not going to happen!" O'Brien says.

"Are you trying to suppress this evidence?" Elmore asks.

"This isn't 'evidence,'" O'Brien says. "We don't know the provenance of these tapes, we don't know their origin, they might very well violate the legal rights of—"

"We don't know until we hear them," Elmore says. "Do you not want them heard, Senator O'Brien?"

"Then we should hear them in closed session," O'Brien says.

"So it's the American people you don't want hearing these recordings," Elmore says. "But I think the people have a right to hear—"

"I want those tapes seized," O'Brien says. "I want them seized and handed over to the US attorney general's office."

"Meaning I'm telling you it's drug money."

"Jesus Christ, are you wearing a wire?"

"Don't be an asshole."

"Are you?!"

"No!"

"Because if you are—"

"You think I'd cross these people? You know who they are, you know what they do."

"Yes, I do. Do you?"

"They'd kill me and my whole family."

"Yes, that's right."

"I'm scared, Jason. I'm thinking of maybe going to the police."

"Don't do that. That's the last *thing you want to do."*

"If this goes south—"

"We're covered. Don't you get that? If it's drug money, if it's Russian money, whatever, we can have any investigation shut down. We're golden now. We're untouchable."

"I don't know . . ."

"Chandler, I needed this fucking loan. My father-in-law needed this fucking loan. Do you know what I'm getting at here?"

Uproar.

Reporters spill out of the room.

O'Brien gavels for order but doesn't get it.

Crosby puts her hand over the microphone and says, "My God, Art."

Keller looks across the room at Marisol, then leans back to the mike and says, "While still in my job, I was asked by both current DEA director Denton Howard and by Senator O'Brien to cease the investigation of Jason Lerner. Mr. Howard, strongly alluding that he was relaying a message from President Dennison, offered that I could retain my position, and also that the administration would support certain liberalizing policies that I have endorsed.

"I refused these offers. Fearing that evidence would be destroyed, I removed tapes and documents from DEA premises and secreted them in a safe location. I am fully aware that in doing so, I have violated certain federal statutes, and, again, I am prepared to take responsibility and accept the consequences. I will leave it to others to determine if O'Brien's and Howard's actions rise to the level of obstruction of justice."

O'Brien gets up and walks out of the hearing room, followed by his staff.

Elmore nods at Keller to continue.

"As a result of this investigation," Keller says, "and with the superb cooperation of the NYPD Narcotics Division, we have destroyed the Caro-Ruiz network and seized vast amounts of fentanyl-laced heroin. Justice for their money launderers, however, has yet to be realized.

"We often point a finger at Mexico for being corrupt," Keller says. "It's too easy because it's too often true. I can personally testify to corruption at the highest level of Mexican government. However . . .

"We also have to look at corruption here in the United States. I just played you a recording that revealed corruption at the very highest levels of American finance and government, by the very people most active in pointing accusatory fingers at Mexico.

"If we do not thoroughly and honestly investigate and prosecute this corruption here at home, we are the worst kind of hypocrites, and we should immediately open the cell doors of every man, woman, and, yes, *child* currently serving time for possessing or selling drugs.

"But the corruption goes deeper than just money. We have to ask ourselves—what kind of corruption is there of our collective national soul that makes us the world's greatest consumer of illicit drugs? We can say that the roots of the heroin epidemic are in Mexican soil, but opiates are always a response to pain. What is the pain in the heart of American society that sends us searching for a drug to lessen it, to dampen it?

"Is it poverty? Injustice? Isolation?

"I don't have the answers, but we must ask the real question—

"Why?"

Cirello sits with a Kingston detective and a state prosecutor.

"It was self-defense," Cirello says. "The guy was raping her and was going to kill her."

"She was hooking," the prosecutor says.

Cirello looks at the detective and knows the interview is going to go down the way it should. He'll ask her the right questions in the right way and leave the DA with nothing to do but write it off as self-defense.

"Please do what you can for this kid?" Cirello says. "She's an addict. She needs help, not prison."

"She's been to rehab already," the prosecutor says. "How many times do you want us to send her to treatment?"

"Until it works," Cirello says.

Jacqui sits at a table in the interview room.

The cop comes in.

"Hey," Jacqui says.

"Hey."

"I'm going to jail now, huh?" she asks.

"I don't think so," Cirello says. "Whatever the cop asks you, you answer yes, okay?"

"I owe you big time," Jacqui says.

"I owe *you* big time."

"Okay," she says, "we owe each other."

"Take care of yourself, huh?"

"You too."

The cop leaves.

Jacqui starts to sing her song to herself.

"When Jacqui—"

Then she stops.

I'm not a little girl anymore, she thinks.

Ric sits in his cell.

There's nothing else to do there until they move him. He's pleaded out for a sentence of twelve years, half the sentence his father took. Ric knows that his dad is never getting out.

But I'll be young, he thinks, in my early forties.

I can still have some kind of a life.

Not like Belinda.

The prison telegraph has already tapped that she's dead, that Iván Esparza executed her for the sin of not killing Ric.

He feels bad about it.

The same prison telegraph told him that Iván has put himself under Tito Ascensión.

So it's over, Ric thinks.

The Sinaloa cartel is done.

You're the godson to nothing.

It doesn't matter, he thinks. The drug thing is over anyway. What you need to do now is to serve your time and get back to your family.

Valeria will be a teenager.

He hears a muffled voice. It sounds like it's coming from the toilet. He bends down and hears, *"Ric? Ric Núñez?"*

"Yeah?"

"What's up? What's up, brother? It's Eddie Ruiz."

Crazy Eddie? Ric thinks.

What the fuck?

"Listen, Ric. We can do some things together . . ."

Cirello gets in his car and heads south on the 87, back toward the city.

Back to the job.

The UC is finally over, Mullen will get him a prime assignment, but he knows that the stink that's on him will never really come off. There'll always be that suspicion, that doubt, the whispers behind his back, the rumors that some of the drug money stuck to him like the crumpled bills you find in your jeans pocket when you take them out of the dryer.

He can stay on, do his thirty, get his pension, but it will never be the same as it was.

When he hits Newburgh, he turns west on the 84.

Doesn't know where he's going, only knows that he's not going back to New York, not going back to NYPD, not going back to being a drug cop.

He's done.

"I have spent my adult life fighting the war on drugs," Keller says.

"I have had many colleagues—some of them fallen—in this war, and I am proud of their sacrifice, their dedication, and their fine efforts to combat what they see as an unmitigated evil.

"They are true believers and truly good people.

"But now I have, sadly, come to the conclusion that we have fought the wrong war, and that it must end.

"The war on drugs has been going on for fifty years—half a century. It is America's longest war. In the process of waging it, we have spent over a trillion dollars, put millions of people, most of them black, brown and poor, behind bars—the largest prison population in the world. We have militarized our police forces. The war on drugs has become a self-sustaining economic machine. Towns that once competed for factories now vie to build prisons. In 'prison privatization'—one of the ugliest combinations of words I can imagine—we have capitalized corrections; corporations now make profits keeping human beings behind bars. Courts, lawyers, police, prisons—we are more addicted to the war on drugs than to the drugs against which we wage the war.

"The war on drugs is a war in more than name. Countless people have been killed because drugs are illegal. You don't see wine or beer or tobacco companies shooting it out to dominate a market, but that's exactly what we see on the corners and in the tenements for control of the drug trade. And, of course, in Mexico. Because drugs are illegal, we send sixty billion dollars a year to the violent sociopaths of the cartels, money that bribes police and politicians and buys the guns that have killed hundreds of thousands of people with no end in sight.

"The 'Mexican drug problem' is not the Mexican drug problem. It is the *American* drug problem. We are the buyers, and without buyers, there can be no sellers.

"We have waged this war for fifty years, and after all those years, all that money, all that suffering, what is the result?

"Drugs are more plentiful, more powerful and more available than ever.

"Fatal drug overdoses are at a record high—we now lose more people to overdoses than to car accidents or gun violence.

"All this while drugs are illegal.

"If that's what victory looks like, I would hate to see defeat.

"We need to end this war.

"We need to legalize all drugs and spend our time, money and effort on addressing the root causes of drug abuse.

"We need to ask and answer the question 'Why?'

"Until we answer that question, we are doomed to repeat the same tragic, repetitive dance of death.

"Hobbes said, 'Hell is truth seen too late,'" Keller says. "I pray that this truth hasn't come too late. Thank you for your time."

Keller gets up and leaves the room.

His arm around Marisol's shoulder, Keller pushes his way through the crush of media outside the Capitol and then helps her into the waiting car.

"Where are we going?" Marisol asks. "Home will be under siege."

True, Keller thinks.

He's exhausted.

The adrenaline from his cathartic speech is draining, his brain is just tired and he doesn't know what's going to happen next. Will I be arrested? he wonders. Tossed in jail? If so, will I ever get out?

"I'd like to go for a walk," he says. "Clear my head."

Marisol looks at him quizzically. "Where do you want to go?"

"The Wall," Keller says. He wants to say goodbye to some old friends, maybe say goodbye to his first war, while he has the chance. "Do you want to come with me?"

"People will see us."

"It will take them a little while to catch up," Keller says.

"Okay," Marisol says. "Let's do it."

Keller tells the driver to drop them on Independence Avenue, between the Tidal Basin and the World War II memorial.

Rollins stays several cars behind them.

"Where is he going?" Mercado asks.

The shooter is nervous, Rollins thinks, watching his foot tap on the car floor. A few nerves are good, too many of them not so much.

They follow Keller's car down Independence.

The car stops.

Rollins watches Keller help his wife out of the car.

"I know where he's going," Rollins says.

The Wall.

Mercado gets out of the car.

A beautiful spring day, the kind that brings thousands of tourists to see the cherry blossoms along the Tidal Basin, the kind of day that makes residents happy that they live in DC.

Keller and Marisol walk along the periphery of the World War II memorial, not wanting to get too close and intrude on the dozens of private moments, remembrances and mourning as groups of veterans escorted by local volunteer guides move along the stones inscribed with the names of battles and campaigns. He remembers they call this program "honor flights," flying in veterans from all over the country to come to the memorial. They're old and white-haired, stooped, some leaning on canes, not a few in wheelchairs, and Keller wonders what they must be thinking as they look at the names of their old battles.

A "good" war, Keller thinks, good against evil, black versus white.

They saved the world from fascist tyranny, and we . . . well, we were told, we were *sold*, the mythology that we were saving the world from communism.

They turn onto a walkway that edges Constitution Gardens Pond. The irony isn't lost on him—one thing all the media seem to agree on is that he's triggered a constitutional crisis.

Mari says, "I'm proud of you."

"Yeah."

"Te amo, Arturo."

"Te amo también, Mari."

They walk around the western edge of the pond, past a small gazebo and a walkway that leads to a restroom, then follow the path to the Vietnam Memorial.

"Target acquired," Mercado says into a neck mike.

"Take position."

One of the work cars is parked along Constitution Avenue. Rollins circles the area, now on Henry Bacon Drive, which runs northeast from the Lincoln Memorial. Mercado moves through the trees and sets up behind the restroom building that overlooks the Wall.

The Wall sits low in the park, hidden like a guilty secret, a private shame.

Keller looks at the names inscribed in the stone. Vietnam was a long time ago, another lifetime, and he's fought his own long war since then. Here and there, mourners have left flowers, or cigarettes, even small bottles of booze.

No battles are inscribed on the Vietnam Wall. No Khe Sanhs or Quảng Trịs or Hamburger Hills. Maybe because we won every battle but lost the war, Keller thinks. All these deaths for a futile war. On previous trips, he's seen men lean against the Wall and sob like children.

The sense of loss heartbreaking and overwhelming.

There are maybe forty people here today. Some of them look like they might be vets, others families; most are probably tourists. Two older men in VFW uniforms and caps are there to help people locate their loved ones' names.

It's a warm spring day, a little breezy, and cherry blossoms float in the air. Sensing his emotion, Marisol takes Keller's hand.

He sees the little boy and the glint of the scope in the same moment.

The child, holding his mother's hand, gazes at the names etched into the black stone, and Keller wonders if he's looking for someone—a grandfather maybe, or an uncle—or if his mother just brought her son to the Vietnam Veterans Memorial as the end of a walk down the National Mall.

Now Keller sees the boy and then—to the right, back toward the Washington Monument—the odd, random glint of light.

Mercado sights in on Keller, moving closer to him now. Puts the crosshairs on his head and says, "Joy."

Hears the command, "Go."

He squeezes the trigger.

Lunging for the mother and the child, Keller shoves them to the ground.

Then he turns to shield Mari.

The bullet spins Keller like a top.

Creases his skull and whips his neck around.

Blood pours into his eyes and he literally sees red as he reaches out and pulls Marisol down.

Her cane clatters on the walkway.

Keller covers her body with his.

More bullets smack into the Wall above him.

He hears shouts and screams. Someone yells, "Active shooter!"

Peering up, Keller looks for the origin of the shots and sees that they're coming from the southeast, from about ten o'clock—from behind a small building he remembers is a restroom. He feels for the Sig Sauer at his hip but then remembers that he's unarmed.

The shooter flips to automatic.

Bullets spray the stone above Keller, chipping away names. People lie flat or crouch against the Wall. A few near the lower edges scramble over and run toward Constitution Avenue. A few others just stand, bewildered.

Keller yells, *"Down! Shooter! Down!"*

But he sees that's not going to help and that the memorial is now a death trap. The Wall forms a wide V and there are only two ways out along a narrow path. A middle-aged couple run to the east exit, toward the shooter, and are hit right away, dropping like characters in some hideous video game.

"Mari," Keller says, "we have to move. Do you understand?"

"Yes."

"Be ready."

He waits until there's a pause in the fire—the shooter changing clips—then gets up, grabs Mari and hefts her over his shoulder. He carries her along the Wall to the west exit, where the Wall slopes down to waist level, tosses her up and over and sets her down behind a tree.

"Stay down!" he yells. "Stay there!"

"Where are you going?!"

The shooting starts again.

Jumping back over the Wall, Keller starts to herd people toward the southwest exit. He puts one hand on the back of a woman's neck, pushes her head down and moves her along, yelling, *"This* way! *This* way!" But then he hears the sharp hiss of a bullet and the solid *thunk* as it hits her. She staggers and drops to her knees, clutching at her arm as blood pours through her fingers.

Keller tries to lift her.

A round whizzes past his face.

A young man runs up to him and reaches for the woman. "I'm a paramedic!" Keller hands her across, turns back and keeps shoving people ahead of him, away from the gunfire. He sees the boy again, still clutching his mother's hand, his eyes wide with fear as his mother pushes him ahead of her, trying to screen him with her body.

Keller wraps an arm around her shoulder and bends her down as he keeps her moving. He says, "I've got you. I've got you. Keep walking." He sees her to safety at the far end of the Wall and then goes back again.

Another pause in the firing as the shooter changes clips again.

Christ, Keller thinks, how many can he have?

At least one more, because the firing starts again.

People stumble and fall.

Sirens shriek and howl, helicopter rotors throb in deep, vibrating bass.

Keller grabs a man to pull him forward but a bullet hits the man high in the back and he falls at Keller's feet.

Most people have made it out the west exit, others lie sprawled along the walkway, still others lie on the grass where they tried to run the wrong way.

A dropped water bottle gurgles out on the walkway.

A cell phone, its glass cracked, rings on the ground next to a souvenir—a small, cheap bust of Lincoln—its face splattered with blood.

Keller looks east and sees a National Park Service policeman, his pistol drawn, charge toward the restroom building and then go down as bullets stitch across his chest.

Dropping to the ground, Keller snake-crawls toward the cop and feels for a pulse in his neck. The man is dead. Keller flattens behind the body as rounds smack into it. He looks up and thinks he spots the shooter, crouched behind the restroom building as he loads another clip.

Art Keller has spent most of his life fighting a war on the other side of the border, and now he's home.

The war has come with him.

Keller takes the policeman's sidearm—a 9 mm Glock—and moves through the trees toward the shooter.

Mercado is freaking out.

He missed the target and now he's lost sight of him in the trees. There are a lot of people down, the sirens are wailing, and he's shot a cop. He loads another clip and then peeks out from behind the building, seeing if he can spot Keller and complete the mission before he bugs out.

But he doesn't see the man.

Looking out toward Constitution Avenue, Mercado sees that escape route is closed—cop cars are rolling up and heavily armed SWAT teams are jumping out of the cars. He looks south to his right and sees more cars speeding down the Mall. A helicopter is circling overhead.

His only chance is to make it out the other way, west to Bacon Drive.

"Target down," he lies into the mike. "Moving toward fallback."

There's no answer.

"Come in," he says, starting to panic. "Come in!"

No answer.

The motherfuckers have abandoned him.

Rollins pulls out from Constitution and drives west toward the Roosevelt Bridge. The plan was for one car or the other to pick Mercado up and do him there, then dump the body, but there's no point in waiting for that now.

The police will take care of Mercado, and if he's captured alive and talks, all he's going to tell them is exactly what he's supposed to tell them.

That Ricardo Núñez hired him to kill Art Keller.

And in the more likely scenario that he's killed first, well, he's just another active shooter.

Thoughts and prayers.

Keller crouches behind a bronze monument.

A nurse cradling a wounded soldier in her lap.

His heart races and blood still flows into his eyes. He wipes it away, takes a deep breath, and charges.

Mercado moves to the other side of the building and looks out.

What he sees freaks him out even more.

A man moving toward him.

At least it might be a man; it looks more like a monster.

Its face wears a pink mask of blood and brain matter, the front of its shirt is red with blood.

It holds a pistol in front of it as it comes toward him.

It's Keller.

But now Mercado knows there's going to be no two million dollars, no entry into La Eme, no privileged status as the man who avenged Santo Adán.

He knows he's been set up.

He's a patsy.

He runs.

He raises the rifle and fires.

Keller runs after him.

More like staggers.

He hadn't until this moment realized that he'd been hit. The pain in his chest is horrific. Or maybe, he thinks, I'm having a heart attack. Either way, he feels weak and dizzy but he keeps moving forward, eyes on the shooter, who's running toward the Lincoln Memorial's Reflecting Pool.

Keller puts one foot after the other.

That's all there is to do now until he can't do it anymore.

Each step sends a stab into his chest. Each step drains him. His breath gets shorter and shorter and he can hear himself rasp. He knows he's bleeding from the inside.

But you've always been, he tells himself.

Bleeding from the inside.

One foot after the other, Keller tells himself.

Until you can't.

Then he sees the shooter.

He's trapped.

The pool behind him, cops coming in from both sides.

He stops, turns and faces Keller.

Raises the rifle and shoots.

Keller aims for center mass, presses the trigger and holds it down.

The shooter falls backward into the pool.

Keller drops to his knees.

Then he falls onto his face, his arms stretched out in front of him.

Epilogue

Adios, my friends, we're leaving El Paso.
The Rio Grande's gone bone dry,
and all the stories have been told.

—Tom Russell
"Leaving El Paso"

Southern California
May 2018

From the hill near their house, where they walk most days, Keller can see Mexico.

Marisol thinks that they make quite the matched pair, struggling up the hill on their respective canes.

The walking wounded of the war on drugs.

And we're the lucky ones, Keller thinks.

We lived.

His recuperation was long, difficult and uncertain, a round having creased his skull, three more having laced his legs. He would have bled out by the Reflecting Pool if the EMTs hadn't already been close.

The toll of the "Mall shooting" was horrific, but not as bad as it could have been. Five dead and fourteen wounded. The aftermath was the usual—thoughts and prayers and talk about gun control and mental health and then absolutely nothing was done.

The new special counsel, appointed by Congress, did investigate the possibility that Daniel Mercado had been hired by the Sinaloa cartel to assassinate Art Keller, but could never prove anything.

He did, however, have enough to bring charges against Jason Lerner, Denton Howard, and Ben O'Brien.

The trials are ongoing.

So are the impeachment hearings.

Dennison and his allies are fighting the charges of obstruction, perjury and corruption like demons.

It's hard to know how it's going to go.

Eddie Ruiz couldn't make a deal with anyone—not the special counsel, not California, not New York. He's back in Victorville, hopefully to stay.

There's been no trial for Keller. No trial and no charges, because no prosecutor would think of bringing the hero of the Mall shooting in front of a jury. And Guatemala, they wanted no part of it—let the dead bury the dead. Keller, guilty Catholic to the end, can't decide if that's right or wrong.

"Accept grace when it's offered," Marisol told him.

He tries to do that.

They bought the little ranch shortly after he got out of the hospital. With his fame—or notoriety—Washington would have been impossible, and they both decided that they wanted a quieter life. Their place has thirty acres of mostly level ground, a grove of live oaks among boulders, and an acre of apple trees. A small town nearby has a grocery store, a bar, and a used bookstore.

It's enough.

Their days are quiet, their nights quieter.

Keller mostly reads history, Marisol has taken up painting, some style called *plein air*.

Althea comes to visit sometimes; Marisol jokingly calls it his harem. Michael came out over Christmas and spent several days. Even Hugo Hidalgo came by to pay his respects, to apologize for what he said, and to tell Keller that he'd caught on with the Bexar County Sheriff's Office. He said he'd finally let go of what had happened to his father.

And I, Keller thinks, have finally let go of Adán Barrera.

He's dead.

Life comes back to you, Keller thinks.

He looks out at the border and wonders what's happening in Mexico. The chaos and violence go on. Rafael Caro is dead and Tito Ascensión is the new "godfather," so brutal and stupid men rule on both sides of the line.

But there's no wall down there, Keller thinks, smiling.

And there never will be. A border is something that divides us but also unites us; there can be no real wall, just as there is no wall that divides the human soul between its best impulses and its worst.

Keller knows. He's been on both sides of the border.

He takes Mari's hand and together they limp back down the hill.

Acknowledgments

A dear friend recently pointed out to me that I have been writing this story for fully a third of my life. What began with a book entitled *The Power of the Dog*, resumed with *The Cartel*, and now concludes with *The Border* has consumed me for over twenty years. A journey of decades isn't walked alone, but accompanied step by step not only by the fictional characters that inhabit its imaginary world, but by real people—long and treasured relationships—without whom this pilgrimage could not have begun, never mind found completion.

I owe these people more than I can ever hope to repay.

Shane Salerno—my friend, fellow writer and agent extraordinaire—was there at the start and is, remarkably, still here at the finish. The word *loyalty* does not begin to describe his steadfastness, belief, counsel and passionate advocacy. Without him and the Story Factory these books—and my career—would not exist.

My son, Thomas Winslow, was a boy when he helped file research materials for the first book. He's now an accomplished young man with (more important) work of his own, and I could not be prouder of him nor more grateful for his role in my life and work.

My wife, Jean Winslow, inexplicably lovelier than even she was when this odyssey began, has endured my obsessions, my moods, and the vicissitudes of a writing life. She has accompanied me on book tours and research trips, literally walking with me to check details of terrain ("Honey, you stand here while I walk over there and see if it's possible to shoot you from that position"), and driven with me to places that were not always the world's garden spots. Her high spirits, sense of adventure and unfailing love are the joy of my existence.

Sonny Mehta edited the first two books, one of which I turned in at two thousand manuscript pages. I will always be grateful for his famously keen aesthetic sense, extraordinary patience and kindness.

David Highfill inherited the final volume, a difficult task to which he brought his considerable talents, sensitivities and skill, for which I am tremendously grateful.

So many people have supported me on this journey.

I would be nowhere without the booksellers, some of whom personally hand-sold hundreds of my books, who warmly welcomed me into their stores and became real friends.

I mustn't neglect the sales forces and marketing people of the publishing houses. They have literally carried my books about with them, they are the unsung heroes and heroines of the writing world, and I appreciate them.

As I do the readers. Without the readers, I wouldn't have this job that I love. They are, after all, the point of all this, and their support, encouragement and appreciation mean the world to me. I can't thank them enough.

To the critics who have written such kind reviews, the journalists who have given me so much exposure, and the fellow authors who have been so generous, I extend my deepest gratitude.

To my mother, Ottis Winslow, for lending me her porch, on which vast portions of these books were written.

To the many friends who gave me help, food, music and laughter—Teressa Palozzi, Pete and Linda Maslowski, Thom Walla, John and Theresa Culver, Scott Svoboda and Jan Enstrom, Andrew Walsh, Tom Russell (America's Bard), M. A. Gillette, the late James Gillette, Bill and Ruth McEneaney, Mark Rubinsky and the late Rev. Lee Hancock, Don Young, Steven Wendelin, the late Jim Robie, Ron and Kim Lubesnick, Ted and Michelle Tarbert, Cameron Pierce Hughes, songwriter David Nedwidek and Katy Allen, Scott and Deb Kinney, Jon and Alla Muench, Jim and Josie Talbert, Neal Griffin, the folks at Mr. Manita's, Jeremy's on the Hill, Wynola Pizza, El Fuego, Drift Surf, The Right Click, and The Red Hen. I couldn't—and wouldn't want to—have taken this walk without you.

To Liate Stehlik at William Morrow—thank you so much for your confidence and trust in me. It means so much.

To Andy LeCount, for your energetic and fine efforts on my behalf.

And to Brian Murray, Michael Morrison, Lynn Grady, Kaitlin Harri, Jennifer Hart, Shelby Meizlik, Brian Grogan, Juliette Shapland and Samantha Hagerbaumer—a sincere thank-you for your unflagging support.

Sharyn Rosenblum and Danielle Bartlett have literally traveled miles with me; we have sat together in traffic jams, train stations and hotel lobbies. Their efficiency, humor and consideration have been a great kindness.

To Chloe Moffett, Laura Cherkas and Laurie McGee I owe a great debt for their detailed, caring, thoughtful and creative work on my manuscript. They have saved me from many mistakes.

To Deborah Randall and all the folks at the Story Factory, thank you so much for all your support and valuable input.

To Matthew Snyder and Joe Cohen at CAA, my sincere thanks for hanging in with me on this long trip.

Cynthia Swartz and Elizabeth Kushel have been unfailingly creative and kind.

To my attorney, Richard Heller, I owe much.

This is a work of fiction. However, any reader at all familiar with the drug scene will recognize that some of its elements have been largely inspired by real-life events. As such, I have consulted many sources.

My deepest appreciation goes out to the many people who have shared their stories and experiences with me. My debt to them is unpayable.

For this volume, I consulted a number of printed sources, including: Sonia Nazario's *Enrique's Journey* and Deborah T. Levenson's *Adiós, Niño: The Gangs of Guatemala City and the Politics of Death.*

Among the journalists' work I looked at were:

Tim Rogers in *Splinter;* Kirk Semple, John Otis, Sonia Nazario, Azam Ahmed, J. David Goodman and Michael Wilson, Sam Quinones, William Neuman, Julia Preston, Wil S. Hylton, and Jeff Sommer—*New York Times;* Laura Weiss—*LobeLog;* Leighton Akio Woodhouse—*The Intercept;* Tyche Hendricks—KQED; Jessie Knadler—WEMC and WMRA; Chico Harlan, David Nakamura, Joshua Partlow, and Julia Preston—*Washington Post;* Rodrigo Dominguez Villegas—Migration Policy Institute; Leon Watson and Jessica Jerreat—*Daily Mail;* Nina Lakhan, Amanda Holpuch, Lois Beckett, Rory Carroll, and David Agren—*The Guardian;* Tracy Wilkinson and Molly Hennessy-Fiske—*Los Angeles Times;* Sarah Yolanda McClure—Center for Latin American Studies; Lorne Matalon—*Fronteras;* Laura C. Mallonee—*Hyperallergic;* Roque Planas, Tom Mills, and Avinash Tharoor—*HuffPost;* Ian Gordon, James Ridgeway and Jean Casella, and Laura Smith—*Mother Jones;* Amanda Taub—*Vox;* Aseem Mehta—*Narratively;* Christopher Woody, Jeremy Bender, and Christina Sterbenz—*Business Insider;* Yemeli Ortega—MSN; Josh Eells—*Rolling Stone;* Duncan Tucker, Luis Chaparro, and Nathaniel Janowitz—*Vice News;* John Annese, Larry McShane, and Christopher Zoukish—*New York Daily News;* Ian Frazier—*The New Yorker;* Kristina Davis and Greg Moran—*San Diego Union-Tribune;* Cora Currier—*ProPublica;* Amanda Sakuma—MSNBC; Claudia Morales, Vivian Kuo, and Jason Hanna—CNN; *La Jornada;* InSight Crime; *Borderland Beat; Blog del Narco; Mexico News Daily;* Univision; *El Universal;* Council on Hemispheric Affairs; and the Associated Press.

At the end of this twenty-year literary hike, I look back with the knowledge that no author has been better served and supported, no author has had better friends or a more loving family, no author has ever been happier in his work. For me, this long walk has been more than worth every step. My fondest hope is this is also true for the reader.